SHARDS OF LAW

SHARDS OF LAW

Book One of the Avanir Chronicles

L. E. DEREKSEN

ISBN 978-1-9994996-0-0 (paperback)

ISBN 978-1-9994996-2-4 (hardcover)

ISBN 978-1-9994996-1-7 (e-book)

Published by SKY STEP PUBLISHING

Author's website: ledereksen.com

For mom:
You showed me how to live.

Contents

Map of the World
THE NORTH SEA
THE WEST ISLES
THE INNER ISLES
MANTUR
TERRYN DAL
MARRENTRY
HON
FOXWYN
MANQUIN
THE TINDANARRA RIVER
ELAMORI
TELLERN
THE ELLENDANDUR FOREST
CALTON
THE MANTURIAN ROAD
TSAVIN
THE BORDER RIVER
TILLEX
TOERN
THE WALL
LENDAHYR
KARTH
LLEWEL
THE EASTWARD OCEAN
THE AETHEN KINGDOMS
KANULF
RANITHGAR
YNAS
EINWYHL
TO THE DESERT

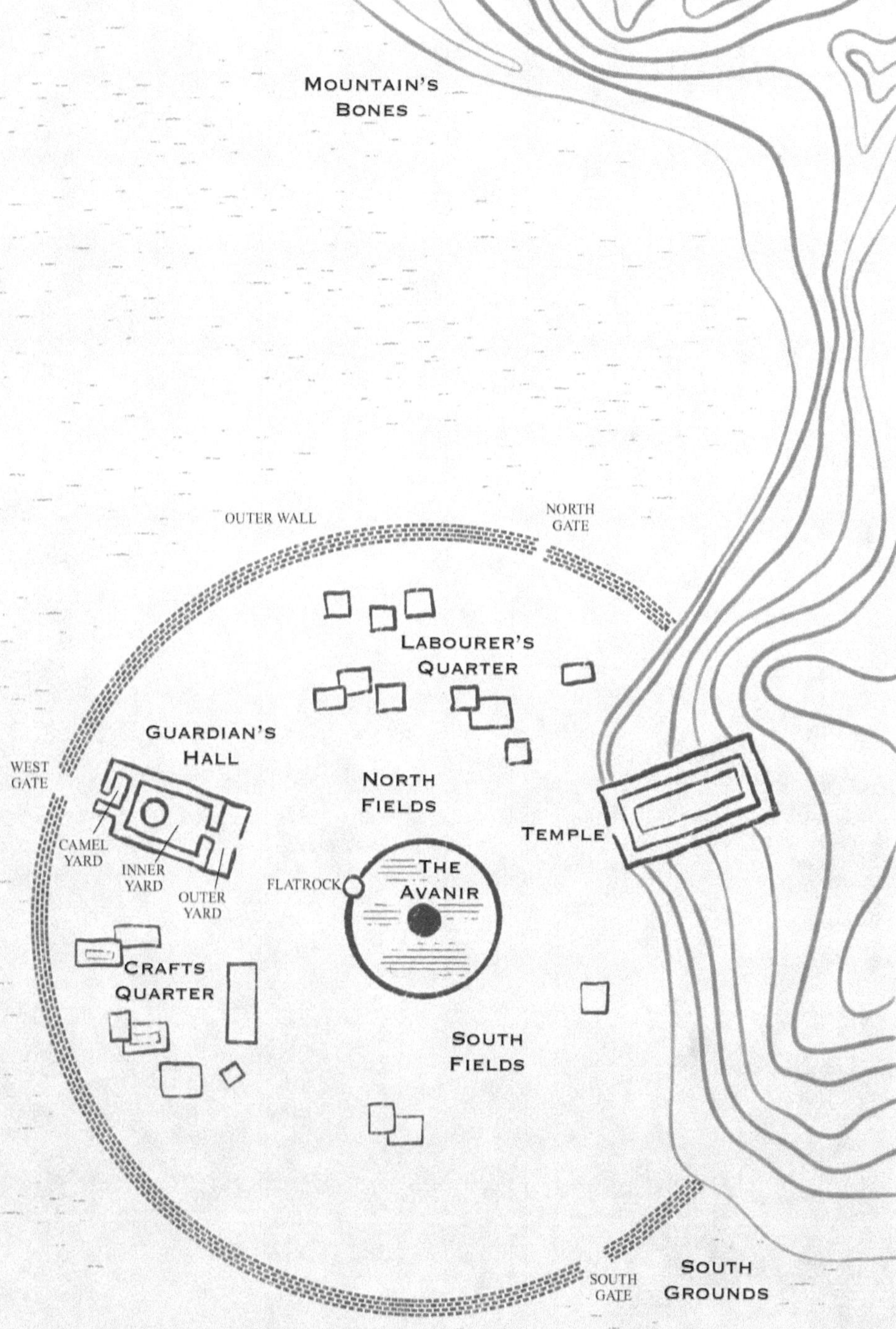

MOUNTAIN'S BONES
OUTER WALL
NORTH GATE
LABOURER'S QUARTER
GUARDIAN'S HALL
WEST GATE
NORTH FIELDS
CAMEL YARD
INNER YARD
OUTER YARD
TEMPLE
FLATROCK
THE AVANIR
CRAFTS QUARTER
SOUTH FIELDS
SOUTH GATE
SOUTH GROUNDS
MAP OF
SHYANDAR

Prologue

The Guardian was old.

He slouched against the black stone, waiting, waiting. It was all he ever did these days. Sitting and peering into the dust, one leg stretched out in front of him. It was not a very Guardian-like posture, but his feet hurt, and the night was long.

He grunted and shivered, pulling his threadbare cloak tighter. It had been red, once. It had been finely made. Now it was tattered, faded, and full of holes. His hair had thinned to a single grey braid, lying limp on the back of his neck. His skin was furrowed with lines. Becoming dust, all dust—except for the sword. His keshu was the last of its kind in Shyandar. Sand-blasted rebels had stolen the rest. Gone. Corrupted by Shatayeth Undying, enemy of the people. Now vanished into the desert to die.

How long until he vanished as well? The shadows would come for him—now, tomorrow, the next night, or in ten long years, if he didn't starve to death first. The shadows, or Shatayeth himself. The wind groaned across the barrenness, whisking sand from one end of the cracked and empty lakebed to the other. He imagined it happening like that. One moment—gone. Nothing. No more Ishtar. No more Guardians. The end. Easy. Then only sand would wait. Then only shadows. And who would welcome the waters then?

"Ishtar," said a voice . . .

The old man leapt to his feet.

"Ab'Adani Al'kah! Forgive me! I was resting my—"

"No, no. You do well," said the figure, though he hung back. His gaunt form was bent, his fingers tense against the edge of his robes. *Something was wrong.*

"Sal'ah Al'kah?"

The man took a sharp breath, as if pained. He turned to face the dry lakebed of the Avanir. "You are faithful."

Ishtar grunted. "I am old, sal'ah Al'kah."

"Are you?" He blinked up at the brilliant ache of the sky. "Stars are old. Sand is old. This rock is old. But you, Ishtar ab'Shatara, are not *old*. You are . . . faithful. You guard the Avanir. Still. Always."

"It will return."

"Will it?"

Ishtar glanced at him in surprise. The man was thin and worn, as they all were. He was dressed in tattered robes, as they all were. But there was a strange energy to him this night. Something restless.

"Seven years," the Al'kah continued, clenching his hands. "Seven years since the water dried up, and no Guardian has seen a drop in three. Still, you wait." He craned his neck. The stone Avanir towered over them, a huge hulking blackness with weird and twisted arms, its crown lost in the shadows above their head.

A shudder passed through the Al'kah. "No," he said.

"No, sal'ah Al'kah?" Ishtar frowned.

"No, no. It's not our place to doubt. We have a duty. Each of us." He spoke with fervent intensity. "And you have done yours, my friend. When the rebels attacked, you resisted. When the Guardians fled, you stayed. You remained at my side, through . . . through *all* of it."

"I swore an oath, ab'Adani Al'kah. I am a Guardian of Shyandar."

"Yes." The man paused, then edged nearer. "Ishtar, let me see your keshu."

Ishtar hesitated. "My keshu?"

"Yes. Would you deny your lord?"

"Never!" Ishtar drew the blade, and its soft light leapt into the space between them. How long had it been? Six months? Seven, since the last attack—since the shadows had taken Lalysha and Ebrynu? A

Guardian did not draw without need, but neither could he refuse the Al'kah, his ruler.

The Al'kah reached out, hands open to receive the blade.

"This is our hope, Ishtar," he said, a tremor in his voice. "We must be strong. New life will return. Do . . . do you believe it?"

Ishtar nodded. "The water will come. If not in my life, then in another's."

"I'm glad you think so." He paused and swallowed. "You do well, Ishtar. You are faithful."

"Thank you, sal'ah Al'kah."

"You are faithful."

Ishtar frowned. "So are you, my lord Al'kah. Is . . . is something wrong?"

"Something? No." He tightened his hands around the blade. "*All* things. If there is no water, who will be Chosen? And if there are no Chosen, who will stop the Breaking of the world? Who, Ishtar ab'Shatara? *Who?*"

Ishtar struggled to hide his alarm. "The Great Tree knows. She will send the water. She must."

"And if she cannot?"

Ishtar said nothing. A darkness crept through him, the one that had always been there, always, beneath his dedication, beneath the waiting and the long hours of supposed hope. He pushed it away. He was too old for those thoughts. He had made his choice, long ago.

"We broke the cycle," the Al'kah continued. "We failed. Not the Tree, not the Avanir. *Us.*"

"There is always hope."

"Yes." The man nodded fiercely, as if trying to convince himself. "Yes, there is. Only I wish . . . I wish . . ."

Ishtar frowned. Something moved in the shadows. Something on his right, circling from behind the Avanir, the huge black pillar. He held up a hand for silence, listening, straining to hear.

"Who goes there?"

No answer.

Ishtar reached for his keshu. It was not there, of course. He had given it to the Al'kah. He opened his hand, gesturing for the man to hurry and hand it back. *The shadows. The shadows had come!*

The figure stepped nearer, and everything in Ishtar tightened. No. Not the shadows. It was a man, robed and swathed like an outrider. Two glittering black eyes.

"Stop!" Ishtar ordered. "Name yourself. Why have you dared to approach the Avanir?"

The man did not stop. His feet were bare against the sand. Bare as they padded forward, circling, drawing nearer. The black eyes regarded him from beneath the wrappings. *Assessed* him.

"Al'kah, my sword," Ishtar said, feeling a flutter of panic. "Hurry." He glanced over his shoulder, still waiting—waiting to feel the smooth grip—and an instant later, he felt the blade drive into his chest.

Ishtar's eyes flew open. The keshu slid easily, up through his ribs, into his heart, punching out his back. A thin spray of blood spattered the rock behind him. The rock he had guarded, watched over, stood by, waiting, waiting . . .

"Al'kah?" he gasped.

Ashkynas ab'Adani Al'kah, last ruler of Shyandar, trembled as their eyes met. "You are faithful," he said. "To death, you are faithful."

The Guardian felt a vague, distant pain. He became slowly aware of it, the pressure building inside of him, squeezing against his lungs, gathering and growing.

"I don't . . ." he spoke thickly. "I don't . . . understand."

"I wish there were some other way. *Any* way. But we are dying, Ishtar ab'Shatara, and this is our hope. Our last hope. Our very last." The Al'kah pressed a hand to the Guardian's face. "You will be for many. I swear to you," his voice caught, "your sacrifice will not be in vain."

Ishtar's eyes swam towards the swathed figure, the stranger, watched as he pulled the wrappings away, as his face emerged from the shadows.

"*You!*" Ishtar choked. Blood flowed hot down his back, bubbling into his throat, soaking his thin robes, pooling and dripping into the cracked and hungry earth. So much. So much. His eyes clouded. *No! He had to warn the Al'kah. He had to . . .*

"Do not . . ." he gasped. "Do not . . ."

The Al'kah stepped back, yanked out the sword, and Ishtar crumpled to the dust. He was unable to move, to cry out, though the pain built and built. The air throbbed. Something was reaching out of the pillar—burning against his mind. A force without substance. A terrifying power.

Not the Avanir. No! Not our good, our hope . . . Not it too!

It clung to him, sucking him out like a husk. Ishtar felt the mawing emptiness, the swirl of hunger and need, reaching, reaching. The end. The ruin of all things, come at last.

"It's working," said the Al'kah, face chiselled in horror.

The other man stepped past him. Bare feet. He walked to the edge of the slithering dark pool. "Faithful," said the voice: cold, measureless, and without pity. "Are you faithful?" He crouched. His fingers dipped into the blood and he paused, waiting for an answer.

Ishtar nodded, even as his vision swam, as painful stars mixed with shadow.

"Always."

"Good," said the man. "Then it's time you were put to some use."

Desert

ISHVANDU AB'ADMUNDI

Year 455 after the fall of Kayr

THREE HUNDRED AND FORTY-THREE YEARS AGO

The desert calls to me.

We are an island, shrouded by emptiness. Dust, sky, dust —I have seen it, beyond the walls. I have seen the world turned in on itself, until the furthest limits of what I knew became the centre. I have stood in the empty world. I, alone, until I was the world. The whole terrifying world.

But for the shadows . . .

I do not speak of the shadows.

Chapter One

It was a bad idea. I knew it from the first, what Koryn was doing, baiting me like a digger rat. Only it didn't seem to matter just then, in the moment. You think I'd have learned by now the moment's a backstabbing little cheat.

I glanced around the stable yard. There were only a handful of us: two Guardians, three Novices, and an audience of unimpressed camels, trudging around the yard to nowhere.

"I don't care if you're a sand-shitting Guardian," I said, "you've no right to beat my Novices."

"*Your* Novices?"

"Mine."

Koryn's nose twitched in a sneer—the same crooked nose I'd broken four years ago. "Where's your keshu?" He asked, tapping his marbled sword hilt.

The question was so obvious, it hurt. "Light and all, Koryn, maybe up your ass. Want to look?"

"Oh, that's right. I almost forgot. You don't have one." He stepped closer. Close enough I could snap his beaked nose between my fingers. "No keshu means no Guardian. Not yet. Maybe not ever. And you have the stones to stand here, eye to eye, and tell me what I can and cannot do?"

I glanced at Bray, where he crouched against the red-stone walls, still tangled up in old hay and camel shit, squinting into the high morning sun. The kid was a year off his Tasking, a sun-blasted idiot, and far too mouthy for his own good, but the swelling eye and the blood smeared across his face had no business being there.

"You're out of line."

Koryn laughed and edged nearer. "You do fancy yourself a Guardian, don't you? You think you're ready. You think you *deserve* it."

"Six years. So yes. Yes I do."

"Prove it."

The challenge was too quick, off his lips before I'd hardly finished speaking. I knew it was a bad idea. "Put a keshu in my hands," I said, "and I will."

"Vanya, maybe that's not—"

"Shut it, Pol," I told my friend.

The older Novice shut it, while, next to him, Bray wiped another slick of blood off his brow. I could tell from the fire in their eyes they wanted a fight. They deserved a fight.

"He can use mine," said Antaru. I glanced at the meaty Guardian, as dumb as he was loyal. Koryn must have put him up to it. You didn't let anyone touch your keshu. Not ever. Only by direct order from a superior.

I smirked. "Yeah?"

"Do it," was all Koryn said.

Antaru gripped his keshu and drew.

The first time I had seen one of the ancient blades, I was ten. The Guardian Lord had been tall, daunting, magnificent. The cloak— fastened with real gold—was the colour of fresh spilled blood. The curved keshu at his side gleamed naked in the dying sun. I had stared, dumbstruck at the sight of a Guardian Lord so close. At his blade. It had answered with a subtle flame of its own, and I must have reached out, because a moment later, the man snatched my hand away.

"Do not," he had said. The force of his grasp could have crushed my bones if he'd wanted.

Nearly eight years later, I was staring at another keshu. It shone with the same subtle glow, and its thick blade was worthy of Antaru's strength. I could hardly believe he was doing this. That *I* was doing this.

I snatched it from his grasp, afraid I might change my mind. Immediately, I felt the weight of the sword—not the heaviness, for it was shockingly light—but the authority of it. It wasn't meant for me, and I could tell. The hilt was too broad. The blade was too long. It was built for long, forceful sweeps. But still, I knew: I was holding the power of Shyandar.

A mistake. And it was too late to back down now.

I heard the draw of Koryn's keshu and leapt back. The point grazed my shirt. I stumbled, scrambling away. My foot slipped in a heap of camel dung. I fell, rolled. I nearly took my own arm off with the keshu. Then I was back up. Koryn was laughing. He could have finished it just then, but that wasn't the point. Now that we both knew how incompetent I was, he was going to wait. Let me settle in. And beat me again.

Or so he thought.

I grinned, testing the keshu's balance, a few double-handed swings, just like I would with a training blade. Only those were clumsy, brittle things. This keshu sang.

I attacked. Maybe it took Koryn off guard, because he doubled back. A safe block. *No.* The keshu slipped, and I had to jump aside to avoid the counter. I ducked. The keshu whistled over my head, nearly trimming the hair from my scalp. Then I twisted for a counter. A ringing clang. Pull in, step back, keep moving.

I could feel myself settling in to the rhythm. I laughed, stepped back again. Straight into the stone wall of the camel yard. I brought the keshu down fast and hard to throw off his swing. The tip cut through fabric as I spun and danced free, breathing hard. Camels scattered and bellowed their annoyance.

"Had enough?" Koryn asked.

"Not until you admit you were wrong."

"Good." He raised the keshu. "I'm rather enjoying this."

"Any time."

"You can take him, Vanya!" Polityr cried.

I couldn't. I was too slow. I was untrained with a keshu. I knew how this was going to end, but I was going to enjoy this while I had it.

We circled each other. Something started to sting. I didn't have time to look, but clearly Koryn's last blow had cut more than my shirt.

Then we closed the distance. I blocked, swung, dodged, leaping back and forth. Koryn was just getting warmed up. I was getting sloppy. I moved in to strike, Koryn knocked me back, and I didn't reverse in time. His keshu glanced along the side of my arm and I twisted away, grimacing. *That* I had felt.

He relaxed—maybe he thought a little scratch was enough to beat me—and I could hear the tense expectation in Pol and Antaru's silence. A tiny window of opportunity.

I lunged, grabbed for Koryn's sword hand. He tried to jump back. My hand closed around the blade instead of his wrist. There was a bite of pain. Deep. But I didn't care. I was going to take this fight. My keshu aimed at this throat. He was trapped. He couldn't defend himself.

A new, slender keshu flashed, spearing a tight cross between us. It snapped down, deflected my blow. Then the attacker closed in, planted a fist in my gut, spun, caught my foot, and I was lying on my back, staring up at the distant blue sky.

A face appeared. It had the same fine-chiselled look as Koryn's, the same condescending tilt. A single thick braid hung over one shoulder and her keshu poked me in the ribs. Atali sai'Neraia. *Tala.* My stomach knotted.

"I appreciate your help, Tala," I laughed, "but I *had* him."

"Idiot!" she snapped. "Umaala's coming this way, and he'll have your guts for rope if he finds you holding a keshu. Drop it. Now."

"What in the name of light is happening here?" a voice thundered.

Tala turned and whipped her keshu into its sheath. It was a single, fluid move. I caught myself staring, and realized too late that I had missed my opportunity.

I swore and leapt to my feet, dropping the keshu as if stung. But one glimpse of Umaala ab'Krushaya bearing down on us, a hand on his sword, red cloak swirling up a cloud of dust as he marched through the camel-yard gate, and I knew I was done.

"Sal'ah." I swallowed, acknowledging him with a Guardian's title of respect.

He glared past me. "You too, Akkoryn ab'Kindelthu. Now!"

Koryn hesitated, glared at me, then obeyed, sheathing his keshu with a quick, firm snap. Polityr and Antaru shuffled uncomfortably. Tala pursed her lips—as she always did when she was worried.

"Someone explain this to me!" The Guardian Lord glanced between Koryn and I, then at my fist, clenched around a torrent of blood. His outrage seared like a furnace off every joint and muscle.

"A . . . a point is being made, sal'ah," I said, desperately hoping he wouldn't hear the tremble in my voice. "Just because someone has the right to carry a keshu, doesn't mean he has the right to beat up a Novice."

"Is that so?"

I glanced at the bloody-faced kid. "Bray wasn't doing anything wrong."

"But you are!" Umaala stepped towards me. I had grown since our first meeting, but the Guardian Lord was still taller than me by a head, his broad arms still capable of crushing me. "How dare you speak of the right to carry a keshu, Novice! Whose is that? Certainly not yours!" He eyed Koryn. "Well?"

"Mine, sal'ah." Antaru stepped forward.

"And how did it end up in the hands of a Novice?"

"I gave it to him. Koryn wanted to fight."

"And you thought that was a good idea?"

"It was just a bit of fun, sal'ah," the Guardian tried to say, but Umaala's crackling eyes should have warned him.

"*Fun?* You gave your keshu to a Novice so he could duel a Guardian. His superior! In the stable yard—in the middle of Kaprash of all times! Like two scrapping boys who don't know any better. Fun? These are weapons, not toys! Yl'avah's might, but I don't know how one of them didn't end up with his guts all over the ground. Pick it up!"

The Guardian hurried to retrieve it, but before he could sheath it away, Umaala shot out his hand.

"Give it to me."

"Sal'ah?"

"Now."

Antaru swallowed and handed over the blade, looking every bit like a chastened Novice himself.

"Since you apparently have no concept of the respect accorded these ancient symbols of authority, I strip you of your right to carry one."

The man stared in horror. "But . . . you can't!"

"I can and I have. And if you want that right back, you'll have to earn it." I had never seen Umaala so furious. I may have actually pitied the young Guardian—only I was next.

"I'm sorry, sal'ah," I said. "I wasn't thinking."

"Blood and light, you're damned sure you weren't. And it's not the first time. Fighting a Guardian! What were you thinking, Ishvandu? You could be a Guardian yourself in a matter of days, and you would risk all that on your blasted pride?"

"My brother put him up to it," Tala said. "Ishvandu was just following orders."

I nodded vigorously.

"Are you willing to stand for that?" Umaala eyed her.

"She can't stand for anything," Koryn said. "She wasn't here."

"I'll speak for myself, thanks," she snapped. "You think I don't know what you're doing? You think the *Circle* doesn't know? You should be ashamed."

Koryn gave a bark of laughter. "Really, Tala—"

"Did you *witness* an order?" Umaala glowered at them in turn.

Tala drew herself up, lips pursed, unwilling to betray her duty with a lie. But I could see her mind flashing through a dozen different responses. She opened her mouth.

"It was Vanya's idea," Antaru interrupted. "He asked for a keshu."

Umaala turned to me. "Is that so?"

Yl'avah's blasted might! I clenched my bleeding fist. *Put a keshu in my hand*, I had said. *Put a keshu in my hand.* I could deny it, but the witness of two Guardians would overrule me. "It might have been . . . sal'ah."

Tala rolled her eyes. "Of course it was. Idiot."

"Enough," Umaala said. "Both of you will spend a night in the holds while we consider what to do about this."

"What? The *holds!*" Koryn spluttered, realizing Umaala meant him as well. "I'm a Guardian, not some green Tasker!"

Umaala whirled on him. "And if you say one word more, I'll hold you fully responsible. Now go! Atali sai'Neraia, see to it!"

"Yes, sal'ah." Tala gave a clipped nod and shot me a look. *Don't you dare open your mouth.* For once I agreed.

Umaala turned and marched from the stable yard. We followed. First myself, then Koryn with a grunt of reluctance, and Tala last of all. She kept a hand on her hilt, not from fear either of us would run —with the Guardian's Hall surrounding us, where would we go?— but as an acknowledgement of her duty. *Nothing personal.*

We pushed through the gates beneath the long, arched hall. It was a brush of shadow: cool and cleansing, as good as a gulp of water. By the time we entered the inner yard, a crowd had gathered. Sparring Novices stopped to stare at us, Guardians glanced and muttered, and even the weapons-master, Tushani'sal, broke off in the middle of a demonstration. Umaala ab'Krushaya commanded instant attention, but Koryn and I, being led towards the red-stone Tower, was a story that leapt fully-formed into their minds. Everyone knew we hated each other. Everyone knew something was bound to happen.

Let them talk. I curled my fist around the dripping blood and marched unrepentant toward the holds.

Chapter Two

The holds beneath the Tower were deep, narrow pits: tunnels boring straight down into the dark earth. Law-breakers were dropped here—and occasionally a rebellious Novice. Which meant this wasn't my first visit. Still, my legs had grown since the last time. They pressed against the far wall, maddeningly close to straight. Sleep would be difficult.

I sighed. My head thunked against the wall. Stupid. *Stupid.* How could I have let Koryn bait me so easily?

"You'll never be a Guardian now," he was saying from the next hole. "I know it. The Circle knows it. Even Umaala knows it. He won't be able to protect you this time, mudfoot. You'll be back digging ditches before tomorrow sunfall, I promise you."

I pressed my lips together. *Don't. Don't react.*

"Tala knows it too."

Tala. Bright, confident Tala. The most promising Guardian of her generation. The daughter of Neraia sai'Kalysa, Guardian Lord of the first kiyah. But most problematic of all—Koryn's sister.

I growled under my breath. "Mind your own sand-blasted shit, Koryn. In case you hadn't noticed, you're in with me too. We'll both get it this time."

"Both?" Koryn said. "There's no *both* here, not for a floor-licking Novice pass-up like you."

"Does it really bother you so much that we're friends?"

"Friends?" Koryn laughed. The jeering sound echoed into the darkness, up and around, dashing into every pit. "You think I haven't noticed? I see the way you look at her. I promise, the moment she finds out, she'll drop you like the roach you are. She's a Guardian now, and she'll have nothing to do with you, just you watch. You're nothing to her. And you'll never be a Guardian either."

I glanced down at my hands, flexing them, curling. My arm ached where Koryn had shaved off a chunk of skin, a keen reminder of the keshu's dangerous edge—undulled since its creation hundreds, perhaps thousands, of years ago. Now blood oozed through the hasty bandage, pooling in the crux of my elbow before dripping onto the clay floor. My fingers had gone numb. My other hand throbbed from clutching Koryn's keshu: a steady pounding, like a second heart struggling to breathe. As long as I kept my fist clenched, it didn't bleed overmuch, but still, I wondered if I was in danger. Blood flowing. Blood, and no water to drink.

Was it worth it?

You'll never be a Guardian. I shut my eyes. I stretched cold fingers, remembering the feel of the keshu. Light, powerful, fast. What would it feel like to train with one every day, to master the sweep and thrust, to feel its weight on my hip, the clearest mark of power in Shyandar? What would it feel like to be one of *them*: rulers, protectors, watchers, outriders and explorers? Guardians.

I wondered now. Would I ever know?

I was young the first time I heard *never.*

Even then, the desert called to me. As soon as my evening chores were done, I hurried off. I was tired of my father's dour silences. Tired of the noise and giggles of the other children as they scampered past, enjoying the precious moments of freedom between intolerable heat and the night's curfew. There was nothing I liked better than my secret place.

Breathing hard, sweat trickling down my face and under my rough-spun Labourer's shirt, I pulled myself up the crumbling heap of stone, up to the very top. It was an old wall. Old and battered and falling apart, worn down by centuries of sand-blasting wind. It was forbidden to cross, of course—but no one ever saw me. In the heat of Kaprash, the Dryness, not many stirred outside their clay hovels, terrified of the desert and its encroaching dust. Terrified of shadows, as if the dark itself could swallow you.

Not many—except for me and a few Guardian patrols.

The wind was in the east, and as I sat there, stretched out on my back along the wall, I could hear snatches of prayer song drifting up from the Temple, like the wind itself, now high and keening, now delicate and calm.

But the singing always drew my gaze out, away from the huddle of civilization and the now-waterless Avanir. Out towards the desert.

It was deadly, that wasteland. I knew it. We all knew it. But still it called to me. Still I sat there. A long time—too long. The shadows cast by the wall stretched beneath me. Longer. Deeper. Cooler. A creature stirred in the sand. A snake? A lizard? I leaned closer. Curiosity pulled at me, and I abandoned my perch, scrambling down the desert-side, shutting out Shyandar, enclosing myself in the empty world.

Silent, I leapt off the lowest rock. A puff of dust rose to greet me, slipping over my tongue and up my nose, gritty, but tasting of open skies. I paused. I waited for it to settle before I crept nearer, crouching as I watched the little creature. Not a reptile, but a hairless rodent. Wrinkled, rough-skinned, with a scaly white tail and long, blunt digging claws. It halted. Its nose twitched, sensing my nearness, feeling it through the particles of sand, each connected to each other, from my leathery soles, through to his leathery paws.

I waited. It was looking straight at me with a milky, sightless gaze. Could it hear me breathe? I held so still, even my heart seemed to slow beneath my skinny ribs. Then, satisfied it was alone, it chirped, turned, and began to waddle off.

I pounced. Fingers clutched at the creature's belly. It squealed and squirmed. Its tail whipped my bare arm, claws scrabbling to get free. I tightened my grip, adjusted one hand under its neck, and gave a quick, hard twist. There was a snap, and the thing went limp.

Food. Real meat.

I stuffed the dead rodent into my shirt, then looked up. The sky was dark. The cliffs were black. It was silent on this side of the wall. Stories sprang to mind: the things that lurked in the desert, far worse than rats and snakes. I wasn't afraid of them. I didn't believe in desert ghosts.

A gust of wind from the north snapped my hair, moaning and whistling along the cliff. My breath caught. I wouldn't run. I faced the darkness, trembling where I stood. Something shifted. Was it my imagination, or had the shadows moved? *No. No it couldn't be.* I took a step closer. I smiled, mocking the dark.

Then I saw it—a blackness against the wall, melting into shadow, there one moment, and gone the next.

If my head didn't believe the stories, my feet sure did. With a gasp, I spun and flew up the rocks, slipping, falling, scraping my legs and arms, and finally hurling myself over the top, sliding the rest of the way.

I landed directly behind a Guardian patrol.

The three men turned to me as one. They stood in their fine, embroidered robes, hair clean and braided, keshu hanging from their sides. I picked myself up, heart thumping as I stared at their bewildered faces. Past curfew, out at night in the middle of Kaprash, caught climbing the wall no less. I'd get a whipping for sure—if they could catch me. I made a dash for the open.

An arm flashed out, seizing my shirt with a jolt.

"Hold it," a voice said. It was calm, almost quiet, but I tried to squirm free, lashing out with my fists. The man just held me at arm's length, my shirt twisted around my ears. The other two chuckled.

"That's a lively shade you caught, ab'Tanadu," said the younger one.

The man frowned. "You have a good reason to be out this late?"

"I was just looking, I didn't do anything, I didn't go into the desert, I was just—"

"We've got rules for a reason, you know, boy. You understand how dangerous this is?"

I swallowed and decided to nod. Vigorously.

"Where do you live?"

"Labourer's quarter, North Fields."

"I can see that. Who with?"

I glanced at the other two. In the dark, I couldn't see their faces, but no one seemed particularly threatening. My father, on the other hand . . .

I considered lying, but there was no one else I knew well enough to trust. "Admundi ab'Adaiah," I said, miserably. "Third turn west from the cistern."

He nodded and, without another word, latched on to my elbow and steered me in that direction. Once or twice I tried to twist away, but he held me firm and walked quickly, forcing me to trot to keep up.

The streets were black and empty. I was glad. This would be humiliating enough without an audience.

"Which one?" he asked as we drew near.

My stomach fluttered, but I scowled to hide my fear. "I guess the one with the light on."

He chose to ignore my tone and marched me in. There was a small dung-fire burning on the stone, enough to cast light on my tangled black hair and the blood trickling down my arms and legs where I'd fallen. My father was up, waiting for me.

His dark eyes moved to take in the scene, myself and the Guardian both, and a frown creased his brow.

"Ishvandu," he said. It was greeting, question, and reprimand, all at once.

"Your son?" the Guardian asked.

My father nodded and rose.

"What has he done this time?"

"We found him climbing the north walls, out past sunfall. Were you aware of this?"

I watched my father's face. There was a slight tightening around his mouth, but not the shock and outrage I had expected. "No," he said. "I was not."

"Then perhaps you could explain to him the danger of his

actions. No one is to be out after curfew, and especially not over the walls. See to it."

"Of course," my father said. "Thank you for informing me."

The Guardian nodded, released me, and disappeared back into the dark. Then there was silence.

My mind churned for something to say. I could feel my father's eyes on me, disapproving, as I stared at the dirt floor.

"I . . . I . . . was just looking," I said. "I didn't go past the wall, I just climbed up. I lost track of time, and I just wanted to see—"

"Stop," he said. "I don't need an explanation. I don't care why, or what brought you there, it will never happen again. Do you understand?"

I glanced up at him. His face was hard. I knew I should just nod and agree, but I found my lips forming something else.

"But why not? Look what I found, Father." I reached into my shirt and brought out the dead, hairless rodent. "I caught it for us."

He snatched the thing out of my grasp and flung it to the ground. "Stupid. Do you know what the penalty is for hoarding? And you told me you didn't go over the wall. Don't you dare lie to me, Ishvandu! Did you go into the desert?"

I stared at my little offering, cast aside like garbage, and my face started to burn. "So what if I did? Nothing happened, and what's wrong with catching a little meat? Rules! Always rules. I'm sick of them."

He struck me, and I staggered back, lifting a hand to my mouth, tasting blood.

"You're too old for that talk, Ishvandu. This Renewal you begin your Tasking. Learn to obey, not question. How many times have you gone into the desert?"

I glared at him. "All the time."

"That stops tonight. Do you understand?"

"No. I don't. It's stupid. Nothing happened. Nothing ever happens."

His face darkened. "Nothing? What do you know, Ishvandu? What do you know of its horrors? It is dangerous, forbidden, and at Kaprash of all times! You could have been killed!"

"But I hate this place! I want to see the desert, like the Guardians do. And I want to see—"

"Don't be a fool! The only thing in the desert is death, and the sooner you learn that, the better. You're not a Guardian, and you never will be."

A tremor ran through me. The word hung there, scornful and taunting. *Never*. He was right, of course.

"You're a coward," I said, looking him straight in the eye. "You're all cowards."

He went still. Still and cold. Then he crossed the room and seized me by the hair, throwing me to the ground. I didn't cry out when he beat me, though the cane made painful welts across my back and arms. I pressed my face into the ground, I covered my head, grit my teeth, let my anger act as a shield—counting each stroke. Seven. Eight. *I hated him. I hated him. I didn't regret my words, not one.*

He paused at last, breathing hard. "How many times?"

"Thirteen." I fought to keep my voice steady. "That's two better than last time—"

He grabbed my arm, shaking me. "How many times, how many times must I tell you? Mind your tongue. Mind your *place*. Everyone in Shyandar has a place, and until you learn *sense*, yours is to do as you're told. You want the shadows to find you? Is that what you want? You want to be roped up as a lawbreaker?"

"Wouldn't you be glad."

I thought he'd hit me again. His breath came out sharp. Then he dropped me with shove.

"Bed. Now. One more word out of you, it'll be two better yet. Ungrateful little rat."

I complied, scrambling to my corner and throwing myself onto the skinny pallet. Only when the thread-bare sheet was over my head did I bury my face in my arms and let a few tears squeeze from my eyes.

Chapter Three

It was dark below the Guardian's Tower. The chill of the holds ate through my skin, as blood dripped, dripped from my wounds. But blast it all, I would *not* call for help.

At first I had tried to sleep, but I woke repeatedly, legs tingling, body aching. I stood and paced—two tight steps one way, two back. This was when panic set in. Confined. Cut off. Skyless dark. Was it night? Day? I couldn't tell.

I leaned against the clay wall. My head was spinning, made worse because I couldn't see. My tongue stuck to my mouth. I groaned.

"What's the matter?" Koryn's voice echoed from the neighbouring hole. "Losing blood?"

"A little."

"Thirsty?"

I laughed. The sick-camel sound grated out of my throat, and that was answer enough.

A moment of silence. Then: "They gave *me* water."

"I hate you."

"I could toss you some."

"Go ram something up your ass."

Koryn chuckled. "You know what your problem is, roach?"

I shut my eyes. Yl'avah's might, there was nowhere to escape. I considered screaming just to drown out the sound of his voice, but I was too parched for that.

"Your problem is you try too hard. You're desperate—everyone can see it. Only you've got it all wrong. You think being a Guardian's about pride, but it's not. Or maybe skill. It's not. Not courage. Not power. Not knowing more or knowing better. You know what it is?"

I focused on breathing. It was getting difficult. It felt like there was a weight on my chest. Like I couldn't quite fill my lungs. Like the dark was circling and circling. Pressing nearer. Reaching for me.

Light and all, no. This couldn't be happening. Not now. Not *here.*

I pressed my arms against either wall, bracing myself. It had been a long time since the memories. They were close—they were always close. But I kept them locked behind an unseen door, studiously avoided. Only the dark revealed it. The confined, lonely dark.

"Koryn, shut up." I was breathing hard.

"Following orders, Vanya. That's the secret. That's all. A Guardian follows orders. A Guardian obeys."

I wasn't listening anymore. I couldn't. I could only feel the shadows. The pressing, reaching shadows. Cold. Cold like fire. No one understood that kind of cold. No one but me.

I started to shake. Loud, tight breaths.

"No." I shook my head. "You're not here. You're *not.*"

"Vanya?" Koryn's voice was distant.

I paced again. Hard. Fast. The space was getting tighter. Tighter with every turn. *No, no.* I had to stop. I folded to the ground, fists tight, clutching my head, trembling. *Focus.* They were whispering to me. I heard them. Slivers in my head. As thin as the cold, as the stars, as hunger, as starlight.

Save us.

"Listen, you crazy mudfoot, there's nothing here. Just shut up. Here. Take it, you useless . . ."

I groaned and covered my eyes. I couldn't breathe. Couldn't . . . The shadows tightened over my chest. I was somewhere else. I was . . . I was . . .

It was coming. I couldn't escape. Couldn't . . .

A scream was building in my chest. I could see them. I called out for help, calling out, over and over—

"Vanya?"

My eyes cracked open. There was light. A new voice. Hot, red light dripped from above. I sucked in a breath, bent double.

"Kylan?" My throat hurt. I must have been shouting. But the light drove back the shadows. The memories. I wiped a hand across my eyes, forgetting the bandages, smearing blood and tears together in a pathetic mess.

A rope slithered down. I heard someone climbing, feet tapping, light and quick. Then he was next to me: a flash of white robes, of bright hair, like fire in the torchlight. "Vanya?"

I swallowed my relief. *It was him, thank Yl'avah.* How did he know? How did he *always* know? They had sent for a healer, and he'd known.

"I'm okay," I said weakly.

He clutched my hand. "You're not. Yl'avah's might, you're not. Doesn't anyone in this blasted Hall know how to bind up a cut? You could have bled to death down here. And you're dry. I can tell. Why haven't you been drinking? Here!"

He seized a nearby water skin—Koryn's. Must have tossed it over.

"Not my water," I scowled.

"Well, it is now. Here."

"No." I pushed him away. "I'm not drinking Koryn's piss."

"You stubborn, delusional ass. It's just water. *Drink it.*"

He shoved it between my lips. It was sweet. It was cool. It was water. Precious, beautiful . . . I spat it out.

For a moment, he just stared. Then he was dragging me to my feet. "One of these days I'm going to say no. They're going to send a camel to fetch me, and I'll just say no. Let him die. He deserves it. He does everything he can to deserve it. He's irremediable."

"What in the blazing sands does that even mean?"

"Past all hope."

"Sounds about right," I said with a weak laugh.

He chuckled. "I know. It's taken me a long time to find the right word to describe you, my friend, so I'm going to use it as often as I can. Now climb."

KULNETHAR AB'ETHANIR, only son of the High Elder and a self-right-eous twat because of it, led me to the room above the holds. It was only marginally better. A rough-spun mat, a low table, and a basin were all that occupied it. Given the present long Kaprash, there was enough water in the basin to soak a rat's paw. I drank anyway. I stuck my whole face in, stopping just shy of licking the bottom.

"Thanks for sharing," Kulnethar said brightly.

"Shut it, white-robe." I wiped my mouth. "I know the treatment you get in that Temple of yours. More than enough water. I was Tasked there too once, in case you forgot."

"Oh, never." Kulnethar dropped his camel-skin satchel onto the table. "But you weren't there during Kaprash, if I recall, so you don't get to talk. Look at it this way: keep it up, picking fights with Guardians and flapping off to them like the brat kid I remember, maybe you'll get to come back." He grinned.

"Does that mean your father's forgiven me?"

"Always, Vanya. But forgotten? Not a chance. Still, maybe he'll let you pull weeds for me. Now sit."

I knelt and held out my dripping arm. It betrayed me. My hand was trembling so hard I could have sifted grain with it.

Kulnethar shook his head. His bright hair and bright blue eyes were the same as ever, as was the worried frown pinching his lips. But he held his silence. He cracked open his satchel and set to work, unwrapping, mopping up the blood, shaking his head, then flushing the wound and binding it back up. The cleansing ointment had a sharp, pungent odour, and I wrinkled my nose.

When he finished, he moved on to my hand and repeated the steps. About half way through, he sighed and opened his mouth.

"Don't," I said.

"Don't what?"

"You know what. That look. That ab'Ethanir look. The one you get right before you tell me something I already know, and you know I know, but you're afraid I don't know *well* enough, hence your burning desire to re-enlighten me. Don't."

Kulnethar's smile was a little thin. "Vanya, you say that you know, but it's the doing that matters. A keshu did this."

"So?" My lip curled. "No, forget I said that. Please. Spare me. Not right before the Circle. I'm going to get it bad enough as it is. Just . . . please."

He gave me a sympathetic glance—almost worse than his cautionary one—and nodded. "Okay, Vanya."

"Thank you."

He finished wrapping my hand in silence. Then he soaked a rag in more of that pungent liquid and held it to my face. "Here."

"No way."

"Vanya, you look like you've been crying."

I snatched the rag and scrubbed my face from my eyes down to my chin. It stung, but felt clean. Kulnethar said nothing else, just gathered his things, took back the rag, and shut his satchel.

"Good luck," he said.

I nodded.

"And Vanya?"

"Yeah?"

"You still owe me a game of jik'u."

I snorted. "Then don't be so scarce. You know where to find me."

"Hopefully not in the holds again. I *hate* that place."

"Me too."

"Good. Stay out of it. I'll be back to check on you in a few days. You better be ready to lose."

"Last I remember," I called after him, "I was up by three."

He held up two fingers on his way out, then he was gone.

Chapter Four

Not long after, they came for me, two grim Guardians of the first kiyah. They led me back to ground level, then up the large, sweeping stairs, passed the sentries, and into the Circle Chamber.

A few members of the Circle sat there around the outer edges of the room, raised on chairs of stone. High arched windows let in the light, silhouetting their forms and bathing the centre of the stone floor in warm, morning sun. The Guardians motioned me forward, then took their positions at the door.

It would be a breach of protocol to glance around me, but from my position, I could see Umaala ab'Krushaya a little to my left, another Guardian Lord out of the corner of my right eye, and Neraia sai'Kalysa, straight ahead. As leader of the first kiyah, she would pronounce the judgments of the Circle. I dropped my head in a deep nod, hands clasped behind my back, as was proper, and waited, hoping I didn't appear as terrified as I was.

"We will be brief," Neraia said. "Your actions were unacceptable, and the latest in a long string of offences. You make an unfortunate habit, Ishvandu ab'Admundi, of rash, unthinking decisions, including apparently the decision to attack a full Guardian, your superior, with a Guardian's keshu."

"I didn't attack him, sal'ah. Koryn—Akkoryn ab'Kindelthu—he wanted to fight."

"You have nothing to say to this Council," she returned.

"But sal'ah," I glanced up, "he was beating one of the Novices for no reason. My friend. How is that—"

"Enough!"

I tightened my jaw. Of course she would take the side of her own son.

"You will be given twenty lashes for your insubordination, and if you step out of line once more, on anything, you will be ejected from this Hall. As such, the earliest chance you have at being named Guardian will be postponed to your nineteenth year."

The blood drained from my face. "A . . . a whole year more, sal'ah?"

"This is not up for discussion. You are dismissed."

THE LASHES WERE PAINFUL, but they didn't sting as much as the humiliation. Stripped and bound in the centre of the yard, I was a spectacle for any passing Guardian or Novice, until someone from the sixth kiyah, the Hall's enforcement, laid into my back with a whip. It was done the same way Guardians did everything: straightforward, serious, and efficient. I ground my teeth and refused to cry out, though every stroke seared my back, ripping off a strip of skin from my shoulders to my ass. But worst of all was Koryn, standing and watching, bearing no sign of any repercussions himself. He stood, arms crossed, head tilted, as if amused. Yl'avah's might, I could have murdered him.

By the time I staggered back to the Novice's quarters, I was angry and sore. My back was flaming from the deep bite of the whip. Part of a Guardian's training was to be above pain, to acknowledge its role, then master it, control it. Groaning and whining would just prove I wasn't ready. Still, when I discovered a few Novices hiding in the hall, seeking shelter from the midday heat, I wasn't in the mood for their gawking stares.

"Get out," I said.

They hesitated, then jumped up and abandoned the hall without a word.

I found my pallet in the far corner of the room and collapsed face first into the pillow. *Light and all, another year!* I was already the oldest in the room. Tala was a Guardian now. So was Antaru, Naomi, Koryn . . . almost everyone I had known as a Tasker in those first years, before I had Come of Age. It was unbearable. And maybe Koryn was right—what would Tala have to do with me now?

Sandals scraped at the entrance. I recognized Polityr's hushed voice, followed by Bray's not-so-hushed one. The same pair of Novices I had defended in the camel yard.

"Vanya?" said Polityr. "It's me and Bray."

"I know. Go away."

They ignored me, and Polityr let out a whistle when he saw my back.

"Sands, Vanya, they really gave it to you this time, didn't they? I told you to let me fight him."

"Idiot. We'd still be picking up pieces of you all over the camel yard."

The big Novice laughed. "Not with a keshu, you dolt. I wanted to *wrestle* him. I mean, don't get me wrong, it was quite the show, but I think you earned this one."

"Does it hurt?" Bray piped in. I turned my head to glare at him. "Alright. Yeah. Stupid question." He flopped onto a mat, one hand tucked behind his curly head, while the other probed his bruised cheek. "I guess I should thank you. Akkoryn would have pounded me to dung if you hadn't stood up to him. You were brilliant."

"Don't count on it again. Next time you open your shitty mouth to someone like Koryn, I won't lift a finger to help you."

Polityr chuckled as he leaned up against the wall, thick arms crossed. "Course you would. I know you. You like breaking the rules too much."

"Blood and light, I mean it, you two! Just do as you're blasting told."

There was a pause, though neither seemed bothered by my outburst. Bray just snickered.

"Did you see the look on Koryn's face when Umaala chastened him like a Tasker? Worth it."

"Not this time," I said.

"What?" Polityr grinned. "A beating never stopped you before. What happened?"

"None of your concern—except I mean it. Either of you get into trouble again, and you're on your own."

Bray seemed to hear me for the first time. He blinked, glanced at me, glanced at Polityr, then glanced back at his toes. "Sorry," he finally muttered. "Didn't mean for this to happen."

"Not your fault," Polityr said. "Koryn's a stupid sack and Vanya was looking for a chance to fight him. You just gave him a good excuse is all."

I said nothing, wishing they would go away. And glad they didn't. They continued to chatter over my head.

"You think Kaprash can go on much longer?" Bray asked.

Polityr shrugged. "Why not? Two years ago, it lasted five months."

"Five and a half," I muttered into my pillow.

"Five and a half," said Polityr. "A blasted long time, far as I'm concerned. It'll only be four this moon."

"But last year it was only three," Bray said.

"Last year we needed it. After the Long Kaprash, our stores were so low we would have died every one of us."

"Does the Avanir know?" Bray asked, wide-eyed.

"Maybe," said Polityr.

I snorted.

"What?"

"You're both idiots."

"Thanks." Polityr grinned. "Why are we idiots?"

"The Avanir is a big dumb rock. Of course it doesn't know. Kaprash will last as long as it lasts, no matter how many die of thirst or disease. It's random."

"Is it?"

I shifted so I could meet Polityr's dark, steady eyes. "Yes," I said. "It is."

"What if it's not?"

"Then whoever's in charge is cruel, stupid, and mean."

"Careful." He laughed. "If the Elders hear you talking about Yl'avah that way—"

"Yl'avah's abandoned us. You think the Maker is watching? You think he cares? No, I'm talking about the Tree, the one who sent us here. Either she's real, and she hates us, or we've thought her up in our heads to give us a reason, *any* reason, for kicking around this desert like rats in trap, just around and around and around. Kaprash, Renewing, Kaprash, Renewing . . . Dying over and over again. And what for?"

Polityr made a sound in his throat. Bray shifted. I glanced at them. "What?"

"They *did* say the shades made you a little crazy," Bray said.

"Hush," Polityr frowned.

"Why?" Bray said. "It's true."

"It is *not* true. Vanya's not crazy."

"Maybe I am," I said. "Maybe I'm two steps from the edge. You're lucky I don't go sand-shit loopy and murder you all in your sleep."

"See?" Bray said.

"Vanya, don't encourage him," Polityr sighed. "Look—you're implying the Chorah'dyn is separate from Yl'avah. But the Elders teach the will of Yl'avah is fulfilled in the Great Tree, so the two are joined. Right?"

"Pol—" I rolled my eyes.

"So," he continued, undaunted, "if Yl'avah's will is carried out through the Chorah'dyn, and the Chorah'dyn's will is bound to the Avanir, then it follows Yl'avah is in the Avanir. Which means you can't argue the Maker has abandoned us."

"Then explain the long Kaprash."

"Explain the Renewing," he returned, dropping to his haunches, leaning forward, eager. He loved a debate. He could argue three sides at once, if he saw fit. "Explain the Choosing—power given *every year* to three individuals. Power to survive the desert. Power to cleanse the Lifewater. Where does the Avanir's power originate, if not the Chorah'dyn?"

"Power isn't everything. Shatayeth had power when he destroyed his own Undying kin."

"True," Pol ceded. "But his power is bound in himself. He can't bestow it."

"Maybe he can, he just doesn't want to."

"Don't you think he would have? A thousand and a half years of Kyre'an power—don't you think he'd have tried something, *anything* to raise an army against Kayr?"

I snorted. "If you believe everything the Elders say, he was busy corrupting Kayr long before its fall. He didn't need armies. Just time. And when you're Deathless . . ." I shrugged, and the motion caused my whole back to arch in pain.

"Fine, fine. Forget that line of argument. We're straying from the point. The Chosen, Vanya. They say the power of the Chosen rivals that of Shatayeth himself—where could power like that come from, but from the Maker and the Tree?"

"I don't know," I grimaced.

"Exactly. The—"

"Pol. Please. I hurt. Just . . . just shut up for a bit, okay?"

He sighed, deflated. "Sands, you know I hate it when you do that."

"I know."

"Fine. But when you're less grouchy, we're going to revisit this."

Then we heard the quick tap of feet on the stone floor.

"You stubborn idiot!" a woman's clear voice rang into the hall. I looked up. Atali sai'Neraia was planted in the entrance, hand on her keshu, chin thrust into the air to make up for her short stature.

Polityr kicked Bray in the shin and they made a quick exit.

"You couldn't just walk away, could you?" she demanded.

"Not a chance."

"He was baiting you, ass-wit. He set you up! And you know what's the worst part? You're so damned full of yourself, you *knew*, and you challenged him anyway."

"So what am I supposed to do?" I pried myself up on an elbow. "Let him get away with whatever he wants?"

"No—just be smart. Think for once! What he wants more than anything is you gone."

"Well, he might get that."

She sighed and strode to the edge of my mat, paced a few times, then found a spot on the wall and slid to the ground, her keshu resting across her knees. "Koryn said you were almost ejected. Was it that bad?"

"Apparently. Next time I step out of line I'm gone, and now I won't have a chance to be Guardian until my nineteenth year."

Tala nodded and leaned her head back against the wall. "Well, that's not so bad, I guess. You just have to behave for another year."

We exchanged glances, I raised a brow, then we both burst out laughing. I buried my face into my pillow, chuckling and groaning in pain, while Tala laughed loudly, letting it bounce off the walls. Doubtless the Novices eavesdropping at the entrance were properly confused.

My mirth faded as I watched her, watched the glint in her eye, the way she threw back her head. Only Tala could berate me one moment and grin with me the next, and every word, every glance was a treasure.

Sands. I frowned. She was a Guardian now. I was a Novice. I had no place even considering it—Koryn was right about *that*. But I had waited my year. Waited in agonizing silence. Waited to be named Guardian. And now . . .

"Just try not to get caught doing anything stupid, Ishvandu ab'Admundi," she grinned. Then saw the look on my face. "What's on your mind?"

You, I almost blurted out. It was easy to be honest with Tala. Too easy. But perhaps now wasn't the best time to make a scandalous confession. "Umaala ab'Krushaya," I said. "He won't let them toss me, I know it."

"You know it?" She raised a brow.

"He . . ." He *what*? Believed in me? It sounded ridiculous, and I wasn't even sure it was true. Except somehow, even when he was tearing a strip out of me, I trusted him. "He's got sense," I said.

Tala chuckled. "Vanya, do you have any idea what an arrogant ass you are? He's got sense enough to keep you, so all the rest on the Circle, my mother included, are just . . . what? Idiots?"

I dropped my head to the pillow with a groan. "That's not what I meant."

"Yes, it is." She grinned and stood up. "But I agree. Umaala's got sense. Just don't count on that going in your favour quite yet, Novice. Take it easy."

I watched her walk down the length of the hall, a red Guardian's sash circling her waist, bringing out the sway of her hips, and all my insides knotted up. *One more year.* Light and all, but I wanted her. If she knew, maybe . . . maybe she would wait. Or maybe, like Koryn threatened, she'd drop me like a bug.

Chapter Five

Only a few days later, and I was sparring again, left hand bandaged, moving slowly to avoid breaking open the scabs on my back. It wasn't working very well. Though a year younger than me, Bretina was quick and she moved in unexpected ways, charging in for a blow when you thought she would take a step back, or dodging right, when you thought she would go left. As the oldest, I was expected to be the best of the Novices, but Bretina was a challenge.

"From your feet, Ishvandu," the weapons-master called as he walked past, tapping the ground with a long, slender staff. "Pull back. That's it. Bend with it. Your whole body is the weapon."

"Doesn't feel like it today, Tushani'sal," I said. Using the weapons-master's given name was a liberty the old man encouraged.

"Why not?" His voice crackled with age, sharp eyebrows pulled into a question. He stopped and watched as we circled each other.

I grimaced. "Do you have to ask?"

"Ah, you mean this?" His staff flashed out and rapped me on the back, not hard, but I gasped in pain and spun, instinctively batting the staff away. There was a crack. Tushani'sal pulled back, swirled the staff, and stabbed with the end like a spear. It caught me in the gut. I staggered back, tried to reposition, but he took a few, simple steps one way, back the other, staff whirling, and before I knew it, one end snapped against my leg. I swiped and missed, and the other cracked into my side, then swept up and tripped the legs out from under me. I landed on my back with a hiss of pain.

"Up," the weapons-master said.

I groaned. "Tushani'sal . . ."

"Up, up. Do you think a Guardian lets himself be caught on his back? You get tripped, you move. Always move. Now. Up!"

I rolled, staggering to my feet, feeling a few fresh cracks open along my back, blood sticking to my robes. He came at me again, and this time I dodged, swinging my training sword one way, then back up, knocking the staff aside, ducking under another blow, moving through the pain. He went for my leg, and this time I swept the sword down, deflecting, leaping back to dodge as he followed through, then lunging in. *Got to get in close.* He blocked my swing, but I twisted and brought my elbow up hard, straight into his face. He grunted, used his weight to push me away. The staff whirled, changed direction, snapped back and caught me in the side of the head.

A moment later I was on my knees, blinking. The weapons-master was beside me, his staff tapping, tapping.

"Better," he said. "Much better."

I bit back an angry retort. Yl'avah's might, that last one hurt! My back was stinging, bleeding, my head pulsing. Tushani'sal's hand appeared next to me and I took it, standing with only a faint grimace.

"Never let pain control you in a fight. It's your body's advice, nothing more." He smiled. "But you're getting faster. When you want to be. Watch that down-swing. You tend to overextend yourself and you leave your side exposed. Keep your movements tight, controlled. Got it?"

"Yes, sal'ah. Move and counter-move." I rubbed my head and checked my fingers for blood.

He chuckled. "You're fine, Novice. Carry on."

Bretina was watching, arms folded, sword dangling from two fingers, like she was bored. "I don't need you to soften him up for me, Tushani'sal," she said with a sigh. "I can do that myself."

"Huh," the weapons-master grunted. "Take what advantage you can, Bretina sai'Anira, when your honour allows."

The old man strode off to the next pair of Novices, half-leaning on his staff, tapping the ground when he had something to say. Even during Kaprash, we trained. Or as Tushani'sal would have said, *especially* during Kaprash. A Guardian learned to train through the heat, through parched throat and empty stomach—through pain. "Every body has its limits," he would say. "You will learn to reach those limits. Then push a little further."

I faced Bretina, her sleek dark hair loose around her shoulders. We weren't allowed to wear Guardian's braids yet, but most kept their hair short or bound. Not Breta. She tossed her head, always managing to look elegant—and a little annoyed.

"So what are you waiting for, Ishvandu? Come on and try me."

My head was starting to throb, but I closed in, lifting my sword again. I thought of what it was like to wield a keshu, for those few, precious moments, the feel of a real blade, its surprising lightness, its strength and reach and deadly precision. Not like these small, blunt training swords. Something about holding that blade had felt good. Right.

I realized I was distracted when I missed Bretina's opening stance. She closed in, faster than I had expected. By the time I hurried to block, readying a counter-blow, she changed directions, spun the other way, slammed the heavy blade into my midsection and as she danced around me, she gave a playful shove from behind. Winded, head still spinning, back fiery with pain, my feet got tangled up and I sprawled into the dust.

Bretina laughed. "I didn't think I pushed that *hard*, Ishvandu."

"Oh, he's just a little sore still, aren't you, Novice?" said another voice. *Koryn.* "Or is that how you normally fight? I can't seem to remember." I pushed myself up onto my elbows and reached for my sword, but the young Guardian kicked it away, sending it skidding a good ten paces across the yard. Past another pair of Novices who glanced up, saw Koryn, and quickly backed away.

"Blood and light, Koryn. Don't you have better things to do?"

He slammed a foot onto my back, shoving me into the dust again, knocking my chin hard enough I tasted blood. "That's *sal'ah* to you now, roach. Don't forget it." His foot twisted, opening more scabs.

"Akkoryn," the weapons-master called, voice calm. "Please stop interfering with my Novice's training."

"Interfering?" He laughed. "A Guardian should know how to fight from this position, too. Don't you think? So, what now, roach?"

He kept twisting slowly, painfully, his whole weight leaning into my back. I gasped, struggling to push myself up.

"Akkoryn, enough."

The foot lifted off my back. "You're right, Tushani ab'Turana. A Guardian would never find himself in such a humiliating position in the first place. My apologies."

He sauntered off.

My hand curled around a stone. I leapt up, chest heaving. *Step out of line once more, on anything . . .* I could see the stone, a quick arc across the sand, then *thwip*—into the back of Koryn's head. My whole body was trembling with the effort to restrain myself. *One more year.* Yl'avah's might, how was I going to do it?

"Careful, Ishvandu," said Tushani'sal, watching. "It's not worth it."

Of course it wasn't worth it. But *sands*, I wanted to. Then I followed Tushani'sal's gaze behind me. Umaala ab'Krushaya was approaching. One glance at Bretina, and the girl sighed and went in search of a different sparring partner. I watched her go, but my eyes were pulled into a fierce scowl, hands tight at my sides.

"It's not fair, sal'ah."

Umaala could have reprimanded me. Instead he rested a large hand around the back of my neck—avoiding the lash marks, I noticed. "I need to speak with you."

"What for?"

He grunted and lowered his head to one side, as he always did when he wasn't amused. Which was often.

I sighed, letting the stone fall. "Yes, sal'ah. Of course. What is it?"

"With me," he said. Then he turned and made for one of the side rooms. The Hall itself enclosed the main yard, while the Tower rose out of the centre, all circled by stark, red stone walls. Umaala strode to one of the storage rooms and I followed, wondering what he had to say that couldn't be shared in public. Normally, the Guardian Lord was blunt and conspicuous. Apparently this was different.

We ducked into the room, only a few eyes following, and the cool shadows closed around us. There was a large water urn by the door. Umaala dipped a cup and handed it to me, and I accepted it with a frown, wiping the sweat off my face and drinking, trying not to wince as every movement rubbed the hemp-weave robes across my stinging back.

"You seem upset," Umaala said gruffly. "Explain."

I snorted. Why under the blasting sun did he want—or need—an explanation? But I seized the opportunity anyway. "Koryn," I muttered. Then glanced at him. "Akkoryn ab'Kindelthu. Sorry, sal'ah. But he does everything he can to humiliate me, and if I so much as breathe in his direction, I get tossed from the Hall. Is that it?"

He grunted. "It is what it has to be. Adapt."

"How is that fair, sal'ah? I mean, what about *his* role in the whole thing? He was the one who started it, knocking Bray around for no reason, getting me to fight him. But he hasn't had to face one consequence, sal'ah, not—"

"Ishvandu, you've made yourself clear."

I tightened my jaw, glancing away to hide the anger bubbling in my eyes.

"You have much to bring to this Hall," he continued. "You have faced things, *seen* things."

I shifted. "That's no advantage, sal'ah."

"It is."

"But no one even speaks of—"

"I'm not finished."

I shut my mouth.

"As I was saying, you have much to bring to this Hall. But that is *nothing* compared to all you have to learn: how to control yourself, for one, and how to take responsibility. Don't forget why you're here. You think you have a right to it? You think you were chosen?"

My face burned. "How could I forget when everyone keeps shoving my face in it? Shouldn't I have a chance to move on? That was years ago."

"Prove it."

I frowned at the dirt floor. *Prove it*, that's all they ever said. Koryn, the Circle, even Umaala.

"How?"

"Show them you're not the undisciplined thieving brat the High Elder dumped on us six years ago. Another year is what you need, and I'll not hear one more word of blame. This was no one's fault but your own. Do you understand? You're lucky something worse didn't come from it."

"So what should I do, sal'ah? What should I do when I see someone like Koryn hurting my Novices?"

"Something that doesn't involve you trampling every rule you can in the process! Think, boy! I don't care that you knew Akkoryn when he was a Novice—he's a Guardian now. There are things you cannot do, and grabbing a keshu to duel him is one of those things. Blood and light! What if you actually hit him with that sword you were so madly waving around? If you had killed him, it would be your own life for his. The ropes, boy. Do you understand? And what would that prove?"

"Koryn's no Guardian," I said. "'Defend the innocent.' Whatever happened to that oath?"

Umaala seized the front of my robes, almost lifting me off my feet. My breath caught. His thundering eyes were close, voice low. "You're not listening, Ishvandu. It's not about Akkoryn ab'Kindelthu, it's about you. Do you understand?"

I nodded.

"*Do* you?"

"Yes, sal'ah." My voice cracked. "It's about me. A Guardian first controls himself."

He released me with a shove. "Besides, I find it hard to believe Ebridyn was as innocent as you claim. He reminds me too much of another Novice I know."

I straightened my shirt, swallowing, saying nothing.

"Now are you ready to listen?"

"Listen, sal'ah?"

"Believe it or not, I didn't pull you aside so I could hear your muttering."

I looked down. "What is it, sal'ah?"

"Right now, as far as the Circle is concerned, you're closer to being a stable hand than a Guardian. This is not about skill or ability. You have to be disciplined, patient, wise, and willing to sacrifice your own interests—your own comfort and safety, and yes, pride—for the good of the Kyr'amanu."

I scowled. That didn't sound like Koryn to me, but I knew if I opened my mouth again it would feel the back of Umaala's hand.

"Wipe that look off your face," he growled. "I don't want to hear a word about anyone else—I'm talking about you. And I would like to think where others fall short, you can do better. Are you listening?"

"Yes, sal'ah."

"Good. Now do you want that chance?"

"Sal'ah?" I glanced at him, confused.

"The chance to move on, to prove yourself. Do you want it?"

I nodded, but warily, not sure what to expect.

"Good. I've convinced the Circle to expand your duties. Starting tomorrow, you will join the fourth on patrol."

I stared at him. It took a full four heartbeats before the meaning sunk in. I didn't believe it. I had already done poorly with the eighth: domestic administration and record-keeping, as much punishment for my wilfulness as anything. Since then, more than a year ago, I'd been given no other assignments, never mind I was getting older. If I had, the seventh or sixth would be the next logical choice. Not fourth. Never fourth. Not with my record.

I swallowed. I looked at the floor. I looked back at him. "Sal'ah . . . h-how?"

"That's not your concern. You will act in absolute obedience. You will show deference to your superiors. You will watch, listen, and follow. You will do nothing else. Is that clear?"

I nodded, breathless at the sudden, unexpected opportunity. "Yes, sal'ah. I will. I . . . I won't let you down."

He grunted, arms folded, eyeing me, as if assessing my sincerity. I wasn't sure what else to say.

"You'll be in the North Fields," he said at last. "Your old quarter. You will know people."

"Is that a problem, sal'ah?"

"Only if you make it one."

"I don't understand. Why . . . why should it matter?"

"Because you've spent most of Kaprash inside this Hall, Novice. You have no idea."

It was then, the way he said it, the lowering of his head, the look in his eye: I knew. There was trouble. The Circle wasn't giving me an opportunity to prove myself. They were giving me an opportunity to fail.

"I can do it," I said, meeting his eye.

"For your sake, I hope so. It's been a long Kaprash."

Chapter Six

Kaprash. The Dryness. It was the time between water. The time of struggling, scrimping, watching, waiting. Waiting to die. I remembered the waiting.

It was the helplessness I hated most. I remembered trudging up the streets of the Labourer's quarter as a child, past the chicken-hutch, all boarded up, a sad, listless clucking from within the only sign of life, past empty urns and cracked pots, past empty faces. A single Guardian stood on watch at the cistern, and already a long line trailed out from him, though the sun had not yet spilled over the Temple cliffs. I sighed and took my place.

Tired faces hovered around me, drooped shoulders, mutterings. Kaprash was getting old. How long had it been? Near three months? How much longer?

The line dragged. No one moved quickly—as a rule. But finally, it was my turn. I shuffled up to the pump. The Guardian on duty, ab'Palinyr, gave me a nod, then looked again. My face was swollen where my father had hit me, and one or two welts were visible below my loose sleeves. Absently, I rubbed at my cheek.

"Talking smart again, Ishvandu?" he asked, his weathered face peering down at me. He took my bucket and started pumping. Water splashed, one careful, dirty-brown drop at a time. "Let me guess. You didn't deserve it this time either."

I scrunched my face. "Never."

"That's the spirit," he chuckled. Then he stopped and handed back the bucket. I stared at it. It was barely half-full.

"Half-measures, I'm afraid. Circle's orders. Use it sparing, and take it easy, now, you hear?"

I wanted to object, but ab'Palinyr was one of the ones I actually liked, and I knew he wouldn't cheat me. Only how could it be half-measures already? I made a face and said nothing. Then I trotted back as quickly as I could without spilling, eager to climb back under my blankets and forget the world.

I turned the corner—and rammed into someone hurrying the other way. The larger weight sent me toppling backwards. I tried to catch myself, but the bucket slipped. I sprawled into the dust, then watched, horrified, as my water leeched into the ground, lost forever.

"No, no, no!" I stared, then craned my neck around. A pale-skinned boy was crouched over me, bright in every way: from his bright sandy hair, to his bright blue eyes, to his white robes. A Temple student.

"Sorry!" he cried, wide-eyed. "So sorry, I didn't see you. Here, let me help . . ."

I shoved him away, scrambling to my feet. My heart was pounding. My water was gone. All of it. Just like that! I imagined the day stretching before me. The lethargy. The sickness. The fuzzy, rough feeling in my mouth as everything became hazy. Would I even have strength to come back tomorrow?

"Look what you did." I couldn't believe it. "Look what you did!"

"I can see." He gave a wry grin.

I leapt at him, seized the front of his robes, and slammed my fist into his nose—three swift blows. Little bones crunched under my knuckles and the boy gave a wail of surprise. Then I shoved him away.

"Stupid, prancing Temple boy! Get out of our quarter!"

His face creased in disbelief as he grabbed his nose. Blood streamed over his lips, down his chin, staining his beautiful clean robes.

"What was *that* for?"

"What do you think, useless white-robe sack?" I shoved my palms into his chest again. "You think water's going to fall from the sky? Don't you even realize what you did?"

"I said I was sorry. Look, I'll get you some more. I can fill it up at the Temple—"

"I don't want your sand-blasted water! Just get out of my face, or I'll hit you again."

"You will, will you?" It was his turn to get angry. He measured me up, one hand still clutching his nose, blue eyes fired. "You think I can't take you?"

"Go ahead and try. I bet you couldn't hit the side of a camel if it was standing—"

His fist struck me in the eye. I staggered back. Then he bowled me over. His weight crushed me into the ground. One bony knee dug into my stomach and his fists flew. I shoved my hands into his face, tried to wrestle him off. We grappled, and whenever I could, I cuffed him in the side of the head, but he was bigger than me and had me trapped. With dawning horror, I realized I was losing to a white-robe. I shouted, struggling harder, grabbing for anything I could—pulling, wrenching.

Then arms were yanking us apart, faces stern. Both of us were bloody and bruised, breathing hard, glaring at each other. Ab'Palinyr appeared and the knot of onlookers parted to let him through.

"Ishvandu, what are you doing? What's going on?"

"My water!" I panted. "What am I going to do? I've got nothing! He . . . ran into me. It was his fault!"

"You ran into me too," the boy shot back.

I tried to lunge at him again, but the Guardian threw an arm across my chest, holding me back.

"Calm down! Both of you." Then he turned to the student. "Kulnethar ab'Ethanir, what are you doing here?"

"I was coming back from Eda's. One of our pots broke, and the medicine won't stay if it's not sealed right."

I felt my face burn. *Kulnethar ab'Ethanir?* It was just my luck to get into fists with the son of the High Elder.

"Ishvandu, I will fill it again," said ab'Palinyr, "but no more fighting. You hear?"

I tightened my jaw, but nodded, and he turned to go. The Temple student did not. "Ishvandu?" the boy asked around his pinched and bleeding nose.

"Go away." I edged towards the pump, but he tugged my arm.

"Hey, you can call me Kylan. No hard feelings, okay? But . . ." he stuck out a finger, pointing to the stinging pain above my eye. "Come by the Temple if you need someone to look at it."

He flashed a grin, then trotted off down the street.

I wasn't sure how long I dozed, but my father's hand shook me awake. It was hot. The dusty strip of cloth I'd pressed to my forehead had slipped, letting the blood drip down and crust into my swollen eye. My whole mouth was dry and sticky.

I grimaced and pressed a hand to my face.

Gently, my father pulled it away, and I could feel his fingers probing the cut. "Come," he said quietly. "Sit up."

I considered shoving him away and turning over—I was still furious with him. But this new incident would need explaining.

I pushed myself up, facing him with one good eye. The bucket was close, as was a small clay bowl with its own thin pool of water. He soaked the cloth in it, not saying anything at first. It made me nervous.

Then he leaned forward and started washing the cut, cleaning the dried blood out of my eye, tilting my head as he worked.

"Ab'Palinyr told me what happened," he said after a moment.

My unease faded, just a little. One less thing I'd have to lie about.

"He spilled my bucket," I muttered.

My father poured another small scoop of water over the bowl and rinsed the cloth. "And you hit him, insulted him, and threatened him. Not just a Temple student, but the High Elder's son."

"I didn't know who he was! And why should it matter?"

He gripped my chin to keep my head from bobbing around, then lifted the cloth again. "It matters. You know it does."

I didn't say anything. He finished cleaning the cut and leaned back, looking at me. I shifted my gaze, glanced at the floor, at the bucket, at my hands. I wasn't sure what he was waiting for.

He sighed. "Tonight, you will come with me to the Temple and apologize for your shameful display."

My eyes snapped back to his face. "What?"

He said nothing.

"But why? *He* was the one who ran into me. I can't go there, I've got nothing to apologize for, I wasn't—"

"Ishvandu."

I scowled as my protests were cut off, knowing it was pointless. It always was.

"You will apologize because I asked it of you. Do not question me further."

WE CROSSED the open sea of sand as the sun sank behind us. The Temple, our oldest structure, was nestled in the sheltering cool of the cliffs, white walls rising on either side of the gate as we approached. I hesitated, but my father's hand rested on my shoulder, urging me on.

I stepped inside, and we crossed into a different world.

Spreading branches gave shade to small greenery below, birds sang sporadically above my head. Even the air smelled fresher. The whole place was still and calm, defying the sun-baked sand outside and the dry lake bed. I felt a pang of jealousy, even as a single keening melody rose up from the depths of the Temple.

I had never seen it so close before. As we meandered through the garden path, the huge white steps and the first tier came into view. Beyond that, each tier was joined by steps cut into the outside of the stone, rising higher and higher. I swallowed, suddenly nervous—but resolved not to shame myself. How many of these coddled students and Acolytes were born here, destined even before their Tasking to join their fathers and mothers in the relatively easy life of study and prayer?

Every child was supposed to go through a full cycle of Tasks, being tested in all the duties of Shyandar. But everyone knew it didn't work like that.

I started up the stairs, my father's hand on my arm, guiding me to the right. We began the large, slow circle, up and around. A few white-robed students and Acolytes hurried past, sending us strange looks. I tried to ignore them.

We were on the third tier when my father caught my arm. "Wait here, Ishvandu. We shouldn't go on without invitation." I frowned, but looked around. A white hall opened beside us, with rooms on either side, and the stairs continued to my right. When I glanced behind, I saw we had already risen above the walls of the Temple, above most buildings in Shyandar. The whole settlement seemed to spread beneath me. I could see the north wall where I liked to climb, and in the distance, the twisting black rock of the Avanir. My stomach churned at the dizzying height.

At last an Acolyte approached, and his nut-brown face seemed kind. "Can I help you?"

My father spoke before I had a chance. "My son exchanged blows with Kulnethar ab'Ethanir this morning. He's come to apologize, if possible."

The man smiled knowingly. "Ah. Was that you? Kind of you to check on him. I'm sure he would be glad to see you. This way."

We continued to climb past the fourth and fifth tiers, each one growing smaller. I tried not to look down, concentrating instead on the man's sandaled feet in front of mine.

Finally, we halted. We were at the very top. "Wait here," the white-robed attendant said, and left us standing there. I swallowed as the wind tugged my loose clothes, threatening to plunge me over the edge. How could anyone live this high above the ground? I stole a look at my father. His bronze face and dark eyes showed nothing. I resolved to look more like that, but as if sensing my fear, he laid a steady hand on my shoulder.

"The High Elder will see you now," the man announced a few moments later.

The High Elder? I wasn't ready for this, but before I could protest, we were ushered through a beaded curtain and into the chambers.

I'm not sure what I anticipated, but this stark room wasn't it.

The ceiling rose high above us, but the furnishings were as sparse as ours, little more than some kneeling rugs, a low table, and two small curtained rooms to the side, where I assumed the High Elder slept—and maybe his son? The greatest extravagance was a window that could be shuttered in a storm, and a potted plant that evidently got sparer rations than us. Its broad green leaves were drooped and folded and a single red flower hung from its crown, withering.

A man stepped from a curtained room and smiled when he saw us. He was younger than I expected, with a neatly trimmed dark beard against fair skin. Blue eyes as bright as his son's twinkled from a kind face, crinkling at the corners.

"Welcome. Yl'avah's peace be upon you."

"And upon you, High Elder," my father said, dropping his head. "Thank you for seeing us. I am Admundi ab'Adaiah, and this is my son, Ishvandu. We've come to apologize and seek forgiveness for the disgraceful way my son acted."

My face burned, but I refused to look away. I waited for the High Elder to glance at me. I met his eye. Then I took a deep breath.

"I'm not asking anyone's forgiveness," I said.

My father's breath echoed like a slap. "Ishvandu!"

"Why should I?" I blazed onward. "Your son ran into me, spilled my water, punched me back. He's no Elder yet—just a student, not even Come of Age. I don't owe him anything. I won't take it back."

My father could barely contain his horror. He clutched my arm. "How dare you insult the High Elder!" he hissed into my ear. "Apologize. Now!"

"I won't!"

He rattled me in panic, and I felt a rush of glee. A little revenge. Oh, I'd get it later, but right now, this was worth it.

Only—the High Elder wasn't upset. In fact he seemed to be *laughing*. He raised a hand. "Now, now. There's no need for that. Your son speaks boldly, but I take no offence. Tell me child, how old are you?"

"T-ten, this Renewing," I replied, still in shock at not being thrown from the room, maybe even the top of the stairs.

"Ten already? Then perhaps we'll have to make a Guardian of

you, with that unrelenting sense of justice!" It was a joke. But I stood a little taller anyway, pleased with myself.

"Jamaala's gone to find my son," the High Elder continued. "He should be here any moment. Would you like a drink? I'm afraid we have only water, but it keeps cooler, near the cliffs." He walked to a basin at the end of the room and dipped two earthen cups as he spoke. By the time he returned, holding out the clean, clear liquid, my father had relaxed enough to release me. We both accepted and drank, though I sensed my father's anger remained. I'd still get it later.

Then the curtain swished behind us.

"It *is* you!" I turned to see the bright-faced boy and took some satisfaction in his swollen nose and bruises. Then amazingly he grinned, and his whole face lit up. "My worthy opponent! Ishvandu, right? Glad to see you again!" He stuck his hand out to be clasped, like an old friend, and for a number of heartbeats, I just stared at it in astonishment, awed by his enthusiasm—and wary.

"Come on!" he cried, then gripped my arm anyway. "No hard feelings, right?"

I was seized by a strange compulsion to like the boy. For a moment, I just stood there, until I realized I was nodding.

"Sure," I said. "Whatever."

The boy's face broke into one of those irrepressible grins, and with that, it was done.

From that day on, Kulnethar ab'Ethanir, son of the High Elder, was determined to befriend me.

My first and strongest instinct was suspicion. No one lucky enough to live in the Temple would bother themselves with a lowly Labourer's son. But he kept finding me anyway. I'd be twining rope to keep my fingers busy, whiling away the boredom of Kaprash and distracting myself from my empty stomach, when he'd come running up with a grin on his face. "Ishvandu!" he would shout. "The Elders say Kaprash will end any day now."

He'd been saying the same thing for a half-month. "It'll end when it wants to," I muttered. "Not before." Once, my father said, it had lasted five months, killing over a hundred Kyr'amanu, and I told him so.

"You're always so gloomy," Kulnethar complained with a laugh. "Don't you think Yl'avah will protect us?"

I shrugged. "He didn't protect my mother. He didn't protect lots of people. He doesn't stop Kaprash. Doesn't sound like he does much."

Kulnethar wasn't sure what to say. It was probably blasphemous to his Temple-ears. But it worked, and he left me alone for a few days after that.

Then, on an especially hot day when I was too weak to even leave the hut, Kulnethar burst through the curtained entrance.

"Ishvandu! I have something to show you. Come on!" He pulled at my arm, but I swatted him away.

"Leave me alone. It's too hot."

"Ishvandu, you have to come." He glanced at my father, who was sitting quietly at the far end of the hut, eyeing us. If I refused, he would scold me. He was afraid of offending the High Elder.

I scowled, but stood up. "Alright. What is it?"

"Just come." He pulled my arm again, then disappeared back into the heat. I groaned.

As soon as I caught up to him, I yanked him to face me. "Look," I said. "I don't like you. I've got nothing to do with you, and you've got no right here. You might have everything you need at the Temple, but I'm hungry, and I'm not running anywhere, so just leave me alone."

Instead of being offended, he just clutched my arms. "I know! We're hungry too, Ishvandu. But Father says we have to be strong." Then he glanced up the narrow street, eyes big, as if afraid someone would be watching. It was empty, of course. All things were empty in Kaprash—especially my stomach. "Come on, there's something I want to show you."

He hurried off, pulling me behind him. He refused to even stop until we left the huts behind and started moving down one of the dry irrigation ditches. The rustling green fields, tops heavy with grain, just waiting for Renewal, stretched around us. There would be Guardians on patrol, but it was easy enough to hide, especially the closer we got to the centre. Finally we dropped behind one of the thick date-palm trunks at the edge of the fields and Kulnethar reached into his robes. He pulled out a sealed flask.

"Look!" he whispered, wide-eyed. "They keep this for the singers. Father says prayers are most important, but I thought . . ." He frowned and a guilty look stole over his face. "I thought maybe we needed it more than Yl'avah. Do you think he'll mind?"

I quickly shook my head, and Kulnethar broke the seal. Inside, smooth, golden cider sloshed around, and my eyes lit up. "Kulnethar ab'Ethanir! How did you get this?"

"I stole it," he confessed. "I'll repent later. But I'm not bringing it back now, right?" He grinned and held it out to me, and with quick, grasping hands, I snatched it up and drank.

I'd never tasted anything so wonderful in my life. My suspicions faded. As I passed the cider back to him, he drank too, and we became co-conspirators. We sat and laughed and started a litany of all the ways we'd get in trouble if anyone found out. I could feel some of my strength returning. All too soon, the flask ran dry, but we stayed for a long time, lounging in the palm's shade, not saying much. The silence was almost comfortable.

I turned to him after a while. "Kulnethar," I asked. "Is it true? Are you my friend?" I wasn't even sure what a friend looked like. I didn't hang around the other boys. But I thought that sharing his pilfered cider was probably something a friend would do.

He laughed. "Of course I am! I said I was, right?"

"But why?"

Kulnethar just shrugged. "Do I need a reason? Everyone needs friends, you know. Even me."

It was a strange thing to say, *even me*. I frowned over that for a moment. Why him? He was the son of the High Elder. He *had* friends. He was important. He mattered.

I glanced out towards the Avanir. It was a lot closer now. The black rock was massive, all the more so because of the empty lakebed. It towered above us, up, up into the painful blue sky, and at the top, its crystalline arms branched at odd angles, bent around each other like a strange, misshapen tree. It was ugly and beautiful at the same time, as compelling as the desert. It was hard to take your eyes off it, once you were looking.

Then I blinked. The sun was hot, and getting higher in the sky, and I had to shade my eyes, but I could swear I had seen something. A glint in the sky, falling from the black monolith.

I grabbed Kulnethar's arm and nearly wrenched it off in excitement. "Look!" Not waiting for him to see, I leapt up and starting tearing down into the dry lakebed, almost tumbling over my own feet.

"Wait, Ishvandu! What is it?" he called behind me.

I didn't stop. I had seen something, I know I had. I prayed it wasn't some cruel trick of the sun. But the sudden whoop of delight confirmed my hopes.

"It is! It is! Ishvandu, you're right!"

Now it was a race. Laughing, we ran as hard as we could, skidding across the cracked and slanted ground. By the time we reached the Avanir, we were panting, trembling, exhausted, but *there!* A little pool of water had formed at its base—fresh, clear, cool water. I got there first and threw myself into it with a splash. Tiny rivulets ran down the sides of the rock and dripped on my face. Kulnethar was a step behind.

"It's over! The Kaprash is over!" He splashed up behind me, laughing, and threw his arms into the air while he danced around the black stone. Then we both drank deeply of the fresh water that had returned like a miracle into the heat of the day.

EVERYONE COME of Age gathered that night for the Choosing— everyone but the children. Hiding from my father never worked, either. It was the Guardian Lord who spotted us, sent us running, the one I would remember for years afterwards: the crimson-cloaked Guardian with his shining sword; the grip that could have crushed my hand; the charcoal-dark skin and the thundering voice.

"Be gone," he said. "This is not your place."

Guardians were always around, overseeing the fields, taking counts, posting sentries, but not the Guardian Lords of the Circle. As I hurried away, Kulnethar urging me on, I kept glancing over my shoulder. I could swear the man's eyes followed me.

"Kulnethar," I said when we were out of sight. "That was a Guardian Lord!"

"I know."

"Did you see his sword?"

"Of course I saw his sword."

"But did you *see* it?" My breath whooshed out. "I've never seen a keshu blade before. It was . . . it shone!"

"I know."

"Like stars!"

"I know, Ishvandu."

We walked in silence for a moment, until I spoke again. "Is it true?"

"What's true?"

"The keshu swords. Do they come from the Old Lands?"

"Yes, of course."

I struggled to repress my excitement. I hated feeling so ignorant. Like Kulnethar knew everything, and I was dull and stupid. But another thought rose up, and before I could stop myself, I was leaning close.

"Do you think it's true? Do you think the Chosen really go back to the Old Lands?"

"Well, of course. It's what the Avanir is for, isn't it?"

"But . . ." I scrunched up my face.

"What, Ishvandu?"

"Well, do they ever come back?"

"Not that I know of."

"So if they don't come back, how do we know it's true? Maybe they just disappear into the desert and die?"

"But the Elders say otherwise."

I huffed. "How can the Elders know what happens to the Chosen if they don't come back?"

"The Elders know. They know lots of things. Have you seen the Library?"

"Of course I haven't seen your sand-blasted Library," I said. I didn't tell him I had no idea what a Library was, and thankfully, he didn't follow that line of questioning.

We walked back towards the Temple in silence. Kulnethar wasn't an idiot, not like the other boys. But sometimes he sure *acted* like it.

"Why do you want to know?" he asked suddenly as we left the Labourer's huts behind.

I shrugged. "No reason." I didn't tell him what I really thought, that maybe one day, just maybe, I would have a chance to go back. If the impossible happened. If, out of all the people in Shyandar, I was Chosen as one of the three. If I got to carry the Avanir's power for myself. Back to the Old Lands. Back to where things like keshu came from, where swords shone like stars and anyone could be a Guardian Lord. If what they said about the Chosen was true.

Or perhaps—my heart pounded just to think of it—perhaps the High Elder hadn't been joking. Perhaps he was trying to tell me. I was his son's friend now. Maybe that made a difference. Perhaps I would be Tasked, even now, to the Hall of Guardians. I could become an outrider. I could explore the desert . . . maybe even the lands beyond. I could make great discoveries, be named a Guardian Lord, maybe even one day Al'kah, and lead a daring expedition back to the Old Lands in the Green East.

My mind danced with possibilities, even while reason held me back. I was just the son of a Labourer. More likely than not, I would never be anything else. And yet . . . and yet . . .

A silly dream.

The moment Kulnethar and I parted, I ran to the north wall. It was dark by the time I got there, but once I climbed up, I could look out across Shyandar, across the clustered huts, all the way to the rock in the distance. Normally black and cold.

But tonight, the most important night of the year, the Avanir was alive. Amidst the dark that had fallen, and the barren sand, and the lifeless, alien stars, far in the distance, where every man and woman in Shyandar gathered, the Avanir was burning like the sun.

IN A WEEK'S time we stood, two dozen of us, huddled outside the Temple walls. The sun was still hidden behind the eastern cliffs, and the air was cool. I shivered. From nerves more than anything.

Some of the boys and girls were talking in low voices, but most were silent like me, shifting from side to side, waiting to hear their fate. We were supposed to be given a chance at all the duties of Shyandar, but from what I'd heard, you were lucky to get two or three different roles in the three years of the Tasking. Your first assignment could last over a year.

Eventually, the gate was thrown open, and a short, ancient-looking Elder shuffled out, joined by four white-robes. We all strained to see him. He just smiled and nodded at us, then began droning on about duty, adulthood, starting on our path to maturity, the joys of serving our people with the gifts Yl'avah had given us. "We each of us are unique, crafted to be one piece of a greater whole, fitted into that place in which no other piece can fit and where no other piece should fit, where you, and you alone, were destined by fate to be fitted. It is our duty, then, to see that you grow in that understanding of your unique abilities and come to the full realization of your potential, that potential that Yl'avah has given to you, and you alone . . . "

I faded in and out, shuffling, watching small insects scurry past my feet, anxious to begin the division. Others were doing the same. I wondered if the Elder thought anyone was actually listening. He seemed to think so, the way his self-important speech puffed out his chest.

"Now, *now* let me begin . . ." he finally announced, and every one of us straightened. Then he produced with a flourish a small scroll from within his robes. Holding it in front of him, he peered at it through narrowed eyes and began to read.

"Kryndia sai'Kylua," he began in a cracking voice. "You will join the Labourers." He gestured to one of the white-robed Acolytes to his right. There was a murmur, and a girl stepped out and made her way to the front.

"Yndeia sai'Itulu, you will join the Temple," came the next one. And then, "Yuvaya ab'Ashvana, you will join the Crafters."

One by one, they were divided into the four Duties. From there, specific assignments would be given, but this was the first and most important step. I held my breath, waiting any moment to hear my name. Most were going to the Crafters or Labourers, as usual. Only one stood for the Guardians. Could it be? I imagined joining him. I imagined walking across the sand, and everyone looking at me in surprise, whispering behind their hands, wishing they had been chosen instead of me.

"Leyana sai'Alyna," he was saying. "Crafters. Karytu ab'Kyrana. Guardians." My ears pricked up. Another! "Ishvandu ab'Admundi. Labourers."

My heart dropped into my feet. As the Elder continued to call out names, I wished a hole in the ground would open and swallow me. Had I heard him right? How could they do this? How could they humiliate me like this? I had been a Labourer my whole life, and they would make that my first Task? I would have done *anything* else. Make me a weaver, for all I cared, just not a Labourer!

Then a scrawny little girl next to me was Tasked to the Hall of Guardians. I looked at her and hated her. It wasn't fair! Why her, and not me? It took everything in me not to shove her to the ground. I could only stand there, unable to move as I should, towards the first and biggest knot of children.

Before I knew it, all the names were called and I stood there alone. The little Elder raised his brow at me over the edge of his list. "Did I not call you?" he asked.

I wasn't sure what to say. I hated him too, and I wanted to jump up and tear his stupid list to shreds. Instead I took a deep breath and lifted my chin. "I think . . . I think there's some mistake, Elder."

His brows shot up again. "I don't believe that's possible, my child. And you are?"

"Ishvandu ab'Admundi," I said. "But I don't think I'm supposed to—"

"Ah, yes! Labourers, it says here. That's Dunava, just to my right. Very good, then. Get to it."

He smiled, pleased to have solved my problem, then turned away without another word and disappeared behind the Temple walls.

No, you don't get it, you stupid old man. I'm not supposed to be a Labourer . . .

I scowled. Of course he didn't get it. I *was* a Labourer, that was all. No one cared about anything else. I trudged over to the group, hanging back while Dunava gave them their assignments, his own little scrap of parchment clutched in a hand.

"Ah," he exclaimed when he saw me. "You must be Ishvandu ab'Admundi. Right?"

I looked up.

"It says here, you'll be Tasked to Admundi ab'Adaiah."

"My *father*?" I blurted out. Everyone stared at me. A few giggled. I shoved the closest one so hard he sprawled in the dust.

"Stop!" the Acolyte grabbed my arm. "What is this?"

"He can't *do* that!"

"It's already been approved."

My face burned with shame, fists tight at my side. Then I yanked myself out of the Acolyte's grasp and whirled away.

"Where are you going? Come back. I must take you to your new place of residence."

I flashed dark eyes at him, voice trembling. "I know the way to my own father's, thanks." Then I hurried away as fast as I could go without running.

I must have wept, because my eyes were burning by the time I stormed back into the dirty little hovel. I found my father mending a patch on one of my shirts, his face as calm as ever.

"I hate you!" I screamed. "I hate you!"

He just looked at me, lifting a single brow as he continued to thread and pull the bone needle. His silence more infuriating than anything.

"Why? How could you do this to me? How could you take away my chance—my *only* chance—to be something? Are you afraid? Jealous? What? Just because *you're* stuck as a filthy Labourer, you think you'll keep me here too? I hate you, and I hate this place! I want out, do you hear me? Tell them I won't stay here!"

My father's face remained untroubled. "You will stay here, until I say otherwise."

"You're just getting revenge!" I wailed. "Because I called you a coward! Well you are one, and I'm not sorry I said it." I was breathing hard, infuriated, more tears threatening to spill out. But he just sat there, saying nothing.

"Then . . . then I'll run away! I'll run into the desert, and you'll never see me again!"

I spun away, but before I could throw myself back into the heat, he spoke. "Ishvandu, stop."

I obeyed, but refused to turn and face him. I never wanted to look at him again.

"Ishvandu, call me whatever names you wish, but for your own safety, if you step foot outside the walls one more time, I will recommend to the Elders you be named a Labourer at your Coming of Age. I know it's what you desire least of all, to follow in your father's footsteps, but you must learn the desert is forbidden. The Elders agree with me in this. I told them what you did, this dangerous habit of yours. No one is allowed outside the walls, except for Guardians and the Chosen themselves. You do not understand, but you must be made to."

I was shaking. A knot formed in my throat. I couldn't think of anything to say, and if I opened my mouth, I would just weep. He did this. Because of the desert. Because of my little haven on the other side of the wall. The place where I dreamed.

But those were silly dreams. I would never be anything. I was just a silly foolish child.

Without a word, I fled, swatting at furious tears before they streaked my face with shame.

Forest

HYRANNA ELDUNA

Year 799 after the fall of Kayr

Let me tell you of Chorah'dyn. She is oldest. Her name means world-root, since before her, there were no Realms—at least, not the ones we have now. Maker breathed, and she called life into place. She led the rivers and mountains. She planted the Dandyri, the red trees of old. She sings snow and summer in their turn. She stands at world's end and tells old things to the dreaming. She whispers of other worlds: seen and unseen, light and void. She is Guardian, she is Mother, and from her, all Life is born.

But for you, my child, she is more.

Interlude: The Last Al'kah

ASHKYNAS AB'ADANI AL'KAH

The desert had an end.

Ashkynas ab'Adani Al'kah, last ruler of his people, knew it. As surely as he was drawn by the burning in his soul. As sure as his need. As sure as the sun baking endlessly into his dark skin and the grains of dust beneath his feet. Just beyond those mountains, and he would find it.

He had to find it. Death did not matter anymore. Sanity did not matter. Only the thing that drew him.

In his mind, he saw light, he saw trees. He saw peace. The Chosen must have lived on, somehow, in the Green East. Must have. For what else drew him? What was this burning? The Chorah'dyn might be dead, but this, *this* was the answer. He would find the Chosen. He would combine his power with theirs. And together . . .

He tripped. The ground struck him in the face. The dust was scalding hot, but his arms and legs had stopped moving. It was good to lie here. It was easy. The ground scorched his skin, and he did not move. The sun burned into the back of his head, and he did not move.

Easy to lie here. How he wished he could. To forget. To let it go— the pain, the guilt, the look in his friend's eyes. *You are faithful. You are faithful.* And the rush of horror, knowing he would do it. That he *had* to do it. That Ishtar ab'Shatara was going to die by his hand. The sacrifice that he, the last Al'kah of Shyandar, was forced to pay.

He clutched the ugly black stone hanging from his neck. The sign of his betrayal—and his purpose. He hated it. It hated him. But it was necessary. Necessary to keep on breathing, to keep on moving. And he *had* to move. It was dying—all of it. The world was Breaking, and he alone could save it.

He hated that most of all.

He dug his hands into the dust, felt the coolness beneath. Wishing, wishing to bury into it, to know relief, to know an end to the endless burning. If only he could lie there and never move again.

Something moved.

Mottled brown shifted beneath a rock. He seized it without thinking.

The scorpion writhed between his fingers and lashed the back of his hand. Over and over again. He felt the pain and twitched. It was good. It made the thing inside come to life, the thing he hated.

Such a little creature, a fierce little spark of life, but enough to kill him. It tried. Ashkynas ab'Adani Al'kah watched as it tried. As the venom spread through his hand like little streams of fire. Then the *thing* woke up, the black stone he had given so much for, and the scorpion began to shrivel. It twisted and cracked and snapped its claws and stabbed.

And then it was dead. A dried-up carapace with stiff, broken legs. He threw it away.

The new fire rushed through him, burning away his weakness. He stood up. One hand still trembled with pain, but he paid no attention. The thing would fix it, as it always did. It would keep him alive, stretch his body long, long past any breaking point. How he hated it!

But if he was going to save the world, he needed all the help he could get.

Chapter Seven

"Get back here, Hyranna Elduna, you miserable excuse for a girl!"

Hyranna whooped as she ran. Her feet hardly touched the earth.

"I'm not doing the stories for you again, I'm not! You'll get it from your ma, if you don't!"

"You'll have to catch me first, Eedi!"

There was no way. Her cousin smacked through every branch and thicket, splashed through the puddles, caught her long skirt, tripped, roared her frustration.

"Hyranna!"

"Thanks Eedi!"

"You're an embarrassment! You hear? An emb—"

Hyranna was too far ahead now. The forest's hush closed around her. She laughed and pushed herself into a sprint, ducking, leaping, almost silent in the morning chill. Her heart woke. It thumped against her chest, beating with the forest and the wild air. She could feel it through her toes: moss and mud, and dew-heavy grass.

She ran as hard as she could, stretching every sense. Knowing every step before she took it. She fell into a rhythm. Lungs opened. Life roared through her. Her black hair streamed out behind her. The short knee-length skirt gave her legs room to fly, and she refused to have it any other way.

By the time she caught up to the hunt, she was winded. She eased into a jog, smiling. She heard voices. Balduin would be happy to see her. He always was.

Then she stopped. The voices were loud, angry.

No.

Her face flashed to a snarl, and she moved into a hunter's run: low to the ground, hand at her knife, silent, quick.

The shouts intensified as she drew near:

"It went that way!"

"It's gone!"

"What happened?"

"*No, no!*"

"Kota!"

And again shouts of, "What happened? What's wrong? Kota, what's wrong?"

A thin shriek rose through the forest like a ghost, just as Hyranna burst onto the scene. A boy was on the ground, clutching his face, wailing, while Balduin knelt next to him—instantly recognizable by his wild, tangled red hair. The other boys were charging towards them.

"Get away from him!" one of the biggest shouted. *Mylar.* He shoved Balduin over, and the scrawny youth sprawled in the dirt.

"Careful, he's hurt!" Balduin cried.

Mylar grabbed for his younger brother, but Kota flinched and pulled away.

"I can't see! I can't *see!*"

"Show me," Mylar said.

The boy shrieked and sobbed, refusing to listen, hands clamped over his face. Had he poked his eyes out with a branch? It wouldn't surprise Hyranna, the way these clumsy idiots ran. But then he stumbled and fell, hands shooting out to catch himself, and she saw his eyes. Both had turned the same lumpy white as curdled milk.

The boys gasped. There was a crowd of them now. Thirteen, including Balduin. And every one of them felt silent with shock.

They didn't even notice when Hyranna pushed through to get a better look. She gaped.

"Maker above," Mylar finally whispered, backing away.

Kota threw his hands over his face and collapsed into a ball, trembling, making pathetic gurgling noises somewhere between a sob and a groan.

"I can't . . ." he wept. "I can't see. I can't . . ."

Balduin edged towards him. "We're here. Kota, we're here. It'll be okay."

"*You!*" Mylar whirled on Balduin. "What did you do to him?"

"Me?"

"Yes, you! You were chasing that elk. You and Kota. I heard you yelling at him. Some wood-witch's curse. What did you do?"

"Nothing. How could you possibly think—?"

"I saw him!" another boy cried, stabbing a finger at Balduin. "I saw him do something with . . . with his hands. It was *his* spear that got the elk. It's his fault!"

"And he touched Kota first after he fell," said another. "He got to him first."

A mutter of agreement ran through the hunting party.

"Don't be ridiculous!" Hyranna marched straight up to Balduin and planted herself next to him. "Back off, Mylar Danu-e! No way you're gonna blame Balduin for this. No way."

There was silence. Everyone stared at her, then at Balduin, then at Mylar, who was still glowering in their direction. A few were brave enough to glance at Kota.

"*Something* happened," one of them said at last. Jerad was the oldest and biggest, though he hung back, watching with furrowed brows from behind his long, neat black hair.

"Yeah, *something*," Mylar said. He grabbed his brother again. This time, the boy didn't resist, but he was shaking so hard the sobs vibrated in his throat.

"We've got to tell Kenan Elduna," said one boy.

"Tell him what?" Jerad asked.

"What we all saw! Isn't it obvious?"

There was a murmur, and Hyranna caught more nervous eyes flashing in their direction.

"Don't bother," Mylar said. "You think he'll listen? As long as his daughter says the witch's bastard is innocent, no one will believe us."

Hyranna growled, but Balduin snatched her hand, pulling her back. "Don't, Anna."

"That's right," Mylar sneered. "You know you're guilty, witch."

"Don't call him that!" Hyranna snapped.

Mylar handed his sniffling brother to Jerad, then faced her, towering over her, fists clenched.

"You know what I think? I think this isn't the first time *something* has happened. Deryn—remember what you saw the other day?"

One of the younger boys nodded. "Yeah, a bird was jumping around on the ground. No wings. Not torn off or anything, just . . . gone."

"That's right. And Jerad *you* saw . . ."

"I remember."

"A huge tree went dead in front of you, isn't that right? All the needles turned brown, you said, one side, then the other, all the way up to the top."

Jerad frowned, as if reluctant to speak of it. "That's right."

"And who showed up a moment later?"

Everyone muttered and turned to face Balduin. "He did," Jerad said. "Balduin showed up."

Mylar let that settle, the murmuring fear punctuated by Kota's whimpers.

Hyranna snorted. "You can't seriously think—?"

"Why not? And there's more, isn't there? Remember Roya?"

Her skin prickled. Balduin took a sharp breath, and the boys stirred uncomfortably, glancing at each other.

"Don't be an idiot, Mylar." Hyranna's voice shook. "Roya has nothing to do with this."

"No? Don't you remember who found her, all sick as she was? Legs useless, just like that, for no reason? But no one questions the fact *he* was there."

Hyranna roared and charged, shoving her weight into him. Mylar stumbled. The boys gasped in shock, leaning forward. Everyone stared at Hyranna.

"Take it back, Mylar Danu-e!" She curled her fists. She was asking for a fight. She was *demanding* one.

"She's just a girl, *get* her!" one shouted.

"Yeah!"

"The Guardian's daughter!" Jerad cried. "Back off!"

"She's asking for it!" Mylar shot back. "*She's* defending the witch."

"Yeah, show her what for!"

"No!" Balduin leapt forward. "Everyone, calm down! We've got to get Kota back. We've got to talk about—"

Mylar punched him. He ducked just in time, taking the fist in his arm, stumbling back. The boys roared their encouragement.

"Get him!"

Hyranna's heart slammed into her ribs. *Maker above, no!* She could feel it: a sudden, dangerous energy. She had to do something. She had to stop this! The boys were hollering over top of each other, edging forward, shaking their spears.

Then three figures materialized out of the forest, and instantly, the clatter froze into silence.

Everyone stopped. Stern faces surveyed the scene. The eldest of the hunters stepped forward. He had long stone-grey hair and black eyes, and he interrogated each boy with a glance.

"What is this?" He finally asked.

"He *did* something to Kota," Mylar said, stabbing a finger at Balduin. "I saw it. We all saw it."

In the silence, everyone could hear Kota's whimpering. He had been forgotten, left huddled against the base of a tree.

The old hunter glanced at Balduin, who was shaking his head, arms spread. "I don't know what happened, Uncle."

"Shit, you don't know," Mylar said. "You cursed him, you mealy bastard!"

The boys muttered their agreement.

"They're lying!" Hyranna said.

"She's just saying that to protect him."

"Enough!" The man threw out a hand. "Jerad Amanti, explain this."

Every eye turned to Jerad—a big oaf as far as Hyranna was concerned—but he had the grace to swallow and flush dark with embarrassment.

"Dal Adis, it's as Mylar says—"

"No. From the beginning."

Jerad glanced at Hyranna. She felt the pleading apology behind his eyes, but he took a breath and began anyway. "We were tracking an elk towards the river. Then there she was, coming out of the forest, a beautiful big creature. We threw. Balduin threw. He was the only one who got a spear in. A good hit. Came out right here." Jerad smacked his collarbone. "I've never seen him hit anything, so I didn't believe it at first. But then he was off, chasing her, shouting something I couldn't hear. Until out of nowhere, he stops. Kota's the first past him. Balduin's shouting at him now, and next we know, Kota's on the ground, and he's screaming, *I can't see, I can't see,* scrambling all over the place. Balduin's holding him. He's got his hands on him, like he's trying to shut him up, and Kota's telling him to stop. Mylar gets there first, pushes Balduin out of the way, tries to help him, and when we finally see Kota, he's . . . he's blind."

There was a hush. Everyone looked at Balduin, whose face was creased with worry.

"Balduin Na-es, what do you say happened?" Dal turned to the boy.

Balduin looked down at his feet. "I don't know."

"That's not a good answer."

"I know, Uncle Dal. But . . . there was something. Something *wrong*. I tried to stop him, and I couldn't. The elk went through it, then Kota."

The boys muttered, and even the older hunters looked wary, except for Dal. "So you didn't hurt Kota?"

"No."

"He's lying."

"Shut it, Mylar!" Hyranna snapped.

"Quiet, both of you." Dal frowned. "We'll discuss this further, but you, Hyranna Elduna, should not be here. You know that."

"Matti said I could go."

"On the Weaving? I doubt it."

"But I *know* the stories! I don't need to sit around and tell them over and over again. I can hunt!"

"Not today. You'll go back. No discussion. Take Kota with you to see your father. And Jerad? Balduin?"

They both looked up.

"I have something to show you."

"What is it?" Jerad asked.

The man's face hardened. "Your elk," he said, and turned back into the forest.

———

Hyranna didn't go back. While Mylar hovered, brooding and whispering to the other boys, she snuck off after Dal and his hunters. The wounded elk had left a blundering trail, and by the time she heard the river, she had caught up to them.

Balduin's tangle of hair was the first thing she saw: it was red as old leaves, unruly and thick, a magnificent mess that he was always shoving out of his face. He was crouched over the elk. His hands were pressed against it, and there were tears in his eyes.

Jerad stood over him, arms crossed. "I don't get it," he said.

"We don't either," said one of the hunters. "It was a fresh kill."

"Not anymore," said Dal.

Balduin sniffed, oblivious to their conversation. His mouth was moving, speaking to the elk as if the soul of the thing could hear him. Hyranna marvelled at him. He was the same age as her—would be fifteen this snow—but sometimes he acted like a child. Didn't he see the way they looked at him? It wasn't just the patchwork skin, milk white and earthy brown all splotched up together like a dyer's mistake, or the wild hair that resisted all attempts at control, or the fact he was taller than any of them at fifteen. Even his strange mother couldn't take all the blame. It was things like this: the way he spoke to the animals like they could hear him, the way he drifted, caught in his own strange world.

"Balduin?" Dal was calling him. "*Balduin.*"

The boy stirred and looked up.

"You said the elk ran *through* something. Can you explain?"

Balduin's blue eyes drifted back into focus. "Explain? No, Uncle. It's just . . . sick."

"It's dead," Jerad muttered.

"Not the elk." Balduin shook his head. "The *forest*. The forest is sick."

Dal's brows sharpened. "What do you mean?"

Balduin just frowned at the elk.

Hyranna edged closer. She could see it now. A flap of hide was peeled back, and the flesh was an ugly grey. Maggots wriggled and squirmed from deep inside. A sour stench hit her, like it had been lying dead for days in the heat. It was rotten.

"Ugh," she said.

Dal sighed, unsurprised at her appearance. "Hyranna."

"I know, I know. I'll go. But is *that* the elk you just killed?"

"Yes," Balduin said.

"Are you sure?"

"Yes."

"Maker above, how?"

"We don't know," Dal said. "But I think we shouldn't touch it. I think we should go."

Balduin nodded. "I'm sorry."

"It's not your fault."

"I know."

There was a pause. Balduin glanced up at Hyranna. "Is Kota okay?"

"How should I know?"

"That was your job," Jerad said. "You were supposed to take him back."

"You honestly think I'm leaving Balduin after you idiots jumped on him like that? *You* look after Kota."

"Hyranna, that's enough," said Dal. "Balduin will be safe with me. Go home. Tell your father and I'll discuss this with him later."

"But—"

"Hyranna."

She sighed. "Fine."

Then Balduin glanced up. "Can I, Uncle? Can I . . . go back with her?"

The elder paused, but gave a curt nod.

"Be at rest," Balduin whispered to elk. "Return to earth and water and the Old Tree."

Then with a swallow and a nod, he straightened and followed Hyranna into the trees.

———

HYRANNA'S PEOPLE had lived in Elamori for years out of count. The caves were deep, and the river wide. Soft muddy banks, cethul stands, and reedy havens gave way to rich soil and neat rows of squash and beans. Cooking smells and laughter drifted up the rocks, birds skimmed the shore, pine trees stood like sentinels across the water. It was, as far as Hyranna could see, the most beautiful place in the world.

The heat was thick and humid by the time they returned, and Hyranna thought of sneaking down to the river for a swim. But she and Balduin barely made it out of the trees before a familiar form barrelled towards them. *Her cousin.*

"Hyranna Elduna!"

Hyranna groaned.

"Sorry," Balduin said. "You know you can't go anywhere with me unnoticed."

"Shut up. They're just jealous."

"Of what?"

"Of your magnificent hair. Who else can build a nest so easily on top of their heads?" Hyranna plucked a tuft of moss out of his curls.

He took both hands, dug them into his hair, and shook it, dislodging a shocking amount of debris. Hyranna ducked and laughed.

"Where have you been?" Eedi's voice slapped through their mirth. "Your mother will skin you this time, on my life, Hyranna Elduna! You're an embarrassment. Why can't you ever do as you're told?" She grabbed hold of Hyranna's shirt.

"Eedi, let go!'

"Why should I? You need my help to do everything! I had to take your place this morning, and what was so embarrassing was I knew the stories better than you. You don't pay attention, you don't care, and you're never where you're needed. You're useless!"

"That's not true!" Balduin leapt to her side. "Anna's the best hunter of us all. She traps and skins and shoots just like—"

The girl laughed in derision. "Men's work! That's not what a woman's for, and if she doesn't grow up and learn, she'll never turn out a woman."

"She's a perfectly fine woman."

Eedi rolled her eyes. "Come on, Hyranna! You're going to find your mother and *apologize*."

Hyranna scowled. Eedi was everything a woman was supposed to be at sixteen: tall, slender, soft-skinned, clear-eyed, and pretty, not to mention promised in marriage in a few moons' time. Hyranna, on the other hand . . .

"Alright, I'm going," she muttered.

MOMENTS LATER, she stood in her family cave, the big one near the river, while Marisela Elduna waved a well-practiced finger through the air.

"You can't just run off like that anymore. You're not a child. You have responsibilities. And you'll be getting more now that you're older. Maker help us! You'll be fifteen this snow, almost an age to marry. What am I supposed to do with a wild girl who won't put shoes on her feet, who runs around the forest half-naked, playing with bows, doing men's work, not even showing up some days until sundown?"

Hyranna rolled her eyes. "Matti, I'm not getting married to one of those stupid boys. I won't."

"Not the way you scoff around, you won't. *Then* what will become of us? Who will be Guardian when your father is gone? Who will be Keeper of the stories?"

"I don't want to be Keeper."

Marisela threw her arms in the air. "You don't get to pick these things like berries off a bush. You are who you *are*. Kenan, tell her!"

Hyranna sighed and turned. Her father sat cross-legged on the floor, eyes intent on his carving while a clever little knife transformed the hunk of wood into something else. Greying hair hung around gentle wrinkles. He had a nose that was a little too big and a face that was a little too round. One dark eye had a habit of squinting, but the other twinkled as he glanced up.

"What do you see here, Anna?" he asked, holding up the half-finished carving. There was a pleasant scratchiness to his voice.

"Papi . . ."

"Oh, come now. It's not *that* bad. You can see it, eh?"

"Of course, Papi. It's Eelun the Dancing Fox."

"And why does he dance?"

"Because he can. That's how he knows he isn't lame."

"But why not crawl on all fours like his brothers? They are not lame."

"It's not the same with Eelun. He limped for seven years, and when he found the Great Tree of Kayr, the source of the Greenwater, it made him well. Now he dances because he can. For every year of sadness when he couldn't run, he wants seven years of happiness because he can."

"And what can we learn from him?"

"That the one who struggles the most for something can be the happiest for finding it."

Kenan smiled. "You see, Mari? She knows one story at least, eh. But Anna, there's something else." He looked at her with a serious face and one twinkling eye. "From Eelun we learn the happiness of everyday things, things we take for granted. Of taking the ordinary, and seeing the extraordinary." He turned the half-finished fox in his hand. "Instead of crawling, we dance."

Hyranna made a face. "You're just trying to tell me to do what Matti says."

"No, Anna-chi. Not at all! I'm telling you whatever you must do, dance."

Her father smiled, and as usual, all his wrinkles lit up.

"But it's not what I *want* to do."

"*Want* has nothing to do with it. We want many things in life we don't get. And many things we don't want, we have. But you know what I've learned? *Want* is fragile. Here today," he blew on the carving, sending a few shavings swirling into the air. "Gone tomorrow. See?"

"Yes, Papi," she muttered.

"Good. Now." He straightened. "I propose a bargain. I will not tell you to act like a little woman and wear shoes and all that nonsense, and you can still go hunting with your friend . . . *if* you promise to do *your* part in being my daughter."

"What part?"

"Well, you should start by recognizing you have a very important place in Elamori. You are my daughter, my only child. That means everything I have will pass to you and the man you choose to marry. The stories, yes, but also the leadership of these people. And leadership requires a very great amount of patience and learning and responsibility. Are you ready for that?"

Hyranna looked down at her toes. "Maybe not."

"Then it's time to start *getting* ready. Eh? I need you, Anna-chi, to start listening to your mother. She knows what's important for you, and if she needs you to be somewhere, or to do something, then *I* need you to take that very seriously. So. What do you think? Is it a bargain?"

Hyranna glanced at her mother. Marisela was frowning, but almost too hard, like she was holding back a smile, the softness that inevitably returned to her eyes.

She sighed. "Alright, Papi. I promise."

"That's my girl." He smiled. "Now ask your mother what you can do to make up for this morning. I have to speak with Dal Adis about what happened, and then Jerad Amanti, and then Balduin Na-es, and then Mylar Danu-e, and then Kota Danu-e, and then Kota's mother, so she knows what happened, and then Balduin's mother, so she won't worry, and then maybe I can come see you again tonight. Eh?"

"Yes, Papi."

He twinkled at her one more time and went out the door.

Hyranna spent the rest of the day mending old blankets and shirts and leggings, and as she did, she recited as many stories as her mother could drag out of her. They sat outside on the open rocks, and from time to time they would have a visitor. Marisela would speak with them about the upcoming berry harvest or answer their questions about Kota.

"We know nothing for certain," she said every time. "Kenan will say when he knows, but I think there was a little accident. Nothing serious."

"I heard it was that boy," one older woman said.

Marisela pressed Hyranna's arm. "We don't think so."

"Well, he's trouble. Everyone knows it. Him and his wood-witch mother."

"Andalina is one of us."

The woman laughed, oblivious to Hyranna's glaring looks.

"One of us? You're so kind, Marisela Elduna. Everyone knows she's a foundling. She's no more Imo'ani than that boy."

"He's got a name!" Hyranna snapped.

"A *southern* name, given by a southern father. The day Alutan left us was a blessing, and the day the boy follows will be two."

"Danita!" Marisela's voice was hard. "You should be careful the things you say."

"Of course, of course. Your daughter's friend—I understand, but we all know *that* won't last." The woman cackled and winked at Hyranna, then toddled off.

"Yuck," Hyranna said. "I hate her."

"Hush, Anna-chi. You shouldn't say such things. Now, where were we?"

"The red trees."

"Ah, yes. The Dandyri." She was quiet a moment. "Can you tell me about Lel-na, last of Kayr, and the red trees—the war against the blackness?"

"The one where the Greenwater was poisoned and all the red trees destroyed?"

"That's right."

"Balduin hates that one. He says it isn't true. He says some of the Dandyri are still alive, and as long as there's a *few* left, then the Greenwater hasn't faded completely. That there's still hope for things to be like they used to be, after the fall of Kayr. When the Imo'ani ruled and spoke with the trees and—"

"Balduin isn't Keeper, Anna-chi. *You* are."

Hyranna sighed, then stuck her bone needle through the fur-lined winter skirt and resumed.

Chapter Eight

Hyranna was up at dawn, released by her mother to spend the day how she wished. She already knew what she would do. She would go hunting, just Balduin and her—and with the start of the high hunting season, they might even catch something. They needed to stamp out yesterday's bizarre incident and remind everyone Balduin wasn't some cursed freak.

She moved from the warm darkness of the cave, through the pine lean-to, and ducked beneath the fur covering the entrance. It was a brisk morning. It smelled of turning leaves and fresh autumn air. She smiled. The snows weren't a long way off, but between now and then, she would savour every day.

She breathed deeply, grasped the nearest swaying rope ladder, and started up.

The cliffs of Elamori were tall and proud: the very heart of the village. They sheltered a honeycomb of caves, some along the shore, some along the cliff face, some tucked between rocks, or high on the tallest points. Looking up, she could see a maze of ropes and bridges, ladders and lean-tos, all grafted onto the surface. The whole thing creaked with comforting familiarity, and as Hyranna climbed, she felt it was speaking to her. The familiar *pop* of the boards. The groan of the ropes. The *tap tap* her feet made along the bridge. She knew the route to Balduin's cave like she knew her own feet.

It was the furthest, smallest cave the Imo'ani could find. When Andalina had returned, heavy with child and bringing Alutan with her—the mad healer, of all people!—Kenan had fought tooth and claw. *She was Dal's sister. She deserved as much as anyone.* But this was the best he could convince them to part with.

Balduin had never seemed to mind. It was quiet, secluded, high on the cliff and near the open forest above the river. It meant the longest trip *down* to the river, but that was not so bad in exchange for a little privacy.

Hyranna arrived breathless from the climb. She stood outside and called. She waited. A moment passed, and then another, and with every one her frown deepened. It wasn't like Balduin to keep her waiting.

She called again, and this time a face appeared in the half-dark.

"Hyranna Elduna." *A woman's voice.* It was deep, entrancing—frightening. It made her think of old things, though the woman half-hidden in shadow was barely thirty.

Hyranna fought the urge to flee. *Don't be stupid.* How could she blame others, if she shrank herself? "Andalina Na-es, is . . . is Balduin here?"

"No, child. He went to the traps."

"Oh." Hyranna frowned, surprised he would go without her, especially today. Maybe he joined Dal Adis? Either way, if she hurried, she could catch up.

"Hyranna . . ." The woman's voice halted her. "Would you come in?"

"I . . . I should be going."

"Please."

Something in her voice, the hint of a plea, of a strange vulnerability, made Hyranna reconsider. Why not? No one else in Elamori would dare come this close—why not go all the way?

"O-okay," she said. She didn't move for a spattering of heartbeats. Then she shook herself. "Okay," she said again.

Instead of coming out to greet her, the woman melted back into the shadows, drawing the entrance open. Hyranna hesitated, then stepped over the threshold and into Andalina's cave.

It was dark and cramped, with a narrow entrance and no cracks for windows. Hyranna could see the woman's shadow moving around, but nothing else, and she stood for a moment, not sure what to do. Then a light flared up, a single tiny flame, and behind it, Andalina appeared. She had dark skin, darker than any Imo'ani, but red hair like her son's. It fell past her shoulders, right down to her waist, in a curling, fiery mass. Beneath all that, her face seemed small and narrow like a fox—her eyes wild. Not the scared, flighty wildness of animals, but a calm, thinking wildness, like the trees, like the scent of pine and moss after a rain.

Andalina placed the candle into a carved nook, and stepped back. "Thank you for your trust."

"What do you mean?"

She laughed. It was a rich sound, but tinged with bitterness. "You think I haven't noticed? This is the first you've stepped in here since you were seven. Since you started to listen."

"Listen?"

"To *them*."

Hyranna huffed. "I don't listen."

"Maybe you should. You could tell me things. You could be my spy."

Hyranna glanced up in alarm, but noticed the hint of a smile across the woman's face. *A joke*, she realized belatedly. "I thought that's what Balduin was for."

"My son barely speaks to me. How can he tell me things when he doesn't speak?"

Hyranna faltered, eyes down, wondering what had happened between them. *That* was not a joke. What explanation had Balduin given for the newest accusations against him? An innocent lie, no doubt, meant to protect his mother, to shift as much blame from her as possible, so well-intentioned—and so pitifully transparent.

"Is he ashamed of me?" Andalina asked suddenly.

Hyranna flushed. "Of course not! You're his mother."

"You think that means anything?"

There was a terrible silence, then the woman dismissed her own words with a toss of her hand. "Forget I asked. I didn't bring you here to pity me. Hyranna—it's coming."

Hyranna swallowed, not sure why those words sent a thrill through her, from her toes up to the ends of her hair.

"What's coming?"

"The emptiness. It came for the Dandyri, and now it comes for you."

"*Me?*"

"Your people, Hyranna. Your world. Everything unfinished since the Greenwater died. Did you think you could escape forever? Kayr fell, and she sent the Dandyri. The Dandyri fell, and she sent Lel-na. And now . . . " Their eyes met, and there was a flash of pain, like a thorn in Hyranna's mind, plucked quickly away.

Hyranna shook her head, confused. "Lel-na was sent to save the Dandyri."

"Was he?"

"That's what the stories say. He failed, and . . . and he died."

"Died?"

The voice was sharp, accusatory. "Well, yeah. Hundreds of years ago. After the Greenwater . . ."

Andalina flipped a hand into the air, dismissing her words. *So this was where Balduin got his strange ideas.* "You think I'm mad. You don't believe me. Of course you wouldn't. You can't see the forest as I can. You can't see the sickness in it, growing, festering."

"That's what Balduin says."

"Does he?" Her eyes lit up for a moment. "He sees so much, but I'm afraid. Afraid for him, Hyranna. Just promise me something. Promise me . . ."

She held out her hand. Hyranna thought there was something there, so she leaned forward. It was empty. Not knowing what else to do, she took it, and immediately the grip tightened.

"I need you, Hyranna Elduna, to look after my son. Can you do that? Can you stand beside him, as you have all these years? He will need you, and you will need him. It's the only way."

"What are you saying?"

"Will you promise?"

Hyranna nodded. "I promise, I won't leave him."

"Good." Andalina squeezed her hand. "Good. Thank you. Now you can go."

The dismissal was abrupt. Hyranna blinked. "What? No. You can't just send me out without an explanation. What's going on? What's all this about?"

"I said you could go."

"But—" She stepped forward, reaching. A light flashed in the woman's eyes. Hyranna hit something and was thrown back. She staggered. The ground trembled—the ground, or perhaps Hyranna. Andalina had drawn herself up, and her billowing hair seemed to move, as if tossed in a breath of wind. In that moment, all the awful rumours about Balduin's mother seemed true. Hyranna stared, too terrified to run.

"He needs you, child. Go."

"N-needs me?"

"Yes, child. Now. *Go!*"

The command shook her. Hyranna nodded, and not knowing what else to do, she fled.

<hr>

THE FOREST BLED PAST HER. She hadn't even stopped to grab a bow from the hunting lodge as Andalina's words rattled through her mind. *He needs you. Now. Hurry, Hyranna. He needs you . . .*

Andalina *was* a little crazy. Even Balduin would admit it. A part of her wanted to laugh off the whole strange encounter, but there was another voice telling her to run, run faster.

She ran. Her bare feet sprang over rocks and roots, legs straining to go faster, faster, though this time there was no joy in it. Her heart was pattering out of control. Her chest heaved, struggling not to panic. She veered up towards the traps. Would he still be there? How long? How long ago did he leave? And who else was with him? Surely he wouldn't be foolish enough to go *alone*? What if . . . ?

Voices began to drift into focus.

"You're stupid, you know?" one of them was saying. *Mylar.* "You should've gone with the grey-heads."

"I just want to be by myself. Is that so—?"

"Hah! Not a chance. You've caused enough harm. You really think we'd trust you out here on your own? We guessed you would come here. Try to curse our traps, would you?"

There was a mutter of disapproval.

"I wouldn't!" Balduin shot back. "I'm not—"

"What did you do to Kota?"

"I didn't do anything."

"Shit, you didn't! He's blind. You hear that?" Mylar's voice pitched higher. "My little brother! Blind! Because of you."

"That's right!" someone else called.

"It was him. We all know it!"

"And who's to say he won't do it again? Eh? Any one of us could be next."

Hyranna ducked behind a bush where she could glare out. There were twelve of them spread around the slope of an open rock, faces dark, muttering and cursing. Balduin stood very still in the middle, shaking his head.

"Mylar, I'm sorry about your brother. I would never hurt him, I swear—"

"You always say so. *Cursed!*" Mylar spat. The jeers rose another pitch. They edged closer, fists tight. Hyranna's heart was slamming against her ribs. Maker's breath, this was bad! She glanced at Balduin. His face was creased with worry, but he was struggling to remain calm.

"Something's wrong," he said. "It's true. I can't explain it, but if we work together, maybe we can figure out—"

"We already know what's wrong."

"You do?"

"Yeah." Mylar paused for effect. "*You.* Don't you get it yet, witch? You're not welcome here!"

Hyranna eyed up the boys. Mylar had gathered everyone on his side, and not for a friendly meeting. She had to do something. But *what?* One wrong move . . .

Balduin nodded, crestfallen, his brief flicker of hope gone. "I see," he said, then glanced behind him, as if noticing for the first time he was surrounded.

"What should we do with him?" Mylar asked.

"Drive him out," said one.

"He'll come back," said another. "I say we sell him to Northmen slavers."

"Idiot," Mylar snapped. "Do you see any Northmen around? We take care of him now."

Balduin swallowed. "If I thought it would solve anything, I promise you, I'd go."

"Then go!" Mylar snarled, fists clenched.

Balduin didn't move. "This is my mother's home. And this . . . this is bigger than me, than any of us. If I go, it won't change anything."

"You see?" one of them shouted. "He knows something!"

"Yeah, it's him!"

"I saw his hand move!"

"He's gonna do it again. Get him!"

Balduin spread his arms, stepping towards Mylar. "I would never—"

"Don't touch me!" Mylar shoved him away, then snatched his hand back as if stung. He stooped and picked something up. A stone.

"You've seen what he can do!" he cried. He was angry, scared. His voice shook. Hyranna noticed now the clearing was full of rocks. Little piles of rocks. "You see how dangerous he is?" He took another step backwards, and another. "We get rid of him now, before he hurts anyone else!"

"I don't want any fighting," Balduin said. "It's not me! It's . . . it's . . . I don't know how, but the forest is sick."

"Balduin, look out!" Hyranna shouted.

The stone flashed for an instant, then struck Balduin in the face. He staggered back. A little bright spot of blood splashed across his forehead.

"Stop it!" Hyranna screamed. Her heart was pounding. "Leave him alone, Mylar Danu-e! He didn't do anything!"

Mylar spun around. His face twisted. "Of course you'd show up! You stay out of this, I'm warning you!"

Her face darkened.

"No, Anna!" Balduin cried. "Stay back!"

She ignored him. Her hand curled around her skinning knife,

and before she could think better of it, she yanked the blade out in challenge.

Mylar's eyes lit up. "Oh, yeah? Is that the way of it, little bitch? Come to finish what you started?" He reached for his own knife. "Just try it! Your Papi can't say anything in a fair fight."

She was trembling, but she was mad enough to do it, mad enough to ignore her own reason as it screamed at her not to be stupid. She gripped the knife tighter. She had never attacked a person before—not in a full challenge. But how hard could it be?

"Anna!" Balduin couldn't believe what he was seeing. He wiped the blood from his eyes, then stumbled forward. "Anna!"

She heard the warning in his voice. She heard the footsteps. Then someone grabbed her from behind. Jerad. He snatched her wrist, giving it a quick, painful twist. She gasped, the knife clattered to the stone, and he hauled her back.

"Let me go!" she screamed. She kicked and twisted, but he held her tight, wrapping both arms around her.

"Stay out of it, Anna!" he said in her ear. "Are you mad?"

Mylar released the knife. "Too bad. I was looking forward to that."

"Stop it!" Balduin's eyes turned fierce. "She's got nothing to do with this. Don't hurt her!"

"Or what? You'll blind us all? Call up the trees with some wood-witch magic?" He backed away and stooped for a handful of stones. The other boys were doing the same, seizing whatever was closest, fear and anticipation naked on their face. *They had planned this.* They had cornered Balduin here on purpose.

"You're done, creep!" one of them shouted.

"Over here!"

Balduin glanced over his shoulder. A stone whistled at his head. He ducked. There was a *thunk* as it struck a pine at the far end of the slope and clattered away.

"No! No, you idiots! Let me go!" Hyranna cried. They weren't listening. She glanced wildly at her friend. He looked scared, but he stood his ground, fists clenched at his side.

"I didn't do anything," he said again, more firmly. "Let's talk to Kenan Elduna. He's the Guardian of Elamori. He decides how to handle these things."

"Hah!" Mylar sneered. "He's been tricked by your witch mother. He should have banished you both years ago! We saw! We saw you attack Kota with our own eyes."

"Yeah! Get him!"

"Run, Balduin!" Hyranna cried. "Run! Just run!"

"I won't run. I didn't—"

A stone left Mylar's hand. Balduin ducked, throwing his arms up. Another came from behind. He jerked forward at the impact, his back arched. Another slapped his arm. The boys jeered, snatching up rocks as fast as they could, hurling them with snarls of triumph, voices edged with fear. Fear whipped the stones from their hands. Hyranna could hear them, the flat, thudding sound they made as they hit his flesh. A hard one smacked the bare skin of his leg, and when he cried out and grabbed for it, another struck the side of the head. He crumpled to the ground.

"Stop it!" Hyranna screamed. They ignored her, throwing even harder. Edging closer. Eyes wild.

"Jerad, let go!"

"I can't."

"They're killing him!"

"I'm sorry, Anna, I can't—"

She tossed back her head and let out a ringing screech, as loud as she could. Jerad clamped a hand over her mouth. She bit down. Hard enough to taste blood. He yelped and let go. She threw her weight back, kicked, and when he lost his footing on the rocky ground, she scrambled free.

She flung herself into the circle. A rock whipped her in the side, surprisingly painful. She gasped. She staggered towards Balduin, falling on him, enveloping him, using her own body as a shield.

"Anna . . ." He groaned. He tried to stir. "Get out of . . . here."

The stones struck her, sharp and painful, one on her leg, another across her back, her thigh, her shoulder. She squeezed her eyes shut.

"Stop!" Jerad shouted. "Don't hurt her, you idiots."

"Someone grab her!" said Mylar.

The missiles stopped. Hyranna leapt up, dragging Balduin to his feet. "Run! Run! Now!"

They sprinted for the trees, barrelling over one of the smaller boys. Two others lunged for them, but Hyranna twisted, lashed out, clawing someone across the face, dragging Balduin with her. They flew over the rocks.

Then they were free. They crashed through the bush, pulling each other along, gasping for breath, falling, scrambling back up, leaping at a sudden drop, hauling themselves over the rocky ground, using hands and knees and elbows.

Shouts followed. Like baying wolves. Snarling, howling, frenzied cries. Hyranna pushed on, the breath tight in her lungs. Branches lashed them as they flew past.

Then suddenly, there was nowhere to go. The ground opened, a scar in the earth, wider than they could jump.

"Look out!" Hyranna dug her heels in. It was too late. Balduin was already tumbling over the edge, and with a jerk, she was pulled after him.

They fell. It was a straight drop into the earth. Only a few trees clung to the sides, and as they crashed through, she clutched at anything that would slow their descent. For a moment there was nothing, just the breath punched from her lungs, the terror of plummeting to an unknown fate, and the world spinning wildly—until she clamped onto a prickly branch.

It was like being wrenched in two. She was jerked in opposite directions, one hand still clutching Balduin, the other scraping down the branch, showering her face with needles and resin. At last it dug into a knot. A moment later, she was sucking precious breath into her lungs. Balduin dangled beneath her.

"Anna!" He coughed. His weight shifted.

"What are you . . . what are you doing?"

"I can almost reach—"

The tree lurched. Hyranna felt its roots let go. She had an instant to panic. Then she screamed and they plummeted together into the dark.

Chapter Nine

Hyranna slammed into Balduin, knee-first, wincing at the force of the blow. She sprawled across him. Her palms hit the ground on either side of his head. It was soft. A thick, spongy carpet of moss.

"Balduin!"

"Shh!" He gripped her, his voice echoing loudly in the narrow space. She froze. Their pursuers were closing in.

"Do you see them?"

"They went this way!"

"I heard them. They were just here!"

"Where?"

"I don't know."

"Damn. We had him, the little bastard. Eh? Now he's gone and hid. Used some wood-witch spell, I'll bet."

"You think it worked? Is he gone for good?"

"Not while *she's* with him."

"What if he comes back? He'll go to Kenan, right off. We're done."

"We're not done."

"It's his *daughter*, damn you. He'll have our skins for a drum!"

"It was the right thing to do, Jerad, and you know it. He's dangerous, him and the witch. It's time we drove them out! Listen to me, all of you! Now we don't let them back for nothing, you hear? If anything moves on the path to Elamori, we take it out. Simple as that, eh?"

"And what about her?"

"She comes back alone, or not at all."

The voices began to fade. Hyranna realized she was shaking, while beneath her, Balduin was lying frozen on his back, chest pounding up and down. She craned her neck and followed his gaze. They'd fallen a long way. The treetops of the forest were just barely visible through the jagged rock. But Mylar and the others had been right there. Hadn't *anyone* thought to look down?

"I think . . . they're gone," Balduin whispered.

She nodded. She had no idea what to say. The horrible thing that had just happened—it was past believing. It was unthinkable. She swallowed. Every part of her was trembling.

Then Balduin shifted, and she realized she was still crushing him. She tumbled onto her back, letting herself lie there for a moment, unable to speak, while Balduin pushed himself into a sitting position.

She felt a hand on her arm. "You okay?"

"Me? Am *I* okay?" She looked at him. There was a nasty cut above one eye, welts and bruises, drops of red everywhere, but the gash on the side of his head was the worst. His hair was thick with blood, dripping down his neck, staining his shirt. "Maker above, look at you."

She reached up a hand.

"Don't!" He snatched it away.

"Balduin, I just . . ."

"I told you not to get involved! You don't listen!" He let her go and slumped back against the wall with a deep, shuddering breath. "I'm sorry," he said in a softer voice. "You could have been hurt, Anna. You shouldn't . . . you shouldn't try to protect me."

"You're my friend!"

"Well, maybe I shouldn't be."

"Don't say that!" Hyranna cried, fists balled at her side. "Damn Mylar and Jerad and those idiots, and anyone else you like, I don't *care* what they have to say. They don't get to decide who and what you are."

His shoulders began to tremble. He buried his face in his hands, struggling not to weep.

"I can't go back. I can't . . . My mother . . . I can't . . ."

Hyranna sidled up next to him and stuck an arm around his bony shoulders. She clutched hard, could feel him trembling, his heart pounding. "Papi won't let them hurt you again."

"But my . . . my . . . I can't . . ."

"And they wouldn't dare. One look from your mother and they'll drop a shit stone, I promise you."

He slapped the tears away, struggling to breathe. "What do I do?" He was breathing fast. "What do I . . . ? What . . . ?"

"I'm with you, Balduin Na-es. You hear? No matter what."

"It's not so simple."

"It is to me. Promise, okay?"

He shook his head, and there were more tears now.

"Balduin, *promise*!"

"What?"

"That you won't listen to them. That you won't let them separate us, or some such nonsense. Promise, okay?"

He said nothing. His shuddering breaths faded into sniffles and then silence. They sat there for a long time. Hyranna had no more words, no answers except her father. *He would help. He would sort this out.*

"I'm scared," Balduin said at last. The words slipped quietly through the cleft. "I don't know what's going to happen. It's all around me. It's wrong, I can feel it, a little more every day. A little more. I never thought . . . Anna, it blinded Kota, just like that, for no reason. Anything could happen."

"Anything," Hyranna echoed. She gazed around the narrow cleft, wrinkling her nose. The air felt different, tasted different. "Balduin, where are we? We've never seen this place before, have we?"

He wiped his face, then pulled away from her, rising on bruised and unsteady legs. He pressed a hand to the stone wall. It was old. It was covered in layer upon layer of moss. Vines clung to the side, and everywhere he stepped, a fragrant, earthy scent sprung up from the spongy ground.

He shut his eyes, and a shiver passed through him. Then he turned and began to walk.

"Balduin?" Hyranna climbed to her feet. "Balduin, where are you going?"

He walked slowly, deliberately. The rock walls rose steeply on every side, narrowing towards a point, where a tremulous shaft of sunlight trickled down. Balduin approached, and her breath caught. The sun touched his wild hair, and for an instant it became a fiery crown, his whole body shimmering with light. Then he passed into the shadows and was gone.

She blinked.

"Balduin?" She hurried forward. "Balduin? Where are you? What—?"

"Anna?"

She almost ran into him. His skinny face popped up beside her, and she screamed in surprise, then smacked him in the arm. "Where did you . . . ?"

"In here." His eyes glinted, and he disappeared again. But this time, she saw where he went. Almost invisible behind the twisted tendrils of old roots, each curtained with moss, was a large crack in the stone. And behind the crack, there was shadow. A deep, waiting shadow.

A thrill prickled down Hyranna's back—the same she'd felt in Andalina's cave. *It's coming, the emptiness.* Something was waiting in those shadows, but she couldn't say what: something beautiful, and something terrible.

They should go back. This wasn't right. Something here wasn't right. It twisted in Hyranna, a strange growing dread. Maybe it was the memory of what had happened, what had *nearly* happened. Balduin—standing one moment, then dropping to the ground like a rock, bleeding, hurt . . .

She swallowed. She was still shaken from the encounter with Mylar. That was all. This was something *new*. Here, under their very feet. Besides, Balduin had already disappeared ahead of her, and she *wasn't* going to be left behind.

She ducked under the roots. A few sticky cobwebs clung to her face. She took a step. Then she took another. She held her hands in front of her, expecting any moment to run into a cold stone wall. It never came. The smell of earth and decay filled her nostrils. She felt a tingle of fear, but excitement too. Something was waiting. Waiting. *Waiting for her*. She blinked. It was like a whisper, come and gone.

"Balduin?" Her voice echoed inward and down, down, into the earth. Her mind filled with strange images of deep, empty halls, and lofty caverns etched with liquid light. She shook herself. "Balduin?"

"Here." He tugged on her, pulling her further in. The shadows were impenetrable. The ground began to slope, and soon they were skidding down on their hands and knees.

"Do you know this place?" she whispered. "It . . . it gives me the willies."

Balduin took her hand and squeezed. "It's okay, Anna. Trust me." There was something in his voice: excitement, anticipation. He knew something, in that strange, sure way of his. Like he knew the forest was sick. He would go on without her if she didn't follow, and she wasn't about to leave him now. Not that Hyranna really *wanted* to go back. The forest was hiding something here, and she was going to find out what.

"Alright," she said. They shifted forward. They could hear stones sliding and falling below them, tumbling off a ledge and plinking below.

"Careful," Balduin said. "It drops here. I'll go first and you hold me, okay?"

"Okay."

Balduin turned and slipped over the edge while she dug her feet in, gripping both his wrists. He hung for a moment, and she could feel him struggling to reach. "Just a little further," he called. His voice echoed into the dark, growing with his excitement.

"It's too far," Hyranna said. "We'll never get back up."

"But I can see something!"

"Balduin!"

"I'm letting go."

"No! Don't—"

He let go of the edge. His hands slipped out of her grasp and he fell. She heard him hit the ground. Maybe he rolled, she couldn't tell. There was a scuffle.

"Balduin?" she called. "Are you okay?"

"I'm here," he said after a moment. "It's not far."

She let out a breath. "The things you make me do, Balduin Na-es!"

"Are you coming?"

It was crazy. No, it was *stupid*. But everything in her was straining to follow him. "Of course I am." She spun around and slid over the edge, holding on to it as long as she could. Fingers dug into the stone. She stretched to her full length, then felt Balduin wrap himself around her ankles.

"That's it," he said. "Let go. I've got you."

She let out a breath—*this was crazy*—and let go. Balduin caught her as she plummeted into the dark. She fell against him, stumbled a few steps, but steadied. Then she saw it.

It was a light. Not sunlight, but a faint, red glow, coming from within the cleft.

"Is that fire?" she breathed.

"I don't think so. The pattern's not right."

"Then what?"

"Let's find out." He took her hand and they went slowly. The ground was smooth now, but the ceiling turned sharply down. They felt above their heads, glancing at one another, faces awash in a rippling red glow. They both grinned, then ducked together toward the light.

The cleft opened into an enormous cavern. Hyranna's mouth hung open. She stared. Every thought was driven from her mind. She might have said something, because her words echoed and flew around her, lifting off into the dark.

And there, in the dark, was a tree.

However massive the cavern was, the tree swallowed it. It was impossibly huge. Its glossy black trunk would have dwarfed her family's cave. Its roots, each as thick as old pines, dug into the earth. But most wondrous was the light. Far above their heads, the tree's branches spread to each corner of the rocky chamber, pressing against the confines of stone like a prisoner testing the bars, seeking the sun, hungry for air and soft wind and rain, and each branch was covered in shining red leaves. They were the colour of maple in autumn, but brighter and fuller, and dancing with light. *Liquid light*, she thought, like sunlight off a still pond.

She let her breath out in a long, slow *whoosh*, as if afraid to make too much noise. It wasn't possible. Something like this just wasn't possible.

There was a flicker of light from above. Hyranna glanced up. One of the red, shimmering leaves was fluttering earthward, carried first one way, and then the other, flipping lazily through the dark. It brushed Balduin's face and landed with a rustle at his feet.

He stirred, as if coming back to himself.

"Do you know what this is?" Hyranna whispered. She wondered if he could feel it too, feel the calling, the waiting, an eager cry in the dark.

He stopped and picked up the leaf, gazing at it in rapturous wonder. "I knew it. I knew they weren't all gone. The Dandyri. The red trees. I knew it, Anna."

"Maker above, those were stories." She shook her head. "Stories I told Matti."

"Yes. But what do you think stories *are*?" Balduin turned. His eyes shone as he thrust the leaf into her hands, pushing back his hair. "Smell it."

"What?"

"Just do it."

The leaf was the size of her head, shaped with seven points, like a crimson star. Holding it, she could feel its thickness, but it looked translucent, as if a light were burning from somewhere within and leaking out the skin in sinewy ripples. Slowly, she lifted it and breathed in.

Instantly, her mind filled with images of dappled sunlight, the smell of good, deep earth, and whispering leaves, the bellow of an elk, the stretching of time—and the tree itself: long, slow, patient, waiting. And there were voices. She couldn't describe them, but they pulled at her, reaching into her soul, speaking things she had no words for, drawing her, pushing, pulling, beckoning. Her mind started to slip, as if into a dream. The ground fell away.

She jerked. Her eyes snapped open. "Maker's breath, what was that?"

"They say the Dandyri could speak." He was grinning from ear to ear. "You know the stories."

"It's a tree," she said. "It can't . . . *speak*."

He frowned at her, and she felt his wash of disappointment. Then he pushed the hair away from his face, like he did when he was trying to be serious, and he held out his hand.

"Here," he said.

Hyranna raised a brow. "Here, what?"

"Here, take my hand. I'll show you."

Balduin's hand was cool and dry, not clammy like hers, and there was such confidence, such assurance in his voice she couldn't help but *know* he was right.

"Close your eyes," he said.

She hesitated, then did as he instructed. He was so serious, yet barely containing his excitement.

"Now follow me and *listen*, Anna."

Hyranna moved forward, stepping carefully. The bare stone beneath her feet was warm and smooth, but as she walked, she felt tufts of grass tickle her ankles. It grew thick, and soft earth began pressing between her toes.

"The ground isn't stone," she said.

"No, it isn't. Keep your eyes closed. Are you listening?"

"I don't hear any—"

"Shh. Here."

He led her a little to the right, then back the other way, and she felt rather than saw a presence rise up before her. The darkness behind her eyes deepened. Balduin lifted her hand and pressed it against something hard and smooth. It was the trunk of the tree; she could smell the fragrant wood, earthy, rich, almost sweet. It was warm to touch, and the longer she stood, the more she sensed something . . . *beneath* the wood. A stirring, a whisper. She still couldn't *hear* anything, but she felt the same joyous thrill she did in the forest, when she ran in step with it—the kind of thrill that burned once, suddenly, opening her soul to a place full of life. It coursed through her now, tingling from her fingers down through everything. For a moment, she thought she heard something. Words. Actual words, on the edge of remembrance. Then it was gone. The feeling snapped shut again, leaving only a dull ache behind.

She opened her eyes. She could see the wood of the tree. It was a deep, dark brown, almost black, and incredibly smooth for something that must be centuries old. The roots twisted around her, some rising above her head before burrowing into the earth, some trailing along the ground in a long, rippling line. She took a step back, letting her eyes lose themselves in the pulsing crimson above her.

"What did you hear?" Balduin asked.

She shook her head. "I don't know."

"But you *heard* it. I know you did, I saw you!" He clapped his hands, then turned and leapt over one of the roots. "A Dandyri, Hyranna! A real Dandyri! A daughter of the Great Tree!"

He ran, whooping and laughing in glee. To think just moments ago, he had been in tears. The horrible thing seemed like another lifetime.

Only it wasn't. Hyranna's face fell. *We have to go back. We have to find my father.* The words pressed against her lips, but she couldn't bring herself to remind him.

Then she heard it. Not the tree. Something else was there. It latched on to her mind, insistent. Tugging. She turned, amazed at how instantly she knew its place. A root dove under the ground, running the wrong way, running parallel to the cavern wall instead of into it. And in the centre, for no apparent reason, there was a bulge.

Balduin remained oblivious to her movements. The ground was thick with grass and moss, and even a few tiny plants sprouted up between the roots. She picked her way over the tangled ground, her heart pounding for no reason she could think of. Then she felt something under her feet. Something cold and hard. She froze.

"What is it, Anna?"

Balduin had finally noticed. Spurred on by a growing certainty— but of *what?*—she pushed aside the grass. It was a jumble of bones. And not just any bones. It took her a moment to piece it all together, to find the pattern. A long time had passed, and the soft tissues were gone, but she was looking at a pair of legs, one bent, the other straight. She had stepped on a human shin.

Her eyes travelled up. The root, she noticed, had wrapped around the person's chest—wrapped so tightly the ribs had cracked and lay in pieces—while the skull leered out at her, mouth hanging open in a scream.

Her benevolent feelings towards the tree vanished.

"Balduin?"

He appeared next to her, hand clutching her arm. "Hyranna, don't."

"What?"

"I don't know, whatever you're going to do. Don't."

"Are you seeing this? Balduin, the tree . . . *killed* someone." She could hear the flutter of panic in her voice. "I don't think we should be here. I don't think . . ."

"Hyranna, you don't know that. It was a long time ago."

"How are you not concerned about this?"

"I'm very concerned. I'm saying maybe you shouldn't touch it."

"Why not?"

"Anna, just . . ." He tugged her arm. "Get back."

There was a shadow under the root—something too dark to be bone. Something solid.

"I think there's something there. I think I can see . . ."

She reached into the gap beneath the root, ignoring the cracked bones and dry grass and dirt, until her hand brushed something, and she stopped. *There.* It was cold and smooth. It was hard, like stone.

"Anna . . ."

She half-expected the tree to come alive and crush her hand, trapping her and whatever was hidden there. But nothing happened. Her hand came free and with it, the thing she'd been seeking.

Hyranna stared at it, and for a moment she wasn't sure what to think. A strange, brooding disappointment fell over her.

It was broken. Whatever she was holding, it was only a piece of something, like a shard of broken pottery. It was dull grey and thin, shaped almost like an arrow-head, sharp along one edge, where it had broken off, and a little rounded at the other. Should she look for something else? For the rest of it?

She lifted the piece of rock and looked more closely, running her thumb over its smooth surface, its jagged edge, flipping it over, feeling the slight bump on the other side. It fit nicely into the palm of her hand, and when she closed her fist over it, one end stuck out from between her thumb and forefinger, like a spike.

"Put it back," Balduin said.

"Why?"

"That's what she's saying. *Put it back.* Please Hyranna. Just . . ."

"She?"

"Yes! You can't have it, Hyranna. It's not yours. She was afraid this would happen, you . . ." He wobbled, shooting a hand out as he swayed.

"Balduin!" She caught him. He sagged into her, gripping her with surprising intensity.

"Sorry," he gasped. "I don't know . . ."

"Here, sit down."

She led him away from the bones. One hand slipped the rock into her pouch, next to her flint and bowstring, while the other helped Balduin to the ground. She leaned him up against a root and pushed his hair back. This time, he didn't resist.

Most of the blood had dried into an ugly, matted mess, but some still oozed out, fresh and thick. Her brows drew together.

"You're still bleeding, you dunce. Here."

Ignoring his protests, she took his knife and cut off the sleeve of her shirt, slicing it into two long ribbons. When she had enough, she leaned forward and circled it around his head, once, twice, as tight as she could, and tied it off. "I need to get you to my father."

He shook his head. "No. I can't . . . I can't leave. You heard them, Anna. If I go with you, I . . . I don't think I'll make it back to Elamori."

"But I can't leave you here."

"Yes, you can." He gave a weak smile. "Don't worry, Anna. I'll be safe. It's a hidden place, like in the stories. Remember? No one will find me."

Hyranna hesitated. There was no water here, nothing to eat or drink, and what if he kept bleeding? Or what if he was hiding an even worse injury? But she had no other choice.

"Okay, Balduin. I'll get my father. He'll put a stop to this nonsense, I promise. I'll come back for you."

She rose to leave, but Balduin reached up and grabbed her hand. "Be careful," he said.

"I will."

"And Anna?"

"Yes?"

"Try behind the Dandyri. I think . . . I think there's another way out. It'll be easier. You'll never be able to . . . climb back out of the cleft . . . on your own."

Hyranna frowned and tilted her head. "How could you possibly know that Balduin Na-es? Have you been here before?"

He smiled, but she could see his eyes were unfocused and his head was wavering. "No. But that's . . . what she told me."

"That's what *who* told you?"

He shook his head, looked like he wanted to say something, but then his head lolled back and his eyes closed.

"Balduin?" she called.

He didn't respond.

"Balduin!" She dropped to her knees, grasping his shoulders. "Balduin, wake up!" She dug her fingers into his arm and tried shaking him. No use. Her heart started to pound. She had to get him help. How could she leave him here? But if she didn't go now, he might only get worse. Could she drag him out herself? Over rocks and roots and who knows what else? She whispered a prayer to the Maker, then rose and hurried to the back of the cavern.

Sure enough, when she picked her way around the giant roots, circling around the tree, she found a promising crack in the stone. One of the roots twisted away from the tree and straight into the rock wall, splintering a hole in it as it went. The crack rose high above Hyranna's head, and widened to twice the span of her shoulders, travelling up, up into the hard earth.

Throwing a last look over her shoulder, she frowned up at the Dandyri. "Take care of him, you hear?"

Then she plunged into the shadow.

Chapter Ten

Hyranna slipped through the forest, silent and low. Her heart pattered like the drums of a bat-tu dance, expecting any moment to be ambushed.

If anything moves on the path to Elamori, we take it out . . .

The red tree under the earth, the shimmering light, the words like a dream: they had faded. She had scraped and clattered up the root's tunnel, until a crack appeared towards daylight, towards the sound of rushing water. A moment later, she had scrambled out into the bright sun. She'd emerged from the cliffs, into the lower forests, just upriver from Elamori. Here the water was fast, tumbling over and over across the rocks, but as she followed the cliffs down, the forest turned dense and marshy.

Soon, she could smell the cookfires and hear the sound of children laughing in the heat of the day. She slowed. She ducked under a fallen tree, skipped around a patch of bog, clambered over a rock, then slipped down the other side. She landed on all fours. Then froze.

The snap of a branch, a rustle. She dropped to a crouch, trying to bring her breathing back under control. Sure enough, one of the boys emerged in front of her. It was Jerad.

Her lip curled as she watched him. He was moving slowly, carefully, scanning the forest as he went, a spear in hand. He hadn't seen her, but any moment . . .

She heard a crunch of pine needles behind her—too late. She swivelled, just as another boy, Calim, leapt at her.

She lashed out, hammering her fist into his nose. He staggered back, but before she could dash free, Jerad grabbed her.

"Let go!"

"Anna, stop! Wait, I—"

She spat into his face. Jerad reared back, but before she could squirm free, Calim recovered, seized her other arm.

"Maker's breath, what's *wrong* with you?" Jerad cried. "Don't you see what's going on here? He's dangerous!"

"What's wrong with *me*? You insufferable toad. Let go of me, or I'll rip your eyes out!"

"Anna—"

"Murderers!"

Her screeching accusation halted them. Jerad stared at her. There was a flash in his eyes—something like fear, like horror. He started shaking his head.

"I never meant—"

"Liar! You would have killed him. You and Mylar and those nitwits he drags around with him. Don't you dare stand there and look at me, Jerad Amanti, and say you *never meant*. Don't you dare!"

Jerad said nothing for an agonizing stretch of heartbeats. His face was all twisted up. He swallowed, and for a moment it looked like he was going to be sick. Then he shook his head. "Anna, he can't . . . he can't stay. What he did or didn't do—look, I don't know. I don't know. But it's not just Mylar, okay? They want him gone."

"*They*?"

"Everyone."

Hyranna knew it, but to hear it so openly, so clearly. She opened her mouth to scream, but instead burst into tears.

"Let her go," Jerad was telling Calim. "Let her go." Then he was leaning close. "Anna, please. I never meant for you to get hurt. I never meant—"

She shoved him, slamming her hands into his chest, throwing her whole weight behind it. "Stay away from me!" she shouted. "And stay away from Balduin Na-es!"

Then she was running. She could barely see through the blur of tears, but she ran and didn't stop until she burst into her father's house like a windstorm.

Kenan was speaking with another man; Marisela was crushing cethul grain. The moment Hyranna skidded into the room, all three turned to stare. Then her mother screamed, and her arms flew into the air with a handful of cethul.

"Hyranna Elduna!" she cried aghast.

Her father stepped around the older Imo'ani and took both her arms, eyes grave. "What in the Tree's name, Anna! What happened?"

Hyranna realized she looked horrible. Both knees were skinned and bloody, one sleeve had been cut away, she'd been hit by stones, her arms and legs were covered with scratches from the fall, and her hands were stained with blood. But she was breathing so hard that for a moment she couldn't get anything out.

"It's . . . it's Balduin Na-es," she finally gasped.

"What happened?" Her father's voice dropped.

"Papi, they tried . . . they tried to *stone* him!"

"*Who* tried?"

"Mylar Danu-e and . . ." The tears were coming fast now. "He didn't do anything . . . anything wrong. He didn't. He *didn't!*"

"Oh, Maker's breath," Marisela said.

Kenan wrapped his arms around his daughter, eyes squeezed shut. "Ah, Anna-chi," he murmured. "You tried to stop them, eh? My brave, brave girl."

"You did *what*?" Marisela's eyes went wide.

"I didn't know what else to do. They were hurting him, and I couldn't just stand there. I . . . I got in their way, and then we ran. Ran and hid. He didn't do anything, it's not him, Papi. Please, don't let them . . . don't let them . . ."

"Now, now." He gripped her. "Anna-chi, my dearest, my brave girl, it'll be alright."

"Don't let them. You know it isn't him, right?"

"Of course I know."

"But Kenan Elduna," the visitor said. "We can't just . . ."

"Not now," her father said over his shoulder.

"But we can't let this go on!"

"Not *now*, Antar! I am with my daughter. You will wait for me outside."

For the first time, Hyranna noticed who was standing in the room. Antar Danu-e, Mylar's father—stiff and grim, fists clenched at his sides. He hesitated, defences and accusations hovering over his lips. Then he turned and stormed out the door.

Kenan waited until he was gone, then he fixed his eyes on her again. "Anna-chi, where is Balduin Na-es?"

"In a hidden place. He's bleeding. They won't let him back."

"Mylar Danu-e?"

"And Jerad! And all the boys. They threatened to drive him out, to sell him to Northmen. They said they'd kill him before letting him close to Elamori again. Do something!"

Kenan drew back and looked at his wife. She was shaking her head, loose strands of black hair swaying across her face. "Oh, Kenan. The poor boy!"

"Mari, will you find Dal Adis? Gather who you can? Tell them to find Mylar at once and bring everyone." Then he turned back to Hyranna, as calm as ever. "You say he's bleeding. How badly?"

"He was hit on the head, right here," she lifted her hand to show. "And he seemed fine at first, but he wouldn't let me see, and then he fainted."

"He's unconscious?"

"When I left him," she nodded miserably. "Please hurry!"

"And he's still bleeding?"

"I . . . I don't know. He was, a little. I tried to bind his head with my sleeve."

Kenan put a hand to the side of her face, just for a moment, eyes grim. "Take me to him."

HER FATHER WAS silent as they moved through the trees, back up the river. If Jerad and Calim were close, they made no appearance. They wouldn't dare come against Kenan Elduna.

Hyranna led him through the marshy parts, up back towards the cliffs, along green-crusted rocks, wet from the Tindanarra's spray. The river roared down the treacherous slopes, crashing into rocks and swirling towards the lower waters. Hyranna spotted the place where she'd climbed out, a nook behind two mossy boulders, close to the spray of the falls.

She hurried and leapt over them, almost twisting her ankle as she slipped across the wet stone and fell headlong into the cliff. Her hands flew out to stop her, one leg skidded beneath her, and she smacked her already bruised knee on the stone. Then she stared. There was nothing. No crack, no tunnel, just slimy, bare rock.

"No," she breathed. She shook her head. This couldn't be happening! Balduin needed her! She knew she hadn't imagined it, it had to be here. "It's here, it's here. Right here, I remember! I was just ..." She slammed her hands into the cliff as if there were a hidden door that would open at her command. "Maker damn you. Don't *do* this!"

A hand fell on her shoulder. "Anna." Her father's voice was calm, controlled, as always, even though he had to lift it above the roar of the river. "What's wrong?"

"It was here!" She hit it again. "Right. Here."

"But now it's not," he said and took her hand, lacing his fingers through hers. "I will look around. What am I looking for?"

She turned and stared at him. "I'm not crazy, Papi! I swear, it was here—"

"I know. I believe you." He smiled. "Sometimes the forest keeps its own mind. Tell me, Anna-chi, what is it hiding?"

"A crack—a tunnel. Balduin's hiding in a cave, one that comes and goes like ... like the hidden places in the old stories."

He nodded, completely calm but for the glint in his eyes. "Is he? Then I will look this way," he pointed towards the river. "You go that way. We'll find him, okay?"

"Anna?"

The voice was small beneath the crashing water, but distinct. Hyranna's head snapped up. A figure stirred in the rocks, and she saw a hand appear, trembling against the stone.

"Balduin!" she cried. She leapt to her feet, rushing across the wet moss, Kenan behind her.

He had wedged himself into a crevice between rock and cliff. Hyranna had no idea how he'd managed to climb out of the Dandyri's cavern on his own, or *why*, but here he was. And he looked even worse in broad daylight.

"Balduin, Balduin!" She bent over him.

For an instant the grey-blue of his eyes were washed clear, as if she could see straight into him. Then they found her and the glint came back.

"Anna?"

She threw her arms around him and squeezed. "Balduin Na-es!"

"*Ow . . . ow . . .*"

"Sorry!" She winced and let go. "Are you okay?"

"I . . . think so. What . . . ?"

"My father's here. He's going to help you."

"Father . . . ?" He shook his head, slowly coming back to himself. "My father was here. I saw him. I saw . . ."

His eyes settled on Kenan, and a frown wrinkled across his brow. "Kenan Elduna?"

"Yes, Balduin Na-es. I'm here."

He struggled to rise. "Your daughter . . . was put in danger, because of me. It's my fault. I'm—"

"No," Kenan crouched beside him. "Look at me."

Balduin frowned at his toes. "I'm sorry—"

"*Look* at me."

He did. But between the blood caking his hair, the cut over his eye, and the grief pulling on his skinny face, he looked utterly wretched.

"My daughter chose to put herself in danger, because she cares about you," Kenan said. "Do you understand? This is not your fault."

"And what about . . . my mother?"

"She's fine. I'll make sure you get back to her. Now I'm going to ask you a few questions. Is that okay?"

Balduin nodded.

"What happened?"

"I told you Papi—" Hyranna tried, but Kenan gave her arm a quick squeeze.

"Let him speak."

Balduin swallowed and looked away. "I don't . . ."

"You don't remember?"

"No, I remember. I . . ."

"Then I need you to tell me. I need to know what happened. Did you fight?"

"No."

"Why not?"

"There were too many."

"Can you tell me their names?"

"Mylar, and . . . and Deryn. Calim. Jos and Meli. Everyone." He paused. "Jerad."

Kenan's jaw tightened. "And what did they do?"

"Called me cursed. Said I was responsible. Said I should go. And when I didn't they . . . they picked up stones."

"Where did they get the stones? Did they find them off the ground or were they gathered beforehand?"

Balduin swallowed. "Gathered."

"Okay." Kenan nodded, took a deep breath. Hyranna had never seen him so upset. A dark look was gathering in his eye. "Can you walk?"

"I think so."

"Good. We're going to get you cleaned up very soon, but first we deal with this."

"They were scared," he whispered.

"I know."

"They were just scared. They weren't thinking. If I were in their place, saw what they did, I'd probably do the same."

"No you wouldn't," Hyranna said. "You're too good."

"Am I?" His brow wrinkled. "I don't want them to be scared. But what's happening, Kenan Elduna, it's not going to stop any time soon. It's getting worse. I can . . . I don't know, I can *see* it. In that flower over there." He pointed to a nearby buttercup, its normally bright, yellow petals turned a colourless grey, like smoke. Neither Kenan nor Hyranna had noticed it until now, but once they saw, they couldn't *unsee*. And the longer Hyranna looked, the more she felt it, like the memory of some half-forgotten task, needling away at the back of her mind. "It's not what it should be," he said. "Nothing's quite what it *should* be; I can't explain it, but it's wrong."

A cloud passed over the sun and Hyranna shivered. She was wet and tired and sore, and nothing made any sense right now.

"I hear you," Kenan said. "Nonetheless, there will be words. I only ask your forgiveness for not speaking them sooner. Come."

Kenan Elduna led them to Elamori's highest point—the peak of the cliff, the gathering place. They crisscrossed the bridges and platforms from one edge of the village to the other, and as they went, eyes followed, whispers chased after them like flies. Feet followed. By the time they crested the top, there was a sizeable gathering.

Kenan Elduna walked straight to the centre, keeping his daughter on his left, and Balduin on his right. He turned and faced the small crowd, almost sixty Imo'ani.

"Mylar Danu-e," he called. Hyranna had seldom heard it so hard, like a layer of crisp autumn ice. "Where is Mylar Danu-e?"

There was a string of whispers. No one said anything. Then Antar Danu-e stepped forward. "What is this about, Elduna?"

Kenan looked at him. "This is about peace in Elamori and good sense. Now where is your son?"

"Not here."

"I would be grateful if you found him. At once."

Antar's eyes narrowed. "Are you saying you'll protect this bastard over my son. Even after what happened to Kota?"

"I'm saying what happened to Kota had nothing to do with Balduin. Now find Mylar and bring him here."

Antar didn't move.

"What's this about?" a voice murmured in the crowd.

Others began muttering, turning to each other. Hyranna heard Balduin's name, and Kota's, and Mylar's, and even her own.

"Are you going to explain this, Kenan Elduna?" an old woman cried, her lips tight with anger.

"When Mylar is here, we will talk."

"What about Kota?" someone else called. "Can he be healed?"

"No," said the old woman. "And what's to say it won't happen again?"

There was a ripple of unease.

Just then, Marisela Elduna stormed out of the trees, black hair flying loose, eyes like coals. Hyranna stared at her mother. She was not alone. Everyone turned to see Dal Adis behind her, his hunting circle materializing out of the trees. Mylar Danu-e was propelled along, next to two others—Deryn and Jos. Dal's grip was firm as he marched the young man straight up to Kenan and shoved him forward. Mylar stumbled, but caught himself and jerked up, eyes blazing.

"Is this who you're looking for?" Dal asked.

"That's exactly who I'm looking for. Thank you," Kenan said quietly. He turned to one of Dal's hunters. "Yanu, can you bring Andalina?" The man nodded and hurried off, but Antar was already scowling, fists clenched.

"What gives you the right, Dal Adis, to drag my son here like a Northman scum?"

"The moment he threatened my nephew without cause. That gives me the right."

"I had all the cause I needed!" Mylar cried. "He blinded Kota. I saw it with my own eyes. We all did!"

There was a rush of murmurs.

"It's true!" shouted the old woman. "Kota is crippled because of that boy. How will you exact justice for this atrocity?"

"By condemning him!" Mylar shouted, stabbing a finger at Balduin. "Cursed wretch."

"Enough," Kenan said.

"Witch's bastard, he's responsible for this. Him or his witch mother." Mylar turned to the crowd. "We should drive them out or stone them now. Not tomorrow, not the day after. Now!"

Kenan struck Mylar in the face, hard enough to knock him to the ground. There was a gasp from those watching. Even Balduin's eyes widened, and Hyranna stared. She'd never seen her father hit anyone. The shocked silence was as heavy as a storm cloud. Mylar cowered on the ground, clutching his face in shock. Antar stared in open dismay. Then he lunged at Kenan.

Dal Adis was faster. He seized the man, dragging him back.

"How dare you strike my son!" the man howled.

"How dare you threaten our Guardian!"

The crowd erupted. It was larger now, a hundred Imo'ani, nearly the full village, and shouts rose on either side—some against Antar, some for him.

"What if it's true?" one cried.

"Is this what happened to Roya? Is this why she died?"

"Don't bring Roya into this!" one of the hunters bristled.

"And what about the fainting sickness? Took three last year! And poor Dem . . ."

"And the blight last harvest?"

"It's the witch's fault!"

"Or *his*."

"They don't belong here. Drive them out!"

Hyranna's gut clenched in horror.

"Papi, do something!" she whispered.

It was Marisela who acted. She hiked up her skirts, leapt onto one of the stones, and threw back her head.

"*Silence!*"

The crowd stilled. They stared, first at Marisela, then at her husband. No one spoke. There was an expectant hush.

Kenan waited, and when the moment was stretched as long as it could bear, he spoke: "I won't hear another word against Balduin Na-es."

The crowd shifted uneasily, muttering and whispering.

"Mylar's right!" one of them called. "It's time for them to go!"

"No!" Kenan lifted his voice, crisp, controlled. "Andalina has been with us since she was a child. Balduin Na-es is an honourable young man. You know them, just as I do! Neither of them is responsible for this, you have my word. And if you can prove otherwise I will take *full responsibility for their actions.*"

He let that hang in the silence. A promise of restitution. From the Guardian himself. His own life laid in balance. Everyone swallowed, shifted, suddenly uncomfortable. Hyranna held her breath.

"Until then," he continued, "no one speaks a word against

Balduin and Andalina, or they'll find it is themselves driven from Elamori."

No one said anything. The tension was thick. Hyranna squeezed her mother's hand, now beside her, realizing she didn't know how this would end.

"I know what you're thinking. I know you're afraid. But this is not the time to lash out in fear. Today, my daughter risked her own safety to protect her friend. That's what we do. We take care of each other, as we always have. And that's what I will do." He put a hand on Balduin's shoulder. "From now on, I will let no one threaten Balduin Na-es or harm him in any way. I will protect him as I would my own son." He looked pointedly at Mylar, who now stood glowering. "I hope you choose to treat him accordingly."

Hyranna stole a glance at her friend. He was staring at the ground, eyes furrowed, a mix of shame and worry running over his face. He wouldn't like this. Balduin never liked accepting help. But what choice did he have? She tried to catch his eye, but he wouldn't even look at her.

"I will do my utmost to learn about these strange happenings," her father said. "They pose a threat to us, but I suspect the threat extends beyond our village. Tomorrow, I will send scouts to Lindys. We will proceed rationally and carefully, and we will need to work together to protect ourselves. Do you hear me?"

"Aye," Dal said quickly, stepping back from Antar. Many echoed him. There were some nods, and some silent, grim faces. Some muttering. A few started to drift away, back to their interrupted tasks. Then there came a shout.

Heads snapped up, alert again, and feet shifted out of the way. Yanu appeared sprinting across the rocky ground. "Kenan Elduna!" he cried, eyes large. "It's Andalina. She's ... she's ..."

"What?" Kenan demanded.

"I think she's dying."

Gasps and muted cries popped up. Faces filled with fear, surprise. Relief. There was a terrible silence—stretched, pregnant with meaning. With horrible meaning.

They heard a choking gasp. Hyranna spun to find her friend. His mouth was parted, chest heaving. He didn't look at her, didn't look at anyone. He squeezed his eyes shut for a moment. Then he took off at a run. Everyone pulled back, whispering, muttering. Hyranna tried to follow him, but her father's hand fell on her arm. "Stay with your mother," he said. "Can you do that?"

"But . . . but . . ."

"I'll see what's happening. You need to get back home and stay there. Do you understand?"

She nodded, feeling miserable and angry and even guilty, as if somehow she had known. Known and said nothing. But how? How could she . . . ?

"Balduin," she whispered, straining to catch a glimpse of him. But he was already gone, leaping down the cliff to find his mother. Kenan Elduna followed, and the crowds parted for him in silence.

Chapter Eleven

Evening dragged towards night. Darkness fell, and the hot, humid day brought ominous clouds in its trail. Still there was nothing, no news, no word from her father. Marisela helped Hyranna clean the cuts and scrapes, and then they shared a small meal of boiled cethul and beans. They lit a candle. It burned low. There was nothing they could do.

"Try to sleep," Marisela said to her daughter. But Hyranna couldn't sleep.

"Why can't I go to him?"

"Because your father told you to stay here."

"I'm not a child. I should be with him. He needs me, Matti."

Marisela looked at her disapprovingly.

"Your father told you to stay here. Let him work."

"But what about Balduin?"

"You're not a child, Hyranna Elduna. Neither is he."

That was the end of it. Hyranna tried to sleep, but her thoughts kept running over and over the bewildering events of the day: her strange encounter with Andalina, the horror of the attack, falling into the cleft and what they found there, and all the confusion since then. Now this.

A few rumbles sounded in the distance. It would start raining soon. Hyranna turned on her side and tried to get comfortable on the thick furs, but everything seemed impossible right now.

Her thoughts drifted back to the tree. Was it true? Was it a Dandyri from the distant past? A survivor, hidden beneath the earth? She closed her eyes and tried to picture it again, and instantly, it leapt to mind. She could see it: the leaves cast a red glow like water, branches spreading to every corner, trembling and whispering and moving with a wind all its own. Her eyes fluttered open and there it was, standing before her, magnificent and strange. But now that she looked again, looked more closely, a darkness rippled across the leaves, obscuring their light, like a wisp of cloud running beneath the stars. She was walking towards it. She was speaking to it, though she couldn't hear her own words.

Hyranna Elduna ellelen-di arama . . . Aktyr.

The whisper touched her mind like the brush of a falling leaf. She was gazing at the tree, but there was something else, another presence. She dragged her eyes away. It was there, hidden, smothered by the roots, pulsing in her mind. *What are you?* She walked towards it. The tree started to move. Roots bulged out of the ground, and she felt earthy tendrils fasten around her ankles. Still she approached. The ground shook and tipped, and she stumbled, but something pulled her forward, insatiable curiosity. No, more than that. A compulsion, a need. The tree started to quiver, and the roots tugged at her feet, dragging her back.

Do not, do not, do not . . .

Hyranna's eyes cracked open. The whispers became quiet voices from the far side of the cave.

She sat up. The curtain had been drawn across the sleeping corner, but she could tell from the close dark that it was still night. Probably old night, not yet dying off to new day.

She crept to the curtain, straining to listen, but she could hear only the swish and drip of a cloth being dipped into water, lifted up, wrung out again.

Then a shadow fell across the curtain. It was pulled back and her father stood there. She couldn't see his face in the dim light, but he dropped to a crouch, and she could smell the sweat on him, mixed with crushed goldenrod and mint.

"Hyranna," he said in a tired, heavy voice.

She knew what he was going to say. She could see past him, and it was all she needed.

Balduin Na-es was cross-legged on the floor while Marisela knelt beside him, washing the blood from his face with a purposeful, gentle hand. The cloth dipped in the water, swirled, twisted. She pushed the hair back from his face and kept cleaning. Balduin just sat there, staring straight ahead, never wincing or pulling back, without any expression at all. Hyranna's chest tightened.

"She's gone," her father said, laying a hand on her shoulder.

"Why?" Her breath squeezed. "How?"

"Her heart. It . . . gave out."

"But she was healthy! I saw her this morning."

"I don't know, Anna. I don't have any answers."

"What do you mean you don't—?"

"Shh. Let it be for now."

She clenched her jaw and rose, walking slowly to her friend's side. He barely looked at her.

"Balduin, I . . ." She knelt next to him and picked up his long, thin hand, with its white-speckled skin. It just lay there in her grasp, not responding. "I'm sorry," she said.

He gripped her hand a little, but said nothing. The cloth swished and dripped. Marisela wrung it out. The water was quickly turning dark with blood. Hyranna couldn't think of what else to say, and the silence stretched out, full and heavy.

Kenan Elduna brought out some extra furs and laid them near the door. Then he turned to a large urn and dipped a cup in it, filling it with cool, fresh water. "You'll stay here tonight," he said as he selected a ceramic pot off one of his medicine shelves. "And then it's up to you." A drop went into the cup, a quick swirl, and he returned, crouching next to Balduin and holding out the drink.

It was as if Balduin didn't see him; he just stared forward.

"You're welcome here, if you wish it," Kenan kept saying. "But you're old enough to keep your mother's home for yourself. It's your choice." He paused. "You would be safer here."

"I don't care about being safe."

"You should," said Marisela.

Kenan nodded. "You may not care right now. I understand. But we do. It's my deepest wish that no one in Elamori is harmed."

"Then why did you let her die?"

There was a shocked silence. Hyranna squeezed Balduin's hand, staring at him.

Kenan only nodded. "I understand how you feel. I would be angry too. But I swear to you, Balduin Na-es, by the Maker and the Tree, I used every skill I had to save her, and I will not let this rest. If harm was caused, I will find who did it. There *will* be restitution—"

"No."

Kenan paused. "No?"

"It wasn't them."

"I hope you're right. An illness maybe, though I've never seen its kind, so sudden, without warning—"

"No," he said again, more firmly. "My mother doesn't *get* sick. She's not like other people. It wasn't illness. It wasn't poison. It . . . it . . ."

"Balduin."

"It *took* her." His voice quivered.

"We don't know what happened."

"It took her. I saw. She was in pain, Kenan Elduna. She . . . she couldn't breathe. Like something was *choking* her. Like something was—"

"Balduin." Kenan leaned closer. "I meant what I said. I will protect you."

"But you can't. Don't you get it?" He spoke it like it was obvious. A fact, not an accusation. "You can't protect anyone. Not anymore."

"Balduin!" Hyranna cried, aghast. She'd never heard him speak like this before. How could he say such things?

Kenan just held up a hand, calming her, one bright eye locked on Balduin.

"You're right. I don't know how she died, but I failed you. I said she was safe, and she wasn't, and now . . . Accept my protection as recompense, or don't. It's your choice."

Balduin said nothing for a moment, though he never took his eyes off Kenan. He was thinking, Hyranna could tell. Weighing everything. Finally he dropped his eyes.

"I hold nothing against you, but if I stay here, I'll only earn you your people's hatred. I'll leave in the morning."

Kenan nodded and sighed. "Very well." He held up the cup again. "Now please, drink this."

"Wait. What?" Hyranna was glancing between them. There were times when Balduin seemed so young, a boy still, fragile, someone she felt responsible for, like the little brother she never had. And then there were times he was something else entirely. Like right now. Her father had spoken to him like an equal, and he'd responded in kind. "Balduin, what do you mean? What you mean, you'll *leave*?"

He let go of her hand and took the cup, glancing into the clear liquid. "What is it?"

"Something to help you sleep," Kenan answered.

"I don't need it."

"You do. You're not well, and your body needs rest. If you want to go anywhere in the morning, short of lying on your back, you'll take it."

Balduin hesitated, but Marisela leaned forward. "No need to be stubborn, child. If you don't take it, you'll be awake all night, with the Maker knows what thoughts running through your head."

Balduin finally nodded and did so, grimacing a little at the taste, while Kenan prepared a fresh poultice. Then he washed the cut again and with quick, skilled hands, applied the poultice and sealed it with pitch.

Hyranna just watched. There was a deep, sinking feeling in the pit of her stomach, like she'd swallowed a rock, and it was sitting there, heavy and cold, making her sick.

Balduin wouldn't look at her, wouldn't meet her eye, wouldn't answer her question. What did he mean? That he would leave and take up his mother's dwelling, or leave Elamori—leave for good? The thought was too much. Surely he hadn't meant *that*. She tried to calm herself, to convince herself she was overreacting. But the look on his face, like he'd glimpsed something, not just for tomorrow, or the next, but something that would come a long time from now, because of one small choice in that moment. Did that explain the sudden ache in her, deep inside where there were no answers?

She wanted to say something, to comfort him, but any words that came to her sounded empty.

So she watched.

<hr/>

When Hyranna opened her eyes, her first thought was a flutter of panic.

"Balduin!" she whispered, sitting up. She didn't know why. It was a dream . . . about him? He was . . . she couldn't remember, but it left her cold with fear.

She shook her head and rose. Even as she climbed to her feet, she couldn't shake the feeling that something bad was happening, or *would* happen. Or already had. She swallowed. Of course something bad had happened. Andalina was dead.

The sleeping corner was empty. She had overslept, worn out by the events of the day before. She could hear someone moving on the other side of the curtain. Maybe it was him . . .

She tossed the curtain aside and saw her mother. She was sorting through a bundle of fresh goldenrod, the yellow flowers in late-summer bloom. One by one, she picked off the leaves, putting them on a flat stone to dry, then plucking the flowers off and dropping them into an old leather sack. She worked efficiently, but there was a little frown between her brows.

"Matti, is he . . . gone?"

Her mother glanced up from her work for an instant, hardly pausing before she looked down again, fingers busy. "He is."

"Did he say where?"

"Back to his mother's hole, I presume. Someone has to take care of the body."

Of course. Hyranna felt a moment of relief. Balduin wouldn't leave without showing the proper respects to his mother: the Darkening prayer, the funeral pyre. But then she thought of his narrow, sombre face frowning in the dark, lit only by the glow of the candle, and she shuddered. She would find him, talk to him alone. He couldn't leave Elamori—he must know that.

"Anna," her mother called as she made for the door. She stopped, turned.

"What?"

"Let him be."

"He's alone now, Matti. He needs me."

"If he needed you, he wouldn't have left so quickly, now, would he?"

Hyranna felt a stab of irritation. "Do we have to do this? Now?"

"Yes."

She paused at the door and considered just walking out, but she knew her mother meant best. "I know what you're going to say, and the answer is, I don't care."

"Oh really? What am I going to say, Hyranna Elduna?"

"That I should keep my distance. That I shouldn't be his friend."

"Hmm." She kept plucking, perhaps a little more intently.

"What?"

"Is that what's happening?"

"What?"

"Friendship."

"Of course! I'm not giving up on him now, because of all . . . this. He didn't cause that elk to spoil, and he definitely didn't blind Kota. It's ridiculous to even suspect him, Matti, and you know it!"

"I know it," she said. "That doesn't change what he is."

"Oh yeah? And what is that!"

Her mother barely looked up from her work. "An outsider," she said.

"What?" Hyranna stared. How could her mother say such a thing? Her *mother*?

Now Marisela did look at her. "You know it's true."

"What about everything Papi said yesterday? He was born in Elamori. Just because his mother is different, just because his father was from outside, that doesn't mean he's like them. He's my friend. My only friend. He's like a brother to me, and I'm not going to turn my back on him now!"

"Like a brother?" She sighed and shook her head. "Last night, when you looked at him, it was not the look you would give a brother."

Something fluttered in Hyranna's stomach, but she pushed it away with a frown. "I don't know what you mean."

"Don't you?"

"No! What are you saying, Matti?"

"That whatever you feel for this boy, you have to let it go. Nothing can happen between you."

"Why not? I'm not going to let *their* fear determine who I spend my time with and what I feel."

"You're not understanding, are you?" Marisela sighed. "Must I lay it out for you? You cannot marry Balduin Na-es."

The words were like a slap. For a handful of heartbeats, she just stared at her mother. The thought had never occurred to her. Not once. Not ever. And yet suddenly she was furious, and terrified, and . . .

"Mother!" she finally cried. "What?"

Marisela laid aside her herbs. "Sit down," she said.

"No! I'm not going to listen to this . . ."

"Sit."

She was trembling, and she didn't know why. She wanted to flee the cave, to run and run and feel the forest around her, but her mother's gaze pulled her into obedience. She sat.

"Good." Her mother reached out and took her hands, catching them firmly, but not too hard. "You'll be fifteen as soon as the snow flies. I didn't understand either when I was your age. It takes time to sort out the feelings."

"It's not *like* that," Hyranna tried to say.

Marisela shook her head. "I am your mother, Anna-chi. Don't think I haven't been watching."

"Watching?"

"I'm telling you now, before you sort out those feelings, so you won't get your heart set on something that cannot be."

"And why can't it be?"

"Do you really need me to explain?"

Hyranna just stared at her hands.

"You're the Keeper," Marisela said. "Your father has no sons. Who will be Guardian when he's gone?"

"I will."

"Your husband will."

"What if I don't marry?"

"That isn't your choice to make."

"Well, it should be!" Hyranna's eyes flashed. "And why can't it be him? He could be Guardian. He's good, just like Papi, and smart, and kind."

"And an outsider. They don't trust him, or understand who he is, or like him, and if they don't after all this time, they never will. Maker's breath, Hyranna, they tried to *stone* him. They would never follow him, and that's why it can never be. Balduin has enough sense to see that for himself."

And then Hyranna understood. She leapt up, furious and mortified. That's what her mother had been trying to say, this whole time. *He cannot stay—because of you.* But what was she supposed to do? Just pretend she wasn't his only friend in the whole village, the only person he had left? He would light his mother's pyre alone, and then, what . . . leave? Leave and go where?

Anywhere but here. He had nothing left in Elamori. He would see himself as a burden to her father, and a danger to her. It made sense. It made *too* much sense, and Hyranna was furious.

"I'm not going to leave him," she snapped, then turned and hurried from the cave.

WHEN SHE MADE it to Andalina's home, that tiny, windowless hole in the rock, she found Andalina, and no one else. The woman had been laid on the floor, her body washed, her vibrant red hair combed carefully and draped across her shoulders. Her eyes were closed, as if in sleep, and once Hyranna got over the shock of seeing her lifeless body, she thought there was an eerie peace to the stillness. She shivered.

Stand beside him. Look after him. The woman's words rang fresh in her mind. It was the only way, she had said. But the only way for what? Had Andalina knew this would happen? Had she seen her own death, pleading with Hyranna not to abandon her son?

Hyranna left the cave, already beginning to smell the decay, despite the oils and spices. Balduin would be back at dusk to light the pyre—she'd seen the ceremony before, sometimes for old, weakened Imo'ani come naturally down death's river, sometimes with the sick or injured. Always the funerals happened at dusk, with the setting sun. Balduin wouldn't be back until then.

Before she could think better of it, Hyranna climbed the last few ropes to the top. She ignored the open stares and sidelong glances and plunged into the forest. She knew exactly where Balduin would be. *If only she could find it.*

She traced her steps from the day before, up towards the traps, and then veering away to the north. Their trampled path remained: signs of escape and pursuit. Her throat tightened at the memory. Was it only yesterday?

And then it was there. It appeared suddenly, like last time, the ground opening in front of her, narrow and steep. She crouched and examined it, and at the far end she saw the jagged, shriven rock giving a few stable footholds down.

It wasn't an easy climb. Rocks shifted under her feet, threatening to plunge her into the shadowy cleft. Gradually, the light was dimmed from above, the sounds of the forest grew distant and muted, as if a blanket were stretched above her head. Then she was there. She leapt into the mossy earth, and paused. She was suddenly afraid to turn around. What would she say to him? What if her mother was right? What if—?

"I knew you'd find me," he said.

She swallowed, and turned to face the dark of the cleft. The shadows seemed thicker this time, but as her eyes adjusted, she saw him sitting against the rock, knees pulled to his chest. Marisela had cleaned him up, but the welts and bruises were now vivid purple, and the cut over his eye had swelled.

"I wanted to see her again," he said.

"Your mother?"

He shook his head. "The red tree. The Dandyri."

"So why don't you?"

He shrugged and looked away. "I just couldn't . . . couldn't go any further. It's like a dream, Anna. Yesterday. Everything. And if I go further . . ."

"The dream vanishes."

He nodded. There seemed nothing else to say, so Hyranna walked over, padding silently across the mossy earth, and slid next to him. They waited. A sliver of light began to creep into the cleft from above —the sun, moving higher.

When Balduin spoke again, there were tears in his voice. "I . . . I was ashamed of her."

Andalina's words cut back to her, harsh and vivid. *Ashamed. Ashamed of me . . .*

"You don't mean that," Hyranna whispered.

"I do. I didn't want her around. I . . ."

His voice broke. He tried to say something, but his whole body began to shake. Painful sobs burst out of him, silently, as tears dripped down his face.

"Balduin!" She watched, shocked and dismayed, then threw her arms around him. He buried his face into her shoulder and wept.

Her friend had a gentle heart—a dead bird would move him to tears. Yet she had never seen him like this. He clung to her. He shook and groaned.

"I'm . . . I'm sorry," he finally gasped when he had breath to speak. He shuddered and pulled away. "I'm sorry." He drew a sleeve across his face, but instead of wiping away the tears and the drippings from his nose, he just streaked it with dirt instead. Hyranna meant to say something comforting. Instead, a snort of laughter burst out of her, and Balduin stared in horror.

"Are you . . . laughing at me?"

"No." She threw a hand over her mouth. "No, I'm not. I'm not."

"You *are!*"He frowned and tried to wipe his face again. It just made it worse. Hyranna couldn't stop herself. He stared at her, blinking, indignant—and then he chuckled. A grin spread across his cheeks, and he laughed with her. It made his face look even funnier, scrunched up and grinning like that, and soon they were both on their sides, laughing for no good reason, mirth mixed up with grief.

Finally spent, they lay on their backs and gazed at the distant treetops and the dancing green shadows. No one said anything for a long, quiet moment, and when Balduin spoke at last, his voice was calm and steady.

"Anna," he said. "I'm leaving Elamori."

"I know," she said.

"You know? You mean, you're just going to accept it? Just like that?"

"I am. Because I'm coming with you."

———

"Anna, no," Balduin said, when the shock had worn off. "You can't!"

"Why not?" She sat up and pushed her hair back. Then gave him the look that said, *I'm the Guardian's daughter, and I can do what I want.* He frowned.

"Don't give me that look."

"Why not?" She grinned.

"Anna, this . . . this isn't some hunting trip. Don't you understand? I'm leaving and I'm not coming back."

"I know, Balduin. Don't treat me like an idiot. I've thought about this, you know." At least, she'd thought about it for a moment or two before the words came out of her mouth, but he didn't need to know that part.

"Look, I know this is hard for you. It's hard for me too, but . . ." His shook his head and took a deep breath. "Anna, my mother said something to me. Right before she died. She looked at me, and she told me . . . she said . . . Anna, she said my father was alive."

"What?" Hyranna stared at him.

"Yes. He's alive out there, somewhere. And I have to find him."

"Balduin . . ."

"No, don't say it! It's true, Anna. I know it."

"How? Why? How could she possibly—"

"She just *does*. She knows it, okay? You don't have to believe me, but that's what I'm going to do, and that's why I can't let you come along. I don't know where this will take me."

"Balduin . . ."

"You can't change my mind."

"No, listen." She grabbed his hand. "Balduin, it's been what, twelve summers since he disappeared?"

"Ten. I was four that spring. I remember."

"Fine. Ten summers. It's still a long time. If he *is* still alive—Balduin, I'm sorry, but you need to ask yourself, why didn't he ever come back?"

Balduin frowned. "I *have* asked myself. Many times."

"And?"

"I was young, I know, but he was a good man. My mother never blamed him. She said it was something he had to do. He wouldn't just leave, and never come back. I *know* he wouldn't. Not unless . . ."

"Unless he died?"

"No! I told myself that for years. It was the only thing that made sense. But now . . . what if my mother's right? What if there's a chance he's still alive out there, and maybe he hasn't come back because he can't. What if I've been waiting all this time for him, but I've had it wrong? What if *I* have to go to *him*?"

Hyranna didn't respond right away. She could see arguing was no use. He was determined, and when Balduin set his mind to something, nothing on the green earth or above could set it back.

"Alright. I suppose it doesn't matter much where we go. You want to look for your father? Great! I'm still coming along."

"Anna . . ."

"Now don't you try to convince *me*!"

"But you have a job to do here. A place. These are your people, and who will take over when your father's gone?"

Hyranna waved her hand dismissively. "Doesn't matter. Eedi can tell the stories, since she's so good at it, and *she* can marry a Guardian, too. That would be Korvin. He's a good enough sort, I suppose. Look, I don't *care* about all that. They want to throw you out, fine. But then they're throwing me out, too, because I'm with you Balduin Na-es. Do you hear me?"

He stared at her, uncomprehending. "You would just give up . . . everything? Your home? Your family?"

Hyranna shrugged, though when he put it like that . . . What *was* she doing? "It doesn't matter. Besides, it's not like we'll never be able to come home. As soon as we leave, and they realize it wasn't you causing all this, they'll welcome us back."

"I don't know, Anna."

"*I* do. Look. Can I, or not?"

"Can you?" He snorted. "You haven't given me much choice."

"Well, I'm giving you the choice now. Can I come with you?"

"And if I say no?"

"Then I'll probably follow you until you give in." Hyranna was grinning, but she meant it too. The idea of losing him was suddenly more than she could bear. What would life be like without Balduin? Tedious sewing and washing and preparing food and gossip and trying to be like her older cousin, Eedi, but never quite being good enough at *anything* except for hunting. And she would learn the stories and tell them over and over again, and eventually they would marry her to someone, probably one of those stupid boys that followed Mylar around, and she would become the Guardian's wife. But what would be the point of any of it? Balduin was her friend, her only friend, and she'd looked after him since they were infants. Abandon him now? She couldn't imagine a more painful betrayal. Besides, she had promised Andalina. *I won't leave him.* So that was that.

Balduin looked at her, with his dirt-streaked face, and his clear, bright eyes, and he smiled. "Yeah," he said. "I guess you can. If you want."

Hyranna let out a squeal of joy and threw her arms around his neck, almost toppling him over in her excitement. She knew it was the right thing to do because just then she was happy, so impossibly happy. The weight in her stomach seemed to lift right out of her and explode in a full, merry laugh. He laughed too, a little incredulously, and her heart leapt at the sound.

Then an impulse seized her. She tilted her head and kissed him.

It was a small kiss. A sudden eager act, born from the moment's euphoria—and perhaps just a little at being forbidden to do it. It lasted only an instant, long enough to feel his lips, first shocked and tight, relax and return the kiss, gentle, unsure of himself. It was sweet, and silly, and awkward, and exciting. It was only an instant—long enough to change everything.

Hyranna pulled away, heart knocking against her ribs, suddenly embarrassed. Balduin was staring at her, blinking.

"Sorry," she said, looking down. Her voice came out a little hoarse and she had to clear her throat. "I don't . . . I don't know why I . . ."

"It's okay." His mouth tilted. "I mean, that was unexpected. But . . . nice."

"*Nice*?" She twisted her face.

Balduin grimaced. "Never mind. I . . . I should go. I need to gather the wood for the pyre, and . . ."

"Wait!" She grabbed his hand, then felt suddenly shy. "Can I . . . can I help you?" It felt odd, asking like that. She would never have asked before; it would've been understood. They were together in everything. But now, something had changed. They were closer, and further away all at once. It was new, and strange, and right now very uncomfortable. It was like she had to learn what to say all over again.

Balduin just looked at her. "Yeah . . . yeah, of course you can help." And Hyranna knew then everything was going to be okay.

Chapter Twelve

Hyranna stood on the river bank beside Balduin, his mother's pyre built up on a raft brimming with wood. Andalina herself had been brought down on a bier of milk-white aspen, carried by Balduin, Kenan Elduna, Dal Adis—the closest thing Andalina had to a family—and his son, Tonu. It was Dal who had found her as a child, wandering the forest alone.

They weren't the only ones in attendance. Marisela was there too, as was Tonu's wife, Lanita, and their baby girl, Josi. Then came Yanu and Nenim, two of the older hunters. Hyranna was touched to see them. There were even a few villagers, come to show respect, though they stood distant, apprehensive, watching Balduin carefully, as if afraid he would turn and curse them if they got too close.

Together in silence, they waited for the sun to set, remembering the stillness, the moment the spirit leaves and the flesh falls empty, its life—gone. Only the sound of the wind could be heard, and the occasional call of a crow, and in the distance, the river as it poured and poured, never ceasing, down towards the sea.

Balduin's face was sombre as he gazed at the pyre. Hyranna reached out to take his hand and he grasped it, holding tight—all the words she needed. Then, as the sun slid below the cliff, she began to sing.

It would be her first time doing the Darkening prayer as Keeper. Her Aunt Nareda had refused to sing for Andalina, and so Hyranna offered to take her place. Now she sang the haunting cry of death: old words she didn't understand, but that flowed off her tongue, beautiful and rich, tasting of a distant time; discordant notes that rose and fell, as if to imitate the mourner's wail; the final note that she had to hold as long as possible, letting it fade out slowly as the light of the sun went out and darkness fell.

It was a privilege to sing for Andalina, and somehow, even though she wasn't very good yet, even though she made mistakes, it was as if the woman's spirit heard and smiled, carried from this realm into the next with that last, long note.

When she was finished, Balduin gave her hand a squeeze, then let go and stepped towards the torch. He lifted it, and, as he moved forward, Kenan Elduna and Dal Adis took hold of either end of the raft, sliding it into the water while Balduin dipped the torch towards the oil-soaked wood. It took only a moment for the flame to catch. Then it began to crackle. All three stepped back, and with long poles, Kenan and Dal pushed the pyre out into the river, and the current took it gently away.

They stood on the shore for a long time, watching the pyre burn as it drifted slowly. The sky grew dark, and the pyre burned brighter. Hyranna thought she could feel its heat. The nights were getting colder, the days shorter. She shivered.

Finally, the Imo'ani turned away: first those who had gathered behind them, and then the inner circle. Dal put his hand on Balduin's shoulder for a moment, and nodded.

Ten summers. Hyranna barely remembered Balduin's father, but it was said he lived a long time near Elamori. Some said he was mad, some a sorcerer from Lendahyr, able to bend the laws of the Three Realms. Sometimes he even healed people, they said, with no more than a touch. So they called him Alutan—an old word for healer, or madman. No one knew where he was from, and no one dared to discover more.

No one except young Andalina. She had *always* been different, so it made sense to the Imo'ani. They didn't question it at first. Why not?

But as time went on, the young woman spent more and more time with Alutan, until one day, she didn't come back.

Here the stories differed, and when Hyranna had asked Dal Adis for the truth, he growled and told her to leave it be. They never spoke of it again. Most agreed, though, that when Andalina returned, she was a changed person. She was heavy with child, but more than that, she was distant and old beyond her years, as if she carried a great secret. Alutan came with her and stayed in Elamori, to the great discomfort of many.

And so Balduin was born. At the very least he was a bastard and the child of outsiders. But there were other rumours. He was conceived with witchcraft, some whispered. He was the mad healer's curse, left to bring evil to them, the payment Alutan would exact for his years of service. And there were even darker tales Hyranna didn't care to recall. It infuriated her, how easily people believed the worst. And yet, there was no denying Balduin's father was a mystery.

Alutan had stayed with Andalina and her son, keeping to himself. For four years, he had stayed. And then suddenly, for no reason anyone knew of, he had vanished.

At first, everyone thought he had returned to the forest. But when time passed, one summer, two, three, and they never saw him, not even once, they wondered if he had gone forever. Whatever the reason, Hyranna assumed he was dead.

She glanced at Balduin Na-es again. Now this was the man they would go looking for? *It didn't matter*. They would probably never find him. He was dead—dead or gone.

She crept near once the others had left, slipping her hand into Balduin's. "You did well."

"You too." He swallowed. "Thanks, Anna."

"For what?"

"For coming. For singing. My mother would have been grateful."

"It's my job."

"It was your aunt's job. You didn't have to do this."

Hyranna shrugged. "Then I guess I wanted to."

He didn't respond right away, but he shifted and looked down at her, brows wrinkled. "Do you still?"

He wasn't asking about the singing anymore. "I'm with you," was all she said.

He smiled. It was a little lopsided, but it lit up his whole face, scrunching his cheeks. "Then meet me tomorrow morning? At the red tree?"

She nodded, paused, and threw her arms around him. She found herself not wanting to let go. The fear returned, sudden and intense. What if . . . ? She squeezed her eyes shut. *Promise me*, she wanted to say, *promise me you won't go without me.* But even in her head, it sounded vain and distrustful. He wouldn't do that to her. Not Balduin. Instead she just whispered in his ear, "I'll see you tomorrow." It wasn't a question. Then she pulled away and hurried after her father.

As soon as they were out of earshot her father gave her a look from the corner of his eye. "Not following your mother's advice, then, eh?"

She decided to play dumb. "What do you mean?"

"Hmm," he said.

"What? I didn't do anything. It's nothing, Papi!"

"Nothing, eh? I've learned that your mother is very wise. I've learned to listen to her when she tells me things."

"She doesn't understand. She thinks Balduin is an outsider."

"He is," her father said quietly.

Hyranna stopped. "How could you say that? Just yesterday, you told the whole village they should treat him like your son. Did you mean it?"

"Of course I meant it, Anna-chi. But not even my words can change what other people see. And to them, he is a curse. He always will be."

"So I can't marry him," Hyranna muttered, echoing her mother's words.

Her father said nothing, and they climbed up to the cave. But just before going in, Kenan paused and looked at her, his round face creased with sorrow. "Anna-chi," he said. "I love you deeply."

She almost burst into tears. Somehow she managed to hold them back, managed to blink them out of her eyes. But her mouth trembled, and if she spoke, she would never be able to keep the tears away.

She was leaving. It hit her. She was leaving, and she would break her father's heart. The tears came anyway, hot and painful.

She grabbed him and hugged him, and he squeezed her back. "I love you too, Papi," she whispered. "I love you so much." But she couldn't say anything else. If he knew, he would try to stop her, and it had to be this way. No matter how much it hurt, it had to be.

"I know," he said quietly.

Then she turned and disappeared into the cave.

***

KENAN WATCHED his daughter turn away, heard the silent words, the ones she couldn't say. And his heart broke.

He waited until she was asleep, until the forest fell to a hush and the night was chill, then he slipped out of the cave. The wind had died. The ropes and bridges barely creaked, except when he pressed a hide-covered foot to them. He moved silently up the side of Elamori. He felt every step. He felt the weight of his people, their fear and uncertainty, their panic. Growing more with every day. Balduin was right. Andalina's death was not at their hands. They were far too terrified for that. It was something else. Something dark. Something coming. It was bound up in everything, Roya and Kota, the strange happenings, and now this.

He came to Andalina's cave and rapped on the door, softly. He waited. There was nothing for a moment, and then a young voice called: "Come in."

Kenan pulled the lever and cracked open the door. It went easily —unbarred, no locks or barricades. Either the boy was foolishly brave, or foolishly trusting. "Don't you want to know who it is?"

"I know," he said. "Besides, if you were Mylar, you wouldn't have knocked."

Kenan grunted. As he entered, he saw a single candle burning on the wall. Balduin stood. He looked sombre, calm, remarkably poised after everything he'd been through. The cut over his eye was still ugly and red, not to mention his other injuries, but he didn't wince or whine. Maker's breath, Kenan admired him! That made what he was about to do even harder.

"Balduin Na-es," he began. "Tell me. Did you think you could steal away my daughter without my knowing?"

The boy had the grace to drop his eyes, brows scrunching together.

"I would never do such a thing, Kenan Elduna," he said.

Kenan paused. A flash of anger rose up, but he wrestled it down, kept his voice calm and controlled. "Lying is beneath you, Balduin. Speak carefully."

"I'm not lying. It's the truth. I'm leaving, and your daughter is coming with me. She insisted, and I won't turn her away."

"You will."

Balduin's head snapped up, clear eyes bursting with unnerving ferocity. "She's no more mine to control than yours. She's a woman now. She has her own mind."

"She is a child. *My* child."

"She's both."

Kenan snorted. "Like you? Too young to understand what you're doing, too old to trust and obey. Is that it?"

"Maybe it's *your* turn to trust Hyranna."

"I trust my daughter implicitly. I do not always trust her choices. And neither would you, if you hadn't let young and fanciful notions of love blind you to the harsh realities you face. You're not a fool, Balduin. Some think the world is a kind place, brimming with opportunity. But you know better, don't you? You've experienced what people are capable of. Sometimes impulses for good, sometimes not. Too often they're ugly, grasping, and scared. Am I right?"

Balduin said nothing, jaw set in a grim line, eyes furrowed.

Kenan went on. "I've tried my best to keep Elamori safe, to keep back the ugliness and encourage people's desire to be good." He shook his head. "I've not always succeeded. I can't change what people are. Yet if you only knew what was out there, beyond our control, you wouldn't rush so heedlessly into danger, bringing my daughter with you. You know better, Balduin Na-es. I see it in your eyes, though you hate it. You hate what you must do. But have you considered? Really and truly? Slavers from the north, raiders from the south, thieves and tyrants and warriors who wouldn't hesitate to stretch out their hands and take hold of you both, two wandering innocents, to do whatever their wickedness desired. They are cruel. I've walked in these places. I've seen things I wish I hadn't, and I've heard worse. You won't be able to protect yourself, much less *her*."

"Stop it!" Balduin's voice quivered. "I know the dangers, but they hate me here. I've got to choose one or the other—"

"And my daughter? What hatred does she face, that she has to throw herself into your very young arms?"

"Please." He almost choked on the word. His face was turning pale. "Don't ask me to do this. I . . . I can't . . . She'd be . . ."

"Devastated. Yes. But better than dead. Better than some Northman's slave." Kenan hated the sound of his own voice, cold and measured and harsh. He hated this more than Balduin, but he couldn't stop now. "And that's just the start. What will you do when the bitter snows blow from the north? We have food, shelter, safety. You won't have any of that. You'll be an outcast, wherever you go, and Hyranna will suffer for it. The world isn't kind to strangers. It's full of war and unrest. Who will shelter you? Will you watch as her fingers turn black from the frost? Will you go cold and hungry, until you'd beg the tyrants of the south to take you in as slaves, just to be free of the cold? What of wolves? What of sickness and injury and infection? Have you the skill—?"

"Stop!" Balduin's voice was small. "I *get* it." Then he folded onto the ground like a leaf, throwing his hands to his face. "I don't want to go. I don't want to. But I have to, don't you see? I have to find my father. He's . . . he's all I have left."

Kenan frowned. "Your father?"

"Yes, my father."

"Oh, child." He shifted, and the hurt slid a little deeper. "I know you don't want to hear this, but . . ."

"He's alive. He *is*."

"Balduin—"

"He *is*." The boy snapped fiery eyes at him. "You have no right to say otherwise."

No right. It had been years since Alutan's disappearance, and regardless of what others claimed, Kenan knew. Alutan had been a good man. He had loved his son. Loved Andalina. Loved them both so desperately, only cruel death could have kept him away. Another mystery, another failure.

Kenan shook his head. "Then I won't say. Only please. Please, my son. If I can't make you reconsider, if you won't trust me or listen to anything I've said, I ask only this: please don't take my daughter with you into the unknown."

He let the words hang in the air. The boy said nothing, didn't even look at him, but he knew it was done. Balduin was an honourable young man. He would do the right thing, no matter how much it hurt.

He waited. Waited for Balduin to come to that conclusion on his own. Waited for him to speak. "I know," he said at last. "I meant to go alone. But she was so happy, and I was . . . Kenan Elduna, I don't want to break her heart."

"You might not have a choice."

Balduin swallowed, then gave the tiniest of nods. *It was enough.*

"So," Kenan said, "here's what we're going to do."

Interlude: The Last Al'kah

ASHKYNAS AB'ADANI AL'KAH

Ashkynas ab'Adani Al'kah huddled in the cleft of the rock. The ground rolled away from him, dotted with grass and shrubs, rustling with a cool breeze. White clouds bunched up against the sky like heaps of unspun wool. This was it. The end of the desert. The far side of the mountains. Life. Hope. But Ashkynas was struck with terror—unable to descend.

There, waiting at the foot of the slope, tending a fire, whistling, happy, wrapped in contentment, was a woman.

Ashkynas stared in horror. Not at the clear evidence of someone else alive in the world—hadn't he always known it? Hadn't he left for this very reason?

No. It was the inconceivable normality of it. As if he hadn't just crossed a world of emptiness. As if living and cooking and being happy were the most natural things a person could do. *Cooking!* As if the world were not in the very throes of death!

He shuddered. The thing in him shuddered. He should go. He should turn back, find another way, flee back up the mountain as fast the thing would allow and cross out of the desert somewhere else.

But she had water. The woman kept it beside her in a large, sloshing canteen. She was cooking meat over the fire, turning it, sprinkling it with a pinch of salt. And every so often, with the audacious carelessness of one accustomed to plenty, she would lift up the canteen and take a hearty slurping gulp.

Ashkynas swallowed. His tongue seemed to grow as he watched, swelling with thirst, filling his mouth with a constant, sticky dryness. The thing sustained him, but no more. They were not on good terms, Ashkynas and the thing he carried. The black stone burned against his bare and bony chest, infusing him with just enough strength to survive. Just that. Nothing more. What would it be like—the sweetness of water? The heaviness of hot meat in his belly? Ashkynas had forgotten.

Yes. It would be good. It would be good, good . . .

But the woman.

He should go. Go now. He whimpered with indecision. A small, involuntary sound. It was enough.

The woman stilled. Her head turned, even as she touched something at her belt. She had a strong, wiry appearance. Strange pale hair danced unbound across her face. She looked straight at Ashkynas.

"*Oelfa gi, shulk,*" she said in a clear, strong voice. Ashkynas pressed tighter against the rock. She repeated herself, beckoning. She used the same alien words. But this time, the thing inside Ashkynas heard, and the meaning was clear.

"Hail, stranger."

Ashkynas gasped in shock. Words. Genuine human words. Not the dark muttering from within him, the mute creature that needled and slipped and clawed inside his mind.

Go, he pleaded with himself. *Flee. Before it's too late!*

But the thing inside would not let him. He could feel it, bending his mind, pulling him towards the living person, hungry and full of aching need.

She beckoned again. "Come. There is room enough by my fire."

Ashkynas rose to a crouch. He edged nearer. Instantly, her face changed. A look of horror and shock. Was he so strange to her? So unsightly? He glanced at himself. Robes draped over skeletal limbs. Hair hung in dark, tattered wisps down the front of his chest. Sandals clung to his feet.

"*Freidtha na!*" she breathed, and leapt to her feet. "You look near death, my friend. Come. Come!" She opened her arms, gesturing to the fire. It was too much to resist. Ashkynas staggered forward, nearer, nearer, yet moving in a wide, sweeping arc—never too close.

The thing woke anyway. It stirred in him. It tightened his chest until he could barely breathe. He forced his eyes away. To the fire, to the hot meat. He folded to the ground, long limbs wrapping together like a shroud.

"This is a far country to wander in," said the woman. "But all are brothers in a far land, as my father would say. What name have you?"

Ashkynas shut his eyes, struggling to think. Why was he here? Why had he come? This woman … this woman …

"I am Ethel," she said. She sat cross-legged on the other side of the fire, easy and relaxed. She drew a knife and began to saw off the leg of the roasting creature. "You must have a mighty hunger, so skinny as you are. Will you eat?"

She leaned over, proffering the leg of meat.

"W-water," Ashkynas rasped through a burning throat. His lips split with the effort, and a little trickle of blood leaked onto his chin.

The woman frowned and withdrew the meat, sinking her teeth into it herself. She chewed. She reached for the canteen.

"You mean this?" she said around a slurping mouthful. "I speak Aethen only, I'm afraid. And a shred of bad Manturian. Just the good words." She gave a lopsided grin. "But this is not useful to us, is it? I have no Lendahyn for such as you. But perhaps …"

She paused. She waved the leg at herself. "Ethel," she said, then waved the leg at Ashkynas.

Now the thing was looking. Really looking. Ashkynas could feel its need, waking and pushing. His fingers flexed against his knees. They curled and bent and straightened, and at their fullest, a shiver ran through him.

"E-thel," the woman repeated, leaning forward, holding out the canteen. "And what name have you?" She pointed. "*You?*"

Ashkynas stared at the canteen. So near. So far away. An insurmountable distance, born of consequence and fear. Yet there he was, already reaching, already grasping, fingers brushing hers—the barest touch. And it was too late.

Ashkynas shut his eyes, afraid to move, to speak, to look. With a blast of cold air, the fire puffed out. Smoke trailed between them.

"*Freidtha na.*" The woman pulled back. There was another rush of wind, harder, stronger, prickling with cold fingers.

"I am the emptiness," Ashkynas said. "I am the *Aktyr.*"

The woman leapt to her feet, backing away as she reached for the axe at her belt, fingers tight and hard. "A daemon," she said. "Freidtha, protect me."

She edged back, but the wind was blowing harder now. Faster. It howled like a dying beast, snapping over rock and hill, whipping through grass. It lashed once around Ashkynas, then seized Ethel.

She screamed. Ashkynas surged to his feet, breathing hard, feeling the burst of impossible, horrible strength. "Stop!" he gasped. "Stop!" He reached for Ethel, but she reared back and slammed the axe into him with brutal strength—straight into his ribs, snapping bone, crushing flesh. Pain howled through Ashkynas, but it didn't stop the thing inside.

His eyes flared. The fire burst through him. "Ending!" his voice pitched to a shriek. "All is ending. All is breaking. All will suffer for our greed. And you!" A finger shot towards her. "You will be first."

He grasped the axe-shaft. The thing inside didn't feel pain as Ashkynas did. Or maybe it didn't care. Or maybe it liked the pain. It wrenched out the blade without a thought, spraying blood across the grass. Ethel scurried back, tried to flee.

"Run, Elbert!" she screamed into the hills. "Run!"

But the wind fastened around her, roaring and pulling. It dragged her back. She kicked. She cried out the names of her gods. Her teeth flashed.

Ashkynas dropped the axe, and the wind hurled her into his grasp. He held her as she howled and writhed, as the wind tore into her, needling through skin and bone. Her eyes bulged. Her teeth stood stark against shrinking lips. Her bones cut through her own skin. She threw back her head and screamed—the most horrible, wrenching sound Ashkynas had ever heard. Then her lungs burst into shreds of flesh, and the dried remains crumpled through his fingers into a withered heap.

The wind died. Ashkynas hunched forward, weeping, shaking.

He was strong again. He was alive. He was bursting with a glut of vigour—more than he even knew what to do with.

"Wretch!" he sobbed. "Cursed wretch! No. *No!* I didn't mean . . . ! I didn't mean . . . !"

He staggered away. He took three lurching steps. And there—crouched behind rock and bush, trembling in horror—two gaping blue eyes.

A boy. Ashkynas stopped, stared, head shaking, shaking.

"No . . ."

The boy burst from the bush. He was brandishing a stick, eyes hot and terrified, screaming battle.

Ashkynas fled. He bounded over the hills, leaping, howling in grief and rage against the thing—the thing he hated, the thing he had become. Heedless of the ground. Heedless of what he left behind. What trailed after him like a shadow . . .

———

THE BOY GROUND TO A STOP, chest heaving, furious and scared, hands trembling around his desperate weapon. He watched the daemon flee, the strips of dirty cloth snapping behind him as he ran, his moans melting into the wind and the grass and the unbound sky.

Then the boy saw the shadow. A crackling scar, a patch of darkness, a creeping line—not in the ground, not in the soil, not in the grass—but in everything. It looked unreal, a thing that should not be. It trailed after the screaming murderer, reaching through the grass, but when the boy looked down, he saw it running between his own legs. He turned. He followed it with his eyes, to the dried heap where his mother had once been. He stared, wide-eyed, frozen with shock. There was a deep, shuddering groan. The crack split wider. Wider. And beneath it was not cold, unforgiving earth. Not even the fires of the under-realm. There was nothing. Only dead, seething emptiness.

When the boy looked up again, the daemon was gone.

Shadow

ISHVANDU AB'ADMUNDI

Year 455 after the fall of Kayr

———

Once, we were Undying. Before the Wars of Rending, before men and women turned on each other, bringing death to themselves, leaving death to us. We are the children of death, and we live in the shadow of death, and death is our legacy.

Once, we were Undying. Once we filled the earth with glory and wonder, with music and law. We spread beauty across the world. We tended all things with love.

Until we found the Half-Being of Light, the Avanir.

It was a gift. It was meant to show us more, to lead us further, bestowed on us by the Chorah'dyn, Great Tree and Guardian of the World.

But the power was too much for us. It changed us. Especially . . . it changed him. Shatayeth Warbringer, the first and greatest of the Undying, and now the Last.

The Chorah'dyn promised us the Avanir's power has changed, that it will come through her alone and be only for a few. I pray she is right. Otherwise, I fear it could destroy us again.

———

From the Chronicles of the Last Age and the Ending of Kayr, set down by Andari ab'Andala, named Al'kah, first of the Age of Exile: scroll 1, lines 1-10

Chapter Thirteen

The sun slanted sideways through the main yard of the Guardian's Hall, reflecting off the walls in a hazy glow, interrupted only by the long shadow of the Tower. Drenched in golden light, the Guardians stood, silent in their long rows, and still. The very air was still, as if listening. Then a high, clear voice, rich with age, rose with the familiar rhythms of the Darkening prayer. I could barely see him from my place at the back with the other Novices, but I knew that voice. The Al'kah and leader of this Hall, speaking the familiar words.

"Wisdom that comes with age," he said. As one, the Guardians moved into first position, feet planted, knees bent just a little.

"Justice that comes with law." Second position: a strong back leg, fists ready to receive.

"Strength against darkness." Shift forward, feet moving, swift, controlled.

"Honour unto death." Twist, hold.

"Grant us these as you will, Yl'avah, great Founder of Good, the Brightsword and High Ruler."

Movement was the heart of the prayer: a careful flow, one stance into the next, controlled, unhurried, then fast, a reverse, in perfect time, a symbol of strength and unity, all moving as one. *An impossible image*. But an important one, especially amongst the Guardians. It wed words to action, oath to movement. How many times had I taken a back stance and thought *justice*, a forward stance and thought *strength*? I moved with them, leading the Novices, younger ones at the back, older in front, even as I watched the eighth kiyah ahead of me, the storehouse guards and record-keepers. We ended in first position again, stepping into a tight stance.

"Let us rule as Keepers of Law and Guardians of the People, for as long as you give us the right, and no longer. May it be so," the Al'kah finished, and with one voice the Guardians echoed: "*May it be so*," a sudden crisp swell of sound, replaced by silence. Then we knelt, heads bowed, knuckles pressed to the earth, a ripple of movement— then nothing. We waited, acknowledging Yl'avah, the great Maker and High Ruler, in perfect stillness.

I never cared much for Yl'avah. Talk of the Maker usually led to talk of our failure, and the Avanir, and our *purpose*, as if dying in the desert was the only thing we were good for—we who weren't Chosen by the Avanir to carry its light. And yet, just as with the Temple prayer songs, there was a peace in this moment, a whisper of rightness and truth that went beyond words, that tugged at my soul, until the sun slipped over the horizon. Then it was over.

We rose in silence and began making our way to the Commons, a long, narrow hall on the north side, next to the storage cellars and the Novice's quarters. It would be a small meal tonight, now Kaprash was dragging into its fourth month, but I was hungry for it all the same. I took a few steps, and like the certainty of sunfall itself, Bray fell into step beside me.

"I heard what happened," he said, glancing around to make sure the other Novices weren't listening. "Light and all, they're going to make you wait another year? A whole 'nother year as a Novice?" Unfortunately, Bray's voice carried like a sounding horn, even when he thought he was being quiet.

"What?" Polityr jumped up and slung his arm around my shoulder, almost knocking me into the ground. "What do you mean, wait another year?"

I sighed. Word was getting around anyway, and better now than after the Renewing, when everyone would expect me to take the oath.

"Koryn set me up for it," I said, digging my elbow into Pol's ribs and pushing him back. "But I *am* going to be a Guardian."

"Of course you are!" Bray said. "It just means you're stuck with us another year. That's not so bad?"

I wrinkled my nose.

"Not so bad? You haven't had to smell yourself."

"Hey!"

"It's true." Polityr chuckled. "Guardians are given soap for a reason, you know. It's called washing."

"Not during Kaprash!"

I lifted one eyebrow, trying to give my best Tushani'sal impression. "*Especially* during Kaprash. Do you think a Guardian lets himself be caught *smelly*?"

Polityr laughed, joined by some of the other Novices. Bray flushed. "You're pulling me. None of *you* lot smell that great either."

"Maybe you've forgot what clean smells like," said Bretina, as she slid up between us.

There was more laughter. Actually, Bray was right. The whole pack of them were rotten by this point in Kaprash. You got used to bathing and washing as a Guardian; we were all expected to do it. I just never realized how much I appreciated that until the Avanir dried up and everyone was put on water rations. Still, it wouldn't kill them to sponge away a bit of the grime, every now and then.

We hurried to the Commons and grabbed our portions of hemp bread, using cups of camel milk to soften the dry, hard cakes. Most of the Novices sat together, kneeling at one of the low tables, laughing and jibing each other. I found myself staring at my cup and half-eaten bread. *Tomorrow*. Tomorrow I'd ride with real Guardians. Outside the Hall. On patrol. Where Labourers young and old would kill for a cup of camel-milk.

"You okay?" Bray whispered from across the table. Loudly.

I shot him a look. "Of course I'm okay."

The boy shrugged. "You don't look okay. You're doing that thing again."

"That *thing*?"

"Yes, where your eyebrows try to fight each other by knocking heads. Like this." He gave a fierce, comical frown, while he wiggled his brows, trying to get them to touch in the middle.

I gave a snort. "You're ridiculous."

"Hey," he leaned in. "We're both off-duty tonight. Want to lose in that stone-game of yours?"

"Me *lose*? At jik'u? Bray, you never even come close to beating me."

"There's always a first." He grinned. "Turn me down, you're a coward."

"Yeah, you big chicken," Polityr added, wiggling his own brows. The older Novice hated jik'u, but he did enjoy giving pointed commentary as Bray floundered around trying to fend off my assaults.

I opened my mouth, then spotted Tala entering the Commons with a small knot of Guardians. She was talking and laughing, so at ease with them, that confident tilt to her chin as she listened. Then her eyebrows shot up and she gave her head a shake.

"No, Jin'sal." She had a cheeky habit of calling other Guardians by their familiar names, but tacking on the honorific as if it evened things out. "You're missing the point entirely! It's not about functionality. It's about predictability. If we change the demands each season, we become unpredictable and therefore untrustworthy." She walked past, the conversation fading again, but I found myself watching her, her easy movements, her poise, the relaxed readiness in her posture, as if she had years of experience instead of just one. She knelt at the table in a quick, graceful motion, then caught my eye and lit up with a little half-smile.

Polityr poked me in the ribs.

"Ow!" I shot him a look.

"You're so obvious sometimes, Vanya, you might as well have a sign hanging off your nose."

"What? What are you talking about?" I bit into the tough bread.

He chuckled. "Tala."

I stopped, mid-chew, then forced myself to swallow as if nothing had happened. The bread stuck in my throat. Yl'avah's might, Pol too? I was going to have to be more careful. I took a gulp of milk. Swallowed, coughing and trying to give a threatening eye at the same time. "Mind yourself, Pol."

"Just saying."

"Don't."

"I mean, you and Tala would be the—"

"I said *don't*." I leaned in. "And that's Atali sai'Neraia to you."

He shrugged. "Like *you* would call her that."

"That's because we're friends."

"Uh huh."

"Just drop it!"

Thankfully, the other Novices had started up their own conversation. Only Bretina was watching us out of the corner of her eye. Had she heard? *Damn*, no one could know about this, not yet. Not for another year at least—if Tala would even have me.

Bray was tipping back the last of his milk, then he poked me across the table. "Alright, a couple matches before sleep, Vanya. What do you say? Come on."

He was already on his feet, and with a shrug I popped the last of the bread into my mouth and rose. "I've got to teach you how to spot that double trap again. You keep running right into it and making the whole sand-blasted thing too easy for me."

"But I've got an idea this time," he laughed. "Just you wait!" Now that he wasn't *trying* to be quiet, every Guardian in the Commons probably heard him.

"Very well. Show me your great idea, and I'll show you where you went wrong."

"What, no faith in me? Just wait! One of these days I'm going to surprise you!"

"I look forward to it." Which was the truth. I was itching for a challenge. The Novices were rotten at jik'u, and the older Guardians had more important things to do. Then there was Kulnethar, who still hadn't returned to check on my injuries. Figures.

"Come on, Vanya! You're as slow as a brick." Bray's voice rang obnoxiously through the corridors. I found myself wondering, not for the first time, how in Yl'avah's name they were going to make a Guardian out of him.

Kaprash ended the next morning.

The Dawning prayer had barely finished when one of the sentries on duty rushed back in, shouting the news like an ecstatic green Tasker: "Water! Water! I see water! Al'kah!"

The Al'kah, marked by a simple collar of gold, turned and paused. An expectant hush fell across the yard. "So be it," his reedy voice declared. "A new year."

The Hall erupted. The eighth kiyah peeled off to count the stores and prepare what we could for a feast. The third kiyah swept towards the walls and the sounding horns. Umaala began to shoulder through the ranks, calling orders. "First, released. Second, stay on active duty. Seventh, you have watch of the Hall. Fourth?" He turned to Tala's kiyah. "You're on patrol. Third, fifth, sixth: released." There was a flurry of activity as the Hall switched abruptly from the tasks of Kaprash to Renewing.

"What about us, sal'ah?" I asked as Umaala paused. *What about me?*

He turned and frowned at the Novices and Taskers, as if wishing he could find something useful for us to do. "Released," he said instead.

"Yes!" Bray shot forward at a gallop.

I snatched the collar of his robe, nearly yanking him off his feet. "Like a *Guardian*, Bray, not a year-calf." Then I hurried after Umaala.

"Sal'ah!"

He grunted. "What?"

"Shouldn't I be joining the fourth, like you said?"

"Not today."

"But they're on patrol. I could—"

"Released," he glowered at me, then softened. "Enjoy Renewal. The assignment will still be there tomorrow."

He moved on, shouting more orders, directing the Hall.

I sighed. Being released meant we could join the festivities at the Avanir's pool, but all my nervous anticipation shrivelled into disappointment. *The fourth.* I would have gone with Tala. I would have stood with real Guardians. Done real Guardian work. With Tala. But not today.

I led the Novices from the Hall. I was eighteen now, I realized. Old enough to be a Guardian myself. I *would* have been, if not for Koryn.

Koryn and my own stupidity.

Umaala was right. I had to stop ignoring my part. The Circle expected me to fail, wanted me to fail. It was up to me to prove them wrong. I could do it. I was ready.

The sun seemed hotter outside the Guardian's Hall. Maybe it was the large swath of barren ground, sloping from the front gates. Maybe it was the openness of it: no storerooms to duck into, no arches, none of the long, cool corridors that lined the Hall with grim efficiency. The Guardian's Hall was the westernmost edge of Shyandar, though for us, it was the centre of everything. From here, we could see the goat stables, the tanneries to the north, the first cluster of Labourers' huts, the fields, and far beyond, the Temple, rising with the eastern cliffs. To the south, it was the Craftsquarter. Most days we could hear the spinning of weavers, the clack of their looms, could smell the flat-breads baking in the deep furnaces at night. During Kaprash, all of that faded—but today was Renewing. Today Shyandar was abuzz. Word spread. Bakers' children ran out of the streets, squealing and laughing. Their parents were close behind. Labourers drifted from the north, their thin, tired faces lit with impossible hope. *Renewing. Water at last.*

We bled together like streams flowing into one pool, all journeying to the heart of Shyandar, following the main road from the Hall to the Flatrock. The fields rose thick on either side, cracked and ready for harvest—but our eyes were drawn forward, beyond the fields and dry irrigation channels, beyond the paths, now streaming with eager feet, beyond the empty lake, forward to what we could all see, from almost every vantage point in Shyandar: the Avanir.

The wait was over. Distant black arms, twisted into the ghost of a tree, shimmered as morning sun danced over water. The Novices could restrain themselves no longer. They broke into a run, whooping and laughing. I didn't join them. I walked properly, back straight.

I thought of how serious and proper the Guardian Taskers had always looked to me as a boy. Now they were just kids, barely old enough to hold a training sword without tripping on it. But as far as the rest of Shyandar was concerned, the image had to hold. We were Guardians—even when we weren't.

I merged with a family of Labourers, an old man, three adult daughters, and a brood of children. The women were carrying the two youngest, and the others trailed beside, too weak to run. One boy, not yet of Age, glanced at me. Our eyes met.

"Uh . . . hi," I said.

A flash of hatred ran across his face. He pressed close to his mother, and the look she gave me was just as cold. They hurried on. I stared after them, speechless. Things had changed since the Long Kaprash. I knew it. Everyone knew it. It hung in the air: an odour of distrust. Too many lives lost, too many fingers pointing, pointing towards the ones in charge. *Their fault*. But even today? Even Renewing?

I wanted to run after them and demand an explanation for their rudeness. Except I already knew. I watched them go, frowning.

"That boy's papa? Dead three weeks past," said a voice. I glanced behind me to see an old Labourer with a pinched face.

"Friend of yours?" I asked.

"Maybe. Does a man get too old for friends?"

"You tell me."

He laughed, revealing a gap-toothed smile, and red, swollen gums. "The old die faster than rats these days. So what's the point? Friendship is for the young."

I thought about this, then shook my head. "I'm sorry anyway."

"*Are* you? One less mouth to feed, isn't that how you folks see it? Or is it two less hands?" He wiggled his knobby fingers. "Don't worry, my useless old gut will follow soon."

I snorted. "The way I see it, if two five-months of Kaprash didn't kill you off, nothing will."

The man guffawed, loud and rickety. I swore I heard his bones cracking. "Maybe so, young blade, maybe so. Never thought of it like that before. Tell me: you have any dead behind those walls of yours?"

"Not this year," I said before the meaning of his words caught up to me.

"As I suspected." He winked, then fell back to his own meandering pace.

I continued on alone in the centre of the path. The Novices had ran on ahead, the other Guardians still at the Hall. I stuck out, painfully clean, painfully fed. A clot of Labourers walked ahead of me, Crafters behind. They seemed suddenly to be glancing at me, whispering, pointing, glowering.

If I had a keshu, they wouldn't look at me that way. I quickened my pace. I tried to ignore them. Except for the man—the old man's winking, knowing look, burned into my mind. None dead in the Guardian's Hall. *As I suspected.*

The look occupied me all the way across the fields, around the Flatrock, and down into the cracked lakebed. Thankfully, the pool's edge was not so grim. Children were laughing and splashing in the shallows. Others were passing out fresh bowls of water, straight from the Avanir's towering black sides. A few Acolytes were singing, one plucking away at a lyre, while the rest clapped and danced and sang along.

I spotted the Novices. They were looking very un-Guardian-like indeed, chasing each other around the pool's edge, then tripping and wrestling in the shallows. But no one seemed to mind. Bray took an especially fantastic fall, spinning on his head and landing with a splash, his feet shooting through the air. *Clumsy idiot.* I found myself smiling.

"Vanya!"

I turned towards the bright mop of hair. "Kylan!" I said. "Where have you been? You were supposed to check on me, remember?" I held up my injured hand, still swollen from the cut running across my palm.

Kulnethar winced. "Sorry, Vanya. The last few days have been . . . difficult."

"What? People dying on you too?"

"Yes."

I swallowed and looked away, annoyed at my own flippant tone. Of course there would be some who died. Kulnethar worked in the healing rooms. He saw the sick and injured from all over Shyandar. Some would live, some wouldn't. It was just the way of it. So why the sudden, stinging guilt?

None dead in the Guardian's Hall.

"Who was it this time?" I asked.

Kulnethar shook his head, saying nothing, so I turned to watch the Avanir again.

Bretina was timing the boys, counting beats to see how long they could hold their breath. They looked ridiculous, crouching down with their faces stuck under the water. One of the Taskers surfaced with a gasp, while a few others laughed and jeered.

I glanced at Kulnethar, ready to distance myself from the Taskers, then stopped. He had a pinched look on his face, hands clenched in front of him, trembling, on the verge of tears.

"Yl'avah's might, what?"

He looked away.

"Oh come on, Kylan. What's so bad you can't even say it? People die. It's a part of Kaprash. It's what happens. You've been a healer for years now, shouldn't you know—"

"Vanya," he whispered. "Shut up."

I frowned and slung my arms across my chest, focusing on the Novices again. Suddenly, their laughter seemed forced. Their games ridiculous. The Acolytes' music painfully out of place.

Then I noticed some Labourer boys with dusty hair and dirt-smeared faces, including the one I met on the road here. The one whose father died. They were watching the Guardian Novices, faces eager, longing to join in, though they wouldn't dare. The Novices were taking over the entire pool, chasing off the others and hogging most of the water.

I rolled my eyes and marched over to them. "What's going on here?" I demanded, trying my best Umaala voice. Apparently it worked, because most of the Novices jerked up, faces and hair dripping, eyes darting around. "Blood and light, you're behaving like children. Umaala ab'Krushaya'sal would have your skin for such a display! Get out!"

Some looked confused. The older ones looked like they wanted to punch me. Only Polityr nodded and obeyed, and enough people liked him soon everyone was splashing out of the water, straightening their tunics, shaking out their hair. Then Bray popped up, gasping and coughing.

"I won!"

"Idiot." Bretina shoved him. He twisted and sent her crashing into the water instead, then danced out of the pool. A moment later, Bretina roared after him.

"You're supposed to be training them or something?" Kulnethar said behind me.

I snorted. "Me? Yl'avah's might, no. I'm just stuck with them."

There was a pause. "They aren't letting you take the oath, are they?"

So he did notice. "Next year." I hurried to change the subject. "Umaala's assigning me on patrol tomorrow. With the fourth."

"Oh? Good news?"

"Yes." I paused. "I think so." I paused again, frowning. "It's just . . ."

"You're worried. About seeing them. About going back."

"Naw." I shrugged. "It'll be fine."

Neither of us spoke for a moment. The noise of the crowd drifted around us, people laughing and shouting, flowing this way and that, people talking, people dancing, people standing silent, like us. Relief and sorrow, joy and fear.

Finally, Kulnethar let out a long, heavy sigh. "I tried to deliver a baby," he said. "My first. The midwife was ill, and the other healers were occupied, and they all think so highly of me. I tried to tell them it isn't true. I'm not what they think I am. I can't . . . I can't do everything. I've helped before, but never . . . never on my own like that. It was supposed to be an easy one. The mother was healthy. It was going fine. Everything was fine. Then . . . it wasn't."

I swallowed, frowning towards the Avanir, anywhere but on Kulnethar's wretched face.

"The baby was so small. It couldn't breathe right. And the mother was bleeding. Just bleeding, I couldn't get her to stop. I called for help, but no one came. There were other emergencies. Other patients. Too few of us. I tried . . . I tried . . ."

"You lost them."

Kulnethar nodded. "Yeah." He paused, struggling against tears. "But it happens right? People die. It's . . . part of Kaprash."

I winced at the sound of my own careless words. "Kylan . . ."

"Sorry." He swiped at his face. "I'm not angry with you. It's not your fault. And . . . you're right. It happens. It's happened before. It'll happen again. It was just . . . my first."

I didn't know what to say, so this time, I decided to just nod and keep my mouth shut. Kulnethar hovered there for a moment, then excused himself: he had things to do, patients to tend to, herbs to sort. He turned away.

"Kylan," I heard myself say. "I'm going to fix it."

He stopped, glanced back at me. "What?"

"This. I'm . . . I'm going to fix Kaprash."

He laughed. "You're delusional, you know that, right? But thanks. I understand."

"I mean it." I clenched my fists. "I don't know how, but . . . we can do better. The Guardians. I *know* we can."

He blinked, as if hearing me for the first time. "It doesn't work like that, Vanya."

Then someone was calling him away, and with a last worried glance, he was gone.

———

TALA JOINED US NEAR SUNFALL, her and the rest of the Guardians. The Taskers, not yet of Age, were sent back.

It was a cool evening. Or maybe that was just the effect of the Avanir's spray, caught up in the swirling wind, the sun casting its last rays across the pool, dancing and sparkling through the water. As a child, watching from the north wall, eyes reflecting back the strange fire at the heart of Shyandar, it had seemed so mysterious, so wondrous. Forbidden, even. Then I had come of Age.

We gathered at the edge of the pool, Labourers, Guardians, Acolytes, all side-by-side, all of us, even the sick and weak and those needing to be carried, near four thousand of us, if the last census was still valid. There would be updates, a tally of the losses, a reapportioning of the stores, same as every Kaprash.

Then the High Elder stepped out, and the soft lull of voices fell into silence.

"Behold, a new year!" he cried in a loud voice, and a cheer went up. A cheer for survival. Ethanir ab'Estaldir had aged since I'd seen him last. His hair was completely grey now, and his shoulders were stooped. But I stood near the front with several of the Guardians, and as he turned, I saw his eyes had lost none of their blue fire.

"This is a glorious day," he continued. "We have passed through darkness and dryness and emerged into the light. The Chosen have triumphed, as we knew they would, with the strength of the Avanir, with the strength they carried from this day, and the Life. They braved the long unknown path back to Ashianys and the Great Tree, the Guardian of the Pillars of Law, back to where it began, and to where the Law was broken by us, threatening all Life with the final destruction."

He paused at that. *Back to Ashianys*. What would it be like to be Chosen? I had wanted it, that first time I stood here. Wasn't that my dream? To go back to the Old Lands? To see Ashianys with my own eyes, and learn of the wonders of our past?

But that was only the first time. Now . . .

I found myself frowning as the High Elder turned, eyes scanning the crowd. "We all know the price of failure. This is what we were sent here to do. To *un*do the horrors of our past. To ensure the cleansing of the Lifewater with the fire of the Avanir, to keep at bay the suffering for which we are responsible. And so our task must go on, the same task that has gone on since that day, given to us by the Great Chorah'dyn—the same task that spurred our Chosen to take up the burden of the power of the Avanir. Because of them, we can see this day again, and because of this day, we can see that Life goes on—we can Choose again."

The speech was over. No cheer this time. As one, we gazed over the High Elder's head, towards the Avanir. And we waited.

The sun slipped lower, until with a wink, it disappeared beyond the horizon. The golden sky darkened into red, and the light that shone over the water went out. There was a hush, a deep breath. No one stirred. No one dared to think, *what if*. But inevitably, as always, the Avanir began to glow.

As if it had gathered up the last rays of the sun, the black stone began to flicker. Everything grew dark, but the Avanir burned brighter. Flashes appeared, licks of fire tracing patterns down the rock. Symbols materialized in the flames, and burnt out. Colours flashed over its surface, and were swallowed up. The water itself ran like liquid gold, and soon the whole lakebed was dancing with a chaos of light.

I swallowed. It was beautiful. No, it was dangerous. I could feel it, pulsing behind my eyes, a terrible, overwhelming presence. Not just light. Not just water. *Power.* Something ancient, beyond memory of time, beyond us, beyond Kayr. Beyond even the desert.

Just a stupid rock.

The High Elder lifted his hand, turned, and gestured into the crowd, his body framed by the fire of the Avanir.

"Who will be first? Who will step forward to test themselves, to see if they are among those Chosen to carry our fate?"

A single woman stepped out of the crowd, red cloak swirling around her heels, hair twisted into intricate knots: Neraia sai'Kalysa. It was tradition for the head of the Circle to go first, though she was never Chosen. She wouldn't be. It was understood, in some sure, unspoken way.

With head high, she stepped into the pool and waded towards the flaming stone, soon dwarfed by its size. One hand rested on her keshu, the other reached out. She passed through the stream of golden water and pressed her hand to the rock of the Avanir. Nothing happened. We watched, waiting as she stood. Then she dropped her hand and turned away. The crowds parted to form a long, clear aisle, and she passed through, her whole body shimmering and dripping with light.

Others followed. They came, one at a time, touching the fiery stone, waiting, then retreating down the long aisle, out towards the edge of the lakebed. There they stood, watching the rest of us, some still glimmering with the Avanir's light, some faded now, barely visible in the dark.

Then it happened.

The thrumming began: beneath my feet, building in my chest, buzzing at the base of my throat. No one else seemed to hear it. Only me. And every time it was the same. I braced myself, knowing what was about to happen.

Light speared the darkness. Everyone threw up their hands, shielding their eyes. I staggered back. There was a twist in my mind, then something was pulling at it, bending. *Reaching, the shadows. Cold. Cold. And pain without end . . .*

I clamped my teeth together to keep from screaming. My mind gaped. I saw the desert. I saw Shyandar. I saw everything, laid out like a game of jik'u, a single, infinite force throbbing at its centre. Connected. Everything. A force that could have crushed me.

Tala gripped my arm, keeping me up. She knew, though I hadn't told her everything. Only that it was linked to what had happened, all those years ago. It lasted a few thundering heartbeats. Then it was over.

I straightened, trying to mask the quiver in my legs, the shortness of my breath, battling back the urge to be sick. The *fear*. Yl'avah's might, how I hated it!

"Look," Tala whispered. "Someone's been Chosen."

I blinked against the pattern of light still burnt behind my eyes and looked up. A man emerged, grey-haired, with a grizzled beard. A Labourer, by his short, tattered old robes. No one knew *why* the Avanir picked the ones it did. It seemed random. Guardians were Chosen least often; Elders and Guardian Lords, almost never. Proportionately, it made sense. And yet . . .

The man was alive with light. It danced and leapt over his body like flames, while in his hand, there was a pinprick of piercing starlight. The Avanir's shard. Unnatural, wondrous, dangerous. The thing, or so they claimed, that would save our lives. Save *all* Life.

He didn't follow the others to the edge of the lakebed. Instead, he took his place next to the High Elder, an unreadable expression on his face. *It was an honour to be Chosen*, they said—yet not everyone was eager for that fabled, unknown fate.

No one spoke. No one moved. Not for a long, hushed moment. And then, one by one, the Kyr'amanu moved forward, just as before. The Choosing continued. One down, two to go.

"Well?" Bray popped up beside me.

"Well, what?"

Tala elbowed me. "You're the oldest now, Vanya. Remember?"

Blood and light, I hated this part.

"Alright." I grimaced. "Let's go." Everyone had to go, eventually, unless all three were Chosen before you stepped up. And *that* wasn't something a Guardian let happen. It was shameful for even Labourers to be left standing, untried.

I stepped out, the Novices trailing. Tala would go with her kiyah, as was traditional. Even still, I found myself swallowing back regret when she didn't stay at my side. Bray followed, as always, and Bretina and Polityr were close behind.

I passed the High Elder in his clean white robes. I couldn't help glancing at him. He was watching me, blue eyes serious, fixed on me, as if he could see my thoughts. He nodded, but I turned away, face burning.

When someone threatened to have you killed, it wasn't a thing you forgot. Did he have it still? Did he carry it with him, the thing he had stolen from me? After all that, they had the nerve to call *me* the thief. *Typical.*

Then it was my turn. I waded into the pool, almost blinded by the ceaseless, dancing light. I tried to steady myself, tried to shove down my fear. *Chosen never came back.* The thought churned inside of me, bothering me, tugging on me. I took another step. But it was true. They were sent off, celebrated as heroes, and never heard from again. No one knew what happened to them. No one even spoke of it—only that they were sent to cleanse the Lifewater and undo the horrors of our past. Whatever *that* meant. I clenched my fists.

No more fear. I stepped forward, pushing the water with my legs, feeling the fountain's shimmering spray as it drenched me with light. It looked like it should burn, but it didn't. It felt . . . clean. I raised an arm. "Don't even think of it," I growled. Then I pressed my hand to the Avanir's surface.

It hit me, as always. It was like a storm wind, rushing through my fingers, blasting me with power. So much power. So big. Sweeping into every part of me, through every Realm. An unstoppable, over-whelming force. *What are you?* The ground opened beneath me. I was falling. I was being swallowed up. I . . .

I jerked back, stumbling, heart throbbing against my chest. My hand peeled away from the stone. Nothing. I felt a wave of relief. I hadn't been picked.

To think I had ever wanted to be chosen by *that*.

I swallowed and took several breaths, trying to gather myself, to pretend I felt the same thing everyone else did. Then I hurried back and followed the others out towards the edge of the lake.

I had barely made it through the crowds when it came again. Tala wasn't there to hold me up. My mind was still fresh from my encounter. I reeled, tripped, and sprawled onto the cracked lakebed, eyes stinging, mind threatening to crack under the strain.

Thankfully, everyone was paying more attention to the Avanir.

A hand slipped through my arm and helped me back up. "You can really feel it, can't you?" Bretina whispered

"Yl'avah's blasted might, it . . . it's nothing."

"I'm not blind, you know."

"I tripped."

"Uh huh. Don't worry, I won't say anything, but—hey!" her head twisted back towards the Avanir. "Look who it is!"

I turned. There was a new Chosen standing next to the High Elder, a thick-armed Novice, dark hair dripping with light.

"Polityr?" I frowned.

"Imagine that," Bretina said. "I've never known a Chosen before."

"Me neither," I said numbly.

It was supposed to be a good thing. An honour. A friend of mine had been Chosen, and he would carry the light of the Avanir. He would leave Shyandar to heal the Lifewater. He would leave and never return.

Strange, how the tightening around my chest was a lot more like grief.

Chapter Fourteen

They say it was the Great Tree, the Chorah'dyn, who exiled us into the desert. They say we broke something—the Pillar of Blood, the foundation of the Seen. Four hundred and fifty-five years ago, they say, give or take a decade.

They say a lot of things.

I didn't always believe them. There were stories upon stories, those days in the Temple. Some made sense to me, others didn't. Some I doubted, while others I listened to in rapt wonder. But some stories, I realized—the most important stories—were the ones they never told you.

My first year as a Tasker was an endless tedium of sweat. I worked side by side with my father, forced into it, under threat of doing so the rest of my life. Sowing, digging, irrigating, tending, cutting, threshing, retting, digging again, and more digging. I hated it.

But for midday break.

On that day, one that began like so many others, I hurried across the North Fields, joined by my fellow Taskers. They chatted together as they walked, but I dashed ahead of them. We Labourers were easy to spot: dirty and sweaty, with short, belted robes, tangled hair, head-wraps bundled under our arms, and the roughest hemp-spun shirts. I wasn't going to stick out more than I had to.

I slowed as I approached the Temple, then plunged into the cool, shaded gardens, down the path, and up the great, wide steps that led to the Commons. It was open to the air on all sides, supported by thick, branching columns and massive blocks of stone, all white-bleached and clean. Tables were laid with food, and we could eat as we came, whatever we liked. Of course, they were always watching. I was convinced this too was a part of our training.

I grabbed a handful of pistachios, a hunk of flatbread, and a fig—simple food, but satisfying. Then I found my way to the far end of the hall. I liked to stare out at the gardens, away from the other Taskers.

"By yourself again, Vanya," Kulnethar laughed, popping up beside me. I rolled my eyes. Not even my father called me that. "Why don't you try the sweetcakes? They're fresh from the bakers this morning. A treat."

I shrugged and munched on another pistachio. Kulnethar could get away with being indulgent, but I wasn't sure I had the same luxury.

In groups and clusters, in knots, in lines, and one by one, the Taskers arrived, from every corner of Shyandar. Students from the Temple, Labourers from the fields and stables. From the Craftsquarter, bakers and weavers and clay-makers.

The Guardian Taskers arrived last of all. They were the smallest group, only eight, and even the youngest walked differently, already trying to carry some pretence of authority. They were dressed in short, simple robes, but of the finest quality; their hair was clean and trim. They were always clean. They didn't shout and push and laugh like the others. They kept apart, eating quietly, talking amongst themselves. At any time, they could be re-Tasked, just like the rest of us, and then—*bam*, they'd be nothing special again. But it happened least with the Guardians. More than anyone else, they were selected, usually the sons and daughters of Guardians themselves, and then they stayed. Stayed to become Guardians—or at the very least to work in the Hall, to tend Guardian camels, cook Guardian meals, run Guardian errands.

Kulnethar chuckled. "You see, Vanya? You really want to be one of those stiffs? As a Labourer, at least you get to do what you want."

I snorted and rubbed at the mud caking my legs. "As a Labourer, I get to dig ditches."

"Father says hard work is ennobling."

"Hah. Your father must not be very noble, then."

Anyone else would have exploded with indignation. Kulnethar just laughed. "I'll tell him you said that."

"Go ahead. Far as I see, the harder you work, the less anyone seems to care about you."

"That's not true."

"It is. Just look. Who gets respect? Elders: they just sit around all day and talk. Who else? Guardians. And Guardians don't work. They tell other people what to do. They decide who gets what and how much and when."

Kulnethar didn't say anything for a moment, but I thought maybe I had won my point. I popped another pistachio into my mouth.

"I don't think . . ." he finally ventured. "I don't think what Elders do is *easy*. They oversee the Temple—the gardens, libraries, musicians, healing rooms. They teach us. They counsel the Chosen. It's not easy, it's just . . . different. Besides, my father respects everyone for what they do. All work is necessary; all work is honoured by Yl'avah."

"Don't talk to me if you're going to spew nonsense. It doesn't work that way, and you know it."

He was about to object, when three Temple Taskers spotted him and came running our way.

"Kylan! There you are. Quick, get the last ones before they're gone!" The boy waved a sweetcake over his head, one stuffed in each fist. Then he glanced at me. "What you are doing, hanging around this dirt-digging loner anyway?" He kicked my mud-spattered leg.

His insult made my point so perfectly I didn't even hit him.

"Yeah, Kylan? What *are* you doing with a hard-working ennobled dirt-digger?" I asked.

My friend's face turned an interesting shade of red. "Listen," he started. "That's not fair. Just because he's a—"

"Oh, come on," the boy interrupted. "Let's go. They're starting soon, and you don't want to be stuck with *him*." He kicked me again.

My point was already made. No use being nice about it. I glared up at him. "Stick your prancing feet near me again, and I'll ram those sweetcakes down your throat and make you choke on them."

Kulnethar leapt up, grabbed the boy's arm, and propelled him away. "Go find Tulli. I'll catch up to you."

The boys wandered off, laughing and mocking my threats, though Kulnethar glanced back at me.

"Sorry, Vanya," he muttered. "They're idiots."

I scowled. "Respect for everyone, though, right? Go on, run after the idiots. I don't mind being a loner."

He hesitated, like he wanted to say something else or make an excuse for their behaviour, but didn't know how to begin. I gave him credit for looking genuinely embarrassed. Then he just muttered another, *sorry*, and ran off.

I had told him to go. Still, it hurt.

I glanced at the Guardian Taskers again. They weren't far from where I was sitting, and I noticed they were watching. One of the older ones leaned over and said something. The others nodded. All except one, a girl with voluminous black hair and a mocking glance. Our eyes met. *Really?* she seemed to say. *You're going to let them get away with that?*

Or what? Punch the idiot in front of everyone, start a fight?

She lifted a brow. *No.* That's not what she meant. That girl would stand up and face him down, and by the force of her gaze alone would squeeze a stammered apology out of him.

If only it were so simple . . .

Then the older one laughed and spoke to her, and she glanced away.

On impulse, I decided I would walk over and introduce myself. Why not? They were Taskers, just like me. Why couldn't I sit with them? I thought about it. I *meant* to do it. But a hush fell before I could act. One of the Elders had just entered the hall, coming down from a higher tier—the High Elder himself.

A whisper ran through the Taskers, there was a quick flurry as everyone grabbed whatever food they happened to be close to and scurried to find their seats. Leaning up against columns or blocks, or just sitting in the middle of the floor, they gathered towards my end of the hall, away from the food and as close to the High Elder as they could. In a matter of moments, there was silence.

The High Elder stood, watching us with a smile on his face. The way his blue eyes wandered, from one to the next, I got the feeling he was really trying to *see* us. To memorize our faces, recall our names. Eventually, his eyes found mine. *Remember me?* I wanted to shout. *Remember I'm supposed to be a Guardian?* Then he started to speak.

"Young Kyr'amanu," he began. "I'm glad to share with you today. Have you heard the stories yet of the Undying?"

There were cries of *yes*, and *no*, scattered throughout the Taskers. Some were in their third and final year and knew more than us, but even the ones who yelled *no*, didn't really mean it. Everyone knew a bit about the Undying, but everyone always wanted to hear more.

I'd heard about Dynaias ab'Kuldayu, the first Al'kah, and the founding of the great city Ashianys in the East, and I'd heard about the rise of our once-great empire. But not much from before. I settled in, savouring the sweetness of my fig while I listened.

"Well," the High Elder said. "Let me tell you a story, a favourite of mine. The Undying, you see, did not grow old and pass away, like we do when the span of our years is up. They would become strong men and women, and stay that way. At first it was good. They lived long and filled the earth with light and beauty. They wrote music. They crafted cities out of living trees. They tended gardens the size of Shyandar itself." He spread his arms, and the audience gasped in wonder.

"How many years passed in such a way? No one knows, save for the Last of the Undying himself—Shatayeth Warbringer. He it was who began the contests: feats of strength and skill and power. But in their growing fervency, something dark began. The contests began to change. The Undying grew stronger, and more skilled in fighting, and more powerful. They began to use that power to take from each other: take lands, titles, objects of beauty. And then—the blow was struck." The High Elder slapped a fist into his other hand. "Shatayeth *killed* a man. He stole his lifeblood. The first to do so in all the generations of the Undying."

His face creased into genuine grief. "There was retribution. The Wars began. They lasted centuries, hundreds of years of fighting and fighting and fighting." We all leaned forward, breathless, seeing in our minds the beautiful, noble people, killing each other in battle. It was sad—and thrilling.

"Until one day . . ." the High Elder paused, letting his voice hang over us. "One of them—one you all know—one who was Shatayeth's most trusted general, had a dream. And in the dream, he was looking out on a great, wide field, marked with thousands of the dead." The High Elder spread his hands, eyes crinkled as they looked over an imaginary graveyard. "And he heard a voice say to him, 'Count the years of the children.' And then he woke up.

"Now this was very odd. But at first the general didn't think much of it. Until the next night he had the same dream, and then again, the night after. Three nights in a row! It was starting to bother him, so he went to his trusted warriors and told them about the dream, but no one knew what to make of it. He started to think, and to watch, and to ask questions about the children. And do you know what he learned?"

"They weren't immortal anymore," a girl piped up from the other side of the hall.

The High Elder smiled. "Very good, Aleya. Yes, they were becoming *us*. Their years were shrinking. The general found no son or daughter born during the Wars who was older than one hundred and fifty years, and many were starting to grow . . . *old*. He went to his king, he went to Shatayeth, and he said to him, 'O great king, have you counted the years of our children?'

"The Deathless King scoffed at the general. 'What should I care about children?' he said. 'My work is blood.'

"The general was troubled by this. But he refused to give up. He went again to Shatayeth. 'O great king,' he said. 'Have you counted the years of our children?'

"Again, Shatayeth laughed at him, but again the general tried. And this time, the king turned to him and said, 'No, I haven't. Have *you*?'

"At last, the general was able to tell him what he'd learned. 'There is no son or daughter born during the Wars who is older than one hundred and fifty years, and many are starting to grow *old*.'

"The king was not happy. 'Hold to fighting,' he said, 'not dream-telling.' But the general grew more and more worried about what was happening. Finally, Yl'avah himself appeared to him in a dream, and this is what he said to the general: 'Because they sought for it, and looked for it, and loved it, Death has come to the children of men. Yet I have called you to a new path. Gather my children and lead them in the way of Life.' And then he gave him a name. Do you know what he called him?"

A dozen voices shouted it out. "Kyrada! Kyrada, our father."

"Yes!" The High Elder looked pleased. "That's right. Kyrada, he was named, Father of Peace, from where we take *our* name. He believed Yl'avah, and he told Shatayeth what he had heard, but the king hated what he said. He tried to *kill* him. So Kyrada fled. For years and years he lived in hiding, moving from one place to another, and everywhere he went, he brought the words of peace. And people joined him! They laid aside their weapons of war. They followed Kyrada, who spoke of their Great Maker, and the way of Life which Yl'avah had called them to walk in. But it was not the Undying who followed him—it was their mortal children. And so began our people."

I listened with rapt attention, and when the High Elder finished that part of the tale, he picked it up again with another story, and another, each telling of the deeds of Kyrada and his people, and how they grew into a nation, how Shatayeth burned for vengeance and sought to destroy them. Finally, he paused. He was sitting cross-legged on the floor now, like many of the children, brows drawn in thought.

"Tell how Kyrada died," one boy called from the back.

The High Elder glanced up, then scratched his beard and sighed. "Not today, Calahyn. That one is special, and should not be rushed."

The Taskers turned and whispered to each other, eager to show off what they knew. *Killed by Shatayeth*, I heard one boy say, and another jumped in: *but he cursed him first.*

No, a girl protested, *Kyrada didn't curse anyone. Shatayeth made an oath with him, and then broke it. That's why his army was destroyed.*

His army—but not Shatayeth himself.

Shh. If you talk about him too much, he'll come looking for you.

Amidst the murmuring, an Acolyte swept by and approached the

High Elder. I watched, curious, as the woman bent and whispered something in his ear. The High Elder's face changed: a tightness, a frown. Then it was gone, and the Acolyte hurried away. Was I the only one who saw?

I leaned forward as the High Elder rose to his feet. It wasn't time yet, but he started to bid us on our way, back to our own duties. Back to pounding dirt. I frowned. No one else seemed bothered by this, and in groups they rose and wandered out.

I hesitated, but when nothing else happened, I sighed and trudged back out into the heat. The sun was still high, and there was a wind now, the dust blowing into my eyes and mouth. I stopped to wrap my head up again, and I wondered if a storm were coming. I scowled. That would make all our trench-digging good for nothing.

The other Taskers went on without me. I was fine with that. I liked the quiet. I walked back through the outlying buildings, back to find my father's hut, hopefully to rest for another sun's breadth before going to the fields.

And then I heard my name.

"Vanya!" I didn't need to turn to know there was a mop of bright hair bobbing through the empty streets. I kept walking. If he wanted to talk to me so bad, he'd have to work for it. I still wasn't sure I'd forgiven him for his idiot friends.

"Vanya, stop! Wait! Hey, wait!" He was running. Within a few moments, he pounced on me, grabbed my arm and threw himself in the way. He was sucking heavy breaths, sweat trickling down his face, but there was a thrill in his eyes. "Yl'avah's mercy, are you deaf?" he grinned. "Look. Something's happened. You've got to come with me."

"What? What are you talking about?"

"Trust me, alright?" He pulled on my arm. "You'll want to see this."

I wanted to go with him. I was hungry for it—for something, anything to keep me from going back to ditch-digging. But if I didn't show up with the other Taskers, my father would be suspicious.

"I can't. I have to get back. You might not have anything to do, but I—"

"Vanya!" There was a sharpness to his pleading. "Just come on. I can't . . . no one else would understand. Look, just come. I'll explain on the way."

I found myself hurrying alongside Kulnethar. It wasn't past midday yet. Maybe my father was asleep. Besides, it was the High Elder's son. Kulnethar didn't know how to break rules—at least not that my father knew. There *was* always that stolen cider flask . . .

Then I realized we were heading back to the north wall. Even from a distance, I could see something was happening. There were camels standing around, and Guardians, and white-robes, and though no one looked panicked, there was an efficient swell of activity.

"What's happening?" I asked as we approached.

Kulnethar grinned. "Someone's gone missing. We just learned a scribe went out into the desert."

"What?" I stopped and grabbed his arm.

He nodded. "No one else knows about it. Well, just a few. None of the Taskers. But I've got an idea. Come on."

The grip of excitement in my stomach was sharp. I ran after him. "Hold on, Kulnethar. What do you mean?"

"I mean you're always talking about being a Guardian, right?"

"I am not."

He laughed. "Just listen to yourself once or twice."

"Whatever, it's not going to happen."

"Maybe not. But at least we can see them off." His blue eyes twinkled mischievously at me.

"See them off?"

"Yeah. They're mounting a search. Three ridings. Real Guardian outriders, Vanya. Don't you want to see?" He didn't wait for me to answer, but ran on ahead. After that, there was no way I was turning back for the fields.

We approached the gate. Everyone here was either a Guardian or a white-robe, and I stuck out painfully, but Kulnethar marched right into the fray. I tried to follow his lead. There were Guardians in outrider cloaks and scarves, faces scarcely visible beneath the intricate wraps, keshu swinging from their sides. There was even the same Guardian Lord I had encountered at the Renewing. He was striding through the men and women, giving orders, speaking with the High Elder, overseeing the effort.

"What happened?" I asked Kulnethar as we found a spot out of the way, against the wall. "Why'd this scribe go into the desert?"

"I heard someone say he stole something. A scroll maybe. Not to mention a camel and all the supplies he would need."

"That's why the Guardians are after him?"

"That, and he'll die if they don't find him. No one survives the desert."

The scarlet-robed Guardian Lord ordered the gate to be opened. The three teams of outriders readied themselves, while two stepped forward to lift the bar. There was pulling, and heaving, and creaking of seldom-used hinges. The Guardians preferred the west gate for their outridings. Then the doors swung open.

The desert appeared. On the other side, sand gusted and swirled, mixing ground and sky in a seamless fog. A bad day for travelling. Which is probably why the scribe picked it. If he really wanted to get away, he'd have a better chance of it in this. If he didn't die himself.

"It's pointless," I said, and turned to Kulnethar. I found myself looking at an outrider, albeit a small one, swathed from head to food in wrappings.

"Kulnethar ab'Ethanir?" I frowned. My friend quickly adjusted his head-wrap, so only his eyes peaked out. "What are you doing?"

"I'm going to follow them," he declared. I could hear the grin in his voice. "Want to come? I pinched another set, if you want—"

"You're crazy!" I looked wildly about, horrified someone would notice. But everyone was busy with their preparations, not paying any mind to the two curious Taskers hovering out of the way. "Little thief! You're supposed to be the good one, remember?"

"Yeah. It helps you get away with quite a lot. So, are you coming? You'd better put this on quick."

I stared at him, then stared at the bundle of robes in his hand, as shocked as I was impressed. I was momentarily tempted: an adventure at last, a chance to see the desert with my own eyes, a shot at joining the Guardians, even if it was just for one desperate mission into the wasteland. Just one. One mission. I thought of my father, his calm voice threatening consequences, and I grimaced. Because that would be the whole blasted extent of my time as an outrider, as *anything* but a Labourer, if I went along with my friend's crazy plan.

"No way," I muttered, though it hurt. "It's the stupidest idea I've ever heard. Sands, you'll be lucky if the Guardians spot you and send you home with a beating. Do you *see* what it's like out there today? Could be a storm blowing in. *Then* what'll you do? You don't know anything about the desert. You're going to get yourself killed."

"You're always so gloomy," Kulnethar laughed. "The wind will die down, and by then it'll be too late for them to send me back. Are you telling me you've never dreamed of seeing the desert for yourself?"

Never dreamed of . . . ? I blinked and looked away. Yl'avah's might. To step outside these walls. To go and never come back. To find the Old Lands, the great city of Ashianys. Surely it was there, still hidden beyond the wilderness, waiting for us to return?

Kulnethar seized my arm. "I knew it!"

"Knew what?"

"I knew you were different. You're not afraid of it. I know you're not. Come on, Vanya, come with me!"

The Guardians were already leading their camels out the gate, the creatures stomping and bellowing and blinking against the blowing sand. I scowled. "I've got work to do. Go on then, but if I don't get back to my father right now, I'm going to get it."

He looked crushed, and I realized how much he'd been counting on me. Maybe he was hoping to shift the blame when he got caught. The thought left a bad taste in my mouth, but Kulnethar wasn't that sort of person . . . was he?

"Fine," he said. "Just don't tell anyone. Promise? Wish me luck."

I nodded, and with that, he slipped up next to one of the camels as they plodded out. As soon as they were past the gates, the sand blew up, already obscuring their numbers, and within a few moments, they were nothing more than a dark blur, moving into the unknown.

Kulnethar was wrong. The wind didn't die down—it grew worse. We were frantic that evening tying canvas over unharvested crop, using ropes and stones and sticks, whatever we could find. When the stinging sand became unbearable, we retreated to our huts and bolted the doors behind us. Then we waited.

The wind beat at our door. It howled and whined and lashed. Kulnethar was probably regretting his decision, but there was nothing either of us could do now. I just hoped he would be okay.

The next morning, everything was covered in a film of dust, myself included. It was in my hair, and between my teeth, and scratching the corners of my eyes. The sun rose hot and merciless, but we went straight to work.

As I feared, the irrigation channels were blocked up again, and some of the shelters had blown off. Tools were scattered. There would be work to do in the fields. But first, we had to restore the flow of water. Back to digging.

It was work as usual. We leapt into the irrigation ditches, scratching and clawing at the bottom, dredging out the muck. Dig and lift. Dig and lift.

"Hey, look who it is!" someone called, interrupting the work.

Everyone glanced up. A white-robed Acolyte appeared, picking his way across the field, looking painfully out of place. The Labourers stared, but the foreman climbed out of the ditch to meet him. They spoke in low voices. Fingers pointed. And then the foreman nodded. "Ishvandu," he said.

Every eye swung towards me. I was dreading this, but expecting it. They had found Kulnethar, and he had blamed it all on me. I knew it.

Face burning, trying to think of all the defences I could make, I hauled myself up the bank and stood before the Acolyte, dripping and breathing hard.

"What is it?" I asked, just as my father loomed behind me. He said nothing, but I felt his hand on my back, steadying me—or perhaps warning me.

The Acolyte glanced at the foreman, and the big man just nodded and jumped back down to his work. "Forgive me," the Acolyte said, voice low. "I wouldn't normally seek you out like this, but there is an urgent matter you might help us with." I could feel my heart beating faster. Damn, Kulnethar! What had he gotten me into?

"Yes?" I said, trying to sound calm and reasonable.

The man frowned. "I'm sorry to say there's been an . . . incident at the Temple. It seems Kulnethar ab'Ethanir has gone missing."

I tried to look shocked. "What?"

"I'm afraid so. And it seems you were the last person he was seen with. At the north gate, yesterday afternoon. Is it true?"

It would be foolish to lie, despite my hovering father. I nodded. "He wanted to show me the Guardians. We just saw them off. That's all." I winced. It had sounded okay in my head, but on my lips it came out defensive.

"And did he say anything to you?"

I paused. "He talked about someone running off. A scribe of some sort, I think. It was interesting to watch them leave—I've never seen so many Guardians all together, and outriders, with their camels! It was . . ."

I trailed off, wondering if my burst of enthusiasm was too much. The Acolyte didn't seem to notice, but he frowned. He was genuinely concerned, and I felt a pang of guilt. Maybe I should have told him.

No. It was too late. If I implicated myself now, whatever blame Kulnethar took, I was sure to get it worse. I kept my mouth shut.

"Nothing else? You're sure of it?"

"I said I had to get back. That's it."

The man nodded, thanked me, and with a worried line between his eyes, turned and trotted back towards the Temple.

My father's hand tightened on my shoulder. "Is it true?" he asked. He was quicker to pick up on my unease than the white-robe.

"Why is it suddenly my fault, just because the High Elder's son went missing?"

He gave me a warning eye.

"And I *didn't* step outside the gates. I promise."

He said nothing. He just gave a stiff nod and patted my shoulder, then turned back to work.

MIDDAY at the Temple was tense. News had gotten around—and now the Temple Taskers were giving me looks, as if somehow it was *my* fault. I just took my food, hurried to my corner, and ate alone.

It was strange without Kulnethar. Usually he found a moment or two to sit with me, and now that he wasn't there, the whole, wide hall was hostile and cold. Eyes accused me whenever they turned my way. I couldn't take it. Clutching my handful of pistachios, I slipped off the back steps and down into the garden, not even caring if I missed the stories.

The worst of it was they were right. If something happened to Kulnethar, it would be my fault. My fault for not stopping him. My fault for not telling his father right away. It was a stupid idea. But if I *had* told someone, Kulnethar would never have forgiven me, and I'd have lost his friendship anyway.

"Stupid," I muttered, kicking a stone. It skittered off the path, into the gardens. The trees were tall here, the greenery thick. Even the flowers were starting to bloom. It was quiet. Peaceful. Yet how could I enjoy it, while Kulnethar was lost in the desert? Maybe forever?

I glanced up at a sound. Someone was coming—not just walking up the path to the Temples, but running. An excessive amount of energy, unless there really was an emergency. I hurried to see. Just as I stepped out, an Acolyte peeled past me towards the Temple, breathing hard, feet slapping up dust from the path. I stared after him.

Then I was dashing in the direction he'd come. Shading my eyes from the bright sun, I strained to see as I burst out of the Temple and down the slopes towards the gate. Sure enough, people were already there. Outriders, camels, two Acolytes.

I almost fell over my own feet as I ripped down the slope. I had to see. I had to. There was an anxious buzz over the gathering. I burst in on them, chest tight with fear. An Acolyte glanced up.

"Stay back," he said, hurrying to put himself in my way.

That's when I saw. There was a person lying on the ground, half-hidden amidst the Guardians. A small outrider, swathed in robes. Very still.

My eyes went wide. "No!" I bounded forward. The Acolyte hurled himself at me. Another grabbed my arm. But even as they dragged me back, I caught a glimpse: pale lips, pale skin, and the head wrap, stained dark with blood. My throat closed up.

No, no, no, no . . .

I fought to break free, squirming, wrestling. I kicked the nearest set of shins. The man gave a yelp and let go, and I wrenched myself out of the other's grasp, hurtling towards the cluster of Guardians. I pushed through them, staring at the body in the dust, mouth forming silent words, demanding how this could have happened, *what* had happened. How my friend, my only friend . . .

A stiff arm, much more powerful than the Acolytes, pulled me back and a Guardian positioned himself in my way. The head-wrap had been loosened, and I saw a dark, grizzled face. The mouth was hardened into a stern line.

"This isn't your concern, boy," he said. "Get out of here."

"It *is* my concern, that's my friend. How could you let this happen? How could you—"

"Vanya?"

The voice pulled me up sharp. My mouth hung in silence for a moment, then a boy stepped out of the other outriders. It was Kulnethar. He was alive. He was unhurt. Though his face was streaked with dirt and tears.

"Kylan! Yl'avah's might, it's you!"

He just nodded.

"What happened? What is this all about?"

"Vanya, not now," he said in a pained voice.

I glanced at the Guardian in my way, at the other, unsmiling faces, then hurried up to my friend. "Kylan, you shouldn't have gone! Everyone's been worried about you. What in all blazes happened? I *told* you it was stupid, but you didn't—"

"Not *now*," he said. "Please. Just . . ." Fresh tears sprang to his eyes. But before I could ask anything else there was a shout from the Temple entrance. It was the High Elder and a half dozen others. Behind them, the Temple gate was thronging with onlookers, while a few Acolytes struggled to restrain them.

If it were my father, I'd have gotten the worst beating of my life. The High Elder just ran and threw his arms around his son and clung to him.

"Yl'avah be praised, you're safe. Don't ever . . . don't ever . . ."

Kulnethar nodded and wept, and I found myself standing apart, a frown forming over my face. Was that it? Wasn't he going to get in trouble?

Eventually, reluctantly, the High Elder pulled away and spoke quietly with the Guardian outriders. They moved in to see the body. I spotted the High Elder kneeling, and as he lifted the head-wrap, I caught a glimpse of the face beneath, mangled, covered in old blood. Then the Guardians gathered in, obscuring my view, and it was just Kulnethar and I, standing awkwardly to the side.

My friend rubbed a dusty sleeve across his face, leaving a smear of snot. He looked wretched, and I told him so. He just nodded, and I didn't know what else to say.

Finally, he gave a heavy, shaking sigh. "I'm sorry. I'm sorry I did it. It's all my fault."

"What do you mean?"

"I mean him." He waved a disconsolate hand. "Trushya. Young Guardian. His first . . . first riding. They thought I was him. He got lost in the storm, and no one heard him. No one missed him. They kept calling me Trushya. And when we stopped, they counted. And I knew, knew what had happened. Knew it was my fault." Tears fell down his face in ribbons. "Vanya, it was horrible. I'm so sorry."

I shook my head. I didn't have any words.

"They were so mad. Of course they were mad. They argued about what to do. And maybe if we'd just turned around to look for him, it would have been alright. He wasn't that far away. But then . . ."

He shuddered, his face turning even paler than usual.

"Then what?" I whispered.

"Then we heard it. A . . . scream. Vanya, it didn't sound human. I mean, it was. But . . ." My eyes went wide, but he fell silent for a long moment. I wanted to press him for more, curious and terrified at the same time. Then he shook his head. "No one went after him. They said it was too late. I didn't understand. At least . . . not till we found him the next morning. He was . . ." He nodded towards the Guardians. "He was dead."

"What *was* it?" I breathed.

Kulnethar looked at me. He didn't say anything. It was the first time I'd ever seen him scared, and a shiver ran through me. *Desert ghosts.* The stories. They couldn't be true. *And yet . . .*

"Kulnethar." The High Elder straightened, his face as white as his son's. "Come. Let's leave these men to their prayers." He nodded at the Acolytes, and they both moved in, probably to help bear the body away. It would go to the Resting House, to be washed and prayed over and prepared for burial. Then it would make the long trek, past the South Fields, out of the city gates, and to the South Grounds. The Guardians would sing the eywah-ka, and his spirit would pass on to the Last Realm.

I swallowed. Kulnethar glanced at me one last time, then he followed his father up to the Temple. I stood alone. I thought of the way the wind howled through my door last night, and then I thought of that face, scarred and bloody beyond recognition. I shivered.

Maybe there *was* something to fear in the desert.

Chapter Fifteen

It was Atali sai'Neraia, Guardian of the fourth kiyah, who met me near the gates of the main yard. She was already mounted. She looked magnificent, with her easy posture, her thick dark braids, keshu resting against her thigh. She sat lightly in the saddle, as if poised to break into full gallop.

"Ready?" she asked.

"Ready."

We rode out. There were four of us: Anajin ab'Anajin, or Jin'sal, as Tala called him, the head of the fourth kiyah, a wiry, keen-eyed man with an easy smile and a hard glance. Tala rode behind him, and I close to her, and last came Antaru ab'Manishu, the same muscly oaf who had lent me his keshu in the camel-yard. I noticed he still hadn't earned it back.

"You understand your role?" Jin'sal asked as we crossed into the grounds beyond the Hall. They were normally empty, but today was the First—not just any First, but the *first* First, the day after Renewing. Labourers and Crafters from all over Shyandar were thronging the gates in expectation. People had this ridiculous notion that water somehow transformed overnight into bread and fruit and eggs. I'd had the notion myself, as a boy, never mind all the harvesting and threshing and sifting I did—the long, tedious process of turning one thing into another. It was startling how quickly that could be forgotten come Renewing. Water was water, and water meant food, and so people came with bright eyes and open hands.

I sighed. If they only knew how carefully the storerooms were managed, how strategic every decision was in accounting for who got what, and how much, and when. The eighth kiyah planned for this week, a celebratory one, but also a flurry of physical activity, a return to hard labour. So they showered bounty on the Kyr'amanu before tightening rations again, a little more every quarter, a little more—until the end of the harvest. It had to be so. Without rations, every one of us would go fat for a half-month, and then starve.

"Ishvandu, are you ready?" Jin'sal asked.

I pulled my eyes away from the crowd of noisy anticipation.

"Yes, sal'ah."

"For what?"

"To watch and listen," I said, recalling Umaala's instructions.

Jin'sal nodded. "Good. Stay close to Antaru. If there's trouble—"

"Do you think there'll be trouble, sal'ah?"

The man smiled. "There's always trouble. As I was saying, if we find it, you'll not get involved. Leave Guardian's work to Guardians. That's all. Let's go."

He spoke lightly, rode lightly, bobbing jauntily on his way. Outwardly, you'd be hard-pressed to find a more extreme contrast to Umaala ab'Krushaya. He seemed actually to enjoy himself, for one. But I wasn't fooled. Don't get involved? Just stand there and do *nothing*? He couldn't have slapped me with a more difficult assignment if he tried. Just hopefully, the trouble would stay out of our path.

We took the north road, the most direct line from the Hall to the Temple, and the dividing line between the Labourer's huts and the fields. It bustled with fresh activity. Foremen were already planning tomorrow's work, stable hands rushed back and forth after their goats, trying to corral them down to fresh water, children were hauling full buckets up from the lake. There were Guardians too. The second kiyah would be out meeting foremen, assessing the needs of the new year. The eighth would have census-takers going down every street, into every house, updating their records, looking for unreported births—or deaths.

Then there was us. What the fourth kiyah did was not so easy to pin down. They patrolled, I knew that much; they kept an eye out for trouble; they watched. But as I rode next to Tala and Jin'sal, I quickly realized it was more complicated than that.

People stopped as we passed. They noticed us, called to us. "Good day, sai'Neraia," said a stable-hand, grinning back at us. "Morning, ab'Anajin!"

Tala lifted a hand in greeting. "Ab'Kalanu. How are your goats?"

"Excellent! Wonderful! So much improved, I'm afraid they're getting into trouble again. See? *Ai!* Jazza, no!" He bounded after his wayward herd, one with her head stuck through a basket, another trying to eat the robes off a Tasker.

We rode on. There were more greetings, more exchanges and nods of recognition. When we turned into the hut-lined streets, we dismounted and continued on foot.

"Here," Tala said, passing me her reins. "Make yourself useful."

"Good idea." Jin'sal tossed me his as well. "That should keep you busy."

"What, *three* camels?" I struggled to rein them in. They jumbled up behind me, bumping and shoving each other, bellowing their irritation.

Antaru pulled alongside me.

"Don't think of it!" I said.

"Need a hand?"

I bristled. "No. I can manage."

"Good." He laughed. "Good luck."

I was so busy wrestling the camels down the narrow gap between huts, it was a moment before I realized what we were doing. I paused. Tala was speaking with an old woman—not the same boisterous greetings as on the road, but leaning close, listening, nodding. She squeezed the woman's hand, then moved on. She greeted the next person by name, and the next. She asked questions, she listened. Sometimes she stopped. I realized I had never seen her on duty before. She was always a Guardian, as we all were; there was no room to be anything else. Yet *here*, amongst the huts and shops, amongst the Kyr'amanu, this was her realm of influence. Her place. And for the first time, I was seeing it.

I watched, mesmerized by her actions, each one so easy, so natural. She listened to one woman, and laughed. She bent next to a little girl.

"How are you feeling, Dima?"

The girl nodded.

"Stronger?"

Another nod.

"What do you have there?"

The girl ducked her head, clutching the treasure against her skinny little chest.

"Ah! Is that a baby?"

The girl frowned, and shook her head. Then she thrust her arms out to reveal a tiny person, twisted from bits of rope and cloth. "No, she's a Guardian."

"Oh, I see." Tala nodded. "Is she strong?"

The girl's head bobbed.

"Is she fast?"

"Yeah."

"Does she fight monsters?"

"Uh huh. And she has beautiful hair, just like you, Tali."

Tala laughed. "Does she have a name?"

The girl nodded, but pursed her lips, blushed, and would say nothing else.

"She calls her Tali," said the mother. "After you . . . if it's not too bold."

Tala laughed in surprise. "Sounds like a good name to me." Then she brushed the girl's head, once, quickly, and stood up.

I found myself frowning, uncertain at the picture that was unfolding. *A waste of good rope*, my father would have said. *Frivolous*. What was Tala doing? When I glanced to the other side of the street, Jin'sal was moving through the people in his own way, asking questions, using names, gripping hands.

"It's what they do," Antaru said, still hovering close to me and the camels. "It's their way, from time to time, checking on everyone. Works as good as any, I suppose."

"Works?"

"Watch and see."

I watched. We moved slowly down each row. We stopped at different huts, sometimes one of them ducking in to check on the inhabitants. And I began to notice what Antaru meant. When the people saw Tala or Jin'sal, their faces lit up, they smiled, they looked pleased, they welcomed them, speaking with them. And when their eyes brushed to Antaru and me, they cooled instantly. It hit me then. I had lived in this place twelve years, ran down these streets, worked with these men and women, even recognized a few. And now, I was the stranger.

"Ishvandu?"

I spun at the voice. An old man was eyeing me, almost more in suspicion than recognition.

"Yes?" I tugged the camels to a halt. I realized who it was: my old foreman, from the year I worked with my father.

The man grunted. "It *is* you. A stable hand then?"

My eyes went big. I almost dropped the camel-reins in shock. "No, I'm a Guardian."

"Novice," Antaru corrected, leaning in.

I wanted to punch him, but decided that wouldn't exactly send the right message. *See?* I imagined telling Umaala. *I can control myself.*

"Novice Guardian," I said.

The old foreman was looking at me doubtfully. I didn't know what else to say. I thought of how Tala and Jin'sal had talked to people, asked about things, knew just the right words. I couldn't even remember the guy's name.

I opted for broad: "How are things? How's . . . being here?" I winced. Antaru winced.

"Things aren't so good."

I nodded. I looked away. The sun was starting to get hot, trickling sweat down the back of my robes. *Yl'avah's might, this was ridiculous!*

"Sorry," I said.

"Let's go," Antaru whispered.

"Yeah." I tried to pull the camels into a fast exit, but managed only to wrench my arm. The camels, it seemed, had decided to stay put.

"Come *on!*" I tugged again. My own camel Yma almost ran me

over, but the other two—nothing. Hooves dug in. Knees locked. A bored, stubborn look dropped over their faces.

"See, he'd make a lousy stable hand," Antaru said. "Come on, then!" He laughed and led his camel easily up the street.

I struggled a moment longer, now trying to pull Yma back, and the others forward, arms stretched to either side of me. "Yl'avah's might, you stubborn—"

I caught the old foreman's eye. He was laughing. He was bent over, tears streaming down his face. Others noticed and joined in. *Light and all, this was mortifying!* I forced myself to smile, to pretend like this was as funny as they thought. Then Antaru clicked his tongue, and all three beasts broke into a trot. I stumbled after them, lost a rein. Jin'sal's camel bounded off ahead of me, then veered down a different street.

"Shit," I said. *I was given one stupid job . . .*

I hurried down the row, dragging the other two beasts with me. The camel quickly disappeared. I heard shouts. I imagined her stampeding through the Labourers, knocking people over, breaking urns, trampling sacks.

I rounded the bend. The camel was nowhere to be seen. Instead, there were two young men. One was clutching something, the other was trying to tear it out of his grasp. They were grappling, faces a hand span apart.

"Let go, Dunya!"

"I won't!" the other dropped his voice. "Back off. Try to stop me, I swear I'll gut you."

"With *Guardians* here?"

"With Guardians."

"They'll rope you."

"You think I care what they do? They *know*, Mal. It's over. They know."

"They don't. Get *off*."

The street wasn't empty. A few Labourers had spotted me, were edging away, trying not to look part of it. The combatants hadn't seen me yet, but any moment . . .

I swivelled my head. There was no time to get Tala and Jin'sal. I could stop this, I could demand to see what they were up to. I could catch them in the act. Be a Guardian.

Don't get involved. I wavered. Surely they hadn't meant . . . ?

No. Jin'sal had meant exactly what he said. There was only one thing I could do. I stepped back behind the camels, craned my neck, hoping to catch sight of Antaru. He could call for Jin'sal, and maybe—

Tala speared past me. "Dunaya! Malishu! What's going on?"

One man peeled off, backing away at almost a run, hands thrown up in surrender. "It wasn't my idea. I didn't ask for this. It's him, all him, I swear. I just found—"

"Liar!" the other screamed. I could see now what he was holding: a wooden shaft for digging or threshing. But on its end was attached a sharpened piece of bone. He clutched it like a spear.

"Look out!" I cried.

Dunya lunged, startlingly fast. Tala was faster. She pushed off the ground in a single leap. Her body slammed into him, even as she caught the thing he held, twisted, spun, feet catching him below. I had experienced that manoeuvre first-hand, and it was difficult to counter. Dunya dropped like a sack. Dust puffed up, once, then settled into awful silence. Tala held the spear aloft, keeping her gaze fixed on its owner.

"Antaru," she said.

The Guardian hurried to her aid, took the spear from her, then passed it to Jin'sal, who held it length-wise, inspecting it. The street had gone deathly quiet. No one dared move. Malishu was stuck in a defensive crouch, as if still expecting Dunya to pounce. A nearby man was shielding a Tasker. Two women had jumped up from their tasks. An adolescent girl stood watching, eyes big. Everyone seemed to be holding their breath, waiting for something terrible to happen.

Jin'sal's easy amiability had evaporated. He looked hard at the shaft, at the bone tip, the sinews lashing it in place. It was too long to be a fine-pointed instrument, too small for chopping, not the right shape for cutting. Its purpose was painfully clear. A weapon.

"I can explain," Dunya said, still on his back.

"You can explain it to the Circle," Jin'sal replied.

"Please, ab'Anajin. It's not what it looks—"

"Yl'avah's might, I hope not."

"It was *his* fault. He set me up."

Malishu's eyes went wide. "No. I wouldn't." He glanced at Jin'sal, then Tala. "Sai'Neraia, you know me. You know I wouldn't."

"Alis," Tala called.

The adolescent girl swallowed and hurried forward. "Yes, Tal—er, sai'Neraia?"

"Is your foreman honest?"

There was another pause. I watched in amazement. It was like Tala already knew what the girl was going to say. Like somehow, she'd known this moment was coming, had planned for it, and was counting on a silent understanding between them.

"No," the girl said. Her voice was cold. Her hands clutched at her sides. "No, he isn't."

Malishu stared at Alis, horrified. "What are you saying, girl?"

"I'm saying I know what you're up to, and—"

"Thank you, Alis," Tala said. "That will be enough for now. Antaru?"

Malishu lunged at the girl, howling in rage. He drove her into the ground. Her head struck backwards, hard. She gasped, even as his hands wrapped around her throat to squeeze. There was a familiar *slick*. Tala's keshu appeared, and in a heartbeat, it was resting against the back of Malishu's neck.

"Consider your next move very carefully," she said.

The man was breathing hard. "I never meant no harm," he said under his breath. "I never meant no . . ."

"Get off her," Tala ordered. "Or I will open your spine."

He backed off. He lifted his hands. He was shaking, though from anger or fear, it was hard to say. "Traitorous bitch. I never meant no . . ."

"Shut up," Tala said.

Antaru dragged the man to his feet, none too gently. In moments, his hands were bound behind him, and Tala was bent over the girl, speaking quietly, earnestly. The girl nodded.

"Ishvandu," Tala said.

I straightened at the sound of my name. "Yes?"

"Give Alis your camel and escort her to the Temple, please."

I glanced at Jin'sal, who nodded grimly. I moved forward. Dunya had risen to a crouch, and I watched his eyes flicker between me, Tala, the girl, and back again. Tala was still helping Alis to her feet. When I drew near, she leaned close, speaking so only the three of us could hear.

"Find Kulnethar," she told me. "Alis may need protection. And she's been hurt."

"Tali, I'm fine," the girl murmured, pressing a hand to the back of her head.

"You're not fine. Ishvandu, you make sure she gets there safe, you hear? Anything happens to her, you'll be choking on your own teeth."

I nodded. "Understood, sal'ah."

THE GIRL SAID little as we hurried out of the Labourer's tight streets. She glanced behind once or twice, watching as Dunya and Malishu were led away, as Jin'sal spoke with those gathered.

Then it was just the two of us. I pulled the camel to a stop.

"Have you ridden before?" I asked.

She looked at me. She tightened her lips, frowning, and immediately I knew she didn't like me. "I'm a Labourer," she said.

"I can see that."

She was unafraid, yet with a wariness I found disconcerting. Her eyes, like flecks of muddy water, were strangely light against the darkness of her skin. Her black hair was chopped short. It stuck out in spiky, abrupt angles.

She lifted her eyebrows. "What? I'm not riding."

"Tala said—"

"Forget it. Not that ugly thing."

I squinted at Yma. She'd gotten the reins between her teeth and was munching noisily, bits of saliva sloshing out of her mouth. She stopped when she heard the insult. "She doesn't mean it," I told the camel, then turned back to Alis. "Look, girl. You had your head knocked in. I can help you up. Yma's a good camel. I *have* to do what Tala says."

"Tali said to give me your stupid camel. She didn't say I had to ride it. I'm fine. I'm walking."

I considered picking her up and throwing her into the saddle, but decided that wouldn't go over well. Besides, she was only a hand shorter than me, if a bit gangly, and the saddle was a long way. I thought of Tala's threats, and sighed.

"Suit yourself. Let's go."

Her lips tightened again. Was she expecting more of a fuss? Well, if she wasn't going to ride, I wasn't going to slow down for her. I turned and pulled Yma into a brisk walk. Sure enough, she fell into step beside me.

We hurried down the road. She had a long, loping stride, though she kept her shoulders hunched, head down. Every now and then, I caught her hand rubbing the back of her head. She kept opening her mouth like she wanted to say something, but always shut it again. Then I noticed her looking at me.

"What?" I finally asked.

"You're not a Guardian."

"I am."

"Then where's your keshu?"

"I don't have one yet."

"Why not?"

"I'm still in training."

"Oh." She touched the back of her head. Shrugged. "Are they going to rope them?"

"I don't know."

"Because you're not a Guardian?"

"I *am* a Guardian."

"So what do you think? Are they going to rope them?"

I sighed. "If the Circle finds they did something wrong? Yeah. Could be."

She looked away. She stuck a knuckle in her eye. "I don't want anyone to get hurt."

"Then why did you speak?"

Her eyes flashed to me, hard, dislike deepening to disgust. "Tali asked."

And that was the end of our conversation.

We passed huts, crackling fields, empty irrigation ditches. The sun was high now—past midday—and most had disappeared indoors. It was painfully hot. Our pace had slowed.

Then Alis stumbled. She righted herself, took two steps, and stumbled again, a hand pressed to her sweaty forehead. I stopped and looked back at her. She was swaying in place, one hand groping for support.

"Here," I muttered. I took her arm, lowered her to the ground, gave her my water skin. The girl drank without question. Yl'avah's might, she wasn't doing well. She was hardly aware of me.

I slapped Yma's rump, and she bowed her legs—front, then back. Alis's eyes lifted. They were watery and unfocused. I had to get her to Kulnethar. Now. No choice about it anymore. Before she knew what was happening, I hoisted her up, turned, and dropped her across the saddle. Then with a click of my tongue, Yma was up and walking again.

"What are you . . . ? What are you . . . ?" She clutched the camel's sides. She started to kick. "Put me down!"

"You can't walk anymore. I have to get you to—"

"Put me *down!*" she screeched, now fully alert again. She kicked. She squirmed. "Put me down, put me down, put me—"

"Be quiet, girl! You're fine."

"I'm not fine! Let me *down!*" She started to scream. She was breathing hard. Panicking. People were looking at us. Then I heard a *thunk*.

I twisted. She'd thrown herself out of the saddle, rolled across the ground. I hurried towards her.

"What in Yl'avah's might is wrong with—"

Her foot cracked into my shin. She threw a terrified glance at me, then vaulted across the open field like a jackrabbit.

"Shit." I dropped Yma's reins and broke into pursuit. She was fast. She flew across the ditch, around field trees. Her long legs ate up the ground. For a horrible moment, I thought she was going to outpace me. Then she stumbled. It gave me the moment I needed. Without thinking, I launched into her.

We hit the ground together and rolled. I pinned her onto her back, grappling her. She was breathing hard, eyes wide.

"Don't," she cried. "Don't, please don't."

"I'm not going to hurt you."

She started to cry.

"I'm not going to— Light and all, just stop. Stop."

"I'm sorry! I'm sorry! I—"

"*Stop!*"

She fell still. She was trembling. Terrified. *Yl'avah's might, this was a disaster.*

"Okay," I said in as calm a voice as I could manage. "I'm going to help you up. You're not going to run. Okay?"

She shook her head.

"Or kick me?"

She shook her head.

"Promise?"

She nodded.

"Okay." I winced. "And please don't tell Tala I tackled you."

She swallowed, but nodded again.

"Thanks."

I got up as slowly as I could, no sudden movements, then reached down.

She hesitated. "Don't make me ride one of those things. Please."

"I won't."

She looked down. She brushed her face, struggling to control a fresh deluge of tears. *Any moment she was going to lose it.* Yl'avah's might, let it wait till I could foist her off on Kylan.

She took a shuddering breath, then gripped my hand and rose. "Where . . . where are we going?"

"The Temple, remember?"

"How come?"

I frowned. "Malishu? Hitting your head? Have you forgotten?"

"Because Tali said?"

"That's right."

She nodded. The woman's name worked wonders, and before long, we were walking again, down the last stretch to the Temple.

It was dark by the time I made it back to the Hall. I unsaddled Yma and passed her off to the stable hand. Then I trudged towards the Novice's quarter.

Tala was waiting for me in the corridor. She was slumped against the wall. Even in the dark, her weariness was apparent.

"Hey," I said.

"Alis?" she asked.

"She's safe. Kulnethar has her now. Says she's mildly concussed and will recover quickly, but he'll keep her as long as you need."

Tala nodded. "Thanks."

"No problem. I mean, I was glad to help with . . . you know, something other than camels."

Tala sniffed. I had the horrible, sinking realization she was crying.

"Tala? You . . . okay?"

"Stupid," she said. She balled her fists. "I was *stupid*. I shouldn't have called her out like that. I had no right."

"You had every right."

"No, *no*. Light and all, she trusted me, and I betrayed her. I could have brought her to the Circle to testify in secret, but no, like a big dumb arrogant Guardian *twat,* I dragged her in front of her family and friends, in front of the whole blasted quarter."

I swallowed. "I think you're being a little hard on yourself."

"Am I? They're going to rope them, Vanya. Both of them."

"Both?"

"Yes. And everyone will think she's at fault, never mind we found hoards of pilfered goods. Malishu was stealing from Taskers, from kids, threatening them, stashing it in other people's homes, ready to rat them at the first hint of trouble."

"You knew this?"

"I had my suspicions. It wasn't the first time I spoke with her. But she was afraid. Afraid the blame would fall to her and her brother."

"Well, it sounds like these assholes are getting what they deserve. What's so wrong with that?"

She snorted and scraped away the tears. "You don't get it, do you? Dunya *is* her brother. When she finds out I can't protect him . . ."

"You mean the guy who attacked us with a spear?"

"He thought he was protecting Alis. It was Malishu he was after, not us."

"Yl'avah's might." I rolled my eyes. "Look, none of this is your fault!"

"It *is*, Vanya. It's my duty to keep peace in Shyandar. I should have seen this coming. I should have done something sooner. I should have—"

"Stop!" I dropped next to her. "You know what *my* job was today? Watch and listen, that's it. That's the only sand-blasted thing they would let me do, apart from herding a bunch of dumb camels, and you know what I saw?" I was breathless, palms bursting into a fresh sweat. "*You*, Tala. You were brilliant, you were *good*, you were—I saw—"

She was staring at me. I trailed off. The words were on my tongue. *Beautiful.* You were *beautiful.* Then I realized I had taken her hand, was grasping it in both of mine, holding it. And it was different somehow. Not how you would take a friend's hand. Certainly not how you would take a Guardian's hand. I was trembling, and she was looking at me. Looking. Her face unreadable in the dark.

I mumbled an apology, and before she could see the pounding in my chest, I released her, jumped up, and dashed into the Novice's quarter. I didn't dare stop to think what I'd done until I found my mat. I lay down. I pulled the blanket over my head. Only then did I wonder. Which words had she heard? The ones I'd spoken, or the ones I hadn't?

Chapter Sixteen

The Circle wasted no time. Dunaya ab'Duani and Malishu ab'Anaasha were sentenced within the quarter. It was the ropes for them.

No surprise, really. Three crimes were punishable by death in Shyandar: murder, rebellion, and thievery. Malishu had been hoarding for a long time, using bribes and extortion to keep people quiet. Alis was only the first speak out, but others followed. Even I was called on to give my witness to the first kiyah. Dunya was a part of it, too, and to make matters worse, he had assaulted Guardians with a weapon. Tala fought for Dunya's exile, but to no avail. In the end, his fate was sealed.

It was rotten luck to follow the jubilance of Renewing with an execution. The Novices were tense. Most of us had seen one before. It happened. But each was a stark reminder of how tenuous our place really was.

The Novices readied themselves for the Flatrock, all silent except for Bray.

"Did you see the spear?" he asked, leaning in. "What did it look like? Were there other weapons? Did he stab someone?"

"No," I snapped, less an answer than a general refusal to talk. The news was fresh, and Bray was curious. He couldn't help himself, but since Pol's departure as one of the Chosen, the kid had hardly given me a moment's peace. Apparently, I was supposed to be his new best friend, or some such nonsense.

"They say Tala showed him pretty good. What was it like, arresting people? Did you get to help?"

"No."

"Is it exciting?"

"Not particularly."

"Did anyone get beat up?"

"Yl'avah's might, a girl got her head knocked on the ground, that was all. Drop it!"

"I've never seen one before."

"What, an arrest?"

"No, an execution."

I frowned at him. At the last one four years ago, Bray would have been just under age. Which was when I realized his bursting enthusiasm was nerves more than anything.

"It's not so bad," I said. "You'll be fine."

"I'm not worried."

"Course you're not."

I remembered feeling the same way, my first execution. Horrified, excited, curious. Yanava. The runaway scribe. The outriding Kulnethar had snuck along with into the storm. The same that ended in a dead Guardian, in Kulnethar's white face as he recounted the screams.

I had been so sure of myself when they finally caught Yanava and dragged him back to Shyandar. "He stole a camel," I told Kulnethar with a laugh. "And rations, and supplies, and scrolls from the Library. He's a thief."

Kulnethar's frown had deepened. "But . . . but I know him."

"You think if you know someone, they'll never do anything wrong?"

"It's not that." We were eating our midday meal in the Temple. Or at least *I* was eating, while Kulnethar rolled a piece of bread from one hand to another, slowly squashing it. "It's . . . I don't know. All this. Is it fair? Someone died because of my stupid, selfish decision. It hurts, you know? And my father was upset, but nothing happened to me.

Yet Yanava takes a few things, doesn't hurt anyone, and you say they're going to execute him. It doesn't seem fair."

"No," I said, crunching down on a nut. "It's not. I wouldn't have gotten away with what you did. But you're Kulnethar ab'Ethanir."

"I don't like that," he said with a burst of anger. "It's not right."

"You want them to rope you up, too?"

"No, of course not! And they wouldn't anyway. I'm not of Age yet. But that's the point, Vanya. If I don't deserve it, then *he* doesn't either."

"I think he does."

Kulnethar stared at me, horrified beyond words.

"Oh, don't be such a child," I rolled my eyes. "It's what it has to be. We can't all steal cider and sneak out of the walls and get away with it. For some of us, at least, there are consequences. So just be glad it isn't you and get back to your happy life, like I'm sure you always do."

"Vanya! That's . . . that's a horrible thing to say."

"Oh, really? You said it yourself. It's not fair. But if I were you I'd enjoy it." I laughed, trying to make light of it, but it came out sounding mean.

His mouth opened, anger sparked in his blue eyes, and he slammed his palms into my chest, sending me sprawling backwards onto the stone floor. "Sometimes, Vanya, you're an ass." Then he stomped off.

It was only the next day I learned Yanava was fourteen. Barely come of Age. Barely old enough to be executed as a thief. The same age as Bray.

I glanced at the gangly kid. He was an annoying little shit, but the thought of him roped up—for anything—sent a jolt of anger through me, startling in its intensity. I swallowed.

"Come on." I grabbed my water pack. "Let's go."

We were the last ones out of the Novice's quarter, though Bretina was lingering beneath the first arch, waiting for us.

"What's taking you so long?"

"Nothing," I said.

"You scared?"

"Not me," said Bray.

I snorted and said nothing. There was a clenching in my gut I didn't like. A feeling like maybe I was going to be sick, maybe not. It wasn't my fault—I kept telling myself, over and over again. If I hadn't been there, it would have happened just the same. But then I thought of Tala, sobbing in the hall: *I betrayed her, I could have stopped it, I had no right. No right.*

The walk down to the Flatrock was a sombre one. Even Bray fell quiet. We passed through the Hall, across the yard, out the front gates, and down, down to the water. Just as on Renewing, there were Labourers and Crafters spilling out of the streets to either side. But there were no smiles this time, no laughter. Even the cold, suspicious looks had vanished. Instead, the Kyr'amanu averted their gaze. The only sound was the shuffling of many feet and the hushed, strained whispers.

When we came to the Flatrock, they were already prepared: two structures, this time, side by side. Sturdy poles were lashed together to support a single, thick rope in the centre of each, mounted at the highest point of the rock. The Flatrock, normally used for retting hemp sheaves, speared out over the lake, rising slowly, pointing like a finger towards the Avanir.

It was around this we spread. I found myself wandering from the other Novices. I looked for Tala, and couldn't find her, so I gave up and chose a place on my own, standing down a little into the half-filled lakebed. The crowds were silent and stern. A grimness hovered over them like smoke. I could almost taste it.

My stomach clenched again. Hard. That's when I saw Tala. She was on Dunya's right, leading him up the rock. The man's face was swollen and bruised, robes stripped away, wearing nothing more than a loincloth. His hands were bound behind him. Had she *asked* to lead him? My fists tightened. "Damn you, Tala. You didn't have to." *My fault*, she was saying.

Then I noticed movement out of the corner of my eye. I glanced over my shoulder. A familiar white-robe slipped out of the crowd and moved to stand next to me. Kulnethar said nothing. I met his gaze and we shared the barest of nods, then both of us turned back to watch.

Malishu came next, also stripped to his skin, flanked by two more Guardians. The red-cloaked Circle followed and took up their place along the edge of the rock. There was an agonized hush.

Then Neraia sai'Kalysa, Guardian Lord of the first kiyah and over-seer of justice, stepped out.

"Before Yl'avah, High Ruler and One-Maker," she began in a firm voice, "before the Avanir, our Hope, and before all Kyr'amanu, with the authority of law, we stand in judgment against Dunaya ab'Duani, who has been found guilty of violence with intent to kill, second-mark theft, and the unlawful possession of a weapon, sentenced by means of witness and testament, and condemned to die. Will the condemned make confession?"

Her question hung over those gathered. No one stirred. I hardly dared to breathe. Dunya's mouth moved, and I saw Tala lean in to speak to him. Her hand pressed his arm. A quick, encouraging squeeze.

The man took a shaking breath. "I . . . I am guilty."

Tala said something else.

"Of . . . of endangering the lives of my fellow Kyr'amanu. Of taking part in baseless theft. Stealing from them. Of . . ." he faltered, but seemed to gather his courage. "I am guilty of cowardice. Of knowing the truth, and . . . and doing nothing. Forgive me."

He glanced up once. Had he seen a face in the crowd? A face he knew? Then with hooded eyes, he dropped his head again, and we were forgotten.

There was silence. Sai'Kalysa nodded, as if accepting his plea. She paused a moment longer, and spoke again.

"We stand also in judgment against Malishu ab'Anaasha, who has been found guilty of first-mark theft, extortion, and unlawful posses-sion of a weapon, sentenced by means of witness and testament, and condemned to die. Will the condemned make confession?"

"Guilty," Malishu snapped the moment she was finished speaking and said nothing else. The Circle waited. The crowd held their breath. No one spoke.

Neraia sai'Kalysa laid a hand on the hilt of her keshu.

"It is as you say. May death come swiftly, and your spirits find passage to the Last Realm."

Tala and the other Guardians led them to the ropes. Two steep, rickety ladders were in place. They climbed. Their chests shone naked in the morning sun. They squinted. Dunya was breathing hard, trembling. Malishu had gone cold. He saw nothing. Heard nothing. Ropes were lowered behind them, then tied to their wrists, still bound at their backs. Heavy stones were strapped to their ankles. There was a low murmur now, running through the Kyr'amanu. My stomach twisted. I was staring at Tala. But she held her post with absolute diligence. And when sai'Kalysa gave the nod, she stepped forward and kicked the ladder out from under Dunya's feet.

The man fell. His wrists jerked up behind him, above his head— breaking his shoulders. He screamed. His feet kicked, held by the stone, while the whole weight of his body pulled, pulled on his wrists, his twisted shoulders, his snapped joints, flesh wrenched out of place. Breathless, sobbing cries bubbled out of him. Nobody moved. Tala didn't even flinch.

A second Guardian came forward. Malishu dropped. This time, I heard the crack of his bones. He jerked in shock, mouth gaping, eyes peeled back. He seemed to have no breath. A heartbeat—maybe two —before he began to scream. He only lasted a few moments before passing out. Dunya remained conscious, cries faded into laboured groans. Silence fell.

We waited. We waited. My mouth had gone dry. I didn't dare reach for my water. I could hear Kulnethar beside me, his breath shuddering.

Then one by one, the Circle turned and left the Flatrock. Only Tala and a handful of Guardians stayed. This would go on for a long time yet, perhaps even to dusk, depending on the strength of the condemned. Perhaps longer. The stones pulled down, while the ropes pulled up, dragging on the dislocated arms, slowly squeezing the air out of their lungs. Suffocating them. It was not a quick, easy death. But the departure of the Circle signalled the end of our obligation. We were free to go.

Some did just that. There was a swell of movement. The Kyr'a-manu left in silence, as grim as they had come. But not all. Here and there, people remained.

"Why?" I had asked my father, as I stood with him, that first execution, when it was Yanava ab'Ashnavas swaying and groaning on the ropes. His body had been limp, hands and shoulders contorted at unnatural angles, now swelling up, dark and splotchy, while blood trickled from his chafed wrists. Every now and then, a tremor would run through him, or he would shift and gasp, straining to pull himself up despite the pain, to get a breath. One more breath. One more.

"Why do people stay?"

"To show respect," my father said.

"To a thief?"

He squeezed my arm. "To a young man. Life is precious. We honour it. We grieve its passing."

So simple, I had thought. But it wasn't. Not for me. And not for the young Guardian who had been watching that day. The one I noticed before leaving with my father. The one with cold eyes, knuckles white around the hilt of his keshu. The one trembling with rage.

"Still want to be a Guardian?" Kulnethar asked, dragging me from my memories.

I snorted. He'd asked me the same question, the day after Yanava's death. And he asked it now. Just as sincere. Just as sure of the answer.

"We all have our duties," I said.

"Like Tala?"

I swallowed. She was standing, still standing, watching as Dunya struggled and gasped. He had bit his tongue, and blood frothed out of his mouth. His whole body trembled.

I gazed at Tala. She was unshakeable. Yl'avah's might, she was formidable. I decided I would stay as long as she. I would stay to the end.

"Tala's not first kiyah," Kulnethar said. "I know how it works. She didn't have to do this. She volunteered."

"She feels responsible."

"She's punishing herself?"

I felt a growl in my throat. "How should I know?"

Kulnethar fell quiet a moment. "She came to see Alis yesterday. The girl. Do you remember?"

"Of course I remember."

"She was kind to her, Tala was. You would be proud."

"I *am*. You think I'm not proud of her? You think I don't admire the blasted sands out of her?"

Kulnethar smiled. "Give it time, Vanya."

His tone struck me. I stared at him. "What do you mean? What did she say? Did she mention me? Did she—?"

"Is now the most appropriate time for those questions, my friend?"

I grunted and turned away. "You brought it up, you self-stuffed white-robe."

"Sorry."

Malishu picked that moment to regain consciousness. He jerked on the ropes and gazed around, as if he'd forgotten where he was. When he remembered, he started screaming again.

It was a pathetic sort of dying. The kind that went on and on. The kind that stripped away any dignity a man had left. Kulnethar was tightening beside me. I could feel it, his disgust, his overwhelming hatred for this, *this*. Over and over again, he'd brought it up. *Why can't they make it quick at least? Yl'avah's mercy, why?*

"I have to go," he said at last.

"I know."

"Sorry, Vanya." He hovered, like he had something else he wanted to say, but the screaming was making it hard for him to think. Then he gripped my arm. "Be careful."

I glanced at him in surprise. "Why should I be careful?"

"I don't know. I don't know. Just . . . Remember Yanava? Remember what happened?"

My jaw tightened. "You don't have to remind me."

"Just . . . just remember. I don't like this. I never did. Pain does things to people, and . . ."

"Okay, I get it. I'll be careful."

He swallowed, nodded, then turned and hurried back across the fields.

Chapter Seventeen

I t was a long, terrible day. I stood in the heat. I watched. I watched two men die. Or more accurately, I watched Tala watching them.

Pain does things to people. Yl'avah's might, he didn't have to remind me. He didn't. He *knew* he didn't!

Remember Yanava?

How could I forget?

I clenched my fists. I drank my water, refilled it at the lake, drank again. Watched.

Kynava. Kynava ab'Ashnavas. You tell them Kynava did this. You tell them . . .

I tried not to think of it, but it came anyway, all tangled up. Every time it was the same. The pain. The screaming. I hadn't always been afraid of the desert. Even now, it wasn't the wilderness that terrified me. Thirst, heat, blacksnakes: they were deadly, but not what curled my insides.

No. It was the shadows.

That day, the black arms of the Avanir had looked contorted in pain, as if warning me, reminding me. I'd spent all day with my father and his crew, digging, redirecting the last of the Avanir's water, repairing breaches and leaks. My back ached and my hands were rubbed raw, despite the calluses I'd been developing. Since the day I was Tasked to him, I had done my work, refused to complain, and nursed my resentment in silence. But I was growing sullen and weary.

"You said I could be Tasked somewhere else if I listened. I've *been* listening. It's been a whole year, I haven't gone over the walls, I swear it, by the Tree."

"Ishvandu, you should not make such oaths."

"But you promised—!"

"Did I?"

I grumbled and kicked at a stone and fell silent.

"You would make a good Labourer," my father continued. "You know how to work hard. You did well today."

"But I don't *want* to be a Labourer."

"I know," he said, frowning, on the edge of saying something more. Instead he just shook his head, looked away, and that was it.

That night, I had trouble sleeping. I imagined the horror of doing this—nothing but this—for the rest of my life. I wouldn't. No. If they tried to name me a Labourer at my coming of Age, I would . . . I would . . .

What? Run away? Flee into the desert? Face the emptiness alone?

Maybe.

The thought scared me, but it was a different sort of fear. A good fear. The thrill of danger.

Anything. Anything but this . . .

I drifted.

I woke. It was still night. My lungs sucked in a breath of alarm, unnaturally loud in the stillness. Not even the wind stirred outside the curtain of our hut. But I sat up anyway, fear clawing at my stomach. *I had heard something.*

"Father," I whispered.

He stirred and rose, a shadow among shadows.

"What is it?"

"I think . . . I think something's wrong."

"A dream?"

"I don't know. I thought I heard something, like . . ." *Screaming.*

I swallowed my words. *Idiot. Go back to sleep.* But my father stood and moved to the curtain. A moment later, it came: a long, distant wail, piercing the silence. The sounding horns of the Hall of Guardians.

The resonance reached down into my gut and pulled—powerful, urgent, compelling. *Arise!*

I scrambled to my feet. "Father?"

He slapped open the curtain and looked out. I could hear others stirring, muttering, calling out questions. My own heart was pattering —I was scared, but something else too. Excited. Fascinated. The same dark wondering that had gripped me at the execution. Anything to break the monotony of my life.

He pulled his head back in, grabbed his robe and threw it over his shoulders, then stabbed a finger at me. "Ishvandu, stay here. Do you understand?"

I nodded, though I had no intention of obeying. Then he disappeared into the night.

"*Up!*" Someone was shouting, getting closer. "Fire at the Hall! Up! Grab whatever you can—sand, dirt, ash. Get to the Hall. Now, now! On your life! Move!"

I crept to the curtain and looked out. It was a Guardian. His keshu swung from his side, a hundred braids tossing as he strode up the street, whirling to face whoever emerged, barking orders. Some were already running, holding blankets and buckets and robes while they dashed past.

"What's happening?" a woman called.

"The rations are burning. Move!"

It took a moment for the words to sink in, then the Labourers broke into action, seizing whatever they could. One man grabbed a bucket of water.

"What are you doing?" the Guardian hollered. "Put that back! No one spills a drop of water, or I beat the skin off his back. This is Kaprash. Are you mad?"

Everyone knew the rules. In Kaprash, water was precious, too precious even for putting out fires. What good was saving our rations, only to die from thirst?

I couldn't just stand there. I grabbed my blanket, gathered it into a sack, and dashed out to join the fray. People were running, scooping sand from wherever the wind piled it, then running again, while the horns whirled and whirled, sending their haunting cries into the night.

I was carried along, caught up in the panic. It was dark. Feet pounded the dust around me. Shouts rang. I was knocked and jostled, but I dove towards a pile of loose sand, filled the sheet, swung it over my shoulder, and hurried on.

Soon, I could see. There was a glow on the horizon, like the sun sinking into the west, red and fiery. But it wasn't the sun. It was the Guardian's Hall. Burning like a torch.

The cries of alarm grew. Everyone could see the blaze now. I clutched my sack and ran harder. Down the tight streets, weaving madly, avoiding the other jostling shadows.

Someone crashed into me from behind. I fell, my sack scattering across the ground, knees and hands scraping on the hard stone.

"Watch it!" I shouted after the fleeing shadow.

Legs tripped over me, someone cursed, and I was almost flattened. I scrambled out of the way, ignoring my scraped knees, struggling to find my blanket-sack. By the time I latched on, it was much lighter, but no time to worry about that now. I leapt back to my feet, running, running.

By the time I dashed out of the Labourer's quarter, my lungs were burning and the blanket-sack dragged at my arms. The open ground in front of the Hall bulged with red light. Labourers, Crafters, Guardians—they ran, dragging sand and dirt, hollering orders, forming chains. Smoke boiled, twisting out of the yard like a living creature. Flames shot skyward. They licked through the walls.

The rations.

It hit me. That was our food. All our food. Our labour. The hard work of a year. If we didn't get that fire out, we were dead. Every single one of us.

A man next to me staggered to a halt. He stood and stared in horror. He collapsed to his knees, face slack. His bucket tipped, the valuable dirt spilling forgotten to the ground.

I seized his shoulders, shaking him. "Get up! Get up! Are you just going to *sit* there?"

He didn't move, didn't even look at me. In frustration, I tossed the blanket-sack over one shoulder, then bent to grab the bucket. It was heavy. I nearly fell over with the weight, but Yl'avah's might, it wasn't doing any good just sitting there. Besides, I hadn't been hauling water all those years for nothing.

I tottered towards Hall, puffing, breathing hard, muscles straining under the heavy sand.

A Guardian woman appeared, hair glowing red in the fire.

"Here!" she cried. She seized the bucket and the blanket-sack, then hurried back the way she had come. The Guardians were forming a chain into the yard, trying to smother the fire with sand. I watched her go. I stood there, empty-handed, lost in the chaos, bodies streaming past me. What now?

More sand. We needed more sand. The ground here was hard and rocky. Where could we find more sand?

I almost laughed. *The desert!* The western gate was there, just on the other side of the Hall, and behind it, there would be dunes of sand, sand piled against the wall, sand rolling, gusting, pushed by the wind.

"The gate! The gate!" I waved my arms. I shouted. I spun. People careened past, heedless of a small field Tasker. "*The gate!*" It was no use. I was drowned out by the chaos.

My eyes fell on an abandoned bucket. *There.* I took a step, and a man hurled into me. I sprawled. Someone stepped on me, and then another, sandals digging painfully into my back, my hand. I bit back a cry and scrambled towards the bucket, clutching it like a shield, feeling a wash of helplessness. What could I do? What could one scrawny boy do?

The gate. The desert.

I swallowed. I waited for the clot of pounding feet to pass, then I dashed across the open ground. Not towards the Hall, but around it. Towards the gate.

The smoke struck me like a wall. It was thick, pungent. It clung to me. It scraped up my nose and into my eyes, coming from every corner of the Guardian's Hall. *At the same time.* Which meant ...

I gasped. A billow of smoke seared into my lungs, and I doubled over, coughing, choking, clutching an arm over my face as I hurried forward. I was blind. I couldn't breathe. My face was burning, my lungs, my chest ...

I burst from the fumes, mind racing. Someone did this. It wasn't an accident. Someone set fire to the rations. On purpose. Yl'avah's might, *why?*

I stumbled out of the smoke, and the western wall of Shyandar loomed out of the dark before me. I saw the gate. And I saw that it was open. The heavy beam was cast to the ground, and a shape was standing there, framed by the entrance, the cold stars beyond. Just standing, watching.

Him. Instantly, I knew. He did this, whoever he was. He was responsible. It could have been Shatayeth Undying himself, but in that moment, anger seared away all sense.

"You!" My voice cracked from the smoke. I coughed, and the figure stirred. He glanced my way, then disappeared beyond the wall. Into the desert.

He had done this! My head was spinning, but I ran, chest heaving, sandaled feet striking the earth. The gate rushed up before me, one of its huge doors thrown inward.

I was going to catch him. No way was he getting away with this! I'd make sure he was caught. I'd see him roped up like Yanava for this. I could be a hero. Just like a Guardian. Then no way they would keep me a Labourer.

I burst out onto the other side.

The chaos and the shouts, the crackling fire, the smoke—it all faded. I stepped into another world. Into the desert. Here, the stars and the moon cast eerie shadows over a barren world. Here, the wind sighed, tugging my hair, and my coughs sounded sharp and loud in the silence.

A chill crept up my skin. Goosebumps peppered my arm. The shadows seemed to move around me, like living things creeping out of the ground. I thought of Kulnethar going into the desert, of how the young Guardian Trushya had been killed, face scarred beyond recognition. I thought of the stories.

I took another step.

And then something cracked into the side of my head.

I collapsed. Pain burst through my eyes, down the back of my neck, rattling through my skull. I gasped, even as hands seized the back of my shirt.

"Meddling boy! What do you think you're doing?"

My head spun. It was hard to think. *A man . . . framed in the gate . . . burning . . .*

"You did this." I coughed.

He shook me, and specks burst in front of my eyes. "Who did you tell?"

I said nothing.

"Who did you tell, boy?"

I was alone. Outside the walls. Alone, but for a criminal. Yl'avah's might, I was a fool!

"Let me go!" I pushed back, struggling—until something cold slid against my throat. It was gleaming with a faint, sharp light.

A Guardian's keshu.

Yl'avah save me, I was going to die!

"Who else?" His breath was hot on my ear. "Who did you tell?"

"You're a . . . a traitor." I gasped. "You burned the rations. What kind of Guardian are you? Without food, we'll die. All of us. Why? Why would you . . . ?"

"Why?" The blade slipped into my skin like loose earth. I never even felt the edge, only the warm blood, trickling down my neck. "Because you're murdering savages, every one of you. You let him die. You *killed* him. And you call this justice? He was a boy."

I shut my eyes, forcing myself to stay calm. "Yanava," I said. *Twisted and groaning, roped up to die.* "Yanava was your friend?"

"My brother."

In a flash, I remembered: the young Guardian I had seen at the execution, his eyes cold, cold with hatred, burning as he watched Yanava die. His brother.

"He was a thief, he . . . he *confessed* it."

"Confessed? Hah! You think that matters? You think it means *anything*? I gave my life to the Guardians, and they took my brother's. This is no more than the lying bastards deserve."

"So you're going to kill me too? I didn't do anything. I didn't kill your brother. I—"

He seized a tangle of my hair, jerking my head back, bending low. "You *are* alone. No one's coming, are they?"

I shook my head, lips tight, refusing to plead. *Yl'avah's might, he was going to kill me.*

"Good," he said, bending close to my ear. "Because eventually they *will* think to look for you. They'll see the open gate. They'll come running. But I plan to be long gone by then. So you tell them, boy. You tell them Kynava ab'Ashnavas did this. You hear? Kynava ab'Ashnavas. Say it. I want to hear you say it."

My breath caught. "You're . . . you're going to let me—?"

"Say it!"

I swallowed. "Ky . . . Kynava. Kynava ab'Ashnavas. He did it."

"So they can watch helpless while their loved ones suffer and die. You tell them. Got it?"

I nodded.

"Good." The blade moved off my neck, though he crouched low, still pinning me to the ground. "Of course, I can't let you run back too soon. I need a head start. Maybe I'll hurt you. Just a little, so you can't move."

I swallowed and glanced up. The bucket was a hand span from my face, lying forgotten. A solid wood bucket.

"Oh, you won't *all* die," he continued. "You'll find a way. This stinking place always does. It goes on and on. Pointless. Stupid."

I eased my hand free, clenching and unclenching, readying.

"Yanava tried to escape, and they dragged him back. Back to mindless drudgery. Back to die. This is just a lesson in their own meaningless brutality."

I shot my hand out, grasping the handle, twisting. It whipped into the man's head. He gave a grunt of surprise and fell back. Then I was on my feet. I lunged for the gate. He dove after me, cursing, spitting. His fingers latched on to my ankle, yanking me back. I slipped. My ankle twisted. There was a jolt, something snapped, and pain shot through my bones. I hit the ground with a thud. I couldn't breathe, my lungs squeezed, gasping, unable to get the air in. I rolled onto my back. Stars spun, high, high above me. A face leered down.

"Stupid boy." I tried to wrestle him off, but my head was spinning, spinning.

I dragged in a lungful of air. "*Help!*" My voice cracked. I took another breath. "He's here. Out here! He's getting—"

He struck me in the mouth. Hard. I gasped, and he hit me again. Then he grabbed a fistful of my shirt, ripped, and stuffed it down my throat. I gagged, helpless as he kicked me over, wrenched my arms behind me. A strand of rope circled my wrists and he yanked it tight. I spat the rag out of my mouth and screamed again, tasting blood. I could see the other side of the gate, the smoke billowing, the shouts in the distance.

No one was listening.

Kynava slammed my face into the ground. I lay there for a moment, stunned. Then he stuffed the bloody rag between my teeth again and lashed a second strip around my mouth. I kicked. Pain stabbed up my leg and I almost choked. Then he was grabbing my feet, roping them up.

"You're not going anywhere, boy. Not just yet." He jerked my injured foot around, tying it to the other. "Oh, they'll find you eventually. Don't you worry about that." He stood and pulled the gate closed, cutting off the noise and smells from the Hall. I twisted and glared up at him, eyes burning. "*Traitor!*" It came out as a muffled shout.

He ignored me. He hoisted a heavy pack, grabbed my injured foot. I shouted again, but he kept walking. He was *dragging* me. My face scraped against the sand. Sand was shoved up my nose and into my eyes. I tried to twist around, to throw myself onto my back, to kick free of his hold, but he marched on, heedless of my struggles. I heard a low whistle. A shadow moved by the wall. A camel.

I finally flipped onto my side, craning my neck to get free of the sand. I blinked and snorted. Between the sand up my nose, and the gag stuffed down my throat, it was hard to breathe. My chest heaved. I was starting to panic. I was choking. My nose burned as I took desperate whiffs of air. How much farther? Who would think to look for a lowly field Tasker, missing in all this chaos?

No one.

He dropped me at last. I lay there, breathing hard. In the dark, I could see him loading up the camel, checking the straps, shrouding his face in a head-wrap. When I looked back at the wall, it was a hundred paces away, at least.

"Don't," I gave a muffled cry. "Don't leave me here. Don't . . ."

He ignored me, and tears stung my eyes. I hated him, hated my own helplessness. I coughed against the gag. I tried to shift, but my ankle burst with pain.

"They'll come," said Kynava with one more glance in my direction. I saw his face, suddenly awash in moonlight. It was a young face, hard and bitter.

Then he leapt onto the camel and was gone.

I WEPT INTO THE SAND. I cursed my own stupidity. I struggled and wept and cursed some more. I coughed through my tears, and when I took a breath, the rag sucked into my throat.

For an instant, I just lay there in shock. Then I realized I couldn't breathe. *I couldn't breathe!* I starting hacking to dislodge the rag. I dragged in breaths through my nose. Tasting blood, dust. My heart was pounding in my ears. All else was silence. It was dark and still. Utter blackness around me. I shivered. Nothing moved. No sound came from over the wall. Had the fire been put out? How long had it been?

I twisted, but couldn't see Kynava anywhere. *Traitor! Murderer!*

My ankle pulsed with pain. It was stiff and sore, and every time I moved, I felt it stab up through my calf.

I lay there for a moment in despair. Maybe someone would come for me. Or maybe they wouldn't. Maybe I would die out here.

Stupid. I would only die if I let myself. I had to make it back. I had to get this gag off. I had to be able to breathe.

I started scraping my face along the ground, pushing it up, lifting, then pushing again, slowly and deliberately, looking for a bump or a stone I could use. It was painful, but I managed to shift the gag. First a little, then more and more as it slipped down to my chin. Finally, it came loose.

Gagging, I spat the filthy, blood-thick rag out of my mouth and sucked in a breath. My face dropped to the ground. My head was spinning and pounding, and my lungs hurt. But I wasn't done yet. I gathered myself for the long, painful crawl across the sand.

Then it came. Up, over the sand, crackling and sharp: an unearthly scream.

My head snapped up. My skin prickled. The scream had not come from the wall.

Trushya . . . an inhuman scream. Kulnethar's story. That face, scarred and bloodied.

It came again. Long, screeching, raw. Close. Somewhere terribly close. Just over the next dune. From the desert. *Kynava ab'Ashnavas.*

The torturous cries raked across the dead landscape, over and over again, rising and shrill. I wanted to block my ears. I wanted it to stop. Tears sprang to my eyes, sheer terror at the thought of so much pain. Suddenly it didn't matter what Kynava had done. No one . . . no one . . .

Then silence. The only sound was a thudding heart.

Yl'avah save me, Yl'avah save me . . .

"Help!" My voice cracked. "Help me! Help! Someone!"

I began pushing myself, one span at a time. My ankle throbbed. I felt sick with pain. Blood dripped down the side of my head, and my face scraped along the ground. A chill was creeping over me, stealing into my lungs, turning my skin to the coldness of naked metal. I paused. I had to think. I couldn't let fear overwhelm me. I couldn't let it win.

Yl'avah's save me, it was cold! I took a deep breath. And another. It was *very* cold—far too cold. I had never known cold like this before. Was I dying? Was this what happened when you died?

I shivered. Something was wrong. *Wrong.* It was more than fear. It was—

There was a rush of wind. No, of something moving, overhead. I gasped and looked. A blackness loomed. A shadow, like shreds of night, gathering into a single, undulating point. My breath caught, stomach tight with terror. It wasn't an animal, wasn't a man, wasn't anything I could name. But it was moving. The shadows gathered and twisted and bulged, like the smoke billowing from the Hall. But this smoke had legs. It was walking towards me. Something reached out, blocking the stars.

And then I *saw*. It was a hand. Lines of light traced its fingers. Long fingers, bent out of joint, reaching towards me. An arm appeared. It was the coldness of the stars, coalescing into the ruined echo of a man. Cold and pitiless. The rest of it emerged, became sharp and clear. And I saw its face. It was twisted, disfigured, eyes like empty sockets, mouth gaping in a wicked smile, skin that dripped from it in flakes of oozing light. It loomed over me. Then its fingers latched under my chin, into my cheeks.

I screamed. The pain was excruciating—cold fire against bare skin, searing it raw. It was leaning closer. I tried to pull away, roll onto my side, but I was helpless, tied so I could barely move. It rushed at me.

The lines of light and shadow smothered me. It filled my eyes so I couldn't see, and my mouth and nose so I couldn't breathe. It pushed into my ears, blocking out everything but a terrible screeching, like metal scraping against glass. Everything was darkness. I could *feel* it. It clawed at my throat, like a rat forcing its way into my lungs. It burned my eyes. *Past* my eyes. Up my nose. Into my brain.

My vision exploded. Colours and lights flooded my mind. Things, people I'd never seen before. They came faster than I could follow. They were hurled against my senses. I could feel every moment, like it was my own. Unbearable pain. All of them ending, burning. My whole body was on fire. Then it was being crushed. My limbs were screaming in pain, twisting, twisting. I hated everyone, everything: hated, longed to devour, to tear apart, to take hold of flesh, to feel it ripping off bone, to devour as my own—an all-consuming lust for what I wasn't, could never be, could never have.

The screeching in my ears. What was it? What a horrible, painful sound! *No, no.* It was my own screaming. Screaming. But a voice not my own. On and on, conscious of every moment. Aware of myself and aware of *it* and powerless to make it stop.

And then it stopped. The thing ripped out of me, raking across my mind as it left, tearing a piece of me with it. The shadow fled.

The voice was mine again, now a babble of weeping—almost words. I gasped for breath. I could hear voices. Shouting. Feet pounding the sand.

"There's someone here!"

"Is it them? The shades? Yl'avah's might, it's a boy!"

The starlight blinded me. The wind was like knives in my flesh.

My stomach heaved. Bile came out, hot, acrid and foul, dripping down my chin. Tasting of blood.

"Don't touch him!" a voice cried. My ears exploded with the noise. I twisted onto my stomach and threw up again. I wept. My body shook.

"He's alive. Stay back! Don't touch him. Don't—"

Arms seized me anyway, pulling me up. I screamed and tried to wrench away.

"Yl'avah's mercy!"

I fell back to the ground, sobbing, gasping for breath. *It hurt. Everything hurt.* My tongue loosened. "I'm sorry," I wailed. "It wasn't me. *It wasn't me!* No, no, no!" I thrashed on the ground. "This is wrong, Illynar! This is . . . *Too late.* No. I can stop them. I can still stop them. I . . ."

Groans rolled over my tongue. The cold swirled. The voices around me—they were crying out. Shouting.

"Get back!"

"Look out!"

I pressed myself into the dust, weeping. My own tears were like fire.

"Over here!" someone shouted.

"There's more of them."

"In rank!"

"*No!*"

A scream. A horrible scream. *Again, again.* It raked across my mind like a knife.

"Protect the boy!"

Someone stood over me. I felt the cold, and the shadows, and the voices. *Save us! Save us, or end. All, all is ending. All . . .*

The screams could not drown out the voices. The voices were inside. In my skin, my lungs, my throat. I heard a sound like tearing fabric, wet and heavy. And laughing, hissing, screeching, a hammer against my skull, rattling my mind, back and forth, back and forth, back and—

All was silence. All dark. The desert closed around me. Pain through every sense. I couldn't move. Couldn't breathe.

Kynava ab'Ashnavas—you tell them. You tell them I did this . . . Kynava ab'Ashnavas.

The stench was thick: of burning and rotting, of blood and piss and shit. It was the smell that clung to me. That dragged me from unconsciousness, thrusting me back into agony.

Bare feet. Bare feet stepped silently over the bodies. *Bare feet?* What Guardian would go into the desert with bare feet? The thought bothered me. It was a hook in my mind—dragging me out of nothingness. Why? How? I wanted to speak. Maybe I did. There was a distant groaning. Desperate and strange.

This one . . . this one . . .

The thought shivered through me, needling, pulsing in my mind, burning behind my eyes.

"Alive," said the voice. It was cool and deep, like a pool. Like a deep, dark pool, speaking softly into the shadows. The bare feet stepped nearer. "This one is alive."

Then hands took me. They hurt. They crushed my skin, bruising with every touch. I groaned. *Stop. Stop.* Something touched my lips. It was fire. It seared down my throat. I gagged and choked. I wanted to scream. But only my eyes moved, blinking madly against the stars. The stranger held the fire to my lips—again, and again. My throat loosened: "*N-no. No more. No . . . Who . . . ?*"

The fire stopped. The stranger bent close to me, hovering. "E'tu-ah," he said. "I am E'tuah."

I groaned. I had no strength to resist, though it hurt, it hurt. Everything hurt.

"It will pass," he said. "If you live."

Then he lifted me. I felt like I was being dragged apart, ripped. One half of my body was being carried, the other left behind. My chest squeezed in panic. But I couldn't move. Couldn't fight. I was nothing, nothing. Nothing but shadow.

Chapter Eighteen

They cut the bodies down at dusk. By then, the only ones left were a handful of Guardians, the corpses, and me. Those who hadn't stood vigil began the long trek to the Resting House, bearing the two dead criminals. The execution was over. I had done it. I had stayed with Tala until her duty was complete.

She strode off the Flatrock. She made it a dozen paces. Then she dropped to her knees and threw up.

"Tala!"

I ran across the ground. I reached her, tried helping her up, but she turned and slammed her hands into my chest, shoving me away.

"Don't touch me! Light and all, Vanya, you idiot, what in Yl'avah's name are you still doing here, are you *mad*?"

The words rushed out of her mouth, cracking and shuddering.

I swallowed. "I waited for you."

"I didn't ask you to!"

"Tala . . ."

"Just leave me alone." She climbed to her feet. Instead of going up the road, she turned and stumbled towards the water's edge, towards the Avanir.

"Tala, where are—?"

"Just go, Vanya."

"But . . ."

"*Go.*"

I hesitated, realizing I had done something wrong, though I had no idea what that was. Another Guardian took my arm, steering me away.

"Come, Novice. You shouldn't be here."

I shook off his hand. "Why not?"

"You missed the Darkening prayer, for one. Go on."

"Darkening prayer." I snorted. But I knew when I wasn't wanted. I started the long march back up the path. Night fell quickly. The stars came out. Soon I was alone on the road, shivering in the sudden cold. I swallowed. *The dark and the cold.*

I quickened my pace. My legs were unsteady from the long day in the sun. I had brought water and filled it up twice, and now it was gone. I realized I hadn't eaten since morning. Tala was right. What was I thinking?

The Hall loomed closer, but so did the shadows. I hurried now. I kept thinking I could see them, out the corner of my eye, the shadows. And the screams. The screams still echoed in my head, mixed with others—darker, wilder.

Save us.

I broke into a run. By the time I made it to the Hall I was gasping for breath. I threw myself through the gate, ignoring the questions of the Watch. They let me go. I staggered through the corridors. I must have taken a wrong turn, because somehow I wasn't in the Novice's quarter. There was a dead end. I doubled back. Another bolted door. I *knew* this Hall. Yl'avah's might, what was wrong with me!

I recognized the signs of my panic.

Steady. Steady. I dropped into a corner, pressing my face to the stone wall.

Kynava. Kynava ab'Ashnavas. You tell them Kynava did this. You tell them . . .

My body trembled with the memory. I bit the back of my hand. I wouldn't cry out. I wouldn't.

Pain does things to people . . .

"Stop," I groaned. "Stop this. It's over."

You tell them Kynava did this.

"I won't."

Save us, said the voices, reaching closer, hovering, whispering. *Save us or die.*

"No!" I pressed a hand to my face. What had it been, one week? Two? Two weeks since the last panic, since they'd put me and Koryn in the holds? I had to learn to control it. I had to. I was going to be a Guardian. I was going to face the desert. I was going to *be* something, and blast everything, I wasn't going to dissolve into a wreck every time a shadow twitched!

"I'm going to be a Guardian," I said aloud. "I'm going to be a Guardian."

I forced myself to breathe. I waited until my heart stopped pattering like a chicken. Then I stood. I traced my way back through the halls, beneath arches, around corners. I found the camel yard at the very back. I stepped out and gazed up into the open stars.

Then quietly, I sat in the middle of the yard, legs folded, and watched the camels cast flickering shadows across the sandy floor.

———

A HAND FELL on my shoulder. I bolted up, eyes wide. Sand stuck to my tongue, between my teeth. I almost gagged, and for an instant, I was there again . . .

"Ishvandu."

It was Umaala ab'Krushaya. I swallowed, blinking against the garish midmorning light. Three camels were only a pace away, staring at my rumpled form.

"Sal'ah."

"We were looking for you."

"Here I am." I grimaced, then turned and spat the dust out of my mouth. "Sorry, sal'ah."

Umaala said nothing, though I felt the grimness of his presence. I was in trouble again. I knew it.

"You stayed to the end."

I nodded.

He crouched to one knee, and his wide, meaty face was suddenly very close.

"Are you okay?"

"Why wouldn't I be?"

"Why did you stay?"

"Do I need a reason?"

"Why did you stay?"

I swallowed, uncertain. "It felt right."

"Because Atali sai'Neraia stayed?"

I shrugged, and Umaala paused, frowning, then glanced up.

"Why are you in the camel yard?"

"Shadows, sal'ah."

There was a long, awkward silence. I looked away, but felt Umaala studying me, watching for something. He knew, of course. Every Novice knew. I never spoke of it, but word spread anyway. New Taskers appeared and already they seemed to know. I was mad. I was a freak. I was ruined by the shadows. But not all of them knew the rest. Not everyone knew what I did. Where I had been. *Alone. Alone in the desert.* Umaala ab'Krushaya knew.

Finally, his gaze broke. He glanced away, more for my sake than his own. "Anajin ab'Anajin gave me his report. Your assignment with the fourth kiyah: you did well."

"I did nothing."

"Exactly."

"Does that mean I get to go again, sal'ah?"

There was a pause. "No."

I glanced up at him, wrestling a flutter of panic. "What do you mean, sal'ah? If I did well ..."

"You won't be joining the fourth again. I've spoken with the Al'kah, and we've decided it's time. We have something else for you to do."

The Al'kah? The Al'kah didn't care about Novices and Taskers. He was the lord of the Hall, the most powerful person in all of Shyandar. Taskers weren't his business. *Never* his business.

"I'm about to share something with you, Ishvandu, and I'm charging you with absolute silence in this matter. You will not repeat this to anyone: not Ebridyn or Atali sai'Neraia, and certainly not Kulnethar ab'Ethanir. Is that clear?"

"Yes, sal'ah."

"Malishu was not only hoarding rations. He was hoarding weapons. Hundreds of weapons."

The meaning was ominously clear. "You . . . you mean a Rising."

"Yes."

I hesitated. The knot of dread was twisting further, sinking deeper. "Why are you telling me this?"

"I think you know. These years have not been kind. The Long Kaprash, the sickness, poor crops, and now again. The people are restless. We are struggling, Ishvandu, and the Al'kah is ready."

The camel yard shrank and grew all at once. I could feel my heart thumping, even as I drifted outside myself. "What do you want, sal'ah?" The words seemed to come from someone else.

"Do you remember what we spoke of, the year you came to this Hall?"

I nodded.

"It's time."

I said nothing.

"Ishvandu ab'Admundi, I need your assent."

I swallowed. I clenched my hands to keep them from shaking. I couldn't look at him. "Ab'Krushaya'sal, I'm not sure I can."

"Are you saying you cannot do what is required of a Guardian?"

"I'm saying that was a long time ago."

"I've already spoken with the Al'kah. He wants you to try. Can you do it, or not?"

I took a deep breath. If I said no, it was over. If I admitted the truth, it was over. "I . . . I can try."

"Good. You will go with the next outriding, and lead them to this valley you spoke of."

I glanced up, horrified as a thought occurred to me. "Not with Koryn?"

"Yes, with Akkoryn ab'Kindelthu. He's one of the best outriders we have. And for your sake, you had better start referring to him as befits his position over you. Now do you understand what this could mean?"

I did. I saw it, as vivid as the day I woke. The lush green. The birds. Life in the desert. Life, surrounded by death.

"Water," I said. "Water in Kaprash."

"Exactly. You will speak of this with no one. His eyes held me, glittering, watching. "You're afraid."

"Yes, sal'ah."

"Good. Then you understand. Be ready."

Aktyr

HYRANNA ELDUNA

Year 799 after the fall of Kayr

Lel-na was the first to fight the darkness. He came at the edge of hope. They say he came bare-foot in the snow, and spoke with the words of Chorah'dyn. He was our champion. He was our voice. He fought to save the red trees. He was the greatest hero of the Greenwater.

But for you, my child, he was more.

Interlude: The Last Al'kah

I am not the thing. I am not the thing.

Ashkynas ab'Adani Al'kah panted the words—over and over again. Grass snapped as he waded through. A ghost. A wind. A daemon.

He stumbled. His feet were bare and cracked. His body hurt. His mouth bled with unending thirst. But he would not—*would not*—call for more.

Let me suffer. Let me feel every torment. He deserved no less. He was a murderer. He had murdered Ishtar. Murdered the woman. Murdered the friend and the stranger both. Faithful. Free. The thing did not discern one from the other. All too soon, the infusion of life had faded and left him cold, hungry, parched. Wanting more. But he would not use it again. Would not. Would not. Not until the end. Not until the last and bitter end.

The end? What was the end? Ashkynas couldn't remember anymore. The thing was curled around his mind, muttering its dark hopelessness, muttering its need. Filling him with one image. One. A red tree. The darkness. Waiting. Something waiting. Waiting in the dark under the tree.

But no. He would not obey the thing. He would fight it. He would throw it aside. He ... he ...

No. He couldn't remember anymore. He groaned as he stumbled and stopped and stumbled on again. He longed for one moment of clarity. One moment. His mind. His plan. What had he hoped for? Why had he done it? Why? What could he possibly do? Him? A lone and ruined wretch?

Ashkynas realized he had stopped moving. He was so weary. His arms, legs, eyes—so heavy. The wind tugged the frayed ends of his hair. He couldn't swallow anymore. Couldn't breathe. Only a dull, gasping struggle. His lungs heaved. His body shook. The sky unrolled above his head—endless untouched blue, a distant canopy, stretching from one corner of his gaze to the next, and he could turn and turn and never see all of it.

Grass bowed, nodding down and down and down to the sky. The blue filled him. It reached into him, deep inside, and went on and on, into the emptiness, running, running, and never filling, until at last he closed his eyes over it, and it was gone.

Chapter Nineteen

Hyranna slept fitfully.

She dreamed she was walking beside Balduin, along wide, muddy banks. She kept trying to ask him something—something *important*—but no matter how many times she repeated herself, he ignored her.

"I'm looking for my father," he would say. "I have to find him. He'll know what to do. Are you with me, Hyranna Elduna?"

Yes, she wanted to say, but couldn't. He walked on. She tried to follow him, but realized her feet were stuck. The mud was thick and wet, and with every step, she sunk deeper.

"Balduin!" she screamed.

He turned back to face her. His eyes were blue, startling blue, the colour of bright sky and sun dappled water. He looked at her. "Why did you take it?"

"I had to."

"Why did you take it? I told you not to take it. I told you."

"Balduin, help!" Something grabbed her ankles. It was pulling her down. She could feel the force of it, pulling, crushing, dragging her.

Balduin stretched out. "Take my hand!"

"I can't!" She couldn't reach. The mud was up to her chest, now almost to her shoulders. She flailed, though it did no good. She was panicking. She was going to die! *No, it's just a dream. You'll wake up.*

"I've got you! Just take my hand!"

But she couldn't see anymore. The mud closed over her head, and everything went black. She was falling. *I'll wake up*, she thought. *I'll wake up.* She was falling.

At first the darkness was thick, like an oozing swamp, but she fell through it, going faster and faster. Then it began to change—she could feel the space moving around her, trying to pull her in every direction, like claws picking at her clothes. Like fish nibbling. She twisted, struggled, but there was nothing beneath her feet, nothing above her, nothing on either side. She was trapped in nothingness. A nothingness that pressed against her, invasive and stifling. She couldn't breathe. Something was squeezing her chest. *Wake up, wake up!* Her lungs sucked in air, but it wasn't air: it was this loathsome blackness, this nothingness that wasn't nothing. *Maker save me!*

Then she heard a voice. Not Balduin's—someone she didn't recognize, and the words were strange to her, like the words of the Darkening prayer. They washed over her, undulating from every side. *Eshta no'ahni, ach'dadian'nu te.* The words came from her left, then her right, wave upon wave. Harsh and cold. She gazed wildly around her. There was only darkness. Only the sound of that voice, growing more insistent. More demanding. *Eshta no'ahni, jah!*

The darkness hurled her back. She stumbled into nothingness. Did she fall? She couldn't tell. She couldn't feel anything. Why couldn't she wake up?

"I don't . . . understand." Her voice was small. Weak.

She felt a pain between her eyes: a pinprick of heat, like an ember pressed to her forehead. It flashed, tearing through her mind, and she screamed and clutched her head.

Then it was gone. And there was silence. Silence, except for her ragged breath, going in and out, in and out. The darkness stilled; the air began to clear. Just a little. Just enough to breathe. Any moment, she would wake up. *Please, let her wake up.*

Then she heard the voice again, a whisper, a breath of frost, and slowly, like someone learning a word, it spoke: "Hyranna . . . Elduna."

HER EYES SNAPPED OPEN. She gasped like she was coming up for air. She sat up. She was breathing hard into the dark—a familiar, comforting dark.

But something was . . . *wrong.*

She glanced down. She was holding something, and it was burning. She was aware, dimly, of pain, but it was distant and unimportant. She just stared at the thing—it was glowing with a strange, burning light, not red, not white, but a pale ghostly grey—a light she had never seen before, never thought possible, like smoke and ash and white-hot fire, all burning in one. And as she stared at the jagged shape, she realized it was the shard of rock. The one from the Dandyri's cavern.

She shrieked and dropped it, and immediately the pain struck her.

"Anna? Anna what's wrong?" Her mother's voice cut through the dark.

Hyranna seized her wrist, too shocked to move, though she knew it was bad. "Just . . . just a dream." Her voice betrayed her. She could hear movement on the other side of the sleeping corner.

"Anna-chi?" Now it was her father.

They would take it from her. They would take it.

"I'm fine. I just . . . just need some air."

She scooped up the glowing stone with her skirt, then dashed out of the cave.

The moment she found the cool air, a groan pushed through her lips. She stared at her hand. The moonlight shone bright and clear, and she could see the outline of the stone, a shocking, angry red, burned into her palm.

How?

She plunged her hand into the rain catcher outside the door. There was sudden, searing pain, followed by a moment of relief.

How? The mountains to the south—fire mountains that spewed out burning rock and dust. That's where the shard was from. *Must* be. And somehow the rock's inner fire had leaked out, and she had reached for it in her sleep, and . . .

The door creaked open. She snatched her hand from the water, curling it into a fist behind her back, just as her father stepped out. *Maker's breath, it hurt!*

"Show me, Anna-chi," he said gently, holding out his hands.

"Show what? I'm fine. I just needed some—"

"Anna." His voice dropped. He reached for her arm, but she pulled away, breathing hard.

"I'm fine. I said I'm fine, Papi! It's nothing."

"I'm having difficulty believing you. Can you please show me your hand?"

Just show him, she thought. But something else flared up, angry and insistent. He would try to take the stone. She wasn't sure why that was bad, but it screamed in her mind. *He couldn't know. No one could know!*

But the burn—it would be impossible to hide the burn. There was no preventing that. She pulled out her hand and let him take. He cupped it gently. His wrinkles deepened with worry. Slowly, he pried open her fingers—every tug on the skin made her want to shriek. But she held her mouth shut, grimacing in silence.

The skin had peeled at the edges, and the palm itself was raw and blistering. Kenan's face opened in shock. "Anna! What did you do?"

"It was stupid. I was at the fires yesterday, and one of the logs rolled out. I just grabbed it with my bare hands. I don't know why I did that."

"What?" he gasped.

"I was so embarrassed, I didn't want to say anything, and with the funeral and everything . . . I must have knocked it while I was sleeping."

"Anna-chi! You should've said something at once. Look how raw it is! It could be infected. I need to clean it out, bandage it. Why would you hide something like this?"

"I don't know. I'm sorry, Papi. I should have told you."

The lie made Hyranna feel dirty, like sinking into the mud from her dream, and it was worse because he believed her. He brought her back inside, and she had to repeat the story to her anxious mother. Her father lit a lantern, cleaned her hand, made a poultice of plantain and honey, and wrapped it up, not too tightly, but snug enough to keep out the dirt. It hurt, but the poultice soothed it, a little.

By the time they were finished, the sky was starting to pale.

"Get some rest before morning," Kenan told her, but as exhausted as she was, she couldn't sleep. She kept seeing herself in the Dandyri's cavern, standing over the human bones. *Don't*, Balduin had said. But she'd taken it anyway. She'd reached out and taken it, and kept it almost without thinking. Why?

There was something wrong with that stone, she realized. And if anyone understood, it would be Balduin.

HYRANNA SNUCK out of the cave before either of her parents were up. *At the old tree*, Balduin had said. She retraced her steps, following the trampled path, and when she found the cleft, she climbed down slowly, wincing with every move of her burned hand. She reached the mossy floor and looked around.

Balduin was not there.

She called for him, and when there was no answer, she realized he must have gone straight to the Dandyri. She found the waiting darkness at the end, hesitated, then plunged into it.

Something was wrong. She knew it the moment she entered. The dream rose up in her mind: the suffocating shadow, the voice, the strange words, rushing on and on, around her on every side.

She should turn back. Something was wrong. Something . . .

But Balduin.

He was waiting for her, and if she didn't come, he would think she had changed her mind. What if he left without her? What if turning back now meant she would never see him again?

It was unthinkable.

She forced herself to breathe, to *think*. She'd had a disturbing dream, but that was all. Just a dream. Would she really let a silly dream keep her from her promise? She moved further in. She went slowly, carefully, and when she reached the big drop, she lowered herself with one arm and jumped the rest of the way. She hit the ground and rolled onto her side, careful not to use her burned hand.

It hurt anyway. She lay there for a moment, breathing hard. Now she could see the red light. It flickered and danced across the stone, but again—something was wrong.

She swallowed.

"Balduin?" she called.

There was no answer. Why was she afraid? She rose trembling to her feet and crept the last distance into the Dandyri's cave.

It seized her breath again—the sheer size of the tree. Bigger, far bigger than the cliffs. Her eyes were drawn up, up into the branches. She was still trying to wrap her mind around it, to figure out *how* the thing was so big, where the branches went, if not into the forest, when movement caught her eye.

The leaves were falling. They came slowly, only a few at a time, drifting, fluttering down, and when she followed them, she saw they littered the ground. She bent and picked up a fresh-fallen one. Last time, the scent alone had triggered the sights and sounds of the forest. Now, lifting it to her face, she smelled only decaying earth. She frowned and dropped the leaf, and its light went out.

What was happening?

"Balduin?" she called again. She took a hesitant step forward. "Balduin, are you here?"

The light rippled. From one branch to another, a shadow hurried across the tree, and for a moment, the whole cavern went dark.

Hyranna's heart beat a little faster. The thought of the lights going out, of being stuck here under the earth, in blackness ...

"Balduin?" She edged forward, gazing around her. *Find Balduin. Get out.* She glanced up at the tree. It towered over her. Its branches curled and swayed, as if touched by a wind. But no. There was nothing. No wind. Maker above, what was going on here?

She hurried forward, circling around the huge tree, suddenly hesitant to touch the roots, unable to shake the sense it was . . . *watching* her.

There! She froze. Something had moved.

"Balduin? Balduin, is that you?" She picked her way carefully around the Dandyri. There was no answer. But she had seen something. And there—there it was again! And . . . *there.*

The ground was moving. No. The *roots* were moving.

Maker above, the whole Dandyri was moving! Balduin was right. It was alive. She gasped and flung herself towards the back of the cavern, towards the tunnel, going up, scrambling and falling, breathing hard as she hurled herself out of the earth. Maybe Balduin was waiting by the Tindanarra. Maybe he was close to the falls. Maybe . . .

Hyranna emerged into the late morning sun, blinking and gasping. Feeling suddenly foolish. Had she just run away from a *tree*?

She forced herself to think. Balduin told her he would meet her by the old tree, but he wasn't in the cleft, and looking around her, he wasn't by the river either. Could he still be back in his mother's cave?

No, he had said he would meet her here, first thing in the morning. He'd *said*. Which meant either Balduin had lied, which was unthinkable, or something had happened to him.

She thought about the roots. She hadn't imagined it. She *couldn't* have. They had moved. She thought about the crushed skeleton. She thought about the stone in her pocket. *Why? Why did you take it?*

Her heart thumped, stomach tightening with sudden dread. What if . . . ? What if Balduin *had* come to the tree? And what if something had happened to him?

She hesitated, then curled her hand over the dark stone and plunged back into the Dandyri's cave.

"Where is he?" she cried, bursting into the cavern. "Did you hurt him? Tell me!"

The ground shuddered. It was faint, yet clear. Hyranna pulled back, breathing, breathing. *Maker above!* This was real. This was happening. The tree was speaking to her.

"What have you done?" She circled the Dandyri. Clutching the stone. Feeling a rush of strength. "Because of this? Because I took this from you?" She brandished the shard, glaring into the red boughs.

The ground moved again, now a long, unsteady trembling. She stared. It *was* the roots. She hadn't imagined it. They flexed, rippling from the base of the tree, down into the rock, rippling and coiling like snakes. She thought of the bones, the crushed ribs, the skull parted in a scream.

"Where is he? If you did something to him . . . If you hurt him . . ." Panic clutched her. A swift, burning anger. "Answer me, old tree!"

She drew herself up and marched towards the tree. Fear burned away. She would get answers. She would—

The ground exploded around her. Roots shot out of the soil, spraying earth and grass and leaves into the air. They came at her, knotting around her chest, her thighs, her ankles. Terrible in their strength. Furious.

Hyranna sprang forward, hands outstretched towards the trunk, clutching the shard, slamming into the wood. *What did you do? What did you do?* Something coiled out of her, furious and wild. It broke through her fingers, through her mind, ripping into the tree.

Her eyes flashed—she saw, in an instant, the vast old world, the red trees, joined in a web of power, a single living thing that grew and pulsed and stretched like a balm over the earth to heal it. *Life, life— sweet life, and clean air.* Words of the first dawn, of the Tree herself, the Chorah'dyn, world's root, the ever-present—

Until the shadow. The sickness spread, and furious groans burst across the web like tremors of a tortured earth. The trees cracked and fell and turned to dust, and she, the last of the Dandyri, felt their dying—a wound in her own flesh, her own spirit. *No!* The dark swallowed her. She was cut off. She was alone. She battled the emptiness, alone—and could not win.

And now! The audacity of the tiny creature in drawing near, in threatening her with the emptiness, in thinking she could demand and escape. After all she had done! After giving her shelter. Opening to her. Trusting her. And now this? *Daring* to suggest that she, *she* would hurt Balduin Na-es?

She had to stop her. She could not let her escape. She could not let her use—

Too late.

Wood broke, booming and crackling through the chamber like a scream, heavy and final.

Hyranna cried out. The roots tore away from her. She fell, scraping across the rocky ground. A force shuddered through her, from the soles of her feet, to the tips of her fingers. It rolled like fire— hungry, eager, exultant. She could feel the life of the tree. It was in her grasp. It was splintering. It was being ripped apart.

"No!" *What had she done?*

She glanced up. A gaping fissure ran through the tree, black and smoking. Something oozed out. It dripped, flowing like blood across the ground, spreading into a pool of blackness.

Maker above, was that her?

"No. No, that wasn't me! That wasn't—"

The light flickered. Once, twice. Darker each time. The leaves of the tree were going out. There was a sound of falling water—the sound of leaves, falling, falling, falling like rain.

Tears sprang to Hyranna's eyes. "No!" she cried. "No, no . . ."

The chamber plunged into blackness. Something sticky began to flow around her. It was thick and putrid, smelling of rotten flesh. She choked. She scrambled to her feet. She had to get out. *Had to.*

There was a flash. Dark light flooded the chamber, illuminating everything for a moment in a grey, ghostly hue. The spectre of the old tree rose one final time, then the greyness rushed together, coming to a point—to her hand, the shard. She dropped the stone and threw herself back, stumbled, fell into the stickiness that was pooling around her feet, and the greyness followed. It enveloped her. She breathed it in like air until it filled her lungs—like the darkness, the nothingness from her dream, it pressed close, suffocating her. Her dream had become a living nightmare! She couldn't even scream.

Then, just like in her dreams, there came a voice.

"Hyranna Elduna." It was low, but with a bright, eager edge. It echoed around her. "Tell me who you are. Are you Lendahyr?"

Her lungs filled with air again, and she gasped. The presence eased away—but she could no longer see. It was completely dark around her. She could feel the ground, and the filthy pool, sticking to her clothes and her hair. She was lying on her back. Then a surge of anger burst out of her.

"You did this!" she screamed into the blackness, pushing herself to her feet. "That was you! You destroyed the tree, the Dandyri. How could you?"

"It would have destroyed you to keep me trapped, but it was dying anyway." He paused. "You are not Lendahyr, are you?"

"What do you mean? I don't—"

"What are you then?" he continued. The voice seemed to float to the other side of her, coming from her left now. "Diat'ti? Manturian?"

He rattled off names. "Llewelyn? Ranithgar? Toernen? Bahna'amanu? Kyr'amanu? Ka-tu-et-ni? Imo'ani?"

She gasped. There was a moment of silence. Then: "Ah. Imo'ani —the mongrel offspring of great peoples." She bristled at his scorn. The voice was in front of her now. "They were young, last I knew. How long has it been, Hyranna Elduna? But you wouldn't know, would you."

"Know what? Who *are* you? What's happening?"

He ignored her questions. "Do you even know what you destroyed?"

Her chest tightened and she took a step back. The stickiness clung to her bare feet. She almost toppled.

"I didn't destroy anything! That wasn't me!"

"That was the last of the Dandyri," he continued. "And now they are gone from this world. Even her. An impressive feat for an ignorant Imo'ani girl-child."

"I don't . . . I don't understand. I didn't do that!"

There was silence, and Hyranna could hear her heart thumping in her own ears, her breath going in and out, in and out. Then there was a splash. The sound of footsteps through the oozing morass.

She froze. They were close. One foot, then the other. *Splash . . . thuck . . . splash . . . thuck.* She backed away.

"Who . . . who's there?" she cried, a tight croak in the dark.

"You have no idea what you're doing, do you?" The voice drew nearer with every step, dripping with disdain. "Just a scared little girl who followed the wrong hole. And now the earth is closing over you, pulling you under, faster than you can escape."

He was close. So close. Something brushed her arm.

"Get away from me! Don't touch me." She tried to jerk away, but her feet got caught in a root and she stumbled. The grip tightened, hauling her back up, clenching hard.

"You're helpless. Weak. A pathetic mistake." He shoved her, and she toppled into the slime again. She landed on her burned hand. The pain slammed the breath out of her lungs, and the only sound she could make was a squeaking groan.

"I . . ." she gasped when she could, "am not . . . *pathetic!*"

"Prove it. Stand on your own two feet, pick it up, and get us out of this stinking hole!"

"I'm not going anywhere with you."

"It's too late for that. You can leave this cavern, but you cannot leave the Aktyr."

"The *what?*"

There came a harsh, biting laugh.

"Hey!" she shouted. "I don't know who you think you are, but I am not pathetic. I am the Guardian's daughter, and my people are a noble people! We keep the stories—and you have no right to insult us!"

He laughed, but Hyranna Elduna was not going to be mocked. She climbed to her feet, ignoring the pain in her hand, ignoring the slime caking her clothes and face, dripping from her hair.

"Explain to me what's happening!" she demanded. "Right now."

There was a pause. "Very well," he said. Then she heard him closing in again, and this time, when he took her arm, she didn't flinch or pull away. His hand slid down, closed around her wrist, and lifted it, her burned hand. He curled her fingers open. The skin cracked and broke. She said nothing. She tried not to show she was trembling, tried not to show how much it hurt. Carefully, almost gently, he unwrapped the bandage and then for a moment, nothing. She found she was holding her breath, waiting, though she couldn't say for what.

Then he spoke. "Your hand is raw—burned no more than a day ago. And this mark—"

"How do you know?"

"Because I can see it."

"But how? I can't see anything! It's –"

"Be quiet! You want me to explain? Then let me speak."

She shut her mouth.

"As I was going to say, this mark was made by a shard of stone. One you picked up, not long ago." He paused. She couldn't see him, but she had the distinct impression he was *looking* at her. "If you have this mark," he continued, "it means it's too late. You stole life through its power. The shard has bound itself to you, mind, body, and spirit. It's a part of you. It is the Aktyr, and it belongs to me."

A shiver of fear ran up her back. "Then who are you?"

"The Aktyr's master. Someone tried to kill me, probably a long time ago. They only partially succeeded. *That* is the power of the Aktyr, for in binding to you, it has given me a way back into your Realm. Through you."

"Through me?"

"Yes. Unfortunately, for now, it seems only through you. While you live, so do I; if you die, then I will perish. So let's not do anything foolish, shall we?"

"I don't . . . I don't understand."

"No, I suppose you wouldn't." He dropped her hand and started to cross through the ghastly pool. "Come," he commanded.

"Wait a moment!" Hyranna's eyes blazed after him. "You can't just tell me what to do!"

"I can, and I will. Now come. You will see."

Her mouth fell open. She muttered a curse under her breath and stumbled after him, trying not to trip over any roots, hands stuck out to keep from falling. She followed the sound of his feet through the muck. When they stopped. So did she.

"Keep going," he said. "A little farther."

She moved forward a few more steps, and then his hand latched around her wrist.

"Good," he said. "Now it's at your feet. Pick it up."

"What?" She recoiled. "No! I'm not touching that thing again." She pulled back, but his grip was strong, holding her in place.

"Hyranna Elduna. You already made your choice. It called, and you answered. You took it into your home. You spoke to it. And by its power, you destroyed the life in this place. Life for power. Like it or not, it's a part of you. Now pick it up."

"You keep saying that, but it wasn't me! I didn't kill the Dandyri! I would never do that."

"Believe what you want, it doesn't change what happened. There was only one person standing beside that tree. You don't understand the Aktyr; you cannot control it; it seems big, and frightening, and overwhelming. I know. But I can help you."

"I don't want your help. Leave me alone!" Hyranna's voice sounded scared in her own ears.

"You are afraid, and with good reason. But there's no going back.

Pick it up! Or if you don't believe me, then try to leave. Go. Walk away! —If you can."

He released her. Hyranna staggered back, stunned that he'd actually done so. She wanted to flee. *Get out.* But the cavern was hopelessly dark. The smell was overpowering her. Rank, putrid, clawing into her throat like sickness itself.

"Eight paces to your left," the stranger said. "There's a wall. Follow the wall until you get to the crack, and follow the crack to the surface. So what are you waiting for? Get out of here! Go!"

His voice was harsh, biting. It frightened her. What was happening? Where was Balduin? *Oh Maker above, let him be okay!*

Trembling, she turned and staggered to the wall. She had to grope with hands and feet, stumbling over roots, into the muck, climbing back up. The nightmarish dark chased after her. She could feel the stranger's eye. His disdain.

She felt like she was going to be sick. Her head reeled. The stench grew and grew. *The sky.* She had to see the sky. To get clean. To get *out.*

She barely remembered the climb. It was horrific and dark. She scraped her skin a dozen times, staggering on hands and knees, clutching her burn to her chest. Tears stung her eyes, but she refused to give in to them. She could smell the fresh air, the pine and balsam and wet rock. It was getting closer. She was almost free! Then came the sound of rushing water, louder and louder. But where . . . ?

She tumbled out of the cliff and onto wet stone. She froze. Her breath stopped. The river's spray, the wind, the rustle of leaves, and the sun's heat dripping across her face: she felt all of it, but saw only blackness. No matter how she blinked her eyes, or squinted, or scratched at the mud caking her face, it made no difference. Like Kota, she was blind.

Chapter Twenty

Hyranna knelt on the rock for a long time, stunned. She felt around her, felt the warmth of the sun, felt it in every pore of her body. Everything but her eyes.

Pick it up, and you will see.

Was it so simple? So brutally simple? She was bound to it, that's what the stranger had said. The Aktyr. The power that had killed the Dandyri. *Oh Maker above, she had killed the Dandyri!* She remembered it tearing out of her, dark and violent. Powerful. She shivered. She didn't want that. Whatever it was, she wanted nothing to do with it. But then what?

Go back.

She ignored the voice. She rose shaking to her feet and took two steps. She didn't even remember falling. Blackness and dizziness blended into the same thing, whirling around her. There was no up or down, no direction. She tried to move, but as she crawled unfeelingly across empty space, her lungs tightened. Pain shot through her chest. She gasped and fell. She was floating in emptiness.

Go back.

"Do you know what will happen to you?" said a voice.

She groaned, but could not speak.

"You will live, and every moment will be excruciating. You will be unable to breathe, to move, to think. The Aktyr will tear out your mind, one piece at a time, until you are mad with it. Until your own name is lost. Until your mind breaks. And then one moment not long from now—though it will feel like centuries—your body will give up, and you will die."

Hyranna moved her lips—laughing. "Is that all?"

"Your efforts are admirable. If I could free you, I would, but I'm not strong enough. Not yet. Do you understand? Our lives our joined, Hyranna Elduna, and while that is true, I will not let you throw yours away. Get up."

She moved her arms. She imagined planting them into the stone, climbing to her feet, turning back to the tree. Back to the shard. Then she realized it was happening, and she could feel stone under her bare, slime-crusted knees. *Maker help me!* She was moving. She felt blindly for the crack into the earth. She started crawling back, shuffling down, down into the dark.

Almost immediately, her strength returned. She could breathe again. The putrid air slapped her across the face. The shard was pulsing in her mind—not just a stone. It had fingers. It was alive. It pulled her and slipped through her thoughts. *Great Tree, help me!* She had no idea what she'd stumbled on, but it was not going to go away so easily. She stepped down into the oozing rot. It closed over her feet, sucking her down. She struggled not to be sick. It was up to her calves now.

She waded through the blackness, knowing exactly where she was going—she could almost see it, the shard. She might not have a choice, but Maker above, she wasn't going to be anyone's slave. She would figure this thing out. She would have answers. And she *would* be free of it.

Her foot brushed something hard beneath the slime. She took a breath. She crouched. Almost instantly, her fingers closed over it, as if pulled there, and she drew it out of the slime. It was hers.

Instantly, the shadows lifted. She brought her head up, and the cavern opened in hues of grey. She saw the dead tree, broken and twisted. She saw the leaves, scattered in careless heaps, some still flickering with valiant light. She turned—and she saw him.

He stood a few paces away, watching her. He was taller than any

Imo'ani. His hair was dark and wound in thick, matted braids. His eyes held her. He stood expectant and intense, as if waiting for her to act, *daring* her to, mouth twitching towards an accustomed snarl.

Hyranna shuddered. This man was a wolf. Wild, dangerous. And yet . . .

"Who are you?" she demanded, holding the shard out, as if that alone gave her permission to speak.

And this time, he answered. "I am E'tuah."

She blinked. Did she know that name? Had she heard it before? It sounded almost familiar. Almost . . .

When she looked again, the man was gone.

———

Hyranna dropped her things, peeled off her filthy clothes, and plunged into the river. She gasped at the cold. She scrubbed her skin until it stung. She scrubbed her hair, raking out the muck with her fingers.

Grey. That's what she saw. Grey trees, and grey flowers, and a white sun staring out of a grey sky.

She scrubbed harder. Grey skin: grey before, and grey now, no matter how hard she—

She stopped. She stared at her hand. The burned skin was raw and sore, and grey, but when she pressed her thumb into it, the pain was distant. Not gone, just not . . . important.

She made a fist and shoved it under the water. What was *happening* to her? What had it done to her, this shard, this Aktyr?

Don't think of it.

She waded to shore, grabbed her clothes, and began to scrub them too, scraping the hides together to purge every sign of what had happened in that cavern. Hot, angry tears burned her eyes, blurring her grey vision. She thought of the tree—the beautiful tree. And then her voice, angry and demanding: *Where is he? Answer me, old tree!*

No. Not her fault. It was the thing. The stone, and the crazy person inside. *He* killed the tree. Not her. Not her!

She sniffed and continued to scrub. Everything was colourless, lifeless. She could feel the sun, but she couldn't see it, not really. She couldn't see the soft golden light, sparkling off the surface of the water. She couldn't see the forest, dappled with green and gold and warm shadow. She couldn't see . . .

She brought an arm to her face, trembling. Maker above, where was Balduin? He still hadn't come. She refused to consider that he might still be in that cave—hurt, unconscious, dead. *No.* It was impossible. He just hadn't come yet. He was packing. He was stuck in his mother's cave. He was waiting for her back at the cleft, at the other entrance.

"Hyranna? Is . . . is that you?"

She gasped and plunged into the water, clutching her clothes to her chest.

"Damn you, Jerad Amanti, I'm *bathing*!"

The youth emerged from the trees, then froze and spun on his heels. "S-sorry!" He took a few paces away, then stopped. "I'm sorry, Anna."

"Stop calling me that. Just stop. I'm not Anna to you. I'm not—"

"Okay, sorry. But, look, I know you don't care much, but . . ."

"No, Jerad. Not right now!" She wiped furiously at her eyes. "Now go away!"

"But . . ."

"Please!"

"But your father . . . You disappeared, and . . . your father asked me to—"

"I don't care!" she sobbed, throwing an arm across her mouth, too late.

There was a pause. Jerad almost turned, but stopped himself at the last moment. "An—Hyranna, are you okay?"

"Yes, just please go away." Her voice broke, betraying her. The tears came, streaming down her face, mixing with the river.

Jerad hesitated, caught in his utter inability to act. "Alright, I'm . . . I'm leaving." He took a few steps, paused, then hurried away, disappearing into the trees.

Once she was sure he was gone, Hyranna struggled back into her wet clothes, stumbled onto the rock, and sat there, fighting to control herself. There was no use pretending anymore—it was a mess. All of it. And where in the green earth was Balduin Na-es?

She squeezed her pouch where she had left the shard. It didn't seem to mind being there. She didn't have to *hold* it. She just had to possess it. And then it wouldn't kill her.

She glanced up, wondering where the stranger had gone, the man who called himself E'tuah—the Aktyr's master, whatever that meant. But she hadn't seen one glimpse of him since the cavern. Good. She was fine with that. Let him stay there. Maker above, she wasn't going to let him near Elamori, if she could help it.

The day was lengthening. It was late afternoon. Jerad was right about one thing—her father would be worried. And then there was Balduin, still missing. She should get back. Satisfied the tears had stopped, and she was reasonably clean, she stood and hurried back towards Elamori.

She made it no further than a single bend of the river, when Jerad popped up from behind a rock.

"Hyranna!"

She screeched. Jerad threw up his hands, ducking a wild fist. "Whoa, hold on."

"What are you doing here! Are you *following* me, Jerad Amanti? How dare you! How—"

"But your father asked me to!"

"What?" She stared at him. "He *what?*"

Jerad winced. "I'm sorry, Hyranna. I wasn't spying or anything, I just had to follow you, to make sure you were okay. That's what your father asked."

"He would never! After what you did? No. *No!*" She shoved past him, storming up the riverbank.

"Wait!"

"Go away!"

"Hyranna, just hear me out, please. Please." He lunged after her, caught her arm.

"Don't touch me!" She shook him off. "I don't want to hear what you have to say."

"I'm sorry!"

His tone of voice brought her up short. She scowled at him, at his outstretched hands, held open in a silent plea, his face wrinkled in shame.

"Hyranna, I swear, I never meant for you to get hurt."

She rolled her eyes. "Really? You think I care a bear's turd about that? You nearly killed him, Jerad Amanti! You *would* have, if it wasn't for me. So apologizing about a few scratches is by far the dumbest thing you could have said to me."

"But I want to make up for what I did. Anna, it wasn't right. I was just trying to look out for you, I swear!"

"I don't need anyone to look out for me!"

"And if I hadn't stopped you from knifing Mylar? How do you think *that* would have turned out? You know the rules. You pull a knife—"

"I know, I *know*. It was stupid, but what else was I supposed to do? You could have helped me, you know. You could have stopped him. You're the oldest. Mylar would have listened to you. It's *your* responsibility. But you didn't. You just stood there. You left him to die. *My friend.* So when I tell you to go away, I damn well mean it, you insufferable ass."

Jerad swallowed. He looked down, letting an appropriate length of time pass before holding something out to her. "Here."

"What's that?"

"Your knife. You . . . you dropped it."

Hyranna growled, then snatched it out of his hand and slammed it into her belt. *It was a good knife.* "Thanks."

"Hyranna?"

"What?"

"Your father said the same thing."

"Good."

"And he's right. I . . . I should have done something. I should have stopped Mylar. I wasn't thinking."

Hyranna glared at him, almost angrier that he admitted it. She *wanted* to be furious. She *wanted* to hate him.

"But that doesn't mean it isn't Balduin," he continued. "He could still be dangerous. We don't know. That's why he had to—"

Hyranna threw up her hands. "Are you serious? Stop, Jerad! Just *stop!*" She turned, took two stomping strides, then pulled up short. "Had to *what*?" She spun back to face him. Her brows slammed into her eyes. "Where *is* he, Jerad? Where's Balduin? What did you do to him?"

"Nothing!" Jerad cried. "I swear it, by the Tree!"

"Then where *is* he? Because he promised to meet me somewhere, and he didn't, and that's not like Balduin Na-es, and . . ." She froze when she saw the look on his face. "What?"

"W-w-well, don't you know?"

"Know *what?*"

Jerad swallowed and looked around, as if scanning for an escape. Hyranna stepped nearer. "Jerad Amanti, if you don't tell me this very moment, I'll put an extra breathing hole in your throat, so—"

"He's gone."

The words washed over her. She stared. She shook her head. "What do you mean *gone*?"

"He left this morning with Dal Adis and the hunting circle. Left for Lindys. Didn't anyone tell you?"

Hyranna felt the ground crumble away from her. *No, no it couldn't be.* After everything. And he had *left*? He had promised her. *Promised.*

She ran. Her feet flew up the riverbank, scattering leaves and sticks, splashing through fresh puddles, smacking across stone. She made it to Elamori and burst into her father's cave, breathless, more furious with him than she thought possible.

"Father!"

Marisela leapt to her feet. "Hyranna Elduna! There you are!" She hurried across the room and grabbed her daughter, almost crushing her, before jerking her out to arm's length. "Maker's breath, child, you can't keep doing this! Not after all that's been happening! *Where* have you been? Your father and I have been worried to the fires over you!"

"Did father send him away?" Hyranna demanded, shocked at the coldness of her voice.

"Yes," said another voice. She spun. Kenan Elduna ducked inside, his face looking more wrinkled than usual. "For his own safety, Anna-chi. They've taken the boats downriver, to Lindys. They'll be back in a few days. And in the meantime, I hope to calm things down here. Find some answers."

"But you never told me!"

"No, I didn't."

"Why not?"

"You didn't need to know. You have other responsibilities here, Anna-chi, like we talked about, remember?"

"You mean you didn't want me to go with them. *That's* why you had me followed! By Jerad Amanti, of all people. How *could* you?"

He said nothing. He looked very sad, and his usually twinkling eye was sombre. Then he reached into his belt-pouch, drew something out, and placed it in her palm. It was Eelun the Dancing Fox.

"I finished it this morning," he said.

Hyranna stared at the little carving. The fox was reared up on his hind legs, balanced, snout tossed back, forelegs batting the air in dance. His ears were pricked up, and his jaws were parted in a mischievous toothy grin. And as she turned it in her hand, she noticed one eye was closed, and the other glinted at her. He was winking.

"It's beautiful, Papi."

"It's for you," he said, and smiled. "So you can remember to dance."

She felt her throat close up. "He's coming back, right? Tell me he's coming back."

She glanced up at him, eyes searching. He looked troubled, his face a mix of tenderness and concern. Then he smiled, and his wrinkles deepened. "I'm sure he will, Anna-chi. Don't be worried. Okay?"

"Okay," she said. She *did* trust her father, and the more she thought about it, the more it made sense. This way, Balduin was safe. He would come back and then they would make their plans. She had only to wait.

Chapter Twenty-One

Waiting, it turned out, wasn't easy for Hyranna.

At least she was kept busy. There were ground-berries to pick, boil, and crush—to pound into berry cakes for the winter. There were hides to scrape. There were shoes and skirts to sew up with fur lining.

Hyranna didn't care for the work, but at least it was *something*. The nights were torturous. Whenever she closed her eyes, she heard dark whispers, and dark thoughts. She would wake feeling like she was coated in slime. The smell of rot lingered, and she would hurry to the river to scrub her hands and her arms and her feet.

And then there was food. Everything she put in her mouth tasted like ash. She choked down as little as possible.

Kenan and Marisela watched her, and sometimes Hyranna caught them speaking together in low voices. But she told no one about the shard. When Balduin came back, she would ask him, and maybe *he* would know what to do. But until then, she tried to pretend the whole horrible thing had never happened.

It was the fourth day her mother finally released her to go fishing. She made plans to go out with her father and little cousin, Justan. But at the last moment, Jerad hurried up to join them.

Hyranna planted her hands on her hips. "Why aren't you out hunting with the boys?"

"My mother needs help with some beams coming loose, but that can wait for the afternoon. I'll help you with the nets. It's a cool morning. Perfect for fishing."

"Yeah, perfect for a swim, too. Take one step onto this raft and that's exactly what you'll be doing."

"Anna!" her father frowned. "There's plenty of room for one more."

It was one of the wide, flat-bottomed rafts. Not as light and quick as the birch-bark canoes, but good for standing and net-fishing on the lake, or spearing in the shallow waters. She rolled her eyes, but soon they were paddling out on the calm waters. Justan sat at the stern, trolling with a little bone-hook and minnow-bait, while her father readied the nets beside her at the prow. Jerad propelled them forward with long, sure strokes. No one said anything, but there wasn't a need. It was refreshing, she thought, after days cooped up with the girls and their endless chatter. She liked the quiet.

She realized she was nodding off when there was a touch on her arm. Her father was leaning next to her. "Ready?"

She nodded.

"Are you sure? If you want to go back and rest—"

"No, I'm fine."

Kenan smiled, but she thought she saw a flicker of worry behind his eyes. "Good. Then you and Jerad can manage the nets."

She snorted. "I came to fish with *you*, Papi, not that meatsack."

"Anna, be kind," Kenan said.

"Why? He showed no kindness to Balduin, he doesn't deserve any himself."

"Maybe not."

Jerad pulled up short, frowning at Kenan's words like he wanted to object, but he had the grace to keep his mouth shut.

"What I've learned," Kenan continued, "is that few of us *deserve* kindness. But if we only got what we deserved, we would never learn how to be better. Isn't that right, Jerad Amanti?"

The young man swallowed. "Yeah," he said. "Yeah, I guess so."

"I've made choices I regret, too, Anna-chi. As have you, I'm sure. Let's practice forgiveness, eh?" He smiled, and his eye twinkled. "Now, I'll leave you two to handle the net, and I'll handle the oar. Even an old man like me should be able to do that, eh?" He chuckled and climbed to his feet, giving a theatrical groan as he did so. Her father wasn't nearly so old as he sometimes pretended, or as his wrinkled face made him look, but she knew she wasn't getting out of this now.

Soon she and Jerad were standing at either end of the raft, letting the net lines run through their fingers.

"Let it out," Hyranna told Jerad, when she felt a jerk.

He shook his head. "We're not deep enough yet, it'll get caught in the rocks."

"It won't get caught. Let it out!"

"Look, Anna. I don't need you to tell me how to fish."

"You do if you're doing it *wrong*. And I told you not call me that. Now let it out."

"Stop bickering," Justan muttered from the other side. "You're scaring the fish!"

Kenan chuckled. "See? At least someone on this raft knows what they're doing." He craned his head around. "Anna, bring it in a bit, and don't be so difficult."

She muttered something under her breath about not catching anything, but tightened the lower line until she was almost even with Jerad. Almost.

It took them a few more tries to settle into a rhythm and get the net covering a wide enough area, but once they got it right, it didn't take long before they felt a tug on the lines.

"Hah!" Jerad shouted. "Haul it in!"

"I know. I got it," she said. She pulled hard. Jerad pulled. They snapped the lower weights shut, trapping whatever fish had wandered inside, then hauled all four ropes in. Not one, but two large whisker-fish flopped onto the raft and a few baitfish wriggled in the net.

"Good work!" Kenan smiled at them.

"At least we got something," Hyranna said. "Let's try again. Come on, Jerad. This time try to keep some space between your lines so they don't get tangled. We just about lost that one."

"Really?" He stared at her, laughing.

"She likes to tell people what to do," Justan giggled, and Hyranna glared at him. Her little cousin wasn't as vicious as Eedi, but he took advantage of the opportunities that came his way.

"Whatever," she muttered. "Come on." They untangled the net and cast it again, keeping at it until their arms and backs were tired. By the time the sun was high, they'd filled the bucket to overflowing, and Justan contributed a few from his line as well. Then they paddled back to shore. Hyranna had to admit, it had been a productive morning, and they'd definitely improved by the end.

"Good fishing," Jerad said, as they hauled their catch back to shore. "You're not too bad, you know? Maybe I'll come along again sometime." He grinned—and just like that, she remembered her anger.

Hyranna dropped the bucket on shore with a thud. "Once with you is enough."

Jerad's eyes flashed hot. He opened his mouth, shook his head, then without a word, turned and marched away.

There was a moment of silence, until Justan cleared his throat and started wrapping up the line. "Well, I can see why the boys don't like you."

"Justan," her father said. "Remember what we talked about?"

"Words are for helping, not hurting. Yes, Uncle."

"Good. You too, Anna."

She stiffened. "I'm not an idiot, Papi. I know what you're doing, and I don't like it."

"Anna-chi . . ."

"No." She turned to face him. "Don't encourage him."

Then she stopped. She swore she saw something, out there on the water. Was it . . . ? Could it be . . . ?

"*River!*" someone called from the clifftop. "*Boat on the river!*"

"They're back from Lindys!" Justan cried, straining to look over the water.

Hyranna flew up the first few rocks to get a better view. Even with her grey vision and the glare from the sun, she could spot the canoe, heavy-laden with trophies from a hunt. It was making its way upstream, and getting close.

Her heart started pounding, though from fear or excitement, she couldn't say. Her feet barely touched the ropes as she vaulted back to the riverbank, then she hit the ground and ran. She splashed up to her knees and stood waiting, straining to catch a glimpse, watching the canoe as it swept the last distance over the still lake. Hyranna's heart was so tight, she felt it was going to burst. She could hear the dip of the oars now. She could see the rowers. Dal Adis was at the back, his son Tonu just in front of him, and Yanu and Nenim paddled at the prow, one on each side. Her eyes swept over the canoe again. And again. Dal and Tonu, Yanu and Nenim, the supplies and catches in the middle, loading down the canoe, keeping it only a hand span above the water. But where . . . ?

A wave of panic rolled over her. And she knew. She knew, even though she refused to accept it. She could feel her heart pounding against her ribs, going faster and faster. Her eyes raked the canoe again as it drew close. Maybe she'd missed something, maybe the greyness was hiding him.

But Dal Adis wasn't meeting her desperate glance. He manoeuvred the craft straight past her and up to the shore, twisting it at the last moment, so it touched the muddy banks along its side, anchoring into the ground. And there could be no question. Balduin Na-es was not with them.

Hyranna waded out of the shallows as if in a daze. She could hardly believe it, but others were noticing the same thing. She heard muttering whispers.

"Is he gone?"

"Who, Balduin Na-es?"

"It looks like he's gone."

"I don't see him."

"No, he's not there. They left him."

"He's gone."

"So it's true. I thought so myself . . ."

Dal Adis leapt onto shore, but Hyranna cut straight to him. He got only a few steps before she threw herself in his way, hands white-knuckled around his sleeves.

"Uncle . . ." was all she managed, unable to form the words. Her eyes said the rest.

Dal shook his head, face hard and unreadable, then pried her hands off and kept walking.

It was Tonu that paused next to her. "I'm sorry, Hyranna," he said. "It was no easy thing, to say goodbye. Especially for him." He nodded at his father's back.

"But . . ." she struggled to speak. "But how could you?"

"It was what Balduin wanted."

"No. No. It wasn't. He . . ."

Tonu gave her a look heavy with pity, then kept going, and Yanu and Nenim busied themselves with hauling the canoe up on shore. Hyranna was trembling. She glanced over. She saw Dal Adis approach her father, and their eyes met. They exchanged a few words, a nod. It was all she needed. She saw the look on her father's face: grim, guarded, but not surprised, not in the least. Fury gripped her, hot and painful, like a stab in her gut.

"No!" Her voice shook, raw and trembling. She didn't care that over half the village was gathered. All she could think of was her father, the look on his face, the nod. "You— you— you did this!" She marched towards him, even as he hurried to meet her, arms outstretched.

"Anna-chi . . ."

"No!" she shrieked, jerking out of his embrace. "You lied to me! You said he was coming back. You said he was coming back, but you did this. You sent him away. And then you lied to me!"

"Anna, I'm sorry. I'm sorry, but it had to be."

"Don't tell me that! Don't you dare tell me that. How could you, after everything you said? After that speech of yours—after saying you would treat him like a son, and then *this*? And that's all you have to say, that it had to be? You're a coward, a coward! A liar!"

"Anna, control yourself!" He gripped her by the shoulders, trying to look her in the eye. "I know you're angry, you can hate me all you want, but right now you need to calm down."

Hyranna met his eye. Grey eyes in a grey face. Suddenly she was calm. Calm and furious and cold, she lashed out, driving her fists against his chest.

She felt it before he did. A jolt racing through her, faster than thought. Kenan staggered back. He stared at her, his wrinkles creasing in confusion, and then worry, and then fear. It all happened in a moment, in a heartbeat. His legs gave way, and he collapsed, sprawling onto the ground, eyes rolling back.

Her mouth worked, but no sound came out. Horror seeped over her, clawing at the back of her neck, tingling down her arms, gripping her gut. Then Dal Adis was pushing past her, shoving her out of the way. He dropped by Kenan's side, one hand pressed against his chest, head bent low.

"His heart," he said. "It's stopped." He shot Hyranna a single, unreadable look. She felt like her own was being squeezed in a vice. She was having trouble breathing. She could see her mother out of the corner of her eye, standing in shock, just as disbelieving as her. Then something broke in Hyranna. She gave a scream. She surged forward, fighting past Dal's arm.

"Stop!" he commanded in a voice like stone. "Stop. He's gone."

"No! He's not. He's not dead. He can't be! He can't . . . Let me go! Let me . . . Dal!" She turned on him, shouting. "Let me go, right now!"

He released her, and she threw herself on top of her father, slamming her hands into his chest. "You can't die! Do you hear me? I won't let you! Damn you, Papi, you can't do this!"

She shoved a hand into her pouch, wrapping her fingers around the shard so hard, she could feel the edges digging into her skin. "Whatever you just did, you take it back, do you hear me? Take it back!" Still holding the shard, she beat on his chest again with both fists, letting her fury, her terror, her wild, inexplicable, stubborn hope pour out of her. And she hit him again, and again. "Take it back! Breathe, Papi! Do you hear me?"

Until it came. Just like before. A jolt, a sizzling burst of grey from between her fingers. It rushed through her.

Kenan jerked. His whole body twitched, from his feet, right up to his head. His mouth gaped, and he raked in a desperate gasp of breath. Hyranna could feel his heart pounding beneath her hands, loud and fast. But she hardly had the strength to be relieved.

She rolled off him and knelt there, her own chest heaving. She glanced around her, saw them staring at her, all those faces, so many faces. Her uncle, his eyes wide. Her mother, stumbling towards her, one hand still pressed to her mouth. Her father. He was breathing, he was sucking air into his lungs, rasping, and choking. And all she could think of was that *she* had done this. She had done this. Hyranna. His daughter.

She clutched the shard, leapt to her feet, and fled.

Chapter Twenty-Two

She made for the thick of the trees and plunged into the dark. Dal's voice followed her, calling her back. Others echoed his cry. "After her!" she heard—and then the trees swallowed her.

She sprang over soft and weedy ground and hit the firm places—root-packed earth, fallen branches, exposed rock. The forest along the river wasn't very big, but it was dense and wild and she knew the places to hide. She ran as hard as she could, until her chest felt like it would explode. Then she veered towards the cliff. Trees clung to the steep rock, but she wouldn't make it to the top. *Hide.* She ducked into a crevice, throwing herself inside and drawing her knees tight to her chest.

Then she sat, and she waited.

She was trembling. Tears streamed down her cheeks. She buried her face in her arms so only her eyes peered out, trying to mask the heavy, gasping sobs. They couldn't find her! She could never go back! How could she face her father again, after the things she had said, after what she had done?

He knew. He knew it was her. He had looked right at her, before he collapsed, and she'd seen the hurt in his eyes, the confusion, the betrayal.

No! She felt another squeeze of anger. It was him. *He* had

betrayed her. He had sent Balduin away, into the wild—alone, defenceless. Then *lied* about it. And now Balduin was gone, and she would never see him again!

The thought brought a fresh wave of panic, and she squeezed her eyes shut, sobs clenching in her gut so hard she was almost sick. *Breathe, Anna*, she warned herself. *Breathe. Stay quiet*. But thoughts kept pouring over her mind: Balduin was gone, he was gone, he'd left without her, and her father had lied to her—*why?*—*why?*—and then she had . . . she'd . . . She saw him in her mind, lying there, utterly still, eyes rolled back, face going slack. For a moment, he had been dead. Because of her.

"Hyranna!" she heard a voice calling her. It sounded like Tonu Adis. She froze. He was close, but the trees were dense enough, he wouldn't find her unless she moved. "Hyranna, come back! Your father's asking for you. He's fine. Everything's fine, Hyranna. Do you hear me? Just come back!" There was a pause. She thought she heard him moving through the trees—he wasn't trying to hide. He called again, "Hyranna!" and his voice was farther away. He passed her and kept going.

She let her breath out in a long, shuddering sob. Then she wept quietly. Her whole life was falling apart. And she felt helpless, swept along by things she couldn't even begin to understand.

"Oh, dear," a voice said, coming from just outside the crevice. "Quite a mess this is."

Her head snapped up, vision blurred into a mess of light and shadow. A shape moved and crouched in front of her.

"You killed him. And with such precision, just a tap on the heart. You surprise me, Hyranna Elduna. But then to bring him back again! With the *Aktyr*? I didn't know it was possible."

E'tuah.

His voice was low and mocking, and this time she heard the hint of an accent, like the Northmen when they tried to speak Imo'ani. It had a strange ripple to it, like music.

"Go away," she snapped.

"Believe me, Hyranna Elduna, if that were possible, I wouldn't hesitate. As it is, we're stuck together. Now tell me. Who is this Balduin Na-es? Someone incredibly important to you. Am I right?"

"I'm not talking about this," Hyranna muttered. "Not with you."

"Why not with me? Keep on like this, and you might have no one left."

Hyranna looked up and met his eyes. They were dark, and keen—unnerving. And despite her best efforts not to care, she felt a flood of shame for her tears. She scowled.

"You saw that? You saw what happened?"

"Of course I did."

"But you weren't there."

"I didn't choose to make myself seen. But wherever you go, I am there. I can see if I wish."

She stared at him. The meaning of his words sank in, and she felt a growing revulsion. She leapt out of the crevice as if stung, scrambling away.

"You . . . you *spy* on me?" she fumed, incredulous. She hated the thought of even Jerad following her, watching her without her knowing. How much worse was this?

E'tuah just sighed, as if bored. "Spy on what? Tedious chores and silly spats with your cousin? I think not."

"But . . ." She swallowed. "But that means . . ." She thought of bathing in the river. She thought of private moments, when she supposed she was alone.

"Oh, please." He rose to his feet with a sneer. "You are a child. And hardly what I find attractive."

The heat rushed to her face. How could he make her feel so worthless? "Fine," she snapped. "Nothing here concerns you. These are my problems, not yours." She turned and marched into the trees, not really caring where she went, so long as it put distance between her and that man.

"Not true at all!" His voice came from directly in front of her, and his imposing form stepped into her path. "Many things here concern me. What if you do something foolish, like throw yourself off a cliff in grief?"

She gave a scream of fury, grabbed a hefty-looking stone, and hurled it at him as hard as she could. It passed straight through him, and he didn't even flinch.

"Really, Hyranna Elduna, I thought you would have figured that part out already."

She glared at him, furious, and helpless to make him go away. "How is this possible? I can see you. But it's like you're not even . . . *there*."

"Watch." He walked towards her. The ground-foliage crunched beneath his feet, but then sprang back up. Untouched. Unbroken. "Whatever you see, whatever you hear, the Aktyr makes it real to you. But only to you. I can have no lasting effect on anything. Except you." He took her chin between his fingers, lifting it. Hyranna jerked away.

"Don't touch me." Her fingers wrapped around the shard and she brandished it like a shield. "Or Maker help me, I'll find out if this has any lasting effect on *you*."

He chuckled and crossed his arms, a spark glinting in his eyes. "Interesting. I admit, I don't know what would happen. Everything around me is dull and dark, unfocused. Except you."

"Good. Then don't do anything to test me."

E'tuah tilted his head, a smile playing on his lips. "Perhaps I was wrong about you. But you still haven't explained who this person is. This Balduin Na-es."

Hyranna was jolted back to the present. Her stomach lurched. She had to battle down another wave of panic, and she found herself backing up, edging towards the cliff again. "I told you already, I'm not discussing that with you."

E'tuah's face changed—a shadow rushed over it, eyes flashing.

"You seem not to like me, Hyranna Elduna. Am I right?"

"I'd say so."

"Good. Then the faster you can get rid of me, the better. Right?"

"Better and better."

He stood there for a moment. Then in an instant—she never even saw him move—he gripped her shoulders and slammed her against the cliff so hard the air whipped out of her lungs. The ridges dug into her back, and one leg twisted as she stumbled. E'tuah gripped her, eyes fierce. Snarling.

"Then perhaps, to make this go faster," he hissed, "you do what I say and answer when I speak to you! You think I want to be trapped like this? Trust me when I say I'm as eager to be parted as you are, so swallow your pride, you foolish, ignorant child, and cooperate!"

He released her and stepped back, and at once his face smoothed out, arrogant and unconcerned, only his smouldering eyes hinting at the deadly rage beneath.

Hyranna curled her hands into fists, more to stop them from trembling. For the first time, she was beginning to understand the danger of her situation.

"Well, now we know one another," she said, and was amazed to hear the steadiness of her voice.

E'tuah stared back at her coldly. "Tell me what happened by the river. Did you mean to kill your own father? Did you *want* it?"

"Of course not! How could you even suggest—"

"Then how did you bring him back?"

"I . . . I don't know."

"So you cannot control it. Not yet. Though it's beginning to bind itself to your desires. Who is Balduin Na-es?"

"Just a friend."

"*Just a friend*," he snorted. "You nearly killed your own father over him. So what? Is he your lover?"

E'tuah's coarseness made her blush, and before she could deny it, he pressed on. "Why do they fear him?"

Hyranna felt thrown off balance. The rapid speed of his questions left her breathless, unable to think. She hesitated.

"The first thing that comes to mind!" He snapped. "Why do they fear him? Answer."

"He's different."

"Different how?"

"I don't know."

"Yes, you do."

"He's . . . just different. I don't know. He can see the forest. He knows it. And he's not really Imo'ani. His parents . . ." Hyranna shut her mouth, suddenly horrified. What if she was endangering her friend?

"Yes, what about his parents?" E'tuah took a step forward.

"They're dead," she said quickly. "He has no one but me, and my father sent him away because the village is afraid what's happening is his fault. But that's just foolishness."

"You mean the strange stories your people keep yammering about? Dead beasts, blindness, withered vegetables?"

"Yes."

He gave a harsh, bitter laugh. "Fools. If they think a single boy, no matter how extraordinary, can cause the decay of the laws, they're more idiots than I thought. It *is* happening. The Breaking. But how long . . . ?" A brooding look crossed his face. "How long has it been since the Dandyri?"

Hyranna stared at him. "I . . . I don't know. Until we found the red tree, they were just stories. Nobody knows, exactly. Hundreds of years, maybe more."

He stopped and gazed at her, as if trying to tell whether she was lying.

"Hundreds of years? *Hundreds?*"

She nodded.

He swore in his own language. "No time. No *time*. I don't have time for this idiocy. If that *fool* hadn't—" He stopped, realizing Hyranna was watching him, then smoothed out his strange robes. "See? I knew you could be cooperative. Now tell me, what do you plan to do next? Will you go back to your village? Or become an outcast like your *friend*."

Hyranna shook her head. Whatever she did, she couldn't look weak. She groaned, brought her hands to her face, and slid to the ground. She was exhausted, and the thought of putting up with E'tuah was almost more than she could bear. "Go away and let me think," she said.

He didn't go away, but he fell silent, his feet pacing slowly back and forth, and every now and then she caught him watching her.

"I can't think with you hovering!" she snapped.

"Yes, you can. And you might as well get used to it. Besides, I thought you were uncomfortable with me . . . *spying* on you. Now you can see me, too. Isn't that fair?"

"That's not what I meant. I don't want you watching me at all."

"We don't always get what we want, do we?"

She growled. "What do I have to do to get rid of you?"

"When I figure that out, trust me, you'll be the first to know." He scowled and picked at his robes again, at the stitching that ran along the hem, the lines that crossed back and forth in complex geometrical patterns. There was a certain elegance to them, Hyranna decided. Even the wide sash looked finely made, and despite her grey vision, she imagined it a bright colour. She tilted her head. But it was all wrong. The robes were long and thin, a fibrous material that would get him frozen to death in the chilly forest nights. E'tuah shook his head. He seemed to be sneering at them.

"You don't like what you're wearing, do you?" Hyranna asked.

He lifted a brow. "Are my clothes important to you for some reason?"

"They're impractical."

"Not where they come from."

"Oh yeah? Where do clothes like that come from?"

He shot her a thin smile. "A desert. A very big desert."

"What's a desert?"

"A place where nothing grows."

Hyranna stared at him in horror. "Why would anyone live in a place like that?"

"An excellent question."

"Lendahyr. That's where you're from, isn't it?" He said nothing. "That's what you first asked me, if I was Lendahyn. Besides, those people are strange enough. After Kayr fell, they thought they could pick up the pieces and build their own little empire, but now with the red trees gone, they barely leave their walls in the south, doing Maker knows what. Is Lendahyr a desert?"

"I'm not from Lendahyr," he said.

"Then from where?"

"South."

"Like the mountains? Are you a southerner like Alutan?"

E'tuah shook his head. "Past the mountains."

"Past the *mountains*?" Hyranna frowned. "I thought . . . ?"

"What? That the world just stopped? That if you kept going you would fall off into emptiness? Stop wasting my time with ridiculous questions. The world is in crisis. The Realms are Breaking. You asked for a moment to think. So *think*. What will you do?"

"Maybe I'll go back." Hyranna watched him carefully, watched his expression. His mouth twitched in a sneer.

"And how that will unfold? Think about it. With Balduin Na-es gone, and your recent wondrous demonstration, who do you think they'll blame next when the harvest goes bad or another heart stops —for no reason."

"My father is the Guardian of Elamori. He wouldn't let them."

"Your father. Yes. The man you almost murdered in front of the whole village. Think, Hyranna Elduna."

She shut her eyes, trying to pretend he wasn't there. Could she really never go back? The thought was so painful, it was hard to consider. Elamori had always been her home. But her guilt, E'tuah's warnings, the fear she might do something like that again—it was all gnawing on her mind, insistent and scary and very real.

"Tell me what it is," she finally said, her voice cracking from weariness.

She glanced up. E'tuah was standing closer than she thought, arms crossed over his chest and looking down at her.

"You would never understand."

"And yet I still want you to tell me."

He paused. He lowered himself into a crouch, eyes strangely distant. "A thorn," he said.

"What?"

"The Aktyr is a weapon. A piece of something very great and very powerful, a remnant of raw creation, the moment before all moments." He reached over and grabbed her hand, opening the palm. "But it doesn't work in itself. It must be chosen. It must be *bought*. And it both shapes and is shaped by the one who chooses it."

"Me," she said.

"No, not you."

"But you said it's . . . it's a part of me, or something like that."

"I did. But you're not its true keeper. It's bound to you now, and there will be . . . effects. I don't know to what extent, or if you could ever learn to control it fully, beyond a vague and instinctual knowledge. Certainly, you could never wield it for its true purpose."

"Which is?"

He looked at her, then dropped her hand and stood up. "Its purpose is mine. So. Have you decided?"

She sighed. Arguing with E'tuah was as useful as knocking her head against a rock. "Right now, I'm going to wait for nightfall. Make yourself useful and wake me if anyone comes."

***

IT WAS dark when Hyranna finally rose and left the crevice. She peered through the night, amazed at how easily her grey-washed eyes could see. She had slept. She had dreamed. She couldn't remember about what, but all she knew was that, when she woke, she understood what she had to do.

A promise.

She began moving through the forest without a word, and sure enough, a shadow appeared beside her, trailing her out of the corner of her eye.

"You've decided," E'tuah said.

She nodded, but said nothing else, and they continued in silence.

The village was dark and still when Hyranna approached. She hovered at the edge of the forest, eyes scanning the lakeside and the garden patch and the open ground beneath the cliff. She even looked into the ropes and bridges. At first she saw no one, but her night eyes were sharp enough to pick out a figure standing at the edge of the trees, not far from her, almost invisible against the shadows. Dal Adis.

Hyranna shrunk back into the dark. She knew her uncle's eyes. If she stepped out into the open, he would see her. She was just lucky she hadn't passed closer to him.

Moving as quickly and as quietly as she could, she used the place where the garden and the tree-line met and slipped between the stakes of squash like a ghost. But once she reached the edge of the garden, she had to make a dash for the thick shadows at the base the cliff. She watched her uncle carefully, but she was too far now to see which direction he was facing.

Taking a deep breath, and crouching low, Hyranna went silently into the open dark. Her uncle's eyes were trained for the furtive quickness of an animal, so she went slowly, opting for silence. Bit by bit, hearing no cry of alarm, she made her way across the open space, holding her breath. The night was absolutely still. Maker above, she'd never felt like the hunted creature herself. It was unnerving.

At last, she fell into comforting shadow. She gazed up the cliffs. There were things she wished she could take with her. Farewells she wished she could make. A last hug—a chance to make things right. But there would be no leaving after an encounter like that. With a loosening of her chest, a little breath out, she started making her way across the base of the village.

It was painful, sneaking out of Elamori like an outcast, but E'tuah was right. The Imo'ani would turn against her, just like they had Balduin, and if that happened, she could no longer trust herself—not with this so-called Aktyr inside her. If it lashed out against her father, who was safe? Besides, there was the promise. Giving up on Balduin was unthinkable.

After a long, slow trek around the edge of the shadows, she found herself crouched near the lakeside lodge, the place where they stored canoes and nets. She would have to use her knife to slit a hole in the back. It would be almost impossible to free a canoe without Dal Adis seeing her, but she had no other choice. She reached for her knife and stepped out of the trees.

Arms grabbed her, yanking her back. A hand clamped over her mouth. She was pulled into a crouch, and someone's breath washed over her. Someone had found her! Someone—

"Hyranna, wait. Don't say anything. It's me."

Jerad? Her mind struggled to rework the image.

"Trust me," he said, breath tickling her ear. "This way. But don't make a sound."

He released her. By the time she turned her head, he'd slipped into the trees. She scowled her annoyance, even as her curiosity trailed after him. What was he up to? Why didn't he shout for Dal?

Then she caught a glimpse of E'tuah, still hovering, and frowning in disapproval. *Well, that settled it.* She hurried after Jerad Amanti.

Trained hunters both, they moved with only a whisper of sound. Their path turned downriver, and every time she tried to get Jerad's attention, his hand came up, motioning for silence.

Finally, he leapt down into a hollow, and she followed him. Her eyes scanned the dark. A small canoe had been stowed up against the root-packed hollow, and next to it a few sacks, water-skins, fishing line, two paddles, and a spear and a bow—her bow. She stared, then glanced back at Jared, unable to speak.

"It's all there," he said. "Food, flint, arrows, extra clothes, some shoes for your feet, though Maker knows you hate them. Everything you'll need. I hope."

"But . . . why?"

"After you ran off like that, I knew."

"So you just . . . packed all this? Tonight?"

His mouth twitched and he looked away.

"What?" she demanded.

"Here's the thing. Most of this wasn't tonight. I'd never be able to get away with it, not with all the excitement. But your father . . . well, he told me you might . . . might try something. He wanted me ready, in case you ran off—"

"Wait, what? You mean you *knew*? You knew this would happen? He *told* you?"

"That's not important." The words rushed out of his mouth. "What's important is—"

"Not important?" Her hands clenched into fists. "Jerad, you were a part of this? Really? After trying so hard to apologize, and then *this*?"

"What's important," he barrelled on, "is that I know where they took Balduin Na-es, and I can help. We can do this together."

She stared at him, then burst into laughter.

"I'm serious, Hyranna. I was speaking with Nenim, and he told me everything you'd want to know. I made some changes to our supplies, gathered a few extra things, got it ready for both of us . . ."

"*Both* of us?"

"Yeah, of course. That's how it's got to be, or I take you straight back to your father. Damn, he would have my hide if he knew I was saying these things."

"You wouldn't!"

"I absolutely would. Shit, Hyranna, it's dangerous for *anyone* to go by themselves. You think I'll just let you run off? A thousand and one things could go wrong to a person in the wild alone. So there—we have to go after Balduin Na-es. It wasn't right to send him away like that, and it wouldn't be right to do that to you either."

"So you just changed your mind? Just like that?" Her voice was heavy with scorn. "Maker's breath, you're as fickle as the winds, and you want me to *trust* you?"

"No, you don't get it! Your father told me to be ready, so here I am. I didn't *change* my mind, I only made it up tonight. Look, Hyranna. I'm trying to offer you the best chance you'll have at finding him. Are you going to turn me down? Because it's both of us, or we don't go at all."

She was close to doing just that. Her mouth was open, and she jabbed a finger up towards him, but changed her mind at the last instant and clenched the hand into a fist. "Damn you, Jerad Amanti!"

"This is a terrible idea," she heard from over her shoulder. She spun around to see E'tuah standing in front of the canoe with his arms crossed, glowering at Jerad.

"What? What is it?" The young man whispered from behind her. "Did you hear something?"

She looked back at him, then looked at E'tuah, then back at Jerad's searching eyes.

E'tuah gave a snort of derision. "He can't see me, Hyranna Elduna. How many times must I tell you? You are my link to this world. Only you can see me, or hear me, or touch me. And right now, you're doing an excellent job at making this boy think you mad."

"Hyranna? Are you okay?"

For a moment, she didn't know what to say, or even where to look. She frowned furiously at the ground, struggling to think.

"Yes!" she finally snapped at Jared. "I'm fine. Now let's go."

"Really?" He looked surprised. Then he gathered himself, nodding. "Okay. Yes. Let's go."

"I told you," E'tuah said. "This is not a good idea. Leave the baggage."

"We need the supplies," she said.

Jerad nodded. "Yes, that's why I gathered it all."

"I meant him," E'tuah sneered.

Hyranna ground her teeth and placed a well-aimed kick at E'tu-ah's shins. She scored a hit, but instead of backing down, the man grabbed her arm, leaning until his face was level with hers. "This will not end well," he said, biting off each word.

"I don't care. I didn't ask you."

"Of course you didn't ask me," Jerad muttered. "And I know you don't care much for me, but right now I'm the only one fool enough to go with you instead of stopping you, so let's make do, eh?"

"Yes. Let's." She glared at E'tuah, and the man finally stepped back in disgust.

"Go on, Hyranna Elduna. But the Aktyr does not make good company. How long before he ends up dead?"

Hyranna ignored him and grabbed one end of the canoe, just as Jerad grabbed the other. She had to admit: carrying the canoe and all the supplies would be far easier with a partner. She just had to find a way to not go completely insane.

Thankfully, E'tuah disappeared, probably to nurse his frustration in some other realm. *Let him*, she thought darkly. And next time she had a chance to talk, she would set some ground rules. No confrontations when she was already in the middle of one!

Sensing her foul mood, Jerad said nothing. They eased the craft into the river and stepped in. Hyranna took the prow, and Jerad the stern, without either saying a word. Then Jerad pushed off. Moments later, they were dipping the sleek paddles in, cutting a path through the water and into the night.

Interlude: The Last Al'kah

ASHKYNAS AB'ADANI AL'KAH

Ashkynas ab'Adani Al'kah was dead. At least he should have been. The breath left his body. The dark closed over his mind. The channels of blood slowed to a sluggish drip.

And still . . . and still . . . Would the thing ever let him die? How long? How *long*?

He came to the edge. The very edge. He peered into the vast and unclaimed nothingness. There was no struggle in that place. No questions. No world to save. No broken Shyandar. No broken people.

But the voices called him back. The voices. He wavered in indecision, straining to hear. They came from behind. From above. From . . .

"Poor sot," said the voice. "Starved or dead of thirst, far as I can see. Poisoned maybe."

"You think he's got anything we can . . . ?"

"What? Loot off him like a Terryn raider? If that's your fancy, go ahead, but who knows what filth did him in."

Let them, Ashkynas thought. Let them take it. Let them empty him of this curse. Maybe then, maybe then he could finally die.

But when Ashkynas looked back over the edge in his mind and considered what he had to do—just a sway, a tiny nudge of momentum—and he would fall and keep on falling forever into the blissful dark . . . When he looked, he saw the dark, and behind it another dark. He saw something else. Something alive. Something reaching. He saw a writhing emptiness. It leaked from him, and it filled the dark, and it came from other places—from many, many places. All growing, and spreading, and reaching, and crackling. Hungry, pressing shadow. And when he looked up, he saw a crack above his head, and there was light, and all the emptiness was reaching for that crack, for the light above, and Ashkynas knew if he let go, if he fell into the dark, it would only grow. It would burst through the crack and spread and keep on spreading until all the world was shrivelled and cold. And Ashkynas knew, knew, knew he could *not* let that happen, for was that not why he'd done it? Why he'd betrayed Ishtar? Sold himself to the thing? Was it not his mission? His last desperate hope?

Fingers brushed his chest. Closed over the black stone. Pulled. The stone came loose. He felt it. It stretched away from him, though it was still in him. Always, always in him. And now outside of him as well. And if it came awake, if the darkness reached the crack above his head before he did, if it stirred, and someone else was touching it—

Ashkynas clawed upward, battling against the shadow, moving through it like thick, blowing sand.

"Question is," said the voice, the same one as before, echoing and growing around him—a woman's voice, a buzzing, drawling voice. "Question is, why'd a dying man clutch a thing like that in his finals?"

"No idea," said the other. The younger one.

Ashkynas reached the light—and so did the shadow. They broke through at the same time. The wind was already shrieking. The grass snapped and bent. Ashkynas tore upright.

He had to stop it! Would not, would not, would not kill again. Never again!

Two figures hurled away from him. He screamed and grasped at the shreds of power, stomping them shut, driving them back into the ground, bolting the emptiness back where it belonged. The strangers crumpled to the grass on either side of him. He clutched his chest. The ugly black stone was gone. Where was it? *Where?* If it bound itself to them, if it sought a second door, a second mind . . .

No!

Frantic, Ashkynas pounced on the woman. She was sturdy and quick. She was already scrambling back to her feet. Ashkynas was faster. He drove her into the ground from behind. He circled her throat, squeezing with desperate fingers.

"Give it!" he croaked. "Give it now. Now! Quick, for your life, woman!"

But his words were strange to her. Kyre'an words. She gasped and grunted, struggling beneath his wiry frame.

"Give me the thing, the Aktyr. You must. It will kill you! It will destroy you! Please, you must give it—now!"

"The stone!" the younger one cried out. "Give him the stone!"

Ashkynas felt the flash of her understanding. She twisted, and he snatched the ugly thing the moment it appeared. The thing he hated. The thing he had—*could it be?*—controlled.

She shoved him away. She reached for something, some weapon. He wanted to cry out a warning, but then it pounded into the sky, a ringing blast, a smoking, rolling punch of power. He fell back in shock. The Aktyr was dampened and sluggish. *Good.* Ashkynas would rather die than kill again. He waited for the pain, the inevitable thrust of the weapon, whatever it was, the thing the woman pointed at him, the thing that smelled of acrid, burning earth.

It never came. She stood, legs planted, pointing and glaring with dark, grey eyes.

"Threaten me, will you? Don't move or I'll aim this next one a little lower."

Ashkynas clutched the stone. He had done it, he had denied the Aktyr, denied it the satisfaction of more lives—and it was almost more than he could take. He trembled with the effort of sitting up, of breathing. It would punish him. It would leech his strength, his one sudden burst of power. What if it woke again? What if it tried to kill these people? He had stopped it once. Would he be able to do it again?

"Hey!" said the woman. "You hear me? Look at me when I'm pointing a gun at you!"

Ashkynas looked at her. She was a seasoned woman, her face

framed with wrinkles and thin grey hair, but she was stocky and strong, and she was not going to be intimidated.

"Good," he said, though the words were unintelligible through his dust-dry throat.

"Is he mad?" said the other one from behind. Ashkynas didn't have the strength to look, but it was a young man, the one who'd first touched the black stone, who'd woken the darkness.

The woman shook her head. "Any fool can see he's not right, somehow." She hesitated, then she lowered the strange, blasting weapon so it pointed to the dirt instead of to Ashkynas. "Mag," she said. "Bring water."

"What?"

"I said water. Now."

The young man hesitated. "But . . . but he's mad or something. Let's leave him and get out of here."

"Now!" she barked.

She didn't take her eyes off Ashkynas. He blinked at her, meeting her gaze. *Water!* She was going to give him water. She was actually going to . . . she was going to . . .

"*Tellit do andi?*" she said in her language. "Do you understand?" Ashkynas couldn't speak, couldn't move. She tried again, with different words. "*Etalli an'du, nek-ko? Imo'ani?* You came from the forest, I'll bet. But . . . no. No good." She tried again. "*Shutni pa? Leunin te mal, dor? Gallwych di eal i me?*" She rattled off different words, over and over again, all running through Ashkynas's head with the same meaning. Not one of the words sounded Kyre'an.

The young man returned with a canteen, and a sour look. "You waste our good water on a corpse, Aunt Tan."

"Maybe," she shrugged and took the canteen. Ashkynas could hear the sloshing inside, the sound of water, of life.

"I think it's a fool idea."

"Fool?" The woman's brows stabbed together. "You're one to speak! Who got us out of Terryn Dal?"

The youth snapped his mouth shut, glowered, and backed away, but kept sharp eyes on them.

The woman uncapped the water, took a small exemplary sip, then held it out. Ashkynas didn't dare move. His eyes followed the canteen. He clutched the black stone. He swallowed painfully. *Water.* But he would reach out. He would touch her. The thing would wake, sensing life. Would he murder her too? Her and the young man, both? Yl'avah save him, this was unbearable!

The woman gave the canteen a shake. She frowned at him. She growled. "Drink, damn you!"

Ashkynas shook himself. The thing inside was quiet. Maybe this was his chance. Maybe . . . maybe . . .

He unfolded a single skeletal arm. He reached for it. His fingers seemed to stretch forever, quivering, terrified, hopeful. *Close! So close!* Then he snatched the water, tore it from the woman's grasp, and upended it. The cold, clear liquid ran over his face, across his cheeks, down his neck—past his lips. A few drops. He tasted them. He felt them slide across his tongue and drip against the back of his throat. He swallowed. He could feel them all the way, running down, down, into his belly. Into the core of him. Life! His burst of rebellion against the thing inside.

The Aktyr awoke.

Ashkynas's lips peeled back. The thing inside had seen. It was laughing at him. Laughing! The harsh, terrible sound grated between his lips, scornful and humourless. "Silly Al'kah. Did you really think? Did you really?"

His stomach clenched—a stab of pain, twisting, wrenching. Ashkynas doubled over. His gut heaved. Sharp, acrid bile burned up his throat. He folded against the ground, he threw up, over and over, wracked with spasms of pain as the thing inside purged him of every drop—a cruel, spiteful denial. *Give me no life, and you will get none.* But he would not, would not, would not—

He was shaking, collapsed onto his side, exhausted, spent. Fists clenched over the stone. He would not. He would not. He would rather die than kill again. He *would* not.

"Forgive me," he gasped. "Forgive me. Forgive me . . ."

The world spun. Head pounding. How had he ever thought . . . ? It was hopeless. All was lost. All was ending. He wasn't strong enough, he couldn't, he couldn't. He *wouldn't.*

He heard voices. They spoke over him. They bent to his side, reaching out, unafraid of his madness. *Leave me*, he tried to say. *Please, leave me!*

They heard nothing, and taking hold of Ashkynas, they bore him away.

Outcast

ISHVANDU AB'ADMUNDI

Year 456 after the fall of Kayr

Ytyri.

It is the first element, the source, the rawness of creation, yet unbound to purpose. For this, we fought. For this, we bled. The possibilities were endless, and so we hoarded it, infinitely more precious than gold. We used it for good. We used it for evil. We stretched the laws of the Three Realms to the uttermost edge of breaking. We created scientific marvels beyond imagining, bending all of our skill to the acquiring and using of ytyri—until it ran out.

Only then did we realize what we had done. We had opened the vein of the world and emptied it. We had destroyed creation itself, and us with it.

From the Chronicles of the Last Age and the Ending of Kayr, set down by Andari ab'Andala, named Al'kah, first of the Age of Exile: scroll 13, lines 86-95

Chapter Twenty-Three

The voices pressed into me like needles. Burrowing deeper. Deeper. *This one is alive. This one, this one . . .*

"Ishvandu."

The name sounded familiar. It sounded like I should know it, like I should know . . .

Save us!

There was more fire. I shivered and turned, calling out. My voice broke through the darkness. I was being crushed. Something was pressing down on me, strangling me, squeezing the air from my chest. I fought and twisted. *A hand.*

"Be quiet. You are safe."

Safe, safe . . . The voice again, the one like water. It rolled over me.

I THRASHED WITH A CRY, trying to beat back the shadows. My skin was burning, peeling. I couldn't breathe. Strong hands grabbed me, but I didn't have the strength to fight. They were killing me!

I groaned and fell back. No . . . no, that was all in my head. It wasn't real. Just another dream . . . another . . .

"Ishvandu."

The water voice.

I paused. I wasn't afraid. I knew that voice. It spoke to me. It drifted through my dreams like a beacon, drawing me back. Into this place. This place smelling of earth and smoke and strange, sharp spice.

"Do you know me?" said the voice.

I nodded. *He had a name. He had a name. Something I had heard before...*

"E'tuah." It slipped through my cracked lips.

A pause. "Good. You are remembering. How many days?"

I shook my head. How many times had he asked me that? It felt like a hundred. It felt like one. Memories floated through me, shattered pieces, still mixed up in thoughts and sights not my own—vivid flashes of another life. Or many lives. I couldn't tell. And pain. There was always pain.

"Water," I rasped.

I felt the stranger move away, and I risked cracking open my eyes. Sunlight shivered across the floor. It made strange patterns. I followed the light, up, up. Palm fronds, woven across a stone entrance, fluttering, shifting. I forced myself to stare. I counted heartbeats: *thirteen, fourteen, fifteen.*

Water dripped from my burning eyes, and I snapped them shut. Why had I counted? It seemed important. It seemed ...

The man returned. I flinched, but this time, the liquid did not burn, and I swallowed with only a little pain.

"More," I said.

"How many days?"

"I ... I don't know."

"Ishvandu. How many days?" The voice was cold, but unhurried. He could wait. He could wait forever.

I groaned, but reached into the dark place in my mind. The nothing place. *Screaming. Screaming without end. And the cold. And the dark. And the shadows, reaching, reaching.*

Tell them, tell them, tell them, tell them ...

"Kynava," I whispered. "Kynava ab'Ashnavas."

"I don't care about Kynava. How many days?"

"Seven."

There was a pause. "Eight," he replied, though I heard a hint of satisfaction. Water followed. It was cold and sweet. It filled me, reaching into every place of me: my throat, my belly, my toes and fingers, my mind. The vicious pounding eased, and I fell back, breathing hard.

"Where am I?" I asked.

"I've already answered that. When you remember, you will know."

"I don't understand."

"Today you remembered my name. The rest will come."

Remember. I remembered everything about the night in the desert. Kynava ab'Ashnavas. The terror, the shadowy creature, lined in starlight, rushing at me, filling me. Every agonizing detail. And then it stopped. And I was here, wherever *here* was.

"How many days?"

"Twelve," I said without hesitation.

"Good."

The water was cool and fresh. When I lay back, I cracked my eyes open. I saw him. Sharp features, and neat, dark hair—tied back without a braid. Not a Guardian, though he was robed like an outrider: long and simple cloth, with a wide belt and open sleeves.

"What did you dream?" he asked.

I told him. *Trees*, I said. But not like the Temple gardens. Like sand was to the desert: green tops, stretching as far as I could see, passing beneath me, running on and on, to distant craggy cliffs, taller than I could imagine—until a wind blew up, and it tore out the roots, stripped the leaves, scattered the greenness, and beat everything into dust. Trees, I said, and the desert swallowed them.

"That is the past you see. The fall of Kayr."

He was always saying such things. *That is another victim. That is an old city. That is the past you see. That is nothing.*

"How? How could I possibly . . . ?"

"The Sumadi."

I'd never heard the word before, but I felt a tightness in my stomach. "Sumadi?"

"Yes. Where do you think they come from?"

"*They*? I . . . I don't know what you mean."

"Ask them. Ask what attacked you."

"Who? I don't . . ."

"Your people. Ask them, when you see them again."

This struck me as odd. *My people.* As if he weren't one of them—but where *was* I? I frowned, realizing I had had these conversations before, but could no longer remember them.

"E'tuah," I whispered.

The man was watching me, curious and unconcerned. He waited.

"E'tuah," I said again. "That's what you call yourself. But that's not a name, it's a title."

"Yes. An old one. Do you know what it means?"

I shook my head. I had heard it before, in the Elders' stories of Kayr. It could be given to the very wise, the very powerful, or the very old; but no one in Shyandar had ever been given such a title.

"So what's your name?" I asked. "Your real name? Real people have real names."

"You think I'm not real?" There was a smile in his voice.

I frowned. What *did* I think? I remembered Kynava—*tell them, tell them*—and then shadow and darkness and screaming. Pain without end. Until: *life.* I shivered. I remembered the bare feet. I remembered the voice. The dark cold, like an endless pool, going down, down . . .

"I don't know who you are," I said at last. "But you saved me."

"I saved no one. You were alive. I came. One is either killed by the Sumadi, or they are not. You are not the first, but you are certainly the youngest. Do you remember?"

"What?"

"Where you are?"

My eyes watered if they stayed open too long, but at least I could sit up. I was in a cave with a low ceiling. Palm fronds twisted over the entrance, while sunlight leaked from behind, tracing shadows across the floor. Jars and baskets lined the far wall, a few tools, and in the centre of the room, a long flat stone for a table. Clouds of some unspun fibre draped off it, sitting next to a bowl full of dates. It was all so . . . ordinary. Yet the silence. For a couple days I thought I might have been in some mysterious corner of the Guardian's Hall. Or maybe a hidden cave near the Temple. But day or night, there were no voices from beyond the woven leaves. No footsteps. No distant shouts, or the bellowing of camels and goats. Nothing but E'tuah. The answer came to me, as obvious as if it were always there. "I'm in the desert."

He nodded.

"But how? How is that possible?"

"You will see."

———

The days shifted together like grain. "Thirteen," I counted for him.

"Fourteen." I touched my feet to the floor. It was cold. It felt like needles through my skin. I ate, though every swallow E'tuah gave me hurt.

"Fifteen . . . sixteen." I was moving in slow circles around the room.

"Seventeen." I could fetch my own water from the urn. *Where did it come from, the cool, clear water?* I could kneel at the table. I twisted a few strands from the untouched fibre. It felt good to do something with my fingers. Still, they shook from the effort.

"Eighteen." *The door.* My gaze wandered to the woven entrance, drawn more and more to it, like a beast to water. Sometimes, when E'tuah was not there, I would stare at it for large silent swaths of time. I longed to break through it—it was only leaves. But it seemed forbidden. Something not to be done. I realized I had never actually seen E'tuah come or go through it. He simply appeared . . . and then vanished. This cave had become my world. A tiny, unreal world, cut off from my life before. To break through the leaves would be to end that world.

So why did I hesitate? Why not go now? I could do it. My feet were unsteady, but the path from one end of the cave to the other was not impassable. Did I like this world so much, this strange place, full of dark dreams and scattered memories and pain?

I scowled. I was afraid. Somehow, I was safe here, and to cross the border was to abandon my safety. To risk death and thirst. To risk the shadows.

The moment I saw my fear, I hated it. I stood. My legs trembled, but using the wall of the cave, I stumbled step by step towards the light.

Tell them, tell them, tell them . . .

I shoved the voice away. Kynava ab'Ashnavas was dead. I was not. I was alive, or at least I *would* be the moment I broke free.

The journey was agonizing and slow. My heart flapped like a bird stuck behind my ribs. Any moment I expected E'tuah to appear, to stop me. *No one is allowed outside the walls. The desert is forbidden. Forbidden. You're not a Guardian, and you never will be . . .*

E'tuah did not appear. The light was close—blinding in its intensity. I blinked and blinked, swatting at the tears. What if it was too much? What if I looked into the light and was struck blind? The thought only deepened my anger. I reached the woven fronds, and without hesitating, I swept them aside and looked out.

The sun was bright. It dazzled me, and for a moment, I could see only flecks bursting across my vision. But slowly, my surroundings came into focus. I wasn't sure what I expected: sand, barren rock, emptiness.

Instead, I found green.

A lush valley opened around me. Palm and fig trees swayed above my head, bushes were clumped along the ground, birds sang noisily, water bubbled and frothed. *Water.* I could hear it. A soft gurgling. And as my eyes adjusted, I saw a long, curving lake, tucked between the rocks, sheltered by steep cliffs and dotted with flashes of colour: red flowers, blue leaves, golden birds skimming across the water, snatching insects out of the air.

My mouth hung open. It was wondrous. It was like a dream. Maybe I was still in the dream. Maybe my madness had descended into complete delusion.

"Welcome to Gitaia."

I spun. A little above me, sheltered beneath a dip in the rock, sat E'tuah. He was cross-legged, a thick green leaf cradled in one hand, while he drew a knife down its side. I wrinkled my nose. A foetid smell was drifting over, while dark, yellow juice dripped from one end and splashed onto the rocks below.

"Have you never seen *aloe* before?"

I drew near, fascinated as the dark skin peeled away beneath the knife. E'tuah turned it, peeled the other side, turned it again. And beneath the green, there was a clear, pulpy mass. I leaned forward. It was almost invisible, like water turned into fruit.

"The desert's gift. One of many your people seem to ignore. Here." He cut off a square and handed it to me.

I frowned but held out my hand, accepting the strange, slippery cube. Then he sliced some off and popped it into his mouth, chewing, watching me, curious. I made a face, raised it to my nose, and sniffed. There was none of the pungent juice left, but the smell lingered.

"This is real," I said, then stared at E'tuah. "*You* are real."

The keen eyes glittered, amused. "You seem surprised."

I was—but why? Hadn't I been speaking with E'tuah all this time? Taking food and drink from him?

"I left the cave," I said.

"Yes." He set the plant aside, stood, and tucked the knife into his robes. Every action was simple, yet they flowed into one another, controlled, deliberate—like a Guardian.

"Come," he said.

I hesitated, overwhelmed, still struggling to grasp what I was seeing. But his voice drew me. I found myself stumbling after him. He led me down the slope, into the thick green. Into the heart of the strangeness, straight to the water's edge.

He pointed to the rocks.

I looked. The gurgling came from the base of the cliff. Clear water sprouted from beneath slippery, dark stone and trickled down, running and running endlessly into the small lake. I felt its spray. It was cool and wet on my cheek. I lifted a hand, brushing numbly.

"Do you see?" he asked.

"What . . . what am I looking for?"

"A reason. A purpose. Do you see one?"

I hesitated. There was a right answer, and I was suddenly desperate for it. I had to show E'tuah. Show him I understood. That I was strong. That I was not just an ignorant dirt-digging Labourer. "It waters the valley."

"It does. But is that why it came?"

I shook my head. "I don't think so."

"Did it spring out because *I* was here?"

"No," I said, gaining confidence. "You came because the water was here first."

"Exactly," he said, and I felt a burst of pride. "Water. It comes for no reason, and life follows it, without reason. Without purpose. Random, virtuosic displays of life. Free from expectation." He paused. "Is it not beautiful?"

My mind stretched to encompass this new world, this valley, perhaps other places, little pockets of life, scattered throughout the desert. Life. Life in the desert! There was a burst of wonder—

Then a fist clenched in my chest. *Impossible.* Shyandar, once the whole of my existence—what was it? What was it, if not everything? I knew it, I *knew* it. I had always known it, yet to see it with my own eyes, to see water. Here in the desert, where there was only emptiness, only death . . .

It wasn't possible. It was a dream. It was—

"Who *are* you?"

The words burst from my lips. This valley. This man. This world. There was no place for them in my mind. Not in the real world. Not in Shyandar. In the cave, I could accept anything. But now the cave was gone, and the terror of the unknown came crashing against me. "Who are you? What is this place? What . . . what . . . what have you done to me? Where have you taken me?"

I took a step back, and fell. I was breathing hard. It was too bright. *Too bright.* Water dripped down my cheeks. I was shaking.

Tell them, tell them . . .

"Kynava," I gasped. "Kynava ab'Ashnavas."

Hands clamped on either side of my face. They were smooth and hard. They were cold, like stone.

"Ishvandu, look at me."

I couldn't.

"Look at me."

The voice—a deep, dark pool. It could wait forever. And if you looked into it, your gaze would go down, and down, and down forever.

"*No . . .*"

"Look at me."

My face was wet, but I forced my eyes open. Just a sliver. The sun was painfully bright.

"Kynava ab'Ashnavas is dead," he told me. "You are not."

I swallowed. I had heard those words before. They were familiar. How many times had he said those words? My stomach lurched. My mouth trembled. "E'tuah," I said. "E'tuah. How many days?"

His face hardened.

"How many days? I don't remember. *I don't remember.*" Tears burst down my face. I could hear screaming in my mind. I could *feel* the screaming. It was coming from my own throat, over and over again, without end. Screaming and screaming. Words I didn't understand. A voice that wasn't mine.

E'tuah released me and, when he stood, I felt his disgust. Or was it my own? *I was weak. So weak.*

His bare feet turned. He was leaving me. I huddled into myself, sobbing so hard my throat hurt. Scrawny arms clutched my knees. I was shaking. Why was I crying? What was *wrong* with me? I couldn't see. I couldn't remember. It was gone. All gone.

I WAS IN THE CAVE. A cool night breeze stirred the fronds across the entrance, while outside, water gurgled.

A silhouette moved in the dark. *E'tuah.* I sat up. When had he appeared? I'd never heard him come in. When my fit was over, he had carried me into the cave and left me.

I flushed with embarrassment at the memory.

"I'm sorry," I rasped.

He made no reply.

"I don't know what happened. I . . . I panicked."

"You think the Avanir is the only source of water left in the world." His voice was cold, quiet. "It doesn't surprise me, the way they speak of it. They are small-minded. They are weak, unable to see the truth of their own enslavement."

I shivered. It was a strange word, yet I knew instantly what it meant, deep inside, in a place no one had spoken to. To be trapped. To be *used*.

"They lie to us," I said. "The Elders say there's only the Avanir. They *lie*."

"For them, it is true. Your people came willingly. They entombed themselves, unable to grasp the horror of their own crimes. And every year the Choosing." He sighed. "Do you really think that will stop the Breaking?"

"The Chorah'dyn calls them . . ."

"Of course she does." E'tuah looked at me, pitying me. "Her instinct is to preserve, to carry on, to fight the decay. She will delay the inevitable—at any cost—but regardless, the end will come."

I frowned at him. He couldn't know the future anymore than the Elders, but the way he spoke . . . as if he knew things.

I rose to the challenge. "How else would we cleanse the Lifewater, if not through the Chosen?"

"That's not the question you need to ask."

"So what question would *you* ask?"

His mouth twitched in a smile. "What would *I* ask?" He settled back. "Now *that* is an excellent question."

I wasn't sure if he was mocking me. I grumbled and crossed my arms, feeling foolish, but E'tuah just continued to stare at me.

"Kayr," he said at last. "Where is Kayr, the once-great empire of the world?"

"It's gone."

"Is it?"

His question stirred something in me: a flash of desire, excitement, fear. I wrestled it under control, trying to sound bored. "Kayr fell. Didn't it?"

He must have heard the longing in my voice, because he gave me another pitying glance. "Oh yes," he said. "It fell. The Kyr'amanu were once the greatest civilization to walk the earth, rulers of the known world, masters of the Three Realms. Now look what's become of you."

Shame burst over me. I knew the stories. We all did, all that we had once accomplished. And now this. Trapped behind our walls, afraid of the shadows.

I shuddered and wrapped my knees to my chest. "So what are you saying? That you can bring back Kayr?"

"I can do nothing of the sort."

"But that was your question," I insisted. "You asked about it like it was real, like it's still out there."

"I did."

"So what's your point? If it fell, and it's gone, then it's over."

"That's small thinking, Ishvandu. Can a thing fall and not get up? Will the broken child never run again?"

I snorted. "I'm not broken."

He just looked at me, mocking my words with a single, cool glance. "Many things must break in order to grow. A seed, an egg, a spring of water. I am not Kyr'amanu. I can only watch and speak. But there is a deep wound in all things, Ishvandu, and the way of the Chosen will not suffice forever."

I frowned. His words picked at me, full of strange energy, whispering of a distant fate. What was he saying? That I could be something? That I . . . ?

It was ridiculous. And thrilling. And wasn't I here, here in the desert—alive?

I thought of the Old Lands, of the long, gruelling journey through sand and rock. And shadow.

I swallowed, shrinking despite the swell of imagination.

"E'tuah?" I whispered.

He said nothing, waiting.

"If this is the desert, then where . . . where are . . ."

"The Sumadi?"

The name crept along the edges of my mind, dark and grasping. "I don't know what that means," I said.

"Yes, you do. You know the Sumadi more intimately than anyone alive. The curse of the Kyr'amanu. The shadows. The creatures that tore open your mind to the Unseen. Yes, you know. And you will know more. More and more, the closer you look. Ask, Ishvandu. When you see your people again, ask."

See my people? What did he mean by that?

"What if . . ." I swallowed, feeling suddenly self-conscious. "What if I don't want to see my people again? What if I want to stay here?"

"That isn't your choice."

"Why not? I don't want to be a filthy Labourer. I don't want to go back."

E'tuah laughed. "You are alive when you should be dead. What more do you want?"

"I want to see the Old Lands."

"And how will you do that, unless you're Chosen?"

"Then I'll be Chosen."

"Be careful what you wish for."

He spoke quietly, yet the words slipped into me, heavy and dark with meaning.

"You've seen them, haven't you?" I asked. "You've been to the Old Lands."

E'tuah didn't respond for a long moment, and I thought I might have actually surprised him. Then his feet slid closer, and he crouched next to the stone where I slept. I could see only his eyes, glinting in the shadow.

"Why would you say that?"

"It's how you speak. Like you know us, but so much more. And . . ." I frowned. "I just see it."

He touched the side of my face. It was a strange gesture, different than his others. Where everything he said or did carried purpose— this, this was a question.

"Your mind is healing," he said. "But not closing. If you seek it, you will walk in the Unseen."

I swallowed, his fingers uncomfortably *present* against my skin, like tiny darts of fire. "I don't understand."

"The shadows have ripped open your mind. Enough to destroy you. To drive you mad. But you are young, and your mind knows how to bend and stretch. Will you let it?"

Fear prickled through me—and something else. Excitement. Wonder. A huge, dark unknown. I nodded.

"Then go back." He stood, and his fingers fell away. The fire passed. "Go back to Shyandar."

"But you said—!"

"You aren't ready. You think you know things? You haven't the faintest idea. Go back. Grow up. Be a Labourer. Learn *strength*. Know a woman. Do all the things of the Kyr'amanu, until they sicken you. Until you know the truth for yourself. Then come and find me."

The words were dismissive, painful, and for an instant I saw myself. I was a wretched thing. A child, starving and half-mad with the dark. Alive, but no use to anyone. Weak. Unwanted. *You're not a Guardian, and you never will be.*

I held myself very still, struggling to keep back the tears. "You're sending me away."

"Yes."

"Back to Shyandar."

"That's what I said."

I considered it—for the first time, my mind touched Shyandar, the possibility of it, of actually seeing it again. My father. His wretched little hut. The scorching fields and the endless work. On and on. Unchanging.

Until I know the truth for myself.

"Okay," I said. It was a small word, but it brought everything crashing back against me. Not the new, exciting world, but the old one. The drudgery. The dullness behind the walls. The world before the shadows. "Okay, I'll go. But . . . but is it true? Are you from the Old Lands? And when I'm ready, will you really take me there?"

E'tuah smiled. "When you are ready, Ishvandu ab'Admundi, you will take yourself."

E'TUAH MADE me wait until I was strong. Until I could sprint from one end of the valley to another without stopping. And he made me count the days. Twenty. Twenty-five. Twenty-eight.

A whole month passed before he declared me ready. It wasn't far, he said, but the desert was still the desert.

"What will they say, when I show up after so long?"

E'tuah looked at me. "They'll call you cursed, or blessed. Either name you will carry the rest of your life."

That didn't sound very promising. I didn't want to go back, but I hadn't asked again since that night. He'd made up his mind, and I was done with looking weak.

I crouched next to the stream to fill my water skins. I had several. E'tuah said he would guide me until I was free of the Bones—the bulbous, misshapen rocks that were strewn like a maze around the valley, hiding it, protecting it. But from there on out, I was on my own. I would need food, water, supplies. I would need to do all this myself. When he told me, I simply nodded and got to work.

E'tuah had grown more distant with every day. He watched me more than he spoke. He almost never helped. I was glad. It was a sliver of dignity: I could do it myself, so I did. I wasn't sick anymore. I didn't need him. Sometimes, I would wake to find him gone, and he wouldn't return for days at a time. I knew better than to ask where he'd gone. He would just look at me, and I knew it wasn't my business.

Still, I burned with curiosity. Whatever else E'tuah was, he *knew* things. He had been places. Seen things. He was brimming with knowledge I could only dream of.

"What are they like, the Old Lands?" I tried to ask once.

He only pursed his lips. "Knowledge is best earned, not given. That is what the Elders do, telling you what to believe, hiding what they are ashamed of. What terrifies them. Look into your own mind. The Sumadi have given you more answers than you know."

It scared me. *The Sumadi.* He spoke of them casually. Without fear. As if they'd given me a gift. But I still dreamed, every night—and every morning, I woke in terror. Heart pounding. Stomach churning. Skin slick with sweat. And the feeling, somewhere deep and hidden, that I'd done things. Seen things. Horrible, unspeakable things, and it was all my fault. Only flashes remained: *water dripping, dripping into the deep, dark pool beneath the earth. Water turning to blood. Blood turning to screams.*

I shook myself. I realized I was holding a water-skin beneath the stream, and it was spilling over.

I straightened. I was ready, and dusk was close. E'tuah said I could make it back to Shyandar if I walked night and day without stopping. He would come with me the first night, but I'd have to make it back on my own before the second if I didn't want to get stuck in the darkness, in the shadows, alone.

"I'm ready," I told him.

He nodded, but didn't move. He just stood, watching me, as if making a decision in his mind. Then he reached into his robes.

"Take this," he said.

He held out his hand. Fingers curled open to reveal a small, stone-like object. It was round and perfectly smooth, milky white, and yet I could see through it. I leaned forward. A tiny flame burned at its centre.

"Like a Guardian's blade," I said, breathless with wonder. "A keshu. Look how it glows!"

"Indeed. The same power forged both, long ago."

"But what is it?"

"It was called Sending. Your Elders forbid even the mention of such things, but your people had power, long ago. Power to bend Blood, Light, and Spirit—the laws of the Three Realms. They knew the ways of ytyri."

"Ytyri?" The word whispered through me, filling me with wonder and dread. The feeling of something opening, something waiting. It was there in my dreams, if I only looked.

E'tuah's eyes seemed to say the same thing. *Stop your wilful ignorance.* But he continued. "This is a Sending stone, because it will send your form to whoever you wish. To me, if you desire. To others. A way to speak with them, as if you were standing face to face."

"I . . . I don't understand. That's not possible."

"It is. I've used it several times on you, and you were never even aware."

"You used this on *me*?"

E'tuah's mouth twitched in a smile. "Take it. It's yours. If you have the courage."

For an instant, I saw the scarlet-robed Guardian Lord with his bright keshu, snatching away my hand. *Do not touch!*

Forbidden—everything was forbidden. But here was E'tuah, holding out a bright and wondrous thing. Like a keshu. Like the Old Lands.

I reached out and took it.

The stone was warm, and surprisingly heavy. I ran my thumb over its surface, fascinated, marvelling at its perfect smoothness.

"Be cautious," E'tuah said. "This thing could get you killed in Shyandar. It's forbidden. Powerful. Proof of what you once were, before the Fall. Let no one see. Now come."

That was all. And as I tucked the stone into the deepest pocket of my Labourer's robes, I hurried after E'tuah, up out of the valley, and then down, down into the shattered mountain that surrounded us.

Chapter Twenty-Four

The sky was dark with stars before us. The camels shifted, eager to be free of the walls. I sat atop mine, clutching the reins, trying not to be sick.

"Ready, Vanya?"

There was a snap, and I shuddered. The memories faded like smoke. Tala was next to me, snapping her fingers, searching for my gaze. "Ready?"

I nodded.

The desert opened on creaking wood hinges. The west gate behind the Guardian's Hall was more than a door. It was a world. It was a Realm as separate as Seen from Unseen. And we were about to cross over.

I stole a last glance at Umaala ab'Krushaya and the few stable hands who had helped us prepare. No one else knew. Not even Bray was allowed to see me off. The Guardian Lord was impassive. He watched us, arms crossed, frowning into the empty sea.

"Let's go," Koryn said. And without another word, we were off.

It was strange, what my memory clung to. The smell was most familiar, not any particular scent, as much as the absence of it. People, food, camel dung, industry, the turning and creaking and burning of everyday tasks: they faded. First the early morning sound of it, then the stench, then even the memory.

Only dust remained.

We were silent. The camels were hushed in their solemn advance. The wind was still. No one spoke. The sky paled behind us, blushing for a moment before leaking into watery blue. Then the sun began its assault.

The heat rose suddenly, viciously, like a wall of fire springing out of the ground. We plodded through it. It was near midday before anyone said anything from beneath their head-wraps.

"There," Koryn pointed towards a down-sloping rock. We made our way towards it. First Koryn, then Tala and myself, and finally the old outrider ab'Tanadu, like a rolling boulder behind us.

We gained the shadow of the rock, dismounted, and took water and food.

"We'll reach the Bones by dusk," Koryn said. "Then it's your turn, roach."

I nodded.

"Nothing else to say? You're unusually tight-lipped."

"So are you."

He grunted. "Neither of us wants to do this. So let's just get it over with. You're not going to give me any trouble, are you?"

"Let him be," Tala said. She was the fourth kiyah's representative, chosen specifically to keep peace between Koryn and me. She was also the fastest with a keshu—an obvious advantage, if *they* appeared. I had been relieved beyond words when Umaala said she'd be joining us. Relieved, and terrified. What if something happened to her? Or more likely, what if she saw me fail?

We rested in the rock's shadow, but no sleep came for me. I would rather race out into the heat now than face the coming darkness. *That*, of course, was beyond choice. Night would come.

I felt sick at the thought. But also—a strange excitement. It was happening. I was going to face the desert shadows again. And this time, I was going to be brave. I was going to be a Guardian.

Koryn, Tala, ab'Tanadu—they all slept. There was nothing to watch for during the day's heat. Still, I watched. I watched the sun arc across the empty sky. I watched the dark ridge on the horizon move and shimmer. I watched the tepid swirls of sand. It was calm, hardly a breath of wind. As long as we were careful, as long as we kept close at night, we could succeed.

As long as I could find the valley.

Yes, I had stood where no other person in Shyandar had been. I had seen water from the earth itself. Wild water. Free of the Avanir. Free of Kaprash. A path to that valley would change everything.

But if they knew the truth, they would never have agreed to this. Not even Umaala.

———

"You want us to go *through* that?"

I nodded.

Koryn glared at the labyrinth of rock sprawling below us—the Mountain's Bones. They stretched as far as we could see in either direction, northwest to southeast, cutting across the desert. Old remnants of an even more ancient landform, perhaps a mountain, perhaps something from before the Wars—a wall, massive beyond imagining.

"South a half-day's ride, there's a pass," Koryn said. "But getting our camels through this is impossible."

My camel Yma gave a sharp yell in agreement, butting her head into my arm.

"No," I said. "It has to be here."

"Why?"

"If we go around, we'll never find it . . . sal'ah." The pause was long enough Koryn could take it as the slight it was. His jaw tightened.

"And why is that, Novice?"

"Ab'Tanadu'sal." I turned to the grim, silent man. "How many outridings have you been on?"

"Huh," he grunted. "I would say forty, forty-five. Maybe more."

"And you've come this way before? You've gone over the pass to the other side of the ridge?"

"Many times."

"And have you ever found a valley filled with water?"

"I can't say that I have."

"That's right, sal'ah. Because it can't be found that way. When I . . . found it, I was going *through* the Bones, but I never passed to the other side. So yes. We have to go this way. Now you said it was my turn, Akkoryn'sal. So is it, or is it not?"

"Depends on whether you plan to lead us to a death-trap," Koryn replied. "Umaala put me in charge; I get the final say. And I don't like this. Can you swear you recall the *exact* location of this passage?"

I made a show of peering over the enormous rocks. From this height, it was deceptive, but I remembered all too well how they over-shadowed me, hemming me in, towering like dead trees, dead fortresses, pressing on every side.

I swallowed. I remembered *that* part. But the valley I was supposed to lead them to . . . ?

"I thought so," Koryn gave a harsh laugh. "You have no idea how to get there. What did you expect? That we'd follow you into this maze and wander blindly around until heat, thirst, or those blasted shades put an end to us?"

"No, I know the way," I said quickly. I *had* to do this. It was my only chance to prove myself to the Circle. Umaala believed in me. This was his idea, and for once I would *not* let him down. "It's through there, and I'll remember it better as we go. I . . . I just need to find my way."

"We have to try," Tala said. "We've come this far, and we knew it wouldn't be easy. Of course Ishvandu doesn't remember everything— it was a long time ago. But he knows we go in there, so we go. Right, ab'Tanadu?"

The old outrider grunted. "Even if we find it, the spring is useless if we can't get the camels through."

"Okay," Tala said. "One problem at a time. We leave the camels here with someone, go in by foot, and find the spring. When we know where it is, *then* we find a route the camels can take."

"We're not splitting up," Koryn said.

"Why not?" Ab'Tanadu looked thoughtful. "Two stay here with the camels, two go in. Use the sounding horns to communicate. Direction won't be easy in the Bones, but if you mark your route, you can always find your way back. We have supplies. We can last a few nights, if need be."

Koryn paced, dark brows lowered. I held my breath. He *wanted* the mission to fail. I could see it. He wanted *me* to fail. But if he turned around without trying, the blame would fall to him.

"Very well," he said at last. "But I'm not going in there under dark. We post watch for the night and break before dawn."

———

I DROPPED INTO A CROUCH, tasting the sweat, the dust, off the inside of my own head-wrap. I yanked it down to drink.

Koryn snatched the water skin out of my hand, spilling three precious drops across the cracked stone between us.

"Enough."

"I'm thirsty."

He capped the skin and looked at me, just looking. Then he shook his head. "Yl'avah's might, you know nothing of rations."

"Nothing?" I stood. "*Nothing?* Twelve years the son of a Labourer. I know more of rations than you could dream of. I'm thirsty, and we have work to do!"

He frowned and glanced up at the sky. It was long past midday. Sunfall had begun, and now barbs of heat struck sideways through the twisting heaps of rock.

"Very well." He flung the water skin at my chest. "I suppose we're done here."

I knew this was coming. I'd watched it gathering in Koryn's jaw from the moment we stepped into the Bones. I'd felt it tightening around my belly like a snake. *Failure.*

"I can do it," I said.

"You can't."

"I can, I *can.* Just give me a chance, give me a sand-blasted chance, Koryn. It's familiar, all of it. I just need time. I need—"

"I've given you time. All day. I've followed you through these rocks, back and forth, and back, and back. And you know what I see? You're lost. You haven't the faintest idea where you are, and don't try lying to me. I know."

I held the water skin, tightening my fingers around the greased leather. He was right. He was so right it was painful, and for the first time I could remember, he wasn't even using petty insults—only facts.

"One more day, Koryn. Please."

"You selfish, shit-scrubbing little roach. You want to get us killed? Is your pride worth it to you? One more day means one more night, and one more night—light and all, you should know better than anyone."

I snorted to mask my tremor of fear. "Are you a Guardian, or not, Akkoryn ab'Kindelthu? Are you an *outrider*, or—?"

"*Don't* question me again!" He slammed a fist around the neck of my robes. "One more word—*one* more word besides 'Yes, sal'ah,' and I will have you roped for insubordination. Is that clear?"

I swallowed. I wasn't sure Koryn had so much authority, but the Circle's warning had been painfully clear. *Step out of line once more, on anything . . .*

"Yes, sal'ah," I muttered.

"What was that?"

"Yes, sal'ah!"

"Good." He released me. "You get one more day."

I blinked. "What?"

"You heard me. One more day. That's it."

"But I thought you didn't believe—"

"I don't. In fact, I'm so dead certain you're lying out of your teeth, I'm going to give you every reasonable chance to prove otherwise. Then, when we get back to the Circle, I will roast you."

I sneered at his ugly, crooked nose. "More blame for me, less for you. Is that it?"

"Exactly. Now if you're done boasting, I doubt you care to spend a night in this maze any more than I do. Let's get back to the ridge."

We retreated through the Bones. The rocks towered around us, some jammed together like frightened hens, with no passage between. Some stood—solitary, leaning figures, bulging at unnatural angles. The ground sloped. From time to time we had to pick our way down sharp descents, following our chalk marks, weaving and shifting through the huge debris. It was dangerous ground. Impossible for camels.

My heart sank a little further with every step, every reminder of my task. Nothing short of dumb, improbable luck was going to save me now.

<hr>

It was dusk by the time we passed out of the Bones, across the gully, and back up the ridge to the other side. Tala was watching for me—or rather, for us, though I liked to think her gaze settled on me longer.

Koryn threw his pack to the ground and drank. I stood there, breathing hard from the climb, wishing . . . wishing . . .

"One more day," I said, in response to her questioning eye.

Tala glanced at Koryn. "Are you close?"

"Yes," I said.

Koryn snorted. "Close to being done here, maybe. Let's set watch for the night. Tala, you get first quarter, then wake Ishvandu. I'll do the last."

Night fell in silence. There was nothing: no wind, no words, only the gradual unfolding of the sky as the stars came out, one by one, into the blackness.

The second night began.

Again, I found it difficult to sleep. The stars kept shifting above me, and I would snap awake, wondering if *they* had come. But as much as I despised Koryn, he was a Guardian, and so was ab'Tanadu, and so was Tala. Their keshu surrounded me. The naked blades gleamed like answering stars, laid bare to the desert, each within reach. Ready. Warning the shadows away.

It seemed to be working. We'd seen nothing the night before, and this night was equally quiet. But Tala didn't know the shades as well as I did. No one did. If they appeared, I would be the first to know.

I listened to their breathing. Koryn and ab'Tanadu were outriders. They knew how to sleep in the midst of danger. I was less practiced. The whole quarter-night, I lay in tense silence, waiting for Tala's hand on my shoulder. Waiting.

It never came.

Had I misjudged the time? But no—a brief study of the stars showed the Tower had already risen, and the Tree was on its side. I hesitated a moment longer, then rose.

Tala was awake, perched on a rock about a stone's throw away, one hand resting on the hilt of her keshu. Her shoulders were thrown back, her body relaxed, but alert, eyes scanning the darkness.

"It's my watch," I said.

She shrugged. "You need to sleep more than I. Ab'Tanadu and I should split the watch, not you."

"Your brother's orders."

"Blast my brother's orders. Go back to sleep."

Instead of obeying, I slipped to the ground next to her. "I can't."

Her silence was as much permission as I could hope for, though she showed no sign of leaving herself. I was glad. Instead, we both stared across the open night, at the clean, cold shadows and the achingly present sky. It seemed closer to us now than in Shyandar, each constellation vivid against the emptiness.

"It's beautiful," Tala said at last. "I've been sitting, sitting and looking, and I can see it."

"See what?"

"What they see. What keeps drawing them back, the old outriders. Ab'Tanadu. Koryn. You."

"Me?"

"Of course."

"But I'm no outrider."

"You've seen more of the desert than most. And you're here now, aren't you?"

"Umaala's orders."

"Maybe." She shrugged. "But you didn't *have to* tell Umaala about the valley. No one would've known. You would never have been sent. Which means when you told Umaala, you *wanted* to return."

I frowned into the dark. It was strange. I'd been more afraid of the idea back in Shyandar, scared enough to feel the panic, the memories, the reaching dark. But now—especially here, with Tala—the desert didn't seem so threatening. Dangerous, deadly, yes. But not the enemy they wanted it to be.

I leaned my head against the rock and gazed into the sky. "Alright," I said. "What do you see?"

"*Yanebashi.*"

"You mean death?"

She smiled. "No, silly. Not death—what waits *beyond* death. What the old ones called the unending. It's the bigness of it all. Like your soul opens for an instant and in that moment, everything makes sense, everything fits. The world is simple, yet it isn't. All around you, these . . . bits of sand, the wind, the creatures that live here, the little plant poking up under that rock: together they make up something as vast as the sky, all the while moving and shifting. Still, yet never still. It's . . . complete. It doesn't want, or need. It just is. And that gives you wonder."

I gazed up at her, feeling a wonder of my own in that moment. "And you got all that from a look?"

"I've a good eye."

"So what about you? If you think you've got us figured out, what gives you wonder?"

"The feel of the keshu in my hands," she said, lifting it slowly so it caught the moonlight, its slender blade springing to life as light called to light. "Not the attack, but the dance—powerful and deadly with the slightest touch. Able to peel the skin from a carrot, or pierce a groundnut without going all the way through."

"Peel a carrot!" I laughed. "You could do that? With one swipe of your keshu?"

"Not a chance." I could hear the smile in her voice. "I'm just making a point."

"What? That your sword's a weapon, or a cooking utensil?"

She whacked me on the back of the head. "Quiet, or you'll find out!"

I chuckled, and we fell silent, staring into the dark. Polityr was out there somewhere, out in the desert. Gone with the other Chosen. He had seemed so at peace with it, but when I thought of the overwhelming force that must be roiling inside of him—the Avanir itself —I shuddered. The others had given their congratulations, thumping him on the back, wishing him well, joking with him, but I'd kept my distance. Too close to Polityr and I *felt* it, pounding behind my eye.

The Avanir's presence. The thing that would keep him alive across the desert. The thing the Great Tree had sent us for. The thing that would cleanse the Lifewater and keep all Life from ending.

"So are you close?" Tala asked. "Are you really?"

I swallowed, shaking myself from my thoughts. I could lie to her. I could tell her something good. Something promising. But when I opened my lips, the truth sprang out of me. "I . . . I don't think so."

"Why not?"

I frowned. *Damn Tala*. She could *do* that. Just by her nearness, her voice. Did she know? Was she lulling me into the truth on purpose? Maybe, but I realized I didn't care. It was Tala. It was *Tala*. I sighed. "I don't remember the way."

"Tomorrow's another chance," she said. "You can try again."

"Doesn't matter."

"Don't say that. You'll recognize something. It'll come to you. I trust you can do it."

"No, Tala, that's just it. I *can't*." I stood, and my fists clenched their frustration. *Shut up, Vanya. Don't! Don't say it!* But I couldn't stop myself. "I won't remember, Tala, because I never found it in the first place."

Silence hovered, but this time it was tense, charged with unspoken questions. Tala was frowning at me. I could feel the sharpness of her eyes, watching me, holding me in place. I wanted to escape and couldn't.

"It's not a lie," I said. "It *does* exist. It's just I . . . I didn't find it."

"Then how do you know it's there?"

I hesitated.

"Ishvandu, *how*?"

I swallowed and looked away, out into the desert. "There was a . . . man."

"Someone from Shyandar?"

I shook my head.

Tala seized my arm, pulling me to the rock beside her, leaning close. "A man from the desert? But Vanya, you *know* what that means."

"I don't."

"Yes, yes you do. An exile. An *exile*, Ishvandu." Her voice was low and sharp. "You met an exile in the desert, you spoke with him, you stayed with him. You shared his food!"

"I'm not sure, Tala. I don't know anything about him, except he saved my life. There . . . there were shadows, and pain. And after . . . all that, I woke up, and I was *there*, in this valley, with water and birds. Trees, Tala! Full, green trees. A whole forest of them! So what choice did I have? I spoke with him, I ate his food. I had no idea what was going on, and for all I knew I was an exile myself. What difference does it make?"

"Yl'avah's bloody might, you fool." She let go of my arm, though I noticed she didn't pull away. We were sitting close. Knees touching. "So you really have no idea."

"Not really, no."

"So you *lied* to Umaala'sal."

I winced. "Not exactly. There *is* a valley. And I know it's around here. And—"

"Does he know about this man?"

"No."

"Then you lied."

Her tone left no room for argument. I felt myself withering inside. *Step out of line once more, on anything . . .*

"Tala?"

"What?" Her voice was sharp.

"Are you going to . . . tell him?"

"Light and all, you think I *want* you kicked out of the Hall—or *worse*? You stayed with an exile, Ishvandu, and then you lied about it. And what am I supposed to say? Nothing. So now you've made me guilty, too. You realize that? Yl'avah's bloody might. Why did you say you could do it? Why, if you had no idea?"

"It was a long time ago. I told Umaala when I was still a Tasker. I was trying to prove myself. Trying to *be* something."

"And you couldn't just fess up?"

"What should I have said?"

"That you were young and stupid, you made a mistake, you can't do it."

"But . . . but what if I can?"

"Vanya, you idiot, have you even *listened* to yourself? You don't know the way. You just said so."

"I know, I know." I groaned. "I wanted to do this Tala. Don't you understand? I want to. I *still* want to. I have one more day. And maybe . . ." I trailed off. "Don't you realize what we could accomplish, if we found water? *Water* in the desert?"

She snorted. "It's not so simple as that."

"I know, but it's a start. It's something different. It's hope."

She softened. Her hand dropped onto mine, resting. My breath caught. *Yl'avah's might, she was holding my hand.* Suddenly, it was hard to concentrate. She was saying something. Of course she understood, but . . . but . . . And didn't I want to be . . . ? And . . .

The rest vanished in a haze. Her touch, her nearness, the rush of desire, so strong I felt sick with it.

"You really mean it," I said. "You won't tell anyone? Not even Koryn?"

"Especially not Koryn. If you can't find it, you tell them you forgot the way—that's what you'll say to the Circle, and that's *all*. Yl'avah's might, Vanya. Why I stick up for you . . ."

My heart swelled. She meant it. She was going to stand for me. She *wanted* me in the Hall.

"I'll find it, Tala. Maybe not tomorrow. But I'm going to keep trying. I can do it, I *know* I can. I won't let you down."

She raised an eyebrow. "Let *me* down? Why would you care what *I* think?"

"Why?" I laughed. "Tala . . ." I trailed off. She was looking at me. And Yl'avah's might, we were so *close*. Our hands . . . our arms touching, her leg against mine . . .

Then I wasn't thinking anymore. I grasped her, pulled her towards me, and kissed her.

Her lips stiffened with shock. Her whole body tensed. Her hand was against my chest, pushing. Pushing me back. But all I could think of was the touch of her, the scent of her, like green gardens and earth. *Any moment, she's going to belt you.* Sanity rushed back in and I leapt up in horror.

"Sorry!" I gasped. "I didn't mean . . . I . . . I shouldn't have . . ."

She punched me. Her knuckles sunk into my eye, exploding

across my face. I staggered back. My foot hit a rock, and I dropped into the sand.

"I'll tell you when you can kiss me, you unbelievable idiot, and not a moment sooner!"

"Tala . . ."

Before I could finish, someone grabbed me from behind.

"You lying roach!" Koryn's voice was a snarl. Horror washed over me. He yanked me to my feet, shaking me so hard my knees buckled. "You dare touch my sister! You *dare*—you filthy, sand-licking Novice."

"Koryn, wait!" Tala tried to intervene, but I was being driven back, back into one of the boulders. My head smacked the stone. I blinked furiously, trying to stammer an explanation through the rush of dizziness, the stars spinning, spinning behind Koryn's face.

"You think I'm a sand-blasted fool? I heard you. *'Don't tell, don't tell.'* Trying to involve my sister in your lies? Well, it's too late for that." Through the blur, I was aware of a tightness around my throat, squeezing, wringing. I grabbed weakly at Koryn's arm, scrabbling for air.

"Little mud-foot filth! Then after your lies, after risking so much for *nothing*, you have the stones to lay a hand on my sister?" Tala's shouts seemed distant. He squeezed harder. His eyes burned into mine, dark and furious enough to do it. He was going to do it.

Lungs started burning. Panic set it. *No, no. It doesn't end this way. It can't!* My vision danced, then faded. I was falling. *Falling . . .*

The dark and the cold. The deep, dark pool. Water dripping, dripping, dripping like blood. Words rolling over me, while I spiralled down and down, into emptiness. Emptiness. Empty. All . . .

Air rushed back in.

I collapsed. I was coughing, gasping.

"You idiot!" Tala's voice snapped into focus again. "You sun-blasted idiot, you could have killed him!" She twisted Koryn's arm, one fist planted into his chest, driving him back. Ab'Tanadu was positioned between us. He glanced at me. My eyes rolled to find him, but then he wasn't there—and then he was. Everything spun.

I groaned.

"Ishvandu. Ishvandu, can you hear me?"

I wanted to nod. I tried. I felt hands shaking me, trying to pull me back.

"You heard him!" Koryn was shouting, somewhere in the blackness. "He lied about this whole thing, just to prove he could do it. Just to make something of himself. And what was that about an *exile*? You heard him, Tala. You said yourself, he's a liar. He's got no right here. So that's it. First light, we're heading back."

"No, you can't do this to him. Koryn, wait. Just listen . . ."

"Ishvandu!" Ab'Tanadu leaned close, shaking me. "Ishvandu, look at me."

Something warm was dripping down the back of my neck. *That didn't go so well.* I slipped to the ground. *Don't . . . don't pass out. Get up. Fix this. Say something.*

I passed out.

A HUGE, spongy wet nose slapped against my head, dragging me awake. Morning light cracked through my eyes. I didn't want to move. It felt like I was tied to the ground.

A harsh bellow, like something dying, blasted into my ear.

"Yl'avah's might, Yma!" I croaked, shoving the camel away. She ignored me and began licking the matted, sticky blood on the side of my head. *Wonderful.* Now I had camel saliva to go with the rest of it.

I planted my hands into the sand, pushing myself up, groaning, trying—and failing—to rise. My mouth tasted foul, and when I swallowed, I felt bruises on my throat.

"I shouldn't have kissed her. Light and all, what a fool. Why did I *kiss* her?"

Yma snorted in agreement, lowering her neck so I could pull myself to my feet. It was hard, but I did it, and stood wavering on my own two legs, waiting while everything spun around me.

I watched them. They were packed already, milling around the camels, sharing a few terse words. Every now and then, Tala glanced in my direction. She was worried. Was that a good sign? Better than *furious.*

"What do you think, Yma?" I asked the creature. She looked at me with big lashy eyes. "Time to give up and go home?"

She stuck out her tongue and bellowed.

"You're right. This is ridiculous. To come all this way for nothing."

"We're leaving," Koryn hollered from across the sand. "Hurry up."

It was morning already. The time to leave was past. They must have been waiting for me. Must have tried to wake me already.

"I look forward to burning what's left of you when we get back," Koryn said. "Now get moving, or get left behind."

I met his eyes. *He would.* This was over. If I went home with them now, I was never going to be Guardian. Anger gave me a moment's resolve.

"I think I will."

"Will what?"

"Stay behind," I said.

He laughed. "You will, will you? Very well. But no one's coming back to collect your corpse." He turned and vaulted onto his camel. "Come on," he said to the others.

Tala stared at me. "*What* did you say?"

"Our friend's finally made a smart choice," Koryn said. "Do what he promised, or don't come back at all."

"We're not leaving him here!" Tala started towards me. "Vanya . . ."

"Don't," I said.

"You're being irrational. You're not thinking straight. You've had your head knocked in!"

"I said I was going to find this valley, Tala, and I will."

"But you don't even have a keshu. Don't be ridiculous!"

"Then I'll do it quickly. I've got Yma. I'll catch up to you by sunfall."

"Then I'm coming with you."

"No," I said.

"Definitely not," Koryn echoed.

"Well, he can't go down there alone!" she cried.

"She's right," ab'Tanadu said. "We can't leave him behind. He's not even a Guardian yet, and—"

"I'm staying!" I cried, glaring at the old outrider, then back at

Koryn. "I'm finding this valley. You promised me one more day. I'm taking it. I can do it." *I have to do it.*

"We should at least try!" Tala said.

"We *did* try," Koryn said. "It's over. I'm the leader of this riding, and I make the decisions. If Ishvandu wants to demonstrate his disregard for authority—again—by throwing his life away, so be it. But I'll risk no one else on his failed pride. Let's go."

Tala marched up to me.

"Vanya, you don't have to do this." Her voice was low. "I asked Koryn not to say . . . about the exile. Even if you can never be a Guardian, it doesn't mean . . . it doesn't mean I . . . that we . . . I mean, there's a chance we could still . . ." She trailed off, brows scrunched, unable to look me in the eye for the first time I had known her. Was she saying what I *thought* she was saying? I gave an incredulous laugh.

"Well, I guess this is a little uncomfortable now, isn't it?"

She shot me a withering glare. "You think this is funny? Vanya, you're going to get yourself killed. You could die, and no one would even know."

"I suppose you'd figure it out eventually."

Her eyes flared, then she slapped me across the face. It was a hard, stinging blow. *So maybe a little furious.* I rubbed my cheek.

"I suppose we would," Tala said. Then she turned and leapt onto her camel without a backwards glance.

I had to pull hard on Yma's reins to keep the camel from following. She paced and bellowed, and shoved me with her nose, but soon they passed over the lip of the next slope and disappeared, leaving me standing in the desert alone.

"Alright, Yma," I said. "I hope you can smell water or something, because this could take a while." But as I packed our supplies and headed down towards the Bones, a smile crept onto my face. Maybe, just maybe, things hadn't gone so badly with Tala after all.

Chapter Twenty-Five

I pressed my palm against the scalding boulder and marked it with a slash of chalk. A white line pointed in the direction I was heading: further into the Bones, further up. I had no memory of these rocks, but I wasn't giving in. I had no choice.

Yma's head drooped beside me. She wasn't pleased with the tangled pattern I was leading her on, weaving through the Bones, this way and that, back and forth. I gave her an encouraging thump, but both of us trudged listlessly. The sun had risen, hot and scalding. And even though it was falling towards evening now, the Bones were like a furnace, trapping and holding the heat, draining my water at an alarming rate. A part of me knew I should find a place to rest, that my life could depend on it. But I wasn't thinking straight anymore. The valley, the passage, proving myself, the triumphant return—*I did it! I found it!*—it was all-consuming.

And likely impossible. I wracked my brain over and over again for a memory of the night E'tuah had led me out of the Bones. It was hopeless. It had been dark. I had hurried to keep up to his long strides, marshalling my courage, ignoring the whispers that chased after us, the twisting shadows, the cold, the terror . . . And the more I thought about it, the torturous twists and turns we took through the rocks, the more I was convinced—E'tuah had complicated our route on purpose.

E'tuah. I hadn't thought about him for years. Not since the Guardian's Hall. Not since being named a Novice at my Coming of Age, my childish hopes of leaving swallowed up into a new reality: becoming a Guardian. The impossible thing, the thing I'd dreamt of all my life, had actually leapt into my grasp. Never mind the circumstances. Never mind I was dumped there by the High Elder, in a last desperate bid to control me. *I would never be a Guardian.* Even in the Hall, I heard it. The Novices said it. The Circle said it. Koryn said it, every sand-blasted chance he could get.

But I was close, and if no one but Umaala knew it, then I had to show them. I had to try. I *had* to. If I found Gitaia, the endless spring, grown almost mythical in my own mind, then no one could deny me. I *would* be a Guardian.

Then it happened. At first I thought I had found something. I turned a corner and the rocks peeled back. *The valley! The passage!*

But when I looked again, I saw the old battered mountainside had fallen away in a heap of rock. The path was gone. The ground itself vanished, torn away by the force of the ridge crumbling and sliding, leaving boulders protruding at all angles from a mass of rock and earth. An impassable landslide.

I groaned. My way was blocked, and even though I had criss-crossed the mountainside around me, not a single boulder or passageway had stirred my memory.

My knees buckled and I sank to the ground, exhausted, on the verge of despair. My head throbbed from where Koryn had slammed me against the rock. My throat burned. My legs were weak. Maybe I should have gone back with them, failure or not. Hadn't Tala been trying to tell me before we parted? That it wouldn't matter to her, that she might even still choose me?

Of course it mattered!

I slammed a fist against the rock. How could I face her again if I came back a failure? How could I face any of them? They would throw me from the Hall, but where could I possibly go after Coming of Age with the Guardians? Not back to the Temple—that door had been closed a long time ago. Not a Crafter—I was too old now to learn. Only back to the fields, digging dirt and hauling water and endless hard labour. I would lose everything, including the hope I could do something, *be* something. It would be stripped away from me. Again. It was all happening again.

A Guardian doesn't give up hope. I could hear Tushani'sal, his staff tapping the ground. *Up, Ishvandu. Up on your feet. A posture of defeat is the first step to defeat.*

I forced myself to stand. A Guardian didn't panic either. I had to look at my options, think about this. I could retrace my path down to the bottom of the slope and try again on the other side, but that would take me past dusk, with nothing gained but a few steps in that direction. I didn't have time for that.

My other option? I could go forward, navigate the treacherous path, despite the risk. I'd have to leave Yma behind. It was a shame, but maybe she could find her own way back down. Once I found the spring—if I found it—I could always turn around and look for her. The biggest problem would be my supplies.

Best get started. I unloaded everything from Yma's back, rearranging things, packing them into a manageable burden, as much as I could carry. Enough for another day or two. Most of the water skins hung from my belt or weighed down my pack, along with some food, a sounding horn in case someone came looking for me, and a sharpened bone-knife. Then I gave Yma a parting scratch and promised to come back for her. At last, I turned and lowered myself over the lip of the broken path.

The rocks were far. I dangled off the edge, hoping to feel the ground, hoping, and hoping—nothing. Then my arms jerked. There was a crack. The edge gave way, and I dropped, hit the ground, and skidded painfully down the slope. My sandaled feet dug into the rocks, stopping my descent. *Careful.*

I stood slowly. I looked around, planning my route across the shattered landscape. From what I could see, there was no safe path. Every rock was a danger. But I had come this far. No turning back.

I took a step. I tested the stone. It wobbled, but held, so I shifted my weight. Then I took another, and another. Yma yelled after me, but when I glanced over my shoulder, I saw her retreating into the shade. *Good for her.* I tested another rock. It seemed to hold. But as soon as I shifted, it slipped. I hit the ground, scraping along the rocks, sending a few stones showering below me. I held my breath, not daring to move. One wrong step, and I would bring the rest of the slope with me. I waited.

Nothing.

I swallowed. I dashed a hand over my brow, wiping the sweat out of my eyes and pulling my head wrap tight again. Keep going. Had to keep going. I stood, wincing as blood beaded along my knee, down the side of my leg.

I kept going. My eyes shifted between the rocks under my feet and the far ledge. It crawled closer. The sun was falling now, blazing out of the west, straight into the ravine. I stopped to drink, then kept going. Then drank some more.

I had to be careful. I needed the water. Tomorrow as well as today.

Tomorrow. I glanced at the sky. It was becoming more and more clear that I had run out of time. I would be lucky to make it out of this ravine and into some quiet, sheltered place before night. And then the long, lonely darkness. I shivered.

Except what if the valley was just beyond? Gitaia was a haven in my mind: water, fruit, plants. I would find it. It would shelter me. It was my best hope now.

One wobbling step after another, and eventually I was there. I gazed up the broken path. A jumble of rocks had piled against the slope. *Just like climbing the north wall as a boy.* I started up. I went carefully, glancing behind to see the ground shrinking away. Yma was a distant mass of shadow, huddled against the rock. I felt a stab of regret. I *would* return for her.

When I finally clawed my way over the lip of the ravine, arms straining, fingers digging into the hard cracks until they bled, pulling and grunting and kicking, I rolled and sprawled in the dust, breathing hard. I was almost fainting from exhaustion. But I had done it.

I lay there. A breath of wind cooled me, drying the sweat off my flushed skin. Cool and refreshing.

A little *too* cool. I glanced up. The sun was sinking fast, disappearing over the distant ridge. I had to keep moving. I pushed my hands into the rock and rose. I took a step.

I was jolted back to my knees. I watched as a crack peeled across the ledge, directly in front of me. I threw myself forward, and in the same moment, the overhang collapsed.

I fell. I grabbed for the edge, my fingers just barely catching hold. The whole weight of my body swung against the rock, slammed hard. I gasped, hung on for a moment, then the earth gave way in a shower of dirt.

Rocks bounced, struck each other, and I followed. I slammed into the ground. I rolled and slid. Everything was breaking apart. A hunk of rock glanced off my shoulder and kept going. It didn't stop. It was tumbling with growing urgency, ricocheting off other obstacles. And everywhere it hit, stones shifted, drawn as if pulled by invisible threads.

Not good. I scrambled back, ignoring the fresh bruises, the pain in my foot, searching desperately for a place to climb out. The ground moved under my feet. I took a step, toppled into a boulder, and leaned, steadying myself. It held for a moment. Then the shapeless mass crumbled away.

It was like opening a barricade on an irrigation river. Stones began to flow, tumbling against each other, setting off other rocks, opening other streams. My feet slid, and I threw myself forward, digging my hands into the morass of stones. *No! Yl'avah's might, no!*

The whole mass began shifting, dragging at the sides, pulling more rocks with it, gathering speed as it went. I had an instant to glance up, to see the horrifying distance between myself and the edge of the ravine, the impossibility of escape—before the crushing force swept the ground out from under me.

I was caught along like a twig in an eddy. The ravine thundered and crashed. *Stay on top!* I clawed at the rubble, sliding helplessly, carried like a sack. *Don't panic. Don't panic.* But I could feel myself turning as I slid. *No.* I had to stay upright!

I dug a foot into the ground, desperate to stop myself from plunging headlong. It was the wrong choice. I was jerked around, sent into a dizzying roll. I bounced down the ravine. Sky and rock and sky again—it flashed by. *I was going to die.* Then I slammed against something hard and the air was punched from my lungs.

I gasped in shock. I was hit again. A rock pummelled my back. I was stuck. *I was going to die.* I threw my arms over my head and curled inwards as more rocks pelted me, bounced off, washed over. Something smashed against my leg. I flinched and cried out. Then the thundering earth closed over me.

I HAD no idea how long I huddled there, gasping as stones hit me, first hard and fast, then in intermittent bursts as the mountain exhausted itself. Pain followed. A deep, aching pain, spreading through every part of me. The rumbling stopped, the earth fell still. I didn't dare move. Dust ground between my teeth, lining the inside of my throat, stinging my eyes until I could barely see.

I had to move. I knew that. I knew I couldn't lie there indefinitely. I *had* to move. But Yl'avah's might, the pain! I was trembling, shaking from head to foot. Shaking like a green Tasker.

Calm down. Think. Don't panic. Guardians don't panic. Slowly, carefully, I shifted my arms, my head. A shower of stones skittered down the slope, but I got one arm loose and poked my head up over the mound of debris.

The sun had vanished below the horizon. The sky was dark.

"No," I coughed. Not good. I had to get free.

I was nearly buried. My ribs ached from where I had slammed into the boulder, but a slab had wedged itself against me, trapping the lower half of my body. Maybe saving my life. I couldn't see my legs, but when I tried to shift them, my left gave a scream of protest. *Yl'avah's might, don't let it be crushed.* It felt crushed. Would I ever walk again? The thought of being crippled, useless—I would almost rather be dead. I could feel my heart beat faster at the thought, more sweat breaking out down my face, trickling down my back. *A Guardian doesn't panic.* Breathe. I had to breathe. Slowly. One problem at a time. Somehow, I had to get free.

I could move one arm. That was enough, for now. Remembering Tushani'sal's training, I pushed away the pain. *Just your body's advice. Master it. Control it.* I grabbed hold of the slab, hoping I could shift it. I pushed, but it was like trying to break a wall with a finger. Nothing budged. I lay back, exhausted, my muscles trembling from fatigue. I would have to squeeze backwards. *Yl'avah's might, my leg!* I tried not to think of the pain. I had to keep moving, before everything seized up. Before I couldn't move at all. *Before the shadows.*

I strained again, pulling on the slab now, trying to leverage myself up. Stones rained down on me, trickling from above. I kept pulling. Then my leg shifted with a jerk and I screamed. I fell back, tears squeezing from my eyes. *Idiot, of course it was going to hurt.* Didn't matter. I had to try again.

Breathing hard, choking back the pain, I pulled. I didn't stop this time. Everything clenched in agony, but I wouldn't stop, wouldn't, wouldn't . . .

A cry tore from my throat, echoing into the ravine, bouncing over my head. It fell away into a sob, and I let go. I collapsed back onto the stone. Trapped. Helpless. *No.* No one was coming to help me. I had to get myself free, or I was dead. It was that simple. *But think!* What else could I do?

I closed my eyes and held my breath, counting heartbeats, then let it out in a long, slow release. I did that two more times. Three. Four.

By the time my eyes opened, I knew what I had to do. In this position, I was stuck. I could pull as much as I wanted, but my legs were not going to move. What I needed was to change position. To dig *under*.

Okay. I could do that.

This one . . .

The words slipped into my mind like a breath. I paused. Had I heard that correctly? Was someone close?

This one. This one.

There was a sigh. A whisper of air, or of words. A stirring in the dark.

We know this one.

This, this is the one. The one who lives. Who sees.

Who hears.

My skin prickled. I felt a brush of cold, and something dark shifted across the ravine like smoke.

Yl'avah's might, it was happening. It was actually going to happen. Here. Now. It was *them*.

I thought I was ready. Since leaving Shyandar, I had been waiting for this. To face my fears. To see them. To be a Guardian. But the wave of terror was almost debilitating. My bladder let go. The warm, shameful liquid ran down my legs. I couldn't breathe. *I was going to die. Going to die. Yl'avah's might, I was going to die . . .*

A hiss peeled through me. Scratching, screeching sounds, one over the other, compounding and growing. They dug into my mind, tearing. Opening. Like an old wound. *Tell them, tell them.* I squeezed my eyes shut, whimpering, struggling to get free. Pulling and pulling, hardly feeling the pain, though it slammed through me in waves. Yl'avah's might, I was going to die. *No, no, no . . .*

He is afraid.

Why does he fight us?

Why does he run?

See us. See us.

The slivering sound: laughter. They were laughing at me.

No. If I was going to die, I wasn't going to cower like a green Tasker. I let out my breath. I clutched the boulder, forcing myself to still, forcing my heart to slow. *Control, control. A Guardian knows how to control . . .*

I opened my eyes. I could see only shadows. But they were moving. They swirled and pulsed, and every now and then—tattered rags of light. Not a *present* light, but like something beyond, something slipping through, from one Realm into another. An echo that pounded in my head, needling through the dark. Hands reaching. Faces leering. Eyes and mouths gaping in need. Brief, hungry flashes. I stared, sickened and fascinated. I turned my head, and turned, and turned, whipping back and forth as the shadows clawed closer. Some slithered along the ground, inching like smoke. Others curled through the air. Some walked upright, pacing around me in slow, deliberate strides. But all, all were closing the circle, tightening like a trap.

Be brave. I had to be brave.

"You didn't kill me the first time," I said, voice shaking. "And you won't now."

He speaks!

He hears us, this one, this one, this living one.

A dark patch separated from the others. It stepped around me, rippling with starlight. Another joined it from behind.

He will save us.

He will give us their lives.

Many lives.

Death is the only way.

"Get back!" My fingers dug into entrapping stone and I felt the slickness of blood smeared from my own nails. I was helpless. They were going to kill me. The pain like fire and cold. The reaching hands. The dark. The screaming. On and on. *Kynava. Kynava ab'Ashnavas.*

I clenched my jaw. Control. Don't lose it.

Something cold touched me. I jerked back. I took a sharp breath and felt the stench of them—like sour, rotting meat. The cold enveloped me. *Now, now they would kill me . . .*

I blinked and saw a face. It was terrifyingly close. It shone as if touched by the moon. A sunken face, disfigured and stretched. Scarred by unknown torment. Smiling. A cruel mouth.

My breath had stopped. I couldn't speak. It settled across my chest, surprisingly heavy for something formless. Fingers clutched at either side of my face. Cold, biting fingers. The cold sunk into my skin, but I didn't move, didn't flinch. Its eyes—they were gone. They were dark, gaping pits, yet they gazed at me, *into* me, while everything else rippled and bulged from shadow, to light, and back again.

You will save us. Its voice cut into my mind. *You will see.*

It bent closer. Its stench was overpowering. Bits of fleshy light dripped and struck me, burning where they touched.

You will save us, or you will die.

Die!

Kill him.

He is ours. He will die.

His life is ours. This one, this one . . .

The voices beat around me. Voices and laughter and screeching cries. My heart thundered in my ears. Other fingers grabbed for me. They were cold, so cold. They scratched and pulled, grasping, hungry.

I shoved my fear down, down. I made myself like a stone. I

refused to shrink. There was nowhere to go. No place I could run. I stared at the one with the sunken eyes. There was something in that, at least. To stare at the source of your terror, to watch as it killed you.

The shadows stiffened, gathering closer, hovering, but in a sudden, strange silence. *This was it.*

The one with the sunken eyes looked up. His teeth barred. *He comes.*

An instant later, I heard a scream. At first I thought it was me, that I was screaming, a horrible, shrill noise. But the shadows exploded around me. They burst into a frenzy.

No!

He comes, he comes . . .

Words dissolved into hissing, shrieking, gagging. There was a rush of cold past my face. Another scream. The one with the sunken eyes was gone, and I found myself staring at a different Sumadi. It was standing over me, lined in starlight. Its arms were splayed out to the side. Its back arched in pain. A horrible, shrill sound was lashing out of it.

Something else dashed over me. Another shadow. Robes snapped. There was a glint of light, just an instant, and the creature fell back, shrieking and clutching its chest. Light burned through it, jumping madly across it as it writhed over the scattered rocks.

A second Sumadi lunged from behind. Its starlit feet hardly touched the ground as it leapt towards—*something*. The new shadow whirled, liquid like the wind. A blade cut the air. The Sumadi spun, a gash across its face, light spraying from it like blood. It fell towards me, then burst into frothing shadow. Its angry cries needled my mind as it fled.

The figure turned. It flew over me, up the rocks, back down, light as dust. My mouth hung open. I had never seen anyone move like that. Faster than the creatures. Faster than my eyes could follow. It struck one down, slashed at another. It turned to the dying one, the one screaming and screaming, like Kynava, endlessly, on and on. The figure lunged, stabbing downwards. There was a burst of light and I shut my eyes, turned my face.

And silence. My breath was the only sound, scraping through my frigid lungs, trembling and gasping. I pried my eyes open.

The figure stood. Turned.

I could see nothing in the dark but an outline—a man whose form did not shift and seethe. A real person.

"Koryn?" I breathed. "Ab'Tanadu? Is that . . . you?"

There was no answer. I was shaking. I tried to shift, to pull at the slab one more pointless time.

"Don't move."

The voice cut through the silence, sharp and stern, and cold, so cold. Like a deep, dark pool. The figure moved closer. Moonlight glanced off bare feet, and a face loomed—a face I thought I would never see again. He stared down at me, unchanged, with the same commanding dark eyes.

"E'tuah?" I gasped.

"Of course." He didn't look pleased.

"But you . . . you killed them."

"I ended them."

"Wha- what happened? How . . . ? How did you . . . ?"

"What are you doing here?"

I stared at him. I was panting for breath, hardly able to think. I was dead and now I wasn't. I was dead. Just a moment ago, I was *dead*. And now here *he* was. Again. Like a ghost himself.

He leaned closer. "Ishvandu ab'Admundi, what are you doing here?" His voice was hard, and cold, and unfriendly. He spoke my name, but with the tone of a stranger.

"What do you think? Looking for Gitaia. Yl'avah's bloody might, how did you *find* me?"

"You brought down half the mountain. This is my home. I know what happens on my own doorstep."

Something was wrong. But as life returned to me, so did the pain. I clenched it down. I took slow, stabling breaths.

"Fine. You're here. Now you can help me out. I'm stuck. My leg. I think it's broken."

He didn't move. "Why do you seek Gitaia?"

"What? Are you serious?"

"Very."

I lay back, panting, trying not to think of the pain in my leg, in my side, pounding in my head, getting worse and worse. "You think I told them. That I was leading them to you."

"Should I?"

"No! Of course not! I . . ."

"Then why do you bring Guardians without warning, leading them to the very edge of my valley? Did you think you could surprise me?"

"I didn't even know you were still alive. How should I?"

"I gave you the means. Have you forgotten?"

"Of course not!"

"And yet you fail to make use of it. Why?"

I clenched my jaw, feeling a wash of shame as I thought of the beautiful shining, white stone. "Because it was taken from me."

"By whom?"

"By the High Elder. The day I returned. He took it from me."

"Then take it back!" His eyes flashed, daring me to disagree.

"I tried. I tried, but I couldn't—"

"The Sending stones are not toys, and I entrusted it to you. Was I wrong?"

I shut my eyes. I was starting to shake. The pain was overpowering, difficult to ignore. Difficult to think past.

"I'm sorry. I'm sorry, E'tuah. I tried, but I was weak and alone, and they threatened me . . ." He stood there, unmoving. "Don't leave me. Please don't leave me. I'm sorry about the stone, okay? Please, don't—"

"Oh, stop."

He held me with his eyes, waiting. *Waiting for what?* Another desperate plea? Then he stepped down beside me. He crouched and plied off the heavy slab, lifting the monstrous thing as if it weighed no more than a hemp sack. It sank into the stones on my right. Some shifted and clattered down the slope, but it held, while E'tuah unearthed my legs. The pressure lifted, and I let out a hiss of pain.

He reached down his hand. "Come."

I hesitated. "They want the water, E'tuah. That's all. No one knows about you, I swear."

"I know."

"But you said . . . you thought . . ."

He shook his head. "That's what *you* said, Ishvandu ab'Admundi."

"And what's that supposed to mean?"

The corner of his mouth twitched. "It means stop talking and get up."

I scowled, took his hand, and managed to stand with his help, but the moment I put pressure on my leg, I collapsed. "Light and all," I gasped, leaning on his arm as pain shot up to my hip. "It's broken. I can't . . ."

"We must get off the slope."

"I'm not sure . . . I'm not sure I can walk . . ."

"What, are you a boy still? I won't carry you this time. Whether you act it or not, you've grown. So walk."

He was right. After seeing him shift that slab of rock, I thought he probably *could* carry me, but that wasn't the point. I wasn't the pathetic whelp who had ran unthinking into the desert six years ago. I was a Guardian now.

I ground my teeth together and limped forward, still leaning on his arm, trying to hop forward on one leg. It hurt, but I refused to say another word. Slowly, excruciatingly, we made our way over the shifting stones. I realized he was leading me back, not forward. Back to the side I had come from. But I had no strength to fight him.

When we finally climbed onto solid ground, I unslung the pack still strapped over my shoulders and collapsed against a rock, sliding to the ground, breathing hard. That hurt, too, and when I pressed my hand to my chest, there was a sharp pain along my ribs.

He crouched to one knee and peeled back the hem of my robe. It was sticky with blood.

"Yl'avah's might." I grimaced. There was an ugly gash on my leg, half-way down my calf. He prodded the wound, peering closely.

"How bad is it?" I asked.

"The force of the blow cracked the bone, and you've twisted it out of place. I will set it."

"What? I don't think—"

He gripped my ankle and pulled. Pain exploded through me. I fell onto my side, clenching my teeth to keep from screaming. One arm lashed the air. I wanted to shove him away, to hit him, to do *something*. I might have passed out. Next I knew, my head wrap was gone, and my tangled hair lay slick with sweat against my brow. I was on my side, and water flowed into my wound, flushing and flushing.

"Not my water," I said weakly. "Not . . ."

"Be quiet." He pushed me back. Now he was lashing something against my leg. He was using strips of cloth, winding it tighter and tighter.

"What did you promise them?" he asked.

"Water." I swallowed thickly. "I promised them . . . water."

"Bold, for an unsworn Novice. You think you can just wander into the Bones and ravage its secrets? These are the consequences, the desert's payment for your audacity. So what will you do now?"

The question struck me as odd. He was here. He had found me. The answer was clear.

"You . . . you will help me. Won't you?"

E'tuah laughed. There was something chilling in that laugh. It shivered through my leg and into my gut, and settled.

"Help you? Give me one reason, Ishvandu ab'Admundi, why I should help you, why I should allow Guardians to invade my peace. One reason."

I had no answer. Koryn would confront him, challenge him, have him hauled back to face the Circle. Ab'Tanadu would agree. Even Tala. It would be the end of his freedom, and—if he *was* an exile—his life. And probably mine too, just for speaking with him.

He jerked the last of the head wrap and knotted it, sending another jolt of pain into my knee.

"I'm sorry," I said, wincing. "I don't know what I thought. I thought you would be gone. I thought . . ."

"You weren't thinking. That's the problem, ab'Admundi. You don't think."

My hands curled into fists. I paused, struggling against the growing pain in my leg, in my ribs. It was becoming a steady, aching throb that spiked every time I moved. "I wanted to do this one thing for them. I wanted to show them what you showed me. That there's more. That they could *be* more. That they don't have to be trapped."

"You think you're trapped?"

"The Avanir."

"What about the Avanir?"

"I don't know. It . . . it gives us water, our way of life, our *purpose*. It even keeps back the Sumadi, but . . . but . . ."

"It needs your utter dependence."

"Yes!" I cried, hearing the words, the *right* words, for the first time I could remember. "It's alive, E'tuah. I can see it. I'm the only one that can see. It's powerful, *deadly*. It would be one thing if there were no Kaprash, but it gives us water, and then just . . . takes it away again. For no reason. Without warning. It makes us desperate, helpless, afraid to go beyond the walls, afraid to push into the desert. So we *hide*. And every year the Choosing. Three people, sent into who knows what. Never to return. Like Pol . . ." I clenched my teeth against the torrent of words, breathing hard. "E'tuah, I don't *trust* it."

"Good," he said quietly. "You're beginning to see. Maybe there's hope for you yet." He reached for my hand. I took it, and he helped me sit up. My leg pounded furiously, but there was a splint on it now. *A splint? Where had that come from?* It was almost familiar. Almost . . . I peered closer. Was that what I thought it was? A piece of Yma's saddle, somehow snapped off the precious wood frame. My mind was muddied, but when could E'tuah have possibly gotten that? Yma was nowhere close. Not that I knew of. Not . . .

I frowned. *Unless he'd known before coming to help me.* Images leapt to mind, unbidden: E'tuah following me through the Bones, E'tuah watching as I climbed into the ravine, waiting until I fell, the rocks closing over me, burying me, and E'tuah seeing my leg crushed. Still waiting. Waiting until the Sumadi. Waiting until the uttermost edge of my need.

I met his eye, his cold, dark eyes, and I saw.

"You've been following me."

"Of course."

"You left me to die!"

"I thought about it."

"But you *left* me there! To face the Sumadi. I could have died. I could have *died!*"

"You didn't."

"What the sand-blasted light and all is *wrong* with you?"

"You needed to see them."

"*What?*"

"They didn't kill you. Did they?"

"I don't know what you're talking about. I don't know what you mean. It's just cruel. You could have done something. You could have helped me."

E'tuah laughed and straightened. "I did."

I leaned against the rock, breathing hard, furious and sore. Feeling humiliated. As if all of this were some joke, and E'tuah knew the answer and I didn't. *Of course* he had saved me. But at the last moment. At the edge of my despair.

"You're not going to let me find Gitaia, are you."

"Of course not."

I nodded. "Okay." I took a few breaths, letting that sink in. "Okay. What . . . what do I have to do?"

E'tuah said nothing. I glanced up through the dark and saw him watching me, his face shadowed by the rocks.

"You think you can bribe me?" he said at last.

"Why not? You're here for a reason. You came from the Old Lands to seek out Shyandar, and you stayed all these years in Gitaia. *Years.* Which means you want something. You want something we can give, and maybe you saved my life because you think I can give it to you. Something I couldn't give you as a child, but now . . . something as a Guardian? A keshu maybe, a . . . a member of the Circle? Am I close?"

E'tuah smiled. "If I wanted something, it wouldn't be had by you."

"Sand-blasted brute." I slapped the stone with my fist, then grunted at the sudden movement and clutched my ribs. "You can't just leave me here. What am I going to do? How . . . ?"

"You have a camel. Somewhere. I'm sure she'll find you. Good luck."

"E'tuah!"

He was turning away. He was leaving me. *Alone, alone in the desert. The dark. The shadows.*

"E'tuah! Wait, wait. Please, just . . . help me get back. I won't ask for Gitaia, just don't leave me."

He paused in the Bones, one more shadow amongst thousands.

"I've done enough. It's time for you to help yourself, Ishvandu. Get back my stone—and then we'll talk."

There was silence. I held my breath, waiting for what else he might say. I peered into the dark.

"E'tuah?" I called at last. "E'tuah?"

There was no answer. Nothing. E'tuah was gone.

———

Dreams took me. Dreams and darkness, and a weariness that lashed me to the ground. I was trapped. A heavy weight pressed on my chest, threatening to crush me. I couldn't get free, but I could hear Tala. She was calling for help.

The shadows!

The Sumadi were coming for her, and I couldn't get free.

"Vanya!"

I pushed at the weight, but couldn't move. Something was stabbing through my leg, pinning me to the ground. I was helpless. *I'm sorry*, I tried to say. *I failed. I couldn't find it. I couldn't . . .*

You are close, the voices whispered. *You hear us.*

Soon. We will come for you . . .

"Vanya!" The voice was stronger, more real. More urgent. I fought towards it, past the burning.

My eyes opened, crusted with grit and tears.

"Tala?" My voice was thick. It was dark, but I could see the perfect outline of her face, the soft point of her chin, the wide, pursed lips.

"Light and all, Vanya!" She put a hand to my face, lifting a water skin so I could drink. I let it flow into me, filling my belly with new life.

"Tala, is it really you? What are you doing here? What . . . ?"

She slammed a hand into my shoulder. "You idiot!"

"*Ow!* Me?"

"Yes, you! I told you it was dangerous, and you didn't listen. Now look at you! What happened?"

"I . . . fell."

"Fell where? Have you seen yourself!"

"I imagine it looks like I fell down a mountainside." I grimaced. "How did you find me?"

"You marked your path. It wasn't hard to follow, but when I found Yma wandering on her own—light and all, I thought you were dead!"

"I nearly was. Turns out rocks are painful when they land on you."

"Huh." She held up the water again for me to drink, and I took it. "We'll get you to Yma. She'll carry you down. Only it looks like you completely dismantled your saddle for that bit of wood. You'll have to use mine, and I'll walk."

I swallowed, nodding, feeling a fresh wash of shame. "Tala," I whispered.

"Mm?"

"I'm sorry."

She snorted. "You'd better be. Koryn threatened to have *me* hauled before the Circle, can you believe it? *Me?* His own sand-blasted sister? But ab'Tanadu took my side. It wasn't right to leave you behind, and even Koryn knew it, that unbelievable ass. Haul me before the Circle indeed. I'd like to see him try."

"Wait, listen Tala." I took her hand. "I made a mess of it. Of everything. I risked your life on my stupid pride, and you were right. I should have told Umaala the truth. I just . . . I want you to know, it wasn't only for me. I wanted to help. I wanted to *do* something. For them. The Kyr'amanu. It was my chance to help."

"Maybe," she said, and softened with the hint of a smile. "But mostly for you." Then she tilted her head. "Did you mean it?"

I frowned. "Of course I meant it! I'm sorry, I really am—"

"When you kissed me, you idiot. Did you mean it?"

I blinked, opened my mouth, then shut it again, searching frantically for words. "What . . . what does this have to do with anything? It was a stupid mistake. I . . . I shouldn't have . . ."

"So you didn't mean it?"

"What? No! I mean . . . yes. I did. But look, forget about that."

She smiled. "I'm not very good at forgetting."

I wanted to say something, but my mouth flapped and nothing came out. It wasn't fair, catching me off guard like this. What was I supposed to do?

She leaned in. Her lips touched mine—a slow, gentle kiss, like a question, the tips of her fingers against my cheek. My heart leapt into my throat. I lifted my hands, not sure what to do. Light and all, where did you put your hands when someone was kissing you? Her waist? Her back? Would that be too bold? Maybe shoulders would be safer . . .

Before I could figure it out, it was over. She pulled back, a glint in her eyes. "There," she said. "Now we're even."

I stared at her. The heat rushed to my face and I managed a few halting syllables that never got far.

She laughed. "But mine was better."

"Does . . . does that mean I owe you another?"

"I'll have to think about it," she said. "Now, let's get you back, before the shades come and finish us both."

Chapter Twenty-Six

SEVEN YEARS AGO

By the time the cliffs and walls of Shyandar rose out of the dunes, I was nearly dead from exhaustion—a scrawny, half-starved boy, screams ringing in my ears, the screams of the dying, my own screams. *Kynava. Kynava* . . . The desert pressed around me, clawing into my mind.

Gitaia was gone. The crisp, cool spring and rustling green was another world. The sun's glare seared my skin. The wind blew hot against my face. I staggered, pressing the tattered remains of my shirt against my mouth and nose, then I pulled them down and took a sip of tepid water. Shyandar was close. I could make it. I *had* to make it.

My bag bowed me over. Stones seemed to hang from my wrists and ankles. I trudged, listless. It was only a day's journey. Only a day. But I could feel my weakness returning, fever pressing at my mind. A month and I was still weak! E'tuah should have made me stay longer. Any moment now. Any moment, I would collapse and the hot sand would blow over me.

I stopped. *No, don't stop!* I stood there, wavering, strength slipping out of me like grain through a sieve. I was close. So close. I could *see* Shyandar. I could make it. I brought an arm to my face, felt the flush, hot skin, my heart fluttering against my ribs. I clutched the water skin, drank. The last drop squeezed down my throat. Then the water skin fell empty into the dust.

I stood there for an agonizing moment. Wondering if my feet had stopped working. *No.* I had to keep going. Had to. Had to.

I stumbled forward. My feet dragged through the sand, one step at a time. I lifted my eyes, fixed them on the shimmering red walls, and promised myself I wouldn't stop moving again until I reached the gate.

It was farther than it looked. It was almost sunfall by the time I fell against the north gate, willing it to open. It was bolted from the inside.

Of course.

I gave a hoarse cry, threw myself against the wood, pounded my fists, shouted and shouted. There was only silence, and my shouts turned to helpless sobs. I sank to the ground, collapsing against the gate, heart pattering, eyes swimming.

There was no choice. My hand travelled to the pocket of my robes, closed over the small, milky-white stone. E'tuah's parting gift. *The legacy of your people,* E'tuah had said. Could I use it? Could I call for help?

I thought of E'tuah. *No.* The man had sent me away. This was for me to do, and I doubted he would help me again.

Kulnethar? My friend in the Temple seemed a distant memory. A flash of bright hair, a ready smile. His palms slamming into my chest as he shoved me over. *Sometimes, Vanya, you're an ass!* Would he understand? Would he help me? I didn't know anymore, and one whispered word to his father about ytyri, and I might as well die here in the desert.

That left my father. He would be furious. He would beat me for going outside the walls. He would never let me be anything but a Labourer. But he would come, I knew it. And he would keep my secret.

I pulled out the stone. Next to the heat, it felt cool and comforting, like a piece of water hardened and pressed into my hand. I stared at it. *Someone help me! Come!*

I ran my thumb over it, just like E'tuah had showed me, letting the smooth stone glide against my touch. There was a faint click, and the light within began to pulse, matched to my own racing heartbeat.

"Father." My voice croaked. "Father, help me, please. I'm at the north gate. I'm here. I . . . I came back . . ."

I trailed off. My voice fell dead into the silence. *Something wasn't working.* A name, maybe. "Admundi ab'Adaiah—"

My mind jerked. It was abrupt, hard, like a hook dug into my thoughts, yanked a world away, turned up, over. Everything rushed by. A confusion of sound and light and place . . .

And then nothing. I was sitting in the dust outside the gate, in the gathering dark, my head spinning and spinning. The world tipped. I threw up. I fell onto my side, shuddering, squeezing my eyes and struggling not to retch again.

Sky and sand settled slowly back into place. I let out a long, groaning breath. It hadn't worked. E'tuah's stone had failed me—or I had failed it. But I was too scared to try again. Trembling hands stuffed it back into my pocket.

"Help," I gasped. "Someone help."

No. No one would find me here, no one would come looking. I was going to die . . . here, on the very brink of Shyandar.

Are you really going to give up? The words burned into my mind, echoing and echoing. I thought I saw him, standing in the red light.

Sunsickness. Dehydration. I knew the signs, same as everyone in Shyandar: seeing things that weren't there, hearing voices on the wind, tricks, cruel tricks for a dying mind.

Keep moving.

"I can't do it," I gasped. "I can't, E'tuah. I can't . . . move."

"Of course you can."

"No. No one's coming. I tried, but it's . . . barred."

"Foolish child. You used to climb into the desert. You did it all the time. Don't you remember? How? *How?*"

"I climbed . . . over the wall. Over . . ."

My eyes snapped open. Blackness clung to the edges of my vision, but I fought it, fought to breathe.

"Stupid . . . Of course. Up the walls. Not far from here . . . if . . ."

I staggered back to my feet. Just a few more steps. I leaned against the wall, stumbling towards the heap of stone. Then I started to climb.

My muscles cramped. My body burned. I hauled myself up the first stone, then the next, then another. Skin scraped against sharp edges. Feet slipped and knees banged against unforgiving rock. But somehow I pulled myself to the top and rolled over the last battered stone with a sob of breath.

I rested for a moment, but the ground was still far below. I tried to slide downwards, from one rock to the next. But all it took was one misstep. My foot slipped, my feet kicked out from under me, I pitched back and my arms shot out for a handhold. There was none.

I hung for a moment in the air, struck something hard, flipped, and landed with a thud of dust.

THE BREATH WAS KNOCKED out of me. I lay there for a moment, too stunned to move, fearing something was broken.

But lying sprawled on the ground wouldn't do any good. I needed to find help. I needed water. I needed . . .

Voices.

I twisted my neck, feeling like the strength of my entire body was concentrated in that move. But yes. There were people walking up towards the Temple. White-robes. Sand-blasted white-robes!

I opened my mouth to call for help—and no sound came out.

I shut my eyes. I was going to die there. There, at the gates of Shyandar.

"*Help,*" I tried again. I shifted my arms and legs. They hurt—but nothing was broken. That was a good sign. This was my one chance. I would never make it up that hill without help.

"*Help!*"

I pushed myself into a crawl. I called out, over and over again. Voice cracking with dust.

"Did you hear . . . ?" The voices shifted.

"*Help!*"

They turned. The white-robes actually turned! They saw me. My strength gave out, and I collapsed onto the ground.

"It's him!" one of the voices was drawing nearer. "He's alive!"

"Impossible!"

The cries cut through my head like knives. Another voice at my elbow: "Come help me, now. There, get his feet."

I shifted and pain lanced through my side. I groaned, pulled my feet in, but hands took hold of me, hoisting me.

"Quick, get the water. And run tell the High Elder!"

Concerned faces swam into view, familiar faces—from another life. They each wrapped an arm around me, bearing me up the hill and into the Temple.

I faded in and out. Familiar sights and sounds I thought I had left behind now washed over me. The deepening green of the gardens. The stir of the evening meal. Voices calling out, sandals slapping against white stone.

It's him! He's back! What? It's him, the boy . . . the boy who vanished.

Ishvandu . . . Ishvandu ab'Admundi . . .

My name rippled through the Temple, following after me like buzzing gnats. I was moved up the steps, brought quickly into the healing rooms. White walls blinded me. Healers bustled here and there. Always busy. Always flowing. Moving in and out of curtained rooms like a dance.

One pushed the others aside. Water splashed my face and I gasped, snapping awake. The healer began stripping off my robes. *The Sending stone . . .*

"No, wait . . ." I clutched at the dirty, torn fabric. She ignored me, soaking it in water and wrapping it around my head, draping it across my shoulders, cooling me off. I fell back, weak and exhausted.

"Drink," said the healer, bringing a cup to my lips. I drank. I could feel myself reviving, just a little.

"Vanya!" Kulnethar burst into the room, throwing himself at me. He clutched my arm, almost wrenching it off in his excitement. "You're alive! You're *alive*! Yl'avah's mercy. Are you okay? Are you hurt? Ynlaii, he's bleeding!"

"Give him space, child!" The healer tugged him away. "That goes for everyone. There should be only two people in this room right now. Me and the boy. The rest—out! Out, out, out!"

Kulnethar fell back, gazing at me like I was a shade myself, eyes wide. There was a shuffle of feet, but when a hush filled the room, he still hadn't moved.

I brought a hand to my forehead. I *was* bleeding, but it was only a trickle down my face, probably from the fall. Ynlaii was already kneeling over me, washing it, checking for other injuries. Her fingers probed along my neck, my chest, my arms. She pressed into my stomach.

"What have you been eating?"

I shook my head.

"Plants, berries, insects? What kind? Depending on what you've ingested, I might have to flush your system, but you need to tell me. And no, I won't believe you've eaten nothing but air and sand for a month." She turned to Kulnethar. "If you're not going to leave, then make yourself useful. Get me yanis and lavender, and fresh bandages. And some lath'is. Hurry on now."

Kulnethar shot me a last worried glance, then disappeared through the curtained entrance.

I let my eyes drift close. I was tired, so tired . . .

I woke several times, sometimes to voices outside my room, sometimes to movement in the dark, water lifted to my lips. I wondered when my father would appear. *Someone* would tell him. He'd want to see me, he would care. Wouldn't he?

But when I woke the next morning, it was Kulnethar sitting in my room, leaning up against the wall, eyes closed, mouth hanging open in sleep.

I sat up. My bandaged head was still spinning, but I felt refreshed. I was alive. I was back in Shyandar. After everything—I had actually made it.

I gazed down, and saw I was wearing clean white robes, just like Kulnethar's. My old robes were gone. It hit me. *My old robes were gone.* Which meant the Sending stone . . . A flutter of panic ran through me. *If they found the stone . . .*

I staggered to my feet, steadying myself against the wall, eyes scanning the small room, looking, looking.

Kulnethar stirred and snapped awake with a gasp. "Vanya!" he cried. "You're up!"

"My things."

He blinked. "What?"

"Kylan, where are my things? My things. My . . . my robe, and my bag, and . . ."

"That filthy old stuff? They're rags now. Vanya, what *happened* to you?"

"I have to find my things." I made for the door.

"Wait! You can't go out there."

"What?"

"You can't . . . you can't leave yet. My father . . . I mean, you have to wait here, until . . ."

"Yl'avah's might, Kylan. What are you talking about?"

He flushed bright crimson, as only he could. "Vanya," he said. "It's been a month."

"I *know* how long it's been. I'm not stupid."

"But a month, Vanya. A month. Where . . . where have you been?"

"In the desert."

"We thought you were dead."

"I was."

"That's not funny."

I rolled my eyes. "Kulnethar, are you telling me I'm not free to go? Because I don't see any Guardians here, and . . ."

"There is."

"What?"

"A Guardian. Just outside your door."

I stared at him. Then I marched to the curtain and thrust it aside. Sure enough, a grim-faced woman stood across the hall. She had a jumble of braids and a keshu, and she met my eye without flinching.

"Yl'avah's might." I ducked back inside. I stood there, just inside the curtain, fists clenched. I could feel my breath quickening. *They had found the stone. I was going to face the Circle.*

"I'm not of Age," I said weakly. "They can't . . . they can't . . ."

"Vanya, she's here to protect you."

"I didn't do anything wrong!"

"I know."

"*I didn't do anything wrong!*"

"I know. I *know.* Just calm down, okay?"

He gripped my arm, pulling me back. "My father wants to speak to you, and we have to know where you were. That's all."

I fell back, collapsing onto the straw pallet. I was shaking. My head was spinning. *A month.* How was I going to explain a month? I couldn't tell them about E'tuah. I couldn't. And what about the shadows? Did they know what happened? Did they know about Kynava? About . . .

Tell them, tell them.

"Kylan, I didn't do anything wrong. I didn't. I *didn't*. It was Kynava ab'Ashnavas. He did it. It wasn't me. It was Kynava. It was . . ."

"Okay. It's okay."

He knelt next to me. His grip was strong, but it was a good sort of strong. Holding me back from panic, from the sudden pressing memories, and the reaching dark, and the screaming. My fingers dug into his arm.

"It's okay," he kept saying, though his voice was distant. "It's okay, Vanya. You're safe. You're in the Temple. Breathe, okay?"

I nodded. I could feel it passing, slowly, bit by bit. My lungs pushed for air. My mind settled. The shadows retreated.

I passed an arm over my face, feeling tiny beads of cold sweat.

"I'm good," I said. "I'm . . . I'm okay."

Then I glanced up—we weren't alone anymore. Beneath dark hair and a silver-flecked beard, beneath furrowed brows, watching me, were eyes as blue as Kulnethar's. He unfolded his arms, revealing a wide blue sash over his white robes. The High Elder. Kulnethar's father.

"Can you hear me, Ishvandu?" he asked. His voice was gentle, and deep with concern.

I nodded.

He knelt next to me, and put a hand on my other shoulder. His eyes came close. He was so intensely close, I wanted to shrink away, but I held myself still, determined not to give the wrong impression.

"Are you able to tell me what happened?"

I thought about it. I could. I could tell him everything: about E'tuah, and Gitaia, and the Sending stone, and . . .

I shuddered. *And the shadows.*

But he wouldn't believe me. He'd think I was mad. He'd question me about the shadows, and then I would have to explain. And I'd have to tell him about E'tuah, and the High Elder wouldn't like E'tuah. I wasn't sure why, I just knew it. But E'tuah had told me about the Old Lands. He'd given me a tool of Old Kayr. And the things he knew—they were important. They burned in me. How could I speak those things to the High Elder: doubts about the Chosen, the Avanir, the Great Tree herself? *No, no, better to keep silent.*

"You don't have to speak now, but there are things I need to know. For your own good and for ours. Do you understand?"

I nodded.

"But take as long as you need."

"I was in the desert," I said.

"We know."

"I didn't do anything wrong. I was in the desert and I came back."

The High Elder smiled, though I caught a flash of concern. "That's what I want to know about. Will you tell me where you were in the desert?"

I swallowed, but met his eye—those keen, bright eyes. Eyes that saw. He knew I was hiding something. *Let him.* I wouldn't tell. "My father," I said instead. "Where's my father? Why doesn't he know? I want to see my father."

The High Elder said nothing. There was a long, terrible pause. I saw the way he looked at me, and then Kulnethar, and then back.

"What's wrong?"

"I think this is not the best time—"

"Tell me," I said. "Tell me what happened. What happened to my father? I have a right to know."

The High Elder didn't flinch. He gripped my shoulder and looked me straight in the eye. "Your father is dead."

The words stuck into me. I realized I knew. I had known since that moment, outside the gates, using the Sending stone and finding . . . nothing.

"Dead," I whispered.

"I'm very sorry, Ishvandu, but when you went missing, he went after you. He went into the desert, alone."

"He went after me."

"Yes."

"He went into the desert. He . . . he came looking for me."

"Yes. By the time the outriders caught up to him, it was too late. They found him a day's ride from Shyandar, near the Bones. They think he was attacked."

"The shadows?"

The High Elder nodded. "So it seems. We buried him in the South Grounds near three weeks ago."

I could see him screaming in pain. Like Kynava, like me. Screaming on and on, without end. His mind tearing itself apart. But unlike me, he was dead. The finality of it struck me. It was hard and cruel, and it was my fault. He was dead, because of me. My father. Dead.

I should feel something. There should be grief, or sadness at least, somewhere inside. Even regret. Instead, my mouth made a hard, firm line, and I felt nothing.

"I'm sorry," I said, though I wasn't sure if I was apologizing for his death, or for the coldness inside.

The High Elder looked at me strangely. "This is not your fault, Ishvandu."

I nodded.

"Do you want to see the place he was buried?"

Did I? A clay marker, a spot of empty ground. The man who had raised me. Beaten me. Confined me. *Died for me.* I swallowed and looked away, shaking my head.

There was a long silence, then slowly, the High Elder stood. "Get some rest. Let me know when you're ready to speak."

I was a prisoner. They tried to say otherwise; they tried to tell me it was for my own good, that I needed rest, that I needed protection. But the desert was in me now, and therefore, I was untrustworthy. So I was contained, kept in my room, in white robes, useless and bored. Waiting for something. For *something*, though I had no idea what.

Kulnethar was my only reprieve. He popped his head in the second day, and, though it was awkward and strange, and neither of us knew what to say, he sat with me and chatted like his old self.

He told me about the fire, and the rations, and how the Guardians saved some, though they would be extra low this year. Kaprash was over, thank Yl'avah, but there was still lots to do, and everyone was working hard to rebuild.

He told me about the Choosing. "Layashi," he said. "One of the gardeners. You would have seen her around. In the gardens."

"So?"

"Well, you say you never know anyone who gets Chosen. Now you do." He smiled.

"Wonderful. Good luck to her I suppose. Saving the world and all. Must be nice to be needed."

Kulnethar ignored my bitterness. His face lit up. "And guess what else is new!"

"What?"

"No, you have to guess."

"You woke up and realized your face was stupid?"

"No, I'm of Age now. I had the ceremony and everything."

"A Temple Acolyte?"

"Yeah." He grinned. "I guess that makes me a man, or something."

I snorted. Kulnethar, a *man*? His legs and arms had stretched, even in the month I was gone, but his face was still boyishly bright, and his yellow hair could have come off a baby's head. I chuckled. "A real man now and everything? Are you sure? Did they check?"

"Hey," he frowned. "It's not funny."

It struck me as funny. I found myself laughing. Kulnethar couldn't help it when I laughed. He giggled even as he shook his head. "It's not funny!"

His voice picked an inconvenient moment to crack, pitching into an unmanly squeak. I roared with laughter, clutching my stomach, tears streaming down my face. Kulnethar had no choice but to join in, and soon we were both doubled over in mirth.

After that, he came as often as his new duties allowed. Sometimes he brought food from the midday meal. Sometimes he would tell me stories about the Old Lands and the ending of Kayr, and the Great Tree—sending us into the desert, sending us to find the Avanir, to find hope. Our last chance to mend the Breaking of the world.

One day he came in clutching a sack. Dozens of little stones spilled out, black and white ones, and a hunk of charcoal.

"Jik'u," he explained, sitting cross-legged on the white floor. He proceeded to draw twelve long lines on the floor, then twelve more going across. It formed a grid. Finally, he arranged the black and white stones in alternating patterns, so no two stones touched. Then he leaned back.

"Move a stone," he said.

"What is this?"

"Fun!" he grinned. "Move a stone. Any black stone. Any direction, until you hit another stone."

"Why?"

"Because. Just do it."

A memory tugged at my mind. Had I seen Temple students doing this, leaning over, peering at the ground like they were reading a scroll? It didn't make any sense, but I shrugged, picked up one of the black stones, and slid it towards the neighbouring white one.

"Good! Now my turn."

He slid a white stone into the black one I had just moved.

"Now you."

"I don't see the point of this."

"Not yet. Just wait."

We kept sliding stones around, and the more they moved, the more confusing and jumbled the board became, with open spaces and closed ones. Finally, Kulnethar connected four of his in a line. He snapped his fingers. "One." Then leaned over and gathered the stones, piling them in front of him.

"What are you doing?"

"I got four in a row. See?" He thought about it, then plunked one of the stones into a new location. "Your turn. But this time, try to make a line."

I tried. I kept moving stones around, but he kept blocking me. He gathered quite a pile in front of him, before I managed to build up a cluster of black stones together. I moved, then Kulnethar leaned over and plucked one of mine off the board.

"Hey!" I grabbed for his hand. "Stop it!"

Kulnethar laughed. "Squares are forbidden. If I force you into a square, I get to steal."

I made a face. "You're making this up as you go, aren't you?"

"It's the rules."

"You could have told me."

"Yeah," he chuckled. "But it's more fun this way."

We played his silly game, slowly emptying the grid of stones. Finally, Kulnethar proclaimed himself the winner—there were a lot more stones piled by his feet than mine—then he collected it all and stuffed everything back in the bag.

"Who cares?" I muttered. "What's the point anyway?"

But when he hurried back to his duties, he left the lines of charcoal on the floor—neat, dark lines. Bored, with nothing else to do, I found myself picturing the little stones and figuring out how I would place them differently. *The point was to make lines.*

The next time he showed up, I pretended not to care when he emptied the black and white stones onto the floor in a heap, but secretly I was thrilled. He coached me through some more rules. The first time, I lost badly, and fast. The second time, I modified my approach. I still lost, but when Kulnethar went to gather everything up, I stopped him.

"One more time."

"I've got to get back to the gardens. I'm helping ab'Ethyru plant the new tanil herbs."

"Just one more." I tried not to sound like I was pleading.

Kulnethar took pity on me. "Fine. But if I get in trouble, it's your fault."

I counted spaces quickly and carefully as I played. I watched how Kulnethar retreated to defend certain positions or moved to intercept mine. I started trying to break his patterns as well, even forcing a few moves. He muttered when he noticed, and, in a few slides, I was able to steal one. The game ended when one of us had fewer than five stones on the board, and Kulnethar counted everything up.

"I beat you by six," he said, sounding relieved as he bent to collect them.

I grabbed his hand. "Leave them."

"What? So you can sit here and do nothing but play and beat me soundly in a week? I don't think so."

"Oh, come on, Kylan. I'm knocking my head against the wall for something to do. Please."

He frowned. "You could also just tell him."

"What?" A chill settled into me. We hadn't talked about why I was here. Not since the first morning. It was like a silent pact between us—one he had just broken.

"You know what I mean, Vanya. My father. You should talk to him. It's been a week and nothing. Do you really want to stay here?"

"Maybe I do."

He sighed and leaned in a little closer. "Vanya, what *happened* to you? The healers talk. They say you're up in the night, screaming. They say—"

"Stop." Everything went cold, from my hands and feet, straight up into my throat.

"Vanya, why? What's the big secret? If something happened, we're here to help, but we have to know."

"*We.*" I snorted. "Is that why you come every day? To soften me up? Pretend you're my friend, until you get all my secrets?"

Kulnethar grew still. He looked at the stones scattered in front of us, then dropped the sack onto the floor. "Keep it," he said. "And if that's what you think of me, you can play yourself."

He stood and marched to the door. I shut my eyes. I thought of the silence, and the small, cramped room, and the waiting.

"Trushya," I said.

He stopped. "What?"

"Remember Trushya?"

I watched his face. It went as pale as milk. Of course he remembered. The young outrider, screaming in the desert—dead, because of him.

"That's what happened to me."

He looked like he was going to be sick. He nodded. Then he turned and hurried from the room.

KULNETHAR DIDN'T COME the next day or the day after that. He was right. The dreams still clung to me—like dying endlessly, like being torn open, like finding the edge of nothing and leaping into it and falling forever and ever. I saw things, but I pushed them away. I didn't want to remember. I didn't want to know.

When I woke, I played jik'u. Day or night. Anything to beat back the fears, the memories, the nothingness. The understanding that my life had become a large empty hole with nothing to put in it.

Then one morning, I looked up. I had a visitor. It was the Guardian. The woman who stood like a statue outside my door, protecting me—imprisoning me.

"You play jik'u?" she asked.

"I'm learning."

"Show me." She knelt across from me.

I set up a new game. My hands shook, though I didn't know why. But the thought that a Guardian, a real Guardian, was choosing to speak with me . . .

We played wordlessly. We each scored some points. She stole one of mine. A few moves later, I stole one of hers. I reached for her stone.

"I know what happened to you."

She spoke quietly, hardly looking at me, but I faltered. My hand hovered over the board.

"The High Elder knows too. We all know. You were attacked by the shades. By the Sumadi. It's not a secret, ab'Admundi. We heard screaming in the desert, and we came. We found you alive, but then the shades were all around us, attacking us. It was horrible." She paused. "They slaughtered us. Everyone but me. I fled."

"You survived too?"

"Not like you. They never got to me. I ran, and by the time we organized ourselves to go look for survivors, you were gone. I failed you. The things you suffer? It's my fault."

I curled my hand over the stone. I was surprised to see it no longer shook. As if by speaking, the woman had made my fears tangible, real—and less powerful.

"Every night, I hear you. I've never known a survivor before. Now I wonder if it's better that way. What I saw that night, what I see now, watching over you, hearing you—it's my punishment. Whatever else you did, however you survived . . . I don't care what you tell them, just tell them something so we can move on. Please."

I found myself nodding. "Okay."

"Thank you."

We finished our game in silence. She beat me by fourteen stones, then left without a word.

———

THE NEXT DAY I asked for the High Elder.

"The desert shadows," I told him. "I tried to stop Kynava. The shadows attacked us, and I don't know how, but I survived. I don't remember what happened. I wandered into the desert and found a valley. I found water and trees. I lived there until I was better, and I came back. That's what happened to me."

The High Elder nodded, watching me with his keen blue eyes. "You survived the shadows?"

"I did."

"And you found this valley all on your own?"

I glanced at him, my heart beating a little faster. "Of course."

"Ishvandu," he sighed. "I'm trying to decide if you're aware of your crime, or if you're just ignorant and scared."

"What do you mean, High Elder?" My voice rang a little shrill. "I'm telling you the truth. I didn't do anything wrong. I don't know what you mean."

"I think you do. I'm sorry for what you suffered, but I need you to start being honest with me."

I swallowed. Did he know? No, he was just guessing. There was no way he could know about E'tuah. No one could know. "I'm telling the truth."

He paused, then he reached into his robes. A moment later, his palm opened, and on it, I saw a small, milky white stone.

"That's mine!" I cried, leaping to my feet.

"Ishvandu, where did you get this from?"

I snatched for it, but the High Elder was faster. His hand pulled back, curling into a fist.

"Give it back!"

His blue eyes met mine, steady and open. "It's not yours, Ishvandu."

"It *is* mine! Give it back."

"Who gave it to you?"

I clenched my teeth, shocked by the directness of his question. *Like he knew.*

"Nobody. I found it in the desert."

"I find that highly unlikely. Who gave it to you?"

"It doesn't matter. I found it."

He shook his head, still holding the stone close. "Ishvandu. I wish you would tell me. I'm not as ignorant as you think. There are those who were exiled by us, sent into the desert for their crimes, and they are dangerous. I would like to know who you met in the desert."

My heart was pounding. Yl'avah's might, this was a disaster! The one thing E'tuah had entrusted to me, the thing he had told me to keep hidden—and not even a day in Shyandar and it was taken from me.

"Ishvandu." The High Elder's voice softened. "I know you're afraid. Perhaps you think you're going to be punished, but that is not my intention. I just want the truth. If you could only understand the severity of this, of what you've done, speaking with an exile, accepting his gifts, not realizing how dangerous this is, how it was stolen from us—"

"You're lying! He's not an exile! He didn't steal it. E'tuah saved my life, he wouldn't—"

I snapped my mouth shut, heat rushing to my face. *Stupid, stupid, stupid!*

The High Elder's jaw tightened. "*E'tuah?*"

I bit my tongue and looked pointedly away.

He grabbed me. His face loomed close, eyes burning into me. Shock had evaporated into anger and he clutched my arm, trembling, hardly able to speak.

"Ishvandu, who did you see? Who did you see in the desert?"

I said nothing.

He shook me. "Ishvandu, *tell* me what he said to you! What did he say, child? What did he say? Did you follow him into the desert? Did you?"

"I've got nothing to say."

"Yl'avah's might and mercy, you have no idea." The man pulled away, pacing to one end of the room and back. "Whatever he claimed to be, it's a lie. Do you understand? That man was exiled from us as a murderer and a rebel; he should be dead. And he *dares* call himself E'tuah!"

I clenched my teeth. The High Elder was lying. He didn't know anything about E'tuah. How could he? It was just a title after all, not a real name. It could be anyone. He stopped pacing and brought a hand to his forehead. He looked troubled. He looked old.

Then he let out a long, tired sigh. "Oh, Ishvandu. I am sick at heart. I'm sorry, child. I'm so terribly sorry. If I had known . . ." He shook his head. "I wish you would trust me. I don't fault you for this; I don't blame you. You are young, and this has been such a horrible thing. I can't imagine the pain you've experienced. Please, speak to me."

I dropped my eyes. "Everyone left me to die. Everyone, but him."

"I know. I know." The man turned to me again. "Ishvandu, please. What did he say? What has he told you?"

"Nothing. He saved my life. He gave me food and water. The stone was a gift. That's all."

"That's all?"

"Yes, High Elder. When I was better, he sent me back."

The man paused, brows furrowed. "Do you know what it means?" he asked at last.

"What?"

"*E'tuah*. Do you know what the name means?"

"I've heard stories. Tensei E'tuah, who went to battle against the wicked mountain tribes; and Karadys sai'Latia E'tuah, who was the first female Al'kah in Kayr—she brought an end to the first Ytyri Wars; and Braga E'tuah, who wasn't Kyr'amanu but was still honoured for his discovery of the ytyri mines in . . . um . . ." I floundered for the name.

"In Ne'adun?" the High Elder prompted.

"Yes! Ne'adun. And . . ."

"That's enough."

I closed my mouth, trying not to look at the High Elder. Even still,

I could feel the intensity of his gaze. He shook his head. "The name means 'One who is Honoured by the Highest.'"

"Highest what?"

"Highest everything: by the leaders of the people, by the wisest and greatest, by Yl'avah himself and the Tree."

I shrugged, trying to sound unimpressed. "It's just a title."

"And do you know the last time we gave someone such a title?"

I didn't.

"Andari ab'Andala, first Al'kah of Shyandar, who led us out of the Old Lands to the Avanir—the last hope of our people. The last man of Shyandar to speak to the Great Tree herself. The last to see the ruins of Ashianys. The greatest man of our age."

"So what?"

"So," the High Elder looked at me sternly. "Imagine a man, an *exile* who gave *himself* this name."

"Maybe he didn't. Maybe that's what people call him."

"You don't understand." The High Elder leaned forward. "This name is *holy*. It is given—only given. It cannot be taken, for to do so commits the worst of crimes: the pride of demanding what must be freely bestowed. Trust me, Ishvandu. If there were a man who deserved such a name, he would not be in the desert."

I nodded, but the answer was obvious to me. If no one in Shyandar had given him this name, then he wasn't from Shyandar. He wasn't Kyr'amanu; he had said so himself. He was from the Old Lands. I knew it. I also knew sharing such insight with the High Elder would get me nowhere.

"Well, I'm here now," I said. "He sent me back. So that's it."

"Is it?" He eyed me. "Was there nothing he told you to do? To look for? Was there no reason he gave you this stone?"

Ask about the Sumadi. When you know the truth . . .

"Nothing, High Elder. No reason."

"Are you sure?"

"Yes, I'm sure. He saved my life. That's all."

The High Elder let out his breath. He was worried. He didn't trust me, that was obvious. But I thought maybe, maybe he was starting to relent. His shoulders sagged a little. I knew it. I knew he was soft. My father would have beaten me raw for my lies, but now he was dead, and the High Elder didn't do that sort of thing. He couldn't keep me here forever.

Now he was dead.

I frowned. He had come looking for me, my father. He had gone into the desert, risked his own life. For me. It made me wonder—had he cared for me? Had he really? He'd never once said so, not in all my years with him. And yet . . .

I imagined him alone in the desert. Night falling. The shadows. The shadows closing in . . .

I shoved the memories away—quickly—before they got too close, and focused on the High Elder again. He had reached into his robes and pulled out a scroll. It was a small scroll, its edges frayed and bent. "Kulnethar tells me you're quite the jik'u player."

I nodded, relieved to hear him say *anything* that wasn't about the desert.

"Do you enjoy playing?"

"Yes, High Elder."

"I'm glad to hear it. Jik'u is about patterns. About seeing. Just like this: take it."

"Take it?"

"The scroll." He was holding it out, reaching it towards me. "Take it. Tell me what you see."

I swallowed and took the scroll, but I could feel a creeping sense of doubt. "I can't read," I said. "You know that."

"I didn't ask you to read. I want to know what you see."

A trap. Some sort of humiliation. But I pushed open the scroll. Sure enough, the parchment was full of unintelligible lines—hooks and swirls joined together to form what I assumed were words, dotted here and there with seemingly random marks. I shook my head in frustration. "I see lines drawn on a page. That's all."

"Really? You see nothing more?"

"Well, this line repeats here, and here, and that cluster of dots looks like this one, but that doesn't help. I . . . I'm just a Labourer."

"You're a Tasker," he replied. "And you have much to learn. Tell me, Ishvandu, do you know what's written in this scroll?"

My face flushed hot. *I knew it. A dumb trick to humiliate me.* "I can't read it, so I don't know."

"And do you think you know more than a hundred scrolls, more than a thousand?"

"I told you what happened, High Elder. I told you the truth."

"No, you told me some of the truth. By accident. Because you think you know better than me. But I know the patterns." He tapped the scroll. "I've spent my life studying the patterns. I understand you're afraid, but I need you to trust me. I can take from a thousand lifetimes' worth of knowledge, and whatever you're going through, whatever you see in your dreams, whatever is eating at you, deep inside, the doubts you're having, and the uncertainties—I can help."

My dreams. He knew about my dreams.

Ask them . . .

I swallowed. I could feel my heart speeding up, my palms turning slick at the memories. But now was my chance. I had an opening. "What are they?" I asked, breathless.

The High Elder raised a brow. "*They*?"

"The things that attacked me. What *are* they?"

He was silent a long moment. Longer and longer, until I wondered if he'd heard me. We could hear healers tapping through the white corridors. We could hear voices calling out. We could hear students and Taskers gathering for the midday meal below, shouts and laughter trickling up through the window. Finally, the High Elder let out a heavy breath. "They are our curse."

I waited for him to explain. He looked at me, and his eyes softened. "We broke the Pillar of Blood, Ishvandu, the laws of the Seen, because we decided we knew better. Better than the Great Tree. Better than the Laws. Better than Kyrada, our Father. You know the story, and you know what happened."

"Kayr fell."

"Yes. Do you know why?" He was falling into his teacher role, into the kindly man who sat at midday meal and told stories. If I humoured him, I might get something—a real piece of information.

"The Realms broke apart," I said. "The Lifewater was tainted, the source of our power."

"What else?"

"The city was swallowed up. Ashianys was the centre of Kayr, so without it the empire fell apart."

"And what else?"

I frowned. "I . . . I don't know, High Elder."

"Do you know what the Breaking of the Pillar of Blood released?"

I shook my head, though something gnawed at my memories, at my dreams, like a shadow in the corner of my eye.

"The Sumadi," the High Elder said. "They are creatures from between Realms, Bloodless, formed of Spirit and Light, and corrupt beyond anything you could imagine. The Breaking of the Pillar released them, and they drove us from Ashianys. They hunted our people. They *still* hunt us. They hate everything with breath and blood, but us most of all for releasing them into this half-life of agony. They feed on us, the only way they can feel alive—in that instant they possess a mind, before tearing it apart. You should have died, Ishvandu."

"But I didn't." My voice was small. "Why not?"

"That's not an answer I can give. But work *with* me, child, and we can learn it together. We can learn about the dreams that plague you. We can learn how to help you. Will you trust me?"

I nodded.

"Then let's start with this: we have only two forms of protection against the Sumadi. The first is the keshu, the blades of the Guardians. The second is the Avanir. Shyandar belongs to us—but the desert? The desert is theirs. Promise me you won't try to return."

"I won't."

He put a hand on my arm. "And if you remember your dreams, will you tell me about them?"

"I don't remember my dreams."

"But if you do . . ."

"I'll come to you first."

"Good. And in the meantime, I trust you'll keep this between us. You never met anyone in the desert. You never found a stone. Is that clear?"

"Of course, High Elder."

He smiled, and I could see it now. He thought he was winning me over. He actually thought I meant it. *Let him.*

"Does that mean I can go back?"

"Go back?" he looked startled for a moment.

"Back to the fields. Can I go back to the fields? I'm strong again. I can do it. I . . . I would like to do something again." *Yl'avah's might, please!* I held out the scroll.

He paused, but the way he looked at me made me uncomfortable, as if any moment he was going to change his mind, have me locked up in the Guardian's Hall, roped up like Yanava, thrown into the desert. Like he wanted to.

Instead he shook his head and pushed the scroll back towards me.

"Take it, Ishvandu. You will study it, learn the patterns. You will work with Ylata ab'Ytanu, one of our scribes, but you will have to learn fast to make any impression on him."

"Learn fast? Why . . . why would I want to impress a scribe?"

"Because I'm Tasking you to one."

"In the *Temple*?" I could barely believe it. "Me, a *white*-robe?"

He nodded. "It's time you tried your hand at something else, and if you can manage jik'u in a week, then this should be easy."

I nodded, but I heard another meaning behind his words. He wanted me close. He would let me out of the healing rooms, but not much further. Not yet. *Fine.* Let him keep me in the Temple all he wanted, this was my chance. Maybe I wouldn't have to be a Labourer after all. Maybe I could learn something. Maybe . . . I glanced down at the scroll. Maybe the truth E'tuah spoke about would be here.

"Thank you, High Elder," I said. "When can I start?"

Chapter Twenty-Seven

I grunted as Kulnethar poked and prodded my broken leg, interrogating me mercilessly.

"What happened?"

"I fell in a rock slide."

"What were you doing in a rock slide?

"I *fell*."

He poked a little harder.

"Ow!" I hissed.

"You can't tell me what you were doing in the desert, and your Guardians won't talk either. Fine. But unless you want to be crippled the rest of your life, you'll tell me every detail about these injuries. Got it?"

"I fell in a rock slide, and rocks landed on me. What more do you need to know?"

Kulnethar looked at me. "Did you feel the worst pain when you landed on the rocks, or when the rocks landed on you?"

"I got trapped, and a big rock crushed my leg. It hurt."

"How did you get free?"

"I pulled. That hurt too, by the way."

"And did you walk on it?"

"I had to get *out* of the rock slide."

His frown deepened, but he said nothing. He inspected the wound, fingers searching carefully along my bruised and mangled skin, then down towards the ankle. "Can you move your toes?"

I made a weak, wiggling effort, not without wincing, but he seemed satisfied. "Tell me if you can feel this." He pressed against the bottom of my foot.

"Yep."

He moved and pressed again. Then again. He touched the inside of my ankle, and I grimaced.

"Definitely there. Yes."

"Okay." He paused, gathering himself for a final assessment. "The rock broke this bone here," he pointed to the inside of my shin, "and you could have stressed the ankle in the fall, but you damaged a lot of tissue when you pulled free and probably worsened the injury. It'll take weeks before you can put weight on this. Do you understand?"

"I have to go back to the Hall."

"No. You have to stay right here, and not even the Circle can refute me. I'll send a messenger."

I groaned. "Kylan, please don't do this to me."

"Do what? I'm keeping you from active duty and saving your leg."

"You're locking me up in a stupid little white room again. I did that already. It was awful."

"Well, maybe you should stop going into the desert. Besides, this way I'll get to see you every day. Just like old times, right?" He grinned.

"Yl'avah save me."

"It's not so bad. Look, you're lucky I don't have to set the bone, and the splint was actually quite effective. You did well, for a medically illiterate Novice. But I mean it. *No weight*. You're on bed-rest until I say so, or you can imagine yourself counting rations the rest of your life."

"So what am I going to do in the mean time?"

He shrugged. "Jik'u? You're getting pretty dusty, playing those dumb Guardians."

"I'll tell them you said that."

He laughed. "I'll check on you later, Vanya. Drink that—*all* of it; I'll know if you don't. And get some rest. Okay?"

Rest.

If only he knew. If only he knew what plagued me every night—since the desert, since staring down my own death in a pair of sightless black pits. The cold, the grasping hands, the whispers scratching through my mind.

Save us, save us.

I smiled. "No problem." But when I glanced up, he was already gone.

IT WAS six years since I'd stepped foot in the Temple, but it was exactly as I remembered. Plain white walls. Healers bustling up and down the corridors, forcing you to drink nasty-smelling concoctions and yelling at you for doing anything productive. The only difference was instead of old, squint-eyed Ynlaii, it was Kulnethar giving orders.

Chief Acolyte of the healing rooms, he'd risen fast: son of the High Elder, clever, too likeable for his own good, and just as infuriating as ever. He seemed to know everything about every herb and root. He could quote passages from two-hundred-year-old plant catalogues. He could rattle off lists of illnesses, their major and minor symptoms, and every possible remedy—even a few impossible ones. And most importantly, he saved lives. No one quite knew how he did it, but he had single-handedly discovered three new remedies and was in the middle of testing a fourth—something to cure infection, apparently.

"I like him," Tala declared on her third visit. I waited eagerly for each appearance, but not once had she brought up our awkward exchange of kisses, or made any move to repeat the experiment. Her announcement made me twist with jealousy.

"What's there to like? He's a white-robed stuffer."

Tala laughed. "You're just jealous."

"I am not. You think I'd want to be stuck in these cramped rooms my whole life?"

"I'm not talking about being a *healer*, Vanya. He's important. You hate that he's important."

I grunted and focused on stretching my leg, wiggling my toes beneath the wood and rope contraption Kulnethar had lashed around it. She was right, of course. She always was.

Then she leaned forward. "You'll have your shine, too. Don't worry, you big suck."

"And if the Circle decides I messed up? If Koryn talks?"

"I told you already. It won't happen."

"But what if it *does*?"

"Ishvandu, I've got it, okay? Trust me. And when you're a Guardian, you'll get your chance. You'll find the valley, I know you will."

I sighed. I had no choice but to trust her. I was stuck here—here with my dark dreams and my doubts and the crushing sense that something bad was going to happen, and there was nothing I could do about it. Nothing I could say. The Circle was deciding my fate without me.

She tilted her head. "How have you been?"

"How do you think? I'm going mad in this cage."

"The dreams haven't improved, have they?"

I shook my head.

"Are they worse?"

I said nothing.

"Okay. So how much worse?"

I didn't want to talk about it. I didn't want to look. But even thinking about it, I felt a chill steal over me. The room seemed to drift, just a little, and a haze crept around the edges of my vision.

"Vanya?"

I shuddered and snapped my eyes back to her. Her honey-dark skin swam into view, eyes like a Guardian's blade, cutting into me.

"Vanya, how much worse?"

"Last night . . ." I trailed off, wishing I could bury it in my mind, never speak of it again. Being Tasked as a Guardian Novice, working in the Hall, training, collapsing exhausted every night—the horror of the Sumadi had almost faded. Almost.

Now it was back and worse than ever. I couldn't pretend the dreams didn't exist. I couldn't pretend my mind was my own. Not anymore.

"I saw them."

"The shades?"

"The Sumadi," I replied. "Not just the shadows, but . . . but the rest of them. The way they look, when you really see them. Shadow and light. They were all around me. They were trying to speak to me. But all I heard, over and over again, were the same words. *Save us*."

"Like from when you were a boy."

I nodded. Tala was the only one who knew. We had been Novices together, and it was only my second year in the Hall when she'd found me curled in a dark corner, weeping in panic as the memories rode over me. Eventually it had passed, and I'd realized it was Atali sai'Neraia coaxing me back to sanity. I was incapable of resisting her questions: I had been then, and I was now.

"Anything else?"

"Yeah." I closed my hands into fists. "But you can't tell anyone."

"Seriously, Vanya. Have I ever?"

"No. But . . . but this is different. This is . . . bad."

She wrapped a hand over mine, and the touch burned into my skin, curling through every part of me. I imagined leaning forward. I imagined our lips touching.

"You can tell me," she said.

Just then the curtain swished, and one of the healers slipped inside. She had more nasty-smelling stuff for me to swallow and fresh bandages for my leg.

"Now?" I snapped. "Does this have to happen right this moment? We're—"

"Alis!" Tala cried, leaping to her feet.

The healer ducked her head, struggling to hide a smile. "Hi, Tali."

Tala gave a very un-Guardian like squeal and grabbed the other woman in a hug. I stared. I had *never* heard Tala squeal. I had barely even seen her hug someone.

"What are you doing here?" Tala cried.

"I'm a healer now."

"I thought they moved you to the South Fields?"

The girl shrugged. "They decided not to."

"But you're over Age!"

"Kulnethar convinced them to keep me here." She bent her head again, but their eyes met, and something unspoken passed between the two women. Tala grinned, then turned back to me.

"Vanya, you remember Alis, don't you?"

The name was familiar, and I had the sinking feeling this was actually important. "Alis," I said and smiled. "Yeah, of course."

The girl rolled her eyes. "He doesn't remember me. It's okay. He's kind of a jerk."

Tala laughed. "Tell me about it."

"Hey, I'm right here!"

The girl raised an eyebrow. "Oh yeah? Then where did we meet?"

I stared in horror. She had dark skin and dark twisty hair, and eyes just a little too light. There was *definitely* something familiar about her, but Yl'avah's mercy, now was *not* the time to humiliate me. Not in front of Tala. "We met in the Temple?" I tried.

She laughed and started yanking the ropes off my splint, none too gently. "See? He doesn't recognize me. Never did."

Then it clicked. "*You!*" I cried, sitting up with a jerk. With her clean white robes, her hair grown out, and a healthy weight to her, I barely recognized her—but it was the Labourer girl, the one who testified against Malishu and her own brother. "You kicked me!"

"You tackled me and made me ride one of those horrible creatures."

"I was trying to get you to the Temple—and," my voice dropped, "I thought we weren't going to talk about this."

"Uh huh." She yanked the splint off, and I swallowed a yelp of pain.

"What's this about?" Tala looked between us.

"Nothing," I said. "It was nothing."

"You told him to get me to the Temple, remember?" Alis said.

"Yes. And I told him not to let anything happen to you. I remember distinctly."

"He tackled me and almost knocked me out."

"Hey!" I cried. "You ran away. What in the sands was I supposed to do?"

"You made me ride a camel, when I said I wouldn't."

"You were being stupid."

"See?" Alis ripped off my bandage. "A jerk."

I clutched my knee, feeling cornered. Tala crossed her arms. "Did you hurt her?"

"It was an accident," I winced.

"What happened?" she looked at Alis.

The woman shrugged. "He picked me up and flung me over the back of a camel, and I fell off. I thought he was going to do it again, so I ran. Probably not my best decision, but I wasn't thinking straight. He chased after me and drove me into the ground. Knocked the wind right out of me."

"Is this true?" Tala stared at me.

"She makes it sound . . . pretty bad. I didn't mean—"

"Ishvandu ab'Admundi, you unbelievable ass! I trusted you! She was frightened. What in the sands were you thinking?"

"Maybe: *oh no oh no,* don't let your charge run away from you?"

Tala's face crackled with anger. "You *forced* her to ride a camel against her will!"

"She was fainting!"

"Then carry her or something. What's *wrong* with you? Yl'avah's might, you're an idiot. This woman is my friend, you hear? You treat her as such, or you'll answer to me. I hear one thing, *one* thing, about you being anything but kind, and it's over between us."

"Over?" My brows shot up. "What do you mean, *over*? What's over? I didn't even know there was something *to* be over, and—"

"Ishvandu?" She lifted a finger. "Shut up. Sorry, Alis. Glad to hear you're doing well. I'll come see you again, okay?" She glared at me, shook her head, then marched out of the room.

As soon as she was gone, I shot Alis a withering look. "You're an evil woman."

She laughed. "Just getting even."

"I would rather you slip poison in my drink."

"I could arrange that too."

"Wonderful. How much longer am I stuck here?"

"Four weeks." Alis tilted her head. "Five if you're mean to me."

"Has anyone told you how delightful you are?"

She smiled. "As a matter of fact, they have."

THE WEEKS CRAWLED BY. I felt each day. Each day I was absent from the Hall was another opportunity to be forgotten. No one came but Tala, and she was increasingly tight-lipped about what went on there. She didn't ask about my dreams again either. She seemed more and more preoccupied, until . . . she simply stopped coming.

"How much longer?" I asked Kulnethar, beating him for the sixth time out of eleven games of jik'u.

"As long as it takes," he replied. "Now show me those stretches again."

I worked aggressively through every exercise. I pushed until it hurt—though over and over again, Kulnethar threatened me with unending tedium if I pushed too far.

"When it hurts, *stop*."

"But it always hurts."

"You know what I mean. There's a line. Don't cross it, Vanya, or you'll be exiled to the Library the rest of your life."

They would never make me a scribe—not anymore. Not after what I did. But the point was there. Unending tedium.

Eventually, I was up and moving. Alis presided over me with an authority I would never have expected from her. "Four steps," she said, holding my arm. "Good. Stop. How does it feel?"

"Wonderful," I said. "Like pillows and clouds."

"I'm going to let go."

"This should be interesting."

"I want you to stand straight. For a count of ten."

She counted, not watching my legs, but my face. She saw every twitch and grimace, no doubt tallying them to report to Kulnethar. Then she made me sit down again. "You're going to do that every day now, and tomorrow you'll add two more steps. When you can do that without pain, we'll add some simple movements."

Two more steps the next day. And four more the day after. Then ten more. Soon I was hobbling triumphantly around the room and up and down the halls, bending my knees, shifting weight, stretching. I was just starting to balance on the ball of my foot, when a Guardian marched into the room. Not Tala, but some rough and grim sixth kiyah hard-ass. I lost my concentration, and my foot jerked. I crumpled like a sand tower.

Alis threw her arm around me and actually held me up, though it didn't save me from an embarrassing few moments of pain. I clutched at her, grimacing as she lowered me onto the nearby stool.

"I'm here from the Hall," said the Guardian.

"Really?" I snorted. "We couldn't guess."

He shot me a look, then turned to Alis. "The Circle says it's time. Ishvandu ab'Admundi is to report to the Hall tomorrow."

I blinked at the man, taking a moment to hear what he'd just said.

Alis got to it first. "Not until Kulnethar ab'Ethanir says he's cleared. Those are the rules."

"This is an order from the—"

"From the Circle? When it comes to the healing rooms, the Chief Acolyte of this ward has more authority than the Al'kah. Two more weeks." Alis stood to her full height.

"That's not going to happen."

"It *is*. He's not ready. He can barely walk, and he certainly can't ride. You'll just have to go back and tell your Circle it's too soon."

"Alis," I said, "it's okay."

"No." She snapped a finger at me. "It is not."

"But—"

"Two more weeks."

I shut my mouth, but watched, fascinated as she stared the Guardian down. There was a bite in her voice I'd never heard before. A surge of defiance. She lifted a brow, daring the man to say otherwise. His nostrils flared, and he glanced at me, eyes dark. Then astoundingly, he stepped back.

"I'll pass your recommendation on to the Circle."

He left without another word. My stomach flipped. What was wrong? What was going on over there? Why hadn't Tala come back?

Alis was frowning, lips pursed tight as her bandages. But when she gripped my arm, her hand was shaking.

"Thanks," I said, before I even knew I was going to say it.

Her brows shot up. "Are you *thanking* me?"

"You're right. I'm not ready."

"Hold on." She stared at me. "Did I just hear what I thought I heard?"

"What?"

"You told me I was right!"

I shrugged. "Even a busted shovel can dig a hole, given enough time and determination."

"Ishvandu, that was almost something not mean! Keep it up, and maybe one day you'll be half-decent."

THEY GAVE me a cane of hardwood, and pushed me out into the gardens. I walked every day. Sometimes Kulnethar and Alis joined me, though I noticed they paid more attention to each other than to me. Alis's prickly edges softened when he was around. She faltered over her words. She smiled too much. Her voice changed.

I preferred the times I would go alone. I liked walking through the greenery, feeling the cool breeze, smelling the yanis blossoms and the figs ripening in the orchards. When I was tired, I would find a lonely place to sit, *lonely* being the important part. Even after all these years, I was still the desert boy who came back broken. The fact I was a Guardian Novice helped not at all. In a strange and worrisome way, it seemed only to make me more untrustworthy. No one spoke to me. They were uncomfortable around me. They avoided me. For that at least, I was glad. I could sit in the gardens, nursing my leg in solitude.

Until *he* showed up.

One day, near the end of my two weeks, a shadow fell across my chosen hiding place. I glanced towards the intruder, only to see a familiar face, now bearded in white.

"Ishvandu ab'Admundi," said the old man.

"High Elder," I replied stiffly.

Somehow, we had avoided each other these many weeks, but accident or not, our silence was broken.

The man smiled. "I've been looking for you."

"And here I am."

"Indeed."

The High Elder paused, as if making a decision, then shifted his old feet across the path and plunked onto the bench next to me.

I tried not to scowl.

"I see you're as fond of me as ever," he said. His voice was scratchier than I remembered, as if fighting back a cough, but he smiled, and his blue eyes shone with the same vigour.

"What do you want?" I asked.

He nodded towards my leg. "Kulnethar tells me you've been healing quickly."

"As well as I can."

"He says you were caught in a rock slide."

"I was."

"In the desert."

I pursed my lips, taking a deep breath before I spoke. "High Elder, I was a Guardian on duty."

"A Guardian?" He eyed me up and down. "Are you really? Then where is your keshu?"

"You *know* what I mean."

"I do. What you mean is you think you're above your promises now."

"It's not about promises, High Elder. I was given an order. How could I say no? Yl'avah's might, *you* sent me to be a Guardian. Did you think this would never happen? That I'd never be asked to step outside the walls?"

"I didn't send you to be a Guardian. I sent you *to* the Guardians. There is a difference."

I let the words settle in me, even as a horrible, creeping suspicion rose. Could it be? Was it his fault all along? Was *he* the one holding me back? I imagined clandestine words to the Circle, passed through a messenger, maybe even Kulnethar himself: *don't let Ishvandu ab'Admundi take the oath.*

I stiffened, and the High Elder felt it. He sighed deeply in his throat, nodding to himself.

"What's in the desert, Ishvandu?"

"You'll have to ask the Circle."

He smiled again, as if all this were a joke.

"Since I care what happens to you, Ishvandu, and since I care what happens to Shyandar, I would advise you: be cautious. But since I know you won't listen, then hear this too: the Elders and the Circle may not be friends, our duties may be distinct, but we help one another. We both have care of Shyandar, in our own way. So if I judge certain pieces of information to be relevant, information about your *past*, about who you spoke with, for instance—I will share them."

"Your care is noted, High Elder."

"I'm glad."

"It won't stop me from doing what I think is best for Shyandar."

"Best for Shyandar?" His eyes went wide, and he gave a weak, croaking laugh that led into a fit of coughs. He leaned into himself, wheezing until the attack passed. Then he patted my shoulder. "You are wonderfully presumptuous, my child. You think you know what's best for Shyandar?"

I looked away, refusing to rise to his bait. He just shook his head, chuckling to himself. "Do you know why I sent you to the Guardian's Hall, Ishvandu?"

"To control me. You never did have the stomach for discipline."

"That may be. But more importantly, I know what you need."

"Oh yeah? What would that be?"

"An impossible goal."

I laughed. "And becoming a Guardian is impossible, is that it?"

"For you? Most probably. From what I hear, you are both closer to it and further away than ever. But don't give up now!"

"I won't." I rose, deciding I'd had enough. I didn't have to sit here and listen to this. I took two limping steps before his voice called after me.

"Ishvandu?"

I growled, but stopped, gripping my cane with crackling knuckles.

"If you manage that impossible goal, don't forget to visit. I have another for you."

I snorted, turned, and hobbled off. But even as I left, I couldn't help wondering what in the blazing suns the old man was plotting.

Chapter Twenty-Eight

"*Blood is the element of the natural world,*" I read aloud slowly, cramped lines squirming across the parchment. I was six months a scribe. I wore clean white robes. I lived in the Temple, away from the hot sun, in the cool of the gardens and the shaded cliffs.

And I had never felt more trapped.

"*Spirit can be shared, Light can be shared, but Blood cannot, for once given, it is spent, never to be gathered up again. For this reason, it is sacred to Yl'avah, perhaps more so than all elements, Seen or Unseen, since it is Life, which our ancestors were so quick to squander in the Wars of Rending. The unjust spending of Blood is . . .*"

I hesitated over the next word.

"*. . . deplored by Yl'avah.*" I didn't know what that meant, but it didn't sound very good. I hurried on. "*Even if the words of Law had not been passed to us through the Chorah'dyn, now handed down by tradition, still this truth is . . . is evident. Every . . . civilization sprung up since the Rending has guarded Blood . . .*"

I sighed and rubbed my fingers into my eyes. Nothing. When I'd found a scroll about the Three Realms, I thought it would have answers. Something about the Breaking the High Elder had mentioned, something about the Sumadi, something about the dreams that still plagued me, even half a year since the attack.

But it was all the same. Boring, useless.

"Ishvandu?"

I dropped the scroll and turned in one smooth motion, using the back of my foot to slip the scroll into one of the hollowed nooks beneath the shelf.

"Yes?"

Ylta peered down the twisting corridor of the Temple's library. His huge mass of black hair made him seem a half-head taller than his already gangly height.

"What are you up to?" He smiled. He was kind. Stupidly kind. Like how he let even Taskers use his familiar name.

I lifted my rag, brought along for a just such a purpose. "Dusting," I said.

"You know Taskers aren't allowed in the inner writings."

"But I can't read any of this stuff anyway. You keep saying it's too advanced."

He narrowed an eye at me. "You can't fool me with that excuse anymore."

Damn. Showing off last week to that stupid white-robe girl, Jeyna, had been a mistake. It was just so hard to believe they'd been Tasked a year and still couldn't read a basic chronicle without stuttering and stammering like idiots. And they had the guts to call *me* half-wit.

I sighed and followed Ylta back out of the inner writings. This place was starting to grate on me. The problem wasn't reading. The problem was they never let me read anything interesting. Rationing lists, surveys, catalogues, dry historical accounts that all sounded the same: long Kaprash, people dying, short Kaprash, not so many dead, shaking sickness, lots and lots of dead, and back to long Kaprash. Seeing all our calamities laid out in a row like a work-list, it was a wonder any of us survived at all.

"Besides," Ylta scolded me in his entirely unthreatening manner. "You're supposed to be copying the lists I sent you this morning."

"Finished."

"Already?"

I shrugged. "Easy. Can't you give me anything more challenging?" *Like an account of the Sumadi, of survivors, of what happened to their minds.* Sleeping was unpleasant most nights. I was getting better at not screaming my lungs inside out, but the other Taskers still whispered.

"The point isn't to challenge you, Ishvandu. Work needs doing, that's all. But if you really want . . ."

"I do."

We passed into the surrounding alcoves that lined the outer reaches of the Library. Here were the scribing tables, the tools, the hutches full of things to be copied and catalogued and filed carefully away into the bowels of the Library, never to be looked at until the next generation of Taskers.

"Here," Ylta said, stopping at his table. "I was working on it, but I believe it fits your request. Something challenging, was it?"

I glanced at the swirling, hooked symbols on the clay tag. "*A Catalogue of Plants in the Three Hundred and Twentieth Year.*" I groaned. "I meant something interesting!"

"Then you should have said something interesting. Ab'Ethyru wants that copied, laid out in neat rows, like I've started, with all the notes put clearly. You'll have to pay attention to the margins. This one wasn't the neatest writer, so they're all over the place, scratched out, redone, added to. A headache, so if you need help, ask. Alright? Well, go on, get busy."

Maybe not so kind after all. I grumbled, but clutched the scroll and hurried off to my table.

I worked right up to sunfall, determined to finish this sand-blasted section. The tallow dripped lower and lower. My fingers were cramping, my feet were falling asleep where I knelt, and there was a little knot of pain forming in the spot where my back joined my hip.

It was awful work, but I found satisfaction in the scratch of the bone-pen. I traced intricate characters for sound groups, simpler ones to add pitches and accents. Each swirled, bent, and dashed across the parchment, joining one to the other. Even something as dull as the properties and benefits of vilgun weed looked beautiful once you put it into writing.

I finished the section and dropped my pen, carefully sealing the leftover ink to keep it from drying out. Tomorrow I would mix more: another of the joyous duties they gave Taskers. But tonight I was done.

I stood and stretched.

There was almost no one left in the Library. A few older scribes carried trough lanterns as they wandered into the inner writings. One or two leaned over a work. I picked up the scroll Ylta had so graciously given to me and walked back to his table, now abandoned for the night.

Then I paused. He had a new work on his table, wound up on a scroll rod and unfastened. He was notoriously forgetful. I bent over and unfurled one end, just a little. Taskers weren't allowed to read without their master's permission, but Ylta never got upset, not really. After being a Labourer my whole life, digging dirt in the hot sun and getting beaten whenever I crossed my father, it was hard not to take advantage of the young scribe's softness.

I slid it open, eyeing the first few lines. The text was difficult, almost unfamiliar. And very, very old. But peering a little closer, I made out the heading scrawled along the side: *The Chronicles of the Last Age and the Ending of Kayr, set down by Andari ab'Andala, named Al'kah, first of the Age of Exile.* It was numbered 72.

My heart started to beat a little faster. I glanced around. No one was watching. A scribe had just disappeared into the pigeon-holed shelves not too long ago. It would be awhile before he returned, and the others were further away, bent over, focused on their texts, not paying any attention to a lowly Tasker finishing up work for the night. I swallowed and read a little more, whispering the words under my breath in a halting voice:

"Here, I will begin the telling of the first year of Exile, following the ruin of Ashianys and the Breaking of the Pillar of Blood. In truth, though the years of Decline and the Last Age are full of horrors of their own, yet this was the most terrible time imaginable for all who lived. The sun itself seemed to hide its face, and at night our guilt and sorrow took shape, agony itself in the form of a man. Fallen, we called them, for so they were: the Sumadi..."

My lips halted, and I went instantly cold. There was no other option. I slipped the scroll off its winding rods, curled it up, and stuffed it into the front of my robes. A moment later, a foot scuffed the floor behind me. I half-turned, heart pounding in terror. The scribe had returned from the shelves, just stopping now to put out the lantern. He wasn't even looking at me. But as he passed he glanced up and frowned.

"Awfully late for you to be here without your master. Where's Yalata?"

"At the meal. I was just finishing up . . ."

The older man grunted. "Well, go on then. Tidy up and be off. He shouldn't leave you here on your own, that man."

I nodded. I didn't dare look down to check if the scroll was visible. Instead, I turned away. The rod was left, lying out, and with trembling hands I picked it up and put it back on the third cubby above the ground, to the right, where Ylta always left it. He might not even realize the scroll was missing. He was so forgetful. He would think he had put it away for the night, like he was supposed to.

I felt a stab of guilt. If anyone found out it was missing, he would be blamed. Blamed for stealing a scroll. *Just like Yanava.*

But it was too late now. Besides, maybe it *was* meant for me. Ylta knew about the attack—everyone did. As a scribe he would have access to information no one but Elders could read. Maybe he'd left it out on purpose, knowing I would find it.

The scribe was still watching me. I tidied up the parchments and inks and syllabaries, ducked my head, and hurried from the library, trying not to look like a thief. I wouldn't go straight down to the meal. Up first, to our sleeping quarters. I'd stash the scroll there—

"Vanya!" The bright mop of hair was coming down the outer steps of the Temple. "You're late! Ylta giving you extra work again?"

His momentum pulled me along the steps—down to the Commons, instead of up, leaving me no choice but to hurry along beside him.

"Just dusty, boring old scrolls about plants." I went for a tiresome tone of voice, hoping Kulnethar was too preoccupied to hear the taut nerves beneath.

"Plants?" he laughed.

"Yeah. You'd love it. I learned all about something called *vilgun* weed."

"*Vilgun*? How old was this scroll? Ab'Ethyru says vilgun died out years ago."

"Shame. Good for stomach pains."

"We have other stuff for that. Still, it's sad when a plant gets lost. Most were carried over from the Old Lands after the Fall, that's what ab'Ethyru says, and . . ."

My stomach knotted up. *Carried over from the Old Lands after the Fall.* The first year of Exile, that's what the chronicler had called it. The first year of the Sumadi. The scroll was practically burning a hole in my robes.

We stepped into the Commons. A girl with soft, dark waves of hair and big eyes came bounding over when she saw us.

"Amazing!" she laughed. "Kylan, you actually managed to drag him down to come eat with us. Mind you, you're hardly better these days." She pouted at him.

Kulnethar laughed as we strode up to the tables. "What do you mean?"

"You know. Doing important things for your father, and all."

"Oh that. Just some messages to write out. A report for the Hall."

"Well, you're late again. Hey!" She brightened. "Did you hear what Vanya did? Go on, tell him."

I clenched my jaw. "Forget it, Jeyna. Leave it alone."

"I didn't think it was possible. Delys was going on and on like a windbag, like he usually does. Saying how great he is at everything. Then out of nowhere, up jumps Vanya, grabs a scroll and whacks it down in front of him. 'Read it,' he says. Just like that." She giggled at her own impression of me.

"I can hear it like I was there." Kulnethar grinned. "Terrific. What did Delys do?"

"Blustered like an idiot. Couldn't get a word out. Called Vanya all sorts of things and told *him* to read it, if he was so good. So Vanya tells him to a pick a place, any place. Everyone's watching, so Delys does. Then Vanya just lets it out. Never heard him string more than five words together, and here he is, expostulating from *Madalar's Commentaries* like an old poet."

"It's called *reading*," I sighed. "Ever heard of it?"

She giggled and grabbed Kulnethar's arm. "I bet *you* couldn't read that well."

"Oh, no?" his chest puffed up a little. "Bring me any scroll you want, and I'll challenge this little scamp right now."

They laughed. *Girls.* I rolled my eyes. Empty-headed and silly, the lot of them, as far as I could see. And worse, Kulnethar was starting to act very strange whenever one of them wandered our way. Especially Jeyna. She was doing a lot of that lately.

I tried to sneak off, but Kulnethar grabbed my arm. "Hey, wait. Where are you going? Tell us what happened next, Vanya. What'd Delys do when you trounced him?"

"It was nothing," I snapped. "Just silly white-robes talking nonsense."

"Silly white-robes? Hold on there, look who's talking. You're one of us now, Vanya. You can't get away with that anymore. Right?" He laughed and tugged the front of my robe.

I shoved his hand away, a little more forcefully than I meant, then yanked the robe back into place. Had he seen? Had it shown? My heart was thudding again, and my palms started to sweat. Kulnethar was staring at me very strangely, but Jeyna was too focused on him to see anything else. Good thing for that.

"Sorry," I said quickly. "I just . . . I just want to be alone for a bit, okay?" Without waiting for a response, I took my bread and cheese and hurried off down into the gardens. *Please don't follow me . . . please don't . . .*

"Vanya, wait!"

I clenched my teeth and kept walking, hoping to lose myself down one of these paths. Maybe he would take the hint, for once.

"Hey!" He ran up and yanked me to a stop. "Vanya, what's going on?"

"Nothing! I just want to be—"

"What have you got there?"

He pointed. Straight at the hidden scroll. I glanced down and swore under my breath. Something had shifted, and now there was a faint bulge under the collar of my robes.

"Nothing."

"No. I saw it. You've got something there, Vanya. Is that a scroll?"

"Just some reading Ylta wants me to finish before tomorrow."

His brow creased. "That's a lie, Ishvandu. Only Elders can take scrolls out of the Library, you know that."

"Look, it's not your concern."

"It *is* my concern. I *saw*. Vanya, you can't—"

"Then pretend you *didn't* see. I want to be alone, now shove off."

"What is it?"

"I said shove off!"

"Show it to me!"

"No!"

He grabbed for it and I tried to twist out of his reach. But his arms were longer than mine. His fingers dove in, snatching it up before I could stop him.

"Careful, careful!" I cried. "It's old. Don't wreck it!"

"Vanya!" He looked aghast as he opened the old scroll, his touch going soft, cradling it like it was made of dust. He ran a reverent finger down its edge, pulling it back so he could read. Then his face went pale as milk. "Yl'avah save you, you know what this is?"

I clenched my fists. "Why do you think I nabbed it?"

"No. No." He shook his head. "No, you have no idea. Where did you *find* this?"

"Ylta's table."

"You took it from *Yalata*? Do you know how much trouble he'll be in?"

"Then he shouldn't have left it out."

Kulnethar stared at me. "Yl'avah's mercy, Yalata's the nicest guy I know, and you were just going to steal this and let him take the blame? What's *wrong* with you?"

"Oh, don't give me that self-righteous flap! I was going to give it back."

"Damn right, you're going to give it back. Right now."

Anger curled through me, thick and black and bitter. "Having fun being the High Elder's son now?"

He shook his head. "What?"

"All the girls hanging off your arm, all the *important* jobs. And now, what . . . you're going to snitch on me, because you know better and you want to look good. Not letting anyone get away with breaking the rules. Not you."

"Vanya, what are you talking about? This isn't about *me*. This is . . . Yl'avah save me, I shouldn't even be holding this right now. I can't believe they let Yalata read it. This is . . . this is . . ." He shook his head, glancing around the twilit gardens to see if anyone was close. The paths were empty. "You found ab'Andala's Chronicles! This is one of our most important texts. Only Elders should be looking at it."

"Why?" I cried, throwing my hands into the air. "Aren't we allowed to know things too? This was written for *us*. For all of us. Not for a handful of stuffy old useless men to hoard up in their holes."

"Of course it's not just for them. Why do you think Elders teach every day? Where do you think the stories come from?"

"*Their* version of the stories. Kylan, this is the real thing!"

"It's *all* the real thing."

"Well, if it's all real, it's all the same. So why can't I read it?"

"Because the Elders know what to teach and how to teach it. Sands, Vanya, what's this about?"

I was shaking. To my horror, I realized tears were burning out of my eyes. "It's got answers. No one will tell me anything, so I've got to learn what I can for myself. Do you have any idea what it's like? Even after all this time? I can't sleep, Kylan! I can't . . ." I stopped. My teeth clenched as the memories pressed back into me, most too scattered to make sense, but there, always there. Pain and blood and screaming. Screaming without end. *Tell them, tell them . . .* Like souls being ripped in two. And blood in the water, and blood on my hands, and blood dripping, dripping from my eyes.

Kulnethar softened, blue eyes crinkling in worry. "I know. They talk about you. I'm sorry, Vanya. I know it's rotten. But there's better ways than stealing. Nothing good will come of it. Sands, you're a Tasker still, so at worst you'll get a whipping. But in two Renewings?" His eyes creased, and I knew he was thinking about Yanava. *The ropes.*

My lips twisted. "Just another beating, so what's that? Go ahead and report me."

"Come on, Vanya. Is that what you think of me? Besides, Yalata would get in more trouble than you, and that's not fair. No, we're going to go up to the Library together and put it back on Yalata's table, and it's done."

"What if I refuse?"

"You won't," he said flatly.

"Why not?"

"Because right now I'm being your friend, Vanya. But if you insist on being an idiot, I'll do what a proper Acolyte should."

"Oh, go get something rammed up your ass."

His jaw hardened. "Vanya, stop this."

"Why? You want to be a sand-blasted proper white-robe, go ahead."

He glared at me for a moment, then grabbed the collar of my robe. I was ready. I shifted and clutched his arm, lunging right back at him. Straight for the scroll.

"Vanya, stop it!" He twisted away.

"Give it back!"

"Stop it!"

I grappled him. He couldn't hold the scroll and fight me at the same time. I stuck my feet behind his. I snatched again. My fingers brushed the parchment, just as he yanked backwards.

He fell. I slammed him into the ground, knee digging into his stomach. I grabbed for the scroll. "No!" he shouted, twisting, throwing an elbow up. I grabbed again. I wasn't thinking anymore. He caught me in the chin, but I hit back. He grunted. I snatched for it.

"No, no, no!"

My fingers closed over it. I pulled. Kulnethar pulled back.

The old parchment shredded. The outside layers tore free, bits of it crumbling away. A swath came off in my grip. We both stared in horror. Neither of us moved.

"Yl'avah's blasted might, Kylan. Look what you did!" My voice was hoarse. "I was going to put it back. What am I supposed to now? *What*? You ruined it!" I slammed the flat of my hand into his chest, shoving him into the ground.

He didn't say anything. But an arm travelled up to his mouth as if he couldn't believe what was he was seeing.

I grabbed what was left out of his limp grasp and leapt to my feet. Turned to go.

I almost ran into Elder Melanyr ab'Kulatyn. The elegant, dark-haired man stared at me, glanced at Kulnethar, then narrowed his eyes at the ruined scroll in my hands.

"What is this?"

Standing there, holding the pieces of the scroll like shattered remnants of an old relic, I couldn't think of a single thing to say.

Then Kulnethar was beside me. "Elder ab'Kulatyn, I'm so sorry!" he cried. "I shouldn't have taken it out of the library."

I turned to stare at him.

"I know the rules," he hurried on. "It's just some old plant catalogue. I wanted to bring it out and compare the descriptions with the real thing, but Ishvandu found it and said I should have left it in the library. There was an accident. We both grabbed it and it's so old, it just started falling apart. I'm so sorry, ab'Kulatyn. I'll copy up another one right away. First thing tomorrow."

He stopped, breathless. I could see he was terrified. The Elder would think he was heartbroken about the scroll. But I knew how much he hated lying. He'd be in as much trouble as me, if not more. I clutched it tighter. No one was prying that thing out of my hands now.

The Elder frowned, stone-faced. "Kulnethar ab'Ethanir," he said. "Do you think your parentage makes you above our laws?"

"No, of course not, Elder." He dropped his head.

"Or exempt from consequence?"

"No, Elder."

The man hovered, frowning, though I caught a hint of satisfaction in his eyes, pleased to catch Kulnethar at something wrong. *That,* I could understand.

"I expect you to follow the same rules in this Temple, and show the same care to our possessions as anyone else. Do you understand?"

"Perfectly, Elder. It won't happen again."

The man grunted. "You will repair this at once—tonight, not tomorrow. And I'll be speaking to your father about this."

Kulnethar nodded, but I could see a tight line in his jaw. I held my breath. Then the Elder gave us one more withering look and moved on.

"Sands," I whispered when we were alone again. "I can't *believe* that actually worked."

"Give it to me," Kulnethar said. I stared at him. He was trembling, but not from fear any more. He was furious.

I hesitated, then found myself holding open my hands. He grabbed the pieces one at a time, breathing deliberately, not saying anything as if afraid of what would come out.

"Find Yalata," he finally said. "Bring him to the Library. Now."

"But we can't tell him. I'll get in trouble."

"*Idiot*," he spat as he turned away. "*Stupid, stupid, stupid blasted idiot!*"

"I didn't ask you to lie for me."

"I wasn't talking about you, alright?"

"Then—?"

"*Myself!* For actually taking pity on your stupid face. Now I can't fix this. I need Yalata. He's a scribe. He'll know what to do. You find him, you tell him everything that happened, and you meet me at his table *now*."

He marched off without waiting for me to respond, and I was left standing in the dark, realizing that my single burst of hope had just been snatched away.

***

THE WORST THING about that night wasn't what happened. And it wasn't Ylta's anger. It was the silence. When he found out, he hardly said anything. His cheery face turned sad. He went with me up to the Library, thanked Kulnethar for his intervention, lit a tallow, and started to work.

He made me sit with him while he shifted through the pieces, copying everything with slow, deliberate strokes. I didn't get to see a shred of it. I didn't even get to work on the stupid plants catalogue. I just watched. And there was silence.

Once I almost dozed off. He simply knocked his hand on the table, a quick *rat-tat*, and I jerked up. I caught his disapproving eye and kept watching.

He stopped a little before dawn.

"Get some sleep, Ishvandu," he said quietly. "Tomorrow night, you'll stay up with me again. And every night until I finish it."

And that was it.

I stood, my back and knees aching from being in the same position all night. I looked at him, hesitated, not sure what to say.

He was about to stand, then seemed to change his mind. "Do you know what it says? About the Sumadi?"

I swallowed, but I could feel my heart thump a little quicker. "No."

"That's why you took it. Because you wanted to know about the Sumadi."

I nodded.

"You could have *asked*, Ishvandu."

I said nothing.

"You could have, but you never once thought of it." He sighed. "I was going to tell you. After I read it. But I'm afraid it's not much help to you. The Sumadi slaughtered thousands upon thousands before some Guardians discovered the keshu, rallied the Kyr'amanu and fought back. There is nothing about someone surviving an attack."

"Then . . . you were able to save it? It's still readable?"

"Parts of it."

"Parts?"

He sighed. "Yes, Ishvandu. And some parts are irretrievably lost."

Lost. Such a little word for something with such enduring consequences. "Ylta." My voice was small in the huge, dark room. "I'm sorry."

He shook his head. "I don't think you are. I'll have to talk to the High Elder about this."

"What?" The fear returned, heart hammering again. "But . . ."

"He'll keep it quiet, I think. But something will have to be done. I don't think I can trust you anymore."

"But . . . but . . . but it was just a stupid scroll. I was going to bring it back. I was . . ."

"See? You don't get it, what you just did. You don't see it as wrong. Reading the scroll isn't the problem. *Destroying* the scroll isn't even the problem. You disobeyed, Vanya. And you did it deliberately. You knew the rules, and you decided you didn't care. You didn't even *try* to find another solution. Yl'avah's might, you could have just *asked*."

"What are you saying, Ylta?"

"I'm saying I don't think I can be your teacher anymore. I don't think this is the right place for you. I'm sorry, Ishvandu."

"You mean . . . you mean they'll send me back to the fields?" I could hardly get the words out. It was all slipping away, all so suddenly. "Back to being a . . . a Labourer."

"I don't know. That isn't for me to say."

"Ylta . . ." I was finding it difficult to breathe. "You can't . . . you can't tell him. Please, don't tell him. I'm sorry. I'm really sorry. I *am*."

"*Now* you are." He stood up. "Me too, Ishvandu. Get some rest."

I WENT BACK to the sleeping quarters, but I didn't sleep. I was afraid—afraid of so many things.

For a while, it felt like I'd been in control of that fear, in control of my own fate. Learning how to read and write. Finding the scrolls. Getting answers. The answers E'tuah had told me to find.

Now it was all gone. Back to being a Labourer. *Back to my father*, I almost thought. Then I remembered: my father was dead.

I swallowed, and for some reason, the thought brought on a fresh wave of loneliness. My father would not have been happy to see me. He would've thought less of me than ever. But at least he would've taken me back. It would have been something familiar—almost something safe.

I took a deep, shaking breath, surprised to find tears in my eyes. Stupid. What was my father to me?

But he had died—because of me. He had tried to find me, and he had been killed by those monsters, and it was my fault. Mine.

I growled and scrubbed my eyes. This was pointless. He was gone, and that was it. So maybe they would Task me to someone else. Maybe someone better to work for, or maybe worse. It didn't matter. I'd been given another chance, and I failed. All because of a stupid scroll.

I scowled. If only Kulnethar hadn't gotten involved. At least he had lied for me. He had tried to protect me. He was my friend, I *knew* he was, even when he was a self-righteous white-robe twat.

Still, I wanted to be furious, to rail at him, to scream myself sick at the injustice of it, but I couldn't. All my anger had shrivelled up into a coldness at the pit of my stomach. I was afraid: afraid of dreaming, of sleeping, of shadows and cold, of my father's memory, of failing, of the desert, of never going back to the desert, of never being anything of any importance.

What now. What *now*?

I took a black stone out of my jik'u sack and rolled it between my hands, back and forth, back and forth, as if holding it would help me think. What to do next?

Dawn light slipped over the high window, brightening the room I shared with five other boys. They all got up, bleary-eyed, sending me strange looks.

"Where *were* you last night, Vanya?" the oldest asked. Jetti.

I didn't respond, just stared at the stone, the possibilities turning in my head as I turned the stone with my fingers.

"Maybe he's finally cracked," said Delys. The one I humiliated the other day.

Bemyn's nasally voice pitched in. "No, he did that a long time ago. Can't blame him. Wouldn't like getting bits of *my* mind eaten by desert ghosts."

They laughed at me, kept taunting me as they tidied up their beds and got dressed. But I could care less this morning. Like squawking chickens.

Jetti slapped my knee as he walked past. "Coming, Vanya?"

"Oh, just leave him," said the annoying one. "If he hasn't moved when we get back, we'll plant him in the garden and see if he grows."

The others left for the morning meal, snickering, but Jetti hesitated. "Hey," he said after a moment. "Vanya. Everything okay? You look . . . well, you don't look very well. You sick?"

Maybe I was. Maybe this new, dangerous idea was just another stage of madness. Maybe they were right. Or maybe . . .

"Hey, whatever." The boy shrugged. "Be a half-wit if you want. Don't say I didn't try." He hurried after the others.

Ylta was probably right. I was good at reading and writing. Better than most here. But it wasn't the place for me. I didn't belong with these white-robes, living in the Temple, copying out plant catalogues and chronicles, learning prayers. And going back to the fields was unthinkable.

Apparently, then, I had made up my mind. Ylta wanted me to sit up again with him tonight while he copied out that scroll. Fine. I would humour him. I would be a model student. But when it was finished, I wasn't going back to bed. I had another idea. A better one. A thrilling, impossible, foolish idea.

I was going to speak with E'tuah.

Chapter Twenty-Nine

The night was black, the moon a bare sliver against the stars, the wind so still, even from the highest tier of the Temple, my white robes hung limp past my ankles. The smallest sound would be heard on a night like this, and so I crouched, hardly daring to breathe, outside the curtained entrance of the High Elder's chambers, my fingers poised to part the beaded threads.

Even now I could change my mind and slink back to my room, defeated, but a new sense of purpose propelled me. I should have done this months ago. I had been lulled into inaction, won over by the High Elder's promise of learning. But I didn't belong here. I saw it more and more every day. What was I doing? What was the point? Only one person understood me, had trusted me with something real. And the High Elder had stolen that from me while I slept. Why should I give him the trust he demanded? No. It was E'tuah I wanted to speak with. His vision that burned in my mind. The desert. *Beyond* the desert. The Old Lands and all the greatness of the Kyr'amanu.

But I was afraid. If the High Elder caught me sneaking into his chambers in the dead of night, there would be consequences. Of course, there were already consequences. What could he do to me, worse than making me a Labourer?

I suppose if I messed this up, I would just have to find out. Taking a deep breath, I parted the curtain, peering into the empty darkness. The chamber was spacious, its furnishings sparse, yet a gentle glow emanated from one of the rooms to the side where the High Elder slept. I frowned. It was the dead of night, too late to be up still, too early for an eager rising—why the candle? They were too precious to be kept on through the night, even for the High Elder. Perhaps it was left by accident. But that seemed like wishful thinking. *Go back*, a voice urged. I ignored it.

I moved forward, parting the curtain as gently as I could. The beads clinked softly, and once on the other side, I held my breath, waiting to see if anyone heard. Silence fell. Nothing. I crept forward. My bare feet made no sound. There was only the thudding of my heart, distractingly loud. Soon I came to the first room, the one with the light. I paused outside the curtain, tilted my head, straining to hear the slightest sound. Again, there was nothing. Not even the heavy breathing of sleep.

Holding my breath in case he was awake on the other side, I put my eye to the curtain, peering between two woven strands. There was a candle-bowl set on the low table, its flame licking up the bottom-most tallow, poised to go out. Yet the room was empty. Hoping to get a better look and feeling a burst of courage, I slipped into the small inner chamber. There was a sleeping pad laid out in one corner, but no one occupied it. Only a few other items decorated the room: a basin for washing, with a clean, soft cloth, a single wall pigeonholed and stuffed with scrolls, a carved wooden chest.

What drew my eye, though, was a tapestry hanging at the far end of the room, bright and colourful, threads dancing across the pattern, forming a tree with roots twisting along the edges, dripping into a deep, dark pool. The pool! The Lifewater! Something clutched inside of me, a stirring, a memory. My heart leapt in terror—

No. I tore my eyes away and started to search. I ran my hand beneath the pallet, under the pillow. I checked among the scrolls, slipping a few out and searching behind. I cracked open the chest, heart pounding. It creaked, and I stopped, waiting. Yl'avah's might, if anyone found me now, I'd be roped up for sure. But nothing. I opened it the rest of the way. There were robes inside, and belts, and a few dusty rugs. Did the High Elder have *anything* of value? I clenched my jaw. I would have to take the candle and search in the other room, and just pray I wasn't caught. He might return at any moment. In fact . . . where *was* the High Elder?

I glanced up. The tapestry was moving. My heart leapt into my throat, and I quickly slammed the lid of the chest, faster and louder than I meant, scrambling to my feet.

Nothing happened. The tapestry moved again. A flutter at the corner. Like it was stirred by a breath of wind. *Time to leave,* a voice insisted. I had tempted fate long enough. And yet why a breeze? I heard it this time, like a sigh, and the tapestry lifted. Just a corner. Enough to reveal blackness behind.

My heart skipped a beat. There was something behind that tapestry. A hidden room. And if the High Elder were hiding a tool of the ancients, that's exactly where it would be.

I walked towards it, not daring to let myself think. I wasn't supposed to be here, and I certainly wasn't supposed to know what lay behind that tapestry. And yet . . . wasn't that what E'tuah had told me to do? Keep my eyes open. Look for answers. Learn the truth. If I wanted to do that, I had to start taking risks.

Compelled forward, I pushed aside the intricate tapestry and found myself staring up a dark, spiralling stair. There was another level, one even higher than these chambers! Definitely forbidden. If I took another step, nothing would excuse me.

I started to climb. I went carefully, quietly, and a faint light began to glow. Moonlight. I was climbing to the very roof of the Temple. I came to the last turn. I peered around it. My breath caught.

I was staring at a chamber with walls that leaned, curving until they met three slender, white columns, an arch connecting each in a circle. In the centre, the roof was open to the sky, and its height was littered with the distant stars.

It was empty. Almost. At the very centre of the wide, open chamber, there was a simple wooden bowl, lifted on a pedestal, and a man stood before it—the High Elder, Ethanir ab'Estaldir himself.

He was facing me, but his head was bent, his dark hair hanging down on either side of his face as he gripped the sides of the pedestal. His whole body leaned forward, drawn towards the basin as if weighed down. A small lamp sat at his feet and gave off a faint, flickering light.

I stood transfixed. I knew I should go. At once. Any moment, he could lift his head and see me. And yet, I couldn't will my feet back down the stairs, entranced by what I was seeing. There was something happening here. Something that made my skin prickle and my head pound, driving out thoughts of the Sending stone.

Then a queasiness lurched in my gut. The room spun. I gasped, almost falling over. I took a stumbling step backwards, one hand pressed to the wall. Something was building, coming from the centre of the room, reaching towards me. Something powerful. I couldn't see it, but it was looming in my mind, clouding my thoughts, drawing me in. I opened my mouth to scream.

Then with a snap, it was gone. I stood, breathing hard, head pounding, leaning against the wall of the stairwell as my legs shook beneath me. Yl'avah's might, what *was* that?

"Do you know, Ishvandu ab'Admundi, what this place is?"

The High Elder's voice carried across the chamber, sounding heavy, thick.

I swore and squeezed my eyes shut. Maybe if I snuck away, back down the stairs . . .

"Don't think of hiding, child. I know it's you."

Damn. I took a deep, steadying breath. Better just to face it. I stepped onto the floor of the chamber, stood as tall as I could, and met his eye. Even from this distance I could see the weariness clinging to him, the sudden age of his face. Was it possible for someone to grow old in a day?

"You said I could come to you if I remembered."

"I said that." He nodded and stepped down, away from the pedestal. "But we both know what you were hoping to find. Not me, I think."

My hands tightened into fists. "You took it from me."

"I took nothing that was yours to keep. I'm sorry you think otherwise, Ishvandu, but you must know. Such things are forbidden." He stepped towards me, hands folded together in front of him. "They are relics of another age, and in coming here, we chose to leave our follies behind. The Sending stones are just one of many. Things born of arrogance, of daring to think the Realms were ours to toy with. Even if I didn't know this E'tuah, he gave you a dangerous thing, and that is evidence enough of his intentions."

"Dangerous or not, it's our inheritance."

The High Elder's lips pursed, a frown creasing his brow. "Is that what he told you? He's wrong. Our rightful inheritance is *death*. We should not be alive to see this haven in Shyandar, but we are here because we were called here. Now stop this foolishness."

"You say it's forbidden, but what's *that*?" I threw a finger towards the bowl at the centre of the chamber. "It did something, and I know what it felt like." *It felt like . . . the Sumadi . . .*

The High Elder was hiding something. I moved past him, taking firm, defiant steps. My sandals slapped across the stone. I was nearly there. I could see the liquid contents of the bowl, glittering beneath the stars.

"Stop!" The High Elder's voice lashed out, commanding and powerful. I had never heard that tone from him before. My feet halted. I could feel my breath escape, like it was punched from my lungs.

"Shameful, that I should have to speak it aloud, but your presence here is utterly forbidden. And since you seem unable to grasp the enormity of your actions, I will make them painfully clear. You have stolen and destroyed an invaluable scroll that wasn't even yours to look at. You have heeded the words of an exile above your own people. You have accepted his gift, a forbidden device of the ancients, and trespassed upon the chambers of the High Elder to recover it, and now . . . *now* you think to desecrate this sacred place and look on things not meant for your eyes! The only thing keeping you from standing before the Circle is a meagre year of age, but if you take one more step, Yl'avah so help me, you shall forfeit your life. Do you understand me, Ishvandu ab'Admundi?"

My face was burning, my back still turned to him.

"Look at me!" he said.

I had no choice. I turned. I was trembling. He meant it. Every word. And if I didn't do exactly as he said, I was going to be executed. I couldn't breathe I was so terrified. And yet at the same time, I felt a heady rush of defiance.

I looked straight at him, glaring at him. Any moment I was going to say something foolish.

"Impossible child! Everyone in this Temple knows their place. Everyone except you. Now I have been exceedingly gracious with you because of your suffering, but you have dismissed me and disdained my compassion. So be it. From now on, you will show me the respect due my station, you will honour our laws, and you will make no further attempt to contact this man from the desert, or the repercussions will be of the utmost severity. Have I made myself clear?"

Anger burned in me, fierce but helpless, threatening to choke me it was so potent. But he was right. I should apologize. I should be desperate to regain his trust, to minimize whatever punishment I would face. And yet standing there, nostrils flared and chest heaving with the angry thud of my heart, I knew if I opened my mouth nothing of the humble sort would come out.

Instead, I glared at him for a few more heartbeats, then turned and fled into the dark stairwell, not stopping until I had passed through the High Elder's chambers, out into the open air again, and down to the level of my room.

"Look who's slept in again!" Jetti's voice cut through the blanket over my head. The five Taskers were up, hovering around me. One of them poked me with his toe.

"Are you dead, Vanya?" That awful, whining voice. Bemyn.

"Sands, I've heard he's been up every night for a week," Jetti said. "I've heard he's in big trouble with Ylta. The scribe's got him locked away in the Library, doing who knows what."

Bemyn sniggered, then gave a yelp of pain.

"Not like *that*, you dunce."

"Then what? What's he up to?" asked Delys. "Come on, Vanya. We know you're not asleep. Come on, tell us."

"Go away." My voice was muffled by the pillow.

"Oh, leave him alone," said Jetti. "Come on, we're going to be late for the morning meal."

The boys chattered amongst themselves, but at least they were retreating, and soon the room was empty again. I didn't move. I was starving, but going down and facing a whole Commons full of buzzing voices and darting eyes was unthinkable. Besides, I was exhausted. I hadn't slept properly in days.

I lay there for a long time, occasionally hearing Taskers or Acolytes down the hall, voices drifting up from below. The sun lifted higher and started to warm the little room. I wasn't sure what I was waiting for. *My sentence*, I thought. Why move at all, until someone told me what would become of me?

The wait was over sooner than I thought. I heard a noise at the entrance, a familiar voice.

"Ishvandu?"

Ylta. I didn't move. I had hoped to be sent from the Temple without having to say goodbye to him, but apparently it wasn't going to be so easy.

"Ishvandu," he said again. He came into the room and knelt next to me. He shook me, but gently.

I pulled away and sat up, blinking in the sudden, sharp light, unwilling to meet his eye.

"Ishvandu, it's time to gather your things. The High Elder wants you gone today." I risked a quick glance at him. Ylta's frowning, uncertain face gave me a bad feeling.

"What? Just tell me, Ylta. What?"

He shook his head. "Come on. You'll see. Grab your things, say your goodbyes, then meet me at the Temple steps, as soon as possible, okay?"

He got up and left, and I was alone again, staring after him and wondering what under the blasting sun was to be my fate. Of course, there was only one way to find out. I snatched up my sack of jik'u stones and ran after Ylta.

He raised an eyebrow when he saw me hurrying down the steps.

"I'm ready," I said.

"Don't you have anyone to say goodbye to?"

"I've got nothing to say to any of them." *Except Kulnethar.* But how could I face him now?

He looked dubious, then just shook his head. "Alright. Come on, then."

Soon we were headed out of the Temple, across the open ground, making for the Labourers' huts. I wondered who I'd be Tasked to this time. I had nobody. No family left, no friends. The sense of sprawling freedom was gone. Instead, Ylta's back was turned in disappointment, the High Elder had threatened me, and my only means of contacting E'tuah had been snatched away. Even Kulnethar was . . . well, he was an Acolyte. He was his father's son. I felt something big and gaping open up—it might have been loneliness.

Then I realized we weren't going to the North Fields.

Ylta was leading me just north of the outbuildings, skirting around the chicken hutch and the storage houses and the goat stable. We walked for a long time, until it was probably midday. Until we passed the Craftsquarter to the south and saw the walls of the Guardian's Hall rise up, stark and lonely on the open hard-pan of western Shyandar.

I stared at it.

"Ylta. Are we going . . . there?"

He nodded, frowning.

"But why?" My mind filled with the High Elder's threats, and suddenly I wondered if he had changed his mind. Maybe I was going to face the Circle anyhow, and *they* would decide my fate. The thought was terrifying. "Am I in trouble?"

Ylta gave an incredulous laugh. "Ishvandu, you are in so much trouble, the High Elder doesn't even know what to do with you."

"So . . . what does that mean?" I felt breathless. My arms and legs tightened, as if ready to run. But that was silly. Where would I go?

The scribe gave a snort. "It means you get to be someone else's problem, as far as I can see it. Come on. Keep up."

I swallowed and hurried after him. His legs were a lot longer than mine, and he wasn't going slowly for me. Soon we were near the front gates. They looked different than usual. But of course—it wasn't quarter month, when everyone lined up for rations. The grounds were eerily empty. Only two Guardians stood at the front gate, looking out, watching. One of them saw us, and he turned and disappeared inside.

By the time we approached, the man had returned. With him was a red-cloaked Guardian Lord, the same man I had seen before, his keshu as bright and deadly as ever. He looked even more intimidating, surrounded by the dusty red entrance to his Hall. He strode out to meet us. With one hand on his keshu, he gave a nod to Ylta, then turned dark eyes on me.

"Ishvandu ab'Admundi." The words rumbled out. "Welcome to the Guardian's Hall. Tushani ab'Turana will show you to the Novice's quarter and answer any of your questions."

I stared at him. "What? But . . . but you mean . . . ?"

"*Sal'ah*. The proper term of respect for a Guardian of higher standing, and whenever possible, you will speak when you are invited, and not before." He paused, frowning at me. "Do not make me regret this decision. Understood? Now move, boy."

I blinked and spotted another Guardian behind him. An older man with a grim face and a balding head. His grey hair still made a few short braids, tied at his neck, but the effect was just as impressive as the Guardian Lord's black mass of hair.

I decided to nod, even though I wasn't sure I understood. It couldn't be what I was thinking . . . could it? I glanced back at Ylta. The man nodded. Then I found myself following the older Guardian, past the outer walls and the sentries, past where I had never even seen before.

"The other Taskers are still at the midday meal, but they will return shortly," the Guardian was saying. "Until then, I will show you where you will sleep, and where you will report for duty every morning and afternoon. Most importantly, you must remember to conduct yourself at all times with the sobriety appropriate to one of this Hall."

I nodded, but when he turned a stern eye to me I stammered a reply. "Y-yes . . . sal'ah."

"Good," he said. "This way."

I could hardly believe what was happening, but with those words, I realized it was true. I wasn't facing trial. In fact, for some inexplicable reason, against all sense, beyond my wildest hopes, I was being Tasked as a Guardian.

Chapter Thirty

The white Temple walls glowed silver in the moonlight. I woke. My leg was aching from the fall in the rockslide, but that wasn't what drew me out of sleep. It was something else. It was *them*. The shadows in the room.

I felt them against my mind, like a dead patch, cold and stiff. They were hovering. I shivered and sat up.

"Go away," I said to the darkness. "You're not here."

The shadows quivered.

I closed my eyes, and I could see them. There were two in the room, outlined faintly against the back of my eyelids. They rippled, shadow upon shadow, but when I looked again, I saw nothing.

I was going mad. Since the desert, I imagined them everywhere. Out of the corner of my eyes. Behind my eyes. In my dreams. Night after night, the sightless pits gazed into me, speaking to me: *see us, save us, look, Vanya. Look.* And all the while, the dreams pressed close —the memories that were not my memories.

I threw off my blankets and stood. Something had happened in the desert. They had seen me, touched me, looked *into* me. I had faced them and survived—for the second time. Not once, but twice! In a strange way, it was like I *had* died, taking my fear with me. At least the visceral part.

The clinging horror. The panic. Now I saw them in my mind, and the fear had changed. It was like they were there, *really* there—but not. Like they were watching. Like they were *in* me. Like I could never escape them.

It was all in my mind. The Avanir flowed freely, still several months from Kaprash. That the Sumadi could be here *now* was impossible.

Either way, I needed to get out of this room. It was tightening around me, strangling me. Yl'avah's might, how much longer would Kulnethar keep me here?

I stumbled into the hall. It was dark, and my cane made *tap-tapping* sounds that echoed, unnaturally loud in the dead of night. The taps seemed to circle around me and come back, to follow after, to sound just a moment too late.

I glanced over my shoulder.

The hall was empty, of course. I snorted and cursed my own fear. That was over. That was past. There were no living shadows in the dark. It was impossible.

See us.

I ground to a halt. I stared forward, behind, looking. My pulse quickened. This was new. Was I sleeping still? Was I dreaming? I shifted my weight, feeling the ache in my leg, and the coldness of the stone under my bare feet, and the familiar smoothness of the cane where my grip tightened.

"You're not here," I said. "You can't be here."

Why not?

My heart leapt into my throat. It was a whisper. The quietest sliver of sound.

"No." I shook my head. "No, no. It's impossible. You can't be here. You can't be here."

My voice pitched louder. I turned and walked quickly, limping towards the edge of the hall, towards the garden, towards—

Where are you going, Vanya?

See us, Vanya.

Look, look . . .

I refused to look. I fixed my eyes onto the white stone floor, going almost at a run. I turned the corner.

I burst into a figure hurrying towards me. She gave a cry of alarm, and I shouted, staggering back, stumbling.

"Vanya!" Alis shot out her hand, seizing me before I could lose my balance. "Vanya, what's wrong?"

"What are you doing here?" I snapped.

"I'm a healer."

"But it's the middle of the night!"

"A healer still has duties, you know. I heard someone moving around. Light and all, what are *you* doing up? You should be—"

"Shh," I clamped a hand over her mouth.

She shoved me away. "Don't *shush* me, you ingrate!"

"Alis, *quiet!*"

"I said don't—"

"Look out!" I pushed her into the wall, holding her, just as the shadow flickered past, brushing over us, slipping from one spot of nothingness into another. It streaked through my mind, cold, so cold . . . and was gone.

"What in the blasted sands is *wrong* with you?" Alis slammed her hands into me, pushing with all her strength. On instinct, I planted my leg—my injured one. It twisted, and though I tried to save myself, hopping, arms wheeling, my balance gave, and I dropped with a crash.

This time, Alis made no move to stop me.

"Light and all!" I cried. "Didn't you see it? Didn't you—"

"See what, Ishvandu?"

I swore and clutched my eyes. They were pounding, pounding. Shapes bulged behind my gaze.

"It's there. Your right. On your *right*, Alis."

The starlight flickered. I saw its face. Its empty, sightless eyes. It stood, watching, hovering.

She turned. She look directly at it. I held my breath, waiting for it to lunge, to reach for her, waiting, helpless to stop—

It snapped back into nothing.

"What are you talking about, Vanya?"

My breath came out in a groan. "Yl'avah's bloody might. I don't believe it. I don't believe it. It can't be. It can't, it can't . . ."

Alis folded her arms, glaring down at me. "Is this a trick, Vanya? Because if it's a trick, it is *not* in good taste."

"I don't know." I shook my head. "It was there. I saw it. It was right there!"

She swore and crouched next to me, throwing a hand over my brow.

"You're burning," she said.

I laughed. "I'm crazy, that's it. I'm just crazy. I'm seeing things. Sand-blasted shades, everywhere, everywhere."

"Ishvandu, hush. Let's get you back to your room, and . . ."

I shook my head. "No!"

"You're not well."

"I can't go back there."

"You have to—"

"I *won't!*" my voice boomed through the corridors, echoed, quivered, and fell silent. I groaned, sagging into the floor. "I'm fine, Alis. I'm fine. I just need the open air. Please. Help me to the gardens. Please."

She pursed her lips. She glowered at me, entirely unimpressed. "Then I'm getting Kulnethar, and I'm describing this incident in exact detail."

I nodded, and my sudden compliance must have finally convinced her. She helped me up, dragged me out to the gardens, and deposited me on the nearest bench.

"Stay here," she said. Then she vanished into the cooling dark.

———

"You saw one," Kulnethar repeated, brows furrowed as he sat next to me. The trees whispered, their voices lilting with the wind—now quiet, now fervent. It was dark, but out here, in this place, the shadows stirred with a wholesome life, masking the emptiness. It reminded me of Gitaia. *Life, life in the desert.*

I nodded. "They've been speaking to me. I thought it was all in my head. I thought I was imagining it. That they were only memories. Now . . . I'm not so sure."

"And this has been going on for . . . ?"

"Six weeks. Since the desert."

"I see."

"What do I do, Kylan?"

He shook his head. "I don't know. Memories like that, they can be powerful. For years, I had nightmares. After Trushya. After what happened. I . . . I thought I could hear him sometimes. Not just in my dreams, but sometimes when I was awake."

"Screaming," I said. "On and on."

"Hitting you here," he stuck a fist into his stomach.

I glanced at him, shocked that he should know. Our eyes met for an instant, then I shook my head.

"This was different." I said. "I saw it. I *felt* it. The thing was standing there, staring at us. Like it was just . . . waiting."

"For what?"

"I don't know."

"Alis told me she saw nothing."

"Maybe because she can't."

Kulnethar shook his head. "Vanya, there's a lot we *don't* know about the Sumadi, but they aren't invisible—at least not when they attack. They appear like shadows, then, the accounts agree, they become bright, visible to all."

"Lined in starlight," I said.

"I suppose you could say that."

"So I'm just crazy. Is that your final assessment?"

"You've always been a little crazy, Vanya." I felt his smile through the dark. "But I believe you."

"So what then? What do we do about it?"

"For now? I have no idea." He sighed. "The truth is, Vanya, I can't hold off the Circle any longer. They're impatient for you."

I snorted. "It's wonderful to be missed."

"I've spoken with them. You're going to be kept on light duty, and every week you'll report to me."

"Okay," I said.

"That's very important. The work you've been doing with Alis. You have to keep up your exercises, your stretches. If you don't—"

"Yes, yes. I'll be crippled the rest of my life, counting rations. I get it."

He nodded, and the silence stretched between us. An odd feeling rose up, and I began to realize what Kulnethar was saying. This was it. I was free. By tomorrow I would be back in the Guardian's Hall. By tomorrow, I would face the Circle.

Fear lashed around my chest, squeezing with a whole new urgency. The Circle. The failed expedition. Unfinished business.

"Don't tell anyone," I said, suddenly breathless. "You won't, will you?"

Kulnethar glanced at me in surprise. "Vanya, this could be important. Do you really want to keep something like this from the Circle?"

"You said it was just memories, just my imagination. So why share it?"

"Because you're confident it's *not*."

"I'm crazy," I growled. "Remember?"

He pressed his hands together, frowning as he leaned forward. "I won't tell the Circle, Vanya, but promise you'll keep me informed. If it gets worse. If something . . . new happens. You'll do that, won't you?"

For a moment, I swore it was the High Elder next to me. I even glanced up, tracing his bright hair against the shadows of the trees. Sometimes I had to remind myself—Kulnethar was one of them. There would be no more pilfered skins of cider. If he saw a stolen scroll, he would send it back.

Then I caught a shadow behind him. Something on the path, coming towards us. Coming fast. I clutched Kulnethar's arm, leaping to my feet, mouth parted in a shout.

Until I noticed the white robes and the bristly dark hair, silhouetted against the moonlight.

Kulnethar chuckled and patted my hand. "It's Alis."

"I know," I snapped.

"What?" She ground to a halt in front of us. "Did I scare you?"

"Yl'avah's blasted might, girl. You really want to sneak up on me right now? What do you want?"

"Making sure you're both still alive." Her teeth flashed white in the moonlight. "I see the shadows haven't got you yet."

"Are you laughing at me?"

"A little," she said with a grin—until her gaze shifted to

Kulnethar. I watched her hands clasp together. I watched her face go through an array of transformations.

"What is it?" Kulnethar asked.

She threw a thumb over her shoulder. "The new guy," she said. "The one with the, uh, crushed foot. He . . . well he hasn't stopped moaning since last night, and now it's getting louder, so I think you'd better come check on him. I . . ." she squinted, as if trying to remember something. "I did the silverwort and the powder goop you like so much, and I gave him . . . er, what's that new stuff?"

"Lyl-"

"Lyllin, that's right! And I checked his dressing, and I tried to talk him through it, and nothing's calming him down, so . . ."

"I'll check on him," Kulnethar said.

"Okay, thanks. I mean, not for me, that would be ridiculous. What do I care?" She gave an awkward chuckle, then realized she might have said the wrong thing. "Wait—but I *do* care, of course I do. I, you know, sympathize with his pain and everything. And . . . and . . ." she winced. "Besides, there's the other patients. And he *is* getting annoying. I mean not annoying to *me*, but oh, damn. Who am I fooling? It's driving me crazy all his howling. Can you please shut him up?"

Kulnethar chuckled. "I'll be there soon."

Alis nodded, stood there for an awkward moment, then fled back towards the Temple.

"Sounds like your kind of healer," I laughed, as soon as she was gone.

Kulnethar nodded, but like he wasn't really listening anymore. He just sat there, frowning, staring after her.

"Kylan?" I nudged him.

He didn't move. I was beginning to think he'd fallen asleep, when he gave a long, heavy breath, and spoke. "I think I love her."

I grunted in surprise. "Alis?"

He nodded, and a pained look came over him. He clutched his hands over his knees.

"What's wrong?"

"Well, do you think she . . . you know? I mean do you *really*?"

"How the blazing sun should I know? I'm not exactly having any luck myself."

"But you've seen her."

"Now and then."

He ignored my sarcasm. "And does she . . . ? I mean, do you think there's anything . . . ?"

"All I know is she goes funny when you're around. Maybe that means she likes you, or maybe not."

"I don't know, Vanya. I don't know. What if she feels she owes me something? I kept her out of the South Fields, I convinced the Elders to make her a healer, against all protocol. What if she says yes just because of what I did?"

"Doesn't sound so bad to me. You did something for her, she gives back."

"Vanya, no! That's horrible. I couldn't!"

"Why not? If she's grateful, isn't that a start?"

"It's not the point! Gratitude isn't love. I *love* her, Vanya! I . . . I don't just want her, I want to *be* something for her. Don't you understand?"

I had never seen Kulnethar so frantic before. I snorted and tried to imagine them together, but Tala popped into my mind instead. Perfect, strong, admirable Tala. Is that how I felt? Did I dare think I could actually *be* something for her? What could Tala possibly need? Certainly not me and my problems. I found myself scowling at the thought, then realized Kulnethar was still talking, going on and on about how he felt, how *she* made him feel, how—

I rolled my eyes. "You could try asking her."

"How would I be sure of the answer?"

It was satisfying to see Kulnethar struggle at something, and I sat back, enjoying the moment. A pleading look came into his eyes.

"Will you help me?"

"*Me?* No way."

"Please, Vanya. Just ask her. I need to know. I need an honest answer, and she'll be honest with you. I know she will."

"I'm not going to ask her."

Kulnethar sat there for a moment, saying nothing, as if pretending to think. Then he rose quietly, smoothed out his robes, and shrugged. "If you ask Alis, I'll ask Tala."

"Dirty little cheat," I muttered.

THE NEXT MORNING I woke without pain for the first time I could remember, as if my body knew: it was time.

I swallowed my nerves and rose. I did my morning stretches. I worked through each exercise. I could make full swivels with my ankle, stand on it, rock from toe to heel, and even pivot. I was making excellent progress. Alis brought me my morning meal and ordered me to do laps around the corridors, then stairs, then more laps, and finally a host of new exercises.

"This is feeling more like the Guardian's Hall already," I smiled.

"Good," she said.

Later that morning, it was Kulnethar's idea to go for one last walk in the gardens. He invited Alis, and together we strolled down to the path.

Then he paused. "Sorry!" he said. "I forgot I'm supposed to meet Elder ab'Itharu today. Go on without me." He gave me a significant look and disappeared back into the Temple.

I growled, but as the cool green closed around Alis and I, I found myself struggling to form the question. We walked. I was gaining speed, though it still hurt if I pushed too fast. Alis was aware of that. She strolled patiently beside me, and I found myself glancing at her, wondering what Kulnethar saw. She was plain. She was small. She had neither elegance nor shape. But I remembered her flash of defiance, staring down that Guardian. I remembered her catching me. She was sturdy. She had spirit.

"Too bad Kylan had to go back," I said, watching for her reaction.

She shrugged. "It's fine. He's busy."

"He's busy a lot."

"Mmhm."

I frowned at my first failed attempt. "I guess we don't need him. I'm getting better. No use for both of you to hang around." I chuckled.

She said nothing.

Damn. This woman wasn't an easy nut to crack. I tried something more direct: "Do you like when he's around?"

Now she was eyeing me strangely. "What's it to you?"

"Oh, nothing. I just don't know how you feel about him. If you . . ."

She stopped and faced me, arms slung across her chest. "Don't even think about it, Ishvandu. I'm not interested."

"But . . ."

"No."

"Come on, Alis. I see the way you act around—"

"Are you blind as well as crippled? I'm not interested, and if you think I've shown the slightest sign of it— Yl'avah's might, I should march over to the Hall this instant and tell Tali. The nerve! After how she feels about you, how you lead her on, though Yl'avah knows what she sees in a miserable brute like you. And you have the stones to stand here and proposition *me*—"

"*What?*" I stared at her. "Light and all, *no*. You think *I'm* interested in you? You're, you're a grouchy old stick at sixteen. No way."

She heaved a sigh of relief. "Thank Yl'avah. You *scared* me, you clot. I thought you were—"

"Wait," I put my hand out, stopping her. "What did you say?"

"Oh, live with it. You insulted me, I insulted you. You deserve it from time to time."

"No, the *other* part. About Tala. What did you say about Tala?"

The girl stopped, then her eyes widened, and a look of horror spread over her face. She lifted her hands. "Me?"

"Yes, you. What did you say about Tala?"

"I didn't say anything."

My face broke into a grin. "Yes, you did! You said . . . *You* said she had feelings for me. I *heard* you."

"I didn't say any such—"

"Yes!" I leapt into the air—a small leap—then quickly regretted it. I came down, stumbled, and my bad leg slipped out from under me. My cane went flying. I hit the ground, even as Alis reached out, too late, to stop me.

But I didn't care. Something grabbed my chest and squeezed, and it felt like joy, or terror, or both at once.

"Are you okay?" Alis cried.

I shook my head, gripping her arm, almost pulling her down with me. "She wants me. She *wants* me. I knew it. Alis, you're wonderful. You're—"

"Hold on there, dasher. She never told me so, okay? You can't say anything to her. You *can't*. She—"

I hoisted myself back to my feet, snatched up my cane, and started hop-running back the way we came.

"Hold on, where are you going?"

"To find Tala!"

"Ishvandu, *no!*"

I spun to face her. "Kulnethar's in love with you. Hurry up and tell him how you feel about him, so he can stop agonizing. Thanks for everything!" And with the girl staring dumbly after me, I raced out of the gardens, out the Temple gate, and west towards the Hall.

Chapter Thirty-One

My enthusiasm waned quickly. My leg was feeling better—but not *that* much better. It began to ache. My limp grew more pronounced, and I had to rest and lean on my cane. Then came the sharp, stabbing pains, like little chips of bone peeling off my shin.

This was a mistake. I should have waited for the inevitable camel, for someone to come and fetch me. But there was no turning back now.

I kept thinking of Tala. *After how she feels about you.* That's what Alis had said. And they were women, and women talked, and they said things to each other, and even when they didn't, they still *knew* things. Which meant Alis had seen something, somehow, in Tala's regard for me, which meant there was still hope.

I let that thought carry me the long trek around the Labourer's quarter, and over the hard pan towards the Hall. I let it carry me all the way up to the gate.

Then I stopped. I was breathing hard. I was fighting not to grimace. I was playing over and over again everything Tala had ever said to me. And suddenly, I was terrified. I couldn't push my feet to go another step. This was a mistake. Tala hadn't told Alis anything; the girl was just wrong, and I was wrong, and if Tala really cared about me, she would have come to see me again. She would have let me kiss her again. She would have made *some* move forward, and . . .

My thoughts were interrupted by the watch at the gate.

"Ishvandu ab'Admundi," he hailed me.

I nodded, hardly able to call back, I was panting so hard. My leg ached, but I *had* to keep going.

Then I realized one of the watch had stepped forward to take my arm. "We were told to bring you directly to the Circle."

"Directly?" My brows went up.

Their brows lowered, and I remembered abruptly where I was, *who* I was—not a Guardian anymore, not even a Guardian-in-training. Inside these walls, I was an ignorant, unsworn Novice, and nothing more.

"Sorry, sal'ahs," I glanced at my feet. "Of course."

"This way," said the watch.

I followed through the outer yard and the second gate, into the main court. The scene unfolded with painful familiarity. As evening gathered, so did the Novices, a few riding around the yard, a few sparring, a few running errands. One of the riders was Bray.

"Vanya!" he cried from atop an uncooperative camel.

"Pay attention," the trainer called, but Bray was already struggling out of the saddle. His foot got caught, and when he hit the ground, he tripped backwards, almost toppling off his feet. His ungainly arms and legs had barely recovered, and he was already sprinting towards me.

"You're back!"

The trainer marched after him. "Ebridyn ab'Branidu, where do you think you're going?"

He ignored her. "You're back, Vanya! Light and all, where have you been? Look at you! What's with the cane? Getting old already? Why are you—"

"*Guardian*, Bray, not a year calf," I snapped at him. "Get back to what you were doing. We can talk later."

He ground to a halt, face falling. But before he could stammer a reply, the trainer descended on him. "Where is your camel, Ebridyn?"

He glanced up. "I just wanted to—"

She struck him in the side of the head, and he staggered back. "Find it! Stay on it. Keep your mind on the task at hand."

Bray scowled and rubbed his temple as he trudged off, and I carried on. With every hobbling step towards the Tower, my uncertainty grew. Why so urgent? It was near Darkening prayer and the evening meal. Surely the Circle had better things to do right this moment than see me? I was just a Novice. I was no one. *Except I had been to the desert.*

I strained for a glimpse of Tala, without luck. She was probably returning from patrol still. But there were the other Novices, sparring under Tushani'sal. Not many would be as eager for my return as Bray, but I did spot Bretina, and as our eyes met, she nodded. Then I passed another pair of sentries, through the Tower door, and into the dark.

They made me wait in the small room again. But I was glad. I sat and rested. I drank deeply from the basin at the door. I stretched my leg. I leaned against the wall. I was exhausted, and I slept so hard I didn't even realize I had dozed off until I jerked awake to a sound at the door.

I struggled through a deep sense of disorientation, and for a moment, had no idea where I was. All I knew was I was stiff, and my leg ached, and I wasn't in the Temple. I had no idea how long I'd slept, but the light outside the door was strong enough to be morning.

"It's time," the Guardian sentry told me. I nodded and rose on instinct, but it wasn't until I limped out of the room that I remembered the Circle. They had left me there all night. And now my fate would be decided.

I gripped my cane and hobbled up the stairs, around and around, into the chamber. The early dawn sun slipped across the floor from behind. They were all present. Every one of them. And they were already in council. In their midst, standing at attention, hands behind her back, stood Tala.

She didn't even break to glance at me. Guardian Lord Jarethyn ab'Torishu was reciting a list of events, and only gradually did I realize what they were:

"He stayed. You went on—after voicing your disagreement—but

by midday, you had convinced ab'Tanadu to side with you, and all three of you turned back in search of Ishvandu. You heard a crashing sound in the distance—what Ishvandu later claimed was a rock slide in the Mountain's Bones, and you personally continued on foot. You followed what you assumed were Ishvandu's markings and found him after sunfall. His leg was presumed broken. Because his saddle was dismantled to make a splint, you gave him your saddle, and helped him ride back to join the others. Then you continued on to Shyandar together without further incident."

There was a pause as I took my place next to Tala. Only then did her eyes flash towards me—just for an instant.

"Atali sai'Neraia, are any of these events untrue, according to the witness of Akkoryn ab'Kindelthu, Tanadu ab'Tanadu, and yourself?"

"No, sal'ah."

"And can you recall Ishvandu's words to you regarding the valley?"

She shook her head. "Ishvandu forgot, that's all. But we can try again. We can—"

"'I never found the valley in the first place,'" quoted Jarethyn. "'I don't know the way, and I've never known the way. I lied.'"

Not my words, but close enough. Which meant Koryn had told them everything—with the exception of the exile. And if either of us contradicted his statement, I had no doubt he would drop the whole truth like a hot stone.

"Did Ishvandu speak those words to you?" Jarethyn asked.

I could almost feel Tala flushing. "He's just an idiot. He was exaggerating."

"Did he say those words?"

She hesitated.

"Atali sai'Neraia, we've been through this before. I would appreciate—"

"I said them." I was frowning at the sun's fire, watching it burn across the floor. "I said those words."

Instantly, the Circle's attention shifted. I could feel their eyes pressing against me—smothering in their intensity.

"And is there a valley with a spring?" Jarethyn asked.

"Yes."

"How do you know, if you never found it?"

"I didn't find the valley. I was brought there."

Jarethyn snorted, but out of the corner of my eye, I saw Umaala stiffen, sitting up in his place.

"By whom?" Neraia asked coldly.

Tala glanced at me. I saw the warning in her eye. *Don't. Don't do it.*

"A bird," I said. "I followed a bird."

I felt the tension release, just a little, like the knot of a cord snapping loose. "A bird?" Jarethyn laughed. "You followed a *bird*?"

"Birds know water."

"Then if you've been there before, why don't you know the way now?"

I looked at him. "Have you ever tried to follow a bird, sal'ah? You spend most of the time looking *up*."

There was a string of laughter. I realized I had won a point, and I felt a burst of hope. Was I actually going to talk my way out of this?

"Nevertheless," Neraia's voice was cold. "Finding the valley was not something you were able to duplicate with any certainty. You knew this, and you agreed to the expedition anyway."

"Ab'Krushaya'sal asked."

"You agreed."

"Because he asked. He said *try*."

"He assumed you knew the way. You *told* him you knew the way. Isn't that correct, Umaala ab'Krushaya?"

Umaala nodded. "Ishvandu approached me with this information the first year he was Tasked to the Hall."

So much for talking my way out of it. The council was galloping ahead, like they had planned every word in advance.

"I was a stupid kid," I said. "I wasn't thinking."

"Were you thinking the day you agreed to the expedition?" Umaala asked. "You never bothered to refute your claims. Or are you still a twelve-year boy without sense?"

I glanced down, shifting my weight, clutching my cane to ease some of the pain in my leg. The eyes were pressing closer, the uncertainty growing again.

"I *was* thinking, ab'Krushaya'sal. I was thinking of what we had to gain. What we could do—"

"And the lives you risked?" Neraia asked. "Were you thinking of them? Were you thinking of the cost we paid for your uncertainty, sending an expedition into the desert so you could play at being hero?"

"It was worth it," I fired back. "It was worth our lives, and more! Water!" I stared at them, pleading with my eyes. "Our people need it more than food, more than safety, more than order and law. They need water, and I saw water in the desert. Water!"

"Ishvandu . . ." Umaala warned.

"What? Isn't it worth a little risk?"

Tala jerked my wrist. *Shut up.* But I had a point—a good point. I couldn't stop myself now.

"Aren't we Guardians? Isn't this what we *do*? Take risks. Explore the desert. Attempt what others wouldn't dare. Or at least we *would*, if we weren't so busy cowering behind our walls."

Umaala sat forward, eyes crackling me into silence, but it was too late.

"You're not a Guardian," Neraia said. "And you never will be."

The words fell into a silent room. I blinked at her, then back at Umaala, then at her. *Had she just—?*

No. It couldn't be.

But the eyes. The circle of cold, unforgiving eyes.

Never.

I swallowed, wondering suddenly if I was going to be sick. Because right then, in that moment, I understood: for all my struggling, for all the long years of proving myself, of trying and trying, and refusing to give up—for all that, I had never once thought the oath was possible. Not ever. Those words. Those horrible, inevitable words. They shot straight into me and settled into the place they belonged. The place they had always been. *Never.*

I stared forward at nothing. My life—my impossible life— dissolved like sand through my fingers, and when I opened my mouth, my throat was too dry to speak. I could only nod.

It was Tala who spoke for me.

"No!" she cried. "No, mother. You can't! You can't let this happen! It was a mistake, but—"

"Atali sai'Neraia, are you contradicting the voice of the Circle?"

"No, I—"

"Are you denying our judgment?"

"But he can do it! He can find the valley. I promised he would have a second chance. Please!"

"A second chance," Neraia frowned. "Perhaps you need to be reminded—this *is* Ishvandu's second chance. Do you think our warning six months ago was for naught? Ishvandu ab'Admundi violated the code by disrespecting the blade of a Guardian and challenging his superior. He committed violence in this Hall. Do you think that inconsequential?"

"No, of course not, but—"

"He was given his chance. He was warned of the outcome if he stepped out of line once more, and now we have here not one breach of conduct, but several. Ishvandu lied and confessed it with his own witness, here in this room, just moments ago. He proceeded to disobey a direct order from his superior. His rebellion nearly cost his own life, and the life of his camel, not to mention *your* life when you followed him in his disobedience—an act for which this council has yet to determine a suitable punishment. Furthermore, he committed a flagrant act of dishonour and a breach of his Novice position."

"What?" Tala cried. "When?"

"He kissed you, isn't that correct?"

"And without your permission," Jarethyn added. "If your brother's account is accurate."

I listened to all this dumbly, still unable to speak, a coldness settling over me like a shroud.

"That's nothing!" Tala threw out her arms. "That's my business, not—"

"You are a Guardian. You took the oath. Your business is our business. Always. And such a relationship is in violation of our codes, for as long as he stands as Novice. You *know* this, daughter."

"But I'm not," I finally managed to say. "I'm not a Novice anymore, am I? I'm nobody."

"You are far from that," said Umaala. "The Hall Hands are in need of hard workers and keen eyes to keep the camels, to ration, to distribute and prepare—"

"To slave for you," I said. "To muck your camel's shit. What else?"

There was a tense silence.

"What else? What other option do I have?"

"Return to your father's house," Neraia said. "As a Labourer."

"Good. I'll take that one."

Tala gripped my hand. Her fingers braced through mine, and in their vicious strength, I heard a thousand words.

"Are you sure?" Neraia asked. "You realize you would never be allowed within these walls again?"

"Fine."

"You would not have the benefits of a member of this Hall."

"I don't need your benefits."

"Very well." She sighed. "Then it's done. Gather your things and exchange your robes. Your new foreman will meet you at the front gates after midday. You are dismissed."

I nodded, turned. Tala's grip yanked me back, and before I realized what was happening, she was kissing me.

I heard the gasp of the Circle. A few clattered to their feet. My heart flew up. It was no gentle kiss, like her experiment above the rocks. Her mouth slammed onto mine. Her fingers clutched the side of my face. She kissed me like she would breathe my lungs into hers.

For the first instant, I was too stunned to respond. In the next, there were Guardians around us, between us. I strained to hold on. But it was over, and I was being hustled from the room like a beast. Prodded, handled, shoved along.

"Get off!" I cried, wrenching free. Then I stood there, outside the chamber, breathing hard in the sudden nothingness. I was looking at people I knew—to whom I was now a stranger, an outsider, a Labourer, a nobody.

Very well. I wasn't going to be them. I was going to be something else. I was going to be something better.

I turned and clattered down the steps and out into the heat.

THE NOVICE'S quarter was empty. I marched inside and stood there, struck with a wave of unreality. It wasn't my place. Six years, and now I was adrift. Again.

"Vanya!" Bray nearly bowled me over, arms and legs tumbling into the big, sparse room. "Vanya, what's happening? Where have you been? They said you went into the desert. With the third! And you were injured, but they wouldn't say how, or what happened. Is it true? Did you really join an outriding?" He slapped his thighs, almost bouncing in glee. "You realize what this means? First the fourth, then the third—Vanya, you're going to be Watch!"

"I don't think so, Bray."

"What else? An overseer? A hearer? *You,* a consultant to the Circle, are you serious? No—no, they would never Vanya. You're a Watch-rider, I know it! It's perfect for you, and they pulled you into the Circle to talk about being a Guardian. You can't keep it a secret!"

"Bray, shut up."

I found my mat in the far corner, my few meagre possessions stuffed into the bottom of a sack. As if ready to go. As if I knew.

"Vanya, what's wrong? Your face! Blood and light, you look like you've swallowed a rat."

Umaala ab'Krushaya appeared in the entrance. He was holding a bundle under one arm, but I turned quickly away, unable to meet his eye.

"Your robes," he said.

I hesitated, then seized my belt, yanked it open, and shrugged off the finely sown Novice's robes, letting them tumble into a heap. I snatched the Labourer's tunic out of Umaala's hands. It was coarse and shapeless. Immediately, it scratched my skin. It was sleeveless. It fell past my waist, though not much further—ending about a hand's span above my knees. Designed for hard work, freedom of move-ment, sweating long days under a hot sun. I belted it shut with the loose cord Umaala handed me. It was done.

Then there was nothing more to do. I stood there, stripped and humiliated, wishing Umaala would just leave. He didn't. He was watching me. Bray was watching, eyes wide in horror.

"Vanya . . . ?"

Umaala's hand shot up, silencing him, and for the first time, I risked a glance in the Guardian Lord's direction.

"You belong here," he said at last.

"But not as a Guardian, is that it? A stable hand, a cook, a store-counter..."

"That was your choice, Ishvandu. One you made when you decided to bend the truth to your liking. I never wanted this. I tried to give you every opportunity."

I snorted. "Well, I'm sorry I failed you. It won't happen again, sal'ah." My voice caught, and before I broke down, I snatched up my bag—the same bag I'd carried into the place six years ago—and turned for the door.

I had an audience. Bretina stood there, Jil, Alynis, Tesh—everyone. Somehow, the news had spread.

"Vanya," Bray said, and reached for me.

I glanced at him, at the worried lines etched across his face, at the sadness. Pol was gone, Chosen, sent somewhere across the desert, and now I was it—his last friend. And I was leaving.

I punched him in the arm. Not quite as hard as I could, but enough to hurt.

"Ow!" he cried.

"Yl'avah's might, Bray, I'm not a sand-blasted exile. When you're on the fourth, come visit. Okay?"

"O-okay," he nodded.

"Good." I turned and stuck the cane under my arm—I wouldn't leave here bowed over like a cripple—then marched for the door. The Novices fell back, and I passed through them without a word.

Journey

HYRANNA ELDUNA

Year 799 after the fall of Kayr

The Greenwater is old. It was the life-blood of the earth. Did you know? It ran once to all the corners of the world. Through the roots, my child! Through the roots of the Chorah'dyn and the red trees. It gave life to the forests and pure fresh air. It chased sickness away. It preserved the Laws of Creation. They say even the animals could talk, though you shouldn't believe everything they say. Some things are just stories.

But for you, my child, the Greenwater is true. It is your heritage. And wherever your path takes you, know this: it is with you, even now.

Interlude: The Last Al'kah

Ashkynas ab'Adani Al'kah wandered through the Unseen. He floated. He moved, rocking side to side, side to side, jostling with a strange lilting motion. He was in a dark place. He was under the earth. He was under the tree. The darkness under the tree. The red tree kept him, watching and watching through untold centuries. Guarding him. Protecting him.

No. That wasn't him. He was Ashkynas. Not the thing inside. He wasn't. *Wasn't.*

"Where is he?" a young voice cried, flinging through the dark. "Answer me, old tree!"

He shuddered. Fire awoke. Fire called to him, deep inside, slipping through his blood. Something was changing. It was happening *now*. It was power. It was life. It was hope and death, all rolled into one horrible cry.

Ashkynas felt the crack. It pounded through him, it burned and shook, tearing through his blood.

There. It was *there.*

His eyes snapped open. He was rocking side to side, side to side. He was in a room. A moving, swaying room. Boards rose all around him, sacks, crates, shelves lined with heaps of unaccountable artefacts. A stack of huge books towered next to him, rocking with him, bumping and shifting, on the verge of collapse.

He sat up. His weakness was gone. His thirst was gone. He examined himself—his shredded robes were still there, but beneath, his flesh had returned. Like he had killed someone and leeched their strength.

Yl'avah's might, no!

He leapt up, and instantly, the rocking motion pitched him to the floor. He fell with a crash. One of the shelves tipped and a sack punched him in the head. It ripped. A strange white powder burst into the air like a cloud, before settling on Ashkynas in a bewildering, choking haze.

He coughed and swatted at the mysterious substance, half-expecting it to choke him with poisonous fumes. Some of it *did* end up in his mouth, but he just spat it out and wiped it off his face, no burning.

The swaying stopped. The room fell still. There were voices outside. Above, and then beside, and then . . .

The door swung open. Light speared into the room, catching motes of white powder, still falling lazily to the floor. The woman was there. The same woman from before, with her thinning grey hair and stout old frame. She peered into the darkness.

"Hello," she said in a crackly, rich voice. Ashkynas was shocked to hear something like—nearly like—his own tongue. Kyre'an.

He glanced up. He considered his options. The thing inside had no need of killing. Not yet. It was strong and satisfied. But that would not last forever. Eventually, it would turn against this woman, and then she would die.

Ashkynas needed to leave.

He gathered himself, standing slowly and carefully, so as not to startle her. The woman just watched. And as she noticed, really *noticed*, her face opened in shock.

"Krunyn's eye!" she gasped in her own tongue. She was seeing him in his strength. She was seeing his skeletal frame transformed with wholeness. The marvel of the thing inside, perhaps something that happened while he slept—a rush of power. But how? And from where?

"You helped me," he said.

The woman squinted in an effort to listen, then she nodded and grunted. "Course I helped you. What's a person to do? Leave you to die in this cursed nowhere?"

She understood him! The thought struck him as odd, until he realized the words he'd spoken were not Kyre'an. The thing was doing something, curling around his mind, filtering both what he heard and what came out of his mouth. And doing it more naturally than ever before. Like it was becoming him. Uniting with him.

Ashkynas frowned, uncomfortable with the thought. He didn't *want* the Aktyr's strength. But then . . . wasn't his mind so much clearer now? He could think and speak. He could move. He could even remember his purpose.

Find the Chosen. That's why he had taken the ugly thing in the first place—to cross the desert, to find whoever was alive beyond the mountains and warn them of what was coming: the Avanir had ceased to flow, the world was Breaking, no more Renewals, no more Chosen. And, if at all possible, he would do his part in cleansing the Lifewater and bringing wholeness back to the world.

"Are you Chosen?" he asked.

The woman gave him a strange, sideways glance. "Am I *what?*"

"Chosen. From Shyandar. The Chosen of the Avanir. Have you crossed the desert?"

"Gods be, I've no idea what you're on about. *Chosen?* All I've been chosen for is a lifetime of pains for my trouble. Name's Tandra. Tandra Yourk."

She stuck out her hand. It was a rough, time-worn hand. An honest one. Ashkynas made no move to take it. Why risk the Aktyr?

"Forgive me," he said. "But if you aren't the Chosen of Shyandar, then I must go. Now."

"Hold on. You don't get to pop up and threaten me and mine, then disappear mysteriously off into naught. I believe you owe us an explanation."

"What's he saying, Aunt Tan?" came the young man's voice from beyond the door, from the blue sky and the open, rolling grass.

The woman just held up her hand, eyes fixed on Ashkynas. She was not going to be moved so easily, he could see.

"You wouldn't understand," Ashkynas replied. "You are not Kyr'amanu."

"Keerama...?"

"Yes. Kyr'amanu."

"Hold a moment. You're not speaking of the Old Ones, now?" She laughed and whistled. "Old Kayr broke up centuries ago. Lendahyn, you mean. Or you're some mad Imo'ani with one too many stories—"

"Lendahyn?"

"That's right. From the south-eastern edge of the forest, far as you can go. Them behind their damned obnoxious wall, like a spike up Krunyn's ass. I always did wonder if they'd have the stones to take that name again."

"Then you know where I can find Kyr'amanu?" Ashkynas leaned forward, eyes flashing.

"Aye," the woman snorted.

"Where?"

"About a thousand years past, give or take a few centuries, they say."

Ashkynas frowned. "You mean... they are dead."

"Well, Kayr's dead, no? So are they. Look, which direction are you heading anyway? If you're from the forest, you should know these things by now."

"I am not from the forest," Ashkynas said.

The woman blinked. "Not from the east at all? Not from Lendahyr? Or from—"

"From the south. I crossed the desert. I crossed the mountains. I will find the Chosen, and restore the Lifewater."

The woman glanced over her shoulder, looking in that direction. Thinking.

"Hold on—"

Ashkynas dismissed her with a shake of his head. "You are not from Shyandar. You wouldn't understand. And the longer you try to keep me here, the greater the danger. Let me go."

"What danger?"

Ashkynas frowned. He could feel the Aktyr waking, looking up, peering into the world. "Push me, and you will find out."

The woman snorted and crossed her arms. "Threats aren't doing you any favours, old boy. So you just hold right on there a moment and tell me, and let me decide if I should let this *danger* walk loose."

Ashkynas felt a spark of admiration. So did the Aktyr. It heard the challenge. It *liked* the challenge. Let the old woman try! It curled around Ashkynas's chest with a dark new eagerness.

Ashkynas tightened his jaw. "There are two dangers. One is threatening the world. It is the Breaking. The end of all things, the darkness that has been growing since the Fall of Kayr and which my people are no longer able to subdue. The second is standing in front of you, and if you insist on pushing it, it will kill you. So please, get out of my way." He enunciated each word carefully. He stepped forward, drawing himself to his full and daunting height. *Yl'avah's might, let the woman back down! Hurry, before it's too late!* But already he could feel it, the wind, the stirring cold.

"Don't take another step!" said the youth. He had leapt through the door. He was holding one of those noisy weapons, clutching it before him, trembling and scared.

"Magellen Yourk, drop it!" the woman cried.

The wind tore away her words. The Aktyr recognized a threat when it saw one. It stirred into action.

No! Ashkynas tried to stop it.

Too late. There was a deafening blast. Two. Three. His body jerked. Something slammed into his chest. Thunder rolled through the confined space, ringing in his ears.

The Aktyr shot out, slamming the woman aside, hurtling toward the boy, the one who dared challenge the Aktyr. It caught him like a bundle of ropes and tore him into the air. The Aktyr pounced. Ashkynas followed, leaping out into the open, landing in the grass. The wind snapped and roared around him.

"No!" he cried. He shot both hands into the air and squeezed around the wind, yanking it back under control.

The boy wheeled and jerked, caught up in the storm, howling in terror. Then he fell. He slammed into the ground, a crumpled, senseless heap.

Ashkynas shoved the thing back down, back inside, wrestling it under control, then hurried across the broken grass. He bent over the youth, clutching the back of his shirt, desperate for a sign of life. Of *anything.* How could he do this again? How? After promising himself, after suffering so much, denying the thing, propelling himself to the edge of death, not once, but over and over again. And now here—had he killed again? Had he really?

The young man was senseless, but breathing. He was alive.

Ashkynas sagged to the ground in relief. He thought he was going to be sick. How he hated the thing. How he hated it! But he felt a strange, grumbling acquiescence from inside. Like it had heard him. Listened. Obeyed. *Impossible.* Could he really? Could he learn to work *with* it? To control it?

He had to. There was no other way to save the world.

Then he blinked. A glimmer of light caught his eye. A small thing, lying in the grass next to the youth. He frowned. He reached forward and curled long, bony fingers around it, lifting it to his gaze. It was a stone. It was a small, milky white orb, strangely heavy, and it glowed with its own faint life. Like a Guardian's keshu. Like ytyri.

Ashkynas's breath caught. He had read the Chronicles. Read them over and over again, until his heart ached with the knowledge. He knew what this was. And even more importantly, he knew what it meant. It meant Kyr'amanu. It meant wherever these two had come from, there would be others. The Old Lands. The Green East.

Ashkynas lifted his eyes, gazing towards the horizon, to the distant smudge of grey against an unbroken plain.

Hope! He surged to his feet. He grasped the small white stone, the Sending stone, and without a second thought, he began to run.

Chapter Thirty-Two

The soft splash of the paddles became a rhythm, the soft glow of light became morning, and with every stroke, Hyranna bore herself further from home.

She had come this way before, to hunt and harvest cethul in the lower waters, but she'd never gone without a plan of return. Before, Elamori went with her; now it grasped at her, clutched at her heels, and tore away, taking a piece of Hyranna with it.

They went in silence, Jerad Amanti at the stern, Hyranna facing forward, thoughts churning as she gazed over grey water, grey forests, grey sky. The river narrowed and deepened. Fists of water rushed and spun beneath their canoe as Jerad began guiding them ashore.

"Let's do this quickly," Jerad said.

Hyranna shot him a look—as if she needed to be told—and leapt out the moment the canoe scraped rock.

She slipped her bow and quiver over her shoulder, and he took his spear. The packs followed, fitting snugly against their hips, while the paddles were lashed to the inside of the canoe. Then they bent and grabbed the cross-beams. Hyranna started to lift, but the weight shifted, and she almost toppled.

"Come on!" she said. "Together."

"Steady, when I say."

"Why when *you* say?"

He rolled his eyes. "Grip . . . brace, and . . . lift."

The craft went over their heads in a single, clean motion, flipping upside down, gunwales resting on their shoulders.

"Ready?" he asked.

"Yes. Let's go."

They bumped and stumbled down the path. It was a short crossing, but not easy. The Tindanarra took a hasty plunge down the rocks, and they had to work together to move the canoe over steep declines.

"Slow down," Jerad kept saying.

"You said to go quickly."

"*Quickly* doesn't always mean *fast*. You'll punch a hole in our canoe, and *then* where'll we be, eh?"

"Well, if you kept up . . ."

Hyranna jumped down another rock. There was a scraping clunk and Jerad swore, jerking them to a halt.

"Hey, what's going on back there?"

"I said, slow down! Maker's breath, girl, you almost pulled me over!"

"Look, any time you want, you can go back. I don't need you!"

Jerad stepped down, then dropped the canoe with a *thunk*, and Hyranna's knees buckled beneath the sudden weight.

"Jerad!" she tipped the canoe off her shoulders. "Maker damn you, what was that for?"

"What do you think?" His voice was hard, chest going up and down from exertion.

"What I think is you're trying to be a hero, or something, but you don't get it! I can take care of myself, so stop treating me like a child, or go back."

Jerad gave a short laugh, then reached behind him, grabbed one of the skins, and took a swig of water.

"What?" she demanded.

He wiped his face. "Look, Hyranna. We need to set some things straight. I know you're perfectly capable of running off on your own, and you could trap and hunt and forage very well without any of *my* help. You could do it alone. It'd be hard, and you might *wish* you had help, but you don't need me. That's not why I'm doing this."

"Then why are you?"

"Because . . ." he paused. "Because no one should have to be alone."

"And what if I want to be alone?"

"You don't," he said simply.

She stared at him. Her face darkened. "What right do you have? You don't know me! Don't pretend to know anything about what I want!"

"You want to be with Balduin Na-es. Isn't that what this is about?"

"No!" she cried, then: "Yes, of course! But that's none of your business!"

"So I'm not wrong."

"What?"

He frowned. "Never mind. Look, some things are just easier with two. Like carrying this. I just want to help. I can be . . . I don't know, a piece of home, until we find your friend. But we have to work together, Hyranna." He paused. "Please."

Hyranna wiped the sweat off her face. He was right, but it was infuriating. She didn't want him here, she wanted Balduin! She wanted . . . everything to be different. She took a shuddering breath.

"Hyranna?" His voice changed. "Are you . . . okay?"

"Yes!"

"What is it? What's going on?"

"Nothing. Let's just keep going."

He looked at her warily. He didn't believe her, not for a moment, but he backed off and nodded. "Okay. Fine."

They went slowly the rest of the way, not saying much, and when they finally made it to the bottom, it was a relief to drop their burdens and step back into the canoe.

THEY PADDLED in silence until the sun rose over the trees, glistening across the grey river, until the heat sapped the strength from their cramping muscles and the sweat dripped from their faces and down their backs.

"We're close to the next crossing," Jerad said.

She just nodded, trying not to feel daunted by the task ahead. But she was hungry and sore and tired, and the enormity of what she was doing was sinking in more and more with every bend in the river.

That's when they saw it.

"Stop!" Hyranna cried, reaching out with her paddle in case they got too close. Just ahead, the water rippled strangely.

Jerad flashed the blade of his paddle backwards and they made a tight, quick turn, just missing it. Except when Hyranna looked, there was no rock, like she feared. There was nothing.

"Maker's breath," Jerad said as they drifted past.

Hyranna struggled to make sense of what she was seeing. It was nothing. It was a hole, going from nowhere to nowhere. Not blackness, not shadow—only a dead space, without shape or texture. But the river didn't flow *into* it, it flowed around, as if eager to pretend the hole did not exist.

"What in all the green earth was that?" Jerad asked.

Hyranna felt queasy. She felt like she'd been playing spin-on-the-stick. She leaned over and clutched the edge of the canoe, thinking she might be sick. Jerad strained to look behind him, to catch one more glimpse, but it was only a ripple again, lost in the current.

"Should we . . . go back? I want to—"

"No!" Hyranna snapped her head up. "No, just . . . just leave it." The thought of even seeing the hole again terrified her.

Jerad just nodded and they fell silent. But there it was—another strange happening, *outside* Elamori this time. Which meant it wasn't just their village. *Except Balduin had come this way too.* She scowled as soon as she thought it. No, of course this wasn't Balduin's fault. It couldn't be!

Hyranna had only been this way once or twice, but as the river pulled them along, faster and faster through treacherously shallow water, Jerad swung the canoe shoreward and brought them into a sheltered bank. It was clear Dal Adis and his hunters had passed not long ago. They'd made no effort to hide their tracks, and some of the plants had been trampled and the mud kicked up. Had they seen the strange thing in the river too?

Hyranna climbed out less enthusiastically than last time. Her legs began to cramp, her arms seized up, but with Jerad's help she got the canoe out of the water. She paused for a moment to catch her breath, then reached for the sack.

"No," Jerad said. "We rest here."

"We can't."

"Yes." He put a hand on her arm. "We have to. Here. Some water first." He held out a skin for her and she drank gratefully.

"I'm not tired," she lied. "I can keep going."

"Well, I can't. There's a good place to rest up here, if I remember correctly. We'll need our strength for this crossing. It's a long one."

She said nothing. He was right, of course, but she would rather not admit it. Once the canoe was safely on shore, they grabbed the packs and their weapons and struggled up the steep, muddy bank. The ground levelled out, hard with roots, but softened with pine needles. The old trees towered above them, dotted with balsam, moss, and fern in the undergrowth. A hush lay over the hot, midday forest.

Hyranna's weariness caught up to her, and before long, she was asleep.

"Hyranna," the voice broke the sweet darkness and she jerked. Everything was sore. Moving was the last thing she wanted, but the gentle hand on her arm was insistent. "Hyranna?" Jerad Amanti bent over her. "I'm sorry, I really am, but we should be moving again. A storm wind is blowing up."

She groaned. How much time had passed? It felt like moments, but even her grey-stained eyes could tell some dark weather was coming.

"Damn," she muttered and pushed herself into a sitting position. "You shouldn't have . . . have let me sleep. Too much . . . time lost."

"You needed it," he said. "And this too."

She blinked. He was holding something out to her, a leaf-wrapped package, and when she took it and peeled back the leaves, she was surprised to see gold-smoked pike.

"Something from home," he said. "Eat."

Her stomach growled plaintively. Everything still tasted like ash, but she devoured the fish anyway, trying to remember the smell of rich, sweet smoke.

Jerad grinned and nibbled on his own piece. "Slow down," he said. "I didn't pack that much. We'll have to gather our own food soon, so enjoy this while you can."

"It's a start, at least," she said around a mouthful.

He nodded and tossed her one of the packs. "You should look through it so you know what you're hauling over this next crossing. Anything you think you don't need, go ahead and dump. I won't care."

She nodded as she opened the oil-rubbed skins. There was warm clothing inside, for the turn of the seasons—thick hide pants, and a fur-lined cloak she could drape around her shoulders and across her chest.

"It'll keep you warm at night, too," Jerad said.

The pilfered gift was almost too kind, but the nights were getting colder, and she knew she should thank him. Instead, she let the silence hang, pursing her lips, and reaching further into the pack.

There were many useful things: more food, neatly packaged, a couple of berry cakes, extra flint, a few lengths of strong tendon rope, bandages and remedies he must have gotten from her father, and even a small sewing kit. A roll of hide unravelled to reveal three bone needles of different sizes, fine thread, a collection of small scraps of hide for patching, and a curved razor for fine work.

But that wasn't all. There was a small wooden object shoved into the bottom. She closed her fingers over it, noticing how . . . familiar it felt, then drew it out. The moment she saw it, her throat closed up. It was her father's carving, his last gift to her: Eelun the Dancing Fox.

Maker above, Papi!

She wanted to scream at Jerad. *How dare he?* He had gone into her cave. Into her things. He had seen this, and guessing her father had made it . . .

Her father. She had nearly killed her own father.

Hyranna gasped, choking back a surge of emotion. Maker's breath, she couldn't let Jerad see her cry. Not again!

She stammered an excuse and fled into the trees.

"Hyranna!"

She ignored him. She ran until she was out of sight, out of earshot, memories swirling against her mind: slamming a hand into her father's chest, stopping his heart, blue eyes looking at her, looking, knowing everything, knowing it was her, knowing she had killed him, that for a single instant, she had hated him enough to . . . enough to . . .

But Balduin! How could he? How could her father send him off like that? Alone? Scared? With nothing and nobody in the world, but a single raving hope that the father who had abandoned him was somehow alive, somewhere. It made her furious. Balduin *deserved* her fury.

But enough to do *that*? No. No. It was too much. Hyranna loved her father. Loved his smile, his kind face, the way he twinkled at her. Loved him so deeply, it hurt. How could she ever go back? How could she face him again, after what she'd done?

She sank against a distant pine, still clutching the little statue in her fist, and wept.

"He makes you feel weak."

Hyranna tightened, shaking her head. She didn't want to deal with that man. Not now. Not him. "Go away," she muttered.

E'tuah crouched beside her, reached for her.

"Don't touch me!" she slapped his hand away, but he seized her wrist anyway, fingers clamping down like pincers.

"He makes you feel weak. Doesn't he?"

"Let go!"

"You aren't weak. The *Aktyr* is not weak. Leave him. Go now."

"That's not going to happen. Now let *go*."

He didn't let go. "His food you do not need. His clothing is wasted on you. His company is tiresome. He is useless to you. The Aktyr can sustain you."

Hyranna gave a short, bitter laugh. "I still need to eat."

"No. Your mind craves food, but your body needs nothing. It can take what it needs from the shard."

She felt a prickle of fear. "That's not possible."

"Many things are possible. More than you can imagine." His dark eyes held hers. "But as long as you have *him* weighing you down, you will never know the fullness of your capabilities. You will never learn all the Aktyr can give you."

"I don't *want* what that thing can give. Not to need food? That's unnatural!"

"Absolutely. But very little about you is natural now. The forest itself is changing, and you know it." His eyes tightened. "What did you see? In the river?"

"Nothing."

"Exactly."

The way he looked at her, eyes burning—it reached into her. It pulled something. Something dark and powerful. *The Aktyr.* His grip hardened.

"There is power here," he said, "just waiting for you. Use it! Leave Jerad Amanti behind and show him *he* is the weak one. I know you want to, Hyranna Elduna. Or would you rather go back to his patronizing protection? He is an insult to you."

She felt a rush of certainty. *Yes! Go. Go now. Show Jerad Amanti what he deserves for trying to manipulate you, trying to make you grateful, make you rely on him, make you weak. You never wanted this! You don't need him.*

The thoughts passed so quickly, so intensely, she gasped and jumped to her feet. E'tuah rose more slowly, watching her, waiting.

"Is it true? I don't even need food?"

"That is true. And more. Would you like to see what the Aktyr can do?"

She hesitated. Then she found herself holding it in her other hand. Was it her eyes? Or had the flat, dull surface become darker?

"I don't care what the Aktyr can do."

E'tuah smiled. "Not even if it can find your friend?"

She swallowed. She felt a strange tingling beneath the shard's surface, as if it were stirring, calling to her, waking up. If she could use it to find Balduin, then she wouldn't need anything from Jerad. The sudden possibility was intoxicating.

"How?" she heard herself demand. "How would I do it?"

He cupped her hand with both of his, leaning forward, drawing as near to the shard as he could. "Hold in your mind everything you know about him. Not just his name, but who he is, his essence. The Aktyr is a thing of all realms, uniting the Seen with the Unseen. Fill your mind with this Balduin Na-es, fix your thoughts on him, and then reach out through the shard. Not only will you learn where he is, but with enough practice, you may even learn to speak with him."

Hyranna felt her heart beating in sudden anticipation. If it were truly possible . . . Her hand turned warm with the glow of the shard and a strange energy ran through her, invigorating and eager, and . . .

"Try it," E'tuah urged, eyes glinting. He closed her hand over the shard. "Try it and see."

. . . and wrong. Hyranna hesitated. Something was wrong. The sudden, hungry fire coursing through her—that wasn't her. And in a flash she remembered the thunderous crack, the splitting tree, the horror of that putrid darkness, dredged up by the thing she held. She remembered the cold, furious violence that gripped her an instant before she struck her father's heart.

She recoiled, jolting back from E'tuah. "Let go," she demanded, annoyed at herself for even considering it.

"There is nothing to fear. I can help you."

"No! I will not let this thing anywhere near Balduin. It's vile and wicked."

"It has potential for more, as you showed when you brought your father back from the edge of death."

"I don't believe you! What do you care about Balduin anyway? I don't trust this thing, and I don't trust you! Let me go!"

"Stop being a fool!"

The shard was burning in her hand, still insistent, demanding, hungry for something to break. Maybe she had just the thing. She dropped the carving and grabbed E'tuah's entrapping fist.

"Let go," she said, voice dark with warning.

He didn't. And so . . . she attacked.

The shard's fire. It was a part of her, a part of her skin, pouring through her, fuelled by her indignation. Everything snapped out of place—everything around her, *jolting* as it seized E'tuah. For an instant, he seemed to grow. The breeze curled around him, instead of through him. He gasped. Then the shard's heat poured out of her. Gone, snuffed out like a candle.

E'tuah staggered back, eyes wide with shock. The hand that gripped her was splayed in pain, fingers bent, twisted. The skin crawled and peeled. Blood vessels burst like ants popping over a fire. His mouth parted in a scream.

He flickered. A shadow rushed over him, flashing over his whole body. And when Hyranna blinked, he was just like before, unchanged, unhurt, except for the look on his face: bewilderment—and then fury.

"What did you do?"

She swallowed, trying to project confidence as she brandished the now cold, dead shard. "That was a taste. Now we know what happens, so don't push me."

"Hah!" A sneer burst out of him. "Using my own weapon against me?"

"That's right! You think you can—"

He seized her wrist, wrenching it so hard the shard slipped from her grasp. She cried out. He grabbed a fistful of her shirt and dragged her to her toes, leaning over her. Whatever power she'd had a moment ago was gone.

"Don't think it will protect you from *me*," he hissed, twisting her arm. "I was trying to open your eyes. But fight me, and I will become your enemy. Is that what you want? *Is it?*"

Pain speared through her shoulder. She gasped, straining on her toes. "Is this what you do? Bully anyone you can't control? I know your sort! You don't . . . scare me."

Frustration rippled across his face. "I'm trying to be patient with you, girl. Do you know what's at stake? If you had any idea—"

"*Hyranna?*" Jerad's voice cut through the forest.

Her heart leapt. "I'm here!"

E'tuah wouldn't give himself away—not yet. His sudden, dark scowl was both satisfying and terrifying. He shoved her away. She sprawled backwards, banging the back of her heel on a rock, tripping, and almost cracking her head on a root. E'tuah paused for a moment, glaring at her, as if wanting to speak, then Jerad loped into sight and the man vanished.

"Hyranna? Are you okay? I . . . I heard a shout." He hurried to her side.

She snatched her arm to her chest, half-expecting something to be broken. It was sore. But as she flexed her fingers and turned her wrist, easing her shoulder around without stabs of pain, she breathed a sigh of relief.

"I'm . . . I'm okay."

"You're bleeding!"

She followed Jerad's eyes. Sure enough, the skin on the back of her foot was ragged. But the sticky substance that oozed out was eerily unlike blood. Grey—like everything else.

"I'll be fine," she said. "I . . . I just tripped." She pressed a thumb to her heel. The cut was deep but she had walked through worse.

Jerad spotted the little carving not far from where she fell. He reached over and picked it up, running his thumb over the ridges. "Look, Hyranna, I . . . I'm sorry. Maybe I overstepped. I just thought you'd appreciate—"

She plucked the fox out of his grasp and seized him in a hug, squeezing with an intensity that surprised even her. "I do appreciate it," she said, then pulled away. "Come on. Let's get moving."

She pushed herself up, reaching for the shard and secreting it away in her pocket before Jerad could notice. But he was too busy staring at her to see anything else. "Well?" she demanded. "Are you just going to sit there? We've got a lot of ground to cover yet, eh?"

"Right." He jumped to his feet. "Okay. Let's go."

Hyranna cast a last glance in the direction E'tuah had gone, unable to shake the feeling that something *important* had just happened, though she couldn't say what. Then she froze.

The place where he stood, not far from her, should have looked untouched. Instead, she saw clear evidence of two heavy feet, feet that had staggered back in surprise, snapping two ferns and scuffing the moss. A shudder passed through her. Whatever else had happened, for a moment, E'tuah had been *present*. Fully in this realm.

Hyranna thought she would do anything to get rid of him, but suddenly she wasn't so sure. She hated the thought of him around, but even more, she hated the thought of him *free*, able to take up *his* weapon, as he called it, and do whatever he wished.

He wasn't just mean, she realized. He was dangerous. And he was keeping something from her. Perhaps it was time to start playing a different game.

Chapter Thirty-Three

The crossing was just as gruelling as she remembered, made worse by the cut in her foot and the persistent pain that kept shooting up her arm. It started the first time she tipped the canoe onto her shoulders, and it just got worse from there.

She tried to hide it from Jerad, but she wasn't very successful. As they were manoeuvring the craft down a steep rock, it tipped. Hyranna's left arm took the brunt, and a stab of pain made her drop it with a cry. It banged on the rocks, knocked Jerad to his knees, and clattered down the hill before it came to rest in a knot of ferns.

"Damn!" she hissed, clutching her arm and glaring at the forest, just in case E'tuah was watching.

"What happened?"

"It slipped."

Jerad put a hand on her shoulder, and she jumped in surprise. "No," he said. "What happened to your arm?"

She looked up at him, saw the frown of worry above his eyes, and felt the urge to tell him everything. But then what? What would he say? He would think she was mad.

"I . . . I must've fallen on it," she said. "I'll manage." She pulled away before he could ask more questions. She was furious with

E'tuah for his thoughtless violence, furious with herself for provoking him, but all she could change was how she dealt with it. From now on, she was going to be more careful.

As they carried on, it began to rain. The day's heat was quickly licked up as the sun went down, and though the canoe kept them relatively dry, the ground became a slippery, muddy mess. Soon the thunder started, and the sky lit up, almost blinding Hyranna's dark-adjusted eyes with every flash.

They went slowly, and by the time they circled back to the river, they were sore and cold and miserable. Hyranna's arm had seized up, and her heel was stiff and swollen, both feet caked in mud. The rain was coming in furious sheets now, and the wind whipped the trees into ominous groans. Cracks rang out. Branches swayed—and snapped.

"Here!" Jerad shouted above the storm. "I have an idea."

They found a sheltered spot and Jerad tipped the canoe against the rocks, shoving the packs underneath. "Come on," he said. "It'll be drier here."

Hyranna had spent more time under the canoe today than she cared to remember, but she was too tired and sore to argue. She crawled into the sheltered space, and though the rain made an incessant pounding over her head, it was better than staying in the open. She was shivering. Her arm was almost immoveable. Sleep seemed impossible, but she curled up on the wet ground, squeezing her eyes shut against her discomforts. Until she realized she was alone.

She glanced over her shoulder. Jerad was sitting outside, knees curled to his chin, while the rain pounded him and ran off his hair and nose in torrents.

"Jerad, what are you doing?"

"It's okay. Get some rest, I'll . . . I'll keep watch."

"Don't be an idiot! No one's going to follow us in this weather. Get in here."

He hesitated. "There's not enough room."

"There's enough."

"No, I don't think—"

She rolled her eyes, crawled back and grabbed his arm. "Come on. You'll freeze to death out here."

"Hyranna, I don't –"

"Then I'll just have to stay out here too." She plopped beside him in the mud and was immediately drenched. A particularly loud crack of thunder shook the ground, and her eyes went blind for a moment. Then Jerad muttered something under his breath.

"Alright, alright."

It was a tight fit, but Jerad pulled out the fur-cloak and they crawled under the canoe together, bumping each other, shifting to find space, turning and squelching through the mud.

"Sorry," Jerad kept muttering. "Sorry."

"Shut up, Jerad."

By the time they huddled under the fur, Jerad's arms were draped awkwardly around her, but despite the storm rattling outside and the damp cold, she was no longer shivering. In fact, she was glad. She would never admit it, but she liked the closeness. She liked the feel of someone next to her, like a wall, a line of protection, however thin, between her and E'tuah.

And if the wall had to be Jerad . . . well, it was better than no one at all.

It took Hyranna and Jerad the rest of the next day, paddling and crossing and paddling again, to finally make it to the slower waters and the hunting grounds. They pulled the canoe up on shore and this time lit a small fire as the sky darkened. Jerad went fishing a little further upstream while Hyranna scavenged fresh berries from the nearby forest. Thankfully, E'tuah made no appearance, but she still felt like she was being watched. Her skin crawled with the thought of invisible eyes, following her every move.

The fire was almost out by the time she returned, and Jerad was nowhere in sight. She was tired and sore, her whole arm frozen up again, her shoulder aching. She barely cobbled together enough energy to toss a few more sticks onto the fire, then she lay back, resting on the cool ground. The grey light above shifted; shadows lengthened. Last night had been a tempest, the forest shaking and swaying, but tonight was still. So still the trees barely rustled as night drew its blanket across the sky. There was a heaviness in her chest. She was weary and scared. What would happen to them? What would happen to Balduin?

The sound of footsteps jolted her awake. She sat up. It was only Jerad, and he was holding a freshly-gutted fish in each hand.

"Ready to eat?" he asked.

It was the last thing her stomach wanted, despite her hunger. *Your body can take what it needs from the shard.* She shoved the voice away and nodded.

Together they roasted the fish and snacked on the berries, but the silence quickly became awkward. What should she say? Hyranna realized she hardly knew Jerad—not really. In fact, she'd spent years doing her best to avoid Mylar and his dupes. Now she was stuck with one.

"I've always liked night," Jerad spoke up. "I like the cook fires, the way the wood glows, like it's alive. And the smell. The forest always smells . . . richer at night."

"Does it?"

"It does to me. What about you? What do you like better?"

"Really?" She rolled her eyes. "Just cook your fish."

"No, serious. Come on, pick one. Night or day?"

She sighed. "Fine. Day, then."

There was a moment of silence.

"Did you say that just because I said night?"

"Maker's breath, Jerad, what do you care?"

"No reason." He grinned. "Well? Why daytime?"

"Because you can *do* things. I like to do things. Go places. See things, you know? I like . . . colours." She frowned and fell silent. She hardly even noticed it anymore, hardly cared that the fire was a whispering grey instead of brilliant red and orange with hints of blue. It made her sad.

"You like hunting, too, right? You're pretty good for a . . ." He trailed off, suddenly concentrating very hard on turning his fish. "Uh, pretty good."

"Pretty good for a *what*? Come on, peas-for-brains, say it! For a girl? Maker above, I'm probably better than you!"

He snorted.

"And what was *that* supposed to mean?"

"Really, Hyranna? I know you trailed after Balduin Na-es a lot, but he's never been great either. He's too soft."

Her face darkened. "You don't know anything about Balduin."

"Maybe I wasn't friends with him, but I still knew him. He talked to animals like they could hear him. He's soft."

"Maybe they could."

Jerad laughed. "Seriously?"

"Yes. Have you seen him coax a fish to the surface, just by talking to it?"

"That's not possible."

"It is. I've seen it."

He raised his eyebrows but said nothing.

"You don't believe me."

"I'd believe almost anything about him. Everyone knows he's not normal."

Her eyes blazed. "You know, for a little while I almost forgot you were as bone-headed as Mylar."

Jerad's teasing dissolved. "I told you, Hyranna, I'm sorry. Sorry I had anything to do with them. Damn it, I thought we were past this! Balduin's not normal, that's the truth. But it doesn't have to be a . . . a bad thing. Would you deny it?" He sighed and forced his face to soften before looking at her again. "I meant what I said. I really hope we find him."

Hyranna wanted to bite off an angry retort, but as she glared up at Jerad, she saw his genuine concern. She swallowed and looked away.

"Yeah," she finally said. "Me too."

There was another silence while they turned the fish. The fire crackled. Somewhere an owl called. A lonely, pulsing hoot.

Jerad glanced up at her, then back down. He cleared his throat. "So . . . so Nenim says they took him overland from here, going west." He pointed over his shoulder to the opposite bank. "Closer to the next village. I think it's called . . . Tellern. An odd one, right along the Manturian road that runs north-south."

Hyranna stared at him. "Why would they go *that* way?"

"Dal Adis told him not to stay. Too many Northmen pass through. But maybe if we ask around, someone will have seen him."

"But why west in the first place? That's leaving Imo'ani lands."

"Balduin's not exactly Imo'ani."

"Well, he's not Northman filth either."

"That's not what I meant."

"You meant he's not one of us. I know. But he's more Imo'ani than anything else. My uncle shouldn't have brought him near that road."

"But if he's looking for his father, better to start there, don't you think?"

Hyranna froze. "What did you say?"

"What? That he's looking for Alutan? Nenim told me that—"

"Wait. Stop." Hyranna's heart skipped a beat. *No, no, don't talk about Balduin.* "He's dead. Balduin's father is dead. Everyone knows that. But fine, we'll go that way in the morning. How's your fish?"

Jerad frowned at her, confused. "What do you mean he's dead? We don't know that, and Balduin *must* have said something—"

"Nothing's wrong. Shut up."

E'tuah laughed behind her. She jumped in fright, then swore under her breath.

"Hyranna?" Jerad peered at her. "Are you sure everything's . . . okay?"

She nodded and tried to focus on turning the fish, but E'tuah crouched beside her, and all she could think of was the fierce, wolfish face.

"You told me Balduin's father was dead, didn't you?"

She said nothing.

"What are you hiding from me, girl? What aren't you telling me? This Balduin Na-es is special, I can see that. So what about his father? What did you call him?" E'tuah glanced back at Jerad. "*Alutan?* Healer? You've used that name before. A southerner, you said. An outcast." He snarled and leaned in. "This could be important. This *Alutan* could be important. Remember what's at stake." His fingers closed over her injured shoulder. "And don't ever lie to me again."

Then he rose and disappeared behind her.

She couldn't move. A shiver of loathing ran through her, and after a few tense heartbeats, she risked a glance over her shoulder, just to make sure he wasn't still hovering. Then she let out a sigh.

Jerad seemed to make up his mind about something. He dropped his fish beside the fire and moved next to her, crouching where E'tuah had been a moment before. He glanced around, then leaned in. "Hyranna," he whispered. "Is . . . is someone following you?"

She didn't answer at first, so focused was she on slowing her heart back down, trying not to look shocked. Then his words began to register. Maybe she *should* look shocked, or maybe puzzled, or amused . . . *Damn.* It was too late. Jerad was already drawing his own conclusions.

"Who is it?" His voice darkened. "What's going on? Did they hurt you? Is that what happened to your shoulder?"

She pursed her lips, not sure what to say. Jerad was a little too perceptive. Maybe it shouldn't have surprised her—after all, he'd figured out she was running away even before she did, then packed for her. Even still, she found herself battling the image of him as one of Mylar's big, dumb brutes. How could she even begin to explain?

"Are you in trouble?" he asked.

"I . . . I don't know."

"What do you mean?" Jerad reached for his knife. "Is there someone here now?"

She put a hand on his arm. "That won't help, Jerad. Trust me, okay?"

"Of course I trust you. Tell me what I can do."

"Nothing. Just . . . just stay close."

"Of course. But can't you tell me what this is about? Is it someone from home?"

"No, Jerad. Not from home. Not from anywhere you would know. I . . . I can't explain right now. Only promise me one thing."

"What?"

"If I tell you to run, do it."

He frowned. "Do I look like some coward? I—"

"Jerad!" she shot him a look. "Maker above, just trust me! I know you want to be a hero, but it's not *me* I'm worried about. There's something going on that I can't explain, and I just need you to promise you'll listen to me."

His jaw made a hard, stubborn line. "I don't like this."

"Of course you don't. But this is one thing I *promise* you I'm right on."

He growled as he sat back, throwing one arm across a raised knee and frowning into the fire. "Huh. Just the one thing?"

She glared at him. "I said *one* thing, not the *only* thing."

"Are you sure about that?"

"Jerad! I'm serious!"

"Okay, okay. Yes, fine. I'll . . . I'll . . . listen to you. Except I'm not leaving you. If I have to keep my distance, I will. Nothing more."

She nodded. "Good enough."

They said little after that, eating their fish in silence and watching as the fire burned low, but Hyranna could tell he was unhappy.

"I'm tired," she announced at last. "I'm going to get some sleep."

He looked at her, then stood and walked out of the hollow, disappearing for a moment. When he returned, he was clutching his short throwing spear from where it lay by the canoe, face grim. "I'll keep watch."

Hyranna shook her head. "No need. Sleep."

"But this person who's following you—"

"Will not harm us. I promise. It's not like that."

"Then what is it like?"

She hesitated. She didn't want to say anything, but Jerad would never be content left in the dark, and she needed him on her side. Measuring her words, she spoke. "He needs something. I'm in a position to help. But until one of us knows more, there's nothing we can do. He's waiting. That's all."

"Then why did he hurt you?"

"I said I fell," Hyranna snapped.

"I don't believe you."

"Believe what you want; do what you want. I'm tired. Good night."

She grabbed the fur cloak, threw it around her shoulders, then huddled next to the fire and dropped her head to the ground. Jerad didn't move for a long time.

She was almost asleep when she heard him mutter. She glanced over to see him laid out on his back, arms folded across his chest. The spear was in easy reach.

"Good night," he said at last.

"Mmhm."

"But wake me if you think, for any reason—"

"Yes, Jerad," she mumbled. If he said anything else, she never heard.

Chapter Thirty-Four

Hyranna woke with a start. Jerad was on his feet, crouched and listening, spear in hand. He motioned for silence. The forest was utterly still in the pre-dawn light, and a faint mist was rolling up from the river. Hyranna shivered. The fire was out, and the damp earth cut straight through to her bones. She waited a moment longer, but hearing nothing, she threw off the fur-lined cloak and stood.

"Jerad, what is it?"

He frowned and tightened his jaw. "I thought I heard something."

"Well, it wouldn't be *him*. I promise, you won't hear him coming."

"I heard *something*," he repeated, but when nothing else happened in the damp hush, he gave up and straightened.

"Maybe it was a squirrel," she muttered as she rubbed her arms and flexed her stiff, cold shoulder.

"It wasn't like that. It came from upriver. It might have been shouting."

"Do you think it's Dal Adis? Do you think they caught up to us?"

"Maybe," he said. "Either way, I don't think we should stay long."

Hyranna nodded, then poked the fire with a half-charred stick. "This won't start again any time soon. The ashes are soaked, just like me. Maker's breath, it's cold."

"All the more reason to get moving. We'll warm up on the way."

They crossed the river just as the sun was starting to crest the horizon. It was wide and fast here, and it took some skilled manoeuvring to get to the other side. They careened close to a few jutting rocks, and Hyranna nearly tipped the canoe when she flashed her paddle out to deflect them, but they finally made it. They dragged the sturdy craft up on shore, much further downstream from where they'd started, dumped out the supplies, then stashed it in the deepest undergrowth they could find.

"Too bad they didn't send Balduin south," Hyranna muttered. "We'd catch up to him in no time with the way the river's racing along now."

"That or smash the canoe," said Jerad.

Not knowing how far it was to the next stream, they retrieved all their empty water skins and filled them with frothing, white water, then drank deeply. Hyranna's stomach was a little tight with hunger, but she pushed it back. The fresh fish from the night before would have to be enough, and they'd keep an eye out for game and berries to eat along the way. It wasn't like she'd never done this before, and she was pleased to be getting something of her appetite back.

Then she stopped. Something was moving down the river. It hit one of the eddies, disappeared for a moment, then resurfaced, and as it rolled towards the bank, it got caught in a low-hanging branch and spun.

"Jerad!" she gave a tight cry. "Jerad, someone's in the water!"

She was already leaping over the rocks, her feet splashing in the shallows as she ran. She reached it first. It was definitely a person—a man, half-submerged. With a cry, she waded into the stream and latched onto one of the arms as he swung close to her. She held on, trying to drag him towards the shore. For a moment his head rolled to face her: eyes shut, mouth slack, skin alarmingly pale, light-coloured hair plastered to his temple. She felt a stab of horror. It was a Northman, a Manturian—giving no signs of life at all.

Jerad was right behind her, and diving in, he stuck his arms around the man's chest and hauled him up, dripping, from the water. He staggered back towards shore and Hyranna helped, taking hold of the feet. They struggled, slipped, almost lost him once or twice, but finally made it onto dry rock and lowered him. Hyranna's breath caught.

There was a large, gaping wound in his side. The gaudy layers of Manturian shirts, vests, and tight, uncomfortable-looking fabric were torn and bloodied, and there were other wounds: a slit down his arm where the skin parted open, pale and deep; bruises to one side of his face; a puncture wound below his collar-bone; and an arrow still protruding from his left leg, just above the knee. Yet despite everything, he coughed when they dragged him out, and water bubbled from his mouth.

"He's still breathing!" Hyranna cried. "He's alive."

Jerad turned the man on his side, and more water spluttered out, followed by groans and coughs and still more water, and then some blood came up too.

Hyranna winced. She had no idea where to begin, or if he had the slightest chance of survival. He let out a few gasps in unintelligible Manturian, and Hyranna glanced up at Jerad. His face had gone hard, his jaw taking on that firm, stubborn line, and when their eyes met, he just shook his head.

She swallowed. The Northman was wretched, probably as good as dead. His wounds were filling with blood again, overflowing onto the rock, and making small rivulets down into the frothing water.

"We have to do *something*," she said.

"Hyranna, I don't think—"

"If my father were here, what would he do?"

"But he's not here. And I don't know much about tending wounds. Do you?"

"A little. Here, press down on this." She pointed to the fist-shaped gouge in the man's side, where blood was flowing out now at an alarming rate. "Hold tight. I'll get my father's things."

Jerad opened his mouth to say something, but she was already on her feet, running back to where they'd left the canoe and supplies. She grabbed her bag, returned, and pulled out the bandages. There were a few long strips. With her knife, she cut a slit down the man's shirt, though he groaned and tried to push her away.

"Relax," she said. "We're trying to help you."

His eyes flickered open. "*Marddin*," he gasped. "*Marddin ne, put.*" Then he coughed and more blood flecked his lips.

"I don't think this is going to work," Jerad said as he pressed on the man's side.

Hyranna ignored him and peeled away the stranger's shirt. Then she rifled through some of the herbs Jerad had packed, trying to remember which ones did what. She only hesitated a moment, then grabbed two and mixed them together with a jar of balsam pitch, slapping it all onto a bandage and pressing it over his wound. Then she wrapped the rest of the strip of cloth around his middle, passing it over his chest, around his back, over again, and again, as tight as she could. When she ran out of length, she looped it through and tied a firm knot. Jerad just watched, helping where he could, or holding the man down when he tried to move.

Finished with his side, Hyranna moved on to his arm, cleaned and bandaged that, and finally turned to his leg. The arrow had pierced straight through above the knee, running through the fleshy part of the thigh. Yanking it out would do more damage than good. Instead, she took a knife and carefully sawed away the barbed point. Only when it was safely off, could she pull out the shaft. The man moaned and twisted, and Hyranna's stomach tightened, but it had to be done. She gripped the end, took a deep breath, muttered an apology, and drew the shaft in a single, strong tug. Then she staunched the flow of blood with more balsam pitch and the last of their bandages, and when it was all done, she washed herself in the river and tried to clean the man's body, while Jerad started a fire. The stranger had gone limp, only the shallow rise and fall of his chest showing he was still alive. They pulled him close to the fire and Hyranna covered him with the fur-lined cloak. Then they waited.

Hyranna felt drained, exhausted. The sun shone for a few moments, drying up the damp ground a little and chasing away the mist, but then clouds rolled in, and a cool wind made her shiver beneath her wet clothes.

Jerad hadn't said much through the whole process, but now he looked at her and gave his head a shake. "You did it." There was a tinge of awe in his voice.

She grimaced. The stranger was even paler than before, some of his bandages were already starting to bleed, and tremors ran through him, shaking him in fits and starts. "I did what I could," she said. "It wasn't enough."

"It was something."

"Maybe it was a waste."

Jerad reached over and gripped her hand. "Don't say that. You tried to help, you did everything you could. That's never a waste."

"Then what do we do now? Balduin's . . . Balduin's not getting any closer with us sitting here."

"I know." He frowned. "What if I build a stretcher? I could drag him behind me or we could carry him to the next village. Tellern isn't far."

"Maybe." She glanced at the arrow she'd plucked out of the man and lifted the fletched end between her fingers. "Except . . . this wasn't a hunting accident, Jerad, and you know it. This is an Imo'ani arrow."

"I know." His voice dropped.

"He might not be welcome in Tellern."

"No. Tellern's on the road. They see Northmen all the time; if there were any place to bring him, it'd be there."

"Then who did this?"

He shook his head and glanced up at her. "If . . . if Dal Adis and his hunters *are* following us, it could be them."

"What? Uncle Dal? He's a hunter not a killer, Jerad Amanti, and Northman or not, my uncle wouldn't hurt anyone unless they were a threat."

"Exactly," was all Jerad said.

She stopped, looked back at the stranger, and thought about it. Few Manturians ever came to Elamori. A couple traders, a couple travellers on their way to the south kingdoms. Once there *had* been a fight, though it was so long ago, Hyranna could barely remember. She didn't think anyone had been killed. Other than that, there were the stories: how Northmen fought each other for no good reason, killing and enslaving their own kind. And sometimes others, too. She remembered rumours of Kaldis in the north, an Imo'ani village that had been completely destroyed, the men killed, the women and children taken. Of course, that was just a rumour.

"Let's wait," she finally said. "Just a little while. See what happens."

Jerad nodded.

After making sure the man didn't pose a threat, Jerad spent the rest of the morning hunting, and Hyranna tended the fire, trying to keep the stranger warm. When it burned low, she left to find more sticks. She foraged as quickly as she could, hating to leave the stranger by himself, but when she returned, a familiar figure stood by the river, arms crossed.

"You're wasting time, Hyranna Elduna."

She deliberately turned away and bent over the fire. "Go away. Your opinions aren't welcome."

E'tuah strode across the rock, coming up behind her. She felt an urge to shrink away, but hated how he made her feel—weak, scared. She held her ground, and he circled around her, standing next to the stranger with a look of contempt.

"You don't know what you're trifling with, girl. What do you know of the world? Nothing but your stories, and those are imperfect at best. Trust me when I tell you, this man is not worth the risk. Leave him to die."

"No one is worth the risk to you," she snapped. "But my father taught me to take care of people who need it. I don't have to *like* Manturians to show them decency."

E'tuah snorted. "I doubt you'd say that if you knew."

"Knew what?"

The man stirred and groaned, interrupting them, and Hyranna moved to his side. His eyes opened, pale and strangely bright.

"*Eetinar, Meeka,*" he rasped in a voice like dirt grinding between teeth. "*Bred keenan nay sarto nefach?*"

She held up some water to his lips and he drank, but E'tuah give a derisive snort.

"He mocks you," he said. "Even while you give him water and bind up his wounds."

"I don't believe you."

"I have no reason to lie. But as you wish. Either way, he's dying. It's just a matter of time."

Hyranna ignored him and offered the stranger a bit of dried fish.

He pushed her hand away. He growled a few unintelligible words, then collapsed, muttering under his breath. Another cough brought up more blood, staining his lips and beard a dark grey.

"'Stupid forest girl. Are you blind? Get your filthy hands off me, and let me die in peace.' Those are the words he uses, or much to that effect. And that's putting it kindly."

Hyranna's jaw tightened. "I didn't ask you to translate. But while you're at it, ask him who did this."

E'tuah gave a harsh laugh. "You already know the answer. What else is he going to say? Your people don't like intruders, Hyranna Elduna, and Manturians don't like your people. Welcome to the world outside your cozy little village."

Hyranna looked at the man. His eyes flickered a few more times, he gave a gurgling cough, then his body went limp. She frowned. The wound beneath his collarbone must have pierced straight through to his lungs. Against that, what could she do? She didn't have her father's skill.

"Damn it," she growled, and wiped a few angry tears from her eyes. "I tried. I did everything I could—"

"Forget him," E'tuah interrupted. "And take my advice. Move on."

Before she could respond, he vanished. But he was still there, still watching. *Still curious about Balduin.* She had to be more careful. Whatever he wanted, the less E'tuah knew about her friend, the better.

THE STRANGER'S breathing turned heavy sometime in the afternoon: not the deep breaths of a sleeper, but the cold, rattling wheeze of a doomed man. By the time Jerad returned, he was dead.

Not knowing what else to do, Hyranna folded the man's hands and closed his eyes, and in a thin, trembling voice, she sang the Darkening prayer.

Then they were quiet. The fire sputtered and went out. A line of smoke trailed into the sky, curling, wafting, then dissolving into the clouds.

"I didn't know anything about him," she said after a while. "Did he have a family? Friends who cared about him, who were waiting for him to come home?" She glanced up at Jerad, but the broad-shouldered youth just shrugged.

"We didn't even know his name," she continued.

"How could we?"

"What about a pyre? Should we make one? We can't just leave him like this . . ."

"Hyranna," Jerad shook his head. "I know you want to help, but we *have* to move on. You've done . . . everything you can."

She nodded, and without a word, they began to pack: stringing the hare Jerad managed to catch, strapping the bags on, and settling in for a long hike.

They would have to travel overland now—a tedious and slow affair—and Hyranna couldn't help feeling daunted by their mission. Exhausted, in fact. How would they ever find Balduin in all the vastness of the forest? If there was trouble with Manturians, had he managed to keep out of it? She heaved a sigh and cinched the hide straps tight. Her shoulder protested, but she shoved the pain away. At least she wouldn't have to paddle anymore.

"Hyranna."

She turned at the sound of Jerad's voice. He was gripping his spear, face grim, but he managed a small, encouraging smile. "We will find him."

"I know. Let's get moving."

They struck out west into the trees. The ground was a little less rocky, but thick with undergrowth: ferns and nettles and small shrubs, competing saplings of pine and spruce. There were aspen stands with tight foliage and old toppled trees. They tried to keep to high ground, and occasionally a long strip of stone would push out of the earth like the back of an enormous creature, furry with moss and lichen. But mostly they trudged through mud and weeds and scratching branches, with uneven ground hidden beneath, just waiting to trip them up. It was slow going. They walked in silence. Hyranna tried to look for signs of Balduin, but no matter how hard she scanned the ground, she saw nothing.

It was the *other* things she noticed: a patch of withered trees where even the ground looked barren, a cluster of sparrows, all crippled and dead, a tree branch that seemed to curl back and grow *into* its own trunk before poking out the other side. She decided not to point that one out to Jerad and he never saw, but it gave her the same lingering nausea she'd felt on the river. The whole world was going *wrong*.

"How much farther to this village?" Hyranna asked when they stopped for the night.

Jerad shook his head. "I haven't been this way before, and I didn't want to press Nenim too closely. Perhaps another day. Perhaps more. We keep going until we find the road, then turn south. That's all I know."

THE NEXT DAY was more of the same, and Hyranna was starting to miss the swift little canoe, the feel of the open air over the river, the fresh breeze. Even though they were going as quickly as they could, it felt like they were losing ground, that as she travelled further from Elamori, so Balduin travelled further from her.

It was mid-afternoon when they came to a little stream. They drank gratefully and refilled their water skins.

"We're three days from home," Jerad said quietly as they sat and cooled their feet in the water.

Hyranna felt a stab of regret. "I wish . . ." she began, then fell quiet.

"What do you wish?"

"Never mind."

"No, tell me. What is it?"

She shrugged and paddled the cold, fresh water with her toes. A tiny minnow swam close to investigate, then darted away. "Well, just that I'd said goodbye to my father. And Matti too. I miss them. I . . . I shouldn't have left like that."

Jerad nodded. "Your father really cares about you, you know?"

"Of course he does. But he still lied."

"And if he hadn't?"

"I would have followed Balduin, and we'd be together by now."

"I think that's what he *didn't* want."

Hyranna snorted and watched the water swirl over a few rocks, making eddies in the shallows by her toes. She knew they should be moving on, but she was sore and weary.

"What happened?" Jerad asked abruptly. "I mean the day you left. Why did you run away like that? Your father fell over, and someone said he wasn't breathing, but I couldn't see. No one really knew what was going on. Then he was up, and you were running, and . . ." He paused. "If . . . if you don't want to say, that's fine. But . . ."

"No," she said. "I don't want to say."

He sat silent for a moment, then nodded and pulled his feet out of the water. "Then I guess it's time to move."

Hyranna sighed into the forest. Had Balduin passed this way? Had he sat at this very stream? The ground showed nothing—no sign of passage, but that didn't mean much. He had an eerie way of slipping into the forest, moving together with the trees and the rock, like they were a part of him—without even trying! Hyranna was good, but she had to concentrate, put effort into it. With Balduin—

Listen . . .

The thought slipped into her mind. She tilted her head, thinking of the Dandyri. *It can speak*, Balduin had told her. *Listen.*

It could speak. She watched the trees. Watched the rustle of leaves, light grey against glaring white. They trembled with the gentlest breeze, winking with a hundred thousand eyes. She could almost imagine the colours: summer green and soft yellow, flashes of autumn.

"Do you know where he is?" she whispered. "Can you see him?"

A breeze sighed through the branches. It stirred around her, inside her, lifting and growing. And then stillness.

She smiled. For an instant, she could almost imagine—*almost*—that the trees had spoken to her. Then she looked again, and blinked.

Two figures materialized out of the greyness, silent as wolves. Their faces were painted with dark whorls and patches of black. One carried a bow, notched and drawn, the other a long, hooked spear.

"Hyranna!" Jerad gave a shout. She scrambled to her feet. There was another behind her. Her bow was only a few steps away. She dove for it, but an arrow punctured the ground a breadth from her outstretched fingers. The painted shaft quivered dangerously. A fourth figure slipped out of the forest to her left, hardly making a rustle in the dense foliage, a glittering, curved knife in hand. She froze, half in a crouch, but caught movement out of the corner of her eye—Jerad's spear-arm poised to throw.

"Don't—!"

Too late, the spear whistled through the air. The warrior jerked back, a swift, light move, twisting him a hair's breadth out of danger, while still grabbing Hyranna. The spear buried into a trunk. Hyranna ducked and wrenched herself free, even as Jerad reached for his knife. Shadows moved through the bush, weapons glinted, bows stretched, and Hyranna saw it in a flash: Jerad dead from the same wounds that killed the Manturian.

"No, wait!" She threw out her arms, backing close to Jerad. He stopped, but he was trembling, his face hard as he brandished the knife.

One by one, the warriors drifted into view, eerily quiet, faces etched dark with paint: some to look like wolves, others with hawk-eyes, or the open jaws of a bear, others with intricate designs Hyranna couldn't interpret, sharp and angular. They were like Imo'ani. They were dressed the same, with hide pants and shirts and wide embroidered belts, but these hunters wore their hair braided, interwoven with strips of cloth, and each had a fierce, terrifying aspect.

"We are Imo'ani travellers!" Jerad said. "And you dare threaten us?"

"You are strangers." A man stepped forward, not particularly tall, but powerfully built, his voice reverberating from his chest. He wore a real wolf-skin cloak, and his face was painted with black, slanted eyes and a canine snarl. Fangs seemed to hang over his mouth, and his eyes shone with a dangerous light. "You crossed the river."

"This is Imo'ani land, from here to the road," Jerad replied. "We have a right to walk freely."

"This is *our* land. We have a right to know who walks it. You pulled the Northman from the river. You gave him medicine, tended his wounds. What is your purpose? Speak now, or find an arrow in your belly."

"That was you!" Hyranna cried. "*You* killed that man."

His eyes narrowed, first at Jerad, then back at Hyranna. "We drove off intruders. That is what the Cay-et do, what we will continue to do, for the sake of the forest. And what of you?"

The name stirred a memory in her mind, as if she'd heard it before, but couldn't remember where. "We're from Elamori," she said quickly. "Three days' travel upriver. We're Imo'ani, just like you— only my people hunt animals, not men."

The warrior stared at her, glanced at Jerad, then began to laugh. It wasn't a particularly nice sound, but the others joined in. Hyranna bristled. "We're no threat to you. We come from a peaceful village. Let us be on our way!"

"No," the man said, and watched her expression change to incredulous anger. Then his eye twitched. A smile tugged at his mouth. "You are hardly a threat." He nodded, and the warriors backed away, spears and bows not quite so near. Only the wolf-masked man stepped closer. "Now tell us your purpose. Why do you seek the Road?"

"We're looking for a friend."

"A friend. Describe your friend."

She hesitated. She didn't trust this man, but he clearly knew the area—and who crossed it. "He speaks Imo'ani, dresses Imo'ani, but looks like an outsider. Hair like red earth, eyes like water, about my age, but tall."

"The spirit-seer," said another. Hyranna glanced at him, heard the tinge of awe in his voice.

"Balduin Na-es," said the wolf-masked man.

"Yes!" Her arms shot forward. "That's him! That's who I'm looking for! What do you know of Balduin? Have you seen him? When? *When*? How long ago?"

"And what do you want with Balduin Na-es?"

"What do I want with him? What sort of a question is that? I've already told you, he's my friend. I want to join him, that's all." He looked at her, and she tensed. "What? What happened? What is it? Tell me! Tell me what happened. Is he okay? If you hurt him, if you did anything to him, I'll . . ."

"No," the man said abruptly. She stopped, but she could feel the shard stirring, prickling through her with an angry flash. She shut her eyes and forced herself to breathe. Attacking these men could be a disaster.

"No," he said again. "I would not hurt him. But you follow too late. Your friend passed six nights ago."

Hyranna's breath caught.

"Where?" It was Jerad who spoke. "Where did he go?"

"To the Road. And from there, I cannot say. He passed from our lands."

"What did he tell you?" Hyranna asked. "Was he okay? Did he say where he was going?"

"He said many things. We spoke at length. He hears the forest; hears what others miss. He may not be welcome in Elamori, but he will always be welcome amongst the Cay-et. He is blessed with sight beyond his years." He paused, then leaned forward. "He too feels the dark season, and reads the signs of a coming ruin, greater even than the fall of the red trees. Do you know, girl, what approaches?"

Hyranna shook her head, feeling a prickle run up her back. "I know the forest is . . . unwell. Balduin spoke of a sickness, but he didn't understand why. None of us do."

The man glanced at Jerad, as if trying to read something beneath the surly jaw and dark eyes. "By the time you are reunited," he said at last, "you may find he understands better. There is a poison in our forest, a disease festering at its heart that must be driven out. Travel to the Road, and you, too, will learn of it."

"What do you mean?"

"What do I mean? Your village would know nothing of peace if not for us. *That* is what I mean."

He nodded, and just like that, the warriors melted back into the surrounding grey.

Chapter Thirty-Five

They walked in silence after meeting the Cay-et warriors, but Hyranna clung to each word, turning them over and over in her mind. The man had spoken with Balduin! He'd called him gifted, instead of cursed. He had listened to him, respected him, and it swelled her heart to hear good of her friend.

But it left her with a strange feeling: that he was apart, different, existing more and more in some other place she didn't belong.

"Spirit-seer," she said aloud. "That's what they called him."

"I heard," Jerad said. He was struggling through the bushes behind her. "But who does that pack think they are, threatening us, treating us like outsiders? This is *our* forest, just as well as theirs."

"Shh," Hyranna glanced into the trees.

Jerad snorted. "Let them hear. What's their deal anyway? Who in the green earth is Balduin Na-es to them?"

"You don't get it, do you? Don't you know the stories?"

"That's your job, Hyranna, not mine."

"Oh, come on Jerad Amanti! Back when the Greenwater flowed, there was a man—a man that could see into the shadow realm, the place of dreams and spirits. Don't you remember? There's a whole cycle of stories about him, how he tried to stop the darkness from destroying the Greenwater. He couldn't, and the forest fell. They say he disappeared, full of grief at his failure."

"Lel-na!" Jerad grinned. "I remember those stories. Who doesn't? The one where he tracked a monster to its lair, only to find it was protected by blood magic. He could have forced his way in, but instead he tricked the monster by telling it stories, right?"

Hyranna nodded. "Each story had the words needed to undo a layer of the spell, but in the end, it didn't matter. The stories were so beautiful, the monster saw the evil it had done and destroyed itself. Yes, that's one of the stories."

"Okay. So what's your point? What does this have to do with Balduin?"

"Lel-na? Don't you know anything?"

Jerad stared at her blankly.

"It means spirit-seer."

Jerad's mouth formed an 'o,' then he frowned. "Doesn't it mean 'bare-foot'?"

"Of course it means 'bare-foot.'" She snorted. "Because that's what we would call one of the greatest heroes of Ellendandur."

"Why not?"

"It's a mishearing. It only means that if you put the emphasis on *na*, and add a beat . . ." She paused. "Or is it the other way around?"

"I was ready to believe you—until just then." Jerad grinned. "So why give Balduin the name of some long-dead hero?"

"The same reason you and Mylar and those idiots drove him out. He's different. He sees things. Maker above, I wish he could hide that better."

"Why should he? The Cay-et seemed pretty pleased with him. Maybe it'll make him friends, wherever he's going."

"Or enemies."

"Maybe that too."

Hyranna groaned. "What if he does this everywhere? What if people start noticing him, calling him things he can never be? *Lel-na?* It's absurd! It's going to get him into trouble. We have to go faster!"

Jerad chuckled. "Has it ever occurred to you that Balduin Na-es may be capable of taking care of himself?"

"That's not the point. Of course he can take care of himself."

"You say that, Hyranna. But you don't really believe it." He shrugged. "Maybe I don't either."

Hyranna felt herself darkening inside. Balduin *needed* her. Why had he left without her? Why would he do something so stupid? And what if . . .

No. That wasn't a possibility.

But even as she thought it, Jerad spoke her fears aloud. "Have you considered the possibility we might find him, and he might not want us?"

"That's ridiculous."

"But what if?"

Hyranna shot Jerad a look. "I didn't want *you* along, did I? And here you are. So there. That's your answer. Now let's hurry up and find this road."

It took two more nights and into another day—their seventh since Elamori—to finally reach the infamous Manturian Road. The ground began to change. The rocks receded into the earth. The trees grew more and more dense. Hyranna had never been so far from home, and the changing scenery unnerved her.

"Do you think we missed it?" she asked.

"How could we miss it?"

"If it was dark? Maybe we mistook it for a game trail."

"I don't know," he sounded doubtful.

"But we've no idea what we're looking for. How big is this thing? How often do people really use it? Maybe it's grown over."

"I don't think so. Let's just . . . keep going."

Hyranna frowned and kept going. But she was growing restless. Something felt wrong. The forest was oddly quiet, yet so dense and thick. Like it was pressing against her, trying to speak to her, to warn her . . .

It wasn't until they emerged from the trees into a sudden, stark wilderness, that Hyranna realized her own naivety.

The road: what an innocuous word for such a merciless piece of devastation. The forest vanished. The land lay desolate, like a carcass hewn open and left to rot. Trees were sawed down and piled off to the side. The earth was scorched, turned over, and scraped into hideous mounds. The air stank. And in the midst of all that, was an unswerving sheet of a thousand tiny stones upon a thousand more.

For several heartbeats they stood, staring across the open ground, unable to speak. Hyranna's only thought was of pain. It was like a wound in her gut. Like her own home lying in rubble and ash. Had Balduin seen this too? Had he stood here, struck by this senseless act of savagery?

"Maker above." Jerad finally stepped out. "What violence is this? How is this even possible?" He picked his way over the scarred earth, a look of disgust on his face. He clutched his spear a little tighter, limbs tense. When he reached the road, he placed a foot to the smooth stone surface and struck it with the butt of his spear. His nose wrinkled.

"This is odd stone. It doesn't belong here."

"No," Hyranna whispered. "No, it doesn't."

"And there's nothing growing, not even weeds. They did something to the ground—do you see this?" He glanced back at her and paused. "Hyranna, are you okay?"

Her fists were shaking. She took a trembling step out of the forest and onto the twisted earth. She stepped over a rotting tree: it had been chopped down and left to lie in the dirt, next to countless others, as far as she could see in both directions. She staggered over another, and another. She tripped on a stump, almost impaling herself on the grasping fingers of a dead branch. She fell against another stump. It had been old. If she counted the rings, she could read its age. Hundreds of years old. Hundreds.

Hyranna swallowed and looked up. Centuries of life had been destroyed. In the span of what—a few years? She imagined the wheels and the clack of industry, trees shattering as they fell, axes chopping, stones grinding. And men. Men stomping across ground that was never their own, breaking it to suit *them*. Northmen.

She was breathing hard. She could *feel* it. Something growing in her. Something strong and hot—like anger. She stumbled onto the road. Not the living stone of Elamori that rose and fell with the land. This stone was cold and dead. It had been chopped into flat little pieces, fitted together into a careless mass. Hyranna took two steps and dropped to her knees.

The forest was groaning. Her fingers dug into the rock. She swallowed and shut her eyes, feeling it inside, the pain, the wound, the furious pain.

The shard. It was pounding in her chest, both her and not-her, demanding restitution, demanding vengeance. She clenched her fingers into the cracks, and for a horrible moment, she saw it: the scar that ran from the sea to the south mountains, the endless marches of severed ground, shattering everything in its path. She screamed and tore up a single chunk of stone, hurling it across the road.

It clattered uselessly away, mocking her. The Aktyr didn't care about lifeless rock. It wanted flesh and bone and pounding blood. *Manturians . . .*

"Hyranna," Jerad came up behind her.

She jerked back, scrambling over a clutter of broken rocks. "Get away from me!" she shouted. "Don't . . . don't . . . I don't want to hurt you . . ."

"Hyranna, I'm sorry. This is horrible. It's ugly and wrong. I had no idea, I . . ."

The greyness darkened around her. The ground faded. *The Aktyr.* It was running away from her, smothering her in a burst of need, of fury, of pent-up purpose, straining everything towards one goal.

"Hyranna?" Jerad's voice sounded distant, with a new note of alarm.

Run, she wanted to say, but the Aktyr was now thick around her, fierce and powerful, eager to consume, destroy. It bent towards the only human presence. And she was going to kill him. *She was going to . . .*

"E'tuah!" she screamed. "Do something! I can't . . ."

Before she could say anything else, the world opened. She could see beyond shadow and light. The darkness fell away. She *was* the darkness. Life pulsed and wavered across the landscape. Tiny things. Tiny compared to the figure standing in front of her, a burning beacon that she would tear apart, consume.

A hand clamped over her wrist, wrenching her to the left.

"Give it to me." E'tuah's voice cut through the layers of distortion. "Do it now!"

She had no choice. The shard responded. Lines of power snapped over him like a trap. Bones broke. Blood burst. There was a vicious shout. For a single moment, she was exultant, powerful, unstoppable. Everything rushed through her, pounding her prey into the dirt. Life poured through her—emptied out of her.

Then it was gone. She fell back, staggering, weak. Power drained from her eyes and she doubled over with a groan.

Oh, Maker above, Jerad!

The shard's edge cut into her hand, black smears of blood dripping from between her fingers. She glanced up. E'tuah had one knee pressed to the ground, face frozen in a grimace of pain, lips peeled back. Sharp black eyes nailed into her. Then he lunged.

"No!"

She fell. Her arm slammed into a rock, and a moment later E'tuah pounced on her, his knee drilling into her stomach. The breath shot out of her. She gasped, even as the shard twisted out of her hold.

Taken from her.

Her stomach lurched. Her mind screamed with pain. E'tuah had her pinned to the ground, and he was clutching it. He seemed oblivious to her. His eyes flared with power and he drew in a long, ragged breath, like he was coming up for air.

And he was *there* again, present, a physical weight crushing her, stinking of sweat and pain. She had attacked him—broken him with the Aktyr—and somehow he had taken that. Used it. He was breathing. The wind tugged at him. He was real and strong, and he held the shard.

He looked at her, as if noticing her for the first time, and smiled.

"You did it!"

She swallowed. She couldn't breathe with his weight on her, and the pain was growing behind her eyes, stabbing and clawing. *The Aktyr.* She needed it back. She . . .

She wanted to be sick. She felt lifeless, empty.

E'tuah ignored her, lifting his eyes, *seeing* the world. He drank it in. His smile widened. "You've gotten stronger. Yes. Much stronger. I can see again. I can . . ." He breathed, relishing the moment.

And then he flickered, his whole body slipped between realms and back. Just an instant. Long enough for the shard to fall through his grasp and plunk into the dirt beside Hyranna.

He stiffened. "No."

Hyranna stared at him.

"No! It's not enough. Not enough." He snarled and grabbed hold of the shard, bending until she could feel his breath on her cheek. "What am I missing, girl?"

She coughed. It was getting hard to breathe.

"What is it? *What?*"

"Get off her!" Jerad cried. E'tuah glanced up, a shadow of surprise darting across his face.

"You!" He stood in a single motion. As soon as his knee lifted, Hyranna gasped and rolled onto her side, sucking in air.

Jerad was only a few paces away, brandishing his spear in one hand, his knife in the other. "You're the one who's been following her," he said. "What have you done?"

E'tuah laughed and stepped towards him. "You are nothing. Your people are nothing. Only a splotch on the sweep of history, smeared off and soon forgotten. Why would I waste words on you?"

Jerad lunged at him, but E'tuah's hand flashed out and, with a crack, the spear snapped in two. Its halves spiralled in opposite directions. The knife clattered to the stone. Jerad's fingers splayed out, bent by some unseen force, while E'tuah closed the distance in two easy strides. His hand wrapped around Jerad's throat, and squeezed.

"Stop!" Hyranna cried, struggling to her knees. But everything was spinning around her. She felt sick and weak. The pain was intense. Like an arrow driving between her eyes.

"You think you can protect her? Fool! You are no warrior. You're the one who needs protecting. She would have destroyed you if I hadn't intervened. She would have snapped your bones like that spear. *I* saved your life. Do you understand?" His voice dripped with disdain. He tightened his grip until Jerad's eyes bulged and the cords stood out on his neck. "Stay out of this, whelp."

He shoved Jerad away, sending him sprawling onto the road, wheezing.

"Hyranna Elduna, I think we're close. So close! Keep trying. Can you smell it?" He shut his eyes and took a deep breath. "The air, the earth! I'm so close!"

He leapt to Hyranna's side and hauled her to her feet, bringing his face within a hand span of her own. "This Balduin Na-es could be the key. *Lel-na.* Spirit-Seer." He laughed, and the sound made Hyranna shiver.

"Balduin has nothing to do with you! Don't even think about it. Or I'll find some way to—"

"You are doing so well, little keeper. Don't ruin this moment, or your *hero* will pay for it. Now . . . or later. It doesn't matter to me. Do you know the things I can do?" He lifted the shard, the point digging into her cheek, burning like fire. "I don't have time for your ridiculous pride. The world is Breaking! Don't you see?" He shook her. "Find Balduin Na-es. Release me, or it will end: I swear to you by that Tree of yours, nothing will survive. Nothing. Do you understand? *Nothing.* I'm the only one who can stop this now."

"Who are you?" she gasped. "How are you doing this?"

He pressed the shard back into her hand, and everything twisted around her. She raked in a breath. The sky opened and life poured into her, shocking in its intensity. She wanted to weep as the pain vanished, as her vision cleared.

E'tuah was already flickering, shuddering like a dying flame. But he wrapped his hand over hers and leaned close, lips brushing her ear.

"*I* am Lel-na."

A shadow rolled over him, he gave a last burning look, then he stepped back and was gone.

Chapter Thirty-Six

The moment E'tuah vanished, Hyranna stumbled towards Jerad. He was struggling to rise, one hand clutching his face as he pushed himself off the road.

"Jerad!"

He shook his head. And when she reached for him, he jerked away as if stung. "Don't!"

"But . . ."

"No." His voice scratched. He rose onto one knee, but kept his back turned, face buried in his arm.

"I'm sorry, Jerad. I had no idea he was capable of . . . Don't listen to him. Don't. He's a lying brute.

"Lying?" Jerad laughed bitterly. "No, he's right. I'm useless. A damned, useless fool."

"Jerad!"

"No! What did I do? What? Nothing!" He wiped something away from his face, and his hand came away bloody.

She started. "Jerad, you're bleeding!"

"I'm fine."

"No, let me see . . ."

He turned his back again, forcing Hyranna to scurry around him.

"Don't be a child, Jerad Amanti. Just show me what . . ."

He lifted his head. A cut ran across his cheek-bone, blood seeping down in dark grey ribbons. She brought a hand to her own face, feeling where E'tuah had pressed the shard's edge to her skin. There was a faint, lingering pain, exactly where Jerad was cut.

She swallowed and closed her fist over the shard. "That brute! Maker damn him." Her fingers reached towards Jerad's face, but he jerked back.

"What just happened, Hyranna? Tell me what's going on. What . . . ?"

"I don't know."

"That's not true. I heard you talking. He said you were close. Close to what? That nonsense about saving the world? About finding Balduin? Is that what this is about?"

"No, never! I'll never let him near Balduin. How could you even *say* that?"

"Hyranna Elduna wouldn't—but you turned around, and you weren't . . . you weren't *you*."

"What do you mean?"

"I don't know, *you* tell me. You were looking at me but your eyes were black—all black, and then everything around you was . . . I don't know how to explain it, like it was bending. Like everything was twisting: the air, the ground, even *you*. And that wasn't even the worst of it. Hyranna . . . ."

"What?" She swallowed.

"Your face. The way you looked at me, like you were going to . . . You wanted to . . ."

"Stop!" she cried. "Jerad, it's not me, I swear to you. There's something else going on, and this is exactly what I was afraid of. I *told* you not to come, but you wouldn't listen!"

"Yeah, well here I am." Jerad shook his head. "This is crazy."

She looked down at her hand. The blood-slicked fingers parted, revealing the shard—black now, black as night, glinting smoothly beneath the grey smears of blood.

Lel-na. That's what E'tuah had called himself. It was preposterous, ridiculous, unbelievable. And yet terrifyingly possible. Whatever this thing was, might it actually be responsible for all Lel-na's stories, the wonders he'd done all those years ago? Who was to say how long

E'tuah had been trapped beneath that old tree, biding his time, waiting for someone to stumble on that passage into the earth. Except the stories had spoken of Lel-na as a hero, and this man was a monster. It couldn't be him. Could it?

It was time. Time to drag this thing into the light.

"This," she whispered, holding up the shard, mouth twisting in revulsion. "This is what's happening. The day you and Mylar and those idiots tried to kill Balduin, we found a place under the earth. And I found *this*."

Then she told him everything. She started with the Dandyri, how she found the shard there, and how she came back, hoping to meet Balduin, but confronted the old tree instead—and destroyed it. How E'tuah appeared, how she'd been compelled to take the thing with her, for the sake of her own life, followed by E'tuah everywhere she went, never truly alone.

"And it's dangerous. Unpredictable." She couldn't bear to meet Jerad's eye. "That's what happened that day by the lake. I . . . I almost killed my own father." Her voice shook. "No, I *did*. But somehow . . . I brought him back. I don't know how, and I don't know if I could do it again. I can't explain it. I tried to run away, to get myself *away* from everyone, but then you were there, and you wouldn't listen to me, so what could I say? I should have told you. But I kept hoping it wouldn't happen again."

She finally looked up, seeing the strain on his face, the furrowed brow as he tried to understand, one hand still pressed against his cheek. "I'm sorry, Jerad. But what he said, he's right. I could have killed you. And if you stay with me long enough . . . The fact is I'm dangerous, and you should . . . you should . . ."

She couldn't bring herself to say it. The thought of being alone was terrifying, but she knew it was the right thing to do. The *only* thing to do. She had to go on alone.

Jerad nodded. It was a small motion, but it twisted inside her, surprisingly painful. Hadn't she wanted this all along? To leave Jerad behind and go her own way?

She slid the shard back into her pouch and rose. She couldn't even look at Jerad. She just gathered her pack, numbly strapping it over her shoulders, then turned south along the road. Tears pricked her eyes, but she strode past him, feet slapping along the sterile road. Soon there was nothing between her and the empty days ahead. Nothing at all.

"Hyranna..." he called hoarsely.

She didn't stop.

"Hyranna, wait."

"Don't, Jerad!" She kept going. "Please don't make this harder than it has to be. Just go."

"Maker's bloody breath!" She heard his feet tapping after her, then he grabbed her and threw himself in the way. "Damn it, Hyranna Elduna, that bastard might be right, but that doesn't mean I'm going to listen to him. I don't know what in the green earth you've gotten yourself into, but Maker help me if I'm going to let you just walk away!"

"Jerad, what's *wrong* with you? Didn't you hear what I just said?"

"Of course I heard you." His shame had hardened back into stubborn lines. "I knew something was wrong from the beginning. So what if I don't understand everything. That's okay. I don't need to. But the point is, why would knowing the truth change what I promised?"

"Why? Because I could kill you! Because I'm bound to an insufferable companion who has no problem hurting you to make a point. And because you don't owe me anything, Jerad Amanti, even if you think you do."

His face bunched with disgust. "Don't you get it, Hyranna? I'm going to help you find Balduin. I'm not leaving you. And if things get hard and complicated and dangerous, all the more reason for me to stick around. I might not be able to do much, but... but I said it and I meant it. No one should have to be alone."

She stared at him. He knew. He knew and he wasn't going to leave her—she couldn't make him leave, even if she wanted to. Her determination dissolved into sudden, stupid relief and she threw her arms around him.

He went rigid in surprise.

"You big stupid ass!" she said. "Thank you."

THE ROAD STRETCHED ON AHEAD of them as they walked. First through the afternoon, heat shimmering off the stone, and then into an eerie dusk.

"I hate this road," Hyranna muttered. "It's dead. It's too quiet. And I feel like I'm being watched."

"You're not used to being in the open," Jerad said. "We could follow it from the trees."

She shook her head. "No, I want to feel every step of ground so I don't forget what those bastards did. It isn't just trees and rocks. It's their mark. Like they have any right to this forest."

"But you don't even know who did this."

"Sure I do," she snapped. "Manturians. Northmen."

Jerad had nothing to say to that, and they walked on until the gloom had deepened to full night.

They found a spot to rest, off the road and hidden on the east side of the trees. Jerad collapsed, falling quickly asleep, but Hyranna lay on her back, staring into the grey branches, restless and uncertain. She was troubled. A dozen different things could've kept her awake: lingering tension, worry over the shard, over what she might do, over what could happen if Jerad stayed with her, the road, E'tuah's needless brutality, his warnings and threats and dubious claims, and all the things she didn't understand.

And yet she found her thoughts turning reluctantly, inexorably, to Balduin's leaving. Why? Why hadn't he warned her? Why hadn't he even *tried* to contact her? Did he—could he, *somehow*—have known of the shard? All this time, she'd been worried about Jerad—but what about Balduin? Would the danger be any less for her friend? Did she think just because she loved him so much, the shard wouldn't hurt him too? The disaster with her father had proved that theory wrong from the start.

For the first time, she felt a sliver of doubt. She was rushing heedlessly towards Balduin, without thought for the consequences. And when she added E'tuah's growing interest in her friend, she began to wonder: was she making a terrible mistake?

She groaned and turned over, finally beginning to see the glaring fault in her own plans. She'd wanted only two things: to protect

Balduin, and to stay with him no matter what. But what if, when the time came, she was forced to choose?

———

BY THE TIME MORNING ARRIVED, Hyranna had stolen only a few moments of sleep, and they left her feeling exhausted. *Light,* she thought. *Light and Spirit, and spilled Blood, and old . . . something old . . .* The nagging thought clung to the back of her mind, then slipped away and was gone.

She had to keep going. She couldn't let indecision paralyze her. Balduin's quest for his father could be her answer as well. Alutan would know things; he could help—as long as he was still alive. Except from now on, she had to keep careful control over herself and E'tuah. As long as he stayed trapped half-way between realms, wher-ever he was now, then he couldn't hurt anyone, and he couldn't use the shard.

She kept her misgivings to herself, afraid Jerad would be quick to point out the dangers. Even now, he looked at her doubtfully, as if he guessed what was on her mind.

"You didn't sleep much," he said.

"It was enough."

He frowned. "Did he show up again?"

"No."

"You'll tell me if he does, right?"

She sighed. "Please don't worry about it, Jerad. As long as he's stuck, he can't do anything, and I'm going to do my best to keep him there."

He was silent a moment, pulling out the last bits of smoked fish. "How's your arm?"

"Not great. Not awful. It's been better since we stopped paddling. How's your face?"

Jerad gave a grim laugh. "I'll live."

The cut had scarred over, but the skin was all puckered and dark. With her grey-shrouded eyes, Hyranna worried she might miss signs of infection.

"How about a deal?" she said. "I'll tell you when E'tuah shows up again and you tell me if your face gets worse instead of better, okay?"

"And if it gets worse?"

"Let's just hope it doesn't get worse."

"What kind of a deal is that?"

"A fair one. I can't do anything if your cut gets infected, and you can't do anything if I see E'tuah. We'll just know to give each other moral support."

"Hah!" Jerad laughed, then grimaced and brought a hand to his face. "A wonderful physician you make. Alright, fine. It's a deal."

As much as Hyranna hated the road, it certainly made for an easy day of travelling. And a boring one. They saw only one variation in the landscape: a little stream that washed across the road, oblivious to the destruction around it. They were glad, since their water had run to almost nothing, yet Hyranna made them walk upstream, back into the forest, to drink from it and fill their skins.

"This ground is poisoned," she said. "I wouldn't touch the water on the other side if I were dying of thirst."

They sealed their water skins and were about to go back, when they both felt something. Hyranna's eyes went wide. The ground was vibrating, like a herd of elk were charging towards them. They dropped to a crouch, silent as ghosts behind some thick bush as they watched the road. A moment later, two huge creatures careened into view. They were as tall as elks, Hyranna thought, but bigger and more powerful. And though they didn't have the spreading antlers of a buck, they had long hair that flowed and streamed behind them as they ran. Even more strange, they each carried a rider.

They were coming so fast Hyranna didn't have time to see who it was, but she caught a glimpse of bright clothing, pale skin, and short-cropped hair. In a matter of moments, they had clattered away and were gone.

"Northmen," she heard Jerad mutter under his breath.

Hyranna's stomach clenched. First roads, now strange beasts? *Intruders*, she thought, and for a moment, tasted the Cay-et's bitterness. Maybe they were right.

They continued on cautiously, staying on the road, but ready to move at the slightest warning. Nothing else appeared. After walking on and on, with no further disturbances, they found themselves beginning to relax.

That was when they heard it: a sound punctured the air, like quick bursts of thunder—a dozen or so cracks coming rapidly, one on top of the other. She thought of cethul popping over a fire. And then nothing. Eerie silence. Until slowly, the noises of the forest resumed.

"What was that?" Hyranna breathed.

Jerad just shook his head and gripped the hilt of his hunting knife. "Nothing good."

They carried on, but Hyranna couldn't get rid of the knot growing in her stomach. It was inescapable. Something was coming. Something had already happened. Or both. It was almost dusk when she learned what it was.

Cresting over a slope in the road, they saw the remains of the riders: three bodies were strewn across the stone, one belonging to those giant beasts and two to Northmen, pierced by arrows and spears. Both of their heads had been sawn off and left standing in the middle of the road, grisly sentinels for those who followed. Blood soaked the ground and spilled between the cracks, and the road itself had been torn up in a deliberate line, from one edge to the other.

Hyranna pressed a hand to her chest. Words vanished from her mind. She couldn't speak. Couldn't breathe. Then before she could stop herself, she heaved her stomach onto the road. She doubled over, shaking, squeezing her eyes shut, still seeing blood and entrails, and the severed, dripping heads . . .

Jerad was tugging her. Pulling her towards the trees. She followed numbly, stumbling into the bush and dropping to her knees when they were out of sight.

"The Cay-et," she said, wiping a sleeve across her face. "They were here. They were . . ."

Jerad crouched next to her. His face was grim, but he said nothing.

Hyranna just kept shaking her head, over and over again, hoping to drive out the images in her mind, thinking of the wolf-masked man and his warnings, thinking of the wounded Northman they had tried to save, and now this. "I don't like this, Jerad. I don't like this. I just want to find Balduin and go home. I just want to . . ."

"I know," Jerad said. "Me too."

"Maker's breath." She swallowed back her fears. Going home was impossible. The shard made it so, and E'tuah, and Balduin's search for his father, and all the inexplicable things happening in the forest. Those things wouldn't just vanish. Hyranna's path was forward, not back. The dread in her gut deepened.

"Should we ... do something?" she asked.

"Like what?"

"Leaving the bodies. It feels ... wrong."

"No." Jerad's voice was hard. "We don't interfere. They almost killed us for trying to save that man's life. Remember? Besides, you're the one who wanted vengeance for the road. This is what it looks like."

"No!" she shook her head. "No, this isn't right. I want them *gone*—that doesn't mean I want them dead. Not like this."

The Aktyr laughed at her. She could almost hear it: a twisting, slavering hiss. *Yes*, it seemed to say. *Yes, exactly like this.* Blood, vengeance, strength—flesh ripping off bone.

She shuddered and swallowed away the thoughts.

"Let's just find this Tellern," she said. "And fast."

Chapter Thirty-Seven

Hyranna and Jerad moved in silence through the trees east of the road, memories of the butchered Northmen still vivid in their minds. Signs of a settlement appeared. Trails wound through the forest. Smells drifted on the air: smoke, roasting meat, animals, and other less pleasant odours.

Then the trees parted. Hyranna found herself staring at a small cleared patch of land and a garden heavy with squash and beans. In the centre of the clearing was a squat building, made of logs, packed tight with earth, while over its roof stretched a grassy knoll of sod.

Hyranna and Jerad exchanged looks as they crouched in the thick brush.

"Should we see if anyone's in?" she whispered.

Jerad frowned. "I suppose it's what we came here to do. No point skulking around when we want to talk, right?"

"Right," she said. "But just in case something happens, stay here."

"What? I'm not staying here. We go together."

"No. Look, a girl all by herself isn't so threatening. And if something goes wrong, you can take them by surprise."

Before he had a chance to reply, Hyranna unslung her bow, left it, and strode towards the house, trying not to look nervous.

She approached the front of the building and risked a look around. There was something familiar about it all—the garden, the earthiness of the structure, the fire-pit, the pile of wood, chopped and waiting to be burned. Yet everything was a little off. A slate-grey pot hung over the smouldering ash, made of some hard, cold metal she'd never seen before, and similar tools were scattered here and there, many of them strange to her. Beyond that, there was a neatness to it all that defied the forest. Grass and shrubs and trees had been cut back, and little wooden spikes were driven into the ground to mark out a place for a goat. The dozy-eyed creature didn't show much inclination to get *out* of the boundaries set for it, though Hyranna thought it could if it wanted to. If she were an animal, there would be no chance in the Maker's creation she would sit idly on a patch of land barely big enough to pace in.

She rolled her eyes and marched up to the entrance: a crooked door in a mud-packed frame. Not knowing what else to do, she knocked. The sound fell flat, like punching a rock, and there was no reply.

She cleared her throat. "Hello?"

Nothing. She glanced at the goat. It chewed back at her without a spark of enthusiasm. "Hello!" she shouted, pitching her voice even higher.

"Eh, right here, girl. Shouting's not necessary," came an aged voice to her left. She spun and found herself eyeing a short man with a heavy-wrinkled face. His hair was streaked dark and silver, cropped in a single severe line around his chin, and his clothing was strange: loose, light pants, like Manturians wore, and a short-sleeved shirt, but with a finely-stitched hide vest belted over top. Then her eyes were drawn down to a pair of thick, heavy boots that swallowed his feet and a quarter of his legs, and seemed grossly disproportionate to his size.

"You can't be Imo'ani!" were the first astonished words from Hyranna's mouth.

The little man calmly raised his brows.

"I am," he said. He had an earthy, crackling voice. "And I dislike being snuck up on. Why's your friend hiding in the bushes, anyway? It's just me. Lonesome and no great threat to you, eh."

Hyranna stared, then stuttered something about not wanting to alarm the man.

He just chuckled, turned, and looked straight at Jerad's hiding place. One of his wrinkled hands flashed a wave.

"From over the river, are you?" There was no question in his voice. "Lindys, Nan-tu, Denan—no." He brought a finger to his temple. "Elamori?"

"That's right. How did you—"

"Ah!" He waved his hand like he was swatting a fly. "I may not look much as your kind, but don't think it makes me slow." Then he frowned, looked very deliberately into the trees, and beckoned Jerad again. He didn't look away until the young man stepped out, an arrow notched to Hyranna's bow and an unhappy look on his face.

The small man *tsked*.

"*Cha, no-ee!* Give not so much credit to an old man. Do I look armed?"

"I'd rather not find out the hard way," Jerad said darkly.

Hyranna frowned at him. "Jerad Amanti, we're not here to threaten, just talk. Put the bow away."

"Not just yet."

The man smiled. "A wise lad." Then he reached into his vest and pulled out a strange tool. It was wood and metal, curved, with a long, hollow cylinder. It looked innocuous, yet the way the old man held it, a smug look on his face, Hyranna was sure it meant something.

"What's that?" she demanded, taking a step back.

He shrugged. "Weapons I don't find much conducive to talk, especially between strangers. If that's all you've come to do, put yours away and I'll put away mine."

"Yours," Jerad echoed, narrowing his eyes. "How is *that* a weapon?"

"*Cha, kay eto!*" The man's eyes widened and he gave another of his wheezing laughs. "Elamori's so truly sheltered? I don't very believe it."

Almost lazily, he flipped up the metal tube, pulled back a little catch, and pointing it toward the garden, squeezed.

There was a deafening crack. Hyranna screamed, throwing her hands to her ears. A branch of peas exploded in every direction, and even her own cries were drowned out by the ringing. A pungent metallic odour curled between them.

"Maker's breath!" She flung a hand to her knife.

Jerad pulled back an arrow, trembling, yet ready. "Drop it! Drop that cursed thing. I know what it is, and you'll not threaten us."

The man looked perturbed. "I may say it's you who's threatening me, not to mention, Maker forbid, my gun's faster. Please. Tell me I didn't sacrifice a stick of peas for nothing, eh? Showing you, is all I meant. See, see."

"I do see. That's a Manturian gun. That's no weapon for an Imo'ani."

The stranger sighed and let the gun dangle from his finger at eye level. "No, *that*," he said, "is self-defence. Welcome to Tellern on the Road." Then he stuffed it back into his vest and spread his arms. "There. Good as you'll get from me, boy. Maker knows why I'm so trusting, but you say you've came to talk, then talk—or be on your way."

Hyranna and Jerad glanced at one another, trying to figure out what to say next. In silent agreement, Jerad lowered the bow.

"Yes, let's talk," Hyranna said. "We're looking for someone."

The little man raised a brow at her, then gave an encouraging nod, like you would to a child. "Yes, and?"

"Well, have you seen anyone pass through? Anyone who doesn't belong?"

The man hobbled towards his garden. "Who doesn't belong? *Cha no!* You think I know every *bunta* traveller passing down this road? Do I look particularly well-situated to greet passersby, eh?"

He chuckled and bent over with a groan to collect some of the scattered pea pods, then promptly stuck one in his mouth. It gave off a snap as he took the first bite.

"You're near the road," Hyranna observed.

"But not on it. One of two things it takes to find me: an Imo'ani, or a very determined Manturian, and so far I've managed to stay nicely out of determined views. Peas?" He held up a freshly fallen pod.

"Uh, thanks," Hyranna took it. It was sweet and crisp. Jerad accepted one too, but he still eyed the man warily. "So," she continued. "You saw no one pass this way? I'm not talking about Manturians, mind you, but a young Imo'ani. Except this one has red hair, blue eyes, skin all funny and mixed up. You can't miss him. The Cay-et said he'd come this way, and . . ."

She trailed off. The man's face had changed. His eyes went wide with horror, then he squinted, shoulders hunching as he snapped his head around, first one way, then the other.

"Really?" he said. "I'm thinking you should come in for a hurry. There's fresh milk and bread baked just yesterday, and as I said, visitors are rare. Come, come."

The man hurried to the big wooden door, set his weight against it, and hauled it open to the tune of a creaking groan. He beckoned them, plastering a smile on his face before disappearing into the dusky dwelling.

Hyranna and Jerad exchanged glances. Jerad shook his head, but she had a sudden stirring sense this was it. The information they were looking for.

"Come on, just for a moment," she said.

"Hyranna!"

She ignored Jerad's protest and stepped past the stranger into a small, cozy space. It was dark at first, but as her grey vision began to adjust, lines emerged from the blackness. She could see a table, two chairs, and a round black object taking up a corner. It had a grate over it and a metal-looking chute running up through the roof. Besides that, there was a bed of furs, much like her own back in Elamori, and numerous sacks and crates and bundles and tools of various dimensions and uses scattered through the small space, some laid out in neat rows, some stacked, one on top of the other, on the verge of toppling, others strewn on the ground or over the table with no seeming care to their placement.

Hyranna shook her head in amazement, wondering how anyone could live in such clutter, but a moment later, Jerad stepped in and the man heaved the door to. The rest of the light snapped out.

"Forgive me if I alarm you," the man said. "But you *saw* them? You *spoke* with them? With the . . ." his voice dropped dramatically, " . . . the *Cay-et*?"

Jerad was on edge again. "Isn't that what she said?"

"*Dack et'ta no-etch*! They are not seen! No one speaks with them but those marked to die." His eyes went big, then he paused and shrugged and tossed a careless hand. "Or so the rumours say. But, ah, what rumours are always true? If they were so, they'd not be rumours, eh? But still, but still. Ghosts they are."

Hyranna thought about the painted faces and the way the warriors had bled out of the forest. "They might seem it," she said, "but they are men. And why should *you* fear them? They hunt Manturians, not Imo'ani."

The man scowled. "In their eyes, we are the same. Fiends! They terrorize travellers on the road, traders minding their own business. Not many they've attacked in Tellern—true—yet they hate us and scorn those who welcome Manturians. They have eyes everywhere, watching, listening, counting themselves judges of our fates. Those who profit most from Northern trade, they'll come upon in the forest, if they can. And you know what they do?"

Hyranna frowned. "Kill them."

"Kill them!" He snapped his fingers. "Open blood on our lands! *Chit-tu ma!* They make business hard, and trouble—they're bringing trouble on us, I very know it!"

Hyranna thought of the gruesome scene on the road and shivered. "What's your point? We saw them and lived. Besides, we all know Northmen don't belong here. Now if you can't tell us anything useful, we'll be on our way."

"No, no!" The little man frowned and brought a hand to his head as if in pain. "You don't understand. I am trying to tell you, if you go into town—no, you can't! You have their look, and if you mention the Cay-et at *all*, you'll be driven out—or worse. Or worse! I'm giving you advice. Good advice. Listen, my young friends, those are *evil* men. Carry not the stench of them, not even their names. Best of all, avoid Tellern if you can. Here, here!"

He jumped and picked his way to the black grated thing in the corner, took something from beside it, struck a flint, and light flared into view with a sizzle.

Hyranna threw her hands over her eyes and blinked, annoyed. She could see through anything, but it took time for her eyes to adjust. Still, she heard the man rifling through one of his crates, heard the bump and shuffle and crash as items fell.

By the time her eyes adjusted to the candlelight, the man had straightened, holding a rolled birch-bark parchment in his hand, slightly crushed, with a few tattered edges.

"Here!" he exclaimed. "You have never seen one of these before, I think, eh? Come look, come look." He motioned them to the table and spread the parchment out, using the heavy brass candlestick to hold one end, and something like a huge, thick cup to tack down the other.

Hyranna blinked and tried to focus her eyes while Jerad came up behind her, looking over her shoulder at the confused lines and symbols.

"It's a map!" he cried. "Hyranna, look. A map!"

"Yes." The man nodded. "Look here." He jabbed a finger towards a cluster of symbols. "This is Tellern. This is where we are, and here's the road." His finger ran up and down a line—the heaviest one, running from the top of the parchment to bottom. But not the only line. Others crisscrossed the map, running parallel to it, or intersecting, far more twisted than the road, more natural.

"These are rivers," she said, as she traced one of them. "Is this the Tindanarra?

He blinked at her approvingly. "Quick, you are. Very well, look here . . ."

She only half-listened as he rambled on about common routes and destinations, and the various geography of each path. She was busy trying to locate the possible site of her own village, compare it with how far they'd come, and guess which way Balduin may have gone. A few other clusters of dwellings were represented, one not far from Tellern. She reached over and put her finger on it, interrupting him.

"Is this a village, too?"

He stopped, mouth hanging open in mid-speech. "Yes, yes," he said. "And if you'd been listening, you would have heard me say already. That is Haiyo-na. But as I was . . ."

"Are they Imo'ani too?"

"Some yes. And some others. But there are very few Imo'ani settling to the west these days. East is the way they go—to your village, perhaps, or to Lindys, and further, into the deep forests. But many now go south, to Calton and the Manturian way of life."

"Manturians are from the north," she corrected.

"Yes, yes, and south now. Both north and south. Everywhere on the road, all the way to the Aethen borders at—"

"And this?" Hyranna pointed to another settlement, one further south down the road. The man heaved a sigh.

"That is Calton."

"Cal-ton," she mouthed the odd syllables.

"Not Ellendi," he said and pursed his lips. "But fine trading partners –"

"Wait." She stared at him. "Not Ellendi? You mean it's a Manturian town? *Here*? In the forest?"

The man gave a shrug. "So hard to believe? Why build a road if not to use it, eh?"

"That's . . . that's absurd. This isn't their place."

"Tell that to them. But if you would just let me finish, I could explain."

She gave a huff. "Then hurry up and explain."

He shot her a look. "Likelihood being what it is, your friend wouldn't have stayed long in Tellern, if he stayed at all. Tellern's not what it used to be: Imo'ani, most, but also Aethen from the south and some mainland Manturians—the kind that come to settle. Honan, they call themselves, and some Yeldin. But see, if your friend happened this way, my guess is he'd make for Haiyo-na—that's west— or if he wants more to seek Manturians, he might have luck in Calton."

"Why not north?" Jerad asked, leaning over the map.

Hyranna rolled her eyes. "Do you see anything north? Look." She ran her finger up the road. It moved in an unbroken line, unspotted with settlements or rivers.

"Truth," the man nodded. "The road north is barren between here and Manquin. Nearly two weeks travel on foot, as the Manturians keep time. Fourteen days, give or take. Less by horse."

"*Horse*?"

He smiled knowingly. "The beasts who carry them overland. Northmen live scattered over a thousand islands. But now they're pushing south, moving to the Wide Lands, bringing roads, horses, wagons, and let's not forget," he patted his vest. "Gunpowder. The force of a hundred hammer falls in a speck of dust. *Bang!*" He clapped his hands and Hyranna jumped.

"Maker's breath, don't speak of that thing! It's ugly and vicious. Just tell me, where would people direct him?"

He shrugged. "Depends."

"On what?"

"On what he's looking for."

Hyranna paused. How much would Balduin have shared? Probably more than was good for him. "He's looking for a man called Alutan. A man who . . . who . . ." She thought of E'tuah and remembered he would be listening, always listening.

"Who what?"

"An outsider," Jerad said, before she could stop him. "Not Imo'ani, not even from the forest, but some other place. Maybe south. He lived near Elamori for a while, had a son, then just left. He . . ."

"It doesn't matter," Hyranna cut in, giving Jerad a withering glare. "Can you help us, or not? All this blathering won't do us any good if you can't tell us where my friend's gone."

The man leaned close, barely a hand span taller than her. "I *can't* tell you where he's gone, because I don't know. I'm afraid you'll have to figure that out for yourself. But two things I can say: if you hear any of my words, stay out of Tellern. If your friend is looking for someone who's not Ellendi, then likelihood being what it is, I would start looking in a place not belonging to Ellendi." He raised his thick, bristling brows and jabbed a finger on the southern town. Calton.

Hyranna gave a nod. "Thank you. Thank you, you've been helpful." She looked at the man, with his shorn hair, wrinkled face, and bizarre blend of Imo'ani and Manturian clothes. A strange flash of gratitude moved her. "Goodbye," she said.

He grinned and nodded. "Banno," he said. "Name's Banno. Good fortune to you."

Banno's hut became two, then three or four, then clusters of seven or eight, and as the trees thinned, Hyranna found it more and more impossible to go unnoticed. There were Imo'ani everywhere: children running through the woods, older folks preparing food as the day wound down to dusk, stoking fires, stretching clothes on lines, or fetching water from an unknown source. Their habits were familiar, even if their clothes and tools were strange.

A child finally noticed them, giving a cry as he pointed in their direction. "Look, *eyno-wa!*"

Instead of a flood of attention, or even someone rushing out to greet them, the child's mother grabbed his hand and pulled him inside a nearby hut. The last thing they saw from her was a flash of suspicious dark eyes.

Jerad snorted. "That man wasn't joking when he said these aren't the friendly type. Maybe we should listen to him. We could turn around, find a way back?"

Hyranna shook her head. "Fastest way south is following that road. If we go back, we'll lose a day or more. We'll never catch up to Balduin at that rate."

Jerad muttered a reply, but they pressed on. The suspicious glances were now on every side. Men and women stopped to stare at them, not saying anything, not even greeting them, just watching, frowning. Hyranna was almost relieved to leave the huts behind.

"Was that it?" Jerad asked. "Was that Tellern?"

Hyranna shook her head. "Listen." Noises drifted up through the trees, voices, shouts, banging doors, the clatter and clang of work. The mutter of sounds was coming from ahead, and soon they glimpsed the road. A moment later, they emerged.

Where the forest should have been, there was a sudden glut of open sky, an expanse of grey above a mottled landscape. Not trees, but row upon row of lifeless plank structures of stone and metal, all warped into stiff square forms with slanted roofs—high enough to house giants. *Tellern.* Hyranna blinked, her eyes stinging from the unveiled white of the sun as it set over the trees to the west.

"Maker's breath, it's bigger than Lindys," Jerad said.

"And barren." The horrible sinking feeling settled deeper, but already the devastation was less painful. The road was the worst, and everything else just sprouted, inevitable, from its trunk. Hyranna grunted and hardened herself to the path ahead. "Let's get this over with."

They stepped onto the road as it dipped into the crowded and treeless tract of land. Buildings rose up on either side, tall and imposing, with square holes for windows and large heavy things for doors. In the forest, the road had seemed gluttonously large. Here, it shrank. The buildings crowded over them, and Hyranna had the unnerving sense of being swallowed into a lifeless beast.

She glanced at Jerad and saw her unease reflected in his eyes. Neither spoke. They continued on. People hurried this way and that, some leading burdened animals, some in groups, and some alone, but no one said a single word to them. The only one who even noticed their passing was a stooped old woman who scowled at them before disappearing behind a door. Voices drifted out, and there were lights in the window, but the woman's parting glance hadn't exactly been welcoming.

"What do we do?" Hyranna whispered.

"Keep moving until we get to the other side."

"Shouldn't we ask about Balduin? Maybe he passed through here and someone knows something. Maybe he's here now."

"I doubt it. You think Balduin would linger in a place like this?"

"We have to at least ask."

A door opened further down the street, and a man stepped out, sighing and shaking his head.

"Hello!" Hyranna called.

He glanced at her, frowned, then quickened his pace, booted feet clacking down the road.

Hyranna felt a surge of frustration. "Hold on there! I'm talking to you! I'm looking for someone, for—"

Jerad took her arm, and she stopped. Her words echoed noisily between the houses, fading into a sudden, eerie silence. The houses cast long shadows like trees, but without the sway and creak of branches, the rustle of animals, or even the soft, still hush of life, the tap of the man's retreating footsteps was the only intrusion into the unnatural quiet. Without even realizing it, dusk had fallen, and Hyranna and Jerad were alone.

"I don't like this place," she whispered.

"This was *your* idea, remember?"

"Oh, stuff it. Let's just keep going."

They had barely passed the next house, when a soft voice called from between buildings. "Who is it?"

Hyranna froze. *E'tuah?* But Jerad turned as well, and the stranger that stepped out of the shadows had a pale, bearded face. Manturian, she thought, and Jerad drew himself up, hovering tight by her shoulder.

"The person you seek," the man said again. "Who is it?"

Hyranna bristled. "How do you know we're looking for someone?"

"How could I not?" The man smiled. "You told half of Tellern. Shouted it, actually."

Jerad glanced at her. "You did."

She dug an elbow into his ribs. "Fine. So what's it to you? Do you know something?"

"I might."

He stepped closer. His hair was longer than most Northmen, clean and combed into a tight braid, his beard just a little longer at the chin. His clothes were strange too—neither Manturian nor Imo'ani, but loose and light, obscured by a long travelling cloak and a pair of heavy, well-worn boots. But as he turned, Hyranna caught the glimpse of a sword hilt sticking up behind his back.

She bristled, hating him at once, though she couldn't explain why. It was a deep gut-sense, a burning instinct that made her recoil. And yet, he posed the best opportunity they'd had so far.

"We're looking for a friend," she said. "A young Imo'ani." She described Balduin carefully, then watched the stranger's reaction.

"What makes you think you would find him here?"

"We were told he might have passed this way. Maybe five or six nights ago."

"Ah." He looked thoughtful. "I'm not sure I'm much help then. I've only just arrived. Maybe you'll have better luck at the wayhouse."

"What's that?"

"Food, drink, beds. A resting stop on the way from one place to another. A wayhouse. Shall I show you?"

"No thanks," Hyranna said, at the same time Jerad said, "Sure."

She frowned at him. "I thought we were going to pass through."

"I thought you wanted to ask around."

"But Jerad, I don't *like* this."

"You mean you don't like *me*," the stranger replied. He was eyeing her, and the closer he looked, the more his gaze made her uncomfortable. He had pale, grey-washed eyes, and he seemed to be looking *inside* her. As if he could see her fears, her struggles, her secret—the deadly thing she carried.

"No," she said. "I don't."

"Hyranna . . ."

"Shut it, Jerad. You heard him. He said he can't help us. Let's just go."

The man nodded. "If you change your mind, you'll need these to stay the night." His hand disappeared into his cloak, and a moment later he pulled something out between his fingers. They were two small circles of metal, not much bigger than her eye, and engraved with a strange symbol.

"What's that?" she frowned.

"Coins."

"We're not spending the night," Jerad said.

"Even still. Take them. If it's information you're after, you'll find people more keen to speak if you put this in their hands. The wayhouse is three buildings up and to your left." He nodded over his shoulder. "Good luck."

Before Hyranna could object, he pressed the metal circles into their hands, one for Hyranna and one for Jerad. A tremor ran through him, like a quick spasm. Then he pulled back, and with a last pitying smile, he strode south into Tellern and was gone. Hyranna stared after him, the knot of fear loosening in her stomach the further he passed.

"Strange," Jerad said. "Very strange." He ran his fingers over the coin, turning it, staring at it. "Who do you think that fellow was?"

"How should I know? Some Manturian on the road."

"Manturian?" Jerad glanced at her. "No way. That was a southerner, from the mountain kingdoms. Aethen. Did you see his sword?"

"What of it?"

"Northmen don't carry swords. Northmen don't wear their hair long either. In fact for a moment, I thought ..."

"What?"

"Never mind. It's just such a long way. I wonder why. Why come so far north?"

"Maybe he's looking for someone too."

"Maybe," Jerad replied, then glanced down the street. "Do you think we should try it?"

"The wayhouse?" She wrinkled her nose. The building he'd indicated was large and grim, and no more inviting than any other, but the dirty windows were lit up from behind. "It's what we came here to do."

"Good," he said. "But this time I get to go first."

Chapter Thirty-Eight

The door creaked open. There was light coming from inside the wayhouse, what looked to be a few greasy lamps and a fire. Barely enough to illuminate the smoke curling around the ceiling, and to highlight a small knot of drinkers at the far end of the room.

Hyranna and Jerad stepped inside, and the door fell closed with a bang. Hyranna blinked, feeling disoriented. Though the room was big—bigger than anything back in Elamori—it felt tight and cloying, and she fought the desperate urge to run.

"Good evening," a voice pulled her back, and she glanced up to see a young woman perched on a massive wooden counter, just to their left. It reached nearly to Hyranna's shoulders and dominated that side of the room, though she couldn't see any use for it, besides looking large and intimidating.

A woman sat on it. She was leaning up against the far wall, feet stuck out and crossed at the ankle, while a lamp hung from the ceiling above her. It cast a dubious glow over something she was holding.

"What are you doing up there?" Hyranna asked.

The woman laughed. "*Golly*, girl, aren't you straight to the point." She stuck a thumb up, pointing to the ceiling. "It's the only damn corner in this place with light enough for *reedin.*"

"*Reedin*?"

The woman guffawed, a loud, obnoxious sound that made the other occupants in the room glance up. "Are you from east? You look right wild, if you don't mind my saying."

"We're Imo'ani," Hyranna said. "And what are you?"

The woman's eyes sparkled. "I'll try not be insulted. We speak the same—isn't that enough?"

Hyranna scowled and eyed the woman. She was rather small, with dark grey skin and black hair, but it was chopped short, and she wore pure Manturian garb: loose pants, a shirt belted at the waist, a tight doublet, and boots reaching nearly to her knees, the cracked leather tops folded down. Hyranna would have mistaken her for a boy, if it wasn't for the fabric stretched tight over her bosom and the rather pretty features that looked down.

"I don't think so," Hyranna said coldly. "No one here looks Imo'ani to me."

The woman laughed and closed the thing she was holding with a snap. "Oh, aye. But live here a month, and you'd start looking like us, too, I warrant. What makes you what you are, dearie? Just your clothes?"

She swung her legs over the counter and sat there, feet dangling, leaning down with a smile. "Now what can I do for you? If you're really from east, you probably don't even know what a wayhouse is. Which figures. Your kind tend to avoid us, keeping your river between, like it's a wall to catch all the unwanted Northman influences. Which means something special has brought you here. Looking to buy a gun?" She tilted her head.

"We just want information," Jerad said, sticking out his hand with the metal piece.

Her eyes lit up and she sucked her teeth, leaning forward a little more. "Pardon me, good sir. Can it be you're more experienced than you look, a little corrupted with Northman ways?" She snatched the piece and held it between her fingers. "A little corruption never hurt anyone, far as I see it. What *can* I do for you?"

As if by some spell, the woman's attention was now entirely fixed on Jerad, and Hyranna found her irritation growing.

"We're looking for someone," she said.

"Well, now. I believe you've come to the right place. Do tell."

"A strange kid," Jerad continued. "Tall, but young, with wild red hair. You can't miss him. Other than that, he'd be dressed like us, talks like us. If our kind are so rare, he should have stuck out."

"Oh, so a *proper* Imo'ani." The woman looked teasingly at Hyranna, then leaned back. "And what if I *had* seen someone of that description?"

"Then I think you ought to tell us," Hyranna said.

"*Ought* I? Tellern doesn't work on *ought* here, I'm afraid, dearie." She raised her eyebrows expectantly.

"Look, woman—"

Jerad tugged Hyranna's arm, interrupting the burst of anger. "Give her the other one."

She had almost forgotten the little metal thing in her hand. Scowling, she held it out, and it disappeared just as quickly as the first. The woman jangled them together in her fist.

"Ah, they *do* sound nicer as a pair, don't they?" she smiled, then jumped down and landed beside them with a loud thunk. She was only a little taller than Hyranna, but much more slender, with ample hips and a full bust. Hyranna narrowed her eyes spitefully. It seemed unfair that she could dress like a boy, but look more womanly than her.

"As a matter of fact," the woman tilted her head back to look at Jerad. "I think an Imo'ani boy passed not many nights ago. *He* was looking for someone, too, if I remember rightly, but I don't think that person was you. A merry little chase, is it?" She laughed.

"Can you tell us anything else?" Hyranna asked. "Did he speak with you?"

"Me? Not much. I got the feeling he didn't care for me. Kinda like you, dearie. But he seemed sweet, all the same. Daryn's the one you want. Right over there." She nodded at the little circle by the fire. Then before waiting for a response, she threw back her head. "*Hoya,* Daryn! I've got travellers that want news on that red-head you almost started a fight with. Remember him?"

"I remember he was an honest bastard, but not much else," the man hollered back. "Who wants to know?"

"Just these."

A chair scraped and an Imo'ani man stood up, thick and broad-shouldered, hair cut short, exaggerating his square forehead and strong, tough jaw. He was dressed like Banno had been, in an odd mix of Manturian and Imo'ani clothes, but the effect was far more intimidating on the big man.

"You friends of that skinny freak?" he asked, puncturing the wood floor with each step.

Hyranna narrowed her eyes. "Call him a freak again and I'll stick a knife in your knee."

The man's eyes widened, then he burst into a laugh. "Ember, do you hear this girl?"

"Uh-huh," the woman chuckled and winked at Hyranna. "A right spitfire she is, all twelve of her summers."

"I'm fifteen."

"I don't think she's joking," Jerad warned. "Did he say where he was going?"

The man thought about it. "Heading south, I think, but I can't be certain."

"How long ago?" Hyranna asked. She realized she was holding her breath.

"Four nights ago, maybe. Or was it five?"

"Four or five!" Hyranna's eyes lit up. "Jerad we're getting closer. Come on!" She snapped out a quick thanks and spun for the door.

"Hold on there," the woman said. "Where're you going? It's getting dark, don't you know?"

"We can see," Hyranna said.

"And where'll you stay?"

"Wherever we find."

"You won't find any place. Unless you want to sleep on the road, that is. And *golly*, but I wouldn't recommend that."

Jerad looked at Hyranna. "She has a point."

"But we don't have anything else to give." She gestured to the metal pieces the woman was still jangling together.

Daryn chuckled. "Really? You gave her two whole marks so *I* could tell you about some kid? She's cheating you. That's enough for a dozen to spend the night, isn't it dear?"

The woman smiled, then stomped on his toe.

"Ow, you brute woman! Just keeping you honest."

"Next time, I spit in your food," she said sweetly. She swung to face Hyranna and Jerad, still clanking the pieces together. Then she rolled her eyes. "Alright, alright." She leapt onto the counter and leaned over, reaching for something behind. A moment later she resurfaced, holding a heavy key between her fingers. "For two marks, you got yourselves a bed. So? What do you say?"

Not long after, Hyranna found herself trying to get comfortable on a creaking wood frame piled with furs, while Jerad stretched on the ground beside her.

"What a strange way to welcome travellers," she muttered, staring at the wood-beamed ceiling. She wrinkled her nose against the musty blankets and scooted them a little further down.

"They're surviving," Jerad said. "Adapting. Let's face it—the world won't look like Elamori, and the sooner we get over that, the better. It's not up to us to decide what others do."

"Sure. It doesn't mean I have to like it. I'll be glad to put Tellern behind us."

"Me too," Jerad said. "The trouble is—is it Tellern that's strange, or just us?"

Hyranna said nothing. She didn't like his point, but everyone looked at them askance—in mockery, or in fear. Like they knew about the gruesome bodies on the road. Like they blamed *them*. Wild. From the east, over the river. Like the Cay-et.

The longer she thought about it, the bigger the world seemed to grow: a cold, unfriendly place, full of guns and boots and musty bed sheets. Was it true? Was Elamori the exception to a world gone mad?

"Doesn't matter," she finally said. "Let's just try to find Balduin. We're getting closer. If we leave first thing in the morning . . ."

Her voice drifted. Jerad had fallen silent, his breath deepening towards sleep. She couldn't blame him. There was nothing else *to* say, nothing they hadn't said a dozen times already. She sighed and tried to relax.

. . . And then she felt it.

"What was that?" she asked.

Jerad stirred. "What?"

"Did you hear that?"

He was silent a moment. And it came again. A sound, like a distant falling tree, popping, cracking. The same sound they had heard on the road.

Hyranna sat up. She could see nothing but a grimy window overlooking the road. "Jerad," she whispered. "I think that was —"

More cracks punctuated the dark—followed by a scream.

Hyranna leapt to her feet and peered out the window. There was movement below, shadows stalking the street like wolves. The shadows stopped by the wayhouse. Voices drifted up. Words she didn't understand.

"Northmen," she hissed. "Outside."

Jerad pulled out his knife and backed against the door. They could hear feet tapping down the hall, movement, voices.

"Manturians!" It sounded like Ember. "From Terryn Dal . . ."

"*Cha, no makai!* What?"

"Find out what they want."

"Are you mad? If they're Terryn raiders, we know exactly—"

"Just *go*! I'll deal with our guests."

Whispers. The door banged. Hyranna jumped as boots stormed into their room. It was Ember, holding a gun, legs planted, silhouetted against a dirty smear of light from the hall.

"What did you bring into my house, you *bunta* filth? There are Terryn raiders at my door. *Terryns!* What do they want?"

Hyranna froze in terror, mouth hanging open—just as Jerad sprang and seized the woman from behind.

Ember shouted. The gun went off. Hyranna screamed and ducked, and the window behind her shattered, blowing shards of glass in every direction. She threw her arms over her head and a few pricked her like nettles.

"Drop it!" Jerad said. "I don't want to hurt you, but if you don't drop that thing—"

Ember's foot flashed, catching him in the ankle. She drove her elbow into his gut. He staggered back.

"Stop!" Hyranna cried, leaping to her feet. "Stop!"

Ember wriggled out of Jerad's grasp, just as Hyranna tackled her. She managed to seize her wrist, twisting the gun as hard as she could. It came free and clattered to the ground, while Jerad wrestled her back.

"Savages!" she screamed. "Let me go!"

"Explain what's happening! Why did you attack us?"

"I'm not attacking you. Let me go! There are Terryns, you fools. Don't you know anything?"

"Stop!" said a new voice.

Hyranna twisted her head. Daryn, the big man from the night before, was standing and holding the gun. *He wouldn't*—would he? Then a knee slammed into her gut, she doubled over, twisted off the bed, even as nails dug into her arm, wrenching her injured shoulder.

"No!" Jerad cried.

"I said stop! You, drop the knife!"

Jerad froze, hesitated. His eyes flicked over to the shattered window. Then his blade hit the ground and he straightened. In the silence they heard breathing, shouting from the street, then another gun went off—once, twice.

"*Chit-tu ma!*" Daryn said. "One of you two explain! What did you bring on our heads?"

"We did nothing," Jerad said. "Whatever you think, it wasn't us, I swear to you by the Maker."

"Then why are they screaming for blood?"

"*Who's* screaming for blood?"

In a flash, Hyranna understood. She saw the bodies on the road. The severed heads. The blood, spilling into the cracks. She felt herself go cold.

"Manturians," she said.

Daryn's head snapped towards her. "What do you know?"

"The Cay-et. They attacked someone on the road."

Ember cursed and jumped to her feet, scrambling away as if afraid to touch them. "Cursed *bunta* fiends! One of *their* lot."

"No!"

Hyranna held up a hand, ignoring the new stabbing pain in her shoulder. "No, we've got nothing to do with them. But we saw. They murdered two Manturians on the road. Maybe more. Left them as a warning . . ."

Daryn shut his eyes and cursed roundly. "Get up!" he said. "Walk to the door."

"I told you already, it wasn't—"

"Shut up! If it's blood they want, we'll give it to them."

"*What*?" Hyranna couldn't believe what she was hearing. Everything spun around her. She swallowed. "No. No, you wouldn't. Let's just stay here, we're all on the same side, we didn't do anything wrong, maybe they'll pass by . . ."

A crash sounded from below, and the wayhouse filled with shouts, angry voices, words she couldn't understand.

Daryn backed away to the door. "They're up here," he shouted. "The ones you want!" He edged a little further, still holding the gun on them, said something in Manturian. There was another bang, closer, and he glanced behind him, down the hall.

Jerad pounced, seized the man's arm, jerked the gun up. It went off, pounding splinters of wood in every direction as Jerad cracked the top of his head into Daryn's face. In the same moment, Hyranna kicked Ember's shin, hard. The woman cried out and grabbed her leg, and Hyranna burst to her feet, hurling herself into her. Ember hit the wall, her breath came out in a whoosh, and sparing no thought for charity, Hyranna slammed the woman's head with her fist as hard as she could.

Ember dropped. Then Jerad snatched Hyranna's hand and yanked her into the hall.

Feet clattered up the steps towards them. Hyranna's heart was thundering, her fists shaking. Bleeding. She was ready to fight, but Jerad tightened his grip.

"Here, here," he breathed. "Next room."

He set his shoulder into the door across the hall and it flew open in a shower of splinters. They leapt in and slammed the door behind them, grabbing the wooden bed-frame and shoving it tight against the entrance.

"Now what?" Hyranna hissed. The space was otherwise useless, identical to their little room, including the table, two chairs, and one grimy square window at the far side.

"Out the window," Jerad said. He strode across the room, grabbed one of the chairs, and hurled it against the glass as hard as he could. There was a dull thud, and the chair bounced off.

"Maker's breath!" He tried again, and again. There was a chink. Again, and the chair splintered. But now the window let out a crackling groan, and the dirty glass became a cobweb of fractures. Jerad seized the biggest piece and threw all his strength into it, once more —it shattered.

The same instant, something banged against the door. Angry words flooded the hall, shouts from the Manturians, from the Imo'ani. A gun went off, deafeningly loud in the small space, louder than Ember's weapon, and for a terrifying heartbeat, Hyranna could hear nothing. Jerad's hand closed around her wrist, propelling her towards the window, even as Ember started screeching.

They peered through the busted glass. It was a long way to the dark below. A long way—but nothing she hadn't jumped before.

More angry shouting blasted through her still-ringing ears. Someone hammered on the door. She swore, then swung herself out the window, wincing as the edges of glass bit into her fingers. She dropped, hit the ground, rolled onto her side. Her injured shoulder screamed in pain, but she bit her tongue and kept silent, scrambling out of the way. Her eyes snapped up. Where was Jerad? Was he coming? The shouts were getting louder, more banging, a crash. Two gun shots split the air, one after the other, and Hyranna's hand flew to her mouth.

No, no, no . . . !

A heartbeat later, Jerad launched from the window. He hung in the air for an instant, before landing with a thud, rolling forward onto his arms.

"Jerad!"

He shook his head, regained his balance, and hauled Hyranna up.

"Come on," he said. "This way. Hurry."

They ran. Not towards the road, but further into Tellern, desperate to put space between them and the cries, the shots ringing on both sides, the clattering of weapons, the fighting. The buildings were crammed together, and not as neatly as she'd thought at first. They twisted between the rows, through the labyrinth of tight muddy spaces, and soon they were both lost, running this way and that, breath coming in ragged gasps, lungs burning, vision spinning from exhaustion.

They ran until the treeline loomed out of the half-light and Hyranna's eyes started to adjust again. They were almost free.

They staggered out of the last line of houses and into the forest, familiar branches and bushes closing around them. They kept going.

Slowly, the sounds of struggle faded, and they stopped to breathe. The sun was just rising. A misty grey was spreading through the trees.

"What just happened?" she gasped.

Jerad shook his head, taking a moment to compose himself. "They thought it was us. What we saw on road. They thought we did that, killed those men."

"I don't know. I don't know. Do you know where we are?"

"Somewhere outside of Tellern. Eastern edge, I think."

"Do we . . . keep going?"

"Or what? We're not going back."

"Yeah. Yeah." Hyranna nodded. She was shaking, and her shoulder stabbed with pain every time she moved it.

"Are you okay?"

She glanced up at him, blinking past the grey wash of light. "*Okay*? Am I *okay*? We were just . . . were just . . . *attacked*. Shot at with those *things*. Maker's breath, am I okay? No, I'm not okay!" She swore again, clutching her shoulder. "The one time I could have used the Aktyr—nothing. Why? Why, when I actually need to protect myself, does the damned thing do nothing?"

"I'm glad," Jerad said. "That was chaotic enough without you turning into that murderous . . . thing. We're alive, that's what matters."

She swallowed, nodding, but the sound of voices brought her up short. They froze. People were coming. Stomping through the trees. Calling out to each other—Manturian voices.

Hyranna turned and pushed through the trees, Jerad hurrying after her, heedless of direction. The trees parted. They found themselves in a clearing, one of the clusters of huts they'd passed on their way to Tellern. They ground to a halt.

"What are we doing here?" Hyranna whispered. "These huts are on the north side!"

"We came out the wrong way. We must have gotten turned around—*wait*, is that . . . ?"

She followed his gaze. There were two bodies strewn on the ground, a man and a child. Dead. She gasped, but couldn't pull her eyes away. The child was covered in blood, splayed across the ground, the man lying close. He was groaning. He was still alive.

"We have to get out of here," Jerad said. "Quickly. Come on."

He pulled at her, back the way they had come. Tears stung her eyes. She followed, branches snapping her face. She felt like she couldn't breathe, couldn't get enough air into her lungs. She was gasping, gasping.

She stopped, bent double, desperate to get a proper breath. But everything was spinning around her. She couldn't see Jerad anymore. The light was toying with her eyes, and she couldn't *see*.

Voices. She spun around, twirling, disoriented. Jerad, where was Jerad?

Shouts echoed through the trees. *Maker's breath, they were close!* More voices. She started to run.

"Jerad?" she screamed. "Jerad, where are you?"

Shouts came from her left, words she couldn't understand. Her heart was pounding again, she stopped, turned, took a few hesitating steps. She couldn't think straight. Then a familiar voice pierced the confusion.

"Hyranna, run!"

She stumbled into another clearing and broke through the trees with a crash. She glimpsed him, locked in a struggle, grappling one of the Northmen, just as two others converged on him from behind. They seized him, dragged him off, started hitting him with their fists.

"Jerad!" Anger burned away her weakness. She sprang forward. Her fingers closed around the shard. *Now! Now! She would kill them! She would—*

A gun lashed out and struck her between the eyes.

ASHKYNAS AB'ADANI AL'KAH

Ashkynas ab'Adani Al'kah was close. He could feel it. *Find me. Find me.* The new fire burned in him, so strong now it was physically painful—but unwavering since the cart. When he closed his eyes, he saw the red tree and the waiting dark, and he knew, *knew* whatever had happened with the tree was sustaining him. Even now.

He ran, and then walked, and then ran again, full of unnatural vigour. He didn't understand, but he knew he had to find the source of this. The Chosen, perhaps? The remnants of the Avanir's power, scattered through the Old Lands? And maybe together, together they could stop what was coming.

And then . . . the trees began.

Ashkynas had dreamed of trees. He had seen the red tree in his mind, the thing waiting in the dark, under the roots. He had heard stories of trees. In Shyandar, there had been tapestries of the Great Tree herself, and of the forests of the Green East. Once, there had even been trees in Shyandar, though that was a lifetime ago.

But he had never seen trees like this. They began in dark, tangled clusters, scattered across the plains. Ashkynas skirted around them, suspicious of their deep and coloured canopies. Some were green, others were golden or red, like the mottled hues of a sunset. They were beautiful, but the thing inside hated them—almost as much as Ashkynas hated the thing.

But soon, Ashkynas could no longer avoid them. The grass fell away, choked by bush and trees and thick, dense weed. If he was going to follow the source of this new strength, he had no choice.

Ashkynas tightened a hand over the ugly black stone, and with a scowl and a deep, shuddering breath, he plunged into the forest.

Oath

ISHVANDU AB'ADMUNDI AND HYRANNA
ELDUNA

Year 456 and 799 after the fall of Kayr

Though the Decline and the Last Age were full of unspeakable horrors, the time of the Breaking was more terrible still. The sun itself hid its face, and at night, our guilt and sorrow took shape, agony itself in the form of a man. Fallen, we called them, for so they were: Sumadi.

In the night, they came. I can still hear the screams of the dying. Our punishment for the crimes we committed against Creation—centuries of distorting ytyri, of stretching the Laws as we saw fit, until the Breaking of the Pillar of Blood itself. We did not guard the Laws. We became them. Had we any right, then, to be surprised when creatures of unlaw, born of our darkest corruption, turned on us, to feast on our souls?

But Yl'avah is merciful. The discovery of the lost armoury of Kat-net brought us one hundred and eight ancient blades, forged from ytyri in the Age of Light. They were good blades, these keshu, masterful in design, pure of purpose, and— praise to Yl'avah and the Tree—effective against the Sumadi.

There were twenty-seven of us trained with the sword. Twenty-seven—and one hundred and eight keshu. Enough for each warrior to train three, as once was the custom. I received this as a sign.

And so, in the thirtieth year of the Age of Exile, the Guardians were reborn.

From the Chronicles of the Last Age and the Ending of Kayr,
set down by Andari ab'Andala, named Al'kah, first of the Age
of Exile: scroll 72, lines 1-19.

Chapter Thirty-Nine

ISHVANDU AB'ADMUNDI

I leapt into the irrigation ditch, landing with a splash in muddy water up to my knees. Pain slivered up my leg, but I growled and shoved it away. *Ignore it. Push past it.*

The water was warm and sluggish, lying tepid in the sun. I braced myself on my good leg and dug in. One shovelful, two, three. My back was cramping from the work, but that was nothing compared to the stabbing ache in my calf, where I'd broken it in the landslide. *Light duty*, Kulnethar had said. So much for that.

Still, there was something satisfying about the pain. It meant I was right. It meant I was justified in my anger. It meant a Labourer worked harder than a sand-blasted Guardian ass-shove any day.

I slammed the spade in and heaved muddy silt up onto the banks. Again and again. A recent storm had blocked up all the channels: sand howling and bursting across the fields like the Sumadi. There was no rest for us now. Not with the swelling Avanir, so much water to direct, and everything backing up in the wrong blasted places.

Yl'avah's might, what was I *doing* here?

The spade dug in, and something shifted on the other side. I felt it *give*. Then the channel burst open at last. Water pushed against my legs, and without thinking I fell into a Guardian's back stance. Then felt ridiculous.

Come at me, ditch water!

I sighed, and once the water evened out, I went at it again, widening the canal a little more with every stroke, sweat sticking beneath my wraps and robes as the day lengthened.

"Ishvandu!" the foreman called.

I didn't even glance up. I wasn't going to climb back out on my aching leg, only to return after midday. I was here. I would finish it.

"Ishvandu, give it a rest. You'll fry your head off in this sun."

"When I'm done."

There was a mutter of voices as the crew passed. I caught one sneering at me out of the corner of my eye—Janaka, the stinking bastard. That one was trouble. Another Koryn, if I didn't watch him, though there wasn't much further down I could go. Part of me wanted to be a brute just for the sake of it, and sands take the lot. Another part, the Guardian part, told me to smarten up: things could get worse if I let them.

I finished the ditch and took my time at it. Then I climbed out stiffly, using my hands and elbows and my one good leg. My cane was waiting for me at the top. I yanked it out of the mud and started the long walk back to the huts.

The sun was burning a hole in my neck by the time I limped into the narrow street. My crew was gathered under their sunshelter—a tattered awning, stitched together from old shirts. They were sharing flatbread, dried figs, and a ration each of jerky. It wasn't unusual for crews to eat together, especially under a foreman like Adar. But all I wanted was the lonely shadows of my hut, some rest, and a bite in silence. I nodded at them as I passed.

"Stuck-up Guardian prod," Janaka muttered, loud enough for me to hear. I stopped. A hush fell over the crew. "Think you're too good to eat with us?"

"I'm tired," I said.

Janaka laughed. "Hear that? The Guardian pass-up is *tired*. Well, isn't that a shock." There was a round of chuckles, a few knowing looks. "They sit up in their fancy Hall, tell us what to do, *or else*—but give 'em a taste of our life, and they roll up like a dead rat. Go on, Guardian. Run into your little hut. Get your rest, now."

I considered doing just that. *Ignore him. Move on.* They would talk.

Of course they would. It wasn't every day an over-age Guardian Novice got dumped into your crew, and the opportunities were ripe for gloating. It made the Hall a little closer, a little more *human*. My weakness was a Guardian's weakness.

Except I wasn't a Guardian. Not anymore.

I grunted, turning slowly to face the crew. There were nine gathered under the awning: four men, including Janaka, four women, as rough and dirty as the others, and Adar, who showed no sign of stepping in. That meant two were missing. And they just happened to be the biggest of the lot—two muscled lugheads, capable of hauling dead camels with their bare hands, should the need arise. My suspicions rose.

"You have a problem with me, Jak?" I asked.

"Maybe I do."

"Then say it now, and be done with it."

"Maybe I should." He stood up.

I glanced at the foreman again. Adar sat on his heels, watching, not saying a thing, though I noticed he hadn't joined in the grinning.

"You think you're above us, don't you," Janaka stuck out his chin.

"Sands, no, Jak. Just above you."

The crew laughed. Janaka's eyes flashed, fists bunched at his sides. "You worthless sot! What right do you think you have, coming in here, trying to show us up, giving lip to the foreman like you're better than him? You know why you're here? Because the man before you dropped dead three weeks ago, that's why. A good man. A friend to all of us. A hard worker. Never complained a day of his life, and they say his heart stopped in the field for no good reason at all. Maybe the same'll happen to you, if you're not careful."

I knew a threat when I heard one. I smiled tightly, trying not to notice the two stomping idiots behind me, flanking me.

"I'm no Guardian, Jak. Not anymore. Threaten me again, and you'll see why."

"Oh, will I? You're going to push me around? *You?* I'd be careful, cripple. You think I'm scared of a one-legged sand-shitter like you? You're in our quarter now. Time to show a little respect."

I shrugged. "Earn it."

That was all he needed. Janaka barged out, fists clenched, roaring his attack. But I caught a shift in his eye. *Left.* I bent my good leg, shifted my grip on the cane, and, just as the Labourer charged from behind, I swung. The hardwood cracked the side of his head and he dropped like a sack. I was already in mid-pivot. The second lugger got in close. I speared the cane into his gut. He doubled over. Janaka grabbed me from behind, trying to throw an arm around my neck, while the other wrenched the cane out of my grasp. I let him take it. I twisted into Janaka, ducked, and hurled the idiot over my shoulder. He fell hard.

I dropped into back stance, strength on my good leg. Now the second sneak had my cane, and he was brandishing it at me like a club. Janaka scrambled back to his feet. They closed in on me, snarling. The cane whistled at my head. I ducked, pounced, threw two swift jabs. The lughead staggered, just as I rammed my other fist up his chin. His teeth rattled, and he toppled straight back, arms thrown out to the sides.

Janaka threw a wild punch at my head. I dodged, grabbed his arm, twisted, and used his own momentum to drive him into the ground. I slammed my weight into his back, pulled his arm up, around—then leaned in hard.

His shoulder popped loose. I heard a gasp of breath, then Janaka gave a curdling shriek.

I didn't let go. I leaned in further. His screams doubled. His legs kicked wildly as he squirmed. "*Leggo leggo!* Aaa! *Aaah!*"

"You want to know why I was kicked from the Hall?"

"P-p-please . . ."

"Rules, Jak. I don't like rules." I bent closer and he howled again. *Just a moment longer.* Let him feel it. Let him *remember* it.

"Ask yourself," I said. "Is that the kind of enemy you want? Is it?"

He blubbered something. It was enough.

I released him with a shove and stood. The man sagged into the ground, whimpering like a green Tasker, while the crew stared slack-jawed. It was only Adar who met my eye.

The foreman stood slowly. An expectant hush fell. Heads swivelled towards him. Necks craned from down the street, wondering what in the sands was going on. A head popped out from one of the curtained huts. Any moment, Adar would denounce me, threaten the Guardians on me. Instead, he nodded, and that was it. *Dismissed*.

I turned, took two shuffling steps towards my cane, bent to retrieve it, then limped off to my hut. This time, no one made a move to stop me.

———

MY DISPLAY DIDN'T EARN me any friends. But it *did* shut them up. At the very least, they left me alone.

I kept expecting a visit from the Guardians. There would be consequences. Halved rations, perhaps. After all, two Labourers had been knocked unconscious, and a third was holed up in the healing rooms, nursing a dislocated shoulder and some severe bruising. But the days passed, and no one came. I should have been relieved. Instead, there was a prickling in the back of my mind, the sinking realization that as far as the Guardians were concerned, I had ceased to matter.

It was three days later when Adar found me. We were dredging the back of the fields, in preparation for the Avanir's rising water. Soon it would reach flood level—the most important stage in the entire crop system—and everything depended on getting these ditches right, flooding and draining in just the right way, for the right length of time, so the crops would last through Kaprash. Our crew was staggered along the back canal, everyone responsible for their own stretch, so when Adar slid into the canal and started digging along next to me, I shot him a glance. He liked to help out where he could, but on jobs like this, it wasn't expected.

"Am I that slow today?"

Adar grunted. "You're slow everyday." It wasn't true. I worked harder than half the slouches on my crew, but Adar would never admit it. Instead he just shovelled along with me in silence, pausing every now and then for a sip of water.

We were over half-finished when he stopped and straightened. "What you did to Janaka—"

"He deserved it."

Adar shook his head. "He was only following my direction."

"What? *You* put him up to it?"

"Let's just say I . . . encouraged him."

I snorted and slammed my shovel into the ground. "I should have guessed. Next time, pick your own fights with me, ab'Dara."

"That wasn't the point."

"Then what was? You like culling your numbers from time to time, or just hoping for a little entertainment?"

The man laughed. "They warned me about you. Said you were hot-headed and proud, unfit for duty, disobedient, and given to violence."

"Is that all?"

"I'm summarizing."

"So what? Are you threatening me? Because you're doing a pretty shitty job of it, if that's the case."

"It isn't. I watched you. You handled Janaka with no more violence than necessary. You were fast, efficient. You kept your head. Proud, yes, but not above using what you could to your advantage. And you looked for my reaction, before and after. You don't like me, but if I stepped in, you would have deferred."

"If only those skills were useful for digging ditches."

"They're not. I want to know if you're a Labourer, Ishvandu, or a Guardian."

I snorted. "I'm digging ditches. Isn't that answer enough?"

"I want to hear it from you."

"Then I'm neither."

He paused, and I felt his dark eyes watching, searching. What in the blasted sands did he want?

He wants a Guardian.

The thought came to me in a burst of understanding. *Rebellion,* Umaala had said. I met Adar's eye, and there—a flash of knowing. A jolt ran up my spine.

"You're not serious."

Adar tilted his head. "I'm not sure I understand. What do you mean?"

"You think . . . you *actually* think . . ." I trailed off, then saw the look in his eye and stopped.

"Think about it, Ishvandu," he said. "Because if you're not a

Labourer, and you're not a Guardian, then what in the blazing sun are you? Now stop gawking and finish this ditch."

———

ADAR'S HINTS left me rattled. As Guardians, we knew there were mutterings and wild, reckless notions going on behind our backs. More often than not, they were small, isolated incidents, easily handled. But Umaala's warnings rose up in my mind like a ghost. Last year's executions hadn't been a simple matter of stealing or hoarding. A failed uprising, he had said. A harbinger of discontent, and the whole reason for our disastrous expedition into the desert.

I found myself wondering. There could be a hundred explanations for Adar's hints and questions. Maybe he just wanted me to be a Labourer, to fit in, to accept my place and move on. Or maybe he genuinely doubted me. Maybe he thought I was a secret Guardian, sent to spy on the Labouring ranks. Who knew? It was ridiculous to suspect a network of rebellion based on nothing more than a look. *And yet . . .*

My doubts lingered. I watched Adar closely after that, and he could tell. He expected it. He pretended nothing was out of the ordinary, but it was the little things I began to notice. The way Labourers knew him and responded to him, never mind they were on entirely different crews. The way he spoke with other foremen. The way he was always *around*. At meals, he was there. In the fields, he was there. If something important was happening, he was there. Once I got up in the middle of the night for a piss, and I noticed Adar strolling along under the stars. But more worrying than anything was the unmistakable sense that he *wanted* me to notice. Something was going on, I knew it. So what in the sands was I going to do about?

Nothing. That was the obvious answer. I wasn't a Guardian anymore, and I wasn't about to crawl back to them a rat. Unfit for duty, they had called me. A *liar*. If I came to them now with unsubstantiated claims of rebellion, they would send me away in disgrace. "Where's your proof?" Umaala would demand, while Jarethyn would sneer at me down his nose.

No, not my place anymore.

Still, when the fourth came around on patrol, I couldn't help watching Adar. He was cool and collected. He gripped ab'Anajin's hand in greeting. He spoke with him. He showed no sign of worry, and even chuckled at one of the Guardian's jokes. *Everything good here.* It was almost too easy. Too friendly. I frowned and turned away. And then I heard it.

Someone was laughing. It was a bright, full sound. It was unmistakable. Everything in me stiffened, and I found myself staring down the street towards the other two Guardians. Why should I be surprised? It was bound to happen sooner or later. It was her job. It was her *place.* But with my hands and feet caked with clay, hair matted, stinking of sweat and hard labour, I felt a wash of alarm.

Light and all, no! Not like this. Not in this place. I wasn't ready!

Tala hadn't noticed me yet. She was engaged with a pair of youngsters. They were telling her excitedly about some event, waving their arms, laughing. A man joined in and Tala shifted her attention to him. It was a nobody, some Labourer, some gap-toothed mudfoot. But in the closeness of her gaze, in her nearness, in the way she smiled at him, I felt a stab of jealousy.

I was being ridiculous, I knew it. But I longed for her eyes to shift. For her to look up and see me. As if in that moment, I would know. My heart was hammering. My throat had gone instantly dry. I strained towards her. And yet as she began to turn, to move, to show signs of lifting her head, everything in me panicked.

I turned and ducked into my hut.

The darkness pooled around me. I limped to the furthest corner and leaned into the wall, clenching my fists, cursing myself. *Idiot!* What was I doing? What was wrong with me? She was there. She was *right there.* I was a coward. I was a fool.

I could hear her. Her voice carried in from the streets, high and confident. She laughed. She spoke. She moved on. Nearer, nearer— then her voice passed and kept going.

Go! Go to her!

I couldn't. I ground my teeth, hating myself, while slowly, gradually, the Guardians moved on, and the sound of their voices faded. Back to midday. Back to hiding from the sun. Back to waiting. And then back to the fields, and the endless struggle to live, on and on.

I slammed my cane into the ground, scowling at the insufficient *thud* it made against the hard-packed earth. Stupid Vanya. Stupid, stupid—

A curtain rustled. My head shot up, and I saw her standing there. Her eyes were sharp, her chin lifted, the line of her body silhouetted against the door.

"Ishvandu ab'Admundi, are you hiding from me?"

My hands shook where they gripped the cane. She was here. Yl'avah's blasted might, she was actually here! Standing in front of me. Was it real?

"Three weeks," I said. "Three weeks, and not once . . ."

"Really?" Her eyes flared. "That's what you're going to lead with?"

"You never came."

"*I never came*. Yl'avah's might, did you even think to ask why?"

"You think I don't know? Mudfoot. Cripple. That's all I am to you now, isn't—"

"Thirty lashes." She crossed her arm. "Thirty lashes and two nights in the holds. Off-duty for three weeks and no—not allowed to leave the Hall. *That's* why I never came."

I stared at her. I tried to imagine someone laying into her, and instantly my mind clouded. Anger boiled up from my belly, into my chest, squeezing hard enough to knock the breath from me. By the time it made it to my throat, it was a tight, trembling gasp. "What?"

"For going back and saving your blasted skin. For trying to defend you. For disrespecting the Circle, or some such nonsense—"

"They did *what?*"

She snorted. "Really, Vanya. You think you're the only one with a price to pay? Get over yourself, you egotistical bastard! You think I care if there's a splash of mud on your feet, if your hair's not braided? You think I've been sitting around the Hall, thinking up ways to *avoid* you? I stood for you! I faced the Circle for you! I fought, and I'm still fighting, and you have the stones to accuse *me* of dropping you?"

"I didn't—!"

"Yes, you did. Look at you. Cowering in the corner, too scared to even look me in the eye, like you think I'll detest you now. Who do you think I am? Look at me, Vanya!"

I opened my mouth, but every word that came to mind sounded

flat and defensive. The silence stretched between us. The distance seemed impassable, three steps—a wall I couldn't cross. There she stood, clean and proud, with long fine robes, a keshu at her side, everything I wanted but could never be. While I stood on quivering legs, dirty and unkempt, bowed over a cane. *Unfit.*

"Tala…"

"Shut up," she said. "Don't. Don't say it. Don't you dare."

"I'm not a Guardian, Tala."

"I know."

"I'm never going to be a Guardian."

"You're right."

She lifted her chin. She watched me, and I felt a blast of outrage, everything in me screaming against my own words.

"That's right," she continued. "Nothing but a filthy Labourer, a nobody. I guess you'll just put your head down and do as you're told and accept *this*, this hut, this dirt, these walls, this place, this, *this*, and say it's enough for you, and you'll never try to be anything again. Yl'avah's might, what kind of an idiot do you think I am? You think I don't know you, Ishvandu? You really expect me to stand here and believe for a *moment* you're just going to roll over and accept that? You're not a Guardian anymore, fine. Well, maybe I don't *want* just another Guardian. Maybe I'm sick of Guardians. Maybe I'm sick of their rules and their systems, the same things, on and on, content to let the world die a little more every day. Maybe just another Guardian is the last thing Shyandar needs. Now drop your blasted pride and get over here and kiss me, or I will walk out of this hut right now, and I swear by the Tree, Ishvandu, you will not get another chance."

I stared at her. She was trembling, radiant. She seemed to fill my hut, pressing back the shadows with a wild, restless hope. For what? For us? No, it was bigger than that. Her words stirred me open. As if reminding me of something I'd always known. But what? But *what?*

I wanted to laugh, to shout, to run over and embrace her, but my feet were rooted to the ground, my body rigid. I opened my mouth, and couldn't speak. Tala took a breath. Her nostrils flared, and I realized something was happening, something was passing, and all I had to do was reach up and take hold of it, but I couldn't. I was paralyzed. My heart was hammering so hard, I thought it would break. Why?

Why? Why was I so terrified? I was looking on something precious, something held out, something *there*, and I knew if I took it, I would fail. I would never be what she wanted. I would never be enough, and she would never be enough, and the churning, reaching discontent would go on and on. But Yl'avah's might, what else?

"Fine," she said. She took another breath. "Fine." She turned.

My heart screamed into my throat. "Tala, wait!"

The words broke something. I staggered forward, then burst across the room. The pain in my leg vanished. I grasped her, pulling her towards me.

She slammed a hand into my chest. "Oh no, you don't! I gave you your chance! I warned you. You can't just stand there like you didn't hear me. You can't make me wait like that, right to the end, to the last possible moment, you unbelievable—"

I kissed her. The words were swallowed up into a gasp of breath, then she dragged me towards her. I drank in the scent of her, the taste of her, the fire in her lips. I could feel her body against mine. The urgency of our movements—nearer and nearer. My head was spinning. I could feel her heart pounding in the space between us, echoing in my own. Her desire, her need, like my own: it was a chain drawing us, binding us together.

—And then movement outside the door, the shift of sandaled feet. "Atali sai'Neraia?" someone called.

The words shot into me like a knife. Tala stiffened. Her breath caught. *No, no, Yl'avah's might, no!*

We clutched each other in silence, hearts slamming together. I grew increasingly aware of her: her body, warm against mine, the swell of her breasts, the rich scent of her, like a garden—like earth and life and sweet yanis.

"Atali!"

She swore under her breath, but I could already feel her pulling away, pulling back, the painful coldness between us. "A moment, Jin'sal!" she called.

I groaned. I longed to hold on to her, to keep her, to wrap myself in her scent, but before I could say a word, she slipped out from my grasp. She yanked her robes into place, smoothed her hair, straightened her keshu.

Ab'Anajin, head of the fourth kiyah, burst through my entrance. "Light and all, is this really the most appropriate thing for you to be doing right now? Your first day since the Circle, since everything?"

"Do I look like I care?" she said.

"Sands, no. But you're on duty." Then he shot me a look, on the edge of speaking. He glanced at Tala. She snorted and rolled her eyes.

"Be nice." Then she ducked under the curtain and was gone.

I stood there, one arm pressed into the wall, feeling like a piece of me had been ripped off. Ab'Anajin crossed his arms, watching me.

"What?" I frowned.

"What do you think?"

"Yl'avah's might, there's no law against it. There's no reason we shouldn't be together."

"I can think of a few."

"Then tell the Circle, if you think it's so wrong. See if they care."

"I wasn't talking about the Circle." He leaned in. "There's a reason you're here, instead of the Hall. You're careless, Ishvandu. Hurt her, and I will see personally to your very long and painful torment."

I thought about this. "Sounds fair."

"Good." Ab'Anajin scowled at me for a moment, then his face broke into a grin and he thumped my shoulder, hard enough to bruise. "I'll remember you said that!"

And with that, he turned, and I was left with a pounding heart, and an ache, and a hope, strong and light, like Guardian's steel.

Chapter Forty

Hyranna was breathing hard through the gag, hands bound behind her. Blood ran down her face, stinging her eyes, filling her mouth with a bitter, metallic taste. She couldn't even spit it out past the filthy rag between her teeth.

Jerad. Where was Jerad?

She strained to catch a glimpse over her shoulder. The sun burned through the treetops, blinding her. Shapes of men loomed everywhere, strange men with strange voices. Her head swam. She couldn't see right.

Too late, she heard the crunch of booted feet. "*Dacka,*" the man said, and kicked her in the ribs. She yelped at the sudden, sharp pain. The man laughed and said something, then marched away.

Hyranna fought back a wave of panic. Where was she? What was happening? Last she remembered, she'd been running with Jerad, fleeing Tellern. Then . . .

Her eyes squeezed shut as she remembered the shots, the screams . . . It all happened so fast. Northmen coming out of the trees. The quick, ruthless blows, her hands groping for the shard, and then . . . nothing.

And then this. This nightmare.

She groaned, but said nothing, too terrified to move. The shots had faded, but somewhere a woman was screaming. She should do something. She had the shard. Why couldn't she do anything?

A man was shouting, giving orders. Harsh, biting words without any music. *Manturian.*

A hand pressed into her back. She jerked. But it was only E'tuah's voice, sharp and urgent in her ear.

"Hyranna Elduna, listen carefully. Are you listening?" She nodded. "Good. I know what you're thinking. But try to use the Aktyr and you'll only get yourself killed. You cannot control it. There's too many of them, and not one of these murdering savages would hesitate to put a bullet through your head. Do you understand?"

Hyranna's gut twisted, but she gave the barest of nods.

"Good," he said. "You want to get out of this alive? Start trusting me. *Now.* Do exactly as I tell you. This will not be easy, but the Aktyr is a potent weapon—wait for the right moment, and you *will* escape. Do you understand?"

Hyranna pressed her face to the ground, forcing herself to breathe, to think clearly. Everything was whirling around her, she was nauseous with fear, and the thought of trusting E'tuah was loathsome. But before she could respond, boots stomped up to her again and gave her a shove.

"*Eet atch in, Meeka. Na?* Get up." There was another kick, a little more impatience. "Get up, I said. *Eet atch in.*" He strode away, then repeated the command to someone behind her.

She struggled to her knees. E'tuah was watching her, eyes furrowed. He wanted an answer, a nod, some sign she understood, but she couldn't. She was afraid, helpless—and Maker's breath, she didn't want to give him the satisfaction of knowing it. She turned away, eyes darting around, looking for a means of escape.

They were in a clearing: there were two sod huts, a garden that had been ripped out, and Northmen everywhere she looked. Seven, eight—no, more. Some were coming up from the town, shoving captives forward at the point of their guns, while others kicked and jostled those already bound and gagged, forcing them into a line. Hyranna found herself at one end. There were maybe a dozen captives. Women, men, children. But where was Jerad? Her neck craned, struggling to see, willing it not to be so. What if they'd killed him? What if—?

No. There. They were dragging him to his feet at the far end of the line. His face was swollen and bleeding, but the stubborn thrust of his chin looked the same. He saw her, and his eyes leapt into flame, his whole body straining towards her.

One of the men struck him across the face, seizing a fistful of his hair, shaking him so hard, Hyranna thought they would snap his neck. She screamed against her gag, but just when she thought she had to do something, *anything*, they released him, and he staggered back. He was breathing hard, nostrils flared, eyes burning with helpless anger. She tried to catch his eye.

Don't, she begged him silently. *Don't try anything. Please Jerad, don't.*

"Well now!" A Northman's lazy voice stretched out the Imo'ani words. He strode down the line, boots grinding the lichen to dust. He was tall. He walked with just a hint of swagger, muscled arms obvious beneath sleeves and a tight-fitting vest. He rested a hand on his dark leather belt and surveyed them. His eyes were cold. Cold and grey. And when they passed over Hyranna, she felt a shiver of horror.

"Now it seems I have your attention." He smiled, flashing white teeth as he dangled a silver-laced revolver from his finger. "Name's Brit Garden, and you'll get to know me real well these coming days—the lucky ones, that is. I've just started teaching you all what it means to cross me. You see, I don't care who's responsible. I don't care who did it. Others maybe put up with your savagery, traders from Yelder, Hon. But you'll find we're not the type, and I will have vengeance for my dead."

"That wasn't us!" one of the women cried. Hyranna was shocked to recognize Ember from the wayhouse. "The others did it, easterners, savages. Not us!"

The man sauntered up to her, and tilted his head just a little. "Excuse me, pretty *pecup*, but you're not a keen listener, now, are you? What did I just say? Just a moment ago, just two ticks of a sec? Mm? Anybody?"

No one breathed a word. The man shook his head and clucked his tongue like he was disappointed, then raised his gun straight between Ember's eyes. She screeched and tried to back away, but one of the men shoved her from behind. He said something to Garden and the man paused.

"Ket here says you're too pretty to kill just yet. So maybe I'll save you for the men."

Ember's eyes went wide, then she snarled and jerked, teeth flashing at Garden. "Just you try, you filthy bastard!"

He struck her with the butt of his pistol, and she went limp. Garden's lip curled. "Get a gag on that one before she comes around."

Hyranna stared. Who *were* these people? What was happening? It was just some misunderstanding. Just . . . She shut her eyes, like maybe she could wake up back in Tellern, but Garden's voice persisted.

"The point is, I don't give a bleeding damn! You understand, *savoes*?" He whirled on the rest of them. "Do you? I don't care who killed my men on the road, far as I know, *you*'ll be the ones to pay. Is that clear? Now! Where *was* I?"

He paused, eyes narrowed at them. Was he looking for an answer? Then his face changed, and the corner of his mouth tilted into a smile. "Ah, yes. As I was saying, while we're here, I might as well bring up the reason I came for a visit in the first place. You see, it was all perfectly innocent to begin with, a friendly exchange of information, a greet and tell. But now I'm pissing mad, and you won't find me as kind."

He tapped the barrel of his gun and paced back up the line. "Now listen close! I'm tracking a pair of thieves, dirt-dumb ingrates who took something what belongs to my mistress, and she's not the forgiving sort. I'm talking about traders. One old woman and a feather-headed young man, with a wagonload of shit to trade and hell to pay. Northmen, so you don't much care for 'em anyway, am I right? I want to know where they went, and I'm thinking perhaps one of you'd be kind enough to tell me what I came here to learn. If so, just step forward into this here space, and we can all see, *seya*?"

There was silence. Hyranna could taste the tension in the air, the anger, the fear.

"Say nothing," she heard E'tuah's voice as he stood next to her. "Stay out of sight, out of mind. Trust me, it will be better."

Hyranna realized she was holding her breath, waiting for something bad to happen. She could feel it.

Then Brit Garden flicked his wrist at one of the men, an older one, with an ugly-looking wound on his hip. Two Northmen came up behind him, slipped off his gag, and pushed him forward. He stumbled and fell to his knees with a grimace.

"You," Garden stopped in front of him. "Are you gonna tell me where the traders went?"

The man's eyes flashed. "Maker damn you, bastard. What do I care about Northmen traders?"

"Oh dear." Garden sighed, lifted his revolver to the man's head, cocked it, and pulled the trigger.

One of the women screamed. Hyranna just stared in horror, too shocked to make a sound as the man jerked and flopped over on his side, dead.

"I hope I've made myself clear," Garden said in a tone of mild annoyance. "Perhaps someone else is itching for a turn, aye?"

His boots tapped the ground, and he looked at each captive in turn, eyes moving up and down, assessing. He stopped in front of Hyranna, and her heart jumped, doubling its rhythm. She forced herself to meet those ice-grey eyes, not to flinch, not to look away. He tilted his head and a smile twitched, then he started back.

He picked a woman next, a little older. *No*, Hyranna thought. *No, don't.* Immediately the woman started shaking, and as soon as her gag was released, she spilled out a flurry of words.

"I don't know. We don't know about any Northmen traders. They came through several days back, and disappeared just as quickly. No one knows where."

"Wrong answer, darlin'."

"Wait!" Hyranna screamed through her gag. Too late. The gun went off, and the woman crumpled to the ground. There were more shouts. One of the younger girls started crying. Someone howled and leapt forward. A man. He threw himself towards Garden, who just lifted his revolver, pulled it to a *click*, and a third shot erupted.

Silence followed. No one dared breathe. Three bodies were strewn on the ground. Hyranna was trembling, eyes wide, staring at them. *He killed them. Just like that. Just . . .* Everyone's eyes were fixed on them—everyone except Garden, whose gaze drifted back and found Hyranna.

Too late, she realized she'd jumped out of line. He tilted his head, swung back to face her and sauntered over.

"Well, well. I *do* like volunteers. They tend to answer me straight, most times."

She thought she was going to be sick. She couldn't feel her own feet, her hands. All she could hear was the thudding in her ears. *He killed them.*

"Fool," E'tuah muttered from behind. "I told you to keep your mouth shut."

One of the Northmen stepped up and ripped off her gag. She swallowed, trying desperately not to gag, then stood trembling and faced Garden.

"Leave them alone," she heard herself say—like it was someone else speaking. "Let them go, and I'll . . . I'll tell you what I know."

Garden laughed—a nasty, dry chuckle that made his eyes gleam. Then he slapped her across the face. She staggered back, lost her footing and sat hard on the ground, blinking and fighting desperately against hot tears. Northmen laughter rippled around her.

"*Kratofan, Meeka,*" Garden said, still smiling as he brought a thumb down over the hammer of his pistol. There was a click. "Let me say. From where I stand, you don't look in any position to negotiate. But I tell you what—sing me your song, little Todaby bird, and I won't pull this trigger, *seya*? How about I give you a beat of three?"

Her heart was already beating its own frantic rhythm, but the man started anyway.

"One."

E'tuah loomed over her, fists clenched. "Say something, girl, for your life!"

Hyranna's mind raced. She knew nothing about Northmen traders, but she remembered Banno's map.

"Two."

She remembered there were two settlements not far from here, one west and one south, and she knew the more commonly travelled road ran north-south. So if she were running from Northmen, she would take the less-travelled road, and the moment her mind leapt to that conclusion she blurted out, "West!" at the same moment the man said, "Three."

She gasped, half-expecting to hear the deafening blast of the gun, but instead Garden paused and lifted his weapon, just a bit. "Say that again."

"West," she said, her voice shaking. "They went west. There's a road that goes west to . . . to Haiyo-na. You have to travel south and turn off from there, maybe you would miss it if you weren't looking for it, but . . . but . . ." she ran out of breath. Her voice squeezed to a stop, then she just waited.

Garden lowered his gun, never taking his eyes off her. "You hear that? Your sorry hides were just saved by a girl. Not so hard after all, was it? But let me tell you, every single one of you is expendable. You know what you are? Extra coin in my pocket, *savoes*—something to trade at the next civilized market we come to, if you last that long. But I don't take kindly to my money talking back, so if any of you think you're gonna be trouble, save us both the grief and step forward right now, so I don't have to haul your ass across the country-side to no good effect. I'm in a particular sort of hurry, this time around."

"You're going to sell us!" a young man exclaimed, horrified.

"*Bingo*! Pin a medal on that man, my friends."

"But we're not slaves!"

"No?" Garden lifted his head, sauntered back. "Let me tell you something, *Karni*. Right now, you're one of two things: either you're a slave, or you're dead. So which is it gonna be?"

There was a heavy silence. Eyes shifted nervously, the young girl was weeping, sniffling. Hyranna trembled from her toes up to her lips, staring, staring without comprehension. She'd seen death before —she'd helped her father tend the sick, and there was always someone who didn't make it. But this was beyond her. Life snatched away: without thought, without remorse. Her stomach twisted, hard, and she swallowed bile.

"I asked you a question," Garden said.

The man flinched and ducked, whispering something under his breath, eyes darting to the bodies.

"What was that? Speak up, boyo!"

"A slave." He growled out the words. "I'm . . . a slave."

"*Kratofan*! Then you'll act like one. Mouth shut, 'less I tell you otherwise, *seya*?" He nodded, and one of the Northmen stepped up and laid a fist into the man's stomach, then grabbed his shirt, dragged him out of line and threw him to the ground.

Hyranna squeezed her eyes shut, brought her knees into her chest, burying her face. She didn't want to see. Didn't want to hear. Dull thwacking sounds filled the clearing, followed by grunts, cries of pain, someone whimpered.

"Anyone else have a problem with our arrangement?" Garden demanded. He let his words hang for a moment and Hyranna could hear his boots pacing up and down. No one breathed a word.

"Good. It's settled then, *savoes*. You." Hyranna's head snapped up, face streaked with tears.

"M-me?"

"Yes, you, darlin'. You know where they went, you lead the way. *Seya*? Now get up. Move."

Hyranna was shaking so hard, she couldn't get her feet under her, couldn't use her arms, still roped behind her. She tried to rise, almost fell, then E'tuah stuck his hands under her arms and guided her up.

"Of course you'd have to play the blasted guide," he snarled in her ear. "You should have listened to me and kept quiet. Do you believe me now? Are you ready to trust me?"

Hyranna stood and faced Garden, trying not to look at the man on the ground, at the three Northmen surrounding him, kicking him. She gave a small nod.

"Good," E'tuah said. "Call him *sir*. There's a strong west-flowing river not far from here."

"I will do my best, sir," she tried to steady her voice, despite the poor man's cries. "But . . . rivers are the best way to travel in Ellendandur."

"Are they?" Garden smiled.

"Yes, sir. Before Northmen came—"

"*Nanif!*" he shouted, cutting her off. Her heart almost stopped from terror. What had she said? Then she realized he wasn't yelling at her. The Northmen ceased their kicking and left the man groaning, curled up and bloodied.

"Apologies, darlin'. You were saying?"

"Uh . . . r-rivers. Rivers are our roads." She forced herself to breathe. Focus on little things, she thought, like standing straight, like breathing, like not looking at the dead bodies, at the beaten man, at the blood. *Maker above.* "F-faster than any road could take you. And there's a strong west-flowing one not far from here."

"A wonderful idea, *Meeka*, but for the fact we have no *boats*. Of course, if you have a suggestion, we're all ears."

"Every Imo'ani village has canoes," she said with as much confidence as she could muster. Tellern was no typical Imo'ani village, but she could only hope these people still had good sense. She glanced over and tried to catch someone's eye—there was a woman, standing taller than the others, her eyes dry and hard, though her face had a strained look to it, like hide stretched out for tanning. Their eyes locked for a moment. *Please*, Hyranna cried silently.

The woman swallowed, then nodded. "Seven," she said, and Garden turned to her. "Seven canoes ready for travel. Three can carry up to eight men, the others are smaller."

"Well done," E'tuah gripped Hyranna's shoulder. "Now take back the lead. Quick."

"See? More than enough, sir," she said.

Garden narrowed his eyes and stepped close to Hyranna, his pistol relaxed, but still alarmingly near. "If I find this is a trick, little *Meeka*, you'll get far worse than a bullet, *seya*?"

"Agree with him," E'tuah continued. "Then say it makes sense for him: the slaves can row and carry. Say it just like that. Keep yourself apart."

"It's not a trick, sir. Doesn't it make sense? The slaves can row and carry the canoes. You and your men just have to watch, and I'll lead the way."

"Well now," he chuckled. "Aren't you eager! Maybe we'll get along fine after all. *Kel it dern andi, Teboes*?"

There was a chorus of cheers from the men, and Garden turned away to snap some orders. Hyranna's breath came out in a shudder.

"You did well." E'tuah's said. "You might just survive. Stay the leader. Stay above the others. Earn his trust. If you're careful, you will get your opportunity."

"I'm not leaving without Jerad," she whispered beneath the shouts of the Northmen.

E'tuah frowned. "Why tie yourself to him? He's as good as dead. It's Balduin Na-es you seek, remember?"

"That doesn't mean I leave Jerad behind! Don't you know *anything* about people?"

"I know," he said darkly. "I also know the Aktyr will defend you, and only you. It will not help your friend. Remember the road? You're more likely to kill him than save him."

She pursed her lips. "Jerad too, or not at all."

"Damn your stubbornness, girl," E'tuah growled. "You may not have a choice."

Hyranna opened her mouth to respond, but snapped it just as quickly. Garden was moving back in her direction. "How far to this river?" he called as he drew close.

"You could be there by dark," said E'tuah, and Hyranna echoed his words.

Garden nodded. "Good. Then let's waste no time, shall we? *Meeka*," he waved his gun at her. "With me. The rest of you, line up, and let's go get these boats, *seya*?"

Wrong way, Hyranna thought, over and over again, as she tromped west into the unknown. Maker above, but she needed to go south. *South*. Toward Calton. Toward Balduin. Why hadn't she said south?

She would have to use the Aktyr. There was no choice. She would use it soon, before something terrible happened. Before they shot Jerad. Before they shot *her*.

But Brit Garden hovered close, and his Northmen were on every side. If she made one wrong move, they would kill her. Her, or others. The Imo'ani staggered under the weight of the canoes, up and over the land, through dense bush, following Hyranna, who followed E'tuah, who seemed to know exactly where he was going.

They rested once. The Northmen passed around some water, but kept the food to themselves. Hyranna didn't care. Her stomach was painfully tight, lurching between nausea and hunger, but she could never have kept something down. *Get what you need from the Aktyr.*

Instead she studied the other captives. There were eleven of them now: the young man who had been beaten, Jerad, six women, two girls, and a small boy, most with dazed looks, like they weren't sure what was happening. But it was already falling out as E'tuah predicted. They were clustered together with the canoes, while she was sitting apart, still uncomfortably close to Garden.

"Take my advice," E'tuah said from behind. "Look too closely, meet their eyes, make friends—it will be harder for you. These are people you cannot save; the less you know of them, the better."

"Unfeeling brute," she muttered.

"What was that, Todaby?" Garden's voice was thick around a chunk of crunching Northman fruit.

She snapped her jaw shut and looked down, studying the patch of moss between her toes. Maybe if she kept quiet, he would ignore her.

"I asked you a question," he said.

She glanced up at him. He was sitting with a half-eaten fruit in one hand, and a knife in the other, elbows resting lazily on his knees, not two paces away. "Nothing," she snapped. "I didn't say anything."

He tilted his head. "That's not what I heard." Then he stood up, a slow, careless motion, like a cat stretching in the sun. His boots clomped towards her, until his leg brushed her arm, then he crouched, filling her nostrils with a sour stench. "I don't like my slaves talking behind my back," he said, still holding the knife, gesturing as he spoke. It flashed alarmingly close to her face, but she refused to shrink away. "You have something to say, darlin', you say it to my face. That's how we get along, *seya*?"

She clenched her jaw, staring straight forward. "Fine. Except I've got nothing to say to you."

He chuckled and leaned a little closer, and she felt cold metal scrape the side of her head. She flinched, then saw he'd picked up a thick strand of her hair, and was drawing the blade gently down its sleek, black length.

"A fascinating thing, this hair of yours," he said. "So straight and thick, it just runs through your fingers, even with your lot sleeping on the ground and crashing through the trees like animals. You'd think it'd be a tangled mess." He gave the knife a little flick, and a moment later he held a chunk of hair in his hand, long enough it draped over his arm. She gasped, but he just let it fall with a shrug and took a bite of his fruit, chewing noisily in her ear.

"I like your spirit, darlin'. *Jipka*, we say—a little bit of cheek. But have a care. If I catch too much, I'll have to break it out of you, and that would be a crying shame, don't you think?"

She said nothing. But a moment later, he snatched her chin and snapped her head around, forcing her to meet his chilly, grey eyes.

"Don't you think?"

She swallowed and nodded, feeling the edge of the blade bite into her lips.

He jerked her chin. "I can't hear you!"

Some of the others were looking at them now, and Hyranna felt a jolt of humiliation. "Yes, sir," she said, though the knife cut her lips as she spoke.

"*Kratofan, Meeka.*" He patted her cheek and straightened, and she let out a breath, realizing every muscle in her body had tensed up. She could feel a trickle of blood run down her chin, but she wouldn't give him the satisfaction of caring. Instead she pressed her lips together and met his gaze. He gave her a twisted smile, took another bite, then turned and shouted out a few orders.

In moments they were being herded to their feet. The break was over. *Good.* Walking, she decided, was less dangerous.

JUST AS E'TUAH PROMISED, it took them until dusk to reach the river. It was wide, wider than the Tindanarra, and the water that swept along it had a dirty grey tinge. The banks on either side were flat and muddy, and some patches were nothing but grass and weeds.

After they picked one of the more open spots, Garden called a rest for the night. The canoes were piled in one place and a long rope was brought out. He led Hyranna towards the other captives, tied the rope around her wrists in front of her, and gestured for another to come. Jerad hurried forward, and the rope looped through his arm. Then Garden gestured again.

"Come on, line up, *savoes*. Next! We don't want you running off on your own, now. We all stick together, *seya*?"

Soon they were all strung in a line, with very little room between them. The rope went around a tree, triple-knotted, with an armed Northman standing guard. Two others lined up to keep watch and Garden strode back up towards the front, looking pleased with his string of captives.

"You okay?" Jerad whispered to Hyranna. He sounded exhausted, one eye was swollen, and the cut on his face had cracked open. She thought she should be the one asking, but she could hear the furious undercurrent in his voice.

She nodded. "I think so."

He was about to say something else, when Garden passed close, and Hyranna elbowed Jerad into silence.

"Congratulations!" Garden said. "You all survived your first day, thanks to our little Todaby bird up here. Now for the rules! Nobody moves too much, or talks too much—I'll leave Turl judge of what's too much." He tossed a hand towards the hulking Northman standing at the end of the line. "And if anyone does, then one of you—I'll let Turl pick—gets a bullet. So we live together, and suffer together, like family, *seya*? Simple rules, no trouble, sweet dreams." He smiled. "Oh, and one more thing. Where's that pretty girl I promised my men? It's been a long, hard day, and they're itching for some fun."

Hyranna stared, horrified, as two men swaggered up to Ember at the far end of the line. The woman stiffened, but didn't struggle as they unbound her. She met their gaze, cold and hard, hating them.

What was this? What now? Hyranna's mouth had gone dry. There was a knife in her stomach, turning and turning. *No.* It couldn't be what she thought. It couldn't.

The men chuckled as they pulled Ember along, across the clearing. Into the darkened trees.

Hyranna turned away. She didn't want to know what happened next. *No.* Her heart shrivelled. She wouldn't consider it. Numbly, she was aware of Jerad clutching her, holding so tightly his hands shook. *Don't*, she thought desperately. *Don't Jerad. Don't say anything. Don't move. Please, don't.*

And then a wave of shame hit her. Shouldn't it be her? She had the shard. Shouldn't she do something, *something*? But E'tuah was right: she couldn't control it. It lay dormant. She felt nothing, though she knew she should. Like her anger over this cruelty should be stronger than her fear.

But it wasn't.

She was helpless, unable to reason, unable to fight. For the first time in her life, she thought she knew what it was to be a coward.

Chapter Forty-One

Kulnethar twisted my ankle, bending it as he dug into the soft spots around my calf. His fingers gripped and pulled. His goal seemed to be causing me as much pain as possible.

"Yl'avah's might, ease up."

"Weekly checks." He shot me a look. "I said light duty, and *weekly* checks. I gave strict instructions."

I winced. "Apparently, no one cares—not when it's a filthy mudfoot on the line. *Ow.*" He twisted it the other way.

"Stop calling yourself that. What you do is vitally important to the lives of every man, woman, and child in Shyandar. More so than any Guardian, if you ask me."

"Yeah, and if I drop dead, they'll find someone else to take my place."

"No one can take your place, Vanya. I don't know a single other person who can gripe and moan like you. Sit up."

I sat up, leaning into my leg as Kulnethar pulled, forcing the muscles to stretch. "It still aches in the morning and by the end of the day. And most of the time in between."

He grunted. "Any sharp pains?"

"Not anymore," I lied.

"Good." He let me relax. "You can probably stop using the cane."

"Already have."

"But you'll want to keep doing these exercises. Every midday. And this time, when I say a week, I mean it." Then he glanced at me. "So what about the other thing. Are you still seeing shadows?"

"I sleep better."

"Ishvandu, that doesn't answer my question."

I sighed. "From time to time, yeah."

"And they speak to you?"

I nodded.

"What do they say?"

"*Save us. See us.*"

"And do you respond?"

"What the blasted sun am I supposed to say?"

Kulnethar shrugged. "Ask them. You'll never know if you don't ask."

"Yl'avah's might, you think I can just talk them out of my head and move on? Kylan, I'm telling you, this is not me. They got *into* me somehow. Worse than before."

"Let's hope that isn't true."

"Hope all you want. I know. Now unless you have some other gleaming shred of wisdom, I've got to get back. Adar wants me on crew this afternoon and he'll never give me a morning off again if I'm late."

Kulnethar nodded. "You know, you're handling this better than I thought."

"Handling what?"

"What do you think, Vanya? The Circle just banished you from the Hall."

"Sands take those ass-shoves. What do I care?"

Kulnethar lifted a brow. "Apparently." He sat back on his heels, watching me. "And what about Tala?"

"What about her?"

"Alis told me you ran off from the Temple in quite a state."

"Did I?" I pretended to pick at the dirt baked onto my robes.

"Uh huh. Right before you announced the depths of my feelings toward Alis. Loud enough for the whole common hall to hear."

I pressed a hand into my chest. "*Me?* No way. I wouldn't do that."

"Then explain how the entire Temple was talking about it by sunfall." He crossed his arms.

I winced. "Alis must have told someone."

"What about me?" The girl popped her head through the curtain. "I heard my name."

"It's you!" I tried to smear on a grin.

Her face darkened. "*You!* Do you have any idea the trouble you got me in?"

"Trouble? I thought I was doing you a favour."

"A favour? A *favour*? You know what they're saying about me? Apparently I seduced Kulnethar, and the only reason I'm in the Temple is because I'm a rat *and* a snake."

"Well, you *were* a somewhat pretty girl in distress . . ."

She rolled her eyes. "Kylan, next time *I* get to do his stretches."

"He'll be all yours." He grinned up at her. "Did you take care of Nenu?"

"New dressings and everything. But I think the goop you're giving him is making it worse. He threw up again."

"Hmm." Kulnethar frowned. "Alright. I'll look into it. Let's change his medicine for now, back to the old one."

"Already did." She glanced back at me. "By the way, Vanya: Tali says you're an insufferable shithead, and she very nearly walked out on you for good, so next time you better show up without the bluster."

I sat up. "*What?* Since when did *you* talk to Tala?"

"Since yesterday." She shot me a smug look, and instantly I knew she knew, probably in excruciating detail. I felt the heat rush to my face.

"You two shouldn't be allowed to talk," I muttered.

Alis chuckled. "Oh no? Then I guess you don't want to hear the rest of her message."

"What message?" I sprang to my feet.

"Naw. I don't think so."

"Alis, wait!" I hurried after her into the hall, limping, ducking through one curtain, and into the next, almost smashing into a white-robe. The man gave a holler of surprise.

"Who are you? What are you doing in—?"

"Alis!" I bowled past without reply. "What message?"

She was picking through a row of medicinal baskets, muttering each symbol to herself before selecting the one for silverwort.

"Alis, please!"

She finally glanced back at me. "Oh, so *now* you say 'please.' I wonder what else I can drag out of you."

"Look, I'm sorry for blurting out what I said about Kulnethar and you. I wasn't thinking straight. I thought it was better to say it and move on, but if I stepped out of line, I'm sorry. I just—"

"Oh, I don't care about that," she waved a hand. "We'll be husband and wife soon, so I suppose you did us *that*, even if you were clumsy about it. People talk. They always do. They'll be over it in a year."

My brows shot up. "You're getting married? You and Kylan?"

"Of course we are. We'll give our oaths before the High Elder next week. So what about you?"

I lurched, feeling a step behind Alis, as usual. "*Me?*"

"Yes, you. Are you going to ask Tali?"

"She's a Guardian!"

"That hasn't stopped you yet."

"Hold on! I'm not falling for this. No way. You think you can wheedle secrets from us and then use them as bribes? I'm not giving you anything."

"Then I guess you don't want her message." She smiled.

I found myself staring at her, horrified at how roundly I was beaten—horrified, and equally impressed.

"You *are* a snake."

"I'll take that as a compliment. So tell me. Will you ask Tali to be your wife? Or are you just flapping your sword, like a lugheaded pubescent?"

"A *what?*"

"A person of budding sexual ability, typically, for males such as yourself, between the ages of sixteen and nineteen."

"You must be learning to read."

"As a matter fact, I am." She grinned. "So?"

I scratched behind my ear, glowering, wondering how to salvage this. "You can't tell Tala."

"That depends on the answer."

"I'm going to say you were fiercely difficult, and she should never send messages through you again."

"You do that. I'm still waiting for an answer. And it better be the truth, because I'll know if you're lying."

"The truth?" I sighed and leaned back against the wall. "Yl'avah's might, girl, you have no idea how much I love her. Everything about her. For years now, since the day I stumbled into the Novice's hall, a gawking white-robed Tasker, everything I'd known shaken upside down like a dumped sack—and there . . . there she was. She's the best, most amazing . . . I mean, when I look at her, there she is. She's strong. She can best any sand-blasted Guardian in a fight. She's smart. Courageous. I was stuck out in the desert, left for dead, and she . . . she came back for me. Believed in me. Stood for me. When no one else . . . And light and all, she's the most beautiful thing, I can't even begin to describe. But . . . but . . . the *truth* is that none of that really matters. What matters is *her*. There's only one of her. No one else." I groaned. "And look at me."

"What's that got to do with it?" Alis asked.

"Have you seen me?"

"Yep. But I thought you said *she* was the part that mattered. So what are you going to do about *her*?"

"Marry her. If she'll have me."

Alis grinned. "Right answer."

I let out my breath. I sagged against the wall, feeling like I had spilled my own blood. Yl'avah's might, I wasn't cut out for this kind of thing! "So do I get her message?"

"I'm sure you will."

I frowned, trying to work out what she meant by that. "Then . . . what is it?"

Alis just nodded. Over my shoulder. Behind me. I had the sudden terrible feeling that I knew exactly what she meant.

"No!" I gasped, wide-eyed and spun around. We were in a storage room, and every corner of it was lined with shelves, baskets, hooks, pots. There was a little alcove to the back, a darkened nook for keeping scrolls, and as I stared, I realized it was occupied. A figure stood against the shadows, and the moment she moved, I knew instantly my fears were correct.

"Yl'avah's might, no!"

Tala slipped out. She met my eye, a sly smile spreading across her face. "You were saying, Vanya?"

My face was like a sun-baked rock. I wanted to wither into a dust heap, but instead of outrage, Tala was chuckling at my discomfort. She sidled closer. "That was quite the speech. Would you ever have said that to my face?"

"Tala, you tricked me!"

"That was Alis, in fact. And very nicely done, I might add. Thank you, dear."

Alis shrugged. "Any time. It was worth the look on his face." She dug an elbow into my arm. "Good luck." Then she turned and pushed back through the curtain.

"You don't trust me?" I asked, when we were alone.

Tala laughed. "If there was a single grain of doubt in my mind about what you were going to say, I would never have done it."

"So you just like humiliating me?"

She drew close, grinning up at me. "Maybe a little. From time to time."

"And you really called me an infuriating shithead?"

"You made me wait, Vanya. You let me stand there for the most agonizing twenty heartbeats of my life. I almost walked out on you, and I swear that would have been the end. Call this my revenge. Besides, it cuts out all the painful parts, like you trying to ask me to be your wife, which let's be honest, would have been a disaster."

"How do you know?"

"You would have spluttered and groaned and put it off more times than you could count. I would have seen it coming for ages. You would still be circling your own tail, and in the end, you would never have said anything half as romantic as you just did, and my answer would still be the same."

"Which is?" The words came out a little breathless.

She tilted her head. "You're an idiot, Vanya. Why else do you think I'm here?"

"But..."

"Ask me." She leaned in. She smiled up at me, hands pressed against the front of my robes.

"I thought you . . . you didn't want to hear me spluttering."

"I changed my mind. Ask me."

I swallowed. There was no turning back now. "Tala, will . . . will you be my wife?"

Her dark eyes pulled me in, gazing at me, glinting in the dim storage room. "Under one condition."

"Which is?" my voice croaked.

"I will not be doted on. I am not your beautiful little woman, your prize, your treasure. Treat me so *once* and I will break every one of your fingers. Is that clear?"

I nodded. "Very."

"Good." She leaned in. "Then, yes. Yes, I will."

I FLOATED BACK to the fields. The huts, hutches, cisterns, streets—they shimmered in the afternoon heat. I felt caught up with them, rising and rising, somewhere above the sand.

I was only barely conscious of a figure coming towards me, calling for me—and then a hand clamped over my shoulder.

"Ishvandu!"

It was my foreman. Adar's nut-brown face and dark eyes slid into focus. He was leaning forward. He was peering at me.

"Where have you been?"

"At the Temple."

"Doing what? You're late! The flood's rising, and we have work to do. You know that."

I blinked at him stupidly. It took me a full few heartbeats to remember where I was, *what* I was. Not a Guardian anymore. The fields. I had work to do. I had a place. A job. *Digging.*

I shook my head, struggling to remember what I had told Adar, why I had gone to the Temple in the first place. There was something. Some reason. An important reason. Something that had nothing to do with Tala . . .

Adar growled and began propelling me forward. I felt a twinge in my leg.

"My leg!" I blurted out.

"I *know* your leg. But how long does it take for that white-robe to look at it? All day? Light and all, I see you working just fine without those prancing bastards poking around."

"Kulnethar had things to say—"

"Here." He was steering me into a hut not my own.

"Yl'avah's might, Adar, what's this about? I'll make it up, I'll work late, whatever."

"Shut up," he said, when we were inside. "I don't care about that."

"So what—?"

He turned and slammed me against the wall. "I want the truth. Are you a sand-blasted Guardian or not?"

I stared at him. Something black coiled in my stomach, and I knew. *I was right.* I steadied myself, every Guardian-trained sense snapping back into focus. Alert. Ready. His eyes were close. I felt tension, a coiled energy, lurking beneath his grip. He was bigger than me, stronger, but it was more than that. I sensed a danger in him—an edge that neither Janaka nor those lugheaded brutes possessed. If it came to a fight between the two of us, I might not be able to take him.

"Adar, this is getting ridiculous."

"Is it?"

I snorted. "You're planning something. I get it. You're in on something. You're hiding something. Fine. You think I care?"

His eye twitched, just for an instant, before his whole face creased in a frown. "What in the blazing sun are you on about, Ishvandu?"

"I don't know, *you* tell me, Adar. Because it happens. Novices get passed up. Guardians get tossed. And if you really think I'm some ratting spy, you've got more paranoia up your ass than is good for you. I'm no Guardian. And even if I *did* smell some ripe-shit mischief, you think I want to go crawling back to them? I don't care. You understand? I don't *care.*"

"But you care about *her.*"

I stiffened. "You leave Tala out of this."

"So it's true."

"What's true? That I have a life outside of some sand-blasted ditch? Yl'avah's might, is it so inconceivable to you?"

"Inconceivable? No. But everyone has loyalties. Where are yours?"

"Loyalties?" I laughed. "I have loyalties to myself, Adar, and the longer you keep your mudfoot hands on me, the less generous I find myself becoming."

The man sneered, and for the first time I saw it: a flash of hatred in those dark eyes. He shoved his weight into me, holding me, hands twisting into the front of my robes. Right then, he wanted nothing more than to beat the sands out of me—out of a *Guardian*. I tensed.

"Do it," I said. "Come on, you roach. *Do it!*"

He twitched. "There it is."

"What?"

"That. *That*. Whatever that is. Guardian or not, you still *act* like one. Like you have all the blasted right in the world." He leaned in. "But I don't care who you think you are, call me a mudfoot again, and I'll have you slobbering on the floor in your own blood and piss, you hear me?"

"You will, will you?" I grinned. "I'm almost tempted to see you try."

"Then say it."

I couldn't help myself. I never could. It was too easy. "Mudfoot," I said.

He narrowed his eyes. He looked at me for a solid three heartbeats. He loosened his grip. Then he struck. His fist shot into my gut, faster than I could twist. It was a smart move. I was expecting the head. Ducking was easy. I was ready for that. I wasn't ready to have the breath knocked out of me.

I doubled over—and *then* he went for my head. Two swift, ringing blows. I hit the ground. I was coughing, struggling to get air. My head was rattling. But I was in for it now. No turning back.

Keep moving. Keep moving.

He fell on me. He yanked my hair back and sent a fist down hard. I threw an arm over my head. I twisted, wrenching myself to the side, grabbing for anything I could get my hands on. His arms flew, but he was leaning into me now, trying to ground me. I bucked. Just hard enough to throw him off balance. I shoved off my knee, ignoring the stab of pain as I spun away and back to my feet, like we had practiced so many times with Tushani'sal. It wasn't the most graceful exit, but it got me out of trouble. I staggered, then found my stance, hands up, leaning into a strong back leg.

He came at me again. His feet moved, shifting right, left, feinting, then he bowled into me. His elbow caught me in the chin, but I shot back with a strong right, then a knee hard into his gut. He didn't back down. He seized my leg and twisted, throwing me off balance. I ran with it, following through with the other foot, slamming my heel into his chest, even as I hit the ground. I heard an *oof*. But by the time I spun to get my feet under me, he was back, swinging. I didn't get my guard up in time. Light flared across my vision. I staggered. There was another swift crack. My arms wheeled.

Shit, shit.

And then I was on my back, staring blankly at a mud roof. Adar's face appeared. He was grinning.

"There he is!"

"Yl'avah's ... bloody might. What ... ?"

"Knocked you out for a few beats, boy. You remember?"

I groaned. My head was pounding, pounding, slamming against the inside of my skull. I thought I might be sick. I swallowed.

He chuckled and wiped his mouth with the back of his hand. It came away bloody. He spat.

"Light and all, kid, I'll admit you're not bad. Kept squirming away, just when I thought I had you."

I nodded. The movement was almost too much, and I had to lay back, eyes squeezed shut. "Yl'avah's might."

"So?" he asked, lifting a brow.

"So what?"

"Anything to say?"

I coughed, tasting blood. "Did I piss myself?"

He looked. "Nope."

"Then nice try, mudfoot, but no luck."

He snorted. He thought about it, then snorted again. Maybe it was the release of all that tension, but what had been insufferable a moment ago, was suddenly and inexplicably funny. I laughed. I rolled over, clutching my stomach, groaning and chortling in quick, interchanging bursts. Adar slid to the ground next to me, holding his own side. I had never heard him laugh before, and suddenly he was *hooting* like a bird—and he couldn't stop. Tears ran down his face. He shook. He hooted again. "You little . . . bastard. I could kill you. Oh. You're something else, you hear? You are . . . you are . . . *hoo hoo hoo*."

I finally crawled to my knees. I slapped Adar on the shoulder, staggering back to my feet, still shaking with laughter. "Shouldn't . . . shouldn't we get back to work?"

"*Hoo*. Maybe that's a good, *hoo hoo*, idea." He nodded. He spat out some more blood. He had a swelling left eye, and one hand stretched across his chest where I had kicked him. Probably a good bruise there, too. I stuck out a hand, and he took it, still chuckling and hooting as he climbed to his feet. "No more days off."

"Kulnethar says every week."

"Sands take that white-robe bastard. No more days off. That's what you get for your lip."

"And Tala?" I gripped his hand. "Are you going to knot up over her too?"

He waved his arm. "Yl'avah's blasted might, what do I care? Maybe I'm just jealous. But go ahead. Poke her all you want, just keep her out of our business. Got it?"

"Fine by me."

"Good. Now go on. Get out of here."

I nodded. I wondered what he would say when Tala and I took the oath, joined for good—but that was another day's problem. And certainly not one that was going to stop me, no matter what Adar and his roaches were up to. I steadied myself against the wall, waited for the spinning to die down, then stumbled out towards the fields.

THE FIELDS HAD BECOME A SWAMP. Trees reached up from the flood plains, bursting through the Avanir's swell. This was it. This was the survival of Shyandar. Three months of flood, and then swift drainage, opening the cisterns, redirecting the water for the planting season. All before Kaprash, if possible.

Our crew monitored the flood, shored up the dams, dredged the ditches. Everyday the same tedious work. We woke. We dug. We rested for midday. We ate. We dug. We slept.

Sometimes we slept.

But there were those other times. *A week from today*, she had said, that day in the Temple. *Wait up for me.*

The week shifted along like an unhurried old codger. Day, and night, and day, and no matter how I threw myself into digging, I couldn't erase the thought of her—her skin like fire, the swell of her breasts, and *her*, the atrocious nearness of our bodies. *Maybe just another Guardian is the last thing Shyandar needs.* She had stood there. She had seen me. And she had pulled me to herself with as much longing as I had. It was there, her desire, crackling between us—and could she really stand there and say *a week*? So rational, a week. So careful. So restrained. So torturously inadequate. A whole week! I even saw her once, on patrol. Our eyes met, and I trembled. Had she really agreed to be my wife? Had I heard her correctly? Or was I imagining it, the delusions of my head reaching out past sleep, past the shadows, into my waking moments? Our eyes met—she smiled at me—and looked quickly away.

That smile. Those dancing eyes. That single, shy glance—it sustained me through the last days of waiting, right up until the appointed time.

I made an effort to wash. I scrubbed off as much dirt and sweat as I could. And then I waited.

I stayed up all night, pacing nervously around the small confines of the room. I waited a long time. I nearly lost hope that she would come. I was sick from fear and desire. What if I messed up? What if I didn't do it right? No one had ever explained these things to me, and all I knew was the jokes and hints I'd gleaned from living in the Hall. I was terrified.

Then she appeared, scattering my fears with the vibrancy of her presence.

"Come on," she said. She seized my hand and I found myself trotting after her into the darkened streets.

"Where are we going?"

"You'll see."

The night was cool. My Labourer's robes felt inadequate, and my skin prickled in the breeze. I shivered. "Tala," I said, as we passed through the narrow streets and into the fields. "What's this about?"

"Here," she said. She pulled me towards the nearest orchard hill, and I climbed in a daze. Fig trees and date palms made little clumped shelters, and Tala drew me into their midst.

Then a white-robe loomed out of the dark. He had familiar bright hair and was trying very hard to look serious.

"Kylan?"

"You owe me a favour, Vanya," he said. "This is ridiculous. Why can't you say your oaths to the High Elder like everybody else?"

"The High Elder doesn't mean anything to him," Tala said with a grin. "You do."

"But I'm not the High Elder."

"That's the point. You're a friend who happens to be a white-robe. That's better than any title. Right, Vanya?"

She shot bright eyes at me, unable to suppress her own excitement. How in Yl'avah's might did she know me so well?

"Right," I said, as a fresh bout of nerves tumbled through my stomach. *This was it! It was actually happening!*

Kulnethar sighed and shook his head. "Very well. But this is serious. No oath should be taken lightly, not though the stars alone be your witness. Do you understand?"

"Absolutely," I said.

"Then give me your hands."

I held out a hand, but Kulnethar swatted it away. "No, not that hand, your *right* hand. Here. With Tala's. No, like *this*." He wove our fingers together. "Light and all, have you never seen marriage oaths before?"

I shook my head. "Should I have?"

Kulnethar just muttered something under his breath, but when our hands were finally locked together under his grasp, he took a deep breath and glanced at us in turn. "Let us begin. What oaths do you bring, before Yl'avah and each other?"

Tala spoke first. "I swear to honour and guard Ishvandu ab'Admundi as my husband, to hold him in esteem, to love him, to work for his good, and to keep his oaths as my own. I offer myself to him, and no other." She glanced up at me, eyes shining in the dark.

"Ishvandu ab'Admundi, do you accept this oath?"

I nodded as my throat closed up. "Yes," I managed to croak.

"Then what oath do you bring?"

I glanced at Kulnethar, then at Tala. "What . . . what do I say?"

"Forget the forms," Tala said. "Speak what's in your heart."

"I . . . I love you," I said.

She laughed.

"That's a start," Kulnethar cleared his throat. "What will you do because of it?"

Right. I was stumbling around like an idiot. I could barely organize my thoughts. "Tala," I said. "I . . . I will— Blast it, I'm no good at this sort of thing. Look, I'm going to make mistakes. I know it, but . . . but you mean everything to me. I will give everything for your good. I will honour you above all others. I will love you as . . . as my wife. You and no other."

"Atali sai'Neraia," Kulnethar said with a smile, "do you accept this oath?"

"I do."

Kulnethar released our hands, mouth twitching in a smile. "Keep hold of her hand, Vanya."

"Okay," I said.

"Don't let go."

"Ever?" I grinned.

"You know what I mean. Just . . . hold still."

Then he pulled out a small leather case from his robes. "I have the symbols of your oaths. Normally, I'd have a bit of help here, but I'll just have to do this myself. Vanya, hold this—Tala, you first." He passed me the case along with a tiny earthen jar, which I had to cradle awkwardly in one hand while still grasping Tala with the other. He pulled out a small, sharp bone needle and a piece of cloth from the case and moved to her right side, first dipping the cloth, then cleaning her ear. Quickly, before I even knew what was happening, he pierced the cartilage along the top of her ear, then reached into the case again, pulled out a simple brass earring, and looped it around. Tala hadn't flinched once through the whole process, but simply gazed at me, serious and steady.

"Your turn," Kulnethar said. He dipped the cloth again as he moved beside me, and I felt the fresh slap of some cleaning ointment. Then the needle. It went in smoothly, with only a pinch of pain. He returned the needle and fished out a second earring, identical to Tala's. It hurt more than the needle, and I could feel a slight burn as he twisted it into place. Then he stepped back, collected his case and jar, sealed them both, and slipped them back into his robes.

"Before Yl'avah and each other you have sworn your oaths. Be faithful to one another. Protect one other. Love in all things. May Yl'avah bless you with many fruitful years together. So may it be."

"So may it be," Tala said, then elbowed me, and I quickly echoed the words.

And it was done.

Kulnethar grinned and slapped me on the shoulder, then gave Tala a quick hug. "Congratulations to both of you. Now I'll get out of your way."

We crept back to my tiny hut, saying nothing, though our hands stayed clasped. My heart was pounding. The ground felt distant and cold. I kept glancing at her, as if to assure myself she was really there, really bound to me. She returned my glance, smiling and saying nothing.

We ducked through the curtain and into the dark. We stood there for a moment, fingers woven together, breathing, letting our eyes adjust. I had no idea what to do next, and for the first time I'd known Tala, she seemed uncertain as well. Or was she waiting for me?

I swallowed, but pulled her close. She stepped nearer. I felt her hand slip out of mine, even as she tugged the cord around my waist. The knot came free. Then she grasped both my hands and guided them to her own sash.

My pulse quickened. But with trembling hands I worked the sash loose. Tala had to help me a little, laying aside her keshu—even here, it was a Guardian's blade, hers alone, and a fresh reminder of what separated us. I pushed aside the spark of bitterness. Tala was here. She had chosen me, and we'd spoken our oaths. Wasn't that enough?

She touched the side of my face, pulling my gaze to her, as if aware of my thoughts. Then she kissed me. Soft, generous. Inviting.

After that, it was easy. We came to each other—hands, lips, breath, skin. Conscious of each movement, each touch, clumsy and unpracticed, yet eager. We sank into each other. She clung to me. The world lifted away, spinning around and around, filling, growing—until our need, our joy, our shared and wondrous surprise burst against us like hot waves of sun.

When it was over, hearts thudding in the silence, we fell against each other, breathing and breathing. Neither of us dared move. There was a shift, a turning, like something vast and immoveable finally clicking into place. We both felt it. We both knew. Such a sudden thing, to change everything. Fates bound. Finished.

She laughed. It was a soft, incredulous sound. She wrapped her arms around me. She pulled me close.

"Tala . . ."

"Shh." She pressed a finger to my lips. "Don't ruin it."

We hovered there, caught up in a strange and alien place, but all too soon, it was time for her to go. She slipped away. I remember lying there, almost in shock, unable to take my eyes off the place where she had been, only moments ago.

But somehow, in spite of everything, I still woke the next morning. I still dressed in the same scratchy robes. I still ate the same gruel. And as always, I trudged out to the fields to dig. Had it been a dream? Had I imagined it all, in the wild drifting night?

The looks they gave me—some grinning, some rolling their eyes—was my only proof, but I clung to it. The rumours had already spread; it wasn't like the tight streets gave much privacy. I pretended not to notice, but inside, for reasons that were still a bit mysterious to me, I was enormously pleased.

Those were the nights I lived for: when Tala was able, when she was on patrol in the North Fields, at night, when ab'Anajin said he would cover for her, and everything worked out perfectly. But each time, the waiting was just as painful. Our time just as short. A week, another week. Another week.

"Why can't I see you sooner?" I asked, intercepting her on patrol.

Three weeks had passed—three painful, euphoric, exhilarating weeks—twenty days, and only two of those with Tala!

"You know why," she said to me in a hushed voice. "I have to be on duty here, and it can't be every time, because that's not responsible."

"What if you didn't have to be on duty?"

"I can't just leave the Hall whenever I want and cross half of Shyandar."

"So what if I came to you?"

She stared at me. "Vanya, don't be ridiculous."

"Not *in* the Hall. What about behind it? Just outside the camel yard, close to the wall. I'll circle around—"

"People watch that side too, Vanya."

"Not as well. Not as many. Maybe I can convince them. There's a supply shed for outriders. We can meet there."

"Convince them *how*?"

"With my natural charm?"

She laughed. "You couldn't charm a camel's ass, Vanya. How do you expect me to believe that nonsense?"

I pulled her close, ignoring the looks people gave us. "Well, it worked on you, didn't it?"

"Don't give yourself too much credit." She pecked me on the nose. "I blame myself."

She wriggled out of my grasp, but there was no way I was letting her get away so easily.

"Three nights!" I called after her, not caring who heard. "Meet me behind the Guardian's Hall in three nights."

She rolled her eyes amidst a chorus of bawdy laughter, but I thought I caught a smile at the edge of her lips. "Two," she said, then hurried away.

I grinned in triumph. I even got a few hearty thumps from some of the crew. It wasn't unheard of for Guardians to mix with Labourers, but from what I knew those were short-lived affairs, the only lasting consequence being the little bastards that sprouted up. Yl'avah knows the North Fields were rife with them. But this was different. This was *going* to be different.

WHATEVER TALA SAID to convince the watch, it worked. By the time I hurried through the night, heart bursting in anticipation, clutching a scandalous cluster of pale fig blossoms, she was waiting for me. It felt good to come to her. I met her in the small outrider's shed, near the western wall, and thrust my gift towards her.

She laughed as she took it. "Idiot. You could get whipped for such wasteful plucking."

"Exactly. It's a demonstration of my feelings for you. The life-threatening risks I would take. The pains I would go through to show my affection."

She snorted. "You just like breaking the rules."

"That too."

And that was the extent of our talking.

This time, Tala lay with me long into the night. There was no rush. There was nowhere to hurry off to. She was mine—for as long and as many times as we could manage. And when our passion gave way to stillness, she stayed, her head resting on my chest, our legs woven together, skin against skin. It was atrociously intimate. It was strange, another presence so close, so close the jasmine-scented sweat of her hair danced in my mind and her heart pulsed against my belly.

Tala.

It was nothing like I had imagined. It was better. It was more than I thought possible. I was holding her. She was in my arms. She had come to me, and I had come to her.

So why the ache, the restless longing, so strong it pained me?

We stayed that way in silence. The night was cold, but neither of us wanted to move—not even to cover ourselves. There was a profound freedom in our nakedness. Even to speak, would seem a betrayal.

Then Tala shivered. The small motion, the tremor of skin, was enough to shatter the moment. She shivered again. She moved, reaching for her robes. Her body stretched against mine, she clambered over me, thighs brushing my chest, but when I lifted my hand, she slapped it away.

"Enough, Vanya," she said.

"Is it?"

"Yl'avah's might, what do you think?" She sat back against my stomach, throwing on her robes. She went to belt them closed, but I grasped her hand and brought it to my lips, kissing the small soft callous along the base of her thumb. She laughed.

"What are doing?"

My lips moved to her wrist. I could feel the sudden rush of her pulse.

"Stop that."

"It's a little late for stopping."

She pursed her lips. "Eventually, I *do* have to go—"

I tugged her arm, and she toppled against me, elbows planted on either side of my face. I pulled her close. She gave way easily—far too easily for someone who was planning to go somewhere—but when I lifted my head to kiss her, her fingers rose up like a wall.

I lay back. "What's wrong?"

"Is this enough?" she asked, her voice strangely distant.

I laughed. "What?"

"Is this enough? *This*. Me. Am I enough?"

"Tala, that's a ridiculous question. You're more than—"

Her knee dug into my side and I yelped.

"Don't lie to me, Vanya!"

"I'm not—"

"Is this what you want? Am I all? Is *this* all? Answer me honestly, Ishvandu."

"Yl'avah's might, what do you want from me?"

"The truth. As always, as with everything between us, from oath to death. The complete and absolute truth. No exceptions."

I swallowed. I gazed at her, at the sudden crackling dark eyes, and I loved her. But I knew the answer, even as she did.

"No," I said.

"Good." She was quiet a moment, though the pressure of her knee did not lift. "So what is it you want?"

I could hardly trust myself to speak. "I don't know."

"Do you want to be a Guardian?"

The thought of it rose up, impossible and unreachable. But there. Still there. Always there. *You'll never be a Guardian.* "Yes," I said.

"And then what?"

"What do you mean?"

"What comes next, Vanya?"

Next? I blinked at her. In my mind, there hadn't been a next. Not really. There had been Tala, but now she was mine. And once there had been the desert, but now it was full of shadows and emptiness. Even being a Guardian—so what? I wanted it. Of course I did. But even if the impossible happened, and I took the oath, what next? Because she was right. It wasn't enough. None of it. It never had been.

I shook my head, feeling something open inside me, a vast uncertainty, like once, *once*, I'd had a purpose, and now it was lost. "I don't know."

She nodded, like it was the answer she was expecting. The pressure on my side eased. She slipped off and belted her robe with a single, careless motion, but instead of leaving, like I feared she would, she stretched beside me. She propped her head up, then spread a hand over my chest, frowning.

"There's an emptiness inside you," she said. "Like the desert. It scares me, Ishvandu. It excites me. It pains me. I can't explain it, but I know if you try to put me there, into that place, I'll be lost. Which is why I can never be all for you. I know that, and I wouldn't want it any other way. Is this making sense to you?"

I nodded, unable to meet her eye. It was making too much sense. She was turning me inside out and speaking of things I couldn't begin to understand, though I knew instantly they were true. I was fiercely uncomfortable, but her hand held me, cold and naked, to the earth.

"I cannot be in you, Vanya. But I meant what I said. I will stand beside you. You and I. Together against the boundless world, the desert, the shadows. Whatever comes: I am with you."

Her words compelled me. I looked at her, letting my gaze fill up with the wonder of her.

"Are you sure you want that?"

She laughed. "Does it matter? We are one, Vanya. You and I. We've said our oaths. We've shared our bodies. The choice is made."

There was something so final about that. It shivered through me, wonderful and terrifying. "Even if I can't be a Guardian? Even if something else ... something ..."

She shook her head. "I meant what I said. I don't *want* just another Guardian. I don't *want* the world as it is. I don't *want* to be content." With each denial, she slapped her fist against my chest.

"So here we are."

"Here we are," she agreed.

I thought I was beginning to understand. She didn't know what she wanted, anymore than I did: but she was drawn to me, with the same burning fascination with which I was drawn to the desert. Once I knew that, there came relief—a kind of painful, humiliating relief.

"Okay," I said. I took her hand in both of mine. I held it against my chest. "Together."

She stayed with me. She even dozed off, her breath deepening in the stillness. But when I woke to the first blush of light, she was gone.

Chapter Forty-Two

The next morning a canal broke. I was late. I ran into the fields amidst bustling chaos. Labourers hurled themselves into the rushing water, shouting, splashing, racing to close the breach.

"Ishvandu!" Adar hollered at me. "Yl'avah's might, where have you been? Brace the wall! Hurry, you mooning slouch, or do you want the whole fields to go dry?"

I leapt into action and joined the chain, tossing heavy bags of dirt from one Labourer to another.

Janaka, on my right, shot me a sour look when he saw me. "Decided to finally grace us, Guardian?"

"Saw him slip off last night, the old goat," said another from my left.

"We'll see how long he lasts."

"What, out in the sun today, or with the girl?" another called.

"Oh, she'll drop him for sure. Give it month."

"Two—she's got to be mad in the first place to pick up an ugly sack like him."

"None of you meat-heads know a thing you're babbling about," I said, unable to help myself. "We're married. See?" I pointed to my ear, still swollen with the jab of the needle.

They roared with laughter, but I didn't mind. I even joined in. Let them think it was a joke.

"Are you really?"

"I don't believe it!"

"That's a fake. You poked yourself, I bet."

"So what if I did? Means the same."

"Did you hear it? Confessed it himself, the hoot! He's lying through his teeth."

"Not the only place he's been lying."

I grinned. "True enough." And they jeered even louder.

Sack after sack we loaded against the canal wall, wrestling each into place, until the gushing stream became a trickle and then nothing. At last, we collapsed into the ditch, dripping and muddy from head to foot. I *was* weary. But in spite of it all, I was happy. I could even imagine the crew being happy for me, if that were possible.

Then I heard a lonely cheer from across the fields. I poked my head up over the edge of the canal and gaped as a gangling Guardian Novice bounded towards me.

"Vanya!"

I groaned.

"Is that your boyfriend now?" one of the Labourers sniggered.

"We won't tell Tali," said another.

"Maybe she won't mind."

"Shut it," I snapped, then clambered up the slope. "Bray, what in the sands are you doing here?"

The kid hadn't changed. He had the same wild, flopping limbs and bursting exuberance.

"Look at me!" he grinned. "I'm on fourth! Just like you said!"

I glanced one way, then the other, scanning the fields. "I don't see the fourth."

"They're patrolling."

"Then what are you doing?"

"Looking for you."

"Why?"

"I wanted to see you, see the work you're doing."

I shook my head. "Bray, you're on *patrol*. That means you have to actually stay with your group. You can't just wander off whenever you feel like it."

"But this *is* on patrol. Tala said I could come find you."

"Did she?"

He nodded. "She said she wouldn't mind seeing you too, if you were able."

The crew snorted behind me and exchanged knowing looks. "Wouldn't mind, would she?"

"I'll bet she wouldn't mind."

"Don't know how to give it a rest, those two."

I glanced at them, at the work to do, at the mess still to clean up and the ditches that needed to be re-dredged, and before I could stop myself I was shaking my head. "Sorry, Bray. I'm on duty, just like you." I wasn't sure why I said that. Maybe I was trying to prove something —to Tala, to the crew, to myself—or maybe I was trying to be a good example for Bray, Yl'avah knows why. But instantly I regretted it. *Tala wanted to see me!* How in the sands had I just said *no*?

Bray shrugged, like it didn't matter to him, and he nodded over my shoulder. "So how's it going?"

"How does it look? We've just stopped up a hole, and now we'll have to dredge it out, shore up the rest. We've got to keep the fields flooded."

"How come?"

I glanced at Bray in shock. "What kind of an idiot are you? Don't you know anything."

"How am I supposed to know when I've never done it?"

"Right." I grunted and steered him away from the crew. "Never worked a day of your damned too easy life. I keep forgetting. Look, it's simple. We need the ground to soak up as much water as possible, everything the Avanir coughs up. So when we plant, the ground is well-saturated and the crops can keep on growing even through Kaprash. We get enough water, the crops survive, and we go on living. We don't get enough water, the crops die, and we have a very unfortunate year. It's as simple as that."

Bray nodded, and I could tell he was actually listening. He had that brightness to his eye. "So your crew keeps the fields flooded?"

"Right now? Yeah, that about covers it. We monitor the canals, the irrigation system on this side of the lake, make sure all the water is where it should be."

"So why do you need the canals at all? Why not just let everything flood?"

"Because we want the water to go where we tell it, where it'll work the most for us. And eventually, we'll need to drain the fields. We want a swift runoff." I pointed along the canal. "Down, towards the cisterns, through the filtering channels, so we can replenish the drinking water before Kaprash."

"Then you plant."

"That's right."

He nodded again and began striding along one of the canals, watching where it went, as if seeing for the first time, then he swivelled, and noticed another channel, this one full right up to the brim. "What's that one for?"

"That's specifically for the orchard. It works differently. See how the trees are higher over there? Those we *don't* want to flood, but we do want a consistent water source. When I was boy, I spent a lot of time hauling buckets up to that blasted orchard, every morning, every evening."

"Sounds tedious." Bray wrinkled his nose.

"No, it was great fun."

He glanced at me, then snorted when he realized I was joking. "It's not all bad, though, is it? I mean look at what you're accomplishing here! You get to work with a crew, together, to produce all this!" He spread his arms. "It's fascinating. You know, I've never been down here before. I've never seen it up close before." He grinned at me. "And think, in a few months, it'll be green. All from nothing. All from what *you* do."

"Thanks, Bray. But you don't have to try to cheer me up. I know what a Labourer does better than you."

He shrugged. "Just trying to be positive. So what are you up to next?"

I glanced over to the crew and realized they were working again, shovelling water back over the dam, re-dredging, while a few hurried off to collect more dirt-sacks in case of another breach.

"Digging," I said. "Same as always. Now get back to your crew, where you should be in the first place. I've got work to do."

He nodded, turned, and took two loping steps, before smacking himself in the forehead. "Right! The message!"

"The message?"

"I was supposed to say—"

"What? From Tala?"

He shook his head. "Umaala'sal."

Instantly, I tightened. I wanted to turn away, to hear nothing. Sands take the Circle and everyone on it—Umaala too! And yet I stopped, leaning forward, heart surging with irrational hope.

"What? What is it? What, *what*?"

"He just says to keep your eyes open."

"To keep my eyes open?"

Bray nodded. "To see."

See us . . .

I swallowed. "See what?"

"He said you would understand."

We were far enough from the crew, I was sure no one had heard—but still, I had to hold myself from turning and glancing back just to make certain. *He knew.* I thought of Adar's suspicions, and suddenly, I wasn't sure they were so wild. What if Umaala had wanted me here all along. What if he had *placed* me here? A backup plan, in case the expedition failed. Or even . . .

No. Now I was just being ridiculous. I scowled and shook my head, refusing to believe Umaala would go that far.

"Alright, Bray. Tell him I get it. And . . ." I paused. "Tell him if he wants a Guardian, he should look up his own ass."

Bray snorted. "You serious? You want me to say that?"

"Word for word."

"Are you *trying* to get me killed?"

"He won't blame you," I said. "But tell him this too: I've got eyes." I clapped him on the arm. "Good luck."

I turned and hurried back to the crew. I couldn't help but notice Adar watching me. He met me. "What was that about?"

"Bray's on assignment. An old friend, wanted to come see what being a Labourer's all about and to pass on a message from Tala."

"I heard." He hesitated. "You sure you don't want to go? If a Guardian calls you away, not much I could say to stop you."

"Look, I'm trying to be responsible here. You're not helping."

Adar laughed. "Good point. Then stop jabbering and get to work, you lazy sot. It's not midday yet."

No, I thought as leapt into the canal. Not midday. Which led to the excellent point: why was Tala's crew on patrol now? What were they looking for, when most of the quarter was in the fields? If Umaala knew, if he *suspected* something, then perhaps Tala's invitation was not everything it seemed.

Idiot. But it was too late to change my mind now. Besides, a satisfied glance from Adar confirmed it. I'd done something right. I was another step closer.

But even as the thought crossed my mind, I began to wonder. One step closer to *what?*

It was a long, gruelling day, but at the end of it, I lay awake, unable to sleep. The euphoria of the night before, of being with Tala, of really *being* with her—not just a stolen moment, but a whole impossible night—it haunted me like a dream, like I was becoming two people: in the fields, a Labourer, a worker, blending in more and more every day, but with Tala, something else. Only what? A Guardian? A spy? A rebel?

Keep your eyes open, Umaala had said, and a part of me wanted to listen. I wanted to get up, slip out of the Labourer's quarter, march over to the Hall, and tell Umaala face to face that there was a plot going on right now under their very noses. It had something to do with Adar ab'Dara, I would say. The details were incomplete, but I was going to figure it out. I was going to earn the foreman's trust and learn everything I could.

But then what? What was I? A Guardian's rat? Or was I something else?

There it was again. Something else, something *else*. Yl'avah's might it burned in me. Isn't that what Tala had been trying to tell me? I didn't have to be a Guardian. She didn't want things to stay the way they were, on and on without end. She wanted me to reach out, to stir up, to make a difference.

A difference.

I turned over and over, restless, missing her, yearning for her, wondering when I would see her again, wondering what she would have told me today if I had come. Had I really turned her down? *Leave me alone*, I'd said. *Let me work.* Yl'avah's might, what an idiot!

The longer the night stretched, the more the denial grew in my head. I'd chosen the Labourers over her. No, I'd chosen duty over her. No, that wasn't it either. It was my pride. Not wanting to be summoned. Not wanting a Guardian to snap their fingers at me. Even if it was Tala. *Especially* if it was Tala.

No, blast it all. It was nothing! I was working, that was all. I couldn't walk away from my work.

"Sleep, you idiot," I muttered under my breath. "Forget it."

But then I had to piss. I groaned, rose, and stumbled out into the cool dark.

The stars were painfully bright. They made me feel naked, standing alone, exposed to their cold fire, their empty shapes—Tower and Tree, Snake and Bear, warriors of Kayr, great Al'kahs, stretching back centuries into the Old Lands. All staring down at me like tombs of the dead.

"You see it too?"

I heard Adar's voice and spun. He stood quietly against the front of his hut, leaning, watching, arms crossed. Of course he would be there.

"See what?" I asked.

"You came to look at the stars?"

"I have to piss."

"Ah. Very well, I won't keep you."

I paused, then found myself edging closer. "What do you mean? See *what*?"

He nodded into the sky. "*Yanebashi.*"

I thought instantly of Tala, of sitting together, gazing into the desert's sprawling emptiness. "The great unending." I frowned. "Do you believe it?"

"I believe things go on, one way or another. But do our souls last forever, somewhere beyond death? I don't know. I don't like the idea of unending, not me, not this head of mine." He tapped the corner of his eye. "It makes me all willy inside."

I nodded. I knew what he meant, but I also knew there was something else, another voice, just as strong. "So if it scares you so much, why do you come to look at the stars?"

Adar laughed. "Good point."

We fell silent. We stood there, neither speaking for a long time, though I felt no desire to slip away.

Then Adar spoke. "You know, the unending—it's not just about where we go, it's about what we do. It's about the effect we have, the imprint we leave behind."

"Is that so?" I pretended not to hear the deepening in his voice.

"Everyone has a choice, Ishvandu: do what you can, or do what you must. And I'm not talking about what some Guardian says you *must*, I'm talking about in here." He knocked a fist to my chest. "You've been to the desert, Ishvandu, and you came back. Why?"

"So you know about that, huh?"

"Word gets around. Besides. We know what happened to your father. We know he went after you, when those miserable ass-shove outriders wouldn't."

"He shouldn't have," I scowled. "He only got himself killed. For nothing."

"For you. He went because he *had to*. You see what I mean? You were his kid, his boy. Everyone said you were dead, taken by the shades, but he knew better."

"Why are we talking about this? I don't care what he did. It was a mistake."

"It was a good mistake, and if he could, he would do it again. Every time."

"What's your point?" I growled.

"My point is, what's *in* you? You survived in the desert, alone, a twelve-year boy for a month—so what the sands are you doing digging ditches, Ishvandu?"

"What? You think I'm going to exile myself out of boredom?"

"Not boredom. *Purpose*. I think you could. I think you *want* to.

There's a world out there, and I see it in your eyes. I saw it in your father's eyes."

"Only Chosen can leave. Every fool knows that."

He laughed. "You believe in the Avanir? Really? You think we're a farm for the Chosen? You're willing to piss your life away, for that?"

"And you have a better idea?"

Adar shrugged. "Not really. But I keep looking for someone who does."

I didn't know how to respond to that. I stood there, frowning into the dark, wondering where this fit into my suspicions, but by the time I thought of something to say, Adar had disappeared back into his hut, leaving me alone in the empty streets.

I sighed and carried on to the latrine, down the winding, narrow alley to the back. I emptied my bladder. I turned.

Save us, Vanya.

A shadow crawled behind my eye. I heard a whisper—a brush of air, something cold creeping along my skin.

I twitched. *No.* There was nothing. Just shadows. Just the sand-blasted shadows. I hurried back, but with every step, I felt something pressing nearer, nearer.

Ask them, Kulnethar had said.

See, said Umaala. *Open your eyes.*

I am with you. Tala promised. *Against the shadows. Against the desert.*

And Adar looking at me. *What's in you?*

I fled into my hut. I paced across the barren room. If I looked, I saw nothing. It was when I didn't look. When I closed my eyes. When I turned away. The tickle at the base of my neck. The flutter in the corner of my eye. I backed against the wall.

"Alright, you bastards," I spoke to the shadows. "Here I am."

There was no answer, but I felt the room stir. Like a wisp of smoke, moving around and around, faint, but present, an undeniable stench, a stinging in my eye.

"What do you want?"

See us.

I growled. The same nonsense. Always the same. Maybe

Kulnethar was right. Maybe it was only a memory, echoing over and over, a piece of horror that my mind didn't know what to do with.

"Well, I'm looking, and I can't even see your rot-ugly faces. If you want me to save anything, you'll have to do better than that."

Silence. I waited. The presence lingered for a moment, then faded. The shadows stilled. The night crept back in. I sagged to the floor and covered my face. I realized I was trembling. Had I really just done that? Had I spoken to the shadows? Had I *challenged* them? Yl'avah's might, what was wrong with me?

And yet, as I crawled to the basin by my door and took long, steadying gulps of water, I felt something shift in me. I wasn't going to run. I wasn't going to be afraid. And I wasn't going to stand around and do nothing. They were right—Tala, Adar, Umaala. It was time to do something. It was time to make a choice. And this time, it was going to be mine.

Chapter Forty-Three

HYRANNA ELDUNA

The day dawned dull and cold. Hyranna felt numb inside and out. She knew she had to keep going, but it was getting harder for her to remember why.

Balduin, she kept reminding herself. She was looking for Balduin. But that objective was slipping away, a little more with every step, her hopes fading as she was dragged mercilessly in the wrong direction.

It had been four days of travelling now: four days of paddling under the sharp eye of her captors, struggling through the pain in her arm, enduring Garden's taunts and torments, trying not to lose heart.

"When?" she whispered to E'tuah whenever she could. "Are you going to help me or not?"

But E'tuah always shook his head. "Not yet. Your chance will come. You have to trust me."

If she wasn't dead first.

It was Jerad she worried about. He was moving slowly, painfully, and though his face had begun to heal, she knew he was masking other injuries. She caught him stumbling, his face drawn and hollow, exhaustion sapping the fight out of him. He was the biggest of them, so they gave him the hardest tasks, the most weight to carry, expected the most, and beat him when he didn't move fast enough.

To make matters worse, Garden had noticed how closely they clung to each other that first night, and they were never put together again. She glimpsed Jerad from a distance now, sometimes passing him and sharing a few whispers, but when they were roped up at night, they were placed at opposite ends, and during the day, Garden kept her tight to him.

Most of her time was spent paddling his small canoe, sometimes with one of the other slaves, sometimes with Ember. The woman's silence was agonizing. Whenever Hyranna glanced behind her, feeling like she should say *something*, Ember would just stare straight ahead, never speaking to her, barely even acknowledging her. She paddled with steady, pointless strokes. Her body moved, but inside, she was hollow.

It made Hyranna cold just to look at her. But she didn't want to think about it. She couldn't begin to wonder what was going on in Ember's mind. So she found herself glaring forward, towards where Garden sat. He lounged against the prow, watching them, or watching the riverbank, relaxed, revolver always within reach.

Her shoulder hurt. Her shoulder always hurt. The first day on the river, she had made the mistake of complaining. Said she needed a break.

Garden hit her, threw her to ground, then hiked up her skirt and beat her with a wooden switch. Her father had never struck her, not once. She thought she could endure it. She tried to be brave. But within a few vicious lashes, she was sobbing. It was the humiliation of it. Her nakedness. Her weakness. The stinging welts across her back and legs. Everyone watching. And when it was over, Garden forced her to paddle anyway.

She kept her mouth shut after that. But her resentment grew, and staring at him, day after day, listening to his insufferable talk—she started to wonder what it would be like to strangle him.

ON THAT COLD, wretched day, Hyranna woke—and realized they had left their packs in the dingy wayhouse in Tellern. She wasn't sure why it struck her so hard, but she thought of the beautiful fur-cloak, the little fox her father had carved, the care Jerad had shown in packing it, now abandoned—and she started to cry. Big soundless tears filled her eyes and rolled down her face, tucked hidden behind her arm.

One of the men stomped up to the line. She swallowed, stiffened her face, and wiped it with a dirty sleeve. The man didn't say anything, just grunted and chucked some dry, mealy bread at her.

She waited until he was gone. Then she peeked out, made sure no one was looking, and quickly nudged the bread over to the girl roped beside her. Hyranna couldn't have eaten it if she wanted to. The pain in her stomach was growing, but she watched the others weaken, underfed and driven hard, while she lost none of her strength. *It was the Aktyr*, just like E'tuah promised—sustaining her, lending her its unnatural abilities. She hated it, but it was the only advantage she had, and Maker's breath, she was going to use it.

The girl stirred as she realized she'd been given food. Then her eyes went wide. She glanced at Hyranna, trembled for a moment, as if fearing a trick, then snatched it up and devoured it.

Don't get attached. Hyranna turned away. The dull ache inside grew, but E'tuah was right. She would never be able to save them.

She heard a shout of Manturian. Her head snapped up, fearing the worst. Had they seen? Would they punish her for it? Would they punish the *girl*? One of the Northmen was marching towards her, finger stabbing the air. Maker, let it not be the girl!

"*Tu! Eet atch in!*" She'd quickly learned the meaning of those words. She swallowed and gathered her feet under her as fast as she could, holding out her arms. The man yanked her up the rest of the way. But instead of hitting her, he undid the rope that bound her to the rest of the captives. She spotted Jerad watching, alert, on edge, as if he could actually do something if they hurt her. Then she was led to Garden.

The man was leaning over a map, a finger-nail picking at something stuck in his teeth, while another waved across the parchment. He saw her and turned his head, slowly, deliberately, the finger swinging towards her.

"Little Todaby," he said. "I have a very important question for you. Are you ready?"

Hyranna nodded, taking a deep breath, as unobtrusively as she could.

The man smiled. "*Kratofan*. Here." He crooked his finger. "Point to the place on this map where you think we are."

She hated getting close to Garden, but she swallowed her distaste and stepped up to the large parchment, dropping to her knees in front of it. He leaned over her. His foul breath filled her space, and it was everything she could do not to gag. She forced herself to stay calm, to focus on the strange lines in front of her. They were different from Banno's map, and it took her a moment to find what she thought was the Manturian Road. She traced her finger along it, stopped at Tellern, and then stared.

Nothing was what it should have been if this was Tellern. The Tindanarra was nowhere in sight, and the western town she had seen on Banno's map was missing. Worse, the river they were supposed to be following looked like it crossed the road south of Tellern and then travelled more north than west.

"I . . . I can't," she said after a moment, and Garden stiffened.

"You can't?"

She shook her head. "It's . . . wrong. Your map is wrong."

Her words met silence. Then very quietly, Garden leaned in. "Is it?"

She swallowed, but watched as E'tuah crouched across from her. For a moment he reached to his side, then stopped and tapped a spot along the road. "You're right. This is Haiyo-na. And this is the river, running close to it."

She nodded. "It's wrong, because this river isn't going where you think it goes. See?" Her finger moved along the small, westward-running line. "Your traders are on this path. We are . . ." she made a wild guess, based on how fast they'd been going, for how long. "About here."

"Really?" Garden laughed. "Just about there? In the middle of nowhere? Why, you are a cheeky lass!" He said something in his own language, and the other two Northmen chuckled.

"Very good. We'll see about that soon enough, then; time for my important question, *seya*? If we're . . . *there*, and my thieves, I'm assuming, did not travel by river—unless they had a big boat tucked into their pretty wagon—then how, might I ask, do you know we're on the right track?"

Hyranna paused. She was trying to work out his question, and how in the Maker's creation she was going to respond, when E'tuah interrupted her thoughts.

"The town is not far from here," he said. "I was waiting for him to ask this. Say you can take him there to speak with the locals. You can be back in a day."

She looked at him, swallowed, then quickly looked away, tapping her finger to the road. "Here," she said, trying to sound confident. "There's a town right about here. I . . . I could take you there myself. We'll ask them, they'll confirm if the traders passed through, and we can turn round and be back at the river by nightfall. Your men get a day off. The slaves can rest, gather their strength, and paddle faster for it the next day, and you get some peace of mind, knowing we're on the right trail."

She was a little breathless by the time she hurried to the end of her speech and she had to slow down, take deep breaths, force her heart not to beat so loudly. *If E'tuah meant what she thought . . .*

Garden's fingers tightened on her shoulder, but he didn't say anything for a moment. He was thinking. Then he leaned forward. "Just the two of us, Toddy, on a little adventure? Is that what I'm hearing?"

"You could bring more if you think I'm a threat," she said.

He chuckled and repeated her words in Manturian, to another chorus of laughter from the Northmen.

"Really, now," he said. "I don't think that's necessary. Though of course, I shouldn't have to warn you about doing as you're told, darlin'. Am I right?"

She nodded, and Garden clapped her on the back. She winced. It was still sore from his beating. Then he was standing up, shouting orders to his men.

E'tuah met her eye. "This is your chance, girl," he said. "As soon as you put some distance behind you, use the Aktyr. You will have to call it up on your own, and I can't help you with that, but I can tell you what to do once you have it. It will not be easy, but I trust you can do it. Kill him, when the opportunity comes, and you are free."

She glanced around her and caught Jerad's eye from a distance. "Wait," she whispered. "What about—"

"Forget him!" E'tuah snarled. "Take this chance and run, Hyranna Elduna. You may not get another."

"No."

"No?" He stared at her. "Foolish child! This *is* the plan. If you want my help, you have to trust me, and I'm telling you, this is how it has to be."

She shook her head and stood up, turning her back on E'tuah.

"Wait!" she called after Garden. The man stopped when he heard her voice. He turned and stared at her. One of the other men made a comment under his breath, and there was a cascade of wicked chuckles. Everyone was looking at her now, including the captives, including Jerad, and she could almost feel E'tuah's disapproving glare on the back of her head. She ignored them and held her ground. "Can I make a suggestion—sir?"

Garden looked far from amused, but he allowed a smile to twist his mouth. "*Another* suggestion? My, aren't you full of bright notions, little Todaby. Alright. Sing."

She took a steadying breath. "I think you have a . . . a slave who isn't well."

His smile stayed put, but his eyes got a little colder. "Do I?"

"What are you doing, girl?" E'tuah hissed from behind her, grabbing her arm. "Keep your mouth shut. Don't try it."

"I was thinking," she kept on. "I was thinking there might be a healer there who could look at him. He . . . he could . . . come along. What does it profit you if someone dies, right?"

Garden's eyes went up, like he was thinking. He stepped towards her, then circled around behind, turning her to face the captives. "Really? *Really?* Let me guess. Is it . . . that one?" His finger pointed towards Jerad, and Hyranna felt herself go cold. Immediately, she knew it wasn't going to work, but she couldn't back down now. She nodded.

"I see," Garden said. His voice had gone as icy as his eyes. "And tell me, darlin'. Do you take me for a fool?"

"No," she said quickly. "No, I don't, I just—"

He spun her and struck her across the face. The stinging blow knocked her back, and she staggered, almost losing her feet. Then, before she could recover, he hit her again. She fell, landing in the mud face first, tasting blood. *Stupid, stupid mistake.*

His knee drilled into her back. A moment later he was leaning over her, one hand yanking back a fistful of her hair, while another flashed a knife in her face, pressing it into her cheek, just below the eye.

"You think you can manipulate me?" he demanded, voice as hard as his blade. "Play me like a *fool*?"

"No . . . no!" she gasped.

"What's your game?"

"Nothing!" His blade moved closer to her eye and she started to panic, could feel paralyzing fear grip her, heart hammering in her throat, threatening to burst out of her. "I didn't mean . . . I just wanted him to get help, I just . . ."

"I *know* what you meant. Thought you could escape, did you? Run off the two of you and tweak your noses at me. But you know, far as I've heard, slaves can adapt just fine to having one eye."

"Please!" A sob hitched her voice. She was shaking so hard she thought he might stab her by mistake. "Please, don't. Please. I . . . I'm not lying to you, I swear."

"You swear." His voice was a sneer. The knife hovered, tickling her lashes as she blinked madly. *He was going to cut out her eye. Maker above, he was going to—*

He flipped the knife around. He showed her the long, jewelled hilt, tapping it against her face. "You see this? It won't hurt, darlin'. I swear."

With a vicious jab, he shoved the hilt between her legs from behind. She was so shocked, she couldn't even cry out. The cold metal went straight inside her, hilt-first. She jerked. She tried to pull away, but his grip was strong, driving her into the ground. He gave the knife a twist, and she wailed.

"Stop!" she heard Jerad scream. "Stop it!"

She tried not to think of the pain, but it was tearing through her. *Make above, it hurt!* Garden just leaned forward, digging the hilt deeper, and she slammed her teeth shut to keep from crying out again.

"We will go," he said, biting off each word. "And if I get the faintest notion any of this is a trick, that you don't know where my thieves are—if, gods above, you've led us in the wrong direction—I will make you *suffer*." He spat the word into her face. "And then I will make *him* suffer. And if you're still alive when I'm through with you, then we'll try this all again, *seyah*?"

He yanked out the hilt. As soon as he released her, she sobbed and pulled her knees into her chest. Garden's boots clomped past her head, he shouted some more orders; there was movement, words exchanged, someone laughed. Then one of the Northmen's smelly sacks landed by her face.

"Come on, Todaby!" Garden snapped. "Time to move, or I'll make you move. We've got ground to cover, yet. Am I right?"

Hyranna choked on her tears. She wasn't sure she *could* move. Pain still lanced between her legs, seizing up her whole body. She managed to pull her knees beneath her, but that was as far as she could get. Then rough hands grabbed her and dragged her to her feet.

Hyranna clamped her teeth together, in part to stop the trembling, and bent to pick up the sack, almost falling over in the process. She managed to stay on her feet, but another burst of pain froze her in place.

"Move!" the man behind her growled. He pulled the catch on his pistol, and shoved it into her back.

For the first time, Hyranna felt the Aktyr stir. Felt a pulse of anger build, feeding off her humiliation and pain, pushing past the helpless panic, demanding vengeance. A part of her wanted to curl up on the ground and weep. Another part wanted to tear Brit Garden to shreds.

The anger gave her strength to take a step, and then another, and grimacing down the pain, fighting back useless tears, she tossed the pack over her shoulder. She wouldn't let him win. She *wouldn't*.

She swallowed back the shard's power—for now—forcing herself to breathe. Her hands were covered in mud, but she used the back of one to wipe her face, and then she started to walk. She caught Jerad's eye as she staggered past the captives. He looked wretched and furious and she thought she saw tears in his eyes. Slowly, he nodded.

Go, he seemed to say. And she realized she would. She was going to take this chance. And when the time was right, she would make sure Garden was the one who suffered.

Chapter Forty-Four

HYRANNA ELDUNA

The hike to Haiyo-na was excruciating.

Every step made Hyranna wince. Soon, she felt blood trickling down the inside of her legs, but with her hands bound tightly in front of her, she was helpless to wipe it away. She heard Whiset, the greasy-looking one, say something, and Garden snorted.

"Stop it!" she shouted.

Whiset gave her a shove. "No talk like this," he said. But she stubbornly kept her feet, planting an elbow into a nearby trunk to right herself.

Garden loped along beside her, not seeming bothered by the dense bush. "Still got a bit of fire in you, darlin', aye?" He shook his head. "I'll admit, I'm impressed, though it'll turn you a rotten slave."

"Then why don't you save us all the trouble and let me go."

He laughed. "Do you know? I rather fancy you, Todaby. Maybe, if this whole thing goes along nicely, I'll just keep you for myself."

Hyranna ground her teeth and said nothing.

"What, that don't tickle you? Wait till you see your options, you won't wear such a scowl. You could manage my house, wear a pretty shirt or two, even come along, if I have need of you. Beats the north-sea mines any day."

"I'd take the mines," she snapped.

"Would you really? It's not for *labour* they'd keep you, darlin'."

Hyranna looked away, refusing to follow his meaning. It wouldn't matter anyway, because she was going to kill him. Soon.

Then she noticed E'tuah tracking beside her through the trees. His hand clenched at his side, and opened, and clenched again. "Foolish," he said. "You were supposed to earn his trust. Now you'll have two men to deal with instead of one. There's no room for mistakes."

She nodded grimly. She knew what she was waiting for. They would find this road to Haiyo-na. Something would catch their attention. Distract them, just for an instant. Then she would reach for the Aktyr.

"It is there," E'tuah continued. "Hovering beneath your mind, sustaining you, making you strong. Find it and hold it."

She said nothing. She was ready.

It was mid-afternoon by the time they found the road: a narrow, weed-ridden version of the one going south. Hyranna hesitated, wondering which direction to go in, and whether Haiyo-na was even on the road, or if she had missed it entirely. She stood, sniffing the air in both directions, looking for a sign.

"Well?" Garden demanded. "You *do* know where you are, right, Toddy?"

She glared at him. "I'm not a walking map! Give me a moment."

He struck her in the mouth. "A little less *jipka*," he said, but smiled, as if he didn't really mind.

Hyranna moved to rub her jaw, causing a fresh rasp of pain along her wrists. Garden's knots were unnecessarily tight. She could feel them chafing, taking a little more skin off as fresh blood continued to stain the cords. The ropes had become little bands of fire. Better to hold still.

She shut her eyes, trying to gather herself, to forget the pain. Focus! Everything depended on this chance.

When she opened her eyes, she saw E'tuah ahead of her, down the road.

"This way," she said.

"You sure?"

She looked at Garden, but just nodded this time, and Whiset gave her an encouraging pat. "Good. See?" The man spoke rough Imo'ani, which was better than most of Garden's thugs. "You learning."

She rolled her eyes. She was going to use the Aktyr. She could almost taste the freedom. She would kill these two and hurry to Haiyo-na to get help. Maybe she could even bring back a force like the Cay-et. Attack the Northmen. Free Jerad.

But Whiset's gun was still close—too close—and his hand was heavy on her shoulder. Garden hovered nearby, quick with his own weapon. One wrong move, and it was over. And what would they do to Jerad when they returned?

She started walking.

For a while the road was desolate. Fallen trees lay across the path, little shrubs were starting to push between the cracks. Some stretches weren't even paved at all, as if the stones had been dug up and used for something else. Hyranna was just starting to worry, when she spotted a path, a well-trodden piece of ground, bushes and weeds trampled into mud. It wasn't as wide as the road they were on, but it was clearly in use. She stopped.

"What is it?" Garden demanded, revolver appearing. His eyes were scanning the forest around him. Was he scared? Was he remembering the severed heads of his men? It gave her the barest thread of satisfaction. *Maker above*, she'd love to see the Cay-et descend on him and take his head off—even if it meant she wouldn't get to do it herself.

"There," she pointed.

Garden sneered. "Why, *that*? Todaby, that ain't big enough for a cart to pass through. It's a game trail."

"No, that's it. It's too big to be a game trail. Trust me, I would know better than you."

His hand went up and she flinched, then hated herself for doing so. The blow never fell. He just narrowed his eyes at her. "If this is a trick."

"It's not. Haiyo-na is just down that path. We don't put stones on our roads like you. Don't believe me? Let's go find out."

He paused, then tilted his head. "I think Whiset will go find out. You and I, we'll stay fine put here. So if something goes wrong, say those people down there recognize you, we won't tempt them to set you loose, am I right?"

Hyranna shrugged, like she didn't care. But inside, her heart leapt. It was better than she could have hoped. She would be alone. One man to worry about. One gun. And Garden at that. Her heart was already starting to pound. Sweat broke out down her back. *Use the Aktyr.* She was going to call it up. She was deliberately going to use it. Maker above, help her!

Then Whiset leaned in and said something under his breath. Garden listened, his face twitching. He wasn't happy, and Hyranna wondered what was going on. After a moment, he growled something back at Whiset.

"Change of plans, darlin'," he said. "You get to stay with Whiset, since the fool speaks piss-poor Imo'ani." He pointed to the far end of the road. "Wait there. And I expect you to be on your best behaviour, now, *seyah*? You say one thing out of line, try anything, and I'll see you regret that, you hear?"

She nodded, trying to appear cooperative, though her heart sank. Whiset? Who was Whiset to her? Even if she managed to kill the creep and escape, Garden would live. He would make it back to the camp. He would punish the slaves. Punish Jerad.

The thought turned her stomach. *No.* It wasn't good enough. But what choice did she have? She had to try. She had to do *something*.

The two Northmen exchanged words, and Garden flashed her a smile. "Hold tight now, Todaby. Try not to miss me."

Keeping his gun held by his side, he turned and sauntered down the path, looking for all the world like he owned it and any fool who happened to be on it. She hated him. Maker's breath, how she hated him! In moments, he had passed into the trees and was gone.

The sudden absence of Brit Garden was like a crack opening in a stuffy cave. A sliver of tension broke off her.

Then she felt a tug on her shoulder.

"You heard—off road," Whiset said. The man had a greasy face and dark greasy hair; his fingers dug into her arm.

"I heard," she muttered and began edging off the road and down into the bush, careful not to move her hands too much. She felt breathless, body tight with anticipation. *Was she ready? Could she do it?* Her heart started to beat a little faster.

Kill a man. She had to. It was her only choice.

She saw the red tree, the beautiful Dandyri—then a thunderous crack rushing through her, pounding the tree, the smell of rot and filth as it died. She winced, shoving the horrible memory away.

This was different.

She saw her father. His eyes wide with shock. The moment he knew—

No, no. Now wasn't the time for doubts. Those things had happened, but they were done now, and this was different. She was fighting back. She was defending herself. She was going to put the Aktyr to its proper use.

"Now is your chance," E'tuah said, appearing like a shadow as they moved deeper into the woods. "Find the Aktyr. Use it."

Whiset's gun was still close, near enough to jab her in the back. She hesitated.

"Find it, Hyranna Elduna. Find it now!"

Whiset stumbled, momentarily distracted by a dip in the ground. E'tuah was right. It was time. She squeezed her eyes shut. *The Aktyr.* She focused on the shard of stone still in her pouch, tried to imagine it burning, like it had at the road, rising up, ripping out of her.

Nothing.

She frowned and tried again. It was there. It *was* there. A moment ago, she had been ready. Back at camp, she had been ready. Maker above, where was it now? *Help me*, she thought to the stone. *Help me!*

"I can't ..." she whispered.

"Yes, you can! You've done it before. It responds to your fury, remember?"

Her fury.

She stumbled as Whiset nudged her forward with the gun. Whiset.

That was the problem. It wasn't Whiset who had shot those

people for nothing. It wasn't Whiset who had beaten her, whose boat she paddled, whose smile mocked her, day after day. It wasn't Whiset who had done that horrible thing to her . . .

Her face darkened. "Garden."

"I know," said Whiset, leaning close. "He is . . . bad man."

Hyranna was too shocked to respond. Had she heard that right? Then he was turning her around, gesturing with the gun.

"You listen," he said. "Yes? No run. No trouble. Promise. Yes?"

Hyranna hesitated, eyeing him, then gave a small nod. "Yes."

"Good."

He pulled out a knife.

She swore and leapt back, heart clawing into her throat.

"No, no, no, no." He waved the gun, a hint of desperation in his voice. "Stop. No." He swallowed, then pointed to her hands. "Rope."

"Rope?"

He nodded. "Rope." He edged nearer. "No run. Rope."

She glanced down at her bleeding wrists. Her stomach twisted. Then before she could respond, he edged forward, slipped the knife between her wrists and quickly sawed off the rope. It hit the grass, all bloody and frayed.

Hyranna swallowed. Her arms hovered in front of her. He had cut her ropes. He had seen she was in pain and freed her.

Her eyes narrowed. "What are you doing? Stay back."

Whiset shook his head. "No, no. Is okay. No run. No run, or I shoot." He brandished the gun, now with two hands, the knife tucked away again. "Sit." He gestured to the ground. "Sit." He hesitated. "Please."

Again, the hint of desperation. He didn't want to shoot her. She saw it now. Saw his eyes for the first time. They were dark and furrowed. He *pitied* her. He actually felt . . . bad.

It couldn't be!

More than all the humiliation and pain, more than the fear of her own helplessness, or the horror of watching people shot in front of her—watching Jerad beaten—more than all that, this sparked a sudden, hot anger.

He *pitied* her.

"How dare you?" Her voice was trembling, sounding soft and

distant to her ears. "How dare you stand there, holding that gun, following that *man*, doing *his* orders, and then pretend you can do any kindness to ease your pathetic little conscience. How dare you, you horrible, filthy, hateful little man!"

He frowned. "Angry? Why angry?" He gestured to her hands. "I cut rope. You no pain."

She laughed bitterly. "No pain? No *pain*? Is that what you think? You think I'm all better now?"

"Listen. I tell you sit, you sit. I cut rope, you sit. Right? Right?" He was starting to get anxious, as if realizing he had made a mistake. "Sit, or I shoot. I tell Garden you give me trouble. Understand?"

He edged closer.

Hyranna edged back. "No," she said. "No. I won't do anything for you."

E'tuah slipped out from behind the man, face grim and sharp. "That's it," he said. "The Aktyr is stirring. Do you feel it now? You won't have another chance like this. He's weak. Do you see him? Do you see how he trembles?"

It was true. The man's arms were shaking, his face pinched. "I want not to hurt you. Just . . . just no run!"

"Don't worry," Hyranna snapped. "I won't force you to shoot me. That would be too cruel of me, wouldn't it?"

E'tuah stepped nearer, as if drawn by the Aktyr's power. "Remember how you felt at the road? These Northmen are all alike—cruel, grasping, heedless of the suffering they cause. Remember how that bastard made you feel, his threats, his insults? He makes you feel like nothing. Like a dog to be beaten. Is that what you are?"

"No!" Hyranna shouted. She could feel it stirring now. There was a rush of anticipation, her stomach rolling and swelling.

Whiset swallowed, mouth pinched. "Stop," he said. She could feel herself edging back. Another step. Another step.

"Stop!"

He cocked the gun. He began to yell at her in Manturian, the words harsh and panicking.

Hyranna realized she could run. She didn't even have to use the Aktyr. She was free. She was at least four steps away now, hands unbound, heart pounding. A quick dodge to the left . . .

She could outrun him. The forest was hers. She could do it.

"Don't!" E'tuah shouted as he saw what she was going to do. He leapt towards her. "Kill him now. What are you—?"

She dashed into the trees. She was fast. She was Imo'ani, born for the forest, for the thrill of the run. She was powerful. The Aktyr was bleeding through her.

There was a crack.

Hyranna stumbled, as if pushed. She righted herself, kept going. The Aktyr laughed, and she was shocked to hear the sound in her own ears—from her own mouth. Harsh and wild.

The Northman cursed, crashing after her. She ran. The gun pounded again. Missed, splintering wood to her right.

She dodged left, flying through the trees, heedless of pain. She was free! She was alive! This was the Aktyr in her. Fearless. Strong. She laughed again as she ran. It felt good to run. To strain with her whole body, balancing left and right, slapping over roots, slipping between trees, leaping off an old stump. She was untouchable. The Northman was slow. He was already falling behind. He was . . .

She stumbled. Something was wrong. Her leg twitched and slipped off a log, and her whole body pitched to the ground. The Aktyr was still burning in her, but there was something else. Some pain. Distant, unimportant. And yet . . .

She slapped at her right thigh, as if to brush away a mosquito, struggling to find her feet.

Her hand came away bloody.

She froze. The pain began to creep into her mind, the realization. A sharp, pinching *wrongness*.

"*Dacka! Dacka, ji ash it nand!*" Whiset cried, as he fell on her. "Stop, *neya?* Stop!"

A roar flew out of her throat. She lashed out, slapping the gun away with a strength she didn't know she had. It spun off into the woods. Whiset didn't even blink. He grappled her, driving her into the ground, screaming at her in Manturian.

"Use it!" E'tuah cried. "I can't help you unless you use it!"

Hyranna barely heard him. A savagery fell over her, darkness and blood. She struck the Northman, she kicked, oblivious to the knife in his hand, heedless of his cries and warnings. He was trying to pin her. Hold her down. Thought *she* was the weak one.

The Aktyr laughed. The man lunged at her with the knife and she caught it. She drove the hilt back, smashing him in the face. Her other hand twisted free. It grabbed a handful of his greasy, dark hair and pulled with inhuman strength. She felt something rip. The man screamed and fell on his side. She rolled with him, driving a knee into his ribs. Her fingers closed over a rock. She wasn't sure what happened next, but she could smell the blood, hear the whimpering cries, feel her body pounding into him.

Then her fingers were around his throat. The Aktyr was panting through her. She could taste it. How it *missed* this! The joy of destruction. The pure glee of it, rushing through her. Her vision cleared and she saw him, face cracked and bloody, eyes staring at her—horrified. His lips trembled as if trying to speak through his smashed jaw.

She smiled, and the Aktyr reached out. Lines of power drove into him, seized him, and ruptured his limbs all at once. Bones snapped. Blood sprayed around her. There was a horrible, shivering pop as his ribs caved in and his lungs burst.

Then silence.

Hyranna realized she was breathing—hard, furious breaths. Sweat dripped off her face. The forest was deathly quiet. The air tense.

She blinked. She still had her hands around a human throat, what *used* to be a throat. The man lay beneath her in a bloody mess. She could smell it—blood, excrement, guts. He was shattered, like a force had collapsed him from the inside out, turning his body to pulp.

A sudden, welling emptiness reached up and wrapped around her. She fell back. She couldn't breathe. She was dark with blood. Her arms were a pattern of cuts, her eyes stung, everything in her was slow, sluggish, aching.

And there he was. Her captor. Dead.

She turned and heaved onto the grass. Nothing came up but bile, but her stomach lurched again, and again. Tears stung her face.

"Maker . . ." she gasped. "Oh, Maker . . ."

E'tuah touched her arm. "Hyranna Elduna, we should go."

She didn't respond.

He shook her. "Garden will have heard the shots. He'll be back any moment. The Aktyr is spent, and I doubt you could call it up again so quickly. We must go. Now."

"Where?" she whispered.

"Away from here."

"No. Where can I run . . . from *that*?" She glanced back at the crushed and bloody mess.

"*That* is the Aktyr."

"That was me."

"You released it, Hyranna, nothing more."

"Really?" Her voice was small. "The Aktyr gave me strength, but I could feel myself doing it. It was my hands that . . . my hands . . ."

"The Aktyr binds itself to you, works through you."

The emptiness inside grew, the feeling that she had done something terrible. That it was the Aktyr . . . *and* her. That somewhere, somehow, she had wanted to do that. Enjoyed that.

No. It was just the Aktyr. Just the Aktyr. Like with the tree. And with her father. And at the road . . .

As if in answer, the clouds broke. Drops started to fall through the trees, landing on her face, her arms, her hair. She took a deep, shuddering breath.

"Maker above," she whispered. "No. Oh no, no . . ."

E'tuah grabbed her and hauled her up. "We are not doing this here. Deal with it someplace else. You are free. So *go!*"

He shoved her. Her leg gave way, and she fell with a cry, clutching her thigh.

"My leg!" she gasped. "My leg. He shot . . . my leg."

"That's what you get for running instead of killing him on the spot. Let the Aktyr deal with it. Run."

"I can't."

"You must."

"*Whiset!*" she heard Garden's voice cut through the forest. "*Whiset, wo an nash? Sa?*"

Hyranna's head shot up, heart pounding. She reached for the Aktyr, but felt nothing. It had retreated, satiated. Besides, the thought of using it again, even on Garden, made her sick with horror. He was going to find her. He was going to take her back, and all this would be for nothing. Wasted. He would hurt her. Hurt Jared.

"No," she hissed, though it came out like a sob. She stumbled to her feet. Her leg was throbbing in pain, but E'tuah was right. The Aktyr was smothering it, dulling the fire. She felt cold. She started to run, at first sluggish and limping, and then faster, heedless of what she trampled underfoot. She ran until her lungs burned, until survival took over and she didn't care where she went.

The rain came faster. Soon she was soaked, her feet slipping through the mud. Rain was pouring down her face. Or maybe those were tears.

She collapsed at the base of a tree, threw her arms around it, and wept. Then got up and pushed on. If she stopped, he might find her. He would see the body. He would go searching for her. She wasn't running anymore, just plodding on through the rain. And if he found her, he would make her suffer for it.

Jerad. Jerad would suffer for it.

She groaned and threw herself into a cluster of thick, twiggy bushes. She crawled inside. The rain dripped and splattered. The dark of the storm fell thicker, closing around her, hiding her, keeping her safe.

But she could still see the body, crushed, burned into her mind. So much blood. So much. The twigs that poked her felt like his fingers, and the cold slap of rain kept jolting her. She was glad she had killed him, glad, glad. And it was done anyway. It was done. He was an ugly wretch who deserved it. If only she'd been able to kill Garden too!

But Jerad! She wasn't going to leave him behind, but she had. And she wasn't going to listen to E'tuah, but she had. She had.

"*Toddy!*" Garden's shout split the night, alarmingly close.

She froze, not daring to breathe. *Oh Maker, let the rain hide me.*

"I'm going to find you, girl, you hear! And you'd better hope I do. You won't even be able look at your man when I'm through with him if you don't show yourself. You hear me, Toddy? I'm going to cut him up good, make him scream . . ."

Hyranna squeezed her eyes shut, trying to block him out. He was coming closer, shouting and cursing at her, mouthing vile threats.

She would kill him. She would murder him if he took a step closer, become that animal, that thing. She would . . .

His voice started to fade. Bit by bit, the rain drowned him out, the sounds of the forest returned. Then nothing.

She wept softly, tears of relief and guilt and fear, until exhaustion took over and she fell into a restless stupor.

Chapter Forty-Five

ISHVANDU AB'ADMUNDI

It was dark. The water swirled around my feet—so much water, rushing and rushing, flowing endlessly from one place to another, dripping through the cavern like rain.

The old man gazed at us, around, on every side. There was something familiar about him. His face was haggard, draped in a cloud-white beard, and he was groaning, reaching—hands dripping.

"*I empty myself, to be filled,*" said a voice.

The knife drove into flesh.

"*I empty myself, to be filled.*"

A second knife, a second pair of trembling hands.

"*I empty myself . . .*"

"*I empty . . .*"

I looked down. My hands were wrapped over the hilt of a knife. A beautiful knife. Laid with gold. Studded with gems. Bound with power. I curled my hands away, longing to see its shape, its form. But the blade was hidden in my own flesh, sunk into my heart. I gaped in surprise. When had that happened? When had I . . . ?

"*I empty . . . empty . . . empty . . .*"

My knees buckled. My hands were dripping with blood. My own blood. I landed with a splash into the cloying stench. Why did he reach for me, dripping with blood? The old man. The cloud-white beard, stained red. Groaning, reaching—horribly familiar.

"*Yanebashi*," the old man gasped. "Is that what you desire?" His robes were torn, stained dark with blood, everywhere, everywhere, leaking blackness into the water. "Fools. You will have it. You will *have it*. Unending dark—unending need—death, death, and bloodless life." Blood bubbled out of his mouth as he spoke. He coughed and folded.

"*I empty myself, to be filled.*"

"Broken." The man wept. He cowered into himself, sinking lower, sobbing, groaning in pain. "Broken."

He died. Each knife burst into flame, tearing through us, spearing into our hearts and shredding us from the inside. I ripped out the blade—but it was too late. The fire screamed, a poison in my blood, roaring, consuming, breaking. I lifted my hands. I watched the flesh melt before my eyes. I was screaming, screaming.

"Save us! *Save us!*"

Then my eyes burst, and the emptiness rushed to consume me.

I WOKE, howling into the darkness. I clutched my face. Fingers dug into my eyes.

"Vanya!" Tala threw herself on me. "Vanya, stop. *Stop.*"

She ripped my hands away. My heart was slamming against my ribs, echoing in my ears, pounding and pounding. I gave a sob of horror, then forced myself to breathe, to come back, to block out the violent cries still raking through my mind.

"Yl'avah's might," Tala groaned, falling against me. "You're okay. It's okay, Vanya. You're safe." She touched my face. "I'm here."

I nodded, still struggling to catch my breath. "I know."

"What happened?"

"I saw it. I *saw* it. The Breaking—Tala, I saw it with my own eyes." I swore and fell back, gazing at the mud roof of the outrider's shed.

"Vanya . . ."

"I know, I know. It sounds crazy, but I know what I saw. In my dream, I could see. And they were there. The Elders who broke the Pillar of Blood. They were there in my dream. And they were . . ."

"Vanya."

"Don't you understand? I could see them. The Elders. They didn't release the Sumadi. They *are* the Sumadi!"

She stiffened, and in the dark, I saw the grim outline of her face. "That doesn't make any sense. There were twenty-four Elders in Kayr. The Sumadi are numberless."

"Are they?"

"Yes."

"Have you seen them? Have you seen them together, *all* of them."

She said nothing.

"I saw them."

"Okay, Vanya. I believe you. It's . . . it's okay." She held me. "Yl'avah's blasted might, I didn't know it was so bad. How long has it been like this?"

"Like this? No. No, this is new."

"But you told me you've been having dreams again. Seeing things. Ever since they found you in the desert."

"Not like this."

"Okay." She nodded. She let out her breath. "Okay."

I sat up. "I have to speak with them again."

"Vanya, what?"

"The Sumadi. I have to speak with them again. I . . . I have to find them and tell them: I *see* them. That's what they keep saying. Don't you understand? They've been waiting for me to ask, to look, to open my sand-blasted eyes and *see* them. And now—"

"Hold on." Tala sat up and gripped my arm. "One thing at a time. You can't just stroll into the desert and ask them what's next."

"I have to try something."

"Why? They've no place in your head. They don't belong. Why can't you—?"

"Because maybe I'm no Guardian, Tala, but Yl'avah's might I've got to be *something*. Isn't that what you were trying to tell me?" I clutched her, leaning close. "And this is it. This is my difference. I'm half-mad. Fine. But what keeps us from the desert, Tala? What keeps us from going, from leaving this place? Is it water? No. We could find water. We could survive. We could find a way, if we had to. It's *them*. And if I can understand them, if I can get into their heads and see what they see, then maybe—"

"Stop."

"Maybe I can figure out how to stop them, Tala. Maybe I can stop them for good. And wouldn't that be better than water?"

"Vanya, stop."

"I could. I *could*. No Sumadi? No shadows? Freedom, Tala. Freedom in the desert. For all our people. Free to explore, to go back, back to—"

She slammed me into the wall, hard enough to knock my head and rattle my teeth, hard enough I bit my own tongue. She leaned close, looming over me, eyes flashing in the dark.

"Ishvandu ab'Admundi, I said *stop*."

I swallowed. "Okay. I hear you."

"Good. I need you to breathe."

"I'm breathing."

"Now slow down. Back up. Are you with me?"

I nodded.

"What are you seeing?"

"You mean the dreams?"

"Yes, the dreams. What *are* they?"

"Memories. From the Sumadi. Things they left in my mind from when I was a boy, but I've never had the courage to look before, Tala, to really *look*. Now—"

"Yes, you're being very brave. Congratulations. That doesn't mean you have to get yourself killed. Do you understand what they did to you?"

I laughed. "What kind of a question is that? Of course I understand! You think I don't know the horror of my own—"

"That's not what I meant. Do you *understand*, Vanya? Do you really get it? Do you know if these things you're seeing, if they're even real? Because if you think one thing is happening, and it's actually something else . . ."

I stared at her. "You think they're lying to me?"

"I don't know. But let's go slowly here, okay? Let's be smart."

I let out my breath, nodding, feeling a shred of sanity return. I fell limp against the wall. "You're right. You're right. I'm sorry, Tala. I . . . I don't know what got into me."

"Those *things* got into you. It's an old wound. A dangerous one. I won't tell you to stop looking, but we're Guardians, and we'll do this properly."

"*You* might be a Guardian."

"Shut up, Vanya. I don't care what robes you wear, you still think like one of us, so don't give me that sulky shit."

I snorted, but felt my chest swell up anyway. *We're Guardians. We. Her and me.* "So what are you thinking?"

"I'm thinking you need to control this. Survivors go mad, Vanya, and maybe the reason you've got half a brain left is because you sealed that part off. We're going to do that again. Starting now."

"It doesn't work like that, Tala. I can't just—"

"Yes, you can. For now. Until we understand more. No more speaking to them, no more challenging them. Tell them you're done. Send them away. *You* are in control, Vanya. Do you understand? Not those monsters."

"But—"

"For *now*." She gave me a look, warning me I had better listen. Two months of being with her, and I was quickly learning to read heaps in a single glance.

"Okay." I nodded. "I . . . I can try."

"Good. Then we're going to walk through what you've seen. Everything you remember, step by step."

"Right. Step by step. You and me."

"And Umaala ab'Krushaya."

"What?" I stared. "*Umaala?*"

"Yes. He needs to know what's going on."

"No way. I'm not letting the Circle into my head. Those sand-shitting sacks can get shoved for all I'm going to talk with—"

Tala punched me in the arm, a sharp, bruising hit.

"Ow!"

"Like their decisions are not, they are the power and protectors of Shyandar, and you still owe them your respect."

I scowled. "When did you jump on their side?"

"Side? Vanya, there's no *side*. Don't be ridiculous. Besides, I didn't say the Circle, did I? I said Umaala. He's responsible for the safety of our people, and have you stopped once to consider who might be at risk? Our decisions could have consequences for all Shyandar; therefore, Umaala ab'Krushaya must be a part of them. No argument."

"Yl'avah's might, you sound like your blasted mother."

"Watch it." She stuck a finger in my face. "You're a step away from sleeping alone for a month."

"You think you could last that long?"

"Right now? I think I could manage."

"Alright, alright." I threw up my hands. "But if this gets me roped, I'm blaming you."

Tala rolled her eyes and sat back, tugging a hand through the long, loose billows of hair. I watched, fascinated as she began to separate out chunks for braiding. "It's almost dawn. I've got to get back, and so do you."

I sighed. "Right. Digging."

For a moment, it had been there: the thrill of leaving, of finding an answer, freedom at last. *But Tala . . .*

"I'll tell Umaala you want to see him," she said. "I'll arrange a meeting. We tell him everything. Do you understand? *Everything.* From there, the decision belongs to him."

My insides squirmed at the thought. But she was right. I couldn't face this alone. I couldn't do anything without her. Even if I wanted to go. Even if I was willing to risk everything. She wasn't. *Not yet.*

I nodded. "Okay."

She stopped and looked at me. I could tell the night was fading, because her cheeks, her lips, the strong curve of her neck, all stood out more sharply against the mud walls of the shack. She softened. "Vanya, I'm proud of you."

"Are you really?" I gave a crooked smile.

"Yes. You're still an infuriating idiot, but this is the right thing to do, even if it's not easy. These dreams, the Sumadi, hearing voices—I wouldn't want to talk about it either."

"Too bad I'm only doing it because I love you."

She blushed and punched me in the shoulder again, a combination that pretty much summed up how she felt about me. I waited until she started braiding her hair, then I leaned in and smacked her with a kiss.

"No," she said, pulling away. "Don't start. Not the right time. Not—"

I kissed her again, and with her hands caught up in her braids, she couldn't defend herself. "Uh-uh," she said, shaking her head, but then she was kissing me back, her lips drawn after mine like a magnet. I pulled her close. I pressed her into the ground, and her body shifted against mine, the urgency of her hair quickly forgotten.

"A month," I laughed. "You couldn't last a month."

"Shut up," she said.

I was late for the fields again. I hurried towards my crew, breathing hard from the run.

It was only when I drew close that I realized they weren't paying any attention to me. Their eyes were fixed up, towards the centre of Shyandar. Towards the Avanir.

"What's wrong?" I asked, panting as I threw myself into their midst.

They all turned to stare at me like I was mad. I saw the circles of their eyes, the shock, the fear bordering on panic, even the anger that I should dare ask such an obvious question. So I glanced up.

The black stone of the Avanir was bare. No water bubbling up. No spray catching the light of the morning sun. It was dry.

"Yl'avah save us," I breathed. "It can't be."

"It is," said Adar.

I blinked towards the fields. They were still flooded, and had to be for another thirty days if we wanted the crops to last. But apparently, the Avanir did not care. It was Kaprash—about two months early.

"Maybe it's a one-day thing," I said.

"You sand-shitting idiot," Janaka snapped. "You ever heard of a *one-day* Kaprash before?"

"There's always a first."

The man threw a punch. It was sloppy and wild. I dodged back.

His foot slipped in the mud. He lost his balance, toppled, and fell face first in the dirt.

No one laughed, not even me. It was far too appropriate an image for what was going to happen to us.

Janaka spat the dirt out of his mouth, and I leaned over to give him a hand. He shoved me away. "Don't touch me, Guardian rat."

Every eye latched on to me, drawing a breath, waiting for what I would do—one of the worst insults they could imagine.

"I'm on your side, Jak," I growled.

"Oh, are you?" He scrambled to his feet. "Running to prod that little bitch of yours, taking your sweet time, you self-entitled smug little shit. You expect us to believe you aren't ratting, just to get between her—"

My roar drowned out the rest of his accusations and I pounced on him, slamming my fists into mouth. He choked and gasped. I hit him again, and again. The crew exploded into action, dragging me back, hollering, throwing themselves between us, shouting me down.

"That's my *wife* you're insulting, you miserable sack!" I bellowed over them. "You say one more thing about her I will *kill* you!"

The shouts intensified. Janaka looked angry enough to burst, though I couldn't hear him over the din. All I could see was his bleeding face, a mouth full of busted teeth, seething at me, pointing.

I never even saw the Guardians. They drove me back. A fist pounded into my side, blasting the air out of my lungs. I coughed and doubled over. Everyone fell away, leaving an instant perimeter around me.

"What in the sands is going on?" one of the Guardian overseers demanded.

Janaka leapt up. "He threatened to kill me!"

There was a mutter of agreement, and I realized how quickly they would abandon me. I couldn't even deny it.

"You insulted my wife!"

"Liar! She's a Guardian—you're a Labourer. You never said no blasted oath! She's a pusher."

I howled, straining against the Guardians, feet drilling into the dirt. "Say that again, say that again, you dirt-licking mudfoot! You—"

"Alright, come on," the Guardian pulled me away, a sturdy strong-limbed woman. "Let's go cool down."

"Good," I spat. I could feel everything in me trembling, straining like a taught cord. If someone let me near Janaka right now, I might just do it. I had never been so furious before. Never.

"This is completely unacceptable," the overseer was saying to the rest of the crew. "Don't we all have better things to worry about? Don't you see what's in front of your eyes? It's Kaprash, sands take us, and we've got work to do!"

Kaprash.

The word snapped me back into focus. Two months early. Two whole months.

"Forget him," said a second Guardian, voice low as he helped steer me away. "The insults of an idiot mean nothing. You want to get roped for him?"

I growled. "My wife. A Guardian. Atali sai'Neraia! Did you hear him?"

"We heard," said the woman darkly. I glanced at her in surprise, but she was already nodding to the other Guardian. "Take him to the holds. Report to Neraia'sal. I don't have time for this now. I'll come and sort it out later. Got it?"

The man nodded, pressing a hand into my back, propelling me towards the road. "Control," he said, shaking his head. "Three months out of the Hall. Three months. Have you forgotten everything you learned?"

That voice . . .

I started. *No.*

I looked up, and instantly, I went cold. It was impossible. It couldn't be . . . The man was a Guardian: from the braided hair, to the robes, to the keshu swinging at his hip. He'd even deigned to strap on a pair of sandals.

But that face, those glinting dark eyes. Yl'avah's blasted might, it was *him.*

He gave a push, and I stumbled forward, too shocked for a moment to speak. We moved off from the other Guardians, away from the shouts and the muttering disapproval, towards the path, towards the Hall.

I shook my head. "Am I going crazy? Tell me I'm not going crazy."

"That, I cannot answer."

"Then what? Blasted sands, you've . . . you've got a *keshu*. Have you been lying to me? Are you really a—? Have you been a . . . a *Guardian* all this time?"

E'tuah answered with a laugh.

"But a *keshu!*"

"Borrowed."

I groaned. "Yl'avah's might, you're going to get us killed."

"Worry not, Ishvandu. When the owner recovers, he'll remember nothing."

I shook my head. I couldn't believe this was happening. How had no one noticed him? How was he *doing* this?

"You shouldn't be here!" I hissed. "They say you're an exile. They say you're dangerous. Is it true?"

"They?"

I swore, realizing my mistake too late. "The High Elder. That's all. He knew the moment he found the Sending stone. But I didn't say anything to anyone else. I—"

"Hush." He gripped my arm. "The High Elder doesn't concern me. He knows who I am, and he knows to keep his mouth shut. I'm not so sure about this woman of yours."

"I didn't tell her—"

"Of course you did. But that's not why I'm here." He paused. He seemed to be thinking, though I sensed he knew exactly what he would say—had probably known for a long time. Yl'avah's might, was there anything he *didn't* know?

We came to the main south road, joining swarms of other people. Some glanced at us, but saw only a Guardian leading a charge to the Hall. They looked quickly away, and we continued north. The closer we drew to the Hall, the quieter the road became.

At last, E'tuah pulled me to a stop. "Ishvandu," he said. "What are you doing?"

"What does it look? I'm digging blasted ditches, is what I'm doing. I could damned well ask you the same!"

He frowned at me. "That's not what I meant, and you know it. You think ditches and droughts are the real problem? You know better, Ishvandu. You *know* what matters. And you're starting to look."

His words ran through me like a dagger. How in the blazing sun did he know? How could he *possibly* know?

"The dreams," I said.

"Yes." He nodded, then glanced up. A clot of Guardians were hurrying towards us. "Keep walking."

We kept walking. The Guardians barely noticed us as they passed, and when we were alone again, he continued. "Ishvandu, this is critical. You must be strong. You have their attention, now. Do you understand?"

"Whose attention?"

"The Sumadi."

My insides curled with dread. I swallowed, forcing one foot in front of the other, trying not to show my fear.

E'tuah saw anyway. "They are gathering. You must not be afraid."

"So this is it? You're finally getting me out of here?"

"No, Ishvandu. You have work to do. You're not ready."

I snorted. "Of course I'm not."

"Face them. Look into the Unseen. *See* them. Everything depends on this. The safety of your people, the future of Kayr, a whole breaking world. *Ishvandu.*" He gripped my arm, his urgency compelling. "You must not fail."

"Fail what? What are you talking about?" I leaned closer. "Is this about the Sumadi being the Elders of Kayr? *They're* the ones who broke the Pillar of Blood. That's what I saw in my dreams. Is it true?"

"If it were, would my *yes* or *no* have any meaning? When you see, you will know, and nothing I say will convince you otherwise."

"Sands take your blasted secrets! What's going on, and why can't you just—"

He brought a hand to my lips. More Guardians, behind us now, approaching on camel. He glanced meaningfully at me. "You will know. Now come."

Chapter Forty-Six

The Guardian's Hall was a swirl of activity—the first day of Kaprash, the news leaping on ahead of us.

E'tuah marched me into the inner yard, as confident as ever, as if he belonged here more than I. And how long had it been? Three months? It was unchanged. I saw camels being herded, Novices sparring in the familiar training grounds, kiyahs gathering for new orders. I saw messengers, red-cloaked Guardian Lords, the tower, even the Al'kah himself coming out with the watch. His high-pitched voice carried easily above the din.

"Are the fields ready? Light and all, has anyone even bothered to *ask*? Where are my patrols? Who's come from there? Someone give me a blasted report!"

His eyes flashed across the yard and landed like a beacon on my mud-caked Labourer's robes.

"You!" he stabbed a finger towards me.

Somehow, I found myself stumbling towards the Al'kah, whose sharp features and beaky nose seemed to dig into me and pull like claws. The fact that I was clearly on my way to the holds seemed to have no bearing on the old man.

"Report!" he said, as soon as I was within reasonable earshot.

I glanced at E'tuah—only to realize he was gone. I was standing alone in the inner yard of the Guardian's Hall. Without an escort.

"The . . . the fields?" I asked.

"Yes, of course the fields. What status?"

"Flooded for sixty . . . sixty-three days, sal'ah Al'kah."

The man pulled up sharp—in response to the number of days, I thought. Until I realized I'd used a Guardian honorific. "Sorry, Al'kah. Old habits."

He snorted. "A little courtesy is appreciated, Novice. I don't know why they do it, toss out well-trained young men, the sort we could use in this place. Was it for pissing in the wrong direction? Huh. Call me *sal'ah* all you want. Once a member of this Hall, always a member, as far as I see it. Sixty-three, you say? Whose crew are you on?"

"Adar ab'Dara."

He grunted and shook his head. "Sixty-three. *Sixty-three.* Not enough."

"I agree, sal'ah Al'kah."

"Then we can't drain the fields, I don't care what it costs us. If we drain the fields, we risk the crop. Precisely. So?"

I blinked at him. "Sal'ah Al'kah?"

"So—what do you propose?"

Propose? I didn't dare glance around me, at the Guardians who had gathered, leaning in to hear the Al'kah's decision—a decision which seemed suddenly to involve me.

"The orchards," I heard myself saying. "The water from the orchards. It's not as necessary as filling the cisterns, so if we dam up the fields and let the water rest instead of drain—just this once—we can redirect the orchard reservoir through the filtering channels, and that should give us a . . . a couple of weeks."

"A couple of weeks?" He narrowed his eyes at me.

"It's better than nothing, sal'ah Al'kah. Though it means spare water rations. And planting in the middle of Kaprash."

"We're already *in* Kaprash. That can't be helped." Then he looked at me, as if noticing for the first time I was a Labourer in the inner yard.

"What are you doing here? How did you get here?"

"I . . . I was fighting . . ."

"So you thought you'd drag yourself to the holds?"

"My escort seems to have . . . slipped off. But yes, sal'ah Al'kah, that was the general idea."

"Huh. You have a name?"

"Ishvandu ab'Admundi."

He narrowed his eyes at me. "Umaala told me about you. You were the boy, the one who promised me water, weren't you? Where's my water?"

"I haven't found it yet, sal'ah Al'kah."

"*Yet*," the man said, and for an instant, our eyes met, and I thought a flash of understanding passed between us. Then he tossed a hand over his shoulder. "Go on, then." And he turned to meet one of the Guardian Lords heading his direction.

That's when I saw Tala.

"Come on," said a Guardian close to me. He tried to hustle me forward, past the watching eyes and questioning glances, but I got only a few steps, before Tala threw herself in the way, Umaala ab'Krushaya right behind.

"Yl'avah's might, Vanya! What are you doing here?"

"Defending your honour."

"What?"

"Some filthy mudfoot insulted you. I may have . . . threatened to kill him."

Tala stared at me, eyes bursting open with fury. "You incomprehensible idiot! Every time I think you might learn—"

"You're my wife. You expect me just to stand by and—"

"Your *wife*?" Umaala loomed over us. "*This* is the sot you married?"

"Yes, my wife. Tala . . . Tala's my . . ." I saw the expression on his face, then glanced at Tala, who flushed dark with embarrassment. She wasn't wearing her ear-band. "You didn't tell anyone? *Two months* and they don't know?"

"Shut up," she said, and pulled me towards her with a quick, fierce kiss. "Stop getting into trouble. Umaala knows. We'll talk."

Then she hurried on into the fray.

Umaala shot me a look. "I don't have time for this now, Ishvandu."

"I know, I know! So someone get me to the blasted holds already."

"Gladly," said my new Guardian escort.

We marched into the tower, past the watch. It was cool inside. The heavy stone walls were lined with steps that wound up to our left, and down to our right, into shadow. We turned, pattering down into the musty hole. Earth and stone, untouched by the sun, closed around us, and the noise of the yard dimmed, a little more, a little more, until eerie silence fell. How long had it been? Almost a year since Koryn's ill-fated duel?

The man uncoiled the rope ladder and dropped it into one of the deep, narrow pits. I hesitated. "You won't forget about me?"

"We'll try our hardest, but right now there's Kaprash on and no end of important tasks, so *get in*."

"How comforting." I scowled into the confining dark. *A chance to test myself. Test my courage.* I climbed into the hole—down, down, down into emptiness, like stepping into a half-world, a place in between, without light or warmth or nourishment. A holding place. The restfulness of death.

"Home at last!" My voice echoed with forced bravado as I reached the bottom. There was a tug on the rope ladder, and when I didn't pull back, it snaked up. The man's footsteps clattered away, and soon, I was alone.

Kaprash. I sagged against the wall. Everything was happening so quickly. The dreams, my decision to tell Umaala, the Avanir drying up, the altercation with Janaka, E'tuah appearing out of nowhere— and now this. Who knows what they would do with me. Probably kick me off Adar's crew, though I couldn't imagine anything worse than digging.

I sighed and pulled my knees into my chest. There was nothing I could do about it now. Now there was only waiting.

WATER FLOWED DARK WITH BLOOD. The hands reached for me. The old man with the cloud-white beard.

You will have it. You will have it.

The hands were dripping. Blood flowed with the water, and the stench rose, thick and sour, bursting through me, spearing to every joint of my body.

Empty myself . . . empty myself . . .

I clutched my face. My eyes were gone. Gone. Dripping down my cheeks like liquid rot. And the screams. On and on, without end.

I was screaming.

No, the man was screaming. The dead man. The man with the cloud-white beard. Screaming as I sunk light-sharp nails into his flesh, deeper and deeper, until *there!* Something soft and hot, thrumming with impossible life. *Save us, save us!*

I pulled.

MY EYES SLAPPED OPEN. I kicked, arms flinging out, finding walls, walls on every side. Everything in me tensed, screaming in panic, breath loud in my own ears.

Don't panic. Don't panic. I stood. Turning as I paced, back and forth, again and again—

No. Not helping. I forced myself to stop, to breathe in and out, hold and release: calm, rolling cycles. I closed my eyes. If I held myself still, in the exact centre of the pit, I could imagine I was somewhere else. The open desert. The sand swirling around my feet. The wind tugging my robes. Rolling dunes and steep, towering ridges. Hidden lakes just out of reach, pockets of life, of fresh, vibrant green. The Green Lands.

I wanted to go. I had always wanted it. To leave Shyandar. To follow E'tuah. And he had come. He had sought me out. He had snuck into Shyandar itself to find me. *Not ready. Not ready.* Of course I wasn't, but something had changed. He'd noticed me. He'd noticed what I was doing in the Unseen, and he had come to . . . to what? *Warn* me? What had that been?

Something prickled under my skin.

"Vanya."

The voice echoed from rock to rock. It was deep and strong. It settled in me, nourishing me.

"Vanya, are you down there?"

My eyes opened. It was Tala, her voice low as she leaned over the edge of the pit.

"I'm here," I said.

I heard a rustle of feet, then a whisper as the ladder dropped into the dark.

"Tala?" I called. "Are you—?"

"Shh."

Her voice bounced between the walls. Sandals scuffed, pattering softly over the knotted rungs.

"Tala, what are you doing?"

"Coming down to you."

"Are you crazy? No! You'll get in trouble. There's no room. Tala—"

"Shut up. You think I'm leaving you alone down here?"

She leapt off the last rung and threw her arms around me. She was breathing heavily, leaning into me, and even in total blackness, I could tell she was grinning.

"Together," she said. "Remember?"

"You're breaking a dozen different rules right now."

"Mmhm. And you love it."

I thought about it. "Okay, maybe I do. But if someone finds you . . ."

"I'll blame it on you." She pressed me against the wall. "Fair?"

I chuckled. "You don't get to chide me for getting into trouble anymore."

"I'll chide you all I want. *I* don't get caught. That's the difference."

She kissed me. My heart leapt at her presence. Tala here—*here*, dropped into the midst of my darkness. Was it a dream? Her scent filled my head, her body close, her lips against mine, banishing the horrors of the night.

"Tala," I whispered.

"Mmhm."

My breath caught in my throat, excited, terrified. "Tala . . ."

"Still my name."

I fumbled, twisting my rough fingers through hers, grasping, holding—holding her back.

"Tala."

She stilled. She hovered close to me, waiting.

"Tala, would you come with me?"

"Where are we going?"

"I don't know. I don't know. But you're right: it's in me, the desert. Not tonight, not tomorrow, but someday, Tala. Someday . . . I can't stay here forever."

"I know."

I heard the softness of her voice, the hesitation.

"Tala? What's wrong?"

"Nothing. Nothing."

"When you say *nothing* twice, I'm less inclined to believe you."

She laughed and leaned against me, holding me, her head resting beneath my chin. "Vanya, I would go anywhere with you. But it's not so simple."

"Why not?" I frowned. "You said yourself, you wanted to make a *difference*. This is what we can do. We can leave. We can follow the Chosen and find the Old Lands for ourselves. Maybe we can take others back with us. Start a new place, free of the desert."

"But you said . . ."

"I know. I know. Umaala, and the dreams. We'll talk. I'll tell him. But . . . they won't do anything. You know they won't. Nothing changes. In the end, it'll be up to us. You and me. We'll have to learn the truth on our own."

She was silent, and this time, I felt her uncertainty. I swallowed, thinking of E'tuah, and the Sumadi, and the dreams, and all the things pulling at me. I couldn't leave Tala. I *couldn't*.

"What's changed?" I whispered.

"Nothing."

"That's not true." I frowned. "Are you ashamed of me? Is that why you haven't told anybody about us? Is that why you sneak out at night, when no one knows?"

"Vanya, shut up."

"Because if there's something else going on—"

"Something *else?*" She pulled back, voice sharp.

"I don't know, some . . . some proper Guardian. Someone better. Like Antaru. Ab'Anajin . . ."

"*Antaru?*" Her voice pitched, hissing out of her mouth like a curse.

"I don't know. I don't know what goes on in here. You haven't told anyone. You don't wear your band. They have no idea. So what's stopping you? What—"

She slammed me into the wall, snapping back my head, rattling my skull.

"How dare you!" she hissed. "How dare you even *think* it! Who do you think I am? What do you think I've been saying all this time? What do you think we've been *doing*? When I said we were one, together, you and I, did that mean anything to you? Did that mean you and I, and some other fool on the side? I wasn't talking about another man, you idiot! I was talking about our child. Yl'avah knows why, but I love you, Ishvandu. Yet so help me, if you ever insult me like that again, I will slit the guts right out of you! I will never lie to you, and I shouldn't even have to say it, but I would blasted-well hope you'd never lie to me either. Blood, light, and all—*Antaru?* You unbelievable ass!"

I groaned as I clutched the back of my head, face hot with shame. "You're right. I'm sorry. I'm sorry, Tala. I . . . wait. *What?*"

I stared into the dark, my addled brain trying to piece together what she'd just said. There was something important in there, something . . .

"Did you just say our *child*?"

"Really? That's what you got from all that?"

"Uh . . . yes?"

She threw up her hands. "Yl'avah's might, I wasn't going to tell you. It's only been a month or more. I can't be certain."

"But you said a child. You think . . . you think . . ." I couldn't finish the sentence. I slid to the ground, my legs crumpling beneath me, mouth hanging open in shock.

"Vanya?" her voice drifted through the blackness. There was a long, embarrassed silence. "I can't see your face. Will you tell me what you're thinking?"

I shook my head. "Thinking? Light and all, Tala. A . . . a *child.*"

"Well, that generally happens when two people make a habit of seeing each other."

"But you look . . . the same. How could you . . . ?"

She laughed, and there was something in the sound, a lightness, a burst of exuberance. It made my stomach twist, though from excitement or terror, I didn't know.

"A child . . ." I repeated.

She sighed and moved. I felt her squeezing into the tight space beside me, draping herself over me, leaning close and brushing a hand to my face. "Don't be scared."

"I don't know if I can do this."

"Me neither." But she smiled as she said it, like it was an adventure, not a disaster waiting to happen.

I shook my head. "Tala, I'm not . . . I can't be . . ."

"Yes," she said.

I frowned, struggling to keep up. "Yes?"

"Yes, I would go with you. I would go anyway. I would walk into the desert, I would stand with you against thirst and shadows, and brave any danger." She paused, and I felt her chest pulsing against mine. "Would you do the same for me?"

"Yes."

"Then be brave with me, Vanya. Can you do that?"

I thought of my father. *How many times?* His sharp, angry words. *Never, Ishvandu. You're not a Guardian. You're not . . . you're not. Stupid, ungrateful little rat.* But he went after me. He went after me, into the desert, rushing into the sands. Had he been angry? Had he been scared? Had he felt like I did now, some twisting, intangible horror: his life no longer his own? I thought of him trudging through the heat, through the night. I thought of the Sumadi. I thought of him screaming. And then—unbidden—came thoughts of my mother. The alien woman I had never known. The woman never spoken of. The empty place. She could have been someone. But she had died. She had died. And my father had held his grief in silence. I saw now, rolled out ahead of me, a life without Tala. The dangers of childbirth. The story that was all too common in the desert. In Kaprash. The unborn babies. The mothers. Gone.

I groaned and pulled Tala close, wrapping my arms around her. "I don't want to lose you."

"You won't."

"But—"

"Vanya, you *won't*."

I nodded. I didn't know what else to say, but I rambled off questions anyway.

"Do you think it's a . . . a boy?"

"I don't know," she said against my cheek.

"A girl?"

"Maybe."

"A little girl?"

"It could be."

"Yl'avah's might, a little girl. Yl'avah's blasted might. I'm not ready. I'm not. I'm *not*, Tala. I can't be a father. I can't be anything. I don't even know . . ."

"Hush," she said smilingly. "I will be here, Ishvandu. Together. You and I. No matter what."

I shut my eyes. I nodded. I imagined a life, a tiny life, moving in the space between us. "No matter what," I said.

TALA STAYED WITH ME, our bodies wrapped around each other like roots. It was impossible to sleep in the cramped blackness. It was dank and cold. We dozed, shivering. Or Tala dozed. I could feel the rise and fall of her chest, the rhythm of her heart—maybe two hearts.

The thought burst through me anew. I tried not to think about it. Not now. Not yet.

I closed my eyes. I saw the desert again, black and strange. Before, it had calmed me, thinking of the desert and the swirling dust. But not now. There was something different about it. Something different.

I felt myself moving through it. If I opened my eyes, I saw the darkness of the holds, I heard the sighing of my wife. But when I closed them, there was the desert. It rushed past me. And I was moving with it: moving, drifting, *searching*. But all black. So strangely black.

That's when I saw it. The stars. There were no stars. No moon. So how could I see? Was this even the desert? Was this even sand? It could be anything. It could be anywhere. It could be . . .

I snapped awake. My heart was beating erratically, a sharp pain pulsing behind my eye. It was dark. Dark and cold.

Tala stirred. "What's wrong?"

"I don't know."

"Did you dream?"

"No. Not like last time. Not . . ."

I shut my eyes, and instantly I saw the blackness, the moving blackness. Shifting, seething, rushing across sand and stone. Drawing nearer.

I sat up. Tala stiffened against me, alert, every Guardian sense at the ready. "What's different?"

"It's not a dream . . ."

I felt her waiting, breath held.

"Tala, it's . . . it's real."

Her grip tightened. "Vanya, what do you mean, it's real?"

"I don't know." I closed my eyes again. I saw the emptiness. I saw the black hole, where the Avanir had been, the light, the light itself— gone out. And now they were searching. They were coming. I saw walls, and with a single leap, the walls fell away. I saw shadows moving. I saw Shyandar.

Save us, save us. This one . . .

I shot to my feet. "It's Kaprash."

"Yes, yes it is."

"The first night of Kaprash."

"Yes."

"Tala, it's *Kaprash*." I gripped her arms. My insides were tying themselves into knots, my head needling with pain. *It couldn't be. Yl'avah save us, it couldn't be.*

But E'tuah had come, had made the effort to sneak into the Guardian's Hall to find me. To warn me. *They are gathering.*

I swallowed and forced my hands to stop trembling. "Tala, can you get to the sounding horns? Can you sound the alarm?"

No, everything in me screamed. *Keep her close! Keep her safe. Her. Her and . . .*

"Of course," she said.

I nodded. Tala could take care of herself, better than I could. "Go quickly. And watch the shadows. If anything moves, stab it."

She squeezed my arm. "Is it them?"

"Yl'avah's might, I hope not. But this is different. I swear this is different."

"Then I'm not leaving you here."

"No," I said. "I have to get to the Circle."

We climbed out, moving silently in the dark, up through the holds, up the winding stair. The tower was empty and cold, but outside the entrance, two Guardian watchmen stood alert and ready.

"We're going to be roped for this," I muttered.

"Not if you're right."

"Are you sure about that?"

She paused. "No. But I'm not leaving you here alone. Not if those *things* show up." Before I could object, she slipped forward, moving between the watch like a shade herself.

They both snapped to attention. "Hold!" one cried. "Who—"

Tala burst into a run.

"Get back here!" They gave chase, abandoning their post. It was everything I could do not to run after them, against the slightest risk they would hurt her.

But that wasn't the point. Tala had opened my way. I slid out, keeping tight to the wall, edging around until I faced the back of the Hall instead of the front. Then I sprinted across the yard.

I moved fast, going as quietly as I could. I heard shouts from the front of the yard. Tala's voice.

Yl'avah's might, no!

I forced myself to ignore them. I dove into the corridor on my left. *Coming. They were coming.* No. My eyes flickered closed and I saw redstone walls. I saw Labourer's huts. I saw flooded fields. I saw the blazing white of the Temple. All at once. Everywhere.

I ran faster, feet slapping the ground in a frantic rhythm, flying around corners, right and left through the kiyahs' sleeping quarters, towards the back, towards the long, narrow passage to the Circle's sleeping chambers.

A guard from the eight kiyah stood at the end of it, slumped against the wall, dozing. I tore past him.

"Hey!" He snapped awake, spun on me. He was fast. His fingers latched around the collar of my tunic, jerking me back. I staggered, grabbed his arm, and twisted, sudden and sharp, just like Tushani'sal had showed us. He grunted, but no sooner had his grip loosened, then a keshu speared the air beside me, cutting me off.

"Umaala!" I hollered. I could feel the needling in my mind, the whispering voices, growing stronger and stronger:

He will save us.

He cannot.

They will die.

All die.

Die!

The guard clamped his hand over my mouth. "What's the meaning of this? What do you think you're doing here?"

I clawed at the hand. "Umaala! Umaala ab'Krushaya'sal, they're here! They're—"

He slammed me to the wall, shoving his keshu against my throat. "Shut it, boy. One more word . . ."

But it worked. I heard stirring in the private chambers, the curtains spread around the room in an arc—close enough every one of them would've heard the racket I was making.

"Blood, light, and all!" I heard a growl from one of the rooms.

At the other end, a face peered out, sai'Lanita. "What's going on here, ab'Keshniya? Who is this?"

"I don't know, sal'ah," said the guard. "But he'll pay dearly for this, I—"

"Let him speak," Umaala's rumbling voice silenced the others. "Ishvandu ab'Admundi, this had better be good."

The guard hesitated, then released me and I pulled away, trying not to tremble at the sudden chance.

"Sorry, sal'ah. Umaala ab'Krushaya. It's not good. Not good at all. They're . . . they're here."

He loomed out of the dark. "Say what you mean, boy! Quickly."

"The Sumadi."

The word fell like a blow. Gasps echoed around me, more curtains were snapped aside, and one by one, the Guardian Lords emerged.

"That's impossible." Neraia's voice was hard.

I shook my head. "Sai'Kalysa, with all respect, I'm the only one in this room that's met one of those creatures and lived, and I'm *telling* you, they're here. We have to mobilize this Hall at once! We have to—"

"Have to?" The words cracked from my right, as Jarethyn ab'Torishu stepped out. "How dare you? You think you have any right to crawl back here, spouting your outrageous lies? How did you even get in? You'll be roped for this!"

"Exactly! You think I would risk that on a stupid lie? I'm telling the truth, Jarethyn. For your own sake. For your life!"

"Get him out of here!"

The guard grabbed the back of my tunic.

"No. No, listen to me—"

He cuffed me in the side of head, and my ears rang. I staggered, but tried to pull away, to dig my feet into the ground. "Umaala'sal! Believe me, they're in Shyandar, in this very Hall. I can see them! I can see them! I *know* they're here, and something terrible is going to happen. You have to believe me. Please, sal'ah!"

As if to echo my words, a wail sounded through the dark, growing and groaning and splitting the air, piercing enough to reach from one end of Shyandar to the other.

The sounding horns! *Tala*.

Umaala's hand flashed to his keshu. "Who ordered the alarm?"

"I did, sal'ah."

"No!" sai'Lanita cried.

"He's mad," Jarethyn sneered. "Get him to the holds."

"Umaala ab'Krushaya, this is real!"

Yes, real. The voice shivered through the room, through my mind, a gust of chill air. A shadow. A shadow moved, laughing, laughing, like a knife behind my eyes. I barred my teeth, trying to pull out of the guard's grip. "There! There!" I cried.

Jarethyn shook his head. "He's lost his mind."

"No." Neraia's keshu was already drawn, head turning through the room. "I saw it."

I sagged in relief, even while the chamber turned sharp with fear.

"Everyone, be ready," Neraia ordered. "Umaala ab'Krushaya, mobilize this Hall. Ab'Keshniya, release him."

The guard obeyed, almost reluctantly, but before I could celebrate my freedom, Umaala's hand landed on my shoulder, propelling me back out.

"Tell me exactly what you saw," he ordered. "When, where. Speak. And quickly, boy."

I found myself jogging down the corridor beside him. "Just a few moments ago, sal'ah."

"These dreams sai'Neraia tells me about?"

"Not that. I don't know how, but ever since I was attacked, I can hear them when they're close."

"And you never saw a need to inform me?"

"Sorry, sal'ah, but I was under the impression you would think me crazy."

He grunted, not missing the sarcasm in my voice. "And when did it start?"

"When I was attacked, the night of the burning—"

"No, fool. Tonight!"

"In the holds, with Tal—" I stopped, glanced away. *Damn, damn, damn . . .*

"With *who*?"

"Sal'ah, she—"

"Excuses later, ab'Admundi. I want your report. Now."

I winced. "In the holds. Tala came to me, and when I heard the Sumadi, she helped me climb out. She's the one who sounded the alarm." Already we could hear movement from the Guardians' rooms, questions buzzing, feet stamping.

"All kiyahs to the main yard!" Umaala thundered as we passed the chambers of the first and second. "Move!" Then he dropped his voice again. "What did you hear?"

"Voices." I shivered. I could hear them now, wispy intangible things. "And I . . . I can see them. In Shyandar. In this Hall. In the fields. Everywhere. I'm afraid . . ."

"What?"

"Afraid they're going to attack."

"They haven't fought us in our strength, on our own ground, not for a very long time. Have they forgotten what it means to cross us? If so, they will remember tonight. *All kiyahs to the main yard! Now, now!*"

"Sal'ah . . ."

"What?"

"It wasn't Tala's fault. I told her I would accept responsibility. All of it. Whatever it might be. Please don't blame her."

Umaala grunted. "Atali sai'Neraia will do as she pleases, and don't try to tell me otherwise. Now is there anything else?" Guardians were rushing out of their rooms, flying past, nodding to Umaala as they went.

"They move like shadows, at first. Then they materialize. When you can *see* them, that's when they're dangerous. That's when they're about to attack. But . . ." I thought of E'tuah, sweeping in amongst them, slicing at the creatures as he danced over the rocks. "But that's when they're vulnerable, too."

"And do you know where they are? Can you see them now?"

I nodded and shut my eyes. "Labourer's huts. North fields, and south too, I think. The Temple. The Craftsquarter."

"Blood and light, if those bastards think they can get the better of us . . ." He glared at me. "Alright, get back to the holds."

"The *holds?* But sal'ah, I can help!"

"You aren't a Guardian, anymore, Ishvandu. You aren't a Novice. You shouldn't even be here."

"But I've faced them before. I can help. I can stay with you. I can watch for them. Let me do something, please!"

"Did you hear me? I gave you an order, boy. Move!"

I swallowed and ground to a halt. My chest was heaving up and down, everything in me screaming to be of use. But Umaala hadn't stopped me from calling him sal'ah. Not once. *A Guardian follows orders*.

"The holds, sal'ah. I'm on my way."

I turned and marched towards the tower, even as Guardians swirled around me, rushing into their kiyahs.

"Wait!" Umaala thundered. I spun, holding my breath. "Get to the Novice's quarter. Warn them and see that they stay there—no matter what, do you understand? You keep them there! I'll send Tushani and whoever else I can spare. Well? Are you deaf? Go, ab'Admundi. Now!"

"Yes, sal'ah!"

Umaala started shouting orders, even as I burst into a run.

"There's been a sighting. The Sumadi have infiltrated Shyandar, numbers and intent are uncertain. Third, to the Craftsquarter. Fourth, South Fields. Sixth . . ."

Muttering swept through the yard. I reached the far end and glanced behind me. The fourth was in motion, sweeping through those still waiting. *Tala.* My stomach clenched as I saw her, falling in line with the others. Umaala was sending her out on patrol, all the way to the South Fields. She would be vulnerable. I should be out there with her. I should be protecting her. I should . . .

Without a keshu? I was being an idiot. I should be grateful Umaala had given me this much to do. The Novices would be clueless, without a keshu, defenceless. What if one wandered off and got killed? I couldn't let that happen!

I threw myself into the corridor. I got two steps. And the cold smacked me in the face like a slap.

See us, Vanya! Come!

I backed against a wall. The whisper was behind me, in front of me, all around, insistent and strong, pulling on my mind. The coldness brushed past me. My chest tightened. Shadows emerged. They pulsed and writhed like smoke, surrounding me, cutting me off. My breath caught. *This was it! This was my death!*

No, no! I had faced them—not once, but twice. I was a survivor. I had seen them. I had looked into their minds and seen them.

"Show yourselves!"

The whispers grew louder—no, *more*. Like they were gathering. Like they were closing around me. "What do you want? Speak to me. Why are you here?"

There was a pressure in my mind, like hands squeezing, pulling. It began to throb and pound. I had to shut my eyes, focus on breathing. I imagined them tearing into me, screaming and screaming without end. *Kynava. Kynava ab'Ashnavas. Tell them . . .*

"I see you!" I cried. "I see you, Elders of Kayr! I see you!"

A flash tore through my mind, strong, like claws. I threw my hands to my forehead, doubling over in pain, coldness twining around and around, tightening, pulling, demanding. The voices were so many now, I couldn't hear them. They were crushing me with their presence. *So many! So many!*

"Speak to me! What do you want? What do you—" I gasped. I forced my eyes open, though the pain almost blinded me. There was thick blackness. They were everywhere. Everywhere! I stepped forward. The darkness moved with me. I lifted my hand, and the shadows swirled around it.

"Show yourselves, you cowards!"

I took another step. And then I was falling. My mind tore open—violent, forceful, a command that couldn't be ignored. The world opened.

I fell.

Chapter Forty-Seven

ISHVANDU AB'ADMUNDI

I never hit the ground. My eyes opened, and I was somewhere else. Somewhere without sound or colour or shadow. Somewhere *alive*. The very air was alive. But in the midst of it, the creatures, like a stain, a pestilence, like broken things in the fabric of space, surrounded me. And I could see them.

The whispers stopped. The strange world rippled with silence. A shifting vastness opened around me, full of presence and power. And impossibly full of them: not shadows, not lines of light, but corporeal things. Bodies. And there were hundreds of them, all watching me, all different. I stood alone in the centre of the living emptiness, and I felt their minds, wrongness and hatred, desperation and pain.

They watched me. Their eyes were almost human, glittering and cold. Their bodies were shrunken, twisted, pathetic. Some wore tattered rags, like the remnants of clothing, while others stood naked. Some looked old, with wispy beards and wrinkled folds of skin, while others seemed young, still bent and deformed, but strong, full of incongruous vitality.

"Traveller-Between. You have come."

It was not a slivering whisper, but a voice like a man. And I saw him. An old one, a bent, corpse-like thing covered in rags, with dark pits for eyes. Dark pits and a cloud-white beard.

It stepped out of the gathering, reaching ahead, clawing the air.

"I can taste your Life," it said. "Hear your blood beating in the Unseen. Alive. Alive. I see you." He stepped towards me.

No more fear. No more.

I held my ground, though I could feel myself shaking, shaking in this place outside the world. Yl'avah's might, what was happening? Had I finally gone insane? Was I babbling somewhere, gazing vacantly into the twisting shadows?

"You are the Sumadi," I said. My voice sounded strange, seeming to grow as it fell away into the silence.

"The Fallen, yes. That is what we are. Since the beginning, so long ago. Forever and forever, and yet a moment."

"What do you want?"

The thing laughed. A cold sound, echoed by the other creatures, crackling into the Unseen.

"Die," one of them said, staggering forward.

"To die," said another.

"To break what is broken."

"To end what is dead."

They shuffled. They pushed at each other, hands twisting in front of them, some reaching towards me. Their eyes shone hungrily.

Yl'avah's might, this wasn't real. It *couldn't* be real.

"Save us," said the sightless one.

I turned back to him. "You are the one who attacked me, all those years ago. The one whose mind I see: an Elder of Kayr."

"Years? Moments? Like the blinking of an eye. Like the unending."

"You left me alive. You could have killed me, but you didn't. Why? For this? So I could speak with you?"

"You are blind."

He stepped towards me again. Every time he moved, the living space around him seethed and shifted, warping him—like an image in a broken mirror.

"I don't know how to save you. Tell me how."

"You must see us."

"I do! I see you."

"No. You are blind."

His blind eyes gazed at me, gazed *into* me. The thing reached for me, the hands getting closer, a finger pointing, hooked, like a talon, with a long, cracked nail scratching at the air between.

"I can!" I cried. "I can see you!"

"You are not looking," he said. "Only when you see, when you truly see, can you end what is Broken. Only then will you understand."

I swallowed. He was drawing closer. *Don't back away. Don't. Don't.*

"I am looking," I said, trying not to panic, though my voice shook. "You are an Elder of Kayr! I saw you. I saw ..."

"Are we? Are we? Are *we?*"

I glanced around me. My breath caught. *Twenty-four.* There were twenty-four Elders, and Tala was right. These were numberless. Hundreds. Hundreds at least.

"Do you see? Do you *see?*"

I shook my head. "You're not just the Elders. Maybe some of you. But others— Who? Who *are* you?"

"You are afraid."

"I don't know what you want."

"Look."

"Blast you, I'm *looking!*"

"Then what do you see?" There was a malevolence in his voice, a growing impatience.

"Stinking corpses," I spat. "Cowards. You hunt my people, killing us off in the desert," *killing my father*, "making us live in fear. You want to know what I see when I look at you? Monsters. Nightmares. You ripped my mind open. You destroyed me. You tormented me. And I asked a simple question, I *try* to see you, to see what in the blazing sun you're whining about, *save you, save you.* And this is what I get? Don't you dare come back here! Don't you dare set foot in my city! These are my people. And if you think you can threaten us, come against us, destroy us, then you will suffer for it!"

The creature sprang at me. Clawed hands reached for my face, closed over my forehead, covering my eyes, so I couldn't see. Talons digging into my skin. *Don't panic. Don't panic. A Guardian never panics.*

"Fool! Your mind is the path we walk. If you will not see us, we will devour them. We will drink their Life. They call to us; they made us; they will suffer for us, and we will join them in Death."

There was a swell of voices: *Destroy them! Destroy their lives!*

I could feel them moving closer.

Hundreds of them, their bodies shuffling in the Unseen, all broken things, all scratching forward. All hungry.

Panic welled in my chest.

"Tell me what you want!" I cried.

"Too late," the thing whispered. "You see nothing. We will choose another."

"Yes," said one of the creatures. "Destroy him."

"Devour them."

"Tear them apart!"

No, no, no . . .

The creature gripped me, its nails cutting the skin around my eyes. I tried to shove my weight, push back, but I couldn't move. My hands were heavy at my sides. My feet leaden. I didn't belong. I was a trespasser, helpless. My head felt like it was being crushed.

"You sought me out!" I cried. "All this time, all these years, and then you don't even give me a chance?"

"What is time?" said the creature. "Time is nothing. Eternity is nothing. You cannot see. You are nothing."

"Someone comes!"

There was a spluttering of laughter.

And then a scream. One of them was screaming. A horrific screeching. Like Kynava. They clawed in a dozen directions, some breaking away from me. Some pressed against me, hands grabbing at my arms and legs, as if to tear them off.

Wake up! I had to wake up. I focused everything on my body. On feeling my toes. My fingers. The pain behind my eyes. Growing stronger.

There was a sharp sting across my face. My eyes flew open.

"Get up, Ishvandu," I heard a voice. "Get up now!"

I was staring at the weapons-master, his eyebrows frowning over me, lit by the glow of his keshu like a star in the dark corridor. A shadow moved behind him, a line of light, a hand.

"Tushani'sal!" I shouted, bolting up.

He spun, moving, lashing out with the shining blade. My mind twisted with the creature's screams, and he whirled back, stepping over me. The keshu split the air. I ducked, and there was a burst of light.

"Up!" he shouted again. "Up, Ishvandu! Move!"

I scrambled to my feet. One of the star-traced creatures dove towards me. I rushed it, throwing my weight into it, half-expecting to go *through* it like smoke. It didn't change fast enough. I slammed it against the wall. Its breath came out in a sharp, hissing laugh. My hand curled into a fist, struck it, sending spears of light flashing from its face. I could hear Tushani'sal behind me, the rush of his keshu as he spun and danced, their screams, their laughter. One keshu—against how many? Light and all, there had been *hundreds*!

Don't think, just keep moving! I struck the creature again, but it melted into shadow and my fist slammed into the wall, sending shocks of pain up my arm. Then something grabbed me from behind, cold and sharp, like blades digging into my flesh.

I hurled myself backwards, into the wall. It let go, and my head knocked against the stone. *Sands take these monsters!* I couldn't even hit them. They were too fast! It drilled into me from the side and I sprawled, hitting the ground, its fingers slicing at the sides of my face. *Coldness and death.* Fingers squeezing. Impossible strength. Trying to dig into my flesh.

"Tushani'sal!" I cried. "Help!"

The creature jerked, hurtling back, then burst with light as it died. The weapons-master stepped over me, staggering, whirling. More shadows formed around us, their shapes leapt out of the walls, converging on a single point.

"Ishvandu," he growled. "The Novices. Go." Another flash. And another. I squeezed my eyes shut, arms thrown over my head. I couldn't move.

Kynava. Kynava ab'Ashnavas. Tell them, tell them . . .

"No!" I wailed.

I felt them. They tore around me. They slammed into Tushani'sal, over and over again. I couldn't move. Couldn't. Couldn't.

The keshu clattered to the ground. Something heavy fell over my legs, grunting. Laughter sliced through my mind—and with a rush, they were gone.

My heart was pounding in the silence. "Tushani'sal?"

The weight on my legs shifted. There was a groan. A cough. A wet, spluttering sound.

"Tushani'sal?" I heard the terror in my voice as I sat up, ignoring the pain. I gripped the man, heaving him over. He was wet with blood.

I couldn't see him, couldn't see anything. It was all dark. But I could hear it: blood gurgled out of his throat, like he was drowning in it. What had they done to him? *Yl'avah save me,* what had they done? Did I even want to know? He trembled as I held him, barely visible, just a shadow.

"I'm sorry," I gasped.

Only wretched sounds came out of him. I gripped his arms; something thick was running over my hands. He gave a shuddering groan, air hissing out his throat. Then he lay still.

I wanted to be sick. The cloying smell of blood filled my nostrils. *Reaching. Hands reaching for me, dripping with blood. Blood in the water. Blood on my hands.*

What now? Yl'avah's blasted might, what now? Where had they gone? Would they come again? The corridor felt empty, but I could hear the whispers, distant and wretched, glorying in death. What had happened? What had I done wrong? I had to fix this somehow, I had to . . .

Tushani'sal's keshu lay on the ground, still glowing with a faint light. I reached for it, scrambling over the man's body, wrapping bloody fingers around the hilt.

"I'll bring it back, Tushani'sal," I said in a tight, shaking voice. "I promise. I'm sorry. I—"

The sword cast a faint light, enough to see. There was a gaping hole in his chest where his heart should have been. He was a mess of blood. I didn't look any closer. I scrambled away and my stomach heaved.

The Novices. That was my job. Those were my orders. No time for grief. No time for weakness. I hauled myself to my feet, took a step, slipped in the blood and fell, banging a knee against the stone. *Up.*

Keep moving. Tushani'sal's voice followed me, snapping in my ear. I was a Guardian, no matter the robes I wore. I *was* a Guardian. I *had* to be. If only tonight.

I was moving again. A shape loomed out of the dark, lit by the keshu, the faint outline of a corpse. *The Sumadi.* Was that even possible? Yes. They died, and they left something behind. Something that shouldn't be there.

I stumbled and ran, down the empty halls, looking for the Sumadi in every shadow. I rounded the corner. A light was on. I heard voices. Saw a silhouette in the entrance.

"We should find out what's happening," called a voice.

"Bray!" I shouted. "Get back!"

"Vanya!" The lanky shadow turned to me. "What are *you* doing here? What in Yl'avah's might is going—" He trailed off when he saw me. His face went pale. I'd never seen him move like that, staggering back, eyes wide in horror.

"Everyone get back!" I ordered. "Light every candle in this room. Stay together."

No one moved. Twenty-two faces stared back at me in the light of a tallow. Shadows were thick in the room. Dangerous shadows. Why was no one moving? Why ... ?

I stared down at myself. I was drenched in blood. Tushani'sal's blood. I gripped his keshu at my side, knuckles white. Blood on the sword. Blood smeared across my legs.

"Did nobody hear me?" I shouted. "Every blasted candle you can get your hands on. Light them, now! And someone, Jil, grab those chests, dump everything out. Breta, help him. And Light and all, Bray stop gawking at me and get back. Yl'avah's might! Are you Guardians-in-training, or Temple white-robes? Now, now you fools!"

For a terrifying moment, I thought no one would listen to me. Eyes blinked, heads turned, muttering. Blast these fools, where was Polityr when I needed him? And then Bretina jumped to her feet, grabbing the big wooden trunk where we kept extra blankets and supplies and heaved it over. Jil, the older, stocky youth I had called on, leapt up to help. Others broke into action, scurrying for their candles, lighting them, slowly pushing back the shadows. I wasn't sure if it would do a sand-blasted thing, but I had to do *something.*

In moments, we had the back of the hall filled with flickering light. Bretina and Jil had hauled over the two trunks and some blankets, and they were making a small fire out of them. Most of the others had retreated to the far wall. Bray was still hovering, staring at me. Then he spoke.

"Light and all, Vanya, what *happened*?"

His voice trembled, but he glanced back at the others. They were all nodding, muttering, eyeing me worriedly. I turned away, trying to keep my back to one of the walls, my eyes fixed at the entrance and the shadows covering that end of the hall. The blood was starting to dry and crack across my knuckles. I gripped the keshu. I owed them an explanation.

"The Sumadi," I said after a moment. "Sand-shitting wretches killed Tushani'sal."

No one moved. No one said anything. Bretina stared up from where she was trying to start the fire, the candle gripped in her hand, forgotten. Jil's face hardened. Then he stood, slowly, glancing over his shoulder toward the hall's entrance.

"And now?" he asked. I was amazed to hear how calm he sounded. *That's because he doesn't understand. None of them do.*

"I don't know," I said. Weariness clung to me. My legs quivered. "I don't know, but my orders were to keep you brainless idiots safe, so that's what I'm going to do."

"Your orders," said Tesh. "What kind of a joke is this? You're a pass-up. A Labourer. You don't belong here."

I looked at him, my insides cramping with fear, though I didn't dare let it show. I tried to stand tall. To stand like a Guardian. Like I actually knew how to use the sand-blasted thing I was holding. "Tonight I do. Tonight, you'll do exactly as I say, or Umaala ab'Krushaya will know why."

I tried not to think of how laughable I was being. I thought of Tushani'sal, how fast he moved, one of the best with a keshu. And they had slaughtered him, torn him apart.

Somehow, I had failed. They had been waiting for me. They had held back, waiting for me to confront them, as if I could actually have done something. But what? Light and all, *what*? What had they wanted from me? To *see* them? What did that even mean?

And Yl'avah's might, what about Tala? If they killed her too . . .

I couldn't even consider it. I gripped the keshu. Anger flared up, hot and invigorating. Yes, that's what I needed. To hate them. To hate my weakness. To drive myself just a little further. *Monsters. Rot-sack filth.* I was going to kill them. I was going to *kill* them.

I was shaking, despite all my efforts to stand strong. I caught some of the Novices watching. They looked worried. They looked scared. *Good.* They should be. I tried not to meet their eyes, or think of the hideous amount of blood covering me, or where it came from.

Bretina finally lit the trunk: the blankets caught, a few tendrils of smoke curled up to the ceiling, then a crackle of heat, a flame. Soon the wood was burning, the precious wooden trunks. But I knew better than to get my hopes up. Jil took his own protective stance on the other side of the fire, and Bretina started pacing in front, hands relaxed at her sides, trying to look like she wasn't afraid. But I could see it in the way she moved, quick shifts of her head, twitching fingers.

"Why are we burning our good trunks?" she asked once they were blazing away—and nothing had happened.

"The Sumadi move in the shadows."

"And you think this will work?"

"Maybe. Maybe not."

I heard whispers from the older Novices. Alynis and Tesh, muttering against me.

"You've a better idea, you little shits? Either of you face a shade before? Huh? Anyone? Anyone have a sand-blasted idea what you're up against?"

"Breta should hold the keshu," said Tesh. "She's faster than you."

"No. Tushani'sal gave it to me. I'm the only one who touches it."

"Vanya?" Bray sidled up behind me. He looked pale, brown eyes wide in fear, though he was trying to hide it. "What are you doing here?"

"I told you already. I came to warn you useless sacks, and Umaala sent me here. So that's it. We wait."

"For how long?"

"Until it's over."

"Maybe it's over."

"No," I said. I could still hear them, *feel* them. The pain in my head, the twisting in the Unseen, like broken things, scratching at my mind. And yet . . . they were getting further and further away. I frowned. "Not yet."

"How do you know?"

"Yl'avah's blasted might, Bray. I know."

"But *how*?"

"Bray, shut up!" said Bretina. Her feet still tapped a nervous rhythm on the stone floor. "Can't you learn when to keep your stupid mouth shut?"

"I just want to know! Besides, maybe we should be doing something to help."

"*You're* going to do something to help?"

"Maybe. Why not?"

"What, are you going to fight them with your stench?"

"Maybe they'd give us some keshu! If the shades are here, in our Hall, we should be fighting them, not hiding like green Taskers."

"Hah!" Jil laughed. "You're practically a Tasker yourself. You can't even hold a training sword straight."

"Can so."

"You'd wet yourself the moment you saw one."

"Stop it," I said, something knotting in my stomach. *No, I thought they were leaving. I thought . . .*

Breta ignored me. "Besides, if they killed the weapons-master, what makes you think *you* stand a chance?"

"Well, if we worked together. Not that you would know anything about that."

"Oh, don't start now, you little prod."

"Shut up! Both of you!" I said.

They fell silent, looked at me. It was getting closer. Something was definitely getting closer. If I concentrated, I could almost *see* it, like a cloud brushing across the stars. It latched on to my mind, pulling itself towards me through the Unseen.

We know this one! This one! This . . .

I crouched into back stance, keshu snapping into guard.

"Get back," I said. "Everyone behind the fire."

"Vanya?" Breta raised a sleek brow, looked around the room. "There's nothing here."

"Blood and light, are you really going to argue with me you stupid girl? Move! Now!"

She shot me a viperous look, then turned her back to me. "Orders or not, Vanya, we're still more Guardian than you. Don't think we'll let you fight alone. Right Jil?"

"Right," the stocky youth nodded. They stayed where they were, standing in line with me, settling into an open-handed attack stance, third position.

"I can take it better without your help. You're going to get yourselves killed."

This one boasts mightily.

A laugh scratched my head, drowning out the other voices. The walls flickered, the stones danced. Which shadows were natural? Which were something else? I took a step forward, keshu held high. I thought I saw movement at the far end.

Much Life here, Traveller-Between. Much to devour!

"Try it!" I shouted at the shadows. "Come out, if you can, you slavering sack, and I'll make you suffer for Tushani'sal. You don't scare me!"

It was a dead lie. I was terrified. And yet I was *more* than that. I was *not* going to let this thing have what it wanted.

It laughed again. *There.* I had seen it, or felt it. One moment it wasn't—and then it was. A shape slinking across the line of shadow at the edge of the hall, peeling out of the dark.

Give us their lives.

"Not a chance."

"Vanya?" It was Bray's voice, coming from behind me, high-pitched and nervous. "Vanya, who are you talking to? There's no one ... here."

"Get back, Bray," I said.

So small. Such simple minds. I can open them.

"You will not."

They will see us.

"No," I said.

Then they will die.

The shadow cut along the wall, twisting with the firelight, flickering between realms.

"There!" Bretina shouted.

I was already dashing towards it, keshu poised, feet ready to spring. Just like Tushani'sal would want.

It slipped into the ground.

I stared. *What?*

Something cold wrapped around my leg, coming out of the stone. I staggered. I slashed down with the keshu, but it dragged my feet out from under me. I fell. The thing burst into shadow, laughter scraping at my mind. I rolled back to my feet and saw it, twisting up with the smoke, clinging to the ceiling.

Which one? Its voice was like the edge of a knife, cutting into my mind. *Which will I take first?*

It fell out of the smoke in sudden, sharp lines of light, driving Jil into the ground, fingers wrapping around the back of his neck. I was already running. I leapt over the fire. Lunged. It disappeared like smoke and I almost ran Jil through, jerking the sword at the last moment.

I twisted back, sweeping the keshu with me. Jil gave a cry of alarm. The creature flashed beside Bretina a few paces away. She spun, lashed out with open hands. One arm materialized, one half of its body, a glimmer of its face, scarred and dripping light. She shoved it aside, twisting around it, coming between us, even as it scraped at her, fingers ripping at flesh. She screamed, stumbled.

"Breta!" I shouted. She ducked and I swung in a wide, swift arc. The Sumadi took the blow on its arm, jerking back with a hiss of pain, bursting into smoke. I expected it to flee. Instead it dove straight for me, past Bretina, materializing a hand span from my face, both fists slamming into my body, hurling me backwards and knocking the wind out of me. I hit the ground, skidding painfully, the keshu clattering out of my hands. The creature's weight pressed into me, a solid, life-like weight, pulsing with wicked force, fingers digging into my ribs. I thought of Tushani'sal, the heart ripped out of his chest. I coughed. Gasped for air.

Then Breta hit it, driving her weight into its side. It screamed in frustration, twisted, burst into shadow, and leaked into the floor. Breta landed on top of me.

"Get off!" I hissed. "Move!"

She rolled and I scrambled to my knees, lunged for the keshu, even as I glanced around me. Where had it gone? Was it finished? Had we beaten it? The other Novices stared in stunned silence. Jil was crouched into a low stance, head snapping around him, trying to figure out where it would come from next.

"Yl'avah's might, Vanya, you okay?" Bray called from the far end of the room. I glanced back at him. He was standing alone, apart from the others, near the shadows. Where I had been standing a moment ago. My stomach flipped. I saw it too late. The thing melted out of the wall, wrapping around him, fingers grabbing for his face.

"No!" I screamed. I was on my feet, throwing myself across the room. But it had the extra moment it needed. The Sumadi dissolved in a rush of light, bleeding into Bray's face, filling his eyes, his nose, his mouth. He stood rigid for a moment in terror. Then he collapsed.

He hit the floor and his eyes went inky black. His whole body convulsed. A scream tore out of his throat.

"Bray!" I dropped to my knees, the keshu clattered uselessly to the ground. "No, no, no, you blasted filth! Get out of him!" I threw myself at him, seizing his head. *Not Bray! No, not him!*

Pain exploded behind my eyes. The creature ripped into him, and I could feel it. Every moment. Every horrible, shattering moment, as it tore his mind apart, fusing itself to him. *Like Kynava. Kynava.* The endless pain, the screaming, on and on, in helpless agony.

"Get out!" I screamed, but the thing clawed at me, dragging me in, laughing, exulting in its prey, threatening to overwhelm me too.

I panicked and let go, jerking back in terror, head spinning. I fought to stay conscious. To think past Bray's wretched, screeching cries.

There had to be something I could do. There *had* to be.

"Bray!" My voice cracked. A useless cry. Useless. I stared at him. He twisted and kicked, grabbed at his own face, nails digging into his eyes, as if to gouge them out. I wrenched his hands away, threw my weight against him, holding him down, teeth clenching as he writhed. He tried to throw me off, jerking in unnatural ways. He wept, he screamed. I'd never felt so useless before. I could feel the Sumadi, feeding off his Life, latching on to him, growing stronger as it tore him apart.

No! Anger boiled up in me. I let go, seized Tushani'sal's keshu, held it in trembling hands. What was I going to do? Kill him? I should. Drive it through Bray's heart. End it. I knew what he was suffering. I knew he was conscious for every moment. Feeling everything. I knew it was the worst agony imaginable. I looked at him.

Yl'avah's might, I couldn't do it!

Tears streaked my face. I just clutched the keshu, kneeling at his side, watching, helpless, as he suffered. The boy clawed at his cheeks, leaving bloody lines, his body arched. The long hall echoed with his cries. No one moved, no one spoke. He gave a gurgling screech, arms snapping out to the sides as he twisted.

Then he fell limp. The ink bled from his eyes, his mouth hung open, he stared at me, vacant. Dead.

My face twisted. A sob of horror built up in my chest, but I wrestled it down. Watched. Waited. A shape began to form over him. Shadow and light was sucked back out of him, and the creature came into view, crouched over his body, like carrion over a desert carcass. I waited. I waited until I could see the silver lines of the Sumadi's face, see its eyes, its hateful triumph. Then I struck.

The keshu sliced into its chest, burrowing deep, fixing the form into place. Its leering face contorted with pain. It screamed and reached for me. I twisted the sword, jerking as hard as I could. Then wrenched it out and stabbed again. I watched as light and shadow flowed from it, oozing into a sticky puddle like blood. I rose to my feet, kicked it over, stabbed down. It yowled, screeched, jerked madly, clawing at the blade, light spearing out of it.

Then it exploded.

The Novices gave a shout of surprise. I didn't even blink. I watched this time as it collapsed onto the floor, light flying over it, as if piecing it back together, moulding its corpse into place, then bursting out. When it was over, I wrenched the keshu out and watched the Sumadi's body crumble into a putrid, stinking mess.

Silence followed. Heavy, thick silence, full of my gasping breath. A whimper somewhere.

I stared down at Bray. Ebridyn ab'Branidu. I didn't want to see, but I couldn't help it. He was just lying there, eyes gazing back at me, accusing me. *You were supposed to keep us safe.*

"No..."

It was Bretina's voice, sounding small and scared. She stumbled to my side, took my arm. I jerked it away.

"You!" I choked out the words.

"Me?"

"Stupid girl." My voice was laced with tears. "If you'd just listened to me in the first place, this wouldn't have happened!"

"Vanya..."

"No!" I whirled on her. "This is your fault."

"*My* fault?" Her face went livid. She took a step closer, fists bunched at her side. "You're going to blame me for this? *He* was the one who wasn't listening. Maybe if Bray wasn't such a clueless idiot—"

I struck her across the face. She gasped. Everyone gasped. Then she looked at me, and lunged, striking me in my ribs. I grunted, dropped the keshu, but grabbed her and spun. I hurled her to the ground. She tried to wrench me off, but I was stronger than her. I trapped her arm. I was shouting something and my fist crunched into her eye, knocking her head back. I dug my knee into her stomach, lifted my fist, hit her again.

"Stop it!" Jil shouted, grabbing me from behind. "Vanya!"

Tesh was there too. He latched onto my arm, dragging me back. I spun and my elbow smashed into his face.

"Don't touch me!" I was on my feet, breathing hard. Jil took a step back, watching me, Tesh was holding his mouth, blood dripping from between his fingers. Bretina scrambled up.

Yl'avah's might, what was I doing? I glanced at the other Novices. Some eyes were nailed open in fear, some were muttering, angry. Some just stared at Bray, only seeing his dead body. Only remembering his screams.

I swore, snatched up Tushani'sal's keshu, and fled from the hall.

I WASN'T sure where I was going, but I stumbled through the dark until I came to the Commons. Long, silent tables greeted me. A faint light leaked through the windows. The Sumadi were gone. I couldn't hear them anymore. Couldn't see them. The shadows were still and empty.

My legs gave way and I sunk into the floor. Then I wept like a green Tasker.

It hurt. Everything hurt. Not physically. That didn't matter anymore. It was the cloying, heart-sick pain of failure, of not being enough. Something had happened with the Sumadi, and somehow, in a bitter way I hardly dared to acknowledge, it was all my fault. If only I knew what I had done wrong.

I cried until my sides ached. Until I thought I was going to throw up. Tushani'sal's keshu rested across my knees and I clutched shaking fingers around it, hard enough the edge bit into my skin and blood dripped to the floor.

Then I heard quiet footsteps. I choked back my tears. I didn't want to look up. I didn't want to acknowledge anyone.

"Ishvandu." It was Umaala ab'Krushaya.

Stand and report, like a Guardian. Be strong. Own up.

I didn't move.

"Ishvandu ab'Admundi."

"I'm sorry," I blurted out. A sob hitched my voice.

"Ishvandu—"

"Tala? Is she okay?"

He grunted. "Fourth hasn't returned yet."

My heart felt like it was being squeezed over a stewing pot. "When?"

"I can't say."

I groaned. My head fell to my chest, tears dripping down my face. "She said there's a child. A child."

Umaala grunted, unsurprised.

"Tell me she makes it back, sal'ah. Please tell me."

"When I know."

I nodded miserably. "Sal'ah?" He didn't respond, so I choked out the rest of the words. "I didn't . . . I didn't act like a Guardian today."

"You followed your orders," he said.

I shook my head. "They killed Tushani'sal. They killed Bray. I couldn't protect him. I was useless. A useless sack. And then I blamed the others. Hurt them just because I was angry. I took Tushani'sal's keshu, but I don't deserve to touch it. I should never have . . . never . . ."

My voice was thick with grief and disgust. I didn't know why I said those things, or how I expected Umaala to respond, but he crouched next to me, one knee to the ground. He reached out and wrapped his hands over my mine where they still dug into the blade. I glanced up through blurry eyes, startled.

"Ab'Admundi," he said. "Acknowledging weakness is a step towards strength. You did what you could. Next time you will do better."

"Next time." I laughed bitterly. "I'm nothing, sal'ah. There won't be a next time. I'm a mudfoot, remember? That's it. That was my chance to be something. My one chance. And I failed."

"We'll see," he said. "Gather the Novices for the Dawning. Tell them we'll tend the dead once the sun is up."

"How many, sal'ah? How many dead?"

"Many," was all he said. Then he rose and left me to the long, empty room. Left the keshu still in my grasp.

What was I doing here? What was he saying? Why wasn't I in the holds?

Somehow I got up again. Somehow I even staggered back to the Novices. I just stood in the entranceway. They were huddled in little groups, talking quietly. Some hadn't moved.

They looked up at me. Silence fell. No one said anything.

"Main yard," I said, voice barely carrying to my own ears. "Sun rises."

I didn't wait for them to respond. I turned and walked out, and one by one, they followed me.

Chapter Forty-Eight

HYRANNA ELDUNA

A shaft of sunlight struck through Hyranna's hiding place, dividing the branches—exposing her.

She flung an arm over her face and lay there, dark memories circling her mind. She didn't want to remember. She didn't want to think about it, to think about anything.

Something shoved her in the leg and she yanked her feet in, trying to disappear.

"Hyranna Elduna, hiding in the bushes will not do you any good."

Anger burst, and fizzled out just as quickly. "Go away," she said.

"Unfortunately, that isn't possible."

She curled up on her side, one hand clutching her leg, shaking. She had torn off more of her dress to make a bandage, but the blood was still seeping through. Was it true? Would the Aktyr heal her? It had dulled the pain, but not completely, and the thought of moving right now was unbearable. She just wanted to be left alone. Couldn't he just leave her alone?

E'tuah gave a frustrated sigh. "We are a long ways out of our way. If you ever want to catch up to Balduin Na-es, you'll have to start walking sooner or later. It might as well be sooner."

Balduin. The name stirred something in her, but how would she ever be able to tell him what happened? *I'm sorry I didn't reach you sooner. But we were captured by slavers. I murdered someone to get away, and I had to leave Jerad Amanti to suffer and die. But I'm here now. Are you glad to see me?*

She gave a bleak laugh. This was a nightmare. She should never have left Elamori. *Balduin* should never have left Elamori. Find his father? It was impossible. Maybe she should give up and go home. The thought of Elamori was a like a dream—peaceful, forested, her father's twinkling smile, her mother waiting for her.

But the Aktyr. This thing. Stuck to her. Waiting to explode. How long? How long before her anger burned against Eedi, or Mylar—or her own father? How long before she murdered them too?

It flashed through her mind: the Aktyr laughing, the stone in her hand, the crack of the man's jaw as she hit him over and over again, heedless of his screams. His eyes, staring. Horrified.

"No," she groaned, pulling her knees in tighter. "No, I can't."

"You have to," E'tuah said. "Put it behind you. Move on."

"How?

"Accept what you cannot change—it's a part of you. Learn from it. Get stronger. Smarter. Adapt. And whatever you *can* change, do."

She pursed her lips, burying her head a little further into her arm. That sounded hard. Sounded like something she didn't have the strength for. "And what *can* I change?" she asked after a moment, her voice sounding small and weak in her own ears.

"To begin with, you can get up. A posture of defeat is the first step to defeat."

Hyranna shut her eyes. *Defeated.* Is that was she was? She felt like it, but she wasn't sure why. Because she'd decided to defend herself, to escape?

E'tuah was right. She was lying here like Garden and his cronies had already won. But they hadn't. Not yet. Maker above, they hadn't won yet. She was free, and that was a step better than the day before. Who said she had to leave? Who said she had to give up on Jerad, without even trying?

She lay there for another moment. She had a choice to make. A very important choice. *Maker above, let me make the right one.* She took a deep breath—and realized she had already made up her mind. It was the only way she could crawl out of this bush with a shred of dignity.

She backed out, trying to ignore the pain in her body: her wounded leg, her shoulder, her swelling jaw, the cuts and bruises on her arms, and between her legs. Tight, tense muscles. Twisting hunger. Cold, raw fingers that refused to bend, even though the sun was struggling to banish the chill.

The twigs poked at her arms and legs, leaving fresh scratches next to the knife marks, but she made it out, sat on her knees for a moment, then climbed to her feet.

"Very good," E'tuah said, watching her. "So what are you going to do?"

She lifted her chin. "I'm going to save him."

E'tuah's look of approval vanished into shock. "Are you mad? Have you lost your mind?"

"We have to help Jerad. If we don't, they'll kill him. Because of me. They'll kill him, and it'll be my fault."

"No," he said firmly.

"No? You saw what I did! The first thing Garden will do is get even. He'll hurt him."

"Most likely. He may even kill someone, but it won't be your friend."

"Why not?"

"They'll need a guide, Hyranna Elduna. That's why. They'll assume he knows the land just as well as you do. And as long as he doesn't say anything foolish . . ."

"Like refuse to help them?"

E'tuah frowned. "There is that danger."

"Like admit we had no idea where we were going?"

"That too."

She glared up at him. "I won't abandon him. If we go now, we could still make it in time . . ."

"To do what? You're useless at controlling the Aktyr. You're one small girl against a dozen slavers, and you almost failed against *one*. What exactly do you intend?"

"Not me," she said. "You."

"Me?"

"Yes. You're going to save Jerad."

He sneered. "Unless you've forgotten, I'm stuck between Realms."

"No, you aren't. Not when I use the shard on *you*. You take it in somehow. You become present. You did it before when you almost killed Jerad, and you'll do it again to save him."

"It doesn't work like that."

"Why not? You keep bragging about how it was never meant for me, it's yours, it belongs to you, oh, the things you can do with it. Well, prove it!"

She took a step towards him, fists clenching. "You owe me that much! Do you know how hard it is to paddle with a bruised shoulder? And then to do it with that disgusting wretch breathing down my neck? And the way you treated Jerad, like he was nothing—Maker above, he deserves better, and we aren't going to leave him. Now I'm going back, and if you want to help me survive, you'll have to help Jerad survive."

He shook his head, like he couldn't believe what he was hearing. "You want to go back? You just escaped from them, and now you want to go *back*?"

"Of course I don't want to go back!" she shouted. "I'm terrified, and I would much rather run in the opposite direction. But I know one thing: I won't be able to live with myself if I don't choose the right thing, right now. And this is the right thing. Even you know it."

Without waiting for him to respond, she marched off in the direction of the river.

He flashed in front of her, barring her way. "Hyranna Elduna, this is foolishness."

She ignored him and tried to push past. He shifted again. She swerved the other way, took two steps, but he lunged forward, seizing her arms.

"No," he said. "I won't allow it."

"I'm not asking your permission. This is how it's going to be!"

"No."

"Yes! Get out of my way!"

His fingers tightened, digging into her arms, just like Garden, just like Whiset. Trying to force her. She'd had enough of that.

"Let go of me!"

"You're not listening!"

"No! *You're* not listening. I'm telling you—I'm going back for Jerad. Now get your rotten claws off me, or I will use it. It may not kill you, but Maker above, I know it'll hurt!"

He laughed, and his teeth flashed in a snarl. "Stupid girl! You think I'm afraid of you, of the Aktyr, my own weapon?"

"Yes," she said.

His face twitched, a hand tugging angrily at the wide sash around his waist. "You have no idea. You want to know what I can do with it? Do you really? Yes, I can save your friend, but are you ready for the consequences?"

He lowered his face, dark eyes blazing into her. "It will destroy them. Every one. Maybe the slaves, too, if you don't free them in time. You will hear them screaming. There will be blood. The Aktyr will drink it in, and you will suffer for it. Every one of those deaths will be on your head. Yours and yours alone. Are you ready for that?"

She thought of Whiset. She thought of crushing him, of shattering his bones and bursting his ribs. She swallowed, but refused to look away. This was it. She nodded. "Yes."

E'tuah look as grim as she'd ever seen him. "Then one last thing."

"What?"

"If we do this, we do it my way. Completely and without question. No arguing. No wasting time. No turning away at crucial moments. You listen to me, follow my lead, do exactly as I tell you, or your hero will be the one to suffer for it. Can you agree?"

She nodded. "Promise to save Jerad Amanti—promise to get him away from those men, alive. Then yes. I don't care how you choose to do it."

"Then we're already falling behind. Let's go."

Chapter Forty-Nine

ISHVANDU AB'ADMUNDI

The Resting House was full of bodies. Bodies laid out on stone slabs. Bodies standing amongst them, hovering over their dead. Ninety-three dead. Not because of Kaprash, not because of hunger or thirst or disease. But because of the Sumadi, every one of them. And my fault.

I stood next to Bray, resting a hand on his pale forehead. It was cold. So horribly cold. Like a slab of clay before firing, supple, but stiff, stuck somewhere between form and use. Bloodless.

I shuddered and pulled away. I had failed him. I hadn't been fast enough. I hadn't been careful enough. First Polityr, lost to the Avanir's will, then my father, and now Bray.

I felt like I was missing something. Like all my life was leading to one thing, one purpose. As if the desert, the shadows, E'tuah, the Avanir—they were all bound up in it, answers without a question, pointing and pointing, without cause. I had suffered and lived, but it wasn't enough. I knew things. I had seen things. And for what?

"Vanya."

I looked up. Kulnethar stood quietly to one side, hands folded, face drawn with exhaustion. I wondered if I looked as horrible as he did, eyes drooping, face lined with grief, spent.

"Alis?" I asked.

"She . . . she's fine." He paused. "Tala?"

"I don't know." She had been sent to the South Fields. Her kiyah still hadn't returned. I could feel it in every muscle, every bone, the agony of unknowing.

"I'm sure she's fine."

"Don't," I said, biting off the words. "Don't say that like you know. Don't."

Kulnethar lifted his hands. He waited, then glanced at Bray. "A friend?"

"He was a dumb kid. Never did as he was told. Probably would have gotten himself killed anyway. Stupid Bray."

My voice caught. I turned. And there was Bretina, watching us with hands clutched tight in front of her. Face swollen from where I'd hit her. Kulnethar saw and slipped quietly away.

"What do you want?" I asked.

Bretina slapped a tear from her face. "Dumb kid," she said.

"Yeah."

"He actually liked you, you know? He looked up to you. Thought you were something else, Yl'avah knows why. Stupid."

"Utterly," I said.

Bretina swiped away more tears. "Shit," she said. And then more tears. "Yl'avah's blasted might, I'm sorry, okay? I feel l-like I failed too, you know? Like I wasn't fast enough."

"Stop, Breta."

"What, so you can be the only one who feels bad? Sands, you're an ass. I'm trying to tell you, Vanya. I'm trying to tell you—it's not your fault."

"You don't know what it was like for him. You have no idea."

"So? It was horrible. We get it. We saw. It's still not your sand-blasted fault. You think everything comes back to you? It doesn't. And shit, *I* wanted to fight too, so I'm not going to apologize for hitting you either."

I snorted and glanced down at my hands, still crusted with Tushani'sal's blood. "No, that one's on me. I shouldn't have—"

New movement caught my eye. I turned, Breta instantly forgotten. Guardians. Guardians carrying their dead—from the South Fields.

The fourth! My whole body strained in that direction. I saw ab'Anajin and Antaru, heaving a bier between them. A fallen Guardian, by the looks of it. It couldn't be Tala. It *couldn't* be. My mind would not allow it. Would not grow in that direction. Anyone but Tala.

I looked. I looked. Hungry for a glimpse of her. There were other Guardians. Other dead. Labourers, too.

She appeared. She was following the others, a hand on her keshu, peering into the dark of the Resting House. Her thick, black braid was loose, face dirt-streaked, robes stained with blood, but I almost burst at the sight of her.

"Tala!"

I pushed through the crowd. Our eyes met, and instantly her face clouded with grief.

I clung to her. We were both covered in blood. Our hands grasped and searched. I felt her face, felt the gush of tears. She dug her fingers into my blood-stiffened shirt.

"Vanya . . ."

"I'm okay," I said. "And you? And you?"

She nodded. "I heard. About Bray. About Tushani'sal. I'm so sorry."

I said nothing. I smoothed a hand over her hair, the most beautiful hair I had ever seen, all crinkly and wild, forever bursting out of her braids. I pulled her aside, away from the crowds, around the outside of the House, and just held her.

We stood for a long time, wrapped in each other, our physical nearness like a balm.

"What happened?" she whispered at last.

I shook my head. "I don't know, but I'm going to find out. I'm going to fix this. I'm going to . . ."

"Vanya."

"What?"

"Not alone."

I nodded.

"Promise me," she said.

"I promise."

She sighed, and this time, her hands clung to me in determination. Her brows already crinkling in thought. "We have to tell Umaala. We have to speak to him."

"Now?"

She nodded. "The Circle—"

A figure loomed over us, and I squeezed her arm into silence. It was Umaala.

"Ishvandu," he said.

"Yes, sal'ah?"

"The Circle is gathering. You will return with me to the Hall and be ready with an exact account of last night's events."

"Now, sal'ah?"

"Yes, now." He glanced at Tala. "You too."

"Sal'ah, she didn't do anything wrong. It's not her fault. It—"

Tala jabbed me in the ribs. "Shut up, Vanya. This isn't about *fault*. I blew the sounding horns. I let you out. Don't you dare try to protect me from my own choices."

"Precisely," Umaala said. "That goes for both of you. Now—"

"Umaala'sal?" I asked.

The man lowered his brows at me. "What?"

"We have to talk. About the Sumadi."

"Save it," he said.

"But I—"

"The Circle will hear. We will all hear." He glanced at Tala. "Let's go."

WE RODE BACK to the Hall in silence. By the time we stumbled into the Circle Chamber, I was limp from exhaustion. I hadn't slept. I had barely eaten. The procession to the South Grounds would begin soon, and the burial would be long and gruelling. I would be wanted on Adar's crew. I had a full night of work ahead of me. And in the middle of all that, the Circle wanted to *talk*.

But it wasn't only the Circle. As I entered, I saw that everyone was in attendance, plus one. A stool had been dragged up, placed just to the right of Neraia, and I found myself staring directly at the Al'kah as I came in.

The man's dark eyes were hooded. Where the Circle sat with straight-backed severity, postures crisp and ready, watching, the Al'kah leaned crookedly. One elbow was planted on his knee, legs spread, chin supported up on a fist. He peered at me with bird-like intensity, a stork perched up on a rock, gazing over the Avanir's lake. I could feel his anger, swelling and churning in the room.

"Ishvandu ab'Admundi." It was Neraia that spoke.

I swallowed. I pulled my eyes away, clasping my hands behind my back.

"Neraia sai'Kalysa. Honoured Circle. Great . . . great Al'kah. How can I help?"

"You can start by telling us everything you know about these creatures, these Sumadi. Start with the night you were attacked as a child."

I blinked. "From when I was a . . . a child, sai'Kalysa?"

"We have been complacent for far too long. We should have sought this knowledge sooner, and we intend to remedy that at once. So tell us. What do you know of these creatures? Everything."

My knees almost gave out. I wasn't ready for this. Not today! Not now! I was trembling with exhaustion, but I was also aware of unfriendly eyes. Including the Al'kah's. So be it. I would give it to them.

"Pain," I said, and immediately it was in my mind, vivid and stark. "The first night in the desert. Darkness rushing—inside, through my nose, my mouth, my eyes." I touched each place in turn. "Down my throat. Filling my lungs. Running through my blood like . . . fire. It was everywhere. In every part of me. My mind, too."

"Your mind?"

I nodded. "I saw things. Memories that weren't mine. I . . . I don't remember them, but they were horrible. The pain was unimaginable. I wanted to die. That's what I remember. Probably what they felt last night, the dead. Everyone who died."

There was a hush. They were looking at me, peering forward, horrified and fascinated, the first time anyone had spoken such an experience aloud. I felt Tala's hand slipping through mine.

"But you survived," said a reedy voice. "Why?"

The Al'kah.

I glanced at him. "I don't know, sal'ah Al'kah. I wanted to die, but I didn't. I lived."

"You lived."

There was silence. I didn't know if he was implying something, but I felt horribly uncomfortable. *My fault. Mine.* No, they couldn't know. Not about what I saw. Not about what I heard. Not yet.

"Am I being accused of something?" I asked.

"We'll see," Jarethyn said. I glanced at the Guardian Lord, but I caught disapproving looks from the others.

"Just tell us what happened next," Neraia said. "You were in the desert a month. Did you see them again?"

"Not at that time. What happened next—it was confusing. My mind was broken. I . . . I must have wandered. I found water, remember? I stayed there, slowly piecing myself back together. The Sumadi did not come again."

"You said not at that time," the Al'kah interrupted. "But have you seen them since? I mean *before* last night?"

"Yes."

There was a murmur from the Circle. They sat forward, just a little further.

"Where?" Neraia asked.

"In the desert. When I was trapped in the landslide, before Tala pulled me out." I glanced at her. "They came to me."

"And they didn't kill you?"

"No."

"Why not?"

"I don't know."

"He's lying," said Jarethyn. "He's hiding something."

"Hiding something," said Neraia. "Yes. But not lying." She glanced at Umaala, and the big man loomed forward.

"Ishvandu, you wanted to speak with me. I think now is the time."

Now. Of course. In front of the entire Circle. "I see them," I blurted out. "I have dreams. Things . . . leftover from when I was attacked. And when they're close, I can hear them. That's how I knew they were coming."

The rush of information was too quick. They didn't understand. They stared at me, then glanced at each other. Then back to me.

It was the Al'kah that broke the silence. "You *hear* them?"

I nodded.

"Then what do they say?" His fists clenched. "What do they *want*?"

His anger flashed—but not against me, I realized. He was thinking of the dead, the weakness of this Hall. He was thinking that before him now, as far as he knew, was his best chance to understand. *I could be that. I could try.*

"Death, sal'ah Al'kah. They want death. Maybe theirs. Maybe ours. I'm not really sure. They speak in . . . in fragments. Disjointed thoughts. I've asked and I've asked, but they never explain. They're bloodthirsty. Driven by some need to latch on to a living person, infest them, and drag them up to the moment of death . . . and past it."

"But they still *speak* to you?"

I nodded.

"Which means they *think*. They are thinking, conscious creatures?"

"In some ways. Yes. Some more than others. Some ask me questions, some even respond."

I could sense the Al'kah's growing excitement. He clutched his knees, eyes bright, desperate to know. "They *ask* you? And you respond? What do you say?"

There was another wave of muttering, but increasingly the Circle was falling away, becoming an audience, while I was alone with the Al'kah.

"I ask them what they want, why they hunt our people, why they cause so much pain."

"And?"

"And over and over again, I get the same response. *See us.* That's what they say to me, sal'ah Al'kah. Over and over again. See us."

"See them? What does that mean?"

"I don't know."

"But you can. You said so yourself. You can *see* them. And do they want others to see them too?"

"Maybe."

"Do they want us to recognize them?"

I thought of my dreams. I thought of the twenty-four Elders and the man with the cloud-white beard. The chamber of water: dripping, dripping with blood. And the screams. *Save us!* The Elders were among them, I knew it. But what of the others? The hundreds of others?

I shook my head. "I don't have any answers. They came to me last night, and no matter how I told them, *I see you, I see you*, it didn't matter. They were mad with rage. They would have killed me, but . . . Tushani'sal saved me."

"At the expense of his own life," Jarethyn cut in.

Everyone turned to him. His face was twisted, hands tight into fists. "You cost him his life. My uncle. And then you dared to lay hands on his keshu."

"I've heard this as well," said a Guardian Lord behind me. "He had no right. The boy isn't even a Novice. He was thrown from this Hall."

There was a murmur of agreement.

"Then how did he get inside in the first place?" asked another.

"He was in the holds," said Umaala. "For a minor offence."

"The holds!" Jarethyn gave a burst of incredulous laughter. "*Was* he? Because he managed to get into our personal chambers easily enough. Did a bird carry you this time too, ab'Admundi?"

"I let him out," said Tala, and every eye snapped to her, murmuring their disapproval.

"Atali—"

"Mother, he heard the *Sumadi*. Here. In our city. And he thought to warn you. Would you rather I'd left him to die in the holds while you slept oblivious through the night?"

"Regardless," said Jarethyn, "he disrespected my uncle's body. He presumed unlawful authority."

"Yes!" I cried. "Yes, I did. Because Tushani'sal was just brutally killed, I was terrified, and there was no one else. No other weapon. No other means of protecting myself and others, so *yes* I took authority into my own hands, because I was under orders to protect the Novices and mine were the only hands around at the time."

My voice echoed through the chamber, sharp and angry.

Jarethyn leapt to his feet. "How dare you speak so to the Circle!

You are a disgrace, ab'Admundi, and now I wonder if you aren't a danger as well." His dark eyes snapped around the room. "You've heard him. He sees the Sumadi. He *speaks* to them. He's connected to them. How do we know he's telling the truth? The Sumadi kept him alive. Didn't he say so himself? They're *using* him somehow, and every moment he breathes is a risk to Shyandar. This was no single appearance. No stray shade. This was an *assault*, and Ishvandu ab'Admundi was at the heart of it. I say we send him to the ropes. Now. This very instant, before night falls and the creatures return."

"I agree," said sai'Lanita from behind me.

"As do I," said another.

I went cold.

"No!" Tala stood forward. "Are you *mad*?"

"Be quiet," Neraia said, rising to her feet. "Jarethyn ab'Torishu, you speak out of turn. Now is not the time for such a decision. We are here to learn the nature of the Sumadi, not pass judgment on ab'Admundi."

"But what more is there to learn? They want death! I say we give it to them."

"You're not speaking sense!" Umaala thundered to his feet. "You're speaking *fear*. Are we a mindless rabble, or are we Guardians?"

"A Guardian's duty is first to protect Shyandar," said another. "That means eliminating danger, even if it comes from within."

"Precisely!" said Jarethyn. "That means—"

"How many dead?" A chair scraped and the Al'kah stood, abruptly taller than anyone else. His voice silenced the room. First Neraia, then Umaala took their seats, then even Jarethyn. The Al'kah turned, dark eyes glittering one way, then the other. "How many dead, my Guardian Lords? How *many*?"

Umaala made a sound in his throat. "One hundred and three, according to our latest count, sal'ah Al'kah."

The old man nodded and eyed the Circle. "One hundred and three souls. In one night. One *hundred* and three." There was silence. "Remember that, my Guardian Lords. Remember that well because it will not happen again." Another pause. "Does anyone disagree?"

No one dared speak. I watched the most powerful figures in Shyandar shrink into their chairs like green Taskers under a scolding.

"Good," he said. He hadn't raised his voice, though it carried through the room, clear and firm. "Then someone explain to me why our best defence against these sand-shitting monsters, the only blasted person in this Hall who knew they were coming, who had guts to sound the alarm when he should have been in the holds, and who dragged you all out of bed so you wouldn't be murdered in your sleep—bloody light and all, *someone* tell me why in Yl'avah's might you would have that boy roped for knowing things, or worse, for taking initiative in the defence of our Novices, the *future* of this Hall, indeed now a much-needed one? Why, in Yl'avah's name, *why?*"

His voice crackled, echoed, and fell silent. My heart was pounding so loud I was afraid the whole room could hear. I didn't dare glance around me, though I had no choice but to meet the Al'kah's gaze as he swung towards me. His eyebrows were stabbing down over his face, eyes carving into me.

"You," he said.

"Y-yes, sal'ah Al'kah?"

"You've survived the monsters three times now?"

I nodded.

"And you were trained in this Hall?"

"Six years," I said.

"And is there any Guardian Lord here willing to vouch for your integrity?"

I opened my mouth, but realized the question was not meant for me. There was silence. The Al'kah turned, ever so slightly, to glance at the Circle.

"Any?" he demanded. "*One?*"

I could hardly breathe. I wasn't sure what was happening. One moment I was on the ropes, the next the Al'kah himself was defending me. But Yl'avah's might, would no one speak?

"I will," Umaala said, rising and actually stepping down onto the floor. "The deaths of last night would have been three-fold were it not for his warning."

I was surprised to hear a murmur of agreement from not one, but two Guardian Lords.

"I will also," said Neraia. My heart surged. *Could it be?*

The Al'kah nodded and crossed his arms. "Then it's settled.

Umaala, you will see to it this boy is on watch every night of Kaprash. If he hears something, *anything*, he will sound that blasted alarm, I don't care if it's a jackrabbit. You will triple the night patrol. You will plan an order of defence, taking into consideration whatever you can learn from him. Jarethyn?"

The Guardian Lord was flushed with anger, but he managed a curt nod.

"In the loss of your uncle, you will take his place as weapons-master and trainer. Double our Novices, even if you have to take them of Age. I want replacements as soon as possible, do you understand? Our top priority now is to drill into each and every one of our Taskers, Novices, and Guardians the best methods of attack against these creatures. And Neraia? Yl'avah's might, make sure this boy gets that oath said. And get him a keshu already. Renewal be damned, do it soon. He's past the age anyway, and if he can survive three encounters without a keshu, I'd like to make sure he doesn't get killed if there's a fourth. Any objections from this Council?"

I watched, stunned, as the Circle remained silent. One by one, they nodded their respect, and with that, it was over.

I was going to take the oath. That's what he had said. I was going to get a keshu. Which meant . . . which meant . . .

My knees went weak. I took a step back and found Tala holding me up, arms tight around my waist.

"Dismissed," the Al'kah said, and without a further word, he marched from the chamber.

"Yl'avah's might," I breathed. "I'm going to be a Guardian."

Chapter Fifty

The day was old by the time she made it. Hyranna staggered to a halt. She was panting from exhaustion. Her leg ached, frozen in pain, though distant, still smothered by the Aktyr. She had run and run to catch up to the slavers, to make it to the camp in time, before they left, before something bad happened. Before . . .

Her limbs shook. She had run so hard. And now this. The thing she'd been expecting, fearing, dreading . . .

The body was painfully obvious. She saw it immediately, lying on the river bank, in the centre of the deserted camp. Just left there.

She clutched her face, stomach churning, breath caught in her throat. Everything tightened.

What if . . . ? What if . . . ?

"Steady," E'tuah said, hand pressed to her shoulder. "It's too small to be your friend."

He was right. Of course he was right. She felt a rush of relief—then hated herself for it.

"I have to see who it is," she said.

E'tuah's grip tightened. "Not a good idea. She's beyond your help now, Hyranna Elduna. It will only cause you grief."

"Yes," she said, voice wooden. "Yes it will." She threw off E'tuah's arm. She moved forward, limping across the bank, over scattered debris and trampled ground. He did not try to stop her. Bare toes squished through the mud. It felt cold to her. Cold and distant, springing back as her foot lifted. As if she were never there. As if she'd become like E'tuah—only half in the world, and half behind it, cut off, stuck between realms.

By the time she knew who it was, she couldn't stop herself. She closed the gap. She stood over the small body, and without a word, knelt and turned it.

There was a single, round hole in the child's forehead. The girl gazed back wide-eyed, face pinched forever in bewilderment. The same girl Hyranna had shared her bread with the morning before. And Garden had killed her. For nothing. No reason. Just because he was mad. Because he could. Because he wanted to hurt Hyranna, and he thought this would do it.

Hyranna wanted to feel something. She wanted to scream. To cry. To wail in grief. She wanted to sing the Darkening prayer, to send the girl's soul to the Last Realm. Instead she just knelt there and felt nothing. Where her grief should have been, there was emptiness.

She knelt for a long time. And then she rose and followed the river west.

***

HYRANNA FOLLOWED THE RIVER—AND she ran.

She ran and ran. She followed E'tuah's rule without question: no rests, no breaks, not even when the cramping became like knives, and her feet bled, and her lungs burned for air. Not even the pain in her leg could interfere. She shut it all off. She kept going. Even when dusk fell, when Garden and his men would have stopped for the night. She didn't need sleep. She could feel it now, just like E'tuah had said she would. She could feel the shard burning in her like a dull flame, lending her strength she didn't have.

Then he appeared in front of her, coming out of the shadows like a grey ghost.

"Stop," he said.

She pushed past him. She'd found a rhythm, and she wasn't going to ruin it now.

He appeared again. "Hyranna, stop."

"You said no stopping." *And he was right.* Stop, and she might not be able to keep going.

"This is important," he said, grabbing her arm.

She was wrenched to a halt. Just as she feared, she staggered and fell. She almost passed out. Then she felt E'tuah's hand on her shoulder, shaking her.

"Hyranna," he said. "Can you hear me?"

She was on her knees. She brought a hand to her face. It was flushed and hot and dry. "I need . . . water." Her voice scratched painfully.

"No, you need to listen to me."

"I . . . am. I'm trying."

"You will burn out if you keep going like this."

"I won't," she said, but even her stubborn refusals sounded weak.

"You are trying, but you're not doing it right."

She buried her face in her hands. She wanted to lie down and never move again. For a terrible moment, she didn't even care about Jerad anymore. Then she thought of his suffering—what he must be experiencing. They hadn't killed him. Not yet. But they could do worse things . . .

She groaned and blinked, forcing herself to pay attention. E'tuah was saying something. There was a chance it might actually be important.

"What?" she managed to say.

"You're not listening."

"I am. I *am.* What am I not doing right?"

"You're not using the Aktyr."

"I *am!*"

"No. You think you are, but that's only the surface. Go deeper."

She gave a bleak laugh. "I can't control it. You said so yourself."

"Sands take what I said!" He was in front of her, crouching, dark eyes fixed on her. "If you actually caught up to Garden in this condition, you'd be dead before you could speak. You have to do better than this. You have to accept it. Let it inside you."

"You said it responds to my fury. When I need to, I can just feel that, and you can do the rest."

"Right now, you can't feel anything."

She sagged. *He was right*. She was dull, half-dead, drifting on some strange will that no longer seemed her own.

"Look at me," he said.

She did. She was surprised to see a glimmer of concern in his eyes. "There are many things I don't understand about the Aktyr, and something like this has never happened before. It's mine, yes—but it's yours too, and it's becoming more fixed to you than I had anticipated. Are you willing to accept that?"

She thought about how she'd overpowered that man, then crushed him, just by wanting it. She nodded.

"Good. Then listen. Have you ever used the shard without anger?"

"No," she said. "It . . . it will work. Just let me—"

"It's a weak control," he said. "Sluggish and unreliable. It almost *didn't* work. We have to try something else. Because when I tell you to use the Aktyr, you have to be ready, and it has to be immediate. You may not get another chance."

She was weary. The thought of trying to call up the shard made her sick. "Now?" she moaned. "We have to do this now?"

"Will there be a better time?"

She said nothing.

He nodded and took her palms, holding them up. They were scarred and bruised. Bloody welts circled her wrists. Blisters had worn into her skin and burst.

She glanced up, meeting E'tuah's eye.

"Tell me exactly what you felt when you healed your father."

She stared at him. "What?"

"On the shores of Elamori. You lashed out at your father and killed him. You stopped his heart. Then—impossibly—you brought him back. What did you feel? In that moment when you started his heart again, what did you feel?"

Hyranna blinked. He was right. It was the only time she hadn't used anger. The only time she'd simply commanded, and it had obeyed.

"I told the shard what I wanted. And it did it."

"That's it? No emotion or feeling?"

"Despair?" she said. "Guilt? Desperation?"

E'tuah was already shaking his head. "That's not it. Those things don't work, or we would have seen the Aktyr respond to them already. You're missing something."

She nodded.

"Try to remember," he said. "Try to remember how you felt in that moment, and then do it again. Do it now; heal your wounds."

She closed her eyes and tried to picture that horrible scene, the panic and desperation of thinking she had murdered her own father. But there *had* been something else. When she broke free of Dal Adis and threw herself on her father, there had been desperation. And then there wasn't. In that moment, when she told the shard what to do, she had just *known*. She had known it would work, because in her mind, in that moment, there was no other option. And then she understood.

"I . . . I can't," she said quietly, opening her eyes.

E'tuah frowned. "What do you mean, *you can't*?"

"I can't because it wasn't an emotion. Not a feeling. I . . . I just knew."

"Knew what?"

"Knew it would work."

"Yes, but *why?*" he gripped her hands.

"I can't explain it," she said.

E'tuah looked as bewildered as she'd ever seen him. He pursed his lips together, thinking, then stood up and began to pace, his robes fluttering around his sash. His hand travelled there again, and she realized she'd seen him do that before, that same motion, as if to grasp something. Like a knife. Or the hilt of a sword.

His hand found nothing and curled into a fist instead.

"Did you . . ." he was fumbling for answers. "Did you sense the Aktyr was telling you to do it?"

She laughed. "Really? If anything it was . . . defiant. It didn't want to bring him back. But I commanded, and it did it anyway."

"And can you repeat that command? Can you *try?*"

"I don't think so. I don't think it works like that."

He growled in his throat. "If you don't even try, Hyranna Elduna, then you *will* fail, and Garden will kill you."

"Maybe not," she said.

He stared at her. "Have you gone mad? That's a real possibility. The power of the Aktyr was never meant for—"

"No," she said. "I'm not mad. What I'm saying is . . ."

She stopped. It was a thought at the edge of her mind, and if she tried to catch and hold onto it, it would just slip away. She had to tease it out. She had to start talking, and hope something would come.

"When I saved my father," she said, "it wasn't a matter of feeling, or even *trying*. I remember thinking, *I can save him. He's not dead.* It wasn't just an empty hope. It was real. I mean yes, there was hope, and anger, and all that confusion. It was horrible. But there was something else that was just . . . *real*. And if I grabbed onto it for a moment, he would be alive. So I did, and the shard listened to me, and he came back."

She glanced up at E'tuah. "Now maybe the same thing will happen again. I don't think it's something I can practice. I think it just is, or it isn't. When I try to manipulate the shard, it does terrible things. But when I see something that has to happen, and *then* I respond, maybe . . ." she trailed off.

E'tuah shook his head. "It's not enough. You have to know you can respond before it happens. You have to *control* it."

"Maker above, I don't want to control it. Don't you get it?" She dug into her pouch and brought out the shard. It was still there, and now it glistened like black glass in the moonlight. "This thing is evil. I felt it when I killed that man. It took me over. It didn't care who Whiset was. I could have done that to anyone. *Anyone*." She shuddered. "All I know is that my friend is in trouble, and he needs me, and this is the only thing I have. And if somehow I can make it do something that's *right*, if I can help Jerad, free all those people, make sure Garden can't hurt anyone again . . ." she shook her head. "I don't know how. I just know this has to happen. Like I knew with my father."

E'tuah looked at her, brows furrowed. He didn't understand, and he would probably never understand. But at last he shook his head, and stood up.

"Very well. That'll have to do."

And that was that. He turned and kept walking, and something in his approval gave her the strength to rise. Her words had been true. She *had* to do this. And in answer, the Aktyr gave her a surge of energy. She put one foot in front of the other, began to walk, and then to run, and with a new burst of hope, she followed E'tuah into the dark.

Chapter Fifty-One

ISHVANDU AB'ADMUNDI

I sat in the dark of the Tower, in the small room below the Circle chamber. I was washed and clean. My dark hair was combed neatly down the back of my neck, despite Kaprash. I was dressed in Novice's robes. I was almost sick with fear.

I was not alone. Bretina sat next to me, and across from us was Jil, Alynis, and Tesh. They were all short of the proper age, Alynis by over a year, but the Circle had decided to make an exception. And so we sat, waiting to be called. Polityr would have been here too, I realized, if he hadn't been Chosen. I felt a twist of regret.

Tala came in, and all five of us turned to stare at her.

"They're ready for you," she said.

I took a deep, steadying breath. I met her eye. Of all the Guardians I had spoken with, of all the Novices, of all the Labourers, even myself, Tala was the only one not surprised. I noticed she was wearing her ear-band again: the symbol of our marriage oaths. She looked at me and nodded.

"Good luck," she said. And she swung the doors wide.

Hot morning sun pooled over us as we stepped into the inner yard. It was full of Guardians, lined from one end to the other, standing with their kiyahs in double rows of six—at least they should have been. The attack had claimed many. One hundred and eight

Guardians strong, shorn down to sixty-nine. Most kiyahs were missing three or four. The third kiyah stood at only five, Koryn amongst them, and old sturdy ab'Tanadu. Everyone had suffered. So much devastation the Sumadi had caused. In one night! I could not let that happen again. That was my job. That's what I was doing here. My only reason.

We stood in the open place in the centre, and behind us, came the Guardian Lords. They made hardly a sound: a rustle of cloth, a scuff of sandal. The whole yard had fallen still. We were not just Novices becoming something else. We were the first of our kind, born out of grim necessity in the midst of Kaprash itself. It had never been done before. It was both an honour and a curse.

The Al'kah came last. He stepped out ahead of us, eyes glinting as he watched each of us in turn.

"You come today as Kyr'amanu," he said, his voice high and clear. "But you will leave as Atala'avah—the hands of God. You will leave as Guardians, sworn to protect and defend, and to uphold the laws. Are you ready to swear an oath of service to the people?"

"We are ready," we answered together.

"Then put aside the garments of your youth."

We stripped off our Novice's tunics, casting the short robes to the ground. We stood in loincloths, Bretina in a loose shift. A moment of exposure, of bearing ourselves before the Hall, symbolic of coming into our new lives, unburdened by the old. I felt the breeze tickle the skin of my chest, even as the sun's growing strength burned into it.

The Al'kah approached and we stretched out our arms. Moving slowly, almost reverently, he draped new Guardian robes over us, going first to Bretina, wrapping it around her waist and tying the wide red Guardian's sash himself as it was handed to him by sai'Lanita. When he was finished, he nodded and continued to me. The robe was slipped over my arms, and immediately I felt the heaviness of the cloth, easily the best I had ever worn, the weight falling comfortably across my shoulders.

As the Al'kah looped the sash around and around, I glanced down and found myself admiring the trim of the robes, the unique embroidered patterns. Mine were complex angles of blue and brown that crossed back and forth down the hem, displayed proudly along one shoulder, across my chest, and along the bottom below my knees. Bretina's had brilliant red flowers, and the long robe flattered her tall, lithe form. She caught me looking, and her mouth twitched in a smile.

The Al'kah tied my sash, and moved on. When all were in place, he took a step back and lifted his hands, palms out as if to receive us.

"You have lived amongst us, seen our ways. You know our laws and our customs, and you know already the great duty that is yours. Before yourself, you will place the safety of your people and their good. You will honour them as fathers and mothers, as brothers, sisters, daughters, and sons. You will do no wrong against them, but uphold justice, seek righteousness, and defend the law. Bretina sai'Anira," he said. "Will you swear the oath?"

"I will," she said, even as she glanced at me.

Neraia sai'Kalysa stepped from amongst the Guardian Lords, circling around so we could see her for the first time. She held an elegant keshu on her open hands. The sword was short, but sleek, with a hilt of milk-white metal carved into a dozen slender shoots, wrapped and braided around each other to form the hilt. It was beautiful, and Bretina gazed in wonder at the shining blade. Then she took the keshu in two hands, one on the hilt, and the other on the blade, palm along the sharpened edge.

"Bretina sai'Anira," Neraia began. "What oath do you give?"

"I swear by this sword, and by my own life, to defend the innocent, seek justice, and uphold the law. I swear to honour and obey the Al'kah, and to serve the people in all things, as long as I shall live. Wisdom that comes with age, justice that comes with law, strength against darkness, honour unto death." Then she slid her palm along the blade, just deep enough to leave a streak of red on the shining metal—blood that sealed her oath and symbolized her life being sworn in service.

"I honour your oath," Neraia said, and it was done. Bretina was a Guardian. The keshu was hers, and she slipped it into the sash at her side and stepped back.

"Ishvandu ab'Admundi," the Al'kah said as another Guardian Lord stepped forward. "Will you swear the oath?"

It was Umaala ab'Krushaya who had chosen to receive my oath. I was expecting it, but seeing the powerful man step towards me, a keshu held on his outstretched palms, for me, my chest swelled with pride at such an honour.

"I will," I said, struggling not to grin. Then my eyes were drawn to the sword he carried.

It was strong, like the one who had chosen it. It was broad from hilt to point, with a sudden, upswept edge, and along the rippled metal was etched the angles of an old Kyre'an script. The hilt was far more simple, made of dark polished wood, long, and overlaid with two thin strands of silver that crossed twice before ending in a pommel. It was, I realized, a blade meant to be drawn.

I stared at it, hardly believing this masterful work was for me. It was old—I could tell from the ancient symbols—old, even to the Guardians of old Kayr, something fit for those long-dead warriors of honour. The tradition of Guardians who came before us, who would have held this very blade, sprawled open in my mind like a long, unbroken thread. And now it was my turn to take it up.

"Ishvandu," Umaala said under his breath. I glanced up, startled. He was waiting for me to take it. I swallowed back a wave of fear. *Be one of these*, he seemed to say, and I found myself struck by the impossibility of it. I was a shadow. We were all shadows. Meagre echoes of something that had once been great. Perhaps could be again.

I took a deep breath and reached for it, closing one hand around the hilt, the other around the blade, lifting it, feeling the weight of it, its ancient power. Umaala nodded, and for a moment, I thought a smile touched his lips.

"Ishvandu ab'Admundi," he said in a loud voice. "What oath do you give?"

"I swear by this sword," I heard myself say, "and by my own life, to defend the innocent, seek justice, and uphold the law. I swear to honour and obey the Al'kah, and to serve the people in all things, as long as I shall live. Wisdom that comes with age, justice that comes with law, strength against darkness, honour unto death." I pulled my palm against the blade, clean and hot. A moment later I was staring at the crimson streak of my oath, sworn into the sword I carried. My keshu. Mine.

"I honour your oath," Umaala finished.

I stepped back, stunned, overjoyed, terrified, full—full of so much I couldn't begin to name. I found Tala's eye amongst the crowd. She felt it also.

I was a Guardian at last. But this—this thing inside me, this fate, this need—it was only beginning. I was going to be a Guardian. And I was going to be something more. One day, I was going to return to the Old Lands, and just maybe, I would not be going alone.

Chapter Fifty-Two

Hyranna forgot what it was like to breathe without shards of glass scraping her lungs. The Aktyr was burning in her, she could feel it, but it didn't take away the pain. It only dampened it, overwhelming it with her *need* to go on.

She hadn't stopped since E'tuah's interruption two nights ago, but she was faltering. Her glimmer of hope had begun to waver. The river was fast, so fast, and Hyranna was starting to doubt her ability to catch up. She should have found them already. A night had passed, and another day, and another night, and she found camp after camp, deserted and empty. How long before she found another body? Another soul discarded to rot? How long before it was Jerad's?

Maker, keep him safe!

She needed to rest. But she couldn't. She couldn't stop. She had to go faster. She had to—

Her foot caught, and she sprawled to the ground. Her hands crashed into a painful patch of thistles. Her breath sobbed out of her lungs.

Hyranna lay there for a moment. *Don't stop. Don't stop!* But her mind was crashing and rolling with fatigue. Two days. She had run for two days, and two nights, and maybe even longer. She couldn't tell anymore.

But she couldn't give up. She *wouldn't*. There was no choice. However fast the river ran, she would just have to run faster. She would dig into the Aktyr. She had no choice.

The nettles stuck into her fingers, stinging her. She pushed away the pain. She pressed her hands to the ground and pushed herself up.

And then she saw. The thistles were dying. They weren't crushed or burned, they were just withering—before her very eyes. A moment later, and she was clutching dead stalks. Then they crumbled through her fingers like dust.

There was a *jolt*. She gave a cry of surprise. Everything seemed to shift, as if for a moment she was standing outside of herself, and so was the birch next to her, and the dead thistles, and the hard earth, and then *snap*—it all dropped into place again.

The shard flared up. She shut her eyes, trying to steady herself, waiting for the burst of dizziness to pass. Waiting for the Aktyr to calm down, to let her think.

"What is it?" E'tuah was by her side, pulling her back to her feet. She rose stiffly.

"I . . . I don't know."

"The Aktyr is waking. What did you do?"

"Nothing. It's not . . . me."

His brows came together, but instead of demanding an explanation, he just nodded. "Then you're sensing him. He must be close."

Hyranna's head came up. "Who's close?"

"The answer to our problem."

"Our problem? You mean the slavers? What are you talking about?"

"You will see."

A gleam rose into his eye, and Hyranna felt a prickle of warning along the back of her neck. Something was wrong. Something was changing. She could feel her body tingling with a strange new energy. She opened and closed her hands, and with every movement, the shard seemed to flex. But it was waiting. Waiting like a wolf circling its prey.

She took a shuddering breath. "I have to . . . keep going." Her feet began to move again—and she was amazed to discover the stiffness leaving them. She could breathe again, and the pain was slipping away, the exhaustion. She almost wept with relief. New strength! New life! The Aktyr was bending to her, and now she could run, now she could catch up to Garden and tear him apart . . .

She came up sharp. E'tuah's was still holding her, fingers tight over her arm.

"Wait," he said.

She stared at him. "*Wait?* But I have energy again. I can run, let me run—"

"Wait. We do this my way, remember? Trust me. Or you're on your own."

His tone left no room for argument. Hyranna clenched her fists. Moments ago, she would have thrown herself to the ground in exhaustion and relief. Now a powerful restlessness was coursing through her. She burned for action. She shook off his arm and began to pace.

E'tuah just stood there, watching, watching with a new intensity. He knew something. He was almost trembling as his fist clenched and unclenched by his side.

"What are you keeping from me?"

He said nothing. He just nodded, gesturing towards the ground. The patch of dead thistles, she realized, was no longer a patch. The deadness was creeping out, moving, crawling over the ground like a column of black ants.

"What . . . ?"

Another *snap*, like the world shifting out of place. She staggered. Pain stabbed through her gut, a queasiness that threatened to turn her inside-out. Her head began to pound. She doubled over.

"What's happening?" she gasped. "E'tuah . . . ?"

"Watch."

Her gaze followed the withering darkness. It latched on to a birch, and before her eyes, the whole thing began to curl. The smooth white bark cracked and peeled, the branches shrank as if pulling away from an unseen fire. A pattering like rain: and the papery leaves curled and fell, landing in a sad pile around the trunk.

Hyranna took a step back. "What is this?"

"A crack."

"A *what?*"

Hyranna flexed her fingers. The tingling power was growing steadily, not a wild burst of strength. This was something else. It was rising, calling. Like something was reaching out of her, and something else was reaching back.

"Your friend, Balduin Na-es. He said the forest was sick, is that right?"

Hyranna nodded, unable to tear her eyes away from the dying tree, from the creeping darkness. "Sick," she said.

"Then this is an oozing sore. A place where the laws of life, of creation itself, are becoming twisted. Twisted to the point of breaking."

"And I caused it," she whispered. "This is me. This is coming from the Aktyr. Just like in Elamori, like all those strange happenings, the rotting elk, the withered berries, Kota's blindness. It wasn't Balduin at all, was it? It was this! The Aktyr. Lying under the red tree!"

She dug a hand into her pouch and brought out the black stone. It was darker and brighter than she had ever seen it. It burned in her hand, pulsing with life.

E'tuah snorted. "The laws were broken long before you—long before *me*. And they are stretching, more and more every day, every moment. The Aktyr is *causing* it no more than a man causes his body to break out in sores. But it will push, it will bend, it will thin. And one step too far, and the Realms will crack."

"So . . . so why now?" Hyranna heard the tremor of fear in her voice. "What's happening, E'tuah?"

He laughed, an edgy, staccato sound more frightening than any of his words. "When I know, I will tell you."

Something moved behind her. Hyranna snapped around, staring into the trees. Something was coming.

She backed away, clutching the shard before her like a shield, heart lurching. Another shift bucked the ground, the world itself rocking out of place, and back in.

"Stop!" she gasped. She pressed a hand to a tree and watched the withering spread, moving faster and faster, sending out tendrils, eating up the grass, sapping the life from the weeds and bushes and trees, and leaving fissures of cracked and dusty ground.

A tendril shot out, faster than the others, and ripped across the forest floor, straight to a pair of bare feet.

Hyranna looked up, struggling through vertigo. There was a man. *Like E'tuah.* He was tall, with a hollow face, dark skin, and dark snapping eyes. He stood in a tattered robe, his black hair twisted free around his face. But there was something about him, something different, a depth of understanding, an otherness, as if he'd stepped out of a distant time.

Then she saw it. Beneath the tatters of fabric, there was a rock hanging from an old, frayed rope. A shard of rock, black and polished to a mirror-shine.

The Aktyr leapt inside of her. Not in murderous rage—but in greeting.

"*Le'ab,*" she said, before she realized what she was saying. *Brother.* The words just flew out of her mouth, and the man's face opened in wonder.

"*Le'sai-ni.*" He reached for the rock around his neck. She had never heard the word before, but instantly she knew it meant *little sister.* "It's you!" he cried, voice raw. "I've found you. I've found you at last!" His knees buckled. He sank to the ground, weary, relieved, like one who had travelled far for this moment.

Hyranna stared in confusion. "Me?"

"Yes! Thank Yl'avah and the Tree, I have come so far. So far! And here you are, the hope of our people, sent across the desert." He clutched the dark stone, trembling in anticipation. "I am not as you. My power is born of emptiness, my strength in destruction, but I had no choice. I was driven by need. The work of the Chosen must continue. Must! The world is Breaking, do you see it? We must seek the Lifewater together, and I will help you. I've come to help you. Yes, yes, I know what I am. I know I am a wretched thing, but I saw it: I saw the power I wield joined with yours in the final moments of the earth. One to break, one to build. It must be so! It must . . ."

He paused, his cascade of words bubbling to a stop. A frown gathered on his brow. "But you. You are not Kyr'amanu. You are . . . so young. How can you be Chosen?"

The words were strange, but the shard didn't seem to care. The meaning was clear, and like it was the most natural thing, she began to respond in his tongue.

"I am Hyranna Elduna, an Imo'ani of the forest."

"But you carry it also?"

She nodded. She uncurled her fingers, revealing the glass-like stone. It was hot, filling her with a strong, heady power, a sense of control, of the whole world spreading out before her. She was dimly aware of a black tendril reaching towards her feet, but it no longer seemed important. "I found it," she said.

"*Found.*" He nodded. "Of course. That would explain the waiting, the lost years. Seven years we've waited. *Seven years.*" He groaned. "So much lost. So much! I am Ashkynas ab'Adani, last Al'kah of my people."

"Al'kah?"

"Keeper of the laws, just judge and ruler. But now my people are gone, scattered."

"Ellendi?" she asked. "From the forest? From the east?" She paused. "From Lendahyr?"

"I know none of those places. I am from Shyandar. From the desert to the south." An image flashed through Hyranna's mind: bright hot seas of sand and rock, stretching without end, not a single tree as far as she could see. The desolation, the *emptiness* of it—it brought tears to her eyes. A desert. The same home as E'tuah.

"Yes," he whispered. "It's an empty world. Dying. Spreading. What my people have suffered, so will all the world if we don't stop it. I've crossed endless sands and mountains to find you."

"Me?" she spread a hand over her chest.

"Yes! Have you heard nothing I've said? You, or rather this stone. This shared power. Before you found it, it belonged to one who was Chosen. The Chosen of the Avanir—"

She laughed darkly. The sound sprang out of her, against her will, wild and fierce. "*Chosen*? No, great Al'kah. I am the Aktyr."

The man's face changed. He blinked, staring at her in horror.

Hyranna clamped a hand over her mouth. "That wasn't me," she whispered. "That wasn't me, I didn't say that."

"But the red tree . . ." he said. "You were with the red tree. You reached out and gave me strength. I felt it."

The Dandyri. She saw it in her mind, pressing her hand to it, the Aktyr ripping through her, the crack, the putrid blackness that ran and ran and ran into the dark.

The man's eyes went wide. "You killed it."

"No." She backed away. "No, that wasn't me. It was the Aktyr. Not me. I couldn't stop it, I couldn't—"

"*No!*" The man staggered forward. "You were the Chosen. You were supposed to be the Chosen. I need the Chosen. I *need . . .*"

Hyranna stumbled back. She swung her head, looking for E'tuah. He was gone. But she could feel the Aktyr—not hers, the man's. It was stirring and rising. It was threatening to lash out.

"Calm down!" she cried.

"I crossed the desert for you!" he screamed. "I came for you. I thought you were our hope, but you're *not*. You're just another like me. Another shard of emptiness. Destroying, murdering wherever you go, tearing apart the land. Don't you understand? We're dying! Everything, everything!"

"I don't know what you're talking about," Hyranna replied, moving back and back, edging away from the madman. The crunch of dead and dying life followed her. The earth groaned and cracked. "I'm just trying to help my friend," she said. "I have to get to him. Just let me go on my way. And you can go yours. Go find your Chosen. And—"

"It doesn't matter!" the man groaned. "My sacrifice is stillborn. All that I've done—for nothing. It will end. All the world will end."

He lurched towards her. The Aktyr in him was growing. She could feel it, like a piece of herself turned against herself, a fierce, wild wind, tugging at her arms and legs, pinching and pulling. *Where was E'tuah?* She gathered her own shard, readying its defence. She would kill him. If he came a step closer, she would.

Somewhere under the earth there was a tremor, a deep shifting.

"Don't blame the girl," said a voice. E'tuah emerged from behind Ashkynas. The man stopped, frozen in shock—and Hyranna knew the impossible had happened. He had heard E'tuah. He had heard him aloud.

"She destroyed a single sickly tree. She stumbled on a power not meant for her. And for all her wonderful ferocity, she's not so important. Let her go."

"Who is that?" Ashkynas demanded. His face had gone stark with fear. He refused to turn around, as if dreading what his eyes would see.

"The Aktyr's master," Hyranna said, with a rush of satisfaction. "The shard belongs to him."

Ashkynas took a trembling step forward. "It can't be! It can't! After all these years?" His eyes were fixed on Hyranna, but he spoke to himself, shaking his head. "But who else has taken it by force? No one. No one but I. And him. Oh, Yl'avah's might, let it not be so!"

E'tuah laughed. "Then you know me, great Al'kah? Do you really?" His eyes brightened. "Do they speak of me?"

He stepped closer, so close he was almost touching. But between him and Ashkynas, Hyranna sensed a wall, something he couldn't cross. Not yet.

Ashkynas groaned, pressing a hand to his face. "Oh, Yl'avah, I am a fool! I crossed the great emptiness for *this*? For *him*?" He reached out a hand to Hyranna. "Listen to me, child. Speak no words to him! He is an outcast of our people, but from long, long ago. A man who spoke to the shadows, who *saw* the curse of our people. That he's even still alive, against all Law—it is testament to his madness, his lies."

"Lies?" E'tuah's voice pitched with scorn. "Murderers and cowards! Too obsessed with tradition to see the truth. Too blind to see your own enslavement." He gave a wild, dangerous laugh. Something in his mind had been triggered, a long-buried memory, painful and exhilarating. Hyranna shuddered, backing away, clutching the shard until its edge bit her skin. Something was happening here, and in a flash, she remembered her conviction. E'tuah could not be trusted. His Aktyr was evil. His purpose was evil. Why had she been so quick to forget? So quick to ally herself with him? Maker above, let it not be too late!

"Don't answer him," Hyranna said, stepping forward, holding out her hand. "Ashkynas ab'Adani, if you are against the Aktyr, then don't make it worse. Don't call up its power. Go." She met the man's eye. "Now."

"What are you afraid of, Hyranna Elduna?" E'tuah asked. "I told you help was coming. Here it is. This is your answer."

"What answer?"

"What you wanted from the very beginning. To be free of the Aktyr. Now you can be."

"And what of our agreement? You promised to help Jerad!"

"And won't that be easier if the Aktyr is mine, fully under my control? I can destroy the slavers without fear of failure. You don't even have to be a part of it. You won't carry the guilt of it. You can take your friend and be free. Isn't that what you want?"

It was exactly what Hyranna wanted. It was so much what she wanted, her suspicions rose up against her hopes.

"How do you expect this man to help?" she asked.

"Simple," E'tuah replied. "Let him turn and see me. Let his Aktyr call out to mine. With his help, I can be free."

Ashkynas shook his head. "I won't."

"What? Because you think you know better?" E'tuah sneered. "Because you think you have the truth? You think *you* can stop the Breaking of the world?"

"No." The man's voice had become heavy. "I can't. But neither can you, without the Chosen."

"The Chosen, the Chosen." E'tuah paced and scowled. "How many years since my time? The girl says *hundreds*. Hundreds of years—"

"Three hundred and forty," Ashkynas said.

"*Three* hundred years, and you still don't see? The Chosen were a lie. A trap. I showed you the truth. I risked everything for you. I sacrificed. I bled." E'tuah slapped his chest. "I wanted only our good—the good of our people—and you dare stand there and denounce me like a common thief, without even deigning to look at me? What are you afraid of? You haven't changed, you Al'kahs, you lords, you *cowards*. Now face me!"

Ashkynas shook his head, his despair as thick as smoke. "It was my curse to be the last. The last Al'kah. To watch the death of the Avanir, the collapse of Shyandar: a thousand years it endured. And now gone. Because of *you*!"

With every word, E'tuah's pacing grew more frantic, eyes burning at Hyranna, threatening, pleading. She tore her gaze away, back to the madman, the one who called himself the last Al'kah.

"How do you know it's the same man?" she asked, hardly daring to breathe.

"Let me ask you, Hyranna Elduna of the Imo'ani: does this Aktyr's master have a name?"

"E'tuah," she whispered, even as she saw the look on E'tuah's face: anger, pride, shame, all boiled together.

Ashkynas laughed. "Is it really? Of course he would. Another blasphemous lie, the sign of his grasping. He would put himself in a place of usurped honour, but he is not what he claims. He was a man once. A simple man. A Labourer and the son of Labourers, who had the misfortune to fall to the shadows. They destroyed him. They whispered secrets not meant for our ears."

"But you remember my name," E'tuah snapped. "Don't you? Three hundred years, and you remember."

"Only because of *that*." He pointed towards the shard in Hyranna's grasp. "Because you stole one, the only one to ever do so. Until me."

"Until you?" E'tuah laughed. "You think your shard is half the strength of mine? What did you sacrifice? What do you know of the Three Realms? You're weak! You need me, great Al'kah! Mine is the only power that can undo the Breaking. The only one who can set things right."

"Stop!" Hyranna cried. "Just stop. While you two are bickering like idiots, the slavers are getting further away. We're going to save Jerad—remember, E'tuah? You promised me! Otherwise, whatever you want from me, I won't do it!"

"You have no choice," E'tuah said. "You've already done your part. Now Ashkynas ab'Adani will do his."

"No," the man shook his head. His eyes found Hyranna's, and she knew what he was going to do. She saw it in an instant, but couldn't get the words out fast enough.

Ashkynas lunged towards her.

"Don't!" she screamed, but it was too late.

The strength of his shard slammed into her. A wind tore up, lashed around her, whipping around and around, flaring the Aktyr's fire. There was a *thud* deep in the earth, like a heavy bone breaking. The ground rocked. Hyranna staggered. She could feel the wind trying to seize her, to tear her apart, but wherever his Aktyr touched, hers latched on, a single power, born of a single purpose. Twining stronger and stronger.

She was bursting with power. The Aktyr was clawing it in, more and more. She hurled Ashkynas away from her. She turned. She tried to flee, but the lines of power wrapped around her, drawn after her, crackling with new strength.

Then E'tuah was standing in front of her. He reached out and grabbed her hand, wrenching it open. And all that horrible, incomprehensible power—he stole it.

The laws that held the Realms together, dictating what should be possible, and what shouldn't—broke. Light streaked into him from both shards. Then he ripped the black stone out of her hand.

Hyranna screamed and clutched at his arm, desperate to take it back, everything wrenching inside of her. E'tuah pushed her away. She fell on her face in the barren ground and tasted dirt.

She spat it out and looked up. Then gasped.

A huge swath of land had been laid desolate, turned into a withered mass. Trees were toppled and dead, grass was shrivelled up, the forest floor was littered with crushed leaves. And directly in front of her, between Ashkynas and her, a crack had opened, a crevice she'd nearly fallen into.

She peered over the edge, lungs tight with shock. Her stomach flipped. Her head spun. It was nothingness. A long, shuddering hole, not in the earth, but in *everything*.

A part of her wanted never to look away—drawn into the *wrongness*, the emptiness, down and down, fascinated by the absence of anything. The stronger half dragged her eyes back up. She fell on her side, stomach heaving. There was nothing to throw up. Not even water. But the painful spasms kept coming, spearing through her like knives.

"No," she heard someone groan. She looked up. Ashkynas was on his back, on the other side of the fissure. "No. What have you done?"

E'tuah was *present* now. He was radiating vitality and dark command. He stepped across the gap without even glancing down.

"Not her. Don't blame her for this," he said, and his voice sounded deeper and stronger. "She tried to warn you, but you were so determined to sacrifice yourself, you couldn't listen to her better sense. You've been driven mad by it. I understand."

Ashkynas struggled to get up. His shard had been drained, his energy spent. The Aktyr's force simply lashed out, grabbed Ashkynas, and hurled him back to the ground, like a rock snapping him in the forehead.

E'tuah strode up to him, bent over, and with long fingers, plucked the shard up from around his neck.

"A child's toy, compared to mine," he said. "I'm surprised you put so much hope in it."

He lifted Ashkynas's shard, wrapped his fist around it, and crushed it. There was another jolt. Hyranna squeezed her eyes shut as the world tilted.

Ashkynas screamed. It was a sickening sound, like a piece of his soul was being torn away. He clutched his head, writhing on the ground. She could feel his pain. And she could only stare in horror. She watched E'tuah stride up to the fissure, open his hand, and let the fractured pieces of black stone fall away like dust into the nothingness below.

And then it was over. Ashkynas lay panting on the ground. Hyranna didn't dare move. Slowly, the man lifted his face, and he seemed to age in a heartbeat, from thirty summers to sixty. First there was fear, then disbelief. Then tears sprang to his eyes.

"You . . . you destroyed it."

"I did."

He paused again. He pressed a hand into the ground, looking weak, old, feeble. He stared up at E'tuah. "You freed me."

A smile touched the corners of E'tuah's mouth. "I did."

"But why?"

"Because I carry it now. All of it. Your power and mine. Because I want you to understand: I have no rival."

Ashkynas stared, bewildered. He tried to rise, a word of gratitude on his lips. Then E'tuah slammed a foot into the man's chest and shoved him back down.

"But you know what happens next. With the Aktyr, there is always a price." His voice was as hard as a blade. "Any last report from Shyandar? Tell me, Al'kah. Did they do it? Did our people break free of the Avanir?"

"*Free?*" Ashkynas's face twisted to fury. "Your *people* brought the ruin of Shyandar!"

"Shyandar was a lie."

"Your words were the lie. You think you're some hero of old? Ishvandu. *Ishvandu.* Your name is a *curse* in Shyandar. The traitor. Ishvandu ab'Admundi. The man who destroyed his own people."

E'tuah snarled. His foot slid up to the man's throat. "You think I care? Before this is over, I will be the hero Kayr needs. The Breaking is mine, and only I can finish it."

"Kayr is *gone!*"

"Is it?" E'tuah pressed his foot down, cutting off the man's breath. Ashkynas struggled against the force of the Aktyr, but it held him, like ropes lashed to his hands and feet.

"E'tuah, what are you doing?" Hyranna cried through a parched throat. "Stop it!"

He paid no attention to her. She stared as Ashkynas's face changed colour, the cords on his neck stood out, his eyes bulged.

"Stop it! You're killing him!"

She staggered to her feet. Pain rolled through her body, vicious and overwhelming. Her energy was gone. The shard's power—gone. But she could feel it, still connected to her, deep inside like a shadow. It was still a part of her. Still bound to her.

"E'tuah!"

She staggered over the fissure, reaching for him, but he shoved her out of the way. She sprawled onto the dry ground. *If only she could grab it back . . .*

Hyranna glanced over her shoulder. Ashkynas's arms and legs began to twitch beneath invisible bonds. E'tuah stood over him, face twisted, crushing the man's life out. *The Aktyr.* She understood that force. She remembered it. The need to destroy. The *joy* of it. And in a flash, she understood. E'tuah was no more the Aktyr's master than she was. It had them. It had them both.

"E'tuah, don't do this. Don't listen to it. You don't have to . . ."

"Be quiet," he said. He was finished with her. Free of her. Did she mean nothing to him now? Would he kill her too?

She buried her face in her hands, tried not to hear the awful, gurgling sounds. *Coward.* She had to stop him. She had to do something. But what? Tears burned against her fingers. The shard. It was still bound to her. He had stolen the power, but not its connection to her. Not yet. If she could just get close enough, then maybe . . .

No. Not maybe. It was like with her father. Either she had to, or she couldn't. She took her hands away. She forced herself to watch the dying man. And then she started to crawl.

E'tuah's attention was fixed on him. He didn't see her. She dragged herself up behind him, dragging her wounded leg, feeling pain everywhere, everywhere at once. She reached out—and touched his foot. The Aktyr pounded back into her. It was a dizzying power, full of authority, full of control. And before she could be swept away by it, she gave a single word, a single thought: *release.*

Ashkynas's limbs jerked. His arms flailed up, grabbed E'tuah's knee, and twisted.

E'tuah wasn't prepared. He staggered, and with a desperate cry, Ashkynas heaved his whole weight against E'tuah's leg, hurling him towards the fissure.

Hyranna watched him fall, heart leaping into her throat. He landed. One arm shot out, gripping the other side of the fissure, his body hanging between. Ashkynas dove at him. They would have fallen together into the nothingness, but the Aktyr flared up, hot and furious.

Ashkynas gave a shout. Like a giant club slamming into him, he was thrown back. His arms and legs wheeled through the air, and he landed with the crunch of bone. He tried to get up, to cry out, but an invisible force slammed him into the ground, and his body broke.

He was instantly dead.

***

AN EERIE SILENCE FOLLOWED, deafening after all the noise and confusion. Hyranna peeled her eyes away from Ashkynas's dead body to see E'tuah had hauled himself up, out of danger, and was climbing to his feet. His chest was heaving up and down in alarm. After being so convinced of his own power—and to come so terrifyingly close to oblivion. He marched towards her.

"I'm sorry," she gasped. "But you didn't have to kill him. You didn't have to—"

He struck her across the face. The force of the blow cracked something in her cheek, a crunch, a bone caving in.

She must have passed out. She fought towards consciousness, pain blooming across her entire face, tasting blood in her mouth. She groaned. She could barely move. Barely lift her head.

Through grey, blurry vision, she saw E'tuah standing over Ashkynas, examining him, as if wanting to make sure for himself he was dead. He heard her, and his head came up.

"Foolish girl," he said, though his tone was quiet, the anger drained out of him. "Your stubbornness could have cost everything." He shook his head and turned back to her, walking slowly. "But I understand why you did it. You heard his lies. You think I'm a monster. That I've done terrible things. Yes. I have. I *have*. But it's not as simple as that."

"You just killed a man," she said, voice slurred from the pain.

"Yes."

"And you didn't have to!"

"Didn't I? You know, Hyranna Elduna. You understand the Aktyr."

She saw herself screaming, driving the stone into Whiset's face, strangling him, crushing him . . .

"But—destroying your own people?"

"You would trust his word? He's been driven mad by the Aktyr, and the story is long and terrible. So much more . . ." He shook his head. "But he's right. I'm not E'tuah. I don't deserve that name—not yet. But when you brought me back, I was afraid I had failed, afraid *Ishvandu* had failed. I made so many mistakes—"

"Ishvandu?"

"My name," he growled. "Didn't you hear him? Ishvandu ab'Admundi."

"You said you were *Lel-na*? I don't understand . . ."

"Lel-na is a title. Just like E'tuah. It can be worn by many. And in time I will be. I will do what I must to stop the Breaking. Which is why—I'm sorry, Hyranna Elduna. This is where I leave you."

Hyranna pushed herself up. Her arms trembled. Pain pounded against her face, against her skull. "L-leave?" She shook her head. "You can't . . . leave."

"I must. You can see for yourself. There will be other fissures like this. The world is starting to break apart. I must stop it. Thanks to you, I'm free to do so."

"But . . ." she craned her neck. "But what about . . . what about Jerad?"

He smiled. He actually *smiled*. "Hyranna Elduna, did you really believe I'd waste precious time chasing down slavers? A whole world is at stake." His smile vanished. "And I have my own enemy to hunt."

"What . . . what do you . . . mean?" Disbelief rose up to choke her. She crawled towards him. "E'tuah . . . don't! If . . . if you take the Aktyr, you'll kill me. Remember? Remember what happened when—"

"Yes," he said. "But the moment it bound itself to you, you were already dead. It can't serve us both, and you can't do what I can. So it's finished. I'm sorry Hyranna. You're stronger than you know. But here is where it ends, where it was always going to end."

She stared at him. She watched him turn and walk away, as simple as that. He was leaving her, and he was taking the Aktyr with him. Anger stirred in her, hopeless, stubborn anger. She tried to struggle up, to crawl after him, but a heaviness struck her. It piled across her back, pulling her to the ground. She sobbed. She could feel the Aktyr stretching away from her, stealing her strength, stealing her eyes. The images around her blurred.

"E'tuah!" she wailed.

There was no reply. The world fell dark. Silent and dark. And gradually, terribly, like finding her own limb severed, Hyranna understood she was alone—and she was dying.

A single traveller strode down a wide, paved road. His blue eyes were turned down, scanning the dust for signs of passage, scanning the trees to either side, scanning the up-turned earth.

Occasionally, he reached and gripped the hilt of his sword, mostly to stop the trembling. The one outward sign of his long suffering. A reminder of what he'd come through and the peril that was still so near.

That's when he heard it: the distant cracking of guns. It was coming from Tellern.

His mind flashed to the two Imo'ani he'd met in the town. The broad-shouldered youth and the girl, that strange girl whose presence unbalanced him. She'd eyed him with distrust and there was something about her. Something familiar. Something dark. Something he'd instantly disliked. Could the gunshots be their fault?

A few screams drifted down with the wind, and the part of him that still cared, the part he could never deaden, was compelled to turn back.

He stopped himself. He had something more important to do. He had something he *had* to do. If he went out of his way to mend every broken bone and free every captive, he'd never be reunited with his son.

And so he kept going. He kept going, even though the guns didn't quit. Not right away. And when he thought they'd fallen silent, they started up again. Three, one after the other, fast and unanswered. *An execution.*

His hand shook.

Those two Imo'ani. They had been looking for someone. A youth of fifteen summers, dressed in Imo'ani skins, with hair as red as fire and eyes of blue, skin all mixed up, fair and dark together, like a dyer's mistake. There was only one person it could be. The age was right, the description accurate, the village achingly close. He would stand out wherever he went. He would draw curious eyes. But loyal friends?

Who would pursue him, if not her? She was the only one he had ever felt safe with.

It had to be her. Her saw her: a small girl with black, braided hair and fierce black eyes, tottering on new legs, shrieking and running after his son. Laughing. It was her, the girl from Tellern. Balduin's only friend.

In an instant, he changed his mind. It was a hard thing, but one of those choices that wasn't really a choice. He had to find her, as he should have done from the beginning. He had to make sure she was safe. Balduin's friend, his only friend. He knew his son—whatever else had passed in ten long years, Hyranna Elduna would always be his friend.

Alutan Na-es turned around, and began hurrying north.

To be Continued . . .

The story continues! Look for **Shadows of Blood: Book Two of the Avanir Chronicles,** now for sale at Amazon, Indigo, and other online retailers.

Glossary of Names

A Note on Pronunciation

Due to the difficult nature of some names found in this book, many of my readers requested a pronunciation guide. This, then, is for you (you know who you are). Good luck!

- *ch* is pronounced *[kh]* as in *character*, never *[tch]* as in *church*
- *y* is pronounced *[ee]* as in *tree*, never *[ai]* as in *why*—the exception is when *y* acts as a consonant, like *[y]* as in *tray*
- *u* is pronounced *[oo]* as in *food*, never *[uh]* as in *mud*
- *ai* is pronounced *[ay]* as in *why*, never *[ey]* as in *way*
- *aa* is pronounced *[a]* as in *father*, though it is held longer than the usual *[a]*
- the symbol (') is not a distinct sound, but represents two words that have been joined into one idea, so *ab'Ethanir* means "son of Ethanir"

Some examples to illustrate these points:

- *Chorah'dyn* is pronounced *[khor-a-DEEN]*

- *Kulnethar* is pronounced *[KOOL-na-thar]*
- *Kyr'amanu* is pronounced *[keer-A-man-oo]*
- *Kayr* is pronounced *[ka-EER]*
- *sai'Neraia* is pronounced *[sai-ner-AY-a]*
- *Vanya* is pronounced *[VAN-ya]*
- *Umaala* is pronounced *[oo-MAL-a]*
- *Hyranna* is pronounced *[hee-RA-na]*
- *Shyandar* is pronounced *[shee-AN-dar]*

Kyre'an Names

A note on familiar names: it is customary in Shyandar for friends and relatives to use a shortened form of a person's name as a way of indicating affection or familiarity. So Ishvandu ab'Admundi would be known by his friends as "Vanya."

- Adar ab'Dara—a foreman of the Labourers
- Admundi ab'Adaiah—a Labourer, Ishvandu's father
- Akkoryn ab'Kindelthu (Koryn)—a Guardian, head of the third kiyah, antagonistic towards Ishvandu
- Alis—a young Labourer, later a healer in the Temple
- Alynis—a Novice in training to be a Guardian
- Anajin ab'Anajin (Jin)—a Guardian, head of the fourth kiyah
- Andari ab'Andala Al'kah—the first Al'kah after the fall of Kayr, led the surviving Kyr'amanu to Shyandar
- Antaru ab'Manishu—a young Guardian of the fourth kiyah
- Ashianys—the first great city of Kayr, built around the Chorah'dyn and the Pillars of Law
- Ashkynas ab'Adani Al'kah—the so-called "Last Al'kah" who left Shyandar with a terrible power
- Atali sai'Neraia (Tala)—a young Guardian of the fourth kiyah, a friend of Ishvandu's
- Avanir—the mystical wellspring that waters and protects Shyandar

- Bretina sai'Anira (Breta)—a Novice in training to be a Guardian, Ishvandu's friend
- Choosing—a ceremony following Renewal in which three people are Chosen to carry the power of the Avanir back to cleanse the Lifewater
- Chorah'dyn—the Great Tree and Guardian of the World, holds all Realms together in harmony and oversees the Laws of Creation
- Ebridyn ab'Branidu (Bray)—a young Novice in training to be a Guardian, Ishvandu's friend
- Ethanir ab'Estaldir—the High Elder of Shyandar, Kulnethar's father
- E'tuah—the mysterious stranger in the desert who calls himself by an honorary title
- eywah-ka—the final rite of passage, sung over the dead to aid their journey to the Last Realm
- Ishvandu ab'Admundi (Vanya)—a Novice in training to be a Guardian
- Jarethyn ab'Torishu—a Guardian Lord of the Circle
- Jil—an older Novice in training to be a Guardian
- jik'u—a game that involves moving black and white stones around to make groupings and score points
- Kaprash—the time of dryness, when the Avanir ceases to flow
- Kayr—the ancient empire, named after its founder, Kyrada
- keshu—the blades of the Guardians, infused with ytyri to remain undulled and effective against Sumadi
- kiyah—a contingent of Guardians (usually twelve), who accomplish a role unique to that kiyah, such as overseeing, peacekeeping, or night-watch
- Kulnethar ab'Ethanir—a young healer in the Temple, son of the High Elder and Ishvandu's friend
- Kynava ab'Ashnavas—a young Guardian who Ishvandu remembers from the aftermath of the fire
- Kyrada—the founder of the Kyre'an people
- Kyr'amanu—the people of Kayr

- Layisha sai'Lanita—a Guardian Lord of the Circle, overseer of administration
- Lifewater—the lifeblood of the world, which flows from the Chorah'dyn and nourishes and sustains all things
- Neraia sai'Kalysa—Guardian Lord of the Circle, overseer of justice in Shyandar
- Polityr (Pol)—a Novice in training to be a Guardian, Ishvandu's friend
- Renewing—the new year, when the Avanir begins to flow again
- Shatayeth—the last of the Undying and the enemy of Kayr, fought against Kyrada in the Wars of Rending
- Shyandar—the last remaining city of the Kyr'amanu, located far south in the desert
- Sumadi—the bloodless creatures of the desert
- Tanadu ab'Tanadu—an elder Guardian of the third kiyah
- Tasking—a period of training that starts at age ten and lasts until age thirteen
- Tushani ab'Turana—an elder Guardian, the weapons-master
- Three Realms—Blood, Spirit, and Light (Seen, Unseen, and that by which we see), together these make up all elements of the world
- Umaala ab'Krushaya—a Guardian Lord of the Circle who oversees defence and order in Shyandar
- Undying—the first people, granted unending life
- Wars of Rending—the period of upheaval in which Shatayeth conquered the Undying
- Yalata ab'Ytanu (Ylta)—a scribe in the Temple
- Yl'avah—the Creator
- Yma—Ishvandu's camel
- ytyri—a mysterious substance of great power, a liquid metal that can be bound into other materials, thus altering them

Imo'ani and Manturian Names

A note on familiar names: it is customary amongst the Imo'ani for women to be called by a familiar name, but this is reserved for only the closest friends and relatives. So Hyranna Elduna would be called "Anna" only by her parents and a select few.

- Alutan Na-es—Balduin's father, missing for ten years
- Aktyr—the name of the black shard Hyranna discovers
- Andalina—Balduin's mother, shunned by the people of Elamori
- Balduin Na-es—Hyranna's friend, shunned by the people of Elamori
- Brit Garden—a Manturian slaver from Terryn Dal
- Calton—a Manturian settlement on the Road, south of Tellern
- Cay-et—a tribe of Imo'ani who have taken it upon themselves to guard the lands between the Manturian Road and the eastern villages
- Dal Adis—Balduin's adopted uncle, leader of the elder hunting party and relative of Kenan Elduna
- Dandyri—the legendary red trees that once covered the Ellendandur forest, thought capable of speech and other powers
- Daryn—a man who works in the wayhouse in Tellern
- Eedi—Hyranna's older cousin
- Elamori—an Imo'ani village in the north, Hyranna's home
- Ellendandur—the name of the vast forest that covers much of the north
- Ember—the woman who owns the wayhouse in Tellern
- E'tuah—the mysterious stranger who appears to Hyranna
- Greenwater—the Imo'ani word for the Lifewater, the lifeblood of the world, which flows from the Chorah'dyn and nourishes and sustains all things
- Haiyo-na—an Imo'ani village west of Tellern and the Manturian Road

- Hyranna Elduna (Anna)—a girl of fifteen, only child of the Guardian of Elamori
- Imo-ani—the people of the Ellendandur forest, Hyranna's kin
- Jerad Amanti—a boy of seventeen, a member of the younger hunting party
- Kota Danu-e—a boy of fourteen who is blinded by mysterious causes, Mylar's younger brother
- Lel-na—a mythical figure who fought against the blackness that eventually destroyed the Greenwater and the Dandyri
- Lendahyr—a secluded land far to the southwest where Kayr used to be
- Lindys—an Imo'ani village close to Elamori
- Manturian Isles—the collection of islands north of the Ellendandur, home to a mercantile and seafaring people
- Marisela Elduna (Mari)—Hyranna's mother, wife of the Guardian of Elamori
- Mylar Danu-e—a boy of sixteen, the "bully" of the younger hunting party
- Tellern—a small Imo'ani town on the Manturian Road
- Terryn Dal—a northern isle in Mantur
- Tindanarra—the river that runs past Elamori

Acknowledgments

Here it is! The culmination of many years, and hopefully the beginning of years yet to come. I'm so thankful to you, my readers, for embarking on this journey with me. Without you, books would live short and selfish lives within the minds of dreamers, but with you, worlds take on colour and form, and strange and wonderful creatures draw breath. Thank you for dreaming with me!

Books, however, are never the product of a single mind. I have many people to thank for helping me along the way. My dear friend, Maria Bergen: you believed in me long before I did, and without you, this book would simply not exist. You know Ishvandu and Hyranna as well as I do. For responding to the anguish of a writer's soul with patience and good sense, and for demanding to read all my drafts—especially the horrible ones—thank you, thank you.

To my beta readers, your work was indispensable, without which this book would be a poor and error-riddled offering. Some of my first eyes were Rachel Siebert, Holly and Devon Berofe, Ari and Julie Dyck, Christine Dyck, and Richard Cavner. Subsequent drafts saw the help of my writer's group, Lianne Riddell and Angela Dunn, while my editor, Kyla Neufeld, supplied her keen insight and challenging perspectives, together with a merciless eradication of unnecessary commas.

Putting words on a page is one thing, but publishing is an entirely different struggle. Over and over again, I found myself in need of skills I didn't have, which is why producing a book takes a community. Thank you to Farideh Saffari for the gorgeous illustrations; to Darrell Dyck for drawing my maps and bringing the cover together with a designer's eye; to Gerald Becker for your technical assistance; and to Christine Dyck for your stunning photography and photo-editing skills.

To my family, your unflagging support means more than you'll ever know. Mom: this is all your fault. You introduced me to Middle Earth and Narnia, then said I could do it too—and believed it. Dad, you fed my curiosity and always spurred me on. You'll never know how much I treasure your words of encouragement! To my brothers, I forgive you for making fun of my panda bear stories. Your friendship enriches my life, and your families bring me oodles of joy.

To my other family, my church: you are the blessing of God. I overflow with gratitude when I consider your kindness, encouragement, prayers, and practical offerings. Food and rides are both essential to a writer's existence. You are too many to name, but I want to especially acknowledge Brenda Charach, Rebecca Gole, Jared Esser, Suzanne Wright, Carolyn Lesey, Matt Klassen, Cameron Kerney, and Tyler Kimball. You upheld me in the difficult times and celebrated with me in the good times. You are what the church is meant to be.

Finally, I want to recognize the grace of Jesus in all I do. You are the beginning and the end, the reason, the hope of the world. All that is good here is from you.

Bless you all! I look forward to sharing the next adventure with you soon.

About the Author

L. E. Dereksen is an emerging author of fantasy. Besides literature, her passions include classical music, board games, and her local community. She also teaches English as a Second Language, where she helps adult newcomers explore language and life in Canada. She lives with her husband Drew and her dog Patrick in the prairies of Winnipeg, Canada.

goodreads.com/ledereksen
facebook.com/ledereksen
instagram.com/ledereksen